VIRAL

"Well thought-out and the characters are interesting and relatable. It is also fast-paced and easy to read. I enjoyed it and am eager to read another of Cook's novels."
—*Mystery and Suspense*

"I love Robin Cook novels and this one is another good one. It incorporates not only COVID but the whole US health care system, which needs a major overhaul to help out every American citizen. The characters and story are well-written and you feel for Brian throughout the story and the plight he goes through." —*Red Carpet Crash*

GENESIS

"With *Genesis*, [Robin Cook] successfully sheds light on genetic genealogy and some privacy concerns involving its ever-expanding DNA databases." —Associated Press

PANDEMIC

"When there's a scientific breakthrough, Robin Cook doesn't just stand up and cheer. He uses his fertile imagination and writes a novel about its possible perils. . . . By graphically showing what could happen were CRISPR/Cas9 to fall into the wrong hands, the author rings a much needed warning bell about gene editing technology."

—Associated Press

CHARLATANS

"Cook has been cranking out best-selling medical thrillers since the mid-1970s, and he long ago worked out a formula that works for his fans. [*Charlatans*] is no exception, proving once again that there is comfort and entertainment to be found in the familiar." —*Booklist*

"Cook fans will keep turning the pages. . . . Makes readers think with long passages about how medical training needs to adapt and how technology is reshaping not only the practice of medicine, but also what it means to be a doctor." —*Chicago Tribune*

"Tantalizing." —*Publishers Weekly*

"In addition to elegant use of language, the carefully planted medical details throughout the book and in dialogue make the plot credible and joyful to read. Cook is aware that the world is quickly changing thanks to the new Internet-based technologies and his plots are evolving as well. . . . A great pick for all thriller fans."

—*Mystery Tribune*

HOST

"Spellbinding . . . *Host* is Robin Cook at his very best."
—*Suspense Magazine*

"Engrossing . . . Cook does a good job of making the medicine intelligible." —*Publishers Weekly*

"A witch's brew of weird science and unbridled greed, Cook's newest medical thriller will boost the blood pressure of anyone facing hospitalization." —*Kirkus Reviews*

"Brutally intense . . . A medical thriller cannot get any better than *Host*." —Associated Press

CELL

"Cook, ever the master of the medical thriller, combines controversial biomedical research issues with critical ethical concerns and gripping suspense. This outstanding and thought-provoking thriller will attract a wide readership." —*Library Journal*

"Cook has found a formula that keeps readers coming back for more." —*Booklist*

NANO

DEATH BENEFIT

CURE

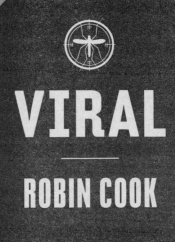

VIRAL

ROBIN COOK

G. P. PUTNAM'S SONS
New York

PUTNAM
— EST. 1838 —

G. P. PUTNAM'S SONS
Publishers Since 1838
An imprint of Penguin Random House LLC
penguinrandomhouse.com

The Library of Congress has catalogued the G. P. Putnam's Sons
hardcover edition as follows:

Names: Cook, Robin, author.
Title: Viral / Robin Cook.
Description: New York : G. P. Putnam's Sons, 2021
Identifiers: LCCN 2021021034 (print) | LCCN 2021021035 (ebook) |
ISBN 9780593328293 (hardcover) | ISBN 9780593328309 (ebook)
Subjects: GSAFD: Suspense fiction.
Classification: LCC PS3553.O5545 V57 2021 (print) |
LCC PS3553.O5545 (ebook) | DDC 813/.54—dc23
LC record available at https://lccn.loc.gov/2021021034
LC ebook record available at https://lccn.loc.gov/2021021035
p.   cm.

First G. P. Putnam's Sons hardcover edition / August 2021
First G. P. Putnam's Sons international mass-market edition / March 2022
First G. P. Putnam's Sons premium edition / June 2022
G. P. Putnam's Sons premium edition ISBN: 9780593328316

Printed in the United States of America
10 9 8 7 6 5 4 3 2 1

*This book is dedicated to the fervent hope
that members of the US Congress will comprehend
the need to enact, at the very minimum,
a viable public healthcare option.*

PREFACE

The Covid-19 pandemic has thrust the virus center stage as a dangerous and dreaded foe similar to the way the influenza pandemic did a century ago. The causative viruses, SARS-CoV-2 and influenza A(H1N1), produce respiratory illnesses that are easily transmittable person to person and thereby quickly swept around the globe. Within months, both scourges sickened millions of people, and many died.

Although these two biologic entities currently dominate the spotlight, there are other viruses that deserve equal fear, concern, and attention, since some of the resultant diseases have a higher lethality as well as the capacity to cause more serious complications. Although these diseases are not transmitted by aerosol and are thereby less communicative, they, too, are spreading around the world at a slower—yet ever-quickening—pace thanks to climate change and human encroachment into previously isolated environments. In particular, a number of viruses have cleverly hijacked the mosquito to ensure their survival. These viruses are responsible for illnesses such as yellow fever, dengue, West Nile fever, and an array of diseases that cause dangerous inflammation of the brain called encephalitis. This includes eastern equine encephalitis virus, or EEE, which is known to have a death rate as high as thirty percent. As climate change advances, aggressive mosquitoes like the Aedes Asian tiger mosquito, which carry these dangerous viruses and which had heretofore been restricted to tropical climes, are progressively and relentlessly spreading northward into temperate regions, currently reaching as far north as the state of Maine in the USA and the Netherlands in Europe.

These other, fearful viruses couldn't have picked a better vector. As obligate bloodsuckers to enable breeding, mosquitoes are high on everyone's nuisance list. Most people can recall a disrupted summer slumber, or evening stroll, or hike in the woods, or barbecue on the beach, heralded by the characteristic whine of the female mosquito. As a creature superbly designed after almost one hundred million years of adaptive evolution (even dinosaurs were plagued by mosquitoes), the female mosquito invariably gets her blood meal or dies trying. For some reason that has yet to be explained, the female Asian tiger mosquito is particularly attracted to human females with blood type O, although other blood types or even human males will do in a pinch.

As a testament to the effectiveness of the mosquito–

pathogen partnership, almost a million people die each year from a mosquito-spread illness. Some naturalists even posit that mosquito-transmitted illnesses have killed nearly half of all the humans who have ever lived.

—*Robin Cook, MD*

VIRAL

PROLOGUE

Although mosquitoes cause more than two thousand human deaths every day, their pernicious impact doesn't necessarily stop there. The deaths they cause can result in further serious societal complications. Such a story of a sad serial tragedy started in the summer of 2020 as the result of a cascading series of events that began in the idyllic town of Wellfleet, Massachusetts, nestled on the bay side of Cape Cod. It all started within the confines of a discarded automobile tire leaning up against a dilapidated, freestanding garage. Inside the tire was a bit of stagnant rainwater where a pregnant female Asian tiger mosquito had deposited her raft of eggs.

On the twentieth of July this clutch of eggs hatched, starting the mind-boggling ten-day metamorphosis from larvae to pupae to adults. The moment the mosquitoes emerged as adults, they could fly, and within three days they followed the irresistible urge to reproduce, requiring the females to obtain a blood meal. By using their highly evolved sense organs, they detected a victim and zeroed in on an unsuspecting blue jay. Unknown to the mosquitoes and to the blue jay, the bird had been infected earlier in July by the eastern equine encephalitis virus. Neither bird nor the mosquitoes cared since birds such as blue jays are a normal host for EEE, meaning they live together in a kind of passive parasitism, and in a similar fashion, the mosquito's immune system keeps the virus at bay. After getting their fill of blue jay blood, the mosquitoes flew off to find an appropriate place to deposit their eggs.

Several weeks later the infected band of mosquitoes had moved eastward toward the Atlantic Ocean. They were now considerably reduced in number from having been prey to numerous predators. At the same time, they were now more experienced. They had learned to favor human victims as easier targets than feathered birds or furred mammals. They also learned the beach was a promising destination in the late-afternoon/early-evening because there were always relatively immobile humans with lots of exposed skin.

At three-thirty on the afternoon of August fifteenth, this cluster of EEE-carrying female Asian tiger mosquitoes awakened from their daytime slumber. They had found refuge from the midday summer sun beneath the porch planking of a building on Gull Pond. A few moments later, ravenous for a blood meal, the swarm became airborne en masse with their characteristic whine. Save for several unlucky individuals, they avoided the many sticky and dangerous spiderwebs and emerged into the sunlight. Regrouping, they set off like a miniature fighter squadron. Instinctively they knew the beach was six hundred yards to the east beyond a forest composed mostly of black oak and pitch pine. Barring being eaten on the way or having to navigate a stronger than usual headwind, it would take the swarm around three-quarters of an hour to reach a crowd of potential targets.

BOOK 1

CHAPTER 1

August 15

Okay, you guys! It's four-thirty and time to get this barbecue show on the road," Brian Yves Murphy ordered, clapping his hands to get his family's attention. His wife, Emma, and his daughter, Juliette, were draped over the living room furniture in the modest two-bedroom cottage they had rented for two weeks across from a hardscrabble beach in Wellfleet, Massachusetts, just beyond the town's harbor. All of them were appropriately exhausted after an active, fun-filled midsummer day that marked the beginning of their final week of vacation. Because of the SARS-CoV-2 pandemic, they'd opted for a road trip vacation rather than flying down to Florida to use Emma's parents' empty condo, as was their usual summer getaway.

"Can't we just recover for ten to fifteen minutes?" Emma pleaded jokingly despite knowing full well that Brian wouldn't hear of it. In truth, she was as compulsive as he in terms of getting the most out of every minute of their vacation while the weather held. On top of that, she was also as compulsively fit and active as he. That morning she had awakened just after dawn and had soundlessly slipped out of the house for a bike ride and to be first in line at PB Boulangerie for their one-of-a-kind, freshly baked almond croissants. It had been a welcome surprise when they discovered the French bakery so far from what they called civilization. As lifelong residents of Inwood, Manhattan, they considered themselves quintessential New Yorkers and assumed anything outside of the city was hinterland.

"Sorry, but no rest for the weary," he said. "I'd like to get to the Newcomb Hollow Beach parking lot before the evening rush to make sure we get a spot." They had found over their first few days that Newcomb Hollow was their favorite Atlantic-side beach, with fewer people and high dunes that acted as partial windbreaks from the onshore breeze.

"But why the rush?" questioned Emma. "We already got a beach parking permit when we got the fire permit."

"The parking permit lets us park, but it doesn't guarantee a spot. Plus, Newcomb Hollow Beach is a popular spot for obvious reasons."

"Okay," she said agreeably. She got up and stretched her shoulders, which were mildly sore from the kayaking on Long Pond they had done that morning, an unusual workout for both of them. Then in the early afternoon she and Brian had done their daily mini-triathlon that involved biking ten miles to Truro and back, swimming for one mile in the bay, and running for five more into the Cape Cod National Seashore. Meanwhile, four-year-old Juliette had spent time with a local high school girl named Becky whom they had luckily found to serve as a daily sitter on day one. The lucky part was that Becky, despite being a teenager, was surprisingly acceptive and attentive to the required testing, mask wearing, and social distancing mandated by the Covid-19 pandemic.

"I'll get towels, the grill, briquettes, beach chairs, and toys and load it all in the car," he rattled off, heading into the kitchen. He'd been looking forward to the barbecue for several days. Although they wouldn't have the sunset like they did every evening over Cape Cod Bay, the Atlantic side was glorious, especially compared to the narrow, seashell-littered beach in front of their cottage.

"Ten four," Emma said. She glanced down at Juliette. The child seemed to already be asleep, although Emma was aware she could be pretending, as she often did when she didn't want to be bothered. With her eyes closed and lips slightly parted, she was clutching her favorite toy and constant companion named Bunny: a foot-long, very floppy, light brown, worse-for wear stuffed rabbit with one missing eye. Emma couldn't help but stare at her with loving eyes, thinking as a mother that Juliette might very well be the world's most beautiful child, with her slightly upturned sculpted nose, Cupid's bow lips, and thick blond hair.

Initially both she and Brian had been taken aback by their daughter's hair as it grew in. The expectation had been that it would either be Emma's flaming red or Brian's blue-black. Instead it had come in as blond as golden corn, establishing from the outset that Juliette was her own person. The same thing happened with her eye coloration. She ended up green-eyed in contrast to Emma's hazel and Brian's blue. But there were some definite commonalities. All three Murphys had pale, almost translucent, Irish skin that required constant application of sunscreen to keep from getting burned. Also similar were their well-muscled and long-limbed figures. Even at age four, Juliette promised to be as athletic and tall as both her father and mother, who stood at six-one and five-eight, respectively.

"Hey! What are you doing?" he questioned as he wheeled a small portable kettle charcoal grill through the living room. He'd caught her hovering over Juliette. "Chop chop! What's holding up the show?"

"I was just momentarily overwhelmed by our daughter," Emma confessed. "We are so lucky she's healthy and so damn cute. In fact, I think she might be the most beautiful child in the world."

Brian nodded but rolled his eyes playfully. "Sounds like a serious case of parental bias. There's no doubt we're lucky, but let's please hold up on our appreciation until we've parked and are on the beach."

She threw the Speedo swim cap she was holding at Brian, who laughed and easily ducked away before pushing out into the front yard, letting the screen door bang behind him. The characteristic noise reminded Emma of the summers she'd spent as a child out on Long Island. Her father, Ryan O'Brien, had done very well for himself and his family after starting a successful plumbing company in Inwood. Emma and Brian had both grown up among Inwood's sizable Irish community and had actually been aware of each other as grammar school–aged children while attending PS 98 even though he was two grades ahead of her.

For her part in preparation for the barbecue, she went into the kitchen, got out the cooler, and after putting in the cold packs from the freezer, filled it with the hamburger patties she'd made the previous day, the fresh de-gritted clams they had gotten earlier that morning at the harbor, a bottle of prosecco, and some fruit juice for Juliette. The unhusked summer corn was in a separate shopping bag, as were the mille-feuille from the bakery.

A half hour later the family was in their Outback Subaru, heading east toward the Cape Cod National Seashore preserve. Juliette was buckled into her car seat next to the cooler, an inflatable boogie board, and three folded beach chairs. As per usual Juliette was holding on to Bunny while watching a cartoon on a screen built into the driver's-side headrest. At Juliette's feet were the rest of the beach toys, including pails, sand molds, shovels, and a pair of Kadima paddles.

After crossing Route 6, both Brian and Emma eyed the Wellfleet Police Department as it came into view. The building was a quaint, gable-roofed white clapboard structure with dormers that looked more like a country inn than a police department.

"I can't help but wonder what it would be like being a police officer way out here in the middle of nowhere," she observed. She turned to get a final glimpse of the picturesque building with a split log fence defining a visitor's parking area. There was not a squad car in sight.

"It is hard to imagine," he said with an agreeing nod. He'd had the same thought simultaneous with Emma verbalizing it. This was a frequent occurrence, and they attributed it to how closely their lives had coincided. Not only had they grown up several blocks apart in the same neighborhood in Manhattan and gone to the same grammar school, but they had both ended up majoring in criminal justice in college, with Brian attending Adelphi on Long Island and Emma going to Fordham in the Bronx. Although they also had gone to different high schools, their transcripts were remarkably similar. Both had done well academically, and had been very active in athletics in high school and college. For Brian it was soccer, wrestling, and baseball, and for Emma it was field hockey, basketball, and softball.

"Compared to our law enforcement experiences, it must be incredibly boring," she said as she faced around to look out the windshield. Both she and Brian had matriculated directly into the New York Police Department Academy after college, serving as patrol officers at very busy NYC precincts. After five years of exemplary service, they had been accepted into the elite and prestigious NYPD Emergency Service Unit. It had been when Emma was a cadet at the ESU Academy that their remarkably parallel lives temporally aligned. Brian, who was a member of the ESU A team, volunteered on his days off to help the ESU Academy instructors. It was his way of staying up to date and in shape, and his reward was meeting one of the few female ESU cadets, falling in love, and gaining a wife.

"Especially off season," he said. "To tell you the truth, I wouldn't be able to do it. No way."

They were now passing through mostly pitch pine and black oak forests. They also passed Gull Pond, which was north but near Long Pond, where they had kayaked that morning. As it was their first trip to Cape Cod, they had been pleasantly surprised by the many freshwater ponds with crystal-clear water so close to the ocean on one side and the bay on the other. They'd asked a local about them and had been told it had something to do with glaciers back in the Ice Age.

Gross Hill Road dead-ended into Newcomb Hollow Beach, and as they pulled into the parking lot, they were encouraged. A lot of bedraggled people were heading from the beach to their cars, carrying an enormous quantity of gear, including beach chairs, sun umbrellas, and impressive coolers that made the Murphys' Styrofoam model seem embarrassingly chintzy. Some were tanned regulars, but most were clearly burned visitors.

"Ouch," said Emma, looking at one adolescent girl who appeared as pale as the Murphys. "She's going to be sorry tonight."

"We're in luck," he exclaimed, pulling into a vacant slot remarkably close to the pathway that led from the parking lot to the beach up over an impressive fifty-foot grass-covered dune. As usual, Juliette was excited at the prospect of being on the beach, so she was first out of the car and impatient as Emma and Brian unloaded. Despite her agitation, she was willing to accept carrying the bag of corn and most of her toys in addition to Bunny. While Emma carried the cooler and towels, Brian handled the grill, the briquettes, and the aluminum beach chairs.

It was late afternoon and the sun streaming over their shoulders painted the entire scene in a rich, golden glow. Everyone they passed leaving the beach was wearing their pandemic mask, as were the Murphys. When they crested the dune, Emma and Brian paused to take in the dramatic sight of the wide, sandy beach and the large expanse of the Atlantic. The breeze was onshore, and it carried the sound of the two-to-three-feet-high waves as they broke. Since the tide was going out, there were numerous tide pools, which Juliette loved, since she was a bit intimidated by the ocean. Capping the impressive scene were large cumulus clouds that hung over the vista like dollops of whipped cream.

"Which way?" Juliette called over her shoulder.

"What do you think?" Brian asked Emma.

"I'd say north," she responded after glancing in both directions. "There's less people. And there's a good-sized tide pool directly in front."

"To your left," he shouted to Juliette, who had already run down toward the water's edge.

They set up their camp about a hundred feet north of the path and up against the steep dune embankment. While Brian struggled with the grill, Emma put sunscreen on Juliette before handing the spray can to him. After tossing Bunny onto one of the towels, Juliette immediately bounded off for the tide pool.

"Don't go in the waves until I'm down there with

you," he yelled to her, and she waved back to signal that she had heard.

"When do you think we should eat?" she asked.

Brian shrugged. "It's up to you. Just give me fifteen to twenty minutes' notice to get the briquettes fired up." He poured them into the grill and closed the lid. "Meanwhile, let's join Juliette."

For the next forty-five minutes they ran in the wash from the surf, either chasing or being chased by Juliette. At one point he managed to get Juliette to venture out into the breakers with him holding her hand, but he could tell she really didn't like it, so they quickly went back to the tide pool. Shortly after, Brian could see that Emma was already back preparing the corn at their campsite, which was now in shadow. Taking the hint, he told Juliette it was time to start the barbecue and that he would race her with him running backward. Delighted at the prospect of beating her father, Juliette took off with a squeal and, mostly thanks to Brian getting a late start, gained a commanding lead.

"I'm afraid we have some unwelcome visitors," Emma announced the moment they came running back.

"What do you mean?" he asked. He glanced around, mostly skyward. On their previous visit to Newcomb Hollow Beach they'd had a run-in with a few very persistent seagulls and had been amazed at the birds' boldness.

"No seagulls," she said, reading his mind. "Mosquitoes."

"Really?" he questioned. He was surprised, considering the significant onshore breeze.

"Yes, really," Emma said. "Look!" She raised her left arm and pointed to the base of her deltoid muscle. Poised and obviously preparing to bite was a black mosquito with white markings, but before the insect could do its worst, she slapped it with an open palm. When she pulled her hand away, she could see that the creature was reduced to a tiny bloody corpse, indicating it had already bitten someone else but still wasn't satiated.

"I don't think I've seen a mosquito like that," Brian said. "Rather distinctive coloring."

"I have," Emma said. "It was an Asian tiger mosquito."

"How the hell do you know about Asian tiger mosquitoes?"

"During one of my ESU Academy medical lectures, we learned about arboviral disease and climate change. The lecturer specifically talked about Asian tiger mosquitoes, which used to be restricted to the tropics, but now have spread widely northward all the way up to Maine."

"I never got that lecture," he complained.

"Times have changed, old man," she said with a laugh. "Remember, you were two years ahead of me."

"What's arboviral disease, anyway?"

"Remember reading about yellow fever and building the Panama Canal? Well, yellow fever is an arboviral disease."

"Yikes," Brian said. "Has there ever been yellow fever in the USA?"

"Not since 1905 in New Orleans, if I'm remembering correctly," Emma said. She abruptly ran her fingers through her hair and then waved her hand above her head. "Uh-oh, I can hear more of the bastards. Aren't they bothering you?"

"Not yet. Juliette, do you hear any mosquitoes?"

Juliette didn't answer, but like her mother, she suddenly waved her hands around her head, suggesting she was hearing them.

"Did you bring the bug spray?" Emma asked with urgency.

"It's in the car. I'll run and get it."

"Please," Emma said. "The sooner the better. Otherwise we are going to be miserable."

With no further urging, Brian grabbed his mask, jogged down the beach, and then went up over the dune. As he expected, he found the can of OFF in the glove compartment. When he got back to the beach less than ten minutes later, Juliette was again in the tide pool.

"I tell you," Emma said as she began to apply the repellent, "these winged bastards were aggressive while you were gone. I had to send Juliette down to the water."

"I tried to be quick." He took the spray and applied it as Emma had done and then called Juliette back from the water's edge to protect her as well.

Once the Murphys had the mosquitoes at bay, they were able to get back to their barbecue. The corn cobs went on the grill first, followed by the hamburger patties, and finally the clams. By the time the food was cooked and served, the entire beach was in the shadow of the dunes even though the ocean and the clouds were still in full sun.

After they had eaten their fill and partially cleaned up,

Brian and Emma relaxed back into their respective beach chairs to finish the prosecco, have dessert, and savor the view. The setting sun, which was out of sight behind them, was tinting the puffy clouds pink. Juliette had retreated back down to the edge of the tide pool to make sandcastles in the damp sand.

For a while neither spoke. It was Emma who finally did. "I hate to break the spell," she said, turning to Brian, "but I've been thinking. Maybe we should consider heading back to New York a little early."

"Really? Why? We've got almost another week with the cottage." He was surprised by her suggestion since coming to Cape Cod for vacation had initially been her idea, and they all seemed to be enjoying it immensely. Even the weather was cooperating.

"I'm thinking that maybe if we were back home we could do something to possibly drum up some business."

"Do you have some new idea of how?" he asked. "What little work we had in the late spring totally dried up in July."

Eight months earlier, Brian and Emma had retired from the NYPD to start their own personal protection security agency, which they appropriately called Personal Protection LLC. They had begun the firm with high hopes of success, considering the level of training and experience they had after being NYPD ESU officers—Brian for six years and Emma for four years, on top of each having been a regular police officer for five years. At the time of their retirement from the NYPD, both were sergeants and Brian had already passed the exam for lieutenant with flying colors. A consulting firm that they had hired at the end of the previous summer to advise them had projected rapid success and expansion for Personal Protection after supposedly taking all potential factors into account. Yet no one could have predicted the Covid-19 pandemic, which had reduced the demand for their services to almost nothing. In fact, during the last month they'd had no work whatsoever.

"No, I haven't had any sudden brainstorms," Emma admitted. "But I'm starting to feel uneasy and guilty about us up here lazing around, enjoying ourselves, not knowing what the hell the fall is going to bring. I know we needed a break after being cooped up all spring with the pandemic, especially Juliette, but we've had our fun. I'm ready to go back."

"The fall is clearly not going to be pretty," he said. "As soon as the United Nations Week got canceled, I knew all our projections went out the window. That week alone was going to put our company on the map." With their professional connections with the NYPD, they had had hundreds of referrals, seeing as United Nations Week was an enormous strain on NYPD resources. Back in December they were concerned about having enough manpower to cover even half of the requests.

"Aren't you worried about how we are going to weather this pandemic with all the talk about a fall surge?" she asked. "I mean, we're already behind on our mortgage."

Both Brian and Emma had been thrifty and fiscally conservative even as children. When they started working for the NYPD, they'd saved more than their friends and colleagues, and also invested wisely. When they had married following Emma's graduation from the ESU Academy and just before Juliette's birth, they'd been able to splurge on one of the few freestanding, Tudor-revival, single-family homes in Inwood, on West 217th Street. It was a mere block away from her parents' home on Park Terrace West. The house was their only major asset besides the Subaru.

"A lot of people are behind on their mortgage payments," Brian countered. "And we spoke with our loan officer. Plus, we do have some cash receivables. The mortgage is not going to cause a problem. I think we've made the right choice to keep our cash to cover our other major business-related expenses, like Camila's salary."

Camila Perez was Personal Protection LLC's only employee. When the pandemic exploded in the New York area, she'd moved in with the Murphys and had been living with them ever since. It was one of the benefits of having a house with adequate living space. Over the course of the spring she'd become more like family than an employee. The Murphys had even encouraged her to come with them to Cape Cod, but she had responsibly declined in order to handle anything that came up in relation to the company. During the previous week, there had been a couple of inquiries about Personal Protection providing security for some high-end fall weddings in the Hamptons.

"You are obviously handling this all better than I am," Emma confessed. "I'm impressed that you're able to compartmentalize so well."

"Truthfully, I'm not doing that great. I'm worried, too," he admitted. "But my worry comes mostly in the middle of the night when my mind can't shut down. Out here on the beach with the sun and surf, thankfully it all seems so far away."

"Do you mind if we continue talking about this now, while we're enjoying this glorious scene? Or do you want me to shut up?"

"Of course I don't mind," Brian said. "Talk as much as you want!"

"Well, what's bugging me at the moment is whether it was a good idea for both of us to leave the NYPD together," she said. "Maybe one of us should have remained on salary."

"In hindsight that might have been prudent," Brian agreed. "But that's not what we wanted. We both felt an entrepreneurial tug to do something creative and outside the box. How could we have decided who would have the fun challenge and who would have had to continue slogging with the same old, same old? Draw straws or flip a coin? Besides, I'm still confident it is all going to be just fine as soon as this damn coronavirus disaster works itself out. And we're certainly not alone. Millions are caught in this pandemic squeeze."

"I hope you are right," Emma said with a sigh, before quickly slapping the side of her head. "Damn! Those mosquitoes are back. Why aren't they biting you?"

"No clue." He reached behind her chair for the can of OFF and handed it to her. "I guess I'm just not as sweet as you," he said with one of his typical mischievous smiles.

CHAPTER 2

August 19

It was the raucous sound of a flock of seagulls loudly arguing with one another out in Wellfleet Harbor that awoke Brian after yet another pleasant night's sleep. Rolling onto his back, he looked out the window through the white sheer curtain fabric, wondering what time it was. He looked at his phone and saw that it was 6:25. Glancing over to Emma's side of the bed, he saw that she was already up, like almost every morning lately, and he smiled in anticipation of the pastries that would be waiting for him once he got out of bed.

With the birds still squawking in the distance, Brian got up to use the cottage's single bathroom, but just before entering from the common hall, a glance into the living room surprised him. He could see Emma fast asleep on the couch. Being that she was an early riser, he guessed she'd possibly had a poor night's sleep, perhaps from worrying about their precarious financial situation, a subject she'd been raising every day since the night of their barbecue. Fearing he was correct, he made it a point to be as quiet as possible. Coming back out of the bathroom, he had another idea that would make it even less likely he'd disturb her. He'd be the one to head out and get the pastries. Whatever the reason was that had her sleeping outside of their bed, he thought she deserved as much time to rest as she wanted.

After silently pulling on some bike shorts and a shirt, Brian checked to see if Juliette was stirring. She wasn't, which he expected. With the amount of exercise she'd been getting combined with being allowed to stay up later than usual in the evening to play board games, she must have been exhausted. Satisfied, he carried his bike shoes while tiptoeing through the living room. As carefully as he could, he closed the otherwise noisy screen door without a sound, pleased he'd managed to leave without waking his wife.

Cycling past the Wellfleet Harbor, he could see the source of the seagulls' frenzy, which was still ongoing. Fishermen were cleaning their catches. Beyond the harbor, Brian passed through the attractive downtown of Wellfleet with its well-maintained period buildings, some of which were hundreds of years old, and he was particularly enamored of those with neo-Grecian Doric columns.

Unfortunately, most of the rest of the trip was on the main highway, which lacked the scenery of the smaller roads. But it wasn't far and there was almost no traffic. To get maximum benefit from the exercise, he cranked up his speed, arriving at the bakery in less than fifteen minutes. Although the shop had yet to open, there were already several people waiting as a testament to its popularity.

Twenty minutes later, Brian was back on his bike, now heading north. When he arrived at the cottage, he returned his bike to the garage and then entered as quietly as possible. To his surprise, Emma was no longer on the couch. Instead, she was now back in their room curled up in a fetal position on the bed, and though her eyes were open, she didn't stir upon his arrival.

"I feel terrible. I had a very bad night."

"I'm so sorry, my sweet," Brian said as he sat on the edge of the bed. "What's wrong?" He was surprised to see her sick, because she was the most resistant of the three of them when it came to winter colds and other ailments. The usual progression was Juliette first, probably picking up something at preschool or at one of her playdates, and then she'd give it to him. More often than not, Emma wouldn't succumb, despite being the major caregiver.

"I just feel awful all around," Emma managed.

"Do you feel feverish?"

"Yes. I've had chills and I've been sweating."

Gently Brian reached out and placed his palm on her forehead. There was no doubt in his mind that she was burning up.

"I've also been vomiting," Emma continued. "I'm surprised I didn't wake you."

"I wish you had," he responded worriedly.

"Why?" she said with seeming irritation. "What would you have been able to do?"

"I don't know," Brian said. "Just be with you."

"There's nothing you could have done," Emma countered. "I also ache all over, and I have a bad headache and a stiff neck. I've never felt this terrible."

"Can I at least get you an ibuprofen?" He reached out and tried to rub Emma's back, wanting to help somehow, but she moved away from his touch.

"I suppose an ibuprofen can't hurt," she said, resettling herself in the center of the bed.

"Have you had a sore throat, cough, or any difficulty breathing?"

"No," she said with force. "I know what you're thinking, but this isn't coronavirus. I can't imagine it could be, from what I've heard about Covid-19. I also haven't lost my sense of smell. Nothing like that."

"Nonetheless, we will have to get you tested for coronavirus," Brian said calmly. "We have to rule it out."

"Whatever," Emma said irritably.

"Are you hungry at all?" he asked. "I've brought back almond croissants."

"I told you I feel sick to my stomach. Do you really think I'd want an almond croissant?"

"Okay, okay," Brian soothed. "I'll get you an ibuprofen. Maybe two." He stood up and went into the bathroom to get the pills, and then into the kitchen for a glass of water. He was a little surprised at Emma's apparent anger. It wasn't like her in the slightest. Whenever she felt under the weather in the past, she never acted irritated. If anything, she tended to downplay her symptoms.

After he gave her the pills, she took the medication and then flopped back onto the bed.

"I'm going to find out where the hospital is out here," Brian said. "Is there anything I can get for you at the moment?" She merely shook her head and closed her eyes.

Out in the living room, Brian opened up his laptop to search for the nearest hospital, thinking that would be the easiest way to get Emma tested for coronavirus. Knowing the variability of the Covid-19 symptoms, he wondered why she was so sure she didn't have it. One way or the other, they needed to know. He also briefly thought about trying to find a local MD but doubted a country doctor could add much to what he already knew. The medical courses he'd taken at the ESU Academy had been extensive, certainly qualifying both him and Emma to be full-fledged EMTs. If he had to guess, he thought that Emma had most likely contracted a case of food poisoning, possibly from the clams they had had for dinner even though he didn't seem to have any symptoms. What he hoped was that within twenty-four hours or so, she would be on the mend.

It didn't take long for him to find out what he needed, and after he had, he returned to the bedroom. She was lying on her back in the center of the bed with her eyes closed.

"Emma?" Brian whispered. If she had fallen asleep, he didn't want to wake her.

"What?" she said without opening her eyes.

"The closest hospital is Cape Cod Hospital," Brian said. "It's in Hyannis, which is forty-five minutes away. I suggest we drive to the hospital as soon as you feel up to it. The sooner you have a coronavirus test, the sooner we'll get the results."

"I don't want to go to some fly-by-night hospital out here in the sticks." She looked up at him with her hazel eyes on fire.

"I don't think you're being fair," Brian argued. "From what I've read online, it seems it's held in reasonably high esteem. Besides, at the moment all we're looking for is a coronavirus test."

"No way! I want to go back to New York. If I need a hospital, I want a real hospital."

"You really want to go home today?" he asked.

"Yes," Emma snapped. "I don't like how I feel and I'm worried I might get worse. This isn't just some cold."

"Okay, okay," Brian said reassuringly. "We'll head back today. I'll pack our stuff, load the car, and strap on the bikes and the kayak. Try to take it easy in the meantime."

CHAPTER 3

Packing all their belongings and loading the car took a lot longer than Brian had anticipated. Part of the problem was having to deal with Juliette. Emma's irritability particularly disturbed Juliette, who didn't seem to understand why she was being ignored by her mother. As a consequence, he had to spend a lot of time trying to console her and keep her occupied. What worked the best was getting Juliette intimately involved with the packing and loading, but the problem was that it then took far longer than if Brian had been able to do it all on his own.

It was just after eleven when they were finally able to pull out of the driveway and start the five-hour drive back to the Big Apple. Since Juliette's car seat was behind the driver's side, Brian was able to lower Emma's seat back to a reclined position. He'd made some sandwiches and stocked the cooler with water and fruit juice for their ride. He wanted to get Emma home as soon as possible.

For most of the way Brian was on his own, as Juliette

was watching cartoons and Emma was sleeping, with her head on the pillow pressed up against the side of the car. A bit of perspiration dotted her forehead, indicating her fever was persisting.

The quiet gave Brian more time to worry anew about the condition of Personal Protection LLC. As he had confessed to Emma, being on vacation in a totally new location had made it possible for him to put work completely out of his mind. But now that they were heading home, all his concerns came flooding back. The reality was that very few wealthy businesspeople who needed security were traveling into the city because of the pandemic, and with the expected fall surge that probably wasn't going to change. All he could hope for was that one of the rare inquiries they'd gotten about the high-profile fall weddings would pan out to be an actual gig. For that reason, he was looking forward to finding out from Camila if there had been any movement whatsoever toward a possible commitment.

Although traffic had only been moderate without any significant delays, he felt definite relief when they reached the Henry Hudson Bridge. It meant they were almost home, and he was anxious to get Emma into bed and take her temperature. A small amount of sweat had continued to dot her forehead for the entire trip, and he also knew that Juliette was nearing the absolute end of her patience while strapped into her car seat.

So when disaster struck, Brian's mind was completely absorbed by the details of how he would manage getting both Emma and Juliette out of the car and into the house efficiently. The first hint of a calamity was a peculiar rhythmic thumping coming from someplace under the car's dash. Within seconds he was aware of movement to his right that coincided with the noise. As his eyes darted in that direction, he realized to his horror that Emma was caught in the agonal throes of what could only be a seizure. Her feet and legs alternately pounded against both the underside of the dashboard and the floorboards of the car. At the same time, she was grotesquely arching her back, straining against her seat belt with her arms wildly flailing and her head slamming again and again against the car's window.

Practically losing control of the car as he ducked away from Emma's pummeling left hand, Brian fought with the steering wheel as the vehicle heaved from side to side, tires screeching. The instant he regained control, he slammed on the brakes and with difficulty managed to pull to the side of the road despite angry honking and rude gestures from other drivers. By now, Juliette was screaming.

From his EMT lectures, he knew he had to keep her from injuring herself until her seizure abated, and thankfully the car's seat belt helped. His biggest concern was her head, which he was able to keep away from the car's metal frame, letting it hit up against the pillow during her violent contractions. With his other hand he tried to keep her powerful legs from injuring themselves against the dash. The fact that she was in such good physical shape made it that much more difficult. Brian had to use all the strength he had.

Although at the time it seemed interminable, finally her contractions lessened and then abated altogether, and Brian could let her sag back against the seat and the car's door with her head against the window. Instinctively he knew it had only been a couple of minutes. A bit of blood trickled from her mouth, suggesting she had bitten her tongue, but he could see that she was breathing normally again.

He straightened up in his seat and quickly unbuckled his seat belt. Juliette was crying uncontrollably in the back, so after leaping out of the car, Brian opened the back door, leaned in, and enveloped his daughter in his arms. He told her over and over that all was okay, that Mommy was fine, and that they would take her to the hospital.

"Now Daddy has to keep driving, okay, sweetheart?" Brian soothed at length when Juliette's tears lessened. Gently he removed her arms from around his head.

Somewhat reluctantly, Juliette let him straighten up. After he gave her shoulder another reassuring squeeze, he got back into the front seat and checked Emma again. She was awake, but seemed disoriented. He told her that they were almost home but that he was going to take her to the hospital, the same hospital where Juliette had been born. He also told her that she had just had a seizure, to which she nodded but didn't respond audibly.

After exiting the Henry Hudson Parkway at the Dyckman Street exit, it was only a short drive to the Inwood campus of the Manhattan Memorial Hospital. Like all New York City boroughs, Inwood had several hospitals.

The Murphys had chosen the MMH, as it was known in the neighborhood, for Juliette's birth because it was where Emma had had her tonsils removed when she was a child. It was also familiar to Brian. During his second year as an NYPD patrolman, he'd been assigned to the 34th Precinct for a number of months to fill in for someone on sick leave and in that capacity had spent quite a bit of time at the hospital, particularly getting some work on many of his days and evenings off. It had been a way for him to make extra money, as the hospital liked having a uniformed officer on-site. He had spent enough time there that he'd even gotten to know a few of the doctors and nurses on a first-name basis.

"Is Mommy going to stay at the hospital?" Juliette asked as Brian turned off Broadway onto the hospital grounds.

"I doubt it," he said. "But we have to see what the doctors say. We just want to make sure she's okay."

Brian drove up to the Emergency Department entrance and pulled to a stop at the ambulance dock.

"Emma, how are you doing now?" he asked. "Are you okay walking into the hospital or do you want me to get a gurney for you?"

"I'm okay," she said in a monotone, speaking up for the first time since the seizure.

"Are you sure?" To Brian she still seemed somewhat disoriented, certainly not herself. Even though she didn't answer, he got out of the car, got Juliette out, and walked around to the passenger side. When he opened the door, Emma made no effort to move, so he reached in and undid her seat belt. He then made sure they all had their face masks on.

"All right," he said. "Let's get you inside." Gently he encouraged her to climb out of the car and with somewhat unsteady legs she walked into the ED holding Brian's hand for support.

CHAPTER 4

August 19

As it was 4:30 and getting close to dinnertime, the Emergency Department was only moderately busy. The Murphys had to stand for a short time at the information counter, but when Brian explained why they were there, a pleasant triage nurse immediately ushered them into a treatment cubicle and encouraged Emma to lie down. As she took Emma's vital signs and got more of a history, a clerk who had accompanied them got their name and health insurance information. The clerk also got Brian to sign a permission-for-treatment form. Once the paperwork was done, Brian and Juliette hurried back outside to deal with the car.

At the car Juliette started crying inconsolably, demanding that she wanted her mommy through near hysterical tears. Although normally quite patient with his daughter, Brian felt unnerved himself, and when she refused to get into her car seat, he had to forcibly control himself. Doing so made him realize that he needed some backup. Although he could have called his mother, Aimée, he chose to call Camila, who'd become almost a surrogate mother for Juliette over the previous five months. As he expected, Camila was horrified when she learned what had happened to Emma and immediately offered to come over to MMH to take charge of Juliette.

"Okay, sweetie pie," he said to Juliette as he disconnected the call. With help on the way, he felt he had a better hold on his emotions. "Camila is coming to take you home."

Juliette greeted this news with even more forceful tears, but Brian took it in stride. He knew she would feel better as soon as she was back in familiar surroundings. He picked up Juliette and held her close to comfort her, and though she continued to cry with less intensity, she still pressed her face into the crook of his neck and hugged him forcibly.

In just a little more than ten minutes, Camila arrived. A moment later she was reaching out for Juliette, who was happy to transfer from Brian's arms to Camila's. "Oh, my poor baby," she said while hugging the child. It was obvious she had a strong maternal instinct, and he greatly appreciated her presence in his life in moments like this.

Camila was a thirty-two-year-old first-generation Cuban American with an engaging, upbeat personality, a ready smile, and frequent laughter. She looked more like a teenager than an adult, especially with her preferred dress being fashionably ripped jeans. She was of medium height and build with long dark hair parted in the middle and an olive complexion that both Brian and Emma coveted, as she never had to bother with sunblock. Like Brian and Emma, she had spent most of her life in Inwood, and they shared some common friends. The difference was that she had grown up on the predominantly Latino east side of Broadway whereas Brian and Emma had been on the largely Irish west side.

Like Brian, Camila had gone to Adelphi University but had majored in business, which was the reason she'd responded to Brian and Emma's employment search. They had specified that they were looking for someone to help with a startup security business. Luckily for both parties, from day one it had seemed a match made in heaven since Camila's business know-how complemented Brian and Emma's law enforcement experience. When the pandemic exploded in the New York area in March, asking Camila to move in was an easy decision, as was her decision to accept. She had several aging grandparents living at home with serious health issues whom she wanted to avoid putting at risk.

"I'll be home with Emma as soon as possible," Brian told her as he gave Juliette Bunny, which she grabbed and enveloped with a bear hug.

"No worries," she said. "I'll grab dinner and make sure Juliette is occupied."

"I can't thank you enough. You're a lifesaver."

After watching Camila drive away and knowing Juliette was being taken care of, he felt significantly more at ease and capable of dealing with the situation. The first thing he did was go back to the check-in counter to ask if there was any information available on his wife, but all he was told was that the doctor would be out to talk to him shortly.

Brian took a seat as far away from other people as he could, which required moving to the end of the room since the ED was already busier than it had been only fifteen minutes earlier. From his previous experience at the hospital as a uniformed patrolman, he remembered there was always a buildup of activity just before and then another after dinner.

The time passed slowly. To entertain himself he took out his phone, and with some reluctance he called his mother, Aimée. He knew that, as the family matriarch, she would be very upset and insist on helping, possibly by offering to come directly to the hospital, even though it would probably cause more stress than good. But he felt an obligation to let her know what was happening. She answered with her lilting and charming French accent, which she had never lost.

Aimée had grown up in the northern part of France—Normandy, to be exact—and had come to the United States forty-one years ago to attend prestigious Barnard College. It was there that she had met Brian's father, who happened at the time to be attending Columbia University on a sports scholarship. Aimée's maiden name was Juliette, a somewhat rare family name even in France, and in her honor Emma and Brian had named their daughter Juliette.

Brian evaded any small talk with Aimée, immediately telling her that he was calling from the MMH ED because Emma had suffered a seizure in the car as they drove into Manhattan following her sudden flu-like symptoms from the morning.

"Oh, my goodness. I'm so sorry to hear," Aimée said with concern. "Is she all right now?"

"There's been no word yet from the doctors," he informed her. "She is being seen as we speak. She walked in under her own power but seemed somewhat disoriented."

"Do you think she has coronavirus?" Aimée asked.

"I hope not," Brian said. "Actually, I don't think so because she didn't have any of the big three symptoms, like cough, difficulty breathing, or loss of sense of smell. But who knows? She did have a fever. We'll have to see."

"And where's Juliette?"

"Camila came to pick her up just a few minutes ago. We've only been here an hour or so."

"How about you? Are you okay?"

"I'm hanging in there," he said. "Though I'll admit it's been a bit unnerving. This is the first time I've ever really seen Emma sick."

"I can well imagine you'd feel out of sorts. Do you want me to come and keep you company?"

"It's not necessary," Brian said. "I'm doing okay now that Juliette is being taken care of. Besides, the hospital is discouraging family visitors with the pandemic going on for obvious reasons. I promise I'll let you know as soon as I know anything."

"D'accord," Aimée said. She had a habit of sprinkling French expressions into her conversations. "I'll call Emma's mother and let her know. Of course, she may want to come to the ED. You know Hannah has a mind of her own."

"Please try to discourage her. I'll let you know the moment I learn anything, and you can let her know."

After speaking with his mother, he debated whether to call his two older brothers or his younger sister, more as a way of keeping his mind occupied than anything else. While he was still debating, he heard his name called out by a tall, slim, relatively young doctor who'd stepped into the waiting room from the depths of the ED. Dressed in rumpled scrubs, a surgical hat, and face mask, he looked the part of a harried emergency physician with a raft of pens jammed into his breast pocket and a stethoscope slung around his neck.

Brian stood up and waved to get the doctor's attention.

"Mr. Brian Murphy?" the doctor questioned yet again as he neared He had lowered his voice considerably. "You are Emma Murphy's husband?" He had a lilting accent Brian associated with people from the Indian sub continent.

"I am," Brian responded. He felt himself stiffen, sensing from the doctor's tone that all was not well.

"My name is Dr. Darsh Kumar. I have important news about your wife."

"Okay," Brian said slowly, bracing himself for what he was about to hear.

"She's going to be admitted to the hospital. In fact, she has to be taken to the Intensive Care Unit."

"Okay," he repeated, feeling increasingly panicked but trying to calm himself. "Why the ICU?"

"She had another seizure while she was being examined," Dr. Kumar explained. "However, we were able to control it rapidly since we already had an IV running. She's resting comfortably now, but is disoriented. We want her to be closely monitored."

Brian nodded. His mind was racing around at warp speed. "More disoriented than when she arrived?"

"Probably, but not necessarily. I can't say for sure."

"Is there a diagnosis? Could this be coronavirus?"

"It's possible, but not probable with these symptoms," Dr. Kumar said. "What we are certain of is that she has some sort of encephalitis, meaning an inflammation of the brain."

"I've heard of encephalitis. I've had EMT training," Brian explained.

"What we don't yet know is the specific etiology," Dr. Kumar continued. "We suspect viral. We did a spinal tap and have sent the specimens to the lab. They will soon let us know what we are dealing with. If I had to guess, I'd say possibly something like West Nile virus or possibly even Lyme disease. Did you have much contact with mosquitoes or ticks while you were on Cape Cod?"

"No ticks, but we did have some mosquitoes during a beach barbecue four or five days ago."

"That could be it, which would favor a viral disease. But there is no reason to speculate at this point. It won't change our treatment."

"What's the treatment?"

"Essentially just supportive. She's on supplemental oxygen. Even though we were able to stop her seizure quickly, her oxygen level fell considerably."

"Can I see her?" Brian asked desperately.

"Not at the moment," Dr. Kumar said. "She's getting an MRI and a CT scan."

"Both? Why both?"

"I leave that up to our radiology colleagues. Meanwhile the business office needs to speak to you about your wife's admission." He pointed across the room to a door that had ADMITTING stenciled on it, and then turned and started to leave.

"Excuse me," Brian called after him. "I would like to see my wife when I can."

"I'll let the nurses know," Dr. Kumar said over his shoulder before quickly disappearing whence he came.

After taking a deep breath to fortify himself, Brian picked up the few things he had brought in with him and walked over to the Admitting office. He had no idea what they wanted from him since he'd already given their information to the ED clerk.

It was a reasonably sized room with several rows of chairs facing two desks. On the cream-colored walls were multiple framed photographs of mostly serious-looking men in business suits although there were several women. He assumed they were hospital administrators. Only one of the desks was occupied, by a middle-aged woman with dark hair and eyes. She was wearing a colorful flower-print dress under a white lab coat.

"Mr. Murphy?" the woman called out as soon as Brian entered. She and Brian were the only people in the room.

"Yes," he said. "Brian Murphy." He could see her name was Maria Hernandez. He approached her desk,

where a large plexiglass shield had been added in recent
months. Like a cashier's window at a bank, there was a
slot for passing papers to and fro along its base.

"Brian Murphy," Maria repeated while tilting her
head to the side to give him a good once-over. "Were you
related to Deputy Inspector Conor Murphy, the commanding officer of the 34th Precinct, by any chance?"

"He was my father," Brian said, surprised that she recognized him with his face mask. Luckily the short time
Brian had been assigned to the 34th Precinct was before
his father had become the CO.

"I knew it the moment you walked in here," Maria
said, as if proud of herself. "You're certainly your father's
son. My husband, Adolpho, who was the sanitation supervisor for Inwood, knew your father very well. In fact,
they shared many an after-hour beer."

"Unfortunately, my father shared far too many beers,"
he responded. He didn't want to be reminded of that
aspect of his father, who ultimately fell victim to the Irish
curse of alcoholism and had died a year and a half earlier.
At the same time, Maria's comment reminded him of the
benefit as well as the disadvantage of living within one of
the many tight-knit New York neighborhoods. Lives
were inextricably intertwined.

"Isn't that the truth," Maria said grimly. "Same can
be said about my Adolpho, bless his soul. Aren't you a
policeman, too?"

"I was. In December I left the force to start my own
business. One of my brothers is a cop and so was my
uncle, grandfather, and great-grandfather." Brian had

loved being a policeman and had longed to become one for as long as he could remember. But part of the reason he left the force was to avoid the trap that had ensnared his father, grandfather, and great-grandfather. The security business had been a way to use his law enforcement background and experience in a new and creative way, without it becoming too routine or depressing.

"And who is this Emma Murphy?" Maria said, holding up the admission papers.

"That's my wife," Brian said. "Emma O'Brien. You probably know her father and mother. Her father started Inwood Plumbing and Heating."

"Yes, I know of her. I'm sorry she's being admitted, especially to the ICU."

"I am, too. What do I need to do here?"

"Just sign these admission forms for me," Maria said. She slid the stack of papers through the slot in the plexiglass.

He leafed through the stack, and he could see it was the usual legalese that he detested and for which he had little patience. It reminded him of income tax forms. "What is all this?" he asked.

"The customary material. It's mostly to give the hospital and our fine doctors and nurses the right to take care of your wife. It also means you are agreeing to pay for the necessary services."

"Does it have our health insurance information?" Brian asked.

"Whatever you gave to the ED clerk, I put in there," Maria said. "Slip it back to me and I'll make sure."

Brian did as he was told. Using her index finger, Maria rapidly flipped through the pages. In a moment she'd found the correct one. "Yes, here it is. Peerless Health Insurance with the policy number. You're fine."

"Okay, good," he said with relief. "Let me sign it."

Maria shoved the pages back through the hole in the plexiglass. While Brian was signing, she asked: "Why do you have Peerless insurance? Why don't you have your official NYC insurance? I mean, you were a policeman for years, right? I still have my Adolpho's plan. It's really terrific."

"When Emma and I left the force to start our company, which was far more expensive an undertaking than we thought, we had to pinch pennies. We couldn't afford the premiums to keep our NYPD insurance, so we turned to the short-term market. Peerless offered what we needed. We felt obligated to be covered because of our daughter. She'd been a preemie." He slid the signed document back through the plexiglass.

"It does seem to be a quite popular company," Maria agreed. "I've seen a lot of it lately. Okay, you are good to go, and I hope Emma gets better quickly."

"Thanks, Maria. Nice chatting with you."

Brian returned to the main waiting area. As someone who was a committed "doer," he found this kind of inactivity a strain. Yet he couldn't leave without having more information and reassurance about Emma's condition. To make certain that the powers that be knew he was still there, he went back to the information desk and essentially rechecked in. He told the clerk that Dr. Kumar had informed the nurses that he wanted to see his wife as soon as her MRI and CT scans were done. The clerk assured him that the nurses would surely let him know the moment they could. With a strong suspicion the woman was merely placating him, he nonetheless took a seat as far away from everyone as possible and committed himself to waiting.

Another hour crept by. Brian watched as an endless cast of characters either walked into the ED or were carried in. Some came with extended family, most of whom were denied entry by the security people because of the coronavirus situation. Under less stressful circumstances he might have found the scene mildly entertaining as a reflection of life in Inwood. He even recognized some of the patients or the accompanying family members, but he didn't talk to anyone, preferring to hide behind his mask and just observe.

"Mr. Murphy?" a voice asked.

Brian turned away from the scene of another ambulance arriving to find himself looking up into the masked and shielded face of Ms. Claire Baxter, RN, as evidenced by her name tag.

"Yes, I'm Brian Murphy."

"Dr. Kumar said you'd like to see your wife before she is transferred upstairs. Come with me."

He quickly got to his feet and followed the nurse back into the Emergency Department's busy hinterland. He was shown into one of the larger treatment rooms, where Emma was seemingly asleep on a gurney with its rails raised. To his great relief she looked entirely normal save for a nasal cannula providing oxygen and a stocking cap covering her red hair. She even had a very slight but healthy-looking tan on her normally porcelain cheeks, which made the IV and an oximeter on one of her index fingers look totally out of place. Dr. Kumar was busy studying MRI images on a flat-screen monitor.

Brian approached the gurney and closed his fingers around Emma's forearm, hoping that she'd wake up. She didn't budge.

"She's sleeping off the considerable medication we gave her to control her seizure," Dr. Kumar explained, speaking rapidly. He quickly moved around to the other side of the bed. "She is still quite disoriented, but I'm happy to say that her oxygen saturation now is entirely normal. That means her lung function is steady, which we feel lessens the chance we are dealing with coronavirus or will be in need of a ventilator. She tested negative for SARS-CoV-2, by the way."

"That's encouraging," he said. "What did the MRI and the CT scans show?"

"Both are consistent with viral encephalitis," Dr. Kumar said. "More importantly I spoke with an infectious disease specialist. She told me that considering the history of you and your wife having just been on Cape Cod and that beach incident you recounted, she'd favor a diagnosis of eastern equine encephalitis rather than West Nile, which we'll be testing for. She reminded me that Massachusetts has seen an uptick in EEE over the last couple of years."

"I've never heard of EEE."

"You and a lot of other people," Dr. Kumar said. "But that's going to alter with climate change. Mark my words."

"Is EEE serious?" Brian asked hesitantly, not sure he wanted to hear the answer.

"Yes, it can be. Particularly when there are neurological symptoms."

"Like my wife is experiencing."

"Like your wife is experiencing," Dr. Kumar agreed. "It's why I want her in the ICU. I want her to be closely observed, particularly for more seizure activity and changes in her orientation and oxygenation level."

"How long do you think she will be in the ICU?" Brian asked. "I think it might stress her out even more."

"With luck, just a few days," Dr. Kumar said. "One of the ICU hospitalists will call you in the morning and let you know how she is doing."

"I appreciate that," he said. "Tell me, is EEE contagious?"

"Not from person to person," Dr. Kumar assured him.

"At least there's that," Brian said.

"It's a mosquito-borne illness, which, simply enough, means it's becoming more and more important to avoid mosquitoes. Especially during evening barbecues like you mentioned. That's when those Asian tiger mosquitoes are out in force."

At that moment several orderlies appeared. Without a word one went to the head of Emma's gurney, where he disengaged the brake, while the other went to the foot and began guiding it out of the treatment room. Brian was able to follow and quickly give her arm one more squeeze before watching her disappear from the room. He couldn't help but wonder when he would be seeing her again, especially since he assumed that ICU visitation was most likely limited these days.

"I can show you back to the waiting room," Ms. Baxter offered.

Brian merely nodded and followed the nurse, passing out through the same door as Emma had just been pushed, but turning in the opposite direction once out in the hallway. He'd hoped to feel more encouraged after seeing Emma for himself, but he didn't. He also didn't respond to the nurse's small talk, too distracted by a wave of anger directed at fate. First it had been the coronavirus that had derailed all their carefully laid plans for their new security business. And now it was this illness he'd never heard of threatening his wife. And to make matters worse, it happened while they were trying to make the best of a difficult situation by having a bit of family fun in the face of the pandemic.

Five minutes later Brian started the short walk from MMH to his home on West 217th Street. Just getting out of the hospital helped his mindset to a degree. Yet he still felt as if he'd run an emotional marathon. Transitioning from yesterday to today boggled him. He couldn't imagine two days being so different. Yesterday he'd been capable of feeling relatively happy despite the obstacles they faced, and today he was overwhelmed with worry about Emma.

When he walked into the house, he was relieved that

Juliette was already fast asleep in bed. He'd been concerned about how he would find the patience to deal with her needs. Camila said she hadn't eaten much dinner but had been eager to go to bed after having a long bath.

"You are more than a lifesaver, you're a godsend," Brian told her after looking in at his peacefully sleeping daughter clutching her beloved Bunny. "You certainly have a way with her that I'm so thankful for. As hard as she was crying at the hospital, I was worried she'd be up all night."

He closed Juliette's door silently to avoid waking her.

"She's a joy," Camila said. "Emma's seizure and then the hospital frightened her, and she just needed to get home to calm down. How is Emma?"

"I only got to see her for a few seconds," Brian said. "She was sleeping off some medication, so I wasn't able to speak with her."

"I'm sure she is going to be just fine. Did they give you any idea when she might be coming home?"

"No, they didn't. I guess we'll just have to see how it goes and keep our fingers crossed." He didn't mention that Emma had had a second seizure. He wasn't sure why, although he guessed it was because he was trying to forget it.

"How about we have some dinner?" Camila suggested. "On the way home from MMH I picked up enough takeout from Floridita for the three of us: pulled pork, black beans, and yellow rice. Juliette didn't do it justice."

"That was thoughtful," Brian said. "The idea of dealing with food hadn't even occurred to me. What did we do to deserve you?"

"I think the feeling's pretty mutual," she said with one of her characteristic laughs. "It's been a real win-win situation."

Over dinner Camila shared some good news. She said that she'd gotten a serious inquiry that afternoon about security needs for a weekend-long wedding planned for the middle of October out in Southampton. "Apparently it's going to be a sizable affair with people flying in on their private jets from all over the country. The man's name is Calvin Foster of Priority Capital. He made the call himself, which impressed me. He asked to speak to you directly and gave me his number. I told him that you would call him back tomorrow."

"Wow," Brian said. "Did he say anything at all about Covid-19 restrictions?"

"He did," Camila said. "Everyone will be required to be tested before arrival, and he's going to have an on-site testing setup."

"Whoa! That is good news," he said. "A big wedding like that will be a significant financial shot in the arm, especially if we will be tasked to take care of some of the guests as well."

"The number to call is on your desk in the office," she said. When Emma and Brian had started Personal Protection LLC, they'd turned the home's formal dining room into a dedicated office with desks for all three of them.

"Did he happen to mention how he got word about us?" Brian asked. The conundrum of publicity from day one had only been made worse by the lockdown. Lately they had only been doing online advertising and not even much of that. With people staying at home, there was simply no real need for security.

"He did. He said he'd gotten the number from Deputy Chief Michael Comstock."

"Really? Terrific! That's encouraging," he exclaimed. Deputy Chief Michael Comstock was the commanding officer of the Emergency Service Unit of the NYPD. Brian had served under him for the six years he'd been with the unit and Emma for four. When Brian and Emma had resigned from the NYPD, they had been mildly concerned the CO was resentful, since he skipped their departure party without any explanation. The fact that he was now recommending Personal Protection was a very good sign.

After dinner, while Brian cleaned up the kitchen, Camila went back to the office to work on their accounts receivable in hopes of scaring up some receipts. A bit later he joined her to do some research on eastern equine encephalitis. After he spent some time reading about it, he wished he hadn't, especially given the paranoia about viruses engendered by the Covid-19 pandemic. EEE was a very alarming illness with a variety of possible consequences, and now that his beloved wife had possibly contracted it, he had a nagging fear that they would be facing a long road to recovery.

CHAPTER 5

August 20

It was one of the worst night's sleep Brian could remember having. He kept waking up, tossing and turning, wondering how Emma was faring in the ICU. He hoped that the heavy medication they had given her to stop her second seizure kept her asleep, so she wouldn't be tormented by the stressful environment. At just after four A.M. he was wandering around the house for the second time, arguing with himself about whether to call the hospital and check on Emma's status. Ultimately, he didn't call, not because he didn't want to but because he doubted he'd get through, and the effort might make him feel even more frustrated and nervous than he already was.

By eight o'clock both Juliette and Camila were up, and while Juliette watched cartoons, Brian and Camila had coffee in the breakfast nook. He told her what a bad night he had had, and she wasn't surprised.

"I think it would be best if you try to keep yourself as occupied today as possible," Camila said in response.

"Make that call to Calvin Foster. It would be terrific for multiple reasons if you could secure us a major security engagement. It would keep Personal Protection moving in the right direction."

"That's the understatement of the year," Brian said. "Good suggestion. I'll make the call for sure. How about you?"

"I think I'll concentrate on keeping Juliette happy and calm," Camila said. "She is going to miss Emma terribly. I know because my mother was hospitalized with pneumonia when I was about Juliette's age, and I still remember how devastated and abandoned I felt."

"She is suffering," he agreed, glancing over at Juliette. "I can tell. I didn't know four-year-olds could get depressed, but she's acting that way. Usually she wakes up a ball of energy. This morning I found her in her bed awake, just lying there and staring into the distance. Let's be more lenient than usual with the cartoons." Under normal circumstances Juliette's screen time was sharply limited, but they needed something to keep her distracted.

"I agree," Camila said. "Since there's nothing for me to do in the office and since it's a nice summer day, I'll take her out to Isham Park this morning to let her get some exercise. She loves climbing on the rocks."

"Great idea to get her out and active," Brian agreed. "I'll make an effort to take her to the Emerson Playground after lunch, which she also likes, particularly the swings."

By nine o'clock, with Camila and Juliette out of the

house, he parked himself at his desk in the home office. The first thing he did was google Calvin Foster and Priority Capital. He was duly impressed. It was one of the larger New York private equity firms and had a stellar record, and Calvin Foster was considered a particularly sharp financier and shrewd investor. Just when he was about to try to call him, Brian's phone rang. It was Dr. Gail Garner, one of the MMH intensivist physicians.

"Mrs. Murphy is doing well. Although she has a low-grade fever, her other vital signs are normal and stable. The problem is that she is still not entirely oriented to time, place, or person, although that seems to be slowly improving. We are pleased that her respiratory status is entirely normal without the need for ventilatory support and, as I believe you already know, her coronavirus test was negative."

"Has a diagnosis been confirmed?" he prodded.

"Yes, it has. As predicted, she's positive for eastern equine encephalitis, or EEE."

Brian swallowed as his throat had suddenly gone dry. After what he'd read on Wikipedia the night before, he'd hoped for a different diagnosis, and the terrifying feeling of serious impending consequences came back in a rush. The fact that she was having neurological symptoms was not a good sign. It seemed unbelievable to him that apparently due to climate change his wife had come down with a serious viral illness he'd never even heard of.

"As required, we have reported this case to the New York State Health Department," Dr. Garner continued. "You might hear from them for more information, although we were able to tell them that the patient had recently been on Cape Cod, Massachusetts, and had reportedly been exposed to mosquitoes. Do you have any questions for me?"

"Can I visit her?"

"I'm afraid that with the Covid-19 situation, visitation in the ICU has been restricted."

"I assumed as much," Brian said. "How long do you think she will be kept in the ICU?"

"Perhaps another twenty-four hours. If she stays stable, we will send her to a normal hospital room. She'll be having a neurology consult today, which might influence timing depending on what they find."

"Will I be kept up to date on her progress?"

"If there are any changes, absolutely," Dr. Garner said. "And I can call again in the morning if you would like."

"I'd appreciate it," Brian said.

After hanging up, he found himself literally shaking at what he'd just found out. He didn't even want to contemplate what could be in store for Emma.

Feeling obligated and with trembling fingers, Brian put in calls to his mother, Aimée, and Emma's mother, Hannah, to tell them what the hospitalist had told him. Both had more questions than he could answer, and he promised he'd let them know as soon as he heard any updates.

After taking a deep breath to try to calm himself, he placed a call to Calvin Foster, desperate to think about something else besides Emma's situation. Luckily it turned out that not only was Calvin Foster seemingly a first-class financier, he was also personable, easy to talk to, and informed. What was particularly helpful was that Brian didn't have to sell himself. After only a few minutes of conversation it was apparent that Calvin knew a great deal about Brian's NYPD background, including his time in the Emergency Service Unit's elite A team.

"How do you know Deputy Chief Comstock?" Brian asked. As the conversation progressed, it became apparent he and Calvin were more than acquaintances.

"I've known Michael since high school," Calvin said jovially. "He's the one who recommended your security firm. I must say, he was full of praise. He said you'd gotten a few awards for exemplary service as a policeman."

"A lot of officers get awards," Brian replied. He was never one to brag or boast, mainly because he always thought he could do better no matter what others thought of him.

"I even heard you won a sniper award when you were an ESU cadet," Calvin commented.

"Luckily that's a skill that doesn't have a high demand."

Calvin laughed. "No, I suppose that's true. Nonetheless, I'm impressed."

"So, how can I help you?" Brian asked, eager to get down to business.

"I'd like to know if your company could cover my daughter's wedding that we've scheduled for the middle of October despite the pandemic. It's kind of a 'hurry-up' affair that we're throwing together but still trying to keep safe. It's going to be outside under an open tent. Kids today live in a different universe than you and I occupied, if you know what I'm saying."

"And it's only getting more different every day. I understand the affair will be at your Southampton summer home?"

"That's the plan. I've been told there will be about fifty guests with about half flying in private, some with their own security. Do you have adequate personnel to handle a job like this?"

"Our business plan is to utilize off-duty NYPD Emergency Service Unit officers, of which there are always a sizable and eager number. I'm certain we could provide the required security."

"Wonderful. What I would like beforehand is a security evaluation and an estimated budget. How soon might you be able to provide that?"

"First, I'd need a guest list with contact information, and I'd have to make a site visit to your Southampton home to view the venue. I can do that in the next few days." Brian welcomed the idea of the diversion, yet he wasn't entirely sure he'd feel comfortable leaving town with Emma in the hospital, even though Southampton was only two hours from the city.

"I'll have one of my secretaries email the Southampton address and guest list to you today, and I'll let my wife know to expect you. She's been living out there along with one college-aged daughter full-time since March, and I've been going back and forth."

After setting up plans to reconnect after Brian submitted his security evaluation and budget, they disconnected the call. The second he put the phone down, concern about Emma flooded back.

"Good God," he murmured, wondering if he could handle this potentially complicated engagement requiring interfacing with other security people while dealing with the stress of worrying about what Emma's status might be in mid-October and without her business input. Personal Protection LLC had always been something they were to do together, but Brian would have to find a way to fare on his own.

CHAPTER 6

August 20

It was after one o'clock in the afternoon when Brian and Juliette started walking home from the Emerson Playground. It wasn't far, only five or six blocks. Try as he might, he had been unable to get Juliette to do anything at the playground. Instead, she sat with Brian on a park bench holding Bunny, content to watch the other children play. To Brian she seemed completely out of character, acting listless and disinterested. Eventually he ran out of things to talk to her about, especially since he had admitted early on that he didn't know when Emma would be coming home from the hospital.

"We're home," he called out the moment they entered the front door. In response, Camila quickly emerged from the dining-room-cum-office to welcome them as they took off their shoes.

"How was your time at the playground?" Camila asked Juliette with forced positivity. "Did you have fun?"

"I want to watch cartoons," Juliette declared, ignoring the question and heading for the kitchen.

Brian and Camila exchanged a concerned glance. "She's not happy," he mouthed. "She didn't want to play with the other kids."

"It was the same this morning at Isham Park," Camila said with resignation. "I'll see if I can interest her in a bite of lunch."

"Any communication from Calvin Foster's people while I was out?"

"Yes, there's an email with the venue address and a preliminary guest list. There was also a call from the hospital."

"Really? Was it one of the doctors?" Brian asked nervously.

"No," Camila said. "It was a Roger Dalton from the hospital business office. He requested a call back as soon as you can. I left his direct-dial number on your desk."

"The business office?" he questioned. He felt relieved but curious. "What do they want?"

"He didn't say. He just said for you to call. Apparently, it is something important."

Brian nodded. He couldn't imagine what it was about since he'd already spoken with Maria Hernandez and had signed the admission papers. Sitting at his desk and with the number in hand, he took out his cell phone and dialed. The line was answered quickly by a commanding, whiskey-baritone voice with a strong New York accent. Brian identified himself and mentioned that he'd gotten the message to call.

"Yes, thank you for getting back to me," Roger said. "I've been assigned as the case manager for Emma Murphy. A problem has developed. I think it is best if you come into the hospital, so that we can discuss it in person."

"What kind of a problem? Is Emma okay?" Brian asked urgently.

"It's a problem with your health insurance coverage."

"I gave all the appropriate information to Mrs. Hernandez and signed the admission papers. Have you spoken with her?"

"This is not about Emma Murphy's admission to the hospital," Roger said. "It's about her visit yesterday to our Emergency Department, and I need to speak to you directly to set up a payment plan."

"What are you talking about? What kind of 'payment plan'?"

"I can explain it far better in person. I see that you live here in Inwood, so it shouldn't be too much of an imposition for you to come in? I will be here all afternoon."

Suddenly Brian realized the line had been disconnected and that the man had hung up. With a sense of impatience, he put the phone down. He didn't know whether to feel irritated or concerned, and what tipped the balance was a mild worry about the possible impact on Emma's treatment if he didn't comply. He didn't think that would really happen, but the mere thought of it made him decide not to make an issue of the situation. Instead, he got up, told Camila that he had to return to the hospital to visit the business office, and set off.

As Brian entered through the main entrance, he could see multiple ambulances pulled up to the ED dock.

The main lobby was moderately full, and he had to wait for his turn at the information desk. From his time at the hospital when he'd done off-duty patrolman work, he knew where the hospital administration offices were, but he didn't know if Roger Dalton's business office would be there as well. He found out quickly enough that it was.

Moving from the impressively renovated but cold marbled lobby into the admin section of the hospital was a stark transition. Now footsteps were muffled with carpet and the forest-green walls were hung with real art. To him the area looked more like a prosperous international corporation rather than the nerve center of a city hospital. There was even a glass-fronted conference room with a large mahogany library table and captain's chairs that looked to Brian more like it belonged in a bank. Next to the conference room was what he assumed was the hospital's CEO's office, outfitted as impressively as the conference room. As a police officer, he'd met the hospital president at the time, a doctor who had transitioned to administrative work, but Brian knew that had changed when the Inwood Community Hospital was purchased by the Manhattan Memorial Hospital corporation eight years earlier and became MMH Inwood. Under new management, it had undergone a major makeover before officially joining the ranks of the hospital chain.

Asking directions from one of the many secretaries, he quickly found Roger Dalton's office, but then he had to wait for a time while Roger finished with someone else. Finally, after nearly twenty minutes, Dalton appeared in his office's doorway and beckoned for Brian to enter.

Brian's first impression was that Roger Dalton didn't look anything like his imposing baritone voice implied. Instead of a commanding figure, he was a tall, thin man whose sports jacket looked more like it was draped over a metal hanger than over a pair of shoulders. His face behind his mask looked haggard, and he had deeply set eyes behind heavy-rimmed glasses. With slicked-back hair streaked with gray, he looked like a man who was either a heavy smoker and drinker or battling a serious illness.

"Thanks for coming," Roger began while taking his seat behind his desk and directing Brian to a chair front and center. "You're probably wondering why I insisted you come in. I'm afraid I have some bad news for you."

Although Brian knew from his call that Roger wasn't talking about Emma, for a second his heart stopped until Roger added: ". . . your insurance carrier, Peerless Health Insurance, has declined to cover your wife's $27,432.88 Emergency Department bill."

"You have already heard from Peerless?" Brian asked. He was astounded by Roger's comment on many levels, but for the moment the speed with which it had been discovered that Peerless wasn't paying took precedence. Emma had only been admitted yesterday, and he assumed the insurance matters took weeks, if not months.

"Yes, we have," Roger said. "As you might be aware, hospitals are being financially stressed through this pandemic. Our usual major sources of operating income such as elective surgery have been curtailed, forcing us to be strict in other areas, particularly the ED, whose operating costs are enormous. I was distressed when I saw that your carrier was Peerless. Our experience with them has been difficult at best, so I wanted to file the claim as soon as possible. True to form, they let us know immediately they were declining the claim, which I'm afraid to say is their normal modus operandi. It seems Peerless often finds creative ways of avoiding paying claims."

"Why would they decline my wife's ED visit?" Brian asked, still perplexed. "That doesn't make any sense."

"As I said, Peerless is particularly creative," Roger said. "But my guess in this particular instance is that the rationale is pretty straightforward. Even some of the big insurers like Anthem and United are getting involved. Here's the deal. There is a lot of talk of the cost of healthcare needing to be curtailed, and that insurance companies have an obligation to put on the brakes or at least appear to be doing so. One area that stands out is the 'emergency' overuse situation. Running emergency departments, particularly Trauma 1 centers like ours, is very, very expensive, and far too many people are abusing them for non-emergency ambulatory care rather than for true emergencies, like heart attacks, strokes, massive trauma and bleeding, and the like. Many insurance carriers feel that they have to put a stop to such abuse by denying claims, especially during normal business hours when patients can see their general practitioners or visit small, independent urgent-care centers."

"You mean that Peerless is saying my wife, who had

suffered a grand mal seizure, shouldn't have come to the MMH Inwood ED?"

"That's exactly what I believe they are saying by denying the claim," Roger affirmed.

"Well, that's preposterous," Brian sputtered. "A grand mal seizure is surely a medical emergency."

Roger shrugged his narrow shoulders and spread his hands, palms up. "I'm afraid that is going to be between you and your insurance carrier. Meanwhile, there is this sizable bill that needs to be addressed. That is why we need to set up some sort of payment plan going forward, especially now that your wife is an inpatient and using significant resources like an intensive care bed."

Brian's thoughts were churning a mile a minute in every conceivable direction. How could this be happening to him? Was his wife's care now in the balance because of their irresponsible insurance carrier? The whole situation was ridiculous, and mind-boggling.

"Well, what has Peerless said about my wife's hospitalization?" Brian managed to ask while trying to rein in his thoughts.

"They have said nothing because they have yet to be billed for that," Roger said. "Here's what I propose. If you were to, say, pay five thousand a month, we would be willing to accept that without adding interest. We realize that this is an imposition to anyone's budget."

"Imposition?" Brian exclaimed. "You don't understand. I don't have that kind of money, and certainly not under these circumstances."

"Well, you tell me what kind of time frame you have

in mind," Roger offered, tenting his fingers, elbows on his desk.

"Well, first, let's talk about this bill," Brian snapped. "Twenty-seven-something thousand dollars! How in heaven's name did the bill come to that? I could buy a new car for that kind of money."

"That's easy," Roger said. "It's par for the course and certainly not out of line. As I mentioned, Emergency Department care is very expensive. Your wife had multiple radiographic studies, a spinal tap, various consults, expensive pharmacological agents, many sophisticated laboratory tests, and her care tied up a number of highly paid nurses and doctors. She also had a seizure while being attended, which had to be treated. It adds up quickly."

"I want to see a copy of the bill," Brian demanded.

"You can request a copy from the billing department. That's certainly your right."

"I want to see a copy right here and now," Brian said. "It's all computerized, so it can be printed out in minutes."

"The way it will immediately print out won't be understandable to you."

"I don't care," Brian countered. "I want to see it."

"Suit yourself," Roger said. He picked up the phone and made a quick call. It was obvious that he was now finding the meeting almost as vexing as Brian.

While Roger was on the phone, Brian tried to calm himself. He realized he needed to talk directly to Peerless. It was absurd to think that a health insurance company wouldn't cover an obviously necessary ED visit even if some other people abused the situation. It had to be some kind of misunderstanding. Maybe they didn't know there had been several seizures involved, as well as a serious diagnosis thereafter.

"Okay," Roger told him, hanging up the phone. "I'll have a copy of the bill in short order."

"Can the ED bill be added on to the bill that will be generated by my wife's admission?"

"No, it can't," Roger said. "The ED bill must be taken care of separately. Can you give me an idea of what kind of time frame you would be able to propose?"

"I'm even behind on my mortgage," Brian blurted. "With the pandemic tying the economy in knots, how the hell do you think I can come up with twenty-seven thousand dollars within any conceivable time frame without being a goddamn fortune-teller?"

"Please, calm down," Roger snapped. "Let's try to have a civil conversation."

"You're right," Brian said. He had to get himself under control. "You'll have to excuse me. I'm just blown over by this whole situation. I never thought about any of this. I've always had good health insurance. I guess I've just taken it for granted. What I need to do is talk directly with Peerless and get them to step up to the plate and take care of this."

"That is a good plan, but you have to do it right away," Roger insisted. "You can't put this off. Talk to your carrier and then get right back to me. As I'm sure you understand, MMH has its own financial responsibilities it has to meet on a daily basis."

After a knock on Roger's door, a secretary came in with a small stack of papers and handed them over to him before retreating. Roger briefly glanced at them and then handed them over to Brian. "Good luck," he said as he did so.

Brian took the papers and glanced through them. It was immediately clear that Roger had been correct. The bill was entirely unintelligible, with every page mostly composed of long lists of alphanumeric entries followed by dollar amounts. Disgusted, Brian tossed the stack onto the desk. "It's not in English. It's all in goddamn code!"

"I warned you that it would be incomprehensible."

"Why is it in code? Why isn't each procedure or product just listed with a price? This format doesn't make any sense."

"Prices are proprietary information," Roger explained. "We have to keep that information confidential for our negotiations with insurance companies."

"I don't follow," Brian said. "Isn't there one specific price for every product and procedure?"

Roger scoffed at Brian's naivete. "There are different prices for different insurance companies. It's all a matter of bargaining. Surely you must know this."

"That's crazy," Brian said. "I've never heard of such a thing. Do I get a chance to bargain?"

Roger genuinely laughed, although he was obviously losing patience. "No, you don't get a chance to bargain. As an individual, you have to pay full freight."

"Why is that? Why do I have to pay more than health insurance companies for the same service?"

"This is how American hospital-based medicine works," Roger snapped. "I don't have time to explain it to you, nor is it my job. It's complicated. But, look, I can have a slightly more comprehensible bill drawn up, which I can email to you if you give me your email address."

"I never had any idea of any of this," Brian said as he dashed off his email address and handed it over. "I'll call Peerless as soon as I get home, and I'll let you know what they say. There has to be a misunderstanding."

"Fair enough," Roger said. "And you'll hear from me as soon as I can get the billing department to expand the bill however much is possible. But I warn you: It still isn't going to be much more understandable than this one. As I told you, hospital prices are proprietary information."

"I'll take my chances." He then added with mild sarcasm: "Thanks for your time."

Leaving the administration area, Brian briefly debated whether to try to visit the ICU because he knew where it was on the second floor. He decided against it for two reasons. One was that it might upset the powers that be, and two, if Emma was still disoriented, she wouldn't even remember he'd visited if he was able to pull it off. Instead, he used one of the courtesy phones in the main lobby and called to see if any of the ICU hospitalists were available, but had no luck.

Brian walked out of the hospital into a warm late summer day, which was beautiful weather-wise but totally lost on him. He walked out to Broadway and turned south as if he were in a trance. Not only was he terrified about the prospects of Emma's condition, he was now discombobulated and mortified about the possibility that he was facing a horrendous bill he could not pay. All he could hope was that Peerless Health had made a mistake, one that could be rectified by a phone call. Yet from Roger Dalton's comments, Brian wasn't all that optimistic. He felt as if he were caught in the outer edges of a whirlpool that had the power to suck him under and drown him.

CHAPTER 7

August 20

The twenty-minute walk from the hospital to his house on West 217th Street was just long enough for Brian to recover, calm down considerably, and think. He had always been a doer who saw adversity as a challenge. By the time he'd turned onto his street, he was back to giving Peerless Health Insurance the benefit of the doubt. He was now progressively convinced that there had to be a major misunderstanding about the nature of Emma's condition, and that a simple phone call to point it out would surely clear things up. With that issue possibly solved, he was able to think more about hospital prices and the incredible amount of money involved in healthcare. It seemed preposterous that it could cost more than twenty-seven thousand dollars for a single emergency visit, yet Roger Dalton obviously didn't think it was at all exceptional. In fact, he had actually said it wasn't out of line.

Back when Juliette had been born prematurely, Brian was vaguely aware of sky-high hospital bills, but that was for more than a month of neonatal intensive care. But even those bills hadn't caused a fuss in his personal expenses, since his and Emma's NYPD health benefits covered it in its entirety. Actually, as Brian turned onto his walkway, what bothered him the most at the moment was Dalton telling him that hospital costs varied depending on which health insurance company was involved and that he, as a nobody, had to pay "full freight." He couldn't imagine what people with no insurance at all had to do.

"What a crazy, screwed-up, unfair system," Brian pondered aloud as he mounted the front steps of his house, one of the very few houses left standing among the myriad of apartment blocks of Inwood, Manhattan.

Once inside, the first thing Brian did was go into the kitchen, where he could hear a cartoon soundtrack. He found Juliette parked in front of the TV and Camila on her laptop at the kitchen table.

"How is everyone?" Brian asked, trying to sound chipper.

"Juliette isn't hungry," Camila said. "I've tried to tempt her with eggs and bacon, which she usually adores, but she doesn't want any."

"How about Bunny?" Brian asked Juliette. Bunny as per usual was tucked in next to her on the banquette. "Is she hungry for bacon and eggs?"

"Bunny has a headache," Juliette said, without taking her eyes off the screen.

"I forgot about that," Camila chimed in. "Juliette says she has a headache."

"I'm sorry," Brian said. "Maybe Bunny shouldn't watch so much TV. Do you think that could be causing her headache?"

"I learned something interesting," Camila said when it was apparent Juliette wasn't going to respond. She took Brian aside, lowering her voice. "I researched whether young children can be depressed. Apparently, they can, but reactive anxiety is more common a problem. I think we are dealing with significant anxiety here with Miss Juliette."

"That makes a lot of sense. Witnessing her mother having a seizure and then being kept in the hospital is certainly enough to cause anxiety. Hell, I'm experiencing it myself."

"I guess we just have to be as supportive as we can," Camila said. "At the moment it means letting her watch TV."

"Agreed," Brian said.

"So, what happened at the hospital? Any word on Emma's condition?"

"No word on Emma. As for the hospital, they're demanding to be paid out of pocket for Emma's ED visit yesterday afternoon."

"Wow! They don't waste any time, do they?"

"And you won't believe the amount they're asking for," Brian said. "It's criminal. As for the speed, I got the sense that MMH Inwood is struggling financially with the coronavirus situation just like we are. Also, it seems the hospital has had a bad relationship with our particular health insurer. True to form, the company already denied the claim. But I'm hoping it's a misunderstanding. I've got to call them and straighten it all out. Are you all right here with Juliette for now?"

"I'm fine," Camila assured him. "Make your call, and good luck dealing with them. Last year I had a terrible time with my grandmother's health insurance company."

Back in the office, Brian searched in the upright file for the Peerless policy to get the policy number and the company's phone number. When he found it, he noticed it was a Manhattan exchange and a Midtown Manhattan address. Sitting at his desk with the information in front of him, he placed the call. As it went through, he vaguely wondered how many of the Peerless employees were working from home and how many were actually going into the office, as it varied from company to company.

When the line was answered automatically, Brian had to listen to a long list of possible alternatives. He chose one of the last: customer service, which resulted in another extensive list of choices. Five minutes later, when he finally got to speak to a real person and explained that he was calling to contest a denial of claim, he was told that he had to speak to the claims adjustment supervisor on duty. Frustratingly enough, that required another wait of almost thirty minutes while Brian was forced to listen to insipid elevator music. As time passed, he struggled with rising impatience.

"This is Ebony Wilson," a strong, compelling, yet mellifluous voice suddenly declared, breaking through the background music. "With whom do I have the pleasure of speaking?"

Brian gave his name and then explained why he was calling, namely to discuss the denial of a claim involving a visit to the MMH Inwood Emergency Department. He went on to say that there must have been a misunderstanding and that he wanted to clear up the situation.

"I'm sure I can help," Ebony said graciously. "Can I please have your Peerless Health Insurance policy number?"

Brian gave the number, enunciating each letter and number so there would be no mistakes and he could get this done as quickly as possible.

"Just a moment, please," Ebony said. In the next instant Brian found himself back to suffering through more background music. He knew that it was supposed to be calming, but under the circumstances it was having the opposite effect. Just when he was ready to figuratively scream, Ebony's assertive and pleasant voice returned. "Okay, Mr. Murphy," she said. "I have the claim here in front of me. It's from Manhattan Memorial Hospital Inwood concerning an Emergency Department visit for Emma Murphy. Is this correct?"

"Yes, that's it," Brian said. In contrast to the elevator music, Ebony's voice had a welcome and distinctive soothing quality. "Out of curiosity, are you in the Peerless Midtown office or are you working from home?"

"I'm in the office," Ebony said. "As a supervisor, it works better for me to be here, same with senior management. Most of the secretaries work from home. Why do you ask?"

"No real reason, just curious. It's such a crazy time,

what with most people working from home if they can. I was wondering how the health insurance world was faring."

"Okay, I have read through the adjuster's report," Ebony said, ignoring Brian's comment. "Everything seems to be in order here. Why do you think there was a misunderstanding?"

"My wife had a grand mal seizure on the Henry Hudson Parkway after feeling ill all day," Brian told her. "As soon as the seizure was over, we drove directly to the MMH Inwood Emergency Department."

"Yes, that is documented here in the claim," Ebony agreed. "But it also says that Emma Murphy walked into the ED without assistance at four-thirty and waited in line to be helped."

"That may be true, but she was disoriented. I could have called for an ambulance, but that would have taken longer. When she had her seizure, we were in our car fifteen minutes away from the hospital."

"I agree perfectly with your assessment, Mr. Murphy. An ambulance surely wasn't needed and would have been an unnecessary expense. But so is the kneejerk reaction to go to a Trauma 1 Emergency Department when your wife should have been seen by her general practitioner, or perhaps an urgent-care center."

"We don't have a general practitioner," Brian interjected. "My wife and I have been in perfect health. We work out every day. For our four-year-old we have a pediatrician, but we haven't needed a GP."

"Doesn't your wife have a gynecologist?"

"Yes, of course she does, for her yearly checkup."

"GYNs frequently function as general practitioners for young women. Your wife could have gone to her GYN, who could have seen her and admitted her to the hospital if necessary."

"That's absurd," Brian practically shouted.

"Calm down, Mr. Murphy. Anger will get you nowhere. Let me explain something to you. Peerless Health Insurance and our CEO, Heather Williams, are responsible members of our community, our city, and our country. We provide health insurance coverage with the lowest-priced premiums possible, but it comes with responsibility on the part of our members. Let me ask you something, Mr. Murphy. Did you read your Peerless policy as carefully as was recommended by our agent?"

Brian glanced down at the thick stack of papers on his desk. The truth was that he had not read the policy at all and didn't know if Emma had, either. He'd never read any of the health insurance policies he'd been given, even while an NYPD officer.

"I glanced at it," he said, embarrassed to admit otherwise.

"Well, you should have read it carefully to know what you were buying," Ebony said. "I recommend you go back and do so now. You see, to make our short-term policies affordable, we have made it a point to spell out specific limitations and define responsibilities of our members. Within our policy it is very clear what will be covered in the Emergency Department, particularly during normal business hours when urgent-care clinics and doctors' offices are open. You see, we take our role seriously in trying to do something about the rise of healthcare costs in the United States."

As Ebony droned on about the overuse of emergency medical facilities and the need to cut down healthcare costs in general, Brian's mind suddenly harkened back to Roger Dalton and how right he'd been. But then Ebony got Brian's attention by saying: ". . . but if you disagree with our adjuster's decision, you have the right to request a review online."

"I'm thinking I will do more than request a Peerless review," Brian snapped. "Denying a legitimate claim like this seems criminal. I think this deserves a review by an attorney."

"Of course, consulting an attorney and even initiating a lawsuit is your right," Ebony said. "But, let me say this, attorneys are very expensive. And in my experience, which is rather extensive, as I do this day in and day out, you'll be wasting your time and money. Peerless Health knows the ins and outs of this business extremely well, which is why we are so successful. We also have in-house counsel to deal with lawsuits. My advice, for what it is worth, is for you to request a Peerless review and see if it changes the situation. Occasionally it comes to light that an adjuster has made a mistake and the claim is reversed upon review. Is there anything else I can do for you today?"

Similar to how he'd felt after his conversation with Roger Dalton, it took Brian a few minutes to calm down enough to think clearly after disconnecting with Ebony

Wilson. He was in no way a litigious person: far from it. As a committed law enforcement officer, he wasn't fond of lawyers. And he recognized Ebony was probably right about the futility of hiring an attorney to try to deal with a company that undoubtedly was "lawyered up" and prepared to deal aggressively with any legal action. He was left with no other option than to request a review.

He brought up the Peerless Health Insurance website to log in, but before he did so, he decided to give the website some attention, seeing as it was basically his second time on there. After a quick glance at the section trying to sell policies to new customers, Brian clicked on the investment section. He learned that the company had had a wildly successful IPO two years ago and that the stock price had doubled since then, making it one of the fastest-growing companies on NASDAQ. It was immediately apparent that the entire success of the company was attributed exclusively to its wunderkind CEO, Heather Williams. Brian looked at the woman's picture. He was impressed with her youth as a CEO of a public company— somewhere around thirty was his guess—and the intensity and imperiousness of her gaze.

Finding himself curious, Brian opened up a new page and looked up Heather Williams. He was surprised by the amount of material available on her and clicked on a recent biographical article. Now he was confronted with a second picture of the CEO that was starkly different from the typical businesslike head-and-shoulder pic on the Peerless website. This was a picture of a painting featuring a haughty Heather Williams in a foxhunting outfit with a horse on one side and a foxhound on the other. Brian's immediate reaction was shock. In his mind foxhunting, like polo, was something reserved for English royalty or those people who aspired to be demonstratively aristocratic. His second reaction was to acknowledge that she'd probably had a very different and a much more privileged upbringing than he had. Beginning the article, he learned that she was the scion of a west Texas oil family, had gone to boarding school in England, and then graduated from Yale undergraduate and finally Harvard Business School.

"Good grief," Brian exclaimed as he read on. She'd been hired by Peerless directly out of business school. At the time Peerless was a small company founded by a group of young entrepreneurs trying to break into the health insurance market by taking advantage of the passage of the Affordable Care Act and the subsidies it offered. Heather Williams quickly and cleverly saw a different path, and instead of relying on politically susceptible subsidies, she strenuously pushed the company to embrace the short-term health insurance market. Within just a few years, thanks to her aggressive and creative marketing, she was elevated to chief financial officer, or CFO, and two years later to chief executive officer, or CEO. In recognition of her single-handedly tripling the company's stock value, she'd become a recognized and applauded darling of Wall Street.

After he finished the article, Brian returned to the picture of Williams in her foxhunting outfit. As he stared at it, he found himself wondering how much her and

Peerless's financial success were dependent on Peerless quickly denying claims, as had just happened to him. After entertaining the thought for a few minutes, Brian decided to move on and return to the Peerless website. He had more immediate concerns, like requesting a review of the claim denial for Emma's ED visit, which he sincerely hoped would result in a reversal and possibly save his family's fortune.

With that unpleasantness out of the way, Brian gave Camila a break from being with Juliette by spending almost an hour reading *The House at Pooh Corner* to his daughter in her bedroom. After finishing the fourth chapter, Brian looked up to discover Juliette had fallen asleep. Being as quiet as possible, he tiptoed out.

"How much information do you want on each of these guests for the potential Foster gig?" Camila asked as Brian came into the office and sat at his desk. She was at her desk on her computer.

"The more the merrier," he said as he booted up his machine. He hoped that the Foster affair would take place despite the growing concern over a second wave of Covid. With that thought in mind, he went online to look at the Personal Protection LLC bank balances to figure out if there were adequate funds to somehow at least appease the hospital while Emma was an inpatient, especially in case Peerless wasn't going to participate. As he expected, the balances weren't encouraging, and they were going to be hard put to cover basic expenses and put food on the table if some significant business didn't materialize during the next month.

"Our cash flow is a bad joke," Brian voiced out loud. It was depressing, and for many reasons he wished he and Emma had not decided to take the vacation on Cape Cod even though they had gotten the cottage for a steal. Continuing in that trend of thought, he wished they had at least avoided the beach barbecue. Things could have been so different.

"As if I didn't know," Camila said. "We're in dire need of some luck. Fingers crossed for this Foster event. One thing I'm going to insist on: Stop paying my salary until things turn around."

"Camila, we couldn't," Brian countered and meant it.

"I know that neither you nor Emma have taken any salary for months. It's only fair, especially since you're giving me room and board."

"At this point you are more like family," Brian said. "How about we defer your salary? I'm willing to consider that under the circumstances."

"That's fine, if that's what you want to call it," Camila said.

With Camila's suggestion of deferring, he looked back at the numbers. From that perspective it seemed possible that Brian could manage five to ten thousand dollars to placate the hospital, provided the bank was willing to continue deferring the mortgage payment on the house. With the mortgage question in mind, Brian decided to put in a call to their banker, Marvin Freeman. As the call went through, Brian thanked his lucky stars that he and Emma had not taken a business loan to start their security company and instead renegotiated the mortgage on their house. After the usual superficial pleasantries, Brian got right down to the reason for the call.

"Our business is suffering, as you might expect with this coronavirus situation."

"You and a thousand other businesses."

"What do you think the chances are that we could renegotiate our mortgage yet again to give us some operating cash to carry us through?"

"We just renegotiated your mortgage not even a year ago, Brian," Marvin said. His voice lost some of its friendliness, becoming significantly more businesslike.

"I was afraid you'd say that," Brian said. "What about a business line of credit? Something to get us cash if we get desperate."

"What kind of collateral are you thinking of offering for a credit line?" Marvin asked. "Do you have any stocks and bonds?"

"No, we don't have any collateral. The house is our only asset."

"Having no collateral ties my hands, my friend. There's no way I could get a line of credit for you without it. Plus, the bank is already allowing you to defer your mortgage payments for the immediate future."

"Yes, and I appreciate that, Marvin. I suppose in a way that is already a line of credit."

"You could look at it that way, but I should warn you that it is not going to last."

"I understand, but thanks, Marvin."

"Sorry I can't be of more help."

Disconnecting from the call, Brian went back to staring at the meager bank balances. After hearing the bank's position, he really didn't think he could pay MMH very much without putting himself, Emma and Juliette, and his fledgling business in jeopardy. Now more than ever, it seemed tragic to live in a wealthy country where basic emergency healthcare could put a decent, hardworking family like his at risk.

CHAPTER 8

August 27

Brian stepped out of his front door a little after eight in the morning, and as he put on his face mask, he surveyed the street in front of his house. The roadway was in the process of being repaved but so far had only been ground down and striated. It was a mess, dangerous to walk on, and he had no idea when it was going to be put back together. In many ways it seemed symbolic of his life in the past week.

Emma was still hospitalized after a week and not doing as well as Brian hoped. During her first twenty-four to forty-eight hours in the ICU, he had been told she'd improved and had regained a reasonable degree of orientation. But then when she was transferred into a normal hospital room and he was able to see her, he found her mental state varied from day to day. Sometimes she didn't even seem to recognize him, and she spent most of her time sleeping. She had continued to run a fever, suggesting that the EEE virus was still active despite whatever antibodies her immune system was making.

But at least being in a normal hospital room made it possible for Brian to see her, and thanks to Camila, his mother, and Emma's mother, he'd been able to spend considerable time doing so while the women took turns taking care of Juliette. His poor daughter missed her mother and was sulky, irritable, and withdrawn despite a lot of effort on the part of all three extra caretakers. To everyone's concern, Juliette wasn't even eating properly. Brian was enormously thankful that taking care of her wasn't on his shoulders alone, as he wondered if he would find the patience it required. Just being with her during the night could be trying enough when she'd wake up crying.

Although he had taken one entire afternoon to run out to Southampton to check out the Fosters' palatial summer home and meet the bride-to-be so that Camila could come up with a budget for the wedding, he spent every other day with Emma. It was his feeling that the nursing staff wasn't spending the time necessary to make sure his wife was being appropriately mobilized. From his EMT training, Brian knew how important it was for a patient not to remain in bed continuously.

Multiple times every day, Brian forced her to get up and walk up and down the hallway despite her constant complaining. While walking with her two days before, he'd noticed a change in her stride. It was a kind of clumsiness that was almost imperceptible at first, but slowly progressed over the next twenty-four hours. Yesterday morning when he got her out of bed, it was definitely more apparent, and he brought it to the attention of Dr.

Shirley Raymond, the hospitalist responsible for Emma's care. She in turn alerted the neurology consult who had been following Emma. This new symptom, labeled by the doctors as spasticity, had raised Brian's concerns, and as he started out toward MMH Inwood, he wondered if he would find Emma even worse today.

Feeling the need for exercise, which Brian wasn't getting, he literally ran to the hospital. The face mask made it a bit more difficult, but he was willing to put up with it. As he entered through the front entrance into the marbled lobby, one of the women behind the information desk called his name. With as much time as he'd been spending at the hospital on a daily basis, he was becoming a known commodity.

"Mr. Murphy! Harriet Berenson would like to see you," one of the pink-smocked ladies said.

"Who is Harriet Berenson?" he questioned. He was moderately out of breath, even though it had only been a little more than a week since he and Emma had done their daily mini-triathlons.

"She's one of our discharge planners. Her office is on the second floor."

Brian was taken aback. He never even knew there was such a position as a discharge planner. And why would a discharge planner want to talk with him—unless they were thinking of discharging Emma? But how could that be, particularly with her developing a new, alarming symptom? After hesitating for a moment to decide whether to go up to Emma's floor first or visit Harriet Berenson, the latter won out. He needed to know sooner rather than later if there was even talk of Emma being discharged. The idea of having to take care of her at home terrified him.

"Ah, yes," Harriet said once he had made it to her office. She picked up one of the folders on her desk and opened it. "Emma Murphy is to be discharged today. I want to arrange for post-hospital services."

"My wife cannot be discharged," Brian stated simply. As far as he was concerned, she was hardly capable of even basic functions. "That's not going to work. Our house is ill-equipped to handle her needs. I'm not even sure she can climb a flight of stairs in her condition and the bedrooms are upstairs."

"That's good to know," Harriet said. "That's what I am here for: to make sure your wife gets the care she requires. We can certainly arrange for extended care in a nursing home."

"But she's developed some difficulty walking," he argued. "And it's getting worse."

"Do you think a rehabilitation hospital would be a better solution?"

"I don't know," Brian stammered. "I hadn't given it any thought. I certainly didn't think she was ready to be discharged. She's still symptomatic from the EEE virus. In fact, she still has a fever as far as I know."

"That's not what Dr. Kathrine Graham thinks," Harriet countered. "She wrote the discharge order this morning."

"Who is Dr. Graham?" Brian asked. He'd never heard the name.

"She is our Chief Medical Officer here."

"Does Dr. Shirley Raymond know that my wife is to be discharged?" He had briefly seen Dr. Raymond around noon the day before, and she'd not mentioned anything.

"I'm sure she does," Harriet said. "As I said, Dr. Graham is our CMO. If your wife needs help regaining strength for things like walking, a rehabilitation hospital would be the proper choice, no doubt. How does the Hudson Valley Rehabilitation Hospital sound to you? It's in Hudson Heights, so it's close by, and it is an excellent facility. We send a lot of our patients there."

"I guess it sounds better than a nursing home," Brian assented. A rehabilitation hospital sounded decent, but he was hardly enthusiastic.

"Okay, then I'll get right on it," Harriet said. "I know Hudson Valley has room because I placed someone there just yesterday. Now, I was told that you must see Roger Dalton right after talking with me. Do you know where his office is located?"

"I do." He didn't like the idea of seeing Roger Dalton again. He'd not spoken to the man since their less than personable visit a week ago and, from Brian's perspective, it was better to let sleeping dogs lie in regard to the outstanding, humongous ED bill. Yet now that there was a possibility of Emma being discharged, it probably wasn't avoidable.

Leaving Harriet's office, he briefly debated whether to see Dalton first or check in on Emma. Reluctantly, he decided it best to get the Dalton meeting out of the way, as he might find it difficult to leave Emma if she became upset about being discharged. Using the stairs, Brian descended to the first floor and entered the administration area.

With Roger Dalton, Brian wasn't so lucky as he'd been with Miss Berenson. Not only was there someone in the man's office, but there was another individual waiting to see him, too. At least the wait gave him a chance to think about Emma's discharge. He still did not like the idea, but he admitted he knew nothing about the Hudson Valley Rehab Hospital other than approximately where it was. Being that it was rehab hospital, maybe Emma would get more attention, but the uncertainty bothered him, as he didn't know what to expect going forward.

When Brian finally walked into Dalton's office and sat, he thought he was prepared for whatever the man was going to say, but he wasn't, especially since the meeting started out on the wrong foot.

"I thought you were going to get back to me about the outstanding Emergency Department bill?" Roger said with a definite accusatory tone.

"I was planning on it," Brian said in his defense. "I have applied for a review of the decision to deny the claim, and I've been waiting for a response."

"You got your response," Roger spat. "You were informed the claim again had been denied by email yesterday. I know because I'd resubmitted the claim when I hadn't heard from you."

For a brief moment Brian let his eyes drift away from Roger's masked face as a minor flash of anger consumed him. He'd developed a distaste for this bureaucrat on their last meeting and his current holier-than-thou attitude was reminding him why.

"I suppose you are going to tell me you didn't see the email," Roger continued derogatorily.

After a short pause to control himself, Brian said: "You are correct. I have yet to see that particular email from Peerless. As it is, I've been busy trying to help my wife, who is not doing all that well. Is the ED bill the reason you asked to see me?"

"No, it is not," Roger snapped.

"Well, perhaps you can tell me what it is then."

"I'm afraid I have more bad news for you. When I was informed yesterday by our Chief Medical Officer that your wife was going to be discharged, I put together a preliminary hospital bill. Because we have had a history of such bad luck with Peerless Health, I wanted to get it to them ASAP. Well, my efforts were rewarded with Peerless informing us that they will not be covering any of the currently estimated $161,942.98 in-house bill, either."

For a few moments of stunned silence, Brian's mind tried to wrap itself around two incredible facts: the sheer size of the in-house hospital bill and the idea that a health insurance company would contend it wasn't going to be involved with a sick patient's required care. He didn't know which was more outrageous.

"What am I supposed to gather from your silence, Mr. Murphy?" Roger demanded. "We have a major problem here. Frankly, we as an institution are finding it very difficult dealing with these short-term insurance policy companies, especially since they have proliferated during this coronavirus pandemic with people losing their employer-based coverage."

"More than one hundred and sixty thousand dollars is a big bill," Brian managed to say, thinking out loud as he tried to conceive of such a number.

"It is not an exceptional hospital bill by any stretch of the imagination in this day and age," Roger said. "Remember, your wife spent several days in the intensive care unit, which, like the Emergency Department, is very expensive to maintain and run. And she has had many tests over the eight days, including several MRIs and a number of electroencephalograms."

"I suppose," Brian said distractedly. Once again, his mind was going a mile a minute, trying to put this cost into the perspective of his life experiences. The only time he'd dealt with such a number was when he and Emma had bought their house. But that was an investment, not a one-time expense, and his wife was still ill.

"Mr. Murphy, please," Roger said. "This is a major problem, and I need your full attention. We have to decide on a course of action."

"Did Peerless give a reason why they wouldn't be covering *any* of the hospital bill?"

"Yes, they did," Roger said. "I was told it had to do with your deductible, all of which was spelled out clearly in your policy. Did you read your policy, Mr. Murphy?"

"Not carefully," Brian admitted, fully aware that he was fibbing similar to the way he'd done during his conversation with Ebony Wilson.

"Well, it sounds like that was a big mistake," Roger said patronizingly.

With some difficulty Brian resisted the temptation to ask Roger how many novel-length, legalese-strewn health insurance policies he'd read in his lifetime.

"I know my policy had a ten-thousand-dollar deductible. Doesn't that mean the insurance company is then supposed to cover the rest?"

"All policies are different," Roger said. "It's up to you to find out. Meanwhile, what do you propose to do about the now $189,375.86 bill that is owed to MMH Inwood? We need to know, or we will have to turn this over to collections."

"I intend to resolve this situation with Peerless today," Brian insisted. "And I'm not going to try to do it over the phone. This sort of money calls for an in-person visit."

"All right, that's up to you," Roger said. "But you must get back to me soon. You can't ignore this situation."

"I'll get back to you right away, but before I go, I need to ask something. What came first: the decision to discharge my wife or the hospital getting word from Peerless that they were not going to cover the bill?"

"I don't think I understand the question." Roger sat back in his chair, wrinkled his forehead, and stared at Brian through his thick-framed glasses.

"I can't help but worry that the reason my wife is being suddenly discharged is because of the outstanding ED bill along with the new fear that her hospital bill might not get paid in a timely manner."

"That is a preposterous accusation," Roger said, taking immediate offense. He rocked forward, glaring at Brian. "The clinical people, meaning the doctors and nurses, make all the decisions about patient care. We on the business side are not involved, ever! All we do is strive to keep the institution solvent. The two do not mix on any level whatsoever."

"Really?" Brian questioned. "There had been no talk of her being discharged as far as I know, and I've made it a point to talk daily with Dr. Raymond, who's been in charge of her care. This all seems very quick and out of the blue. And my wife has recently developed a new symptom of spasticity. From my vantage point, she's no better off now than when she was admitted."

"Let me tell you something, young man," Roger said as he used a mildly crooked index finger to point repeatedly at Brian. "This hospital never allows financial concerns to affect patient care decisions. Never! I'm offended you would even suggest such a thing."

"I wonder," Brian questioned while provocatively raising his eyebrows. He was getting a smidgen of pleasure from being the cause of Roger's apparent indignation and discomfort. After a pregnant pause, he added: "Who actually is Dr. Graham, this supposed chief medical officer? I've never met her, and I have been coming here every day for more than a week to see my wife. Is she more on the clinical side or the administrative side?"

"What on earth do you mean?"

"What I'm wondering is whether she is more concerned about patient welfare or institutional welfare. It's as simple as that."

"Dr. Graham is part of the administration, but she is also a doctor," Roger sputtered. "Once you are a doctor, you are always a doctor. That should be plenty obvious."

"I hope you're right," Brian said. He stood up, knowing that the chances of getting a straight answer were slim. "Meanwhile, I expect to get a copy of the hospital bill, and I'd like it in English. Even the second ED bill you sent me seemed like it was done on an Enigma machine."

"I'll see what I can do," Roger said. "But let me warn you in advance: The hospital bill will definitely be more complicated than the ED bill, especially the part involving the ICU. And the bill from MMH Inwood is not the only bill you will be getting. You'll also get bills from individual doctors not employed by MMH who saw your wife during her stay."

"What kinds of doctors?" Brian demanded as he sat back down. This sounded like insult added to injury or, more accurately, like a kind of extortion.

"Specialists of various kinds," Roger answered vaguely. "Some of the consults are independent practitioners."

"Is this the surprise medical billing I've vaguely heard about?"

"It is," Roger admitted.

"Well, get me what you can," Brian said while regaining his feet in preparation of leaving. "Meanwhile, I'll be back to you after I have a face-to-face visit with Peerless Health, which will hopefully be today."

As he rode up in the elevator, he couldn't get the concern out of his mind that Emma was being discharged on account of economics, which was an infuriating thought. When he walked into Emma's room, he found her asleep, which was happening more frequently of late. Instead of waking her, he let her be and returned to the nurses' station. Over the preceding week he'd gotten to know many of the day-shift nurses, including the charge nurse, Maureen O'Hara, whose brother Brian knew well. They'd shared a class in grammar school and had attended the NYPD Academy together.

"So, Emma is being discharged," Brian said when he managed to get Maureen's attention. She was a no-nonsense, squat, and powerfully built woman just like her brother, and she ran the fourth floor with an iron fist. She, like most of the floor nurses, was wearing a plastic face shield as well as a mask.

"That's what I've been told," Maureen said. "To tell you the truth, it took me by surprise."

"Do you think it's appropriate?"

Maureen shrugged. "We're not doing all that much for her. In fact, you are doing more than we are, even more than physical therapy. The thing that I am most concerned about is the seizure monitoring."

"Me, too," he said. "What's the story with this Dr. Kathrine Graham?"

"What exactly do you mean?"

"I'm not sure. I was just told she was the one who wrote the discharge order."

"That's not surprising," Maureen said. "She does that a lot."

"What kind of doctor is she?" Brian asked. "I've never met her."

"She doesn't often come to the floor. She has an office in admin. My understanding is that she was an internist before becoming the Chief Medical Officer."

"What about Dr. Raymond? Where is she today?"

"She's back in the chart room. I saw her go in there not five minutes ago."

Knowing full well he was overstepping his bounds to a degree, Brian went to the door to the chart room and pushed it open. Instead of being full of charts as he was expecting, the room was made up of countertops and computer monitors. Dr. Raymond and several other people were busy entering data. The only noise was coming from the keypads.

"Excuse me, Dr. Raymond," he called out self-consciously. "Could I please have a word?"

To Brian's relief, she immediately stood up and came to the door. Speaking in a whisper, she asked what he needed.

"I've just heard my wife is being discharged," Brian whispered back.

Dr. Raymond graciously stepped out of the chart room, allowing the door to close.

In contrast to Maureen, Dr. Shirley Raymond was rail thin and imbued with a nervous energy. "Yes," she said. "I was informed of the discharge plans this morning."

"So, this wasn't your decision?" Brian was surprised to learn that she hadn't been involved in the order.

"No, it wasn't. It's apparent to me that Emma still has an active viral infection. She also seems to be somewhat drowsier and more confused. And, as far as I know, neurology hasn't finished evaluating the spasticity that's emerged."

"The current plan is to send her to Hudson Valley Rehabilitation Hospital."

"Oh, I didn't hear that," Dr. Raymond said. She shrugged. "That will work, I guess. She should be under a seizure watch since the encephalitis is still obviously active, and they're capable of doing that at Hudson Valley. Although, if it were up to me, I'd keep her here in an acute care facility."

"I was told she was discharged by a Dr. Graham. Do you know her?"

"Of course. She's one of the kingpins around here."

"Is she a good doctor?"

Dr. Raymond laughed nervously. "That's a strange question. Yes, I guess she is a good doctor."

"To be frank, I'm a little worried. Do you think there is any chance that finances influenced the decision to discharge my wife?"

She shook her head. "No. That's not how we practice medicine. There must be a valid reason Dr. Graham gave the discharge order. Perhaps it's to free up beds for the expected Covid-19 surge."

"That's reassuring coming from you. Well, thank you for talking with me and thank you for taking care of Emma."

"You're very welcome. And good luck. I'm afraid you are in for a long haul with Emma. EEE is a persistent illness."

"Yes, I've gotten that impression," Brian muttered and turned to return to Emma's room, significantly more confused and daunted by these conversations than he was expecting.

CHAPTER 9

August 27

It was just after two in the afternoon when Brian walked out of the Hudson Valley Rehabilitation Hospital and paused on the steps to regroup. He was feeling out of sorts. It had been a stressful morning. Emma had resisted the idea of leaving MMH Inwood, but there had been little he could do, and it was true to an extent that MMH wasn't doing very much in terms of therapy. It was also true that Emma had not had another seizure since the one in the Emergency Department, so maybe the need for seizure monitoring was less important. Plus, the term "rehabilitation" had a nice ring to it as far as Brian was concerned, and he hoped that there would be more opportunity for Emma's walking difficulties to be addressed. But that was before he had seen the hospital.

During the admission process, Brian again had to sign papers giving the name of their insurance carrier and committing to being responsible for all charges. Knowing what he did about Peerless, it was obvious he was accepting even more debt despite having no possible way to come up with the money he already owed.

And if all this wasn't bad enough, Hudson Valley Rehabilitation Hospital had been a disappointment. In sharp contrast to the renovated MMH Inwood, the building was aged and shabby, especially Emma's room. And worse still, the number of patients per nurse was significantly higher than at MMH, meaning Emma probably wasn't going to be receiving a lot of seizure monitoring or monitoring in general. Luckily she seemed oblivious to the nature of the hospital surroundings and had fallen into a deep sleep almost immediately after she'd been put in her bed and her vital signs were taken. The transfer procedure had been stressful for her even though MMH had arranged an ambulance service, and she had been moved in and out of both institutions on a gurney. The ambulance ride itself had been only fifteen or twenty minutes, and Brian had been able to ride with her.

From his perspective, this whole experience of Emma contracting a disease that he had never heard of from an innocent barbecue had been a rude awakening. As a conscientious hard worker who followed the rules, he'd always felt reasonably in control. Now it was the exact opposite. It was as if he and Emma had been poised on a precipice and didn't know it, and now that Emma had slipped off, Brian and his family were only holding on by their fingertips. To make matters worse, he'd never had any inkling that the cost of a week's stay in a hospital could potentially upend his life thanks to an unscrupulous health insurance company. It seemed criminal that he was now almost two hundred thousand dollars in debt and counting.

Pulling his phone out of his pocket, Brian made a quick call to Aimée to let her know that Emma had been moved and to ask her to let Emma's mother know as well. He then passed along the current visiting restrictions and requirements. Toward the end of the call, he experienced a sudden and unexpected surge of emotion, bringing him almost to tears.

"Are you okay, Brian?" Aimée asked, detecting a catch in his voice.

"This is all more stressful than I could have imagined," Brian managed after a pause. He'd not shared any of the financial problems with his mother, nor his worry that Emma might have been discharged from MMH because of the bill. "I hope this Hudson Valley Rehab Hospital works out."

"I'm sure it will," Aimée assured him. "I've had a number of friends who have been hospitalized at HVR, and they did well. It's not the Ritz or even MMH, but the staff is friendly and caring."

"They better be, or there's going to be hell to pay." As quickly as his surge of emotion had appeared, it metamorphosed into anger, and he was reminded of his planned visit to the Peerless Health Insurance offices. "Mom, I'm sorry, I've got to go."

"Okay, dear," Aimée said. "I'll let Hannah know that Emma is situated at HVR, and we'll plan out a visiting schedule. You get home and take care of that darling daughter of yours. She needs your attention, too."

Brian disconnected the call, eager to make the visit to Peerless. The question was: How to get there? With his anger ramped up and wanting to get it over with quickly, he decided on the subway. From Inwood it was by far the fastest way to get to Midtown Manhattan.

Ten minutes later he was on the A train thundering south, and as he rode, he thought about the hospital bill that Roger Dalton had emailed to him and that he'd glanced at briefly on his phone while waiting for Emma to be discharged. As Roger had suggested, it was mostly incomprehensible and in code similar to the ED bill, but there were some bits of it that were perfectly understandable and that riled Brian to no end. One of those was an outlandish charge of $970 for a supposed "physical therapy evaluation session."

From the date of the service, Brian distinctly remembered the episode. A young, bouncy, and very friendly woman had appeared at Emma's bedside, gotten her out of bed, and proceeded to merely walk her up the corridor exactly as he had done fifteen minutes earlier. Another was a thirty-dollar charge for a single ibuprofen tablet that Brian had requested for Emma on that same day when she complained of a headache. From Brian's perspective, if such charges were representative of the entire bill, the whole thing bordered on being absurd, if not out-and-out fraud.

From the Columbus Circle express stop it was a relatively short walk to the building on Sixth Avenue where

Peerless Health Insurance had their home office. He found it strange to be walking the streets of Midtown Manhattan and seeing so few people. Like on the subway, most of the few people he encountered were masked. Reaching the proper building, Brian thought it a coincidence that it happened to be a few doors down from where Priority Capital was located. Thinking about Priority Capital and Calvin Foster made Brian hope that his proposed budget for the fancy Southampton wedding was being well received, and that he could be on the verge of securing some income.

He had purposely not called ahead to schedule a meeting with Peerless, as he doubted that they would be willing to see him. These days, companies limited physical contact, often preferring phone or, better yet, impersonal email exchanges. Dealing with an unhappy customer like Brian was far easier at a distance, particularly online. Of course, there was still the problem about physically accessing the Peerless Health Insurance office with the security Manhattan commercial office buildings invariably employed. But Brian still had his duplicate NYPD shield and ID. The fact that his ID card had RETIRED under the photo hardly limited its effectiveness in providing access to most everything in the city. Besides, he also knew that many of the NYC commercial office buildings employed retired NYPD officers as guards.

As he negotiated the revolving door, he withdrew his wallet to have it ready. Similar to the street outside, the interior of the building was almost deserted. As he approached the security desk, he was encouraged to see, seated behind a plastic shield, a well-groomed, silver-haired, mildly overweight gentleman who looked the part of a retired cop with his crew cut and mustache. With practiced nonchalance, Brian flashed his ID quickly and the two men exchanged a convivial, knowing greeting, like members of a private club.

"How are you, my friend?" Brian said.

"Fine, thank you," the security man replied with a broad smile. "Are you with Midtown North Precinct?"

"No, ESU."

"Oh, wow!" the guard said. The ESU was highly regarded by the entire NYPD, since they were the ones called in whenever the regular patrolmen confronted a major problem. "How can I help?"

"How about yourself? What was your last command?"

"I retired from Midtown North. It's how I got this job."

"Good for you, but it looks like you're not very busy these days."

The security guard laughed. "It's unbelievable," he said. "It's like a morgue around here. It makes me wonder if it's ever going to go back to normal. So, what can I do for you?"

"I need to talk to someone at the Peerless Health Insurance office," Brian said. "Are many of them here or are they all working from home?"

"A few of them come in. Mostly the brass. None of the secretaries or grunts."

"How about Ebony Wilson?" he asked. "Do you know her, by any chance?"

"Of course I know Ebony. She's one of the ones who comes in every day. Treats me like a person, and always says hello. Not like the Peerless boss lady."

"Are you talking about Heather Williams?" The eccentric and rather outlandish image of the woman in the pretentious foxhunting outfit popped into his mind.

"I don't know her name," the guard said. "I made a point of not wanting to know it."

"Why is that?"

The guard looked to both sides as if to be sure no one was listening, even though the expansive lobby was otherwise deserted. A janitor who'd been wiping down the turnstiles with disinfectant when Brian had first entered had disappeared. "She's extremely snotty and thinks she's better than everyone else. That's my personal assessment. Not only does she not say hello, but she doesn't even acknowledge that I exist. She waltzes through here with her entourage like she's the pope."

"What do you mean, 'entourage'?"

"She's always surrounded by three or four people rushing around her doing this and doing that, fawning over her. It's ridiculous. She doesn't even push her own elevator button. And several of them are armed bodyguards. I know because I had a conversation once with one of them. He's a former marine."

"Armed guards? That's rather surprising," Brian observed. "But are you sure about that? Don't you think maybe this former marine was pulling your leg?"

"I swear on a stack of Bibles," the guard promised. "I'm not exaggerating."

"But why?" It seemed excessive, to say the very least.

"The ex-marine I spoke to says she's become really wealthy. He bragged she's been making ten million a year."

"That can't be true." The idea that the CEO of a small, up-and-coming health insurance company could make that kind of salary seemed ridiculous.

"It's not out of line," the guard insisted. "As a small-time investor, I happen to know that some of the CEOs of the big health insurance companies that I've invested in make upward of twenty million a year."

"Really?" Brian questioned. He never knew that such salaries existed in healthcare, though Emma's astronomical hospital bills were beginning to make more sense. Someone had to benefit.

"It's true. Health insurance companies are good investments. Mark my words."

"I'll give that some thought," Brian replied for lack of another response. He wondered if the security guard was exaggerating. Twenty million for running a company that sold health insurance seemed preposterous.

"You learn a lot being one of the security guards in a building of this size," the guard added.

"I bet you do. How about today? Did you see Ebony Wilson?"

"Oh yeah," the guard said. "She's upstairs."

"Well, she's one of the people I need to talk to."

"Is she in trouble?"

"No, no," Brian said quickly. "I just need to chat with her about Peerless. What floor?"

"Fifty-fourth. Do you want me to call up there and let her know to expect you?"

"I'd rather you didn't. You know the trick. It's often better to catch certain people unawares, because you might learn more."

"Gotcha." The guard gave him a knowing look and a thumbs-up. "Use the turnstile farthest to the left."

"Will do," Brian said as a youthful, casually dressed man in jeans, polo shirt, and tennis sneakers entered through the revolving door. As he passed, he flashed a card at the security guard and headed for the turnstiles.

"Hello, Mr. Bennet," the guard called out. Then to Brian he whispered: "He's with Peerless."

"Now, that might be handy," Brian said, making a rapid decision. Quickly he headed for the visitors' turnstile and pushed through. Hurrying after Mr. Bennet, who had boarded one of the elevators that served floors forty through sixty, he was able to catch the elevator door before it closed.

"Sorry about that," Brian apologized as he stepped in.

"Not a problem," Mr. Bennet replied graciously.

"The guard happened to mention that you are with Peerless Health," Brian said, making it sound like a casual statement.

"I am indeed," Mr. Bennet agreed. "Director of sales. And you?"

"I run a security firm," Brian said. "I'm impressed, and I hope you don't find this offensive, but you look more like a college student than a health company executive."

"I'll take that as a compliment," Mr. Bennet replied with a laugh, tossing a bit of his blond hair out of his eyes.

"I've heard that Peerless is doing very well."

"You heard correctly."

"So, you think the stock is a good investment?"

"It's an excellent investment," Mr. Bennet said. "Especially with the coronavirus pandemic, we're selling short-term health policies like no tomorrow. I'd certainly advise you to pick up some stock if you are in the market."

"Maybe I will," Brian said, nodding his head. "Thanks for the tip."

"You're very welcome."

The elevator came to a stop on the fifty-fourth floor and Mr. Bennet got off. Brian followed right behind. With an entry card, the man unlocked the door into the Peerless suite. A moment later they were standing in front of an empty reception desk in a posh lobby furnished with high-end leather furniture and with a view to the west over Sixth Avenue that included a tiny wedge of the Hudson River. But by far the most dominant object in view was the near life-size painting of Heather Williams dressed in her foxhunting finery.

"Excuse me," Mr. Bennet said, turning to face Brian. "Who are you here to see, if I may ask?"

"Ebony Wilson," Brian answered distractedly. It was hard to take his eyes off the painting, especially remembering the security guard's impression of her personality and narcissism.

"Is she expecting you?"

"Absolutely," Brian assured him. "Can you tell me where her office is?"

"Of course. Follow me!"

After skirting a number of empty secretarial desks, Mr. Bennet stopped at an open door and leaned in. "Ebony, there's someone here to see you."

"Who is it?" Brian could hear her ask.

Mr. Bennet turned to Brian, raising his eyebrows questioningly.

"Brian Murphy," Brian declared as he advanced to the doorway and looked in. In sharp contrast to Roger Dalton, whose deep baritone voice belied his appearance, Ebony Wilson and her assertive voice were well matched. She was an athletic-looking African American woman with a smattering of freckles over her face. Her dark hair was done in a braid, and she was sitting behind a monitor.

"Nice chatting with you, Mr. Murphy," Mr. Bennet called out before continuing on to his office down the corridor.

"Likewise," Brian called after him.

Ebony leaned back in her chair and removed wireless earbuds she used for her phone conversations as a claims adjustment supervisor. She tilted her head to the side as she gave him a studied look. "Brian Murphy?" she questioned. "Do I know you?"

"Somewhat," Brian said vaguely. He stepped into the small office and sat down uninvited in one of two side chairs. "We spoke on the phone about a week ago."

"I speak to people all day every day. You'll have to be more specific. Are you an employee of Peerless?"

Brian laughed mockingly. "No, I'm not an employee of Peerless, and we certainly have never met. We spoke about Peerless denying a claim for an Emergency Department visit at MMH Inwood for my wife. You advised me to request a review, which I did, and which has again been denied. But that's not why I am here."

"How on earth did you get in?" she demanded as she straightened up in her chair.

"I walked in," he said.

"I don't mean how you physically got in. I mean how did you get past security and into our office suite?"

"Mr. Bennet was nice enough to get me in the office," Brian said. "As far as building security was concerned, all I did was show the guard my NYPD ID. Would you like to see it?" Brian leaned forward to allow him to get out his wallet.

"No, I suppose not since you are already here. Okay, so you are a Peerless customer. If you are not here about a claim denial, why exactly are you here?"

"I didn't say it wasn't about a claim denial," he corrected her. "In fact, it is. It's just not about the Emergency Department claim we spoke about. It's now the inpatient hospital bill that I'm concerned about. I've been told today that Peerless will not be covering that either, and I want to know why. This situation is the reason my wife and I made sure we had health insurance: in case one of us had to go to the hospital."

"Maybe you better show me your NYPD ID," Ebony said. "None of this makes sense."

Brian complied, flashing the ID the way he'd done for the security guard, but she wasn't to be fooled, and she demanded to see it up close.

"I see. So you are retired," she said, handing it back. "You hardly look old enough to retire."

"My wife and I started a security company," Brian explained. "She was also an NYPD officer."

"Which I assume is the reason you purchased a Peerless policy."

"That's correct. We were trying to be responsible because we couldn't afford the COBRA premiums that would have allowed us to stay covered by the NYPD health insurance."

"Do you have your Peerless policy number with you?"

"I do," he said, and he gave it to her. She used her computer to bring up the record. As she read, Brian glanced around at the surroundings. Even this small office was opulently decorated, making him wonder what kind of sumptuous, over-the-top quarters Heather Williams occupied. It also made him wonder how such extravagance could be supported by the mere two-hundred-dollars-a-month premium he and Emma had been paying. But then he remembered that when they had bought the policy in December, they'd been told such policies like theirs were selling like hotcakes because a huge number of self-employed people couldn't afford standard health policies that commercial businesses were buying for their employees. And that was before some twelve million Americans lost their jobs and their employer-based health insurance during the pandemic. Even if just a million of those people bought Peerless policies, that could mean $200 million a month revenue for the company.

"Okay, I found your case and have read through the latest adjuster's decision. It's actually pretty simple. Did you carefully read your policy like I suggested during our phone call about the Emergency Department bill? I remember you said you hadn't when you purchased it."

"No, I haven't," Brian admitted. "My wife's illness has taken precedence since we talked."

"Okay, tell me this. Are you aware your policy has a sizable deductible?"

"Of course," he said. "The sales agent let us know that it was ten thousand dollars."

"How about the amount that Peerless would pay per day for hospitalization?"

"I'm not sure I remember that."

"It clearly states in your policy on page thirteen that Peerless will pay a thousand dollars a day after the deductible is satisfied."

Brian suddenly felt embarrassed, realizing what fools he and Emma had been. Although a thousand dollars a day had sounded like a lot of money when they bought the policy, Emma's stay in MMH Inwood had been well over twenty thousand dollars a day.

"So now let's talk about the deductible," Ebony continued. "Are you aware how the Peerless deductible works?"

"I assume so," Brian said. "It means that we are responsible for the first ten thousand dollars. After that, Peerless steps in."

"No, that's not how the Peerless short-term policy deductible works. This is why you should have carefully read your policy, Mr. Murphy. With Peerless Health Insurance the deductible relates to Peerless payments, not to the policy holder's payments."

"I don't follow," he said, confused by all the semantics.

"Peerless doesn't pay the thousand dollars a day until it would have paid ten thousand if there was no deductible. Essentially that means the hospitalization has to be for more than ten days. Starting on the eleventh day, Peerless pays a thousand dollars a day. It is a permutation of the deductible concept devised by Heather Williams, our esteemed CEO, when she was our chief financial officer."

"But that's totally crazy," Brian managed. "That's the opposite of what everyone understands about a deductible."

"Excuse me, but it is very clearly explained in the policy. It's the reason you were advised to read it carefully. All our salespeople make a big point of making sure our customers understand their policies. And it is all spelled out in our extensive promotional materials, which I'm certain you were given."

"Maybe it was described," Brian admitted, yet he still felt cheated and incensed. Actually, he barely remembered how he and Emma had ended up with their Peerless Health Insurance in the first place. Was he the one who had found it or had it been Emma? He didn't know. All he could recall was talking with her about the need to have something for the rare "just-in-case" possibility and that they needed to look into the short-term policies the government was pushing. In many ways they were between a rock and a hard place thanks to a screwy healthcare system dependent on corporate or government employment.

"Is there anything else I can help you with?" Ebony asked. He could tell she was at the end of her patience with his unexpected appearance. "I really have to get back to work, and I have at least a dozen people on hold."

"I have a few more questions," Brian demanded, his rising anger causing him to flush. "I'm staring at a nearly hundred-and-ninety-thousand-dollar bill and counting, which boggles my mind. I had no idea hospitalization was so expensive. But you and your friends here certainly knew since you're in the damn healthcare business. Here's my question: Above and beyond the screwy deductible business, how the hell can you people possibly justify selling a policy that's going to bankrupt a family by only paying a thousand dollars a day? I mean, in contrast to all of us common folk with limited experience with hospitals, all of you insurance types surely know that a thousand dollars a day for hospital costs is equivalent to pissing on a forest fire."

"Just a minute, Mr. Murphy!" she stammered with obvious indignation. "I'm not going to sit here and allow you to verbally abuse me."

"Maybe I should be complaining to someone higher up," Brian said, reining in his anger by recognizing he was talking with a mere functionary. "I apologize for singling you out. But try to understand my situation. I'm facing financial ruin, and maybe the details of my insurance coverage were spelled out in the small print, but as a member of the general public, this seems to amount to a type of fraud. Maybe I should file a complaint of unfair and deceptive business practices with something like the Better Business Bureau."

"Filing a complaint or even instigating a legal action is your right, as I told you a week ago on the phone," Ebony said, partially mollified by his apology and the change of his tone. "But, as I also told you, the chances of anything like that going anywhere positive are just about zero. We here at Peerless are filling a needed niche, as the government has encouraged us to do, at the lowest possible price. Anyone can get health insurance that pays a higher portion, if not all of hospital costs, but insurance is like anything else: You get what you pay for."

"What about arranging for me to have a talk with this esteemed CEO of yours? She's the one who needs to have an idea of what she is doing to real people buying her policies."

Ebony's jaw dropped open in mock shock. "Now, that would be an interesting confrontation," she choked out. "Let me tell you something: Heather Williams is riding the crest of a wave and doesn't talk to mere mortals. I'm doing well with this job and I'm appreciated, but there is no way that even I could arrange to have a meeting with her. Even high-flying investment types often have to pay for her time."

"She sounds charming," Brian said sardonically, also remembering the security guard's description.

"She's a piece of work, no doubt about it. But she is extraordinarily good at what she does. I have to say we are all appreciative of the ride she's engineered for us, especially with the employee stock she's doled out to encourage company patriotism."

Fifteen minutes later and more irritated and strung out than he ever remembered feeling, Brian left Ebony's office. He felt as if he'd accomplished nothing. Reaching the empty Peerless lobby with its vacant reception desk, he collapsed onto one of the leather couches, wondering how much of the expensive piece of furniture his and Emma's premiums had paid for. Adding insult to injury, he found himself staring again at the haughty foxhunting portrait.

A sudden clamor of voices at the far end of the long hallway caught his attention. A few moments later a throng of five people entered the room, heading for the door out to the elevators. Leading the pack was none other than the woman in the painting herself, perhaps having aged maybe five or ten years. In Brian's estimation, she appeared to be maybe a year or two younger than Emma's thirty-four. As she swept past with a determined, rapid gait, she glanced in his direction. For a moment a look of mild disdainful bewilderment flashed across her thin-lipped, carefully made-up face, but she didn't slow down.

"Excuse me! Heather Williams?" Brian called out on

a whim. "I need to talk to you. I think you're in need of some moral advice." His unplanned outburst surprised even himself, but it had the desired effect. The Peerless CEO came to a stop at the threshold of the lobby door that had been opened for her. She turned to treat Brian to a shocked but clearly contemptuous inspection.

"You are going to give *me* advice?" she questioned with a disbelieving tone. "Who the hell are you?" Her voice was shrill. She was obviously unaccustomed to being accosted by a stranger, especially in her own office. "Do you know it costs a thousand dollars a minute to talk with me?"

"That sounds like a bargain to me," he said as he leaped to his feet. He wanted to take full advantage of this serendipitous encounter by looking at her eye to eye. "I was guessing more like two or three thousand at the very least."

In spite of her obvious irritation, Heather laughed. Apparently, Brian's mocking humor appealed to her narcissism. From the vantage point of his six-foot-one stature, he guessed she was somewhere around Emma's five-eight but of much slighter build. What he didn't expect was that his sudden standing up alarmed two of the four men in her entourage, including the one who had rushed ahead to open the lobby door. Both of these men were dressed in dark, ill-fitting suits and wearing prototypical aviator sunglasses. Instantly it occurred to Brian that the two older men were the bodyguards the building security guard had described.

As the two men started toward him, reaching under

their lapels presumably for their firearms, Brian instinctively went for the P365 Sig Sauer nine-millimeter automatic pistol holstered in his waistband, which he carried religiously ever since he'd been a cop. Brian was a firearms expert par excellence, particularly with a handgun, which he had trained with on a regular basis and was fully licensed to carry. Luckily, in this instance, a potentially bad situation was averted by Heather, who snapped her hands out laterally to restrain her overeager escorts. Brian relaxed the fingers wrapped around his gun's grip.

"I repeat: Who are you?" Heather demanded. "And what makes you possibly think you can give me advice?"

"I'm a very, very dissatisfied Peerless Health Insurance customer," Brian answered. And then while poking his index finger accusatorily toward Heather's face, he added: "You should be ashamed of yourself for designing and selling your worthless policies."

Reacting to Brian's possibly threatening hand gesture, the two bodyguards surged forward once more only to have Heather restrain them for the second time. There was little doubt that in his angered state he could more than handle these two mildly overweight, out-of-shape men who looked more like bouncers at a small-town bar than proper security personnel. In his aggravation, he would have actually enjoyed giving in to his bottled-up emotions and taking them down.

"Worthless?" Heather questioned in an overly mocking tone. "I beg your pardon, but thousands of extremely happy investors would tell you how wrong you are. How in God's name did you get in here, anyway?"

"You're the second person who has asked me that question," Brian said, imitating Heather's sarcastic tone. "I merely walked in, which means that not only are you selling morally suspect crap, it seems that you are in dire need of some professional security advice. Luckily, I happen to be an expert in that realm, and I'd be happy to give you one of my cards if you are interested."

"Get the hell out of here!" Heather snapped, pointing to the door to the elevator lobby. "And if you ever venture to come within a hundred yards of me again, I won't restrain my pit bulls."

Despite himself, Brian laughed while glancing briefly at the two supposed pit bulls. "I hope that's a promise, not a warning. But I can tell when I'm not appreciated, so I'll take your suggestion and leave. But, your threat notwithstanding, I have a sense that you are going to hear from me again very soon. You, your attitude, and your company continue to ruin my life. It's just not right, and I'm going to do something about it."

Without looking back, he walked to the door, deriving a bit of satisfaction from the shocked silence his little speech had engendered. Unfortunately, when he got there, he couldn't open it and had to wait until one of the younger men in Heather's entourage came over and used a magnetic card.

"Thank you," Brian said with forced dignity as he strolled out into the elevator lobby.

CHAPTER 10

August 31

Brian awoke Monday morning way before he intended but instantly knew he would not be going back to sleep. It was the characteristic whine of a mosquito that had rudely awakened him. Sitting bolt upright in bed, he listened intently. The sun had yet to come up, but dawn's twilight filled the room with more than enough light for him to see. A moment later he caught sight of the insect as it landed on his upper left arm just above his elbow. For a split second he watched as it prepared to bite. He noticed that it was the same species that had plagued them at their beach barbecue, an Asian tiger, with its characteristic white marks on its black body and legs.

With fear-fueled speed, Brian slapped the insect with enough force to make his arm sting. The blow reduced it to a smudge of blood, suggesting it had already feasted. After using a bedside tissue to wipe off the remains, he bounded out of bed to check the open window. Sure enough, one corner of the screen was not fully engaged in its track, providing an opening to the outside. Brian quickly pulled it in tightly and set the small spring lock in place. With his heart racing, he climbed back into bed on his side and pulled up the covers, marveling at the fact that the Asian tiger mosquito could haunt such a highly urbanized area.

When he'd gone to bed just before midnight, he'd been totally exhausted both mentally and physically. The five or so hours of sleep he'd gotten clearly weren't adequate, yet the confrontation with the pesky mosquito started him thinking. It was depressingly clear to him that there was no guarantee that things were going to improve as he faced another difficult week ahead. Rolling over onto his back, he stared up at the blank bedroom ceiling to make sure no other mosquitoes had gotten in. Although he knew more sleep was out of the question, he didn't get out of bed, preferring to wallow in self-pity and lament his life. He'd never realized how tenuous it had been. Friday had started out bad, when a call from Calvin Foster's executive secretary came in informing him that the October wedding had been canceled until further notice, meaning that even that modest potential income was off the table.

Right after that bit of disappointing news, Juliette had a meltdown while Camila tried to make her eat some breakfast. As if that wasn't bad enough, then Brian started getting a flurry of calls on both the business landline and his mobile phone as well as multiple emails from a company called Premier Collections, which was threatening both a lawsuit over the $189,375.86 MMH Inwood bill and a sharp decrease in his credit rating if he didn't immediately set up a payment plan. The harassing communications had shocked him after having had a face-to-face meeting with Roger Dalton just the day before. When he'd tried calling him for an explanation of why it was happening so quickly, he'd had to leave a voice message.

Continuing to stare up at the ceiling with unseeing eyes, Brian wondered how his bill was so astronomical, especially when he considered that MMH Inwood hadn't really done anything besides just watch Emma go downhill. Except for handling the seizure in the ED, they hadn't really treated her, and they certainly hadn't cured her. In many ways, she was worse off when discharged than the day she walked into the Emergency Department. And then to truly add insult to injury, he had gotten three more non-hospital bills by email. The smallest invoice was from the ambulance company, Adultcare, who had had the nerve to charge nine hundred dollars to drive Emma about twenty blocks from MMH Inwood to the Hudson Valley Rehabilitation Hospital. At the time the MMH discharge people had arranged the transportation and if Brian had been given any warning about the cost, he would have driven Emma himself.

And then worse still were two other much larger bills from doctors. The biggest was from the neurologist who was not employed by MMH Inwood but had been asked to see Emma. The cost of his evaluation was $17,197.50. The second bill was for an out-of-hospital cardiologist in the amount of $13,975.13 after a nurse had possibly detected a few extra heartbeats when taking Emma's pulse. In the end, Emma's heart function was determined to be entirely normal, and all this meant was that his debt had reached a staggering $221,448.49.

The blaring of a horn accompanied by an angry shout out on West 217th Street briefly interrupted Brian's thoughts, but a moment later he was back to his musing, specifically about how financially predatory and overly expensive the healthcare industry had become, particularly the hospitals. What he realized was that most people with good insurance, like he and Emma had had when employed by the NYPD, were ultimately complicit in allowing this ridiculous situation to happen. If hospital bills got paid, and of course they did, who cared or questioned how much the costs were, especially if trying to figure them out was practically impossible? Now he saw that such an attitude over time had contributed to allowing prices to climb exponentially, making it a recipe for disaster when someone lost their insurance or had bad insurance like the short-term policies Peerless offered. From his perspective it all amounted to a type of tolerated fraud, seeing as hospitals like MMH Inwood could create their own demand and then charge whatever they pleased. On top of that, less than ethical companies like Peerless could latch on and enjoy the ride while making a fortune.

As bad as Friday had been, Saturday was even more upsetting for Brian. It had started encouragingly enough when Aimée had called early and offered to come over and help with Juliette, whose behavior was getting worse.

In many respects Juliette was as attached to her paternal grandmother as she was to her mother, and with Aimée present she'd eaten a decent breakfast for the first time in several days and for a while was her old self and content watching her cartoons. The reprieve gave Aimée and Brian a few moments to talk, which he used to share the disturbing news about Emma's astounding hospital bill. Shocked at the amount, Aimée had suggested he contact a medical billing advocate.

"What the hell is a medical billing advocate?" Brian had asked. "I've never heard of such a person."

"Apparently they help people with hospital bills," Aimée had responded. "I hadn't heard of them, either, but a friend of mine had a problem with an MMH Inwood bill and told me a billing advocate had helped her. The advocate's name is Megan Doyle, and she has an office here. You should let her help you."

Following that relatively pleasant morning and with Aimée entertaining Juliette, and Hannah expected to join them, Brian had gone to Hudson Valley Rehabilitation Hospital with the intent of spending the day with Emma. His plan was to get a true idea of how much rehabilitation she was actually receiving. But similar to what had happened at MMH Inwood on Thursday, as soon as he had entered HVR, he was told he needed to see Antonia Fluentes in the business office immediately.

With some trepidation Brian complied, but the moment he entered the woman's office, he knew from her body language that trouble was afoot, and she confirmed it immediately.

"It's been brought to our attention that your MMH Inwood bill is outstanding with no payment plan arranged," Antonia said. She stared at him expectantly with dark, piercing eyes framed with equally dark glasses.

"It's only been a few days since my wife's discharge," Brian said evasively.

"But we also have learned that your account has been turned over to collections. As you can imagine, that is not encouraging for us."

"It's not great for me, either," he responded.

"We've also not had a good experience with your insurance carrier, Peerless Health."

"That doesn't surprise me," Brian added.

"I'm sure you can see our dilemma. Due to the pandemic, Hudson Valley Rehabilitation Hospital has been struggling financially, like most healthcare facilities. To be perfectly honest, we are going to need upfront coverage for your wife if we are to continue with her rehabilitation."

"I see," Brian said, feeling like he was taking yet another low blow. "Exactly what kind of figure do you have in mind?"

"Minimally we are looking for two thousand dollars a day for the first ten days. At that point we can reassess the situation and her progress."

"I'm afraid we don't have a spare twenty thousand lying around." He could hardly keep the sarcasm out of his voice.

"I figured that might be the case, so I spoke with our chief medical officer, Dr. Harold Spenser," Antonia continued. "Medically he doesn't see any reason your wife cannot be discharged and have her rehabilitation carried out at home by local physical therapists who will be up to you to retain."

"What about somewhat of a lower advance, say, in the five-thousand-dollar range?" Brian said. "This would be a gesture of good faith to keep my wife here as an inpatient."

"I'm afraid not. Your wife's current bill is already almost five thousand dollars."

At that point the conversation went downhill as he became incensed that Emma's charges could already be at the five-thousand-dollar mark, considering she'd only been there two full days, the shabby state of the facility, what seemed like a lack of staff, and that she'd essentially received no treatment. In the end, it was decided that Emma had to be discharged, and to avoid another thousand-dollar ambulance bill, Brian had to drive her home himself.

Although getting Emma into the car had been a struggle, once they'd gotten underway, she perked up. "Being discharged was unexpected, but I'm looking forward to getting home," she'd said. She was out of breath from the effort of climbing into the car's front seat. There was no doubt her spasticity was worse.

"I can well imagine. We are all going to be thrilled to have you, especially Juliette, who's really missed you."

"I've missed her, too," Emma confessed. "And how about the business? I've been afraid to ask."

"Not good," he told her regretfully. "There was a

possibility of a wedding in October out in the Hamptons, but just yesterday it was canceled. Camila is constantly trying to scare up some business with social media."

"How are our finances?" Emma asked.

"Also not good, I'm afraid," Brian said with a wince. He'd not mentioned anything to Emma about the problems with Peerless or the hospital bill and didn't intend to until she was fully recovered, seeing no reason to stress her out.

At first Emma's homecoming had been well received, especially since both Aimée and Hannah were there to greet her with Juliette and Camila. Juliette was obviously thrilled, at least initially. But the bonhomie didn't last, as Emma's physical limitations and precarious emotional state put the festivities to a quick end. She quickly tired, had no patience with Juliette, who needed constant attention and reassurance, and soon just wanted to go to bed and sleep. Getting her up the stairs to the master bedroom became an exhausting ordeal for everyone; although she could walk on the flat with some difficulty, the stairs were almost impossible.

For him it had been the night that was by far the most difficult part, when he was left alone with his ailing wife. Although Emma had slept most of Saturday afternoon and evening, at night she was mostly awake, emotionally unstable, and rather restless, putting Brian's patience to a true stress test. She even managed to fall out of bed around four A.M. On top of that was the difficulty of getting her from the bed to the toilet on multiple occasions.

He'd barely slept a wink, and it also made him understand why it had been far better that he'd become a policeman rather than a medic, a notion he had entertained for a short time as a teenager.

Sunday had been spent trying to make the home situation tolerable for everyone. Luckily Hannah had an acquaintance with a late husband who'd been chronically sick and had required a hospital bed with guardrails for the last years of his life. Since she no longer needed the bed, she'd graciously offered it to Brian to install in the second-floor guest room, across from Camila's room. To his great relief, Hannah had insisted she'd spend the night with her daughter to give him a break and a good night's sleep.

The sound of the front door chimes ringing shocked Brian from his recollections of the past few difficult days, and he leaped out of bed, grabbing his robe in the process. As he headed for the stairs, he wondered who in God's name could be ringing his doorbell before eight on a Monday morning.

Grabbing a mask off the console table in the front foyer and looping its strings around his ears, he pulled open the door. His wild rush had been hopefully to prevent whoever was there from impatiently ringing the doorbell yet again. About eight feet away, standing on the top step of a mini flight of stairs in the middle of Brian's front yard, was a white-haired, moderately well-dressed gentleman in a white shirt, poorly knotted tie, and sports jacket. Despite only seeing the man's forehead and his blue eyes through rimless eyeglasses above his face mask, Brian sensed that he vaguely knew the person. The man was holding an envelope in his right hand, although his arms were limp along his sides.

"Can I help you?" Brian asked, trying not to be irritated. It wasn't a convenient time to be bothered, especially with the possibility of rousing Emma and Juliette. Thanks to phones and email, house visits of all sorts were rare these days, especially with the pandemic.

"I apologize," the man said with a mild Irish accent. "Really I do."

The combination of the sound of the man's voice and the other visual cues brought some memories back. "Grady?" Brian questioned, tilting his head to the side to get a slightly different view. "Grady Quillen?"

"Yeah, it's me. Sorry to bother you like this at the crack of dawn."

"It's not a problem. It's not that early, Grady. I was awake, although the rest of the brood is still asleep. What's up?" He recognized him as one of the patrolmen of the 34th Precinct when Brian's father had been the commanding officer. He also knew Grady lived not that far away, on Payson Avenue in an apartment overlooking Inwood Hill Park.

"Believe it or not, I have to ask you if you are Brian Yves Murphy."

"Is this some kind of a joke?"

"I wish," Grady said, looking sheepish.

"How's the family?" Brian asked. "Everybody staying well in this crazy time?"

"Yeah, we're fine and healthy. Thank you for asking,

but you are making this harder for me than it needs to be. Are you Brian Yves Murphy?"

"Okay, yes, I'm Brian Yves Murphy. Are you happy?"

"Hardly," Grady said as he handed him the envelope. "After I retired from the NYPD five years ago, I sat around for a few months and drove my wife batty. You know the expression: 'for better or worse but not for lunch.' Then I took a job as a process server for Premier Collections. It's kept me married and pays for the Jameson. I'm sorry, Brian."

"So, I guess I've been served?" He looked at his name typed on the front of the envelope, and with his background in law enforcement he knew full well what it meant. The fact that Grady had become a process server didn't surprise him in the slightest. Like being a commercial building security guard, being a process server was common for retired New York City patrolmen.

"I'm afraid so," Grady said. "It's a complaint and a summons. I apologize for being the bearer of bad news, but I couldn't refuse just because I know you."

"If you have a few minutes, let's sit and chat," Brian suggested while pointing down toward the ground. "Sorry I can't invite you inside, so this will have to do." He stepped out and sat on the single step leading up to his front door. Moving more than the mandated six feet away, Grady sat on his step and turned sideways. It was pleasant enough with the morning sun and mild temperature, surrounded by Brian's shrub-and-tiger-lily-filled front yard.

After briefly leafing through the papers Grady had

provided to confirm what they were, Brian replaced them in the envelope and looked up. "Please don't feel in any way responsible for this. My getting served is not unexpected except for the speed involved. If this was going to happen, I thought I'd at least have the usual thirty days."

"It's been my experience that MMH Inwood has been progressively aggressive with collections over the last few years," Grady said, "but with the pandemic throwing a monkey wrench into the hospital's finances, it's gone through the roof."

"So I've heard."

"To give you an idea, just since March they've had me running ragged, averaging ten to fifteen services a week. And I'm not the only Premier process server. There's three of us."

"Are you guys serving just people in Inwood?" he asked, taken aback by the numbers from just one community.

"The vast majority," Grady said. "There's always a few from Hudson Heights."

"How do you know it's the hospital behind the uptick and not the collections people themselves?"

"That's easy. The hospital actually owns Premier Collections. They are part and parcel of the same organization."

"You're kidding?" Brian questioned, even more shocked by this than by the numbers. Learning that MMH Inwood was in the collection business meant that the hospital was even more predatory than he thought.

"I'm not kidding in the slightest," Grady said. "It's all the brainchild of the hospital CEO, Charles Kelley."

"How do you know?"

Grady gave a short, sardonic laugh. "I know because he's a cult figure around Premier Collections and with the hospital admin people, too. They all think he's a financial genius. He's also liberal with the MMH stock with higher-up employees, meaning, of course, I've been out of luck. I tell you, if I had any extra cash, I'd buy some of the MMH stock because I hear that it's a winner, constantly going up."

In an uncomfortable way, Charles Kelley and his tactics were sounding rather similar to Heather Williams's business model.

"I'd like to meet this Charles Kelley sometime," Grady continued. "I've heard his compensation is more than five million per year. Can you imagine? I think the only hospital CEO who makes more is the guy who runs the University of Pittsburgh Medical Center. He gets over six million. It's crazy."

Knowing the ridiculous amount of money he owed from Emma's seven days of hospitalization, he could now believe it rather easily. He'd never had any idea what an impressive gold mine medical care could be.

"So, what are you going to do about this situation?" Grady asked. "As a friend, I want to make sure you know you have to respond to the summons within thirty days or there will be a summary judgment against you."

"Yeah, I know," Brian said.

"Obviously I couldn't help but see that MMH Inwood is suing you for almost one hundred and ninety thousand dollars. Who in your family needed hospitalization?"

"My wife, Emma," he told him. "She caught a bad mosquito-borne illness while we were on Cape Cod. It isn't contagious, if you are worried."

"I'm not worried," Grady said. "What a bummer. How is she doing?"

"So-so," Brian admitted, unwilling to provide any specifics. "At least she's home."

"I'm glad to hear it. What's the story with your health insurance? I heard you and your wife were with the ESU."

"We were until we retired in December to start our own security company," Brian said. He was getting tired of explaining. "When we retired, we lost our city insurance and were forced to rely on a short-term policy that's not worth the paper it's printed on. They aren't contributing a penny."

"Ouch," Grady said. "Have you talked with a lawyer?"

"Not yet. That would cost more money."

"Money well spent," Grady said. "Take my word."

"I think I'll go back and try to reason with the MMH Inwood business office and come to some understanding."

"From my vantage point the chances of that helping are piss poor. You need a lawyer, because Premier is dogged. I'm telling you: They won't give up, and they'll go after everything, including your house. By the way, this is one of the nicest houses in Inwood."

"We were lucky to get it."

"I'm serious about Premier being hard-nosed. You might know a neighbor of mine, Nolan O'Reilly."

"I know the family," Brian recalled. "What about him?"

"I had to serve him. He ended up losing everything, and his and his wife's salaries have been attached from now until hell freezes over."

"Was that a hospital bill, too?" he asked.

"It sure was, about twice yours. It involved surgery on their son, and to make matters worse, the kid died."

"That's awful."

"I know a lawyer," Grady continued. "He's down on Broadway. A local kid, and he's really good. I gave his name to my neighbor, and he fell over backward trying to help him."

"Is this the neighbor who lost everything?" Brian asked.

"Unfortunately, yes."

"That's not a very good advertisement for your lawyer acquaintance," Brian countered.

"I know it sounds that way, but my neighbor had failed to respond to the original summons, and there had been a summary judgment. When that happens, it's almost an impossible uphill struggle, so please respond!"

"I'll definitely take care of it. What's the lawyer's name?"

"Patrick McCarthy."

At that moment, he saw Aimée turn into the walkway, carrying a white bag from CHOCnyc, an Inwood French bakery. Both Brian and Grady immediately got to their feet. She stopped when she saw Grady, and like Brian had done earlier, she tilted her head and wrinkled her forehead, obviously recognizing him on some level but struggling to place him.

"Hello, Mrs. Murphy," Grady said to help her. "It's Grady Quillen."

"Oui, Grady Quillen," Aimée repeated. "So nice to see you again."

"I'm sorry about Deputy Inspector Murphy's passing," Grady said, bowing his head.

"Thank you," Aimée responded kindly. "It was a shock to us all." Brian's father had died of a heart attack a year and a half earlier while on the job as commanding officer of the local precinct.

After a few minutes of small talk, Grady went on his way, saying he had more work he needed to do. After he was out of sight, Aimée turned to Brian. "What was he here for so early?"

He waved the envelope. "He's a process server, and he served me. I'm afraid MMH Inwood is already suing me for Emma's care."

"C'est terrible," Aimée said, worry creasing her face. "Why so soon?"

"It is terrible," Brian said, mimicking his mom's French accent. "I feel like my life is coming apart at the seams, and I don't even know where to begin to try to fix it."

CHAPTER 11

August 31

It was just after eleven o'clock in the morning when Brian slowed his running pace as he neared MMH Inwood and then jogged up the driveway. As religious as he'd been about keeping himself in superb physical shape with weight training and cardiovascular exercise since high school, he seriously missed his daily workouts and hoped that with Emma at home and Aimée and Hannah offering to help, he could get back to some semblance of a routine. His mother and Emma's mother certainly had helped that morning and had allowed him and Camila to spend a few hours in the home office brainstorming potential ways to drum up business for Personal Protection LLC. While they were strategizing, several more harassing calls came in from Premier Collections, confirming Grady's assessment of their persistence.

After having been duly served with a complaint and summons, Brian had been eager to see Roger Dalton in the hopes of stopping the collection process, so as soon as he could, with Aimée's and Hannah's blessings, he'd set out. Now as he entered, he wondered if his visit would turn out to be worthwhile. After Grady's estimate that the chances of reversing anything were "piss poor," he wasn't optimistic, but he couldn't see any harm in trying.

As he entered the hospital's swank admin area, he was reminded that he'd always thought of MMH Inwood as a positive asset to the community. Now he was thinking the opposite, especially knowing how many other Inwood residents were being pursued for collection of most likely seriously inflated hospital bills.

Brian had not called ahead, preferring just to show up and plead his case. But he soon began to think he'd made a mistake, as he was subjected to a considerable wait. When he was finally ushered into the office, Roger added to his pessimism by announcing that Brian had better make it quick, as he didn't have much time.

"I'll try to be fast," he said, struggling to control his emotions. He was beginning to hate this thin wasp of a man. "I'm shocked and disappointed that my case has already been turned over to Premier Collections and they are already hounding me. From my memory, that's legally questionable. Besides, you and I have been in continuous contact, and you know that I am taking this situation seriously enough to have made a personal visit to Peerless Health Insurance late last week."

Sighing with boredom and annoyance, Roger tented his skinny, gnarled fingers. "To be honest, I didn't have any choice, not under these trying times. Turning a case over to collections immediately has become standard policy dictated from above when it's obvious the situa-

tion is futile, which is what you have led me to believe.
You refused to set up an agreeable payment plan. Case
closed."

"I can't set up a payment plan in this financial environment with the pandemic going on," Brian said irritably. "My company's income these days is zero."

"That's my point precisely," Roger said. "You are not
going to agree to a reasonable payment plan. So we
agree."

"What exactly do you mean, 'dictated from above'?"

"Exactly as it sounds," Roger answered.

"How far above?"

"The top."

"Let me ask you this," Brian said. "Does MMH Inwood own Premier Collections?"

"Why do you ask? What difference does that make?
You owe what you owe."

"I think it makes a lot of difference," Brian argued.
"And your response certainly confirms my suspicion.
When you say policy is dictated from the top, I assume
you mean the CEO, Mr. Charles Kelley?"

"Obviously," Roger said as if progressively bored by the
conversation. "He is the chief executive officer, after all."

"So he must be really hands-on if he's concerned
about the nitty-gritty goings-on in the hospital, like collections and speeding up the process."

"Oh, yes," Roger said with emphasis. "Mr. Kelley is
the man behind MMH's financial success and massive
building campaign. Both this campus and MMH Midtown have been totally renovated, bringing everything

up to twenty-first-century standards. All that takes money, so Mr. Kelley has made us, the Business Department, feel as essential to the hospital mission as any other department. Charles Kelley is a superb businessman. Mark my words!"

"I'm beginning to think 'ruthless' might be closer to the truth than 'superb,'" Brian said. "Did you know that I have already been served?"

"I did not," Roger said. "But I'm not surprised. Once an account is moved to collections, I'm no longer involved."

"I'd like to get you reinvolved and hold up the legal maneuvering. Why don't you and I go back to talking about some kind of goodwill payment to carry us through this pandemic?"

"That's not possible." Roger shook his head firmly.

"Why not?"

"Mr. Kelley, the superb businessman he is, has insisted that Premier Collections operate as a separate entity even though owned by MMH Inwood. For accounting and tax reasons, Premier has bought your debt. I'm no longer involved, so you have to deal with them from now on."

"But if Charles Kelley were to give you license to get reinvolved, would that work?"

"Obviously," Roger said with a dismissive laugh, as if that was the most ridiculous idea he'd heard all day. "But that's not going to happen."

"How often does he come here?" Brian asked. He'd noticed that on all his recent visits to the MMH Inwood admin area, Charles Kelley's office and its neighboring fancy conference room were empty.

"Not that often. Maybe once or twice a week. He's mostly at his MMH Midtown office, which is a facility four times the size of this one."

"Is he approachable?" Brian asked. "I mean, could I set up a meeting with him? As good a businessman as you think he is, maybe he should hear from someone in the community being adversely affected by his policies. Ultimately, he must be concerned about the hospital's image in the community, which I think is suffering. I've learned I'm not the only one being sued."

Roger laughed even harder than he had a moment earlier. "You would not be able to arrange a meeting with Charles Kelley," he scoffed. "No way. His time is inordinately valuable. Besides, he doesn't have the time to get involved with individual patient accounts."

"Maybe he should be," Brian insisted. "As a business-man in a service industry, I would think he'd be very interested in the hospital's image. What do you think about me approaching him on my own?"

"He wouldn't waste a minute talking with you," Roger said. "I'm telling you: He's a very, very busy man. Besides, you'd be taking a risk going up to him unannounced."

"How so?" Brian asked.

"He has an armed driver."

"Why would a hospital CEO need an armed driver?" Brian asked. As a security-minded individual, Brian was legitimately interested.

"Because he is an inordinately important man running several large institutions," Roger said impatiently. "It's to protect him from people like you, if you want to know the truth. What a ridiculous question."

"Okay," Brian said, trying to maintain his composure. "Let's move on to another issue. Did you or anyone here make it a point to contact the Hudson Valley Rehabilitation Hospital and report that my wife's hospital bill had been turned over to collections?"

"I can't imagine. It certainly wasn't me, if that is what you are implying."

"Someone did," Brian said. "Last week I was dragged into their business office and presented with an ultimatum: Either I came up with a twenty-thousand-dollar advance or my wife was going to be booted out for the second time because of nonpayment of exorbitant hospital charges."

"I resent that statement," Roger said irritably. "It seems you're implying that your wife was discharged from here because of nonpayment of her bill and that our charges are not appropriate. Both statements are patently untrue, as I've told you before." He stood up. "This meeting is over. I want you to leave, or I am going to call security, and they will throw you out."

For a brief moment of irrationality, Brian fantasized about refusing to leave in hopes of having a half-trained hospital security person or two try to throw him out. Instead, feeling chagrined at being summarily dismissed after he'd made a sincere effort to come in and resolve the hospital bill problem, Brian stormed out of Dalton's office. Cursing under his breath and feeling a searing anger at a system designed to make money more than anything else, he strode toward the door leading into the hospital lobby. But on his way out he couldn't help but stop and stare in at Charles Kelley's empty office and fancy glass-walled conference room.

Motivated by morbid curiosity, Brian walked in through the open office door. He was looking for the equivalent of Heather Williams's ostentatious foxhunting portrait, and he wasn't disappointed. Hanging above a faux fireplace was a nearly full-sized painting of a blond-haired middle-aged man in a three-piece business suit, arms folded, leaning up against an impressive desk similar to the real one in the room. Just to be certain, Brian approached to read the engraved plaque. It was indeed Charles Kelley. Although pictorially tame in contrast to Heather's outlandish portrait, Charles's painting conveyed the same sense of entitlement and privilege, with an equally haughty, superior-than-thou smile. "Two birds of a feather," Brian observed out loud as he shook his head in disgust.

"Excuse me!" a voice called. "What are you doing? You are not allowed in here!"

Brian turned to face a secretary clearly outraged at his violation of Charles Kelley's inner sanctum.

"Just enjoying the artwork," Brian said with a fake, innocent smile.

A few minutes later as he was passing out through the main entrance's revolving door, with his irritation and anger still at a boiling point, Brian thought again about the two CEOs and how they seemed to be poster children for what was wrong with American medicine and unbridled entrepreneurial capitalism. And as a doer, he knew he couldn't just passively allow their greediness to go unchallenged and dictate the unraveling of his life. He had to do something. He just didn't know what.

CHAPTER 12

August 31

As Brian turned from Park Terrace East onto West 217th Street and slowed to a walk on his torn-up street, what was becoming progressively clear to him was the need to retain a lawyer despite the added cost. The question was: Should he use the counselor Grady suggested, who had some experience dealing with MMH Inwood, or should he use a lawyer from the white-shoe firm he and Emma had employed to set up Personal Protection LLC? As he climbed the stairs in the middle of his front yard where Grady had been sitting that morning, he decided to give Patrick McCarthy a try, as the cost would undoubtedly be appropriately and remarkably less. But that wasn't the only reason. Brian also thought that Patrick's experience with MMH could be significant in addition to his being a local boy. In a community like Inwood, being part of the neighborhood made a difference.

Reaching the top step and despite his preoccupations, he paused. He couldn't help but appreciate his surroundings. He was standing with his profusion of riotously beautiful orange tiger lilies flanking both sides of the walkway, which had been planted by the house's previous owners in lieu of a minuscule lawn. After admiring the flowers, he then looked up at his home with its striking Tudor revival mixture of brick and stonework. He and Emma loved the house and had admired it during their childhoods. Brian was proud that they owned it, but now, with MMH Inwood's Premier Collections on his case, he knew that the property was potentially in jeopardy. The thought shocked him back to reality and reawakened the anger he'd felt in Roger Dalton's office, forcing him to try to think about something else.

The something else was what he would be confronting once he entered through the front door. The one positive thing that he hoped would have resulted from Emma's being kicked out of two hospitals was that her presence at home would have drastically improved Juliette's attitude and behavior. But that hadn't happened. If anything, Juliette's apparent anxiety was even worse because Emma's illness made it difficult for her to meet her daughter's needs. As a result, Juliette was back to refusing to eat, was again voicing vague bodily complaints, and was displaying frequent temper tantrums.

Brian's worst fears were substantiated the moment he entered through the front door. Standing in the foyer and removing his shoes, he could hear both his wife and his daughter distantly sobbing and complaining, one from the kitchen and the other from the upstairs guest room. Flipping a mental coin of which situation took precedence, he first went into the kitchen. Juliette was sitting in the breakfast nook and Camila was at the sink washing a frying pan. For a brief moment Brian and Camila exchanged a glance and Camila rolled her eyes.

He slid into the banquette alongside Juliette. In front of her on a plate was a freshly made grilled cheese sandwich. "What's the matter, my sweet?" Brian asked. Juliette cried harder.

"She said she was hungry for a grilled cheese," Camila said. It was obvious her patience was being tested. "Now she won't eat it." Camila finished with the pan and then turned to face the room, leaning back against the sink arms akimbo.

"Why are you not eating?" he asked his daughter.

Choking on her tears, Juliette managed: "I don't feel good."

"I'm sorry, sweetheart," Brian said. He looked over at Camila, who was at her wits' end. "Why don't I spend a little time with her?"

"I'd appreciate that," Camila said, and immediately left the room.

"If you don't want to eat, what do you want to do?"

"I want to watch cartoons with Bunny." Bunny was propped up against her as per usual.

"Why don't you?" He pushed the TV remote in Juliette's direction.

"Camila said I couldn't until I finished my sandwich."

Brian guessed there had been a mini test of wills, which wasn't uncommon or unusual considering both individuals' personalities. He took the remote and turned on the TV. "What do you mean when you say you don't feel good?" Brian was curious about Juliette's ongoing long list of mild complaints, which had started with Emma's seizure and hospitalization, and had only gotten worse since her homecoming.

Juliette rubbed her hand vaguely around her stomach, which is what she'd done previously when he had asked for specifics. "And my head hurts."

"I'm sorry you are not feeling well. Does Bunny have the same symptoms?"

Juliette nodded.

"The more I check out that grilled cheese sandwich, the better it looks," Brian said. "Do you mind if I have a bite?"

Juliette pushed the dish in his direction. Brian took a bite and chewed thoughtfully. "Not bad! Actually, really good! Maybe you should let Bunny give it a try."

After offering the sandwich to Bunny to take a bite, Juliette took one herself. Brian purposefully didn't comment. Instead, he was content to just sit with her and enjoy a portion of a *Curious George* episode. As they watched, Juliette toyed with her food without eating any more, until Camila eventually returned.

"I'm sorry," Camila said. "I don't know what came over me."

"Don't be silly," he said, waving her apology away. "I understand completely. We're all under stress."

"I think you'd better see if you can help Aimée and Hannah. They're having a difficult time with Emma."

"Right!" Brian slid out from the breakfast nook. The

whole time he'd been in the kitchen, he'd occasionally heard distant sobbing and raised voices. With some apprehension about what he was going to face, he climbed the stairs. If both Aimée and Hannah were struggling, he thought the chances he could help were mighty slim.

The hospital bed was in the center of the room with the head pressed up against the wall between the two windows that looked out over the driveway and the neighboring house. The guest room bed, where Hannah had spent the night, had been pushed back against the common wall with the hallway. Aimée was on one side of the hospital bed and Hannah on the other, while Emma was lying in the bed with her upper body on a towel. Her face was streaked with tears, and a basin with soap and water was on a stool on Hannah's side. As Brian entered and approached the foot of the bed, Hannah draped a towel over Emma's midsection.

"She's refusing to let us bathe her," Hannah explained with irritation.

To Brian it was clear that everyone in the room was emotionally overwrought. The question was: What to do?

"I want to take a shower," Emma complained, her voice catching. "They won't let me!"

"It's too dangerous," Hannah lectured. "You are not walking right, and you might fall. Then you'd be worse off than you are now."

"It's true," Aimée added.

"How about a bath in the master bathroom?" Brian offered. It was clear Emma was feeling ganged up on, and the guest room bath only had a shower.

"That might work, but only if she lets us get her there and then back to bed," Hannah stated as the domineering mother she'd always been.

"How about you guys take a coffee break?" he suggested, trying to be diplomatic toward Aimée and Hannah. Since he was highly dependent on their help, the very last thing he wanted to do was offend them in any way. "I think I'd like to have a few moments with my wife."

Aimée and Hannah exchanged a questioning glance, then reluctantly agreed. They filed out without another word. Hannah, who was the last to leave, closed the door behind her.

"I don't want to be here," Emma said, surprising Brian. Over the last few days, she'd been suffering various stages of confusion. But now she sounded not only oriented, but lucid and almost like her old self. "I feel that I'm getting worse, not better. I need to be back in the hospital so I can be treated to get back to normal."

Brian nodded but struggled with what to say. After he had read that the vast majority of encephalitis survivors ended up with serious neurological deficits, he was reluctant to bring up the issue of what getting back to normal was going to mean. He also wasn't prepared to explain to her why it wouldn't be possible to get her back into MMH Inwood, even if that was what she preferred and even if it made the most sense medically. The whole situation was much too complicated and heartbreaking.

"Besides, I'm a big burden being here at home," Emma continued as new tears formed in the corner of her eyes.

"You are not a burden," Brian said, trying to protest but knowing in many ways that her presence was more difficult than he had expected. He gave her a hug and then gripped her hand. "And your mother and my mother are thrilled you are here. They see it as an opportunity, certainly not a burden. They're happy to help."

Taking advantage of her sudden lucidity, he broached the subject of Juliette. Brian could tell that she was horrified to learn that her actions since arriving home on Saturday had exacerbated Juliette's behavioral problems.

"I had no idea," Emma said regretfully. "I hardly remember anything since I've been here, which is scary."

"She's missed you terribly. If I had to guess, I think it's mostly from having witnessed your seizure in the car. That's frightening for anyone, especially a four-year-old who's as close to her mother as Juliette is to you."

"Oh, gosh! I'll have to make it up to her. It just makes me feel awful, the poor thing. She's been through a lot."

"It's certainly not your fault," Brian said. "But anything you do or say will undoubtedly help."

Without any warning, Emma pulled her hand away from his and slapped her palm to her head, gripping herself hard enough that her forehead wrinkled and knuckles blanched. At the same instant, her other hand noisily grasped one of the bed's metal guardrails. Shocked by the sudden motion and noise, Brian blinked and retreated a full step backward.

"What's going on? What happened? Are you okay?"

Emma withdrew her hand, blinked, and looked over

at him. "Wow! That was strange. I guess I'm okay. I just had a sudden jolt, and now I have a headache."

"Do you want me to get you something? An ibuprofen?"

"No, I'm okay. I just feel a little odd, and the headache is already going away."

Brian moved back alongside the bed and gripped Emma's arm. "Are you sure?"

"Yes, I guess." She blinked several times. "What I'd like to do is get this ridiculous bath conundrum over with. As much as I hate to admit it, my mother is correct about it being dangerous to try to shower in my current state. I don't want to fall, nor do I want to burden them with giving me a bed bath like I'm a child."

"Okay, I'll run the bathwater," he said. "And then can I call the mothers back? They are desperate to help."

"I guess. Sure. Call them back! Meanwhile, put down one of the guardrails so I can sit here for a few minutes on the side of the bed to adjust to being upright. What will you be doing while I take a bath?"

"If you don't mind, I'll spend a little more time with Juliette."

"Good idea," Emma said, sounding like her old self. "Tell her that I look forward to seeing her after my bath."

"I'm sure she'll like to hear that," Brian said, giving his wife's arm a reassuring squeeze.

CHAPTER 13

August 31

After spending nearly a half hour with Juliette watching *Ask the StoryBots* and getting her to eat the rest of her grilled cheese sandwich, Brian was glad she seemed back to near normal. When she and Camila began coloring together, Brian had checked on Emma's situation before retreating to the home office. His plan was to try to get an idea of what they would be able to cover with their current depleted cash reserves if they were forced to endure the entire fall season with few or no security gigs, which was how it was beginning to appear. The reality was that by the New Year, they were going to be in bad shape even with Camila gracious enough to be willing to defer receiving her salary. The thought of losing her, especially under the current circumstances with Emma and Juliette, was painful.

While deep in his depressing thoughts, a sudden nerve-shattering, shrill scream reverberated around the room, sending a shot of adrenaline through Brian's body and propelling him out of his desk chair and into the hallway. Instantly he could tell the continued shouts were coming from above, although already there was an answering softer wail from the kitchen. Brian hit the stairs at a run and within a blink of an eye he'd reached the guest room. Inside he found both Aimée and Hannah frozen like statues with their hands clasped over their mouths and eyes thrown open to their limits.

Within the hospital bed Emma was in the throes of yet another full-blown seizure, with her back arched grotesquely and her arms and legs thrashing. Most disturbing of all, her head was repeatedly hitting against the bed's protective metal rails and making a horrific clamor. Without a second's hesitation Brian rushed to the bedside and pulled his convulsing wife more into the center of the bed to prevent any head trauma. With Brian's arrival, the mothers' screams trailed off.

"Thank God you came," Aimée wailed. She stepped closer to the bed. Hannah stayed away, her hand still clasped over her mouth.

"What happened?" Brian managed as he forcibly kept Emma away from the bedsides and struggled to roll her on her side, so she didn't choke. As muscular and athletic as Emma was, it took all of Brian's considerable strength.

"I don't know! Nothing particular. She'd had her bath, and we'd managed to get her back into the bed, which wasn't easy. It did make her really upset. Could that have caused this?"

"I can't imagine," Brian said, struggling to keep Emma centered in the bed and on her side. He noticed she was turning slightly blue from her breathing being suppressed.

"Should I find something to put in her mouth so she doesn't bite her tongue?"

"No, it's not necessary," Brian said. "That's an old wives' tale. It's enough to keep her on her side and keep her from injuring herself."

"Should one of us call an ambulance?" Hannah asked frantically. She'd recovered to a degree but still hadn't moved from where she had backed up.

Brian didn't answer immediately because he didn't know what to do and keeping Emma centered was taking all his attention. He assumed the seizure would stop just as it did when she'd had a similar fit in the car on the way back from the Cape. But as the minutes ticked by, Brian got progressively frantic, especially since she was only getting bluer in the face.

"Hannah!" Brian yelled over his shoulder. "Go ahead and call an ambulance!"

Glad to have something to do, Hannah struggled to get her phone out of her pocket. She hit emergency and dialed 911, then put her phone to her ear.

"Tell the operator it could be a status epilepticus!" Brian shouted. "Tell them that an ALS ambulance is needed."

"What's an ALS ambulance?"

"Advanced life support!" Brian shouted back.

Since Emma's convulsions were still making considerable noise in the hospital bed, Hannah stepped out into the hallway. A moment later, with the phone still pressed against the side of her head, she returned and called out to Brian: "How long has the seizure been going on?"

"I don't know," Brian cried. "Say five minutes."

Hannah left again but was back quickly to stand next to Aimée. "Okay, an ALS ambulance is on its way."

Brian didn't answer. His concerns were quickly mounting as his wife was even more blue than she'd been just a few moments earlier. "Hurry, please!" he said under his breath.

"C'est très inquiétant!" Aimée said, catching Brian's words despite the noise Emma was making.

"Of course it's worrisome!" Brian responded irritably at what he thought was a foolish thing to say.

Suddenly a pitiful scream crying "Mommy!" penetrated the clatter Emma was making in the bed. All eyes turned to the doorway to see Juliette's form silhouetted against the backlight.

Aimée was the first to react, and she rushed to the doorway and guided Juliette away with soothing words. A moment later Camila appeared, taking in the commotion. "I'm so sorry," she blurted out. "I turned my back just for a second, and Juliette was out of the kitchen."

Brian didn't answer. As the seconds ticked by and Emma's lividity deepened, he was getting more and more concerned, since Emma's seizure was now at least twice as long as her first. "Someone should go down to the front door and let in the ambulance medics!" he shouted to no one in particular.

"I'll go," Camila said quickly, glad to do something

to appease her guilt. She disappeared before anyone could respond.

"Will the medics be able to stop the seizure?" Hannah asked nervously. Though clearly still distraught, she'd recovered enough to come around the bed and was standing across from Brian.

"Who the hell knows!" Brian snapped insensitively. He was becoming so concerned himself that he wasn't thinking properly.

After what seemed like hours but had been only ten to fifteen minutes, undulating sirens could be heard. It was music to Brian's ears. From the sounds he could tell there was more than one vehicle, which surprised him. Quickly the sirens reached a crescendo, and then trailed off and stopped, indicating the vehicles were outside. A few minutes later four medics, one woman and three men, rushed into the guest room carrying a wide variety of equipment, including a stair chair used to get patients up and down flights of stairs. All of them were outfitted in full protective gear due to the pandemic.

The woman, clearly in charge and taking command, crowded Brian to the side. The noise from Emma's thrashing became louder. "I'm Alice, a paramedic, and this is George, my partner," she said quickly, motioning to the man who had gone to the other side of the bed. He was carrying an instrument case. "How long has the patient been convulsing?"

"I'm not sure," Brian admitted, but he knew it was important to give an answer. "Probably more than twenty minutes." Brian, along with Hannah, backed up into the doorway leading out into the hall.

"Okay!" Alice said, looking at George. "Break out the Arrow Intraosseous drill."

"What do you want for the injection?" George yelled as he opened the case and took out what looked like a normal carpenter's drill.

"Versed, five milligrams," Alice said. Then, looking at the two other medics, she added: "Tom, I need a glucose! And, Bill, set up an oximeter! She's looking way too cyanotic. And set up oxygen with a nasal cannula."

"I can't watch this," Hannah said, and fled to find Aimée, Juliette, and Camila.

Brian stayed riveted where he was. Although worried sick about Emma, he couldn't help but be impressed and reassured with the speed and confidence the medics were displaying. Most impressive was how much modern medics could do in the field. In olden times, meaning just a decade or so earlier, ambulance drivers were just that: drivers. They went out and brought victims to the hospital for care. Nowadays it was totally different, with paramedics starting lifesaving treatment right at the scene just like they were doing here. He was hopeful that they'd be able to stop the seizure quickly.

To Brian's great relief, within only a minute or so after the intraosseous injection, Emma's agonizing full-body contractions slowed and then mercifully disappeared altogether. Quickly the medics took her vital signs. Alarmingly, Brian could see that Emma hadn't regained consciousness despite the seizure having stopped.

"Pulse is steady and blood pressure is low," Alice said, removing her stethoscope from her ears. "How about her oxygen level?"

"Not great," George said. "Below ninety but she seems to be breathing okay."

"Let's hook up an ECG and get her into the stair chair," Alice said. "Come on! Move it! We have to get this one to the ED now!"

Tom and Bill picked up the stair chair and brought it next to the hospital bed, which gave Brian an idea of the hierarchy with the medics. Alice and George were paramedics, manning the ALS ambulance, and Tom and Bill were EMTs probably manning a BLS ambulance, or basic life support. As Tom and Bill organized the safety straps in preparation for securing Emma in the carrier, Alice and George collapsed the hospital bed's rails in unison. The moment they did, almost as if in response, Emma exploded into another full-blown seizure.

"Draw up another ten milligrams of Versed!" Alice barked while she and George made sure Emma didn't convulse herself off the bed now that the side rails were lowered. A few seconds later Alice was handed the appropriately filled syringe, which she used to inject the drug into the cannula still positioned into Emma's marrow cavity. Emma's convulsions immediately began to slow and then stopped. Alice was pleased until she tried to take Emma's blood pressure, at which point she realized that Emma had no blood pressure and no pulse, even though the ECG that George had attached was showing a slow but regular heartbeat. She wasn't breathing, either.

"Good lord!" Alice exclaimed. "We're looking at PEA. Start CPR stat!"

George climbed up onto the bed to start chest compressions. Alice took an ambu bag from Tom, attached the oxygen line to it, and then started respiring Emma.

Brian was horrified at this sudden turn of events, watching his thirty-four-year-old wife being given CPR and knowing she was at death's door. It was as if he was caught in a nightmare and couldn't wake up. Nor could he even move.

"How the hell could she have PEA?" George demanded between compressions.

"I don't know for sure, but I suspect loss of vascular resistance," Alice said. "Tom, draw up one milligram of epinephrine and give it stat."

"Circulatory collapse from anoxia?" George asked. He paused momentarily to allow Tom to connect a syringe to the tibial cannula.

"Yes," Alice said. "This is the kind of case where I wish to hell we had the capability for some kind of emergency electroencephalographic tracing to be one hundred percent, but that's my guess. Well, more than my guess. It's the only explanation."

Despite feeling like he wanted to run away and hide, Brian couldn't move. Knowing things had just gone from bad to worse, he was desperate to at least understand what was happening, so he managed to lean toward Bill, who for the moment was idle. "What's PEA?"

Obviously distracted, Bill still turned to Brian. "Pulseless electrical activity," he said. "The heart's trying to beat, but it can't. It usually means there's little or no blood coming into the heart because it's all pooled peripherally due to circulatory collapse."

Before Bill could explain more, Alice called out to him to run down on the double and bring up the Lucas CPR, a battery-driven cardiac compression device. As Bill headed out the door, he had to dodge Hannah, who was on her way in. Fearing what she was about to see, Brian intercepted her, blocking her view of the spectacle taking place.

"What's happening?" Hannah said, trying to peer around Brian's body. "How is Emma doing? Has the seizure stopped?"

"It's important for you and everyone else to stay out of the way," Brian cried out, purposefully evading Hannah's question. "Where is Aimée?"

"She's in the kitchen with the others. I just want to be sure Emma is okay."

"They are attending to her," Brian said evasively. "Really, it's better for you not to be here." To back up what he was saying, Brian herded Hannah out the door into the hallway. At that moment Bill was rushing up the stairs carrying the Lucas device, and he squeezed past into the guest room. "They'll be taking Emma to the hospital very shortly," Brian added. "You join the others. I'll go along with Emma if possible, and I'll call you guys just as soon as I can."

"All right," Hannah said reluctantly, and backed up a few steps. She then fled down the stairs.

When Brian returned to the guest room, he could

hear from Alice's order that Tom was giving yet another dose of epinephrine, a major cardiovascular stimulant, meaning the first dose probably hadn't had any effect. Stepping over to the foot of the bed, Brian spoke to Alice, who, with George, was rapidly setting up the Lucas. "I've had EMT training," Brian said. "Can you tell me what's happening here?"

"Sorry. We've got to get this patient out of here. I don't have time to explain."

Once they had the Lucas machine giving the chest compressions, they transferred Emma from the hospital bed to the stair chair. It was obvious to Brian that these people had prior experience working together since everyone knew their role without a lot of talk or direction. Then with Alice walking alongside and doing the breathing, Tom and Bill maneuvered the stair chair out of the guest room, down the stairs, and out the front door. George brought up the rear carrying the rest of the equipment. Brian followed, grabbing a face mask off of the foyer's console table and putting it on. Outside, a few of the neighbors who'd come out of their homes in response to the sirens silently watched as Emma was rapidly loaded into the ALS ambulance. For Brian there was a sense of unreality about the whole scene, especially with everyone wearing face masks. It was as if he were participating in a science-fiction horror movie. Alice leaped in the back to ride with Emma. George started for the cab, but Brian grabbed his arm.

"She's my wife," he rasped. "Can I ride in the ambulance?"

"Of course," George said. "Hop in!"

As Brian climbed into the front of the ambulance, he felt even more like he was caught in a nightmare that he couldn't escape. The fact that his wife was in the back, fighting for her life, seemed so far-fetched that it couldn't possibly be true.

CHAPTER 14

August 31

Riding in the ambulance with the siren wailing was a true déjà vu for Brian, reminding him of countless trips he'd made in one of the ESU heavy vehicles speeding out to handle some kind of disaster like an active shooter or a hostage incident. When you were a member of the NYPD ESU, most every call was a serious event, which required being prepared for the worst. The good and bad part of that was it was never boring like being a patrolman could be. As the ambulance drew closer to MMH Inwood, he found himself wishing he was back on the force and in an anonymous ESU transport, as it would mean Emma wasn't in the back struggling for her life.

George and Alice had used the radio to let the MMH Inwood Emergency Department know what they were facing, namely a patient in extremis and receiving CPR. Brian heard the back-and-forth exchanges with growing alarm. What tormented him was Alice's request for an emergency electroencephalogram with neurological consult. He knew that was out of the ordinary for someone with a run-of-the-mill cardiac arrest and receiving CPR.

At the ED receiving bay, a group of doctors, nurses, and orderlies, all in full personal protective gear and face shields, were waiting, including a rugged-looking, slim, white-haired man and the ranking emergency physician on the shift, Dr. Theodore Hard. By the time Brian had quickly climbed out of the ambulance's cab, Emma was already on her way inside with the Lucas apparatus pumping and Alice still respiring her with the ambu breathing bag. Brian had to run to catch up. He knew he probably wasn't supposed to follow, but he did anyway, and in the commotion, no one questioned his presence despite the fact that he was the only person without an impermeable protective gown and face shield.

The entire group raced into one of the Level 1 trauma rooms, where Emma was transferred from the ambulance gurney to the table. Brian stayed in the background while Dr. Hard yelled orders to set up an ECG, place an oximeter, and start an intravenous even though the tibial cannula was still in place. The oximeter gave a reading of 95 percent, suggesting that the CPR had been effective. The moment the electrocardiogram blip appeared, tracing across the monitor, everyone could see there was electrical activity, but it was obviously not normal. It was also quickly determined that when the Lucas was switched off, there was no pulse and no blood pressure. Instantly they reinstated CPR with manual compressions while Alice, who had not stopped using the ambu bag, quickly summarized for Dr. Hard what had happened in the victim's home and in the ambulance, listing the medications that had been given and the approximate duration of the initial seizure. She made a point of emphasizing how cyanotic the patient had been, and then described how surprised she was to be confronted with pulseless electrical activity after the second seizure and what she thought it meant.

"I think you are probably correct," Dr. Hard said. He'd been nodding as Alice had related what they'd done. After Alice finished her rapid synopsis, he took a small penlight from his pocket, bent over, and checked Emma's pupils. "Uh-oh! No reaction whatsoever," he stated as he straightened upright. "That's not encouraging, to say the least. It suggests no brain stem reflexes. Okay! Let's get the neuro guys down here and do an emergency electroencephalogram. Meanwhile, continue the CPR and draw blood for electrolytes, glucose, and troponin just to be sure."

As the only person in normal street clothes, Brian felt that he stood out like a sore thumb and was expecting to be asked to leave at any moment. Taking advantage of a new flurry of activity, enacting Dr. Hard's latest orders, Brian glanced around the trauma room, quickly spotting a long, white doctor's coat hanging on the back of a door. Trying not to garner attention, he walked over, lifted the coat from its hook, and slipped it on. It was unreasonably snug, but he couldn't be choosy. He was aware there was a name tag, but he couldn't make it out upside down. So attired, he felt considerably less out of place and only hoped no one asked him any difficult medical question, which would surely expose him as an outsider.

A few minutes later Alice and George informed Dr. Hard they had to call in their home base and be available for their next run. After they'd gathered their belongings and said goodbye to all, George recognized Brian despite the white coat and approached.

"Wait a minute, are you a doctor?" George asked, momentarily confused. He leaned forward and read the name tag on Brian's doctor's coat. "Dr. Janice Walton? I don't think so. I'm sorry, but you really shouldn't be in here."

Brian started to desperately explain that he needed to be with his wife.

"Sorry," George repeated. "I can only imagine how wrenching this must be for you, but you aren't allowed back here." He called out to one of the ED nurses named Tamara Reyes, who came over immediately. George explained that Brian was Mr. Murphy, the patient's husband.

"Good lord! Have you been watching all this?" Tamara said, eyeing him as he struggled out of the doctor's coat and returned it to its hook. "You poor, poor man. How did you get in here? Oh, never mind. Follow me! I'll take you out to the lobby. You should have gone out there to sign in your wife."

Resigned to having been discovered and mildly surprised he'd managed to stay undetected as long as he had, Brian followed Tamara. Out in the lobby there was a line of people waiting to check in, but Tamara ignored them and called out to one of the clerks. She introduced Brian as Mr. Murphy, the husband of the CPR victim, and told her to get all the info and a signed release pronto.

For the next fifteen minutes he gave all the usual information, including the Peerless policy number. As he did so, he wondered how Peerless might try to evade covering this emergency visit since Emma certainly hadn't walked in. He also wondered if the hospital computer would immediately spit out that he owed the institution almost two hundred thousand dollars when the clerk entered his name. If it had, the clerk didn't let on. After Brian signed what he needed to sign, he was free to find a place to sit. He chose a spot at the far end of the room, as far as possible from any other people.

Time dragged. Minutes seemed like hours. At one point he took out his phone to call home, more just to connect than anything else since he didn't have anything yet to report. As he held his phone, he noticed his hand was trembling. Try as he might, he couldn't stop it, and he realized it was because every muscle in his body was contracted. Changing his mind about calling anyone, he used his phone to check his email, but he did so with unseeing eyes. He couldn't concentrate. What he was really attempting to do was occupy his mind so as not to think about what was going on back in the trauma room, yet it was impossible. In his mind's eye he kept seeing the horrifying image of Emma being given CPR. From his EMT training and experience as a police officer, he knew all too well what that could mean if the patient didn't respond immediately.

In an attempt to avoid thinking the worst, Brian let his eyes wander around the ED waiting room. It was moderately busy as per usual. In contrast to him, no one seemed to be in an agitated state, which only made him feel worse. Then he suddenly saw Dr. Hard, who had just materialized from the depths of the Emergency Department. The doctor paused, and after a moment surveying the room, his eyes locked on to Brian's. He then immediately headed in his direction with a determined stride.

Assuming the man was coming to see him, Brian quickly rose to his feet. As the doctor approached, Brian's mind, which was trying desperately to divert his attention away from reality, decided that without his protective gown and with his lean and lanky body the man looked more like a cowboy hero in an old Western movie than a doctor in a New York City Emergency Department. Yet, unfortunately, he didn't appear as if he was coming to save the day. With his mask covering most of his face, Brian couldn't see the man's expression, but the way he was walking suggested a disturbing gravity. Fearing the worst, he tried to steel himself.

Dr. Hard stopped six feet away. "Are you Brian Murphy, husband of Emma Murphy?" he asked. He spoke with an aura of seriousness and empathy that cut to the chase.

"I am," Brian managed. His throat had gone bone dry.

"I'm afraid I have very bad news for you," Dr. Hard said. "Would you please come with me?"

BOOK 2

CHAPTER 15

August 31

Squinting his eyes, Brian walked out of the MMH Inwood Emergency Department into the glare of the late summer sun and then hesitated on the sidewalk. He was overwhelmed and had never felt so much in a daze in his whole life. Was he locked in a terrifying dream with no escape? If it was reality, was he depressed or furious? It was difficult to decide as his mind flipped back and forth from one extreme to the other.

Just an hour before, Dr. Hard had led him back into the depths of the Emergency Department, coming to a stop outside of the trauma room where the paramedics had taken Emma. After telling Brian he had very bad news for him, he'd not said anything until that moment. Brian had known what was coming and had tried to brace himself.

"We ran an emergency EEG, which is an electroencephalogram, on your wife, which is a recording of brain waves."

"I know what an EEG is," Brian had said irritably, not yet ready to hear what else the doctor had to say.

"Your wife had a flatline EEG, including no activity from the brain stem, which is responsible for basic life function. What we believe is that her status epilepticus had gone on too long, depriving her brain of oxygen for a protracted period."

Although Brian had suspected as much, Dr. Hard's words were like lightning bolts and suddenly the meaning was clear: Emma was dead. A seizure caused by brain inflammation from a disease carried by a mosquito had killed her. To him, the odds seemed impossible. Was human life really so fragile and tragic? The question kept reverberating in his mind, as did Emma's last wish to be readmitted to the hospital, where she could have been treated immediately for her third seizure and thereby might still be alive.

At that point Brian had been permitted to view Emma's body in the trauma room. Gazing down at the pale, lifeless form on the table with an endotracheal tube protruding from her mouth and an IV line going into her arm was an image straight from a nightmare. It was hard to believe that someone in her prime, with such vitality and strength, could be so easily brought down by an insect, which seemed so tiny and inconsequential in comparison.

After viewing Emma's body, Brian knew he had to make some decisions. In a kind of a trance he remembered the funeral home that had handled his father's funeral a year and a half prior. After a quick call, it was arranged, and he couldn't believe the finality of it all. Brian was told that after Emma was seen and cleared by a medical examiner investigator, her remains would be picked up by the Riverside Funeral Home. Then after signing some forms, he was told that he could go home.

The wail of a siren yanked Brian out of his momentary trance as he watched an ambulance race up the hospital driveway and then make a rapid three-point turn to back against the ED receiving bay. He watched the doors open as a patient was extracted, similar to the way Emma had been handled a few hours earlier. Had it really only been a few hours ago?

After taking a deep breath, Brian pulled out his phone. He'd been putting off calling home to report the news, but he knew he'd have to do it at some point. Of course, he could wait until he got back and do it in person, but he thought that was somehow unfair since he'd promised he'd keep everyone informed. Involuntarily he shuddered at the thought of having to tell Juliette that her mother was gone and never coming home. Considering how much she had suffered when Emma had been hospitalized, he knew this was going to be devastating.

Marshalling his courage, Brian opened his contacts and was about to tap on Aimée's number when he paused. Something arresting caught his attention. About a hundred feet away, a uniformed, mildly overweight driver carelessly flicked a cigarette butt onto the sidewalk. Equally attention-grabbing was the vehicle whose front passenger-side fender the chauffeur was leaning up against. It was a gleaming black Maybach parked in a clearly marked no-parking zone directly in front of the hospital's main entrance. Although Maybachs and other luxury cars were common in some areas of Manhattan, particularly Wall Street and Midtown, in Inwood they were scarcer than hen's teeth. Brian pocketed his phone and, desperate for a diversion from the paralyzing sadness, headed over to get a closer look. As he approached, the driver went through the ritual of lighting another cigarette, and after doing so, he proceeded to toss away the used match with the same disregard he'd exhibited with his cigarette butt. He then crossed his arms and assumed a posture of boredom and haughtiness that truly rubbed Brian the wrong way. The man had a face mask, but it dangled uselessly from an ear.

Without any particular plan in mind, Brian approached. The driver eyed him with a kind of colonial disdain as if Brian was a native of a distant, semi-civilized part of Manhattan. Feeling a tidal wave of anger at this individual's self-satisfied superiority as clearly a member of the capitalistic world that had also created Peerless Health and the MMH hospital chain, Brian tensed. From his experience as a police officer, he could see the man was wearing a shoulder holster from a characteristic bulge in his overly tight chauffeur's uniform. Even the fact that the man thought it necessary and appropriate to be armed for his visit to the "wilds" of Inwood struck him as offensive.

In fact, he was about to tell the man that he had to pick up his cigarette butt and used match, which he was certain the man would refuse, when a sudden realization popped into Brian's head. Up until that moment it hadn't occurred to him to question who the owner of the Maybach might be.

"Quite a nice set of wheels," Brian voiced, nodding toward the Maybach's imposing hulk.

The driver didn't respond but rather eyed him with hooded eyes that Brian could just make out through the man's aviator sunglasses. He was wearing a chauffeur's hat, but it was jauntily sitting back on his shaved head.

Purposefully being provocative while maintaining the required six-foot distance, Brian walked directly up to the Maybach's rear passenger-side door. With almost every muscle tensed in his six-foot-one, nearly two-hundred-pound frame, he quickly rapped on the window with his knuckle. As he expected, it made almost no sound, confirming his suspicion that the Maybach limo was armored.

The snobby chauffeur was caught off guard by Brian's actions. He straightened up, flicked away his half-smoked cigarette, and spoke in a strong Brooklyn accent: "Don't touch the car!" It wasn't a request but rather an order.

With his body taut like a high-note piano wire, Brian was fully ready to take the man down. But the driver did not follow up his threatening order with any gesture whatsoever. Instead, he added, "Please step away."

With some disappointment, Brian relaxed a degree and then said: "An armored Maybach! We don't get to see too many of these babies around here in Inwood."

"I'm surprised you haven't seen this one on occasion. It comes up here maybe two or three times a week." He then leaned back against the car's front fender and looked off into the distance as if Brian didn't deserve any more of his time.

Brian bent down and looked at the rear tire. "Wow! Run-flat tires, too." He stepped back from the vehicle so he could see both passenger-side tires at the same time. "Yup. Run-flat tires, front and back." He was now reasonably sure who the owner of the vehicle was, especially if this person visited the hospital two or three times a week and could afford an armored Maybach. It had to be the MMH Inwood CEO, Charles Kelley.

Turning his attention from the car, he looked over at the main entrance to the hospital. It seemed to him, particularly in his current state of mind, that fate might be providing him with a rare opportunity to address his pent-up anger at Emma's avoidable death. If she hadn't been discharged, she would have been under seizure watch and likely still alive. Suddenly there was little doubt in Brian's mind that Charles Kelley and Heather Williams bore significant responsibility not only for Emma's passing, but also for his future bankruptcy, the possible loss of his home, and the ruin of his life.

With a new sense of purpose, Brian turned his attention back to the snotty driver. "Tell me. Could this impressive armored vehicle belong to the one and only Charles Kelley?"

A slight but detectable smile briefly turned up the corners of the driver's lips as he turned to look condescendingly at him. "I'm not allowed to say exactly who it is I chauffeur."

To Brian the driver's response was the equivalent of admitting what Brian suspected, and the effect was immediate. As if propelled out of a cannon, he bolted for the hospital entrance, shocking the driver out of his staged indifference. "Hey!" the surprised driver shouted. "What the hell? Where are you going?"

Brian didn't slow or respond. He was a man on a mission. Having visited Roger Dalton's office so many times and even Kelley's office once, he knew exactly where he was going. Because the hospital had instituted visiting restrictions due to the pandemic, he was confronted the moment he navigated the revolving door by a woman with a clipboard who asked if she could help him. Besides her clipboard, she was holding a number of face masks for those who needed them.

Without slowing since he was already wearing a mask, Brian just called over his shoulder that he had an appointment in administration with Mr. Charles Kelley. That was sufficient for the greeter, who merely nodded and waited for the next arrival.

Although his decision to confront Kelley had been spur of the moment, now that he was on his way, he became progressively determined to follow through with his plan. He knew he'd undoubtedly be considered a persona non grata, but he was committed to saying his piece. As he pushed through the door separating the vast, marbled hospital lobby and the carpeted admin area, he made a beeline for Kelley's office after seeing that the conference room was clearly empty.

"Excuse me!" a receptionist-cum-secretary called out

as Brian swept by, heading for the closed door. "Where do you think you are going? You can't go in there!" She was the same individual who had unceremoniously escorted Brian out of Kelley's office on his previous spur-of-the moment visit. Swiftly she picked up her phone and frantically punched in a series of numbers.

Reaching Kelley's office door, he didn't bother to knock. Instead, he tried the knob, which was unlocked, and burst in. Inside Kelley was clearly having a meeting with five of his underlings, including Roger Dalton, all seated on the oversized leather couch or occupying assorted side chairs. Kelley was standing behind his massive desk, apparently in the middle of a PowerPoint presentation. There was a flat-screen wall-mounted TV displaying RAISING COLLECTIONS ON ACCOUNTS RECEIVABLE DURING THE COVID-19 CRISIS.

For a moment time stopped, allowing Brian to get a good look at Charles Kelley and to appreciate the skill of the painter who had done the man's portrait hanging over the faux fireplace. True to life, Kelley was a handsome man with high cheekbones, sharply defined features, carefully coiffed sandy-colored hair, and an expensive business suit. Unlike the portrait, he was darkly tanned, and his hair was streaked with golden blond as if he'd just returned from a Caribbean vacation despite the pandemic. To Brian he looked like a model in a top-of-the-line menswear advertisement. The only thing that surprised him was Charles's height, which Brian guesstimated to be somewhere in the six-foot-eight realm.

"Who the hell are you?" Charles demanded, having finally recovered from his momentary stunned silence at Brian's precipitous arrival. His tone was condescending, as was the facial expression he quickly assumed, reminding Brian of Heather Williams.

"I'm an aggrieved customer and a long-term resident of this community," Brian snapped as he strode toward Kelley, pointing his finger up at his face. "I need to talk to you about this hospital and its mission, and you need to hear me out."

Roger Dalton struggled to his feet from where he'd been sitting in the deep couch and leaped forward to intercept Brian. "He's Brian Murphy," Roger called out, positioning himself between Brian and Charles Kelley. "His account is seriously in arrears and has been turned over to collections."

Brian was briefly taken aback by the audacity of the rail-thin Roger Dalton. "Sit down, Roger!" he ordered, pointing back to where Roger had been. "You are not personally responsible for this travesty, unlike Mr. Kelley."

"Yes, sit down, Roger," Charles echoed. "Okay, Mr. Murphy. Exactly what do you think you can tell me that I don't already know and know invariably far better than you?"

"Fat chance you know it better than I!" Brian sniped, approaching closer to the desk while continuing to jab his index finger up into Charles Kelley's tanned face. "Do you have any conception whatsoever of what your profit-oriented leadership is doing to families like mine, struggling to get through this pandemic? My wife just died minutes ago from encephalitis after being discharged from this hospital while still ailing with EEE, all because I couldn't pay an outlandish and incomprehensible bill."

"I am sorry to hear about your wife's passing," Charles offered, casually crossing his arms. "But I can assure you that her discharge and her passing did not have anything whatsoever to do with your ability to pay. At MMH all patients are treated with the same attention to clinical detail and are given the finest care possible."

"Bullshit," Brian countered. He could tell stock language when he heard it and what Charles had just said certainly wasn't at all what he and Emma had experienced. "Here are the facts: My wife needed to be under seizure watch because she was still suffering brain inflammation, yet she was discharged even though neither of us wanted that. If she had remained in the hospital, she wouldn't have died. It's as simple as that."

At that moment two hospital security guards dressed in dark suits came flying into Charles Kelley's office, clearly responding to the distress call by the secretary. Without waiting to assess the degree of danger Brian represented, they made the mistake of rushing at him.

Reacting by reflex and using his tested skills, Brian made quick work of both security guards, throwing them ignominiously to the floor and pulling their jackets up over their heads. As they struggled to free themselves, Charles's demeanor changed dramatically as he sensed real danger from Brian. Uncrossing his arms, he grabbed his wheeled executive chair and stepped back from his desk. Brian, for his part, had now moved up to the desk and was leaning on it with both hands, glaring up into Charles's alarmed face.

"Here's what I think in a nutshell," Brian said with vehemence. "I think you are running what amounts to fraud with your health insurance coconspirators by taking advantage of this country's laissez-faire healthcare situation to maximize your profits. In the process, you and your collections people are bankrupting me and hundreds of others."

Before Charles could even respond to this denunciation, the limo driver doubling as a personal bodyguard came flying into the office in a manner similar to the hospital security people. Making the same mistake as they, he came at Brian at a run. On this occasion, not only did Brian throw him to the floor, pull his jacket over his head, and rip it in the process, but he also disarmed him.

By now the first two security people had managed to disentangle themselves from their jackets and had gotten to their feet. Thinking of trying their luck with him a second time, they took a step forward but then hesitated upon seeing that Brian was holding the limo driver's Glock pistol. But to their surprise and relief, Brian merely emptied the gun, tossing the shells into the corner of the room, where they clattered against the bare floor and hit up against the wall.

"I'm here to talk, not fight," he warned, looking both security men directly in the eye to make certain they got the message and were willing to stand down. "I need to get off my chest what needs to be said about what this hospital is doing to this community." With a particularly large clatter that made everyone in the room jump, he tossed the gun into a wastebasket beside the desk.

Intent on trying their luck again with Brian, both security guards took yet another step toward him, but now Charles held up his hand, intuitively sensing that Brian was more than capable of holding his own. "Stand down!" he ordered. "Let the deadbeat have his say."

"Thank you," Brian said insincerely, sensing that Charles was merely humoring him. "Until recently I had good health insurance, so I never concerned myself with hospital bills, like when my daughter was born prematurely. I now think that was a big mistake. Everyone, myself included, is guilty of giving you people free rein, and your greed and your secrecy has had no bounds. You are all new age robber barons."

Brian was just getting warmed up in giving this haughty, unprincipled businessman a dressing-down when he was again interrupted by the arrival of additional security. On this occasion it was an older uniformed patrolman who, like Brian had done years ago, was clearly earning some extra money covering the hospital on his day off. As he ran into the room, keeping the various police paraphernalia attached to his service belt from falling out, he pulled up short when he saw him. Almost simultaneously they recognized each other.

"Brian Murphy?" the officer questioned with shock. He'd been warned that a deranged individual had broken into the hospital CEO's office.

"Liam Byrne?" Brian questioned. He'd not seen Liam

for almost two years, and the man had gone prematurely gray. Plus, the face mask made recognition more difficult.

Charles immediately pricked up his ears at this interaction between apparent old acquaintances. Speaking scornfully to Liam, he said: "Do you know this trespasser?"

"Yes. He's with the NYPD, like myself. In fact, he's a member of the elite Emergency Service Unit. And his father, rest his soul, was commander of my precinct."

"That's a shock," Charles said with a mixture of disgust and disbelief. "A policeman! It's hard to believe with the way he's carrying on. He should have known better. Well, you've saved him from himself, but get him the hell out before I have him arrested for trespassing and criminal intimidation."

"Yes, sir," Liam said. He stepped up to Brian and whispered, "I think it's best I walk you out of here with no arguments."

For a moment of indecision, Brian looked back and forth between Charles Kelley and Liam Byrne. He had a lot more that he wanted to say to Charles, but seeing a community friend, particularly one who'd known his father, shocked him back to a sense of reality. In his confused state of mind brought on by Emma's death, the last thing he should have done was rush into Charles Kelley's office and make accusations. He shuddered to think of what might have happened had the limo driver drawn his gun before coming into the room or if the other security people had been armed. Someone could have been killed, and there was a chance it could very well have been him.

Suddenly feeling embarrassed, he locked eyes with Liam and said: "Okay! You're right. Let's go."

Liam grasped Brian's upper arm, and the two of them walked out. The secretary didn't say anything as they passed her desk, but her expression suggested she was satisfied that her quick thinking had saved the day. They started down the hallway, but behind them they could hear Charles ranting and raging about how the hell such a miscreant had been able to saunter into his office.

Brian and Liam didn't say anything until they'd reached the hospital lobby, where they knew they could talk without being overheard.

"What on earth were you doing in there mouthing off to the hospital CEO?" Liam asked in a forced half whisper, sounding truly concerned. "He's a bad dude from what I know."

"My wife, Emma, died about an hour ago. I wasn't thinking," he said after letting out a deflating sigh.

"Mary, Mother of God, I'm so sorry. What was it, an accident? Or Covid?"

"No, neither." He struggled against tears and had to take a few breaths in an attempt to keep them at bay. Despite his best efforts his eyes brimmed and a few tears ran down his cheeks, which he wiped away with the back of his hand. "She died of a viral disease called eastern equine encephalitis," he added when he could.

"I've never heard of it," Liam said, putting an empathetic hand on Brian's shoulder.

"I hadn't heard of it, either," Brian admitted. He took

a deep breath. "But apparently we are going to hear a lot more about it in the coming years thanks to climate change. It's transmitted by mosquitoes that used to live in the tropics, but because it's getting warm, they're now all the way up to Maine and beyond."

"Another virus we have to worry about besides coronavirus?"

"I'm afraid so," Brian said with another sigh.

"Were you really mouthing off to Charles Kelley about climate change?" Liam asked.

Despite his precarious mental state, Brian let out a brief laugh and shook his head. "Hardly," he said. "No, I wanted to make sure he knew that there was a chance my wife died after she had been discharged while she was still sick because I couldn't pay any of her nearly two-hundred-thousand-dollar insane hospital bill. At least that's what I'm afraid happened. I've been learning a lot of shady things about hospitals and health insurance companies the hard way. They're in this together, sucking money out of the system like there's no tomorrow."

"What about our great health benefits as members of the NYPD?" Liam said. "How did you end up owing so much money?"

Although he was tired of once again explaining, Brian went ahead and described how he and Emma had retired from the NYPD to form their own security company and ended up with Peerless Health Insurance, which he described as legalized fraud. "These short-term health policies collect your premiums but then figure out a way of avoiding paying for most everything. Of course, I didn't read the policy. I mean, nobody reads their health insurance policies."

"You got that right," Liam said.

"The hospital is already suing me," Brian went on to elaborate. "And as I understand, that kind of aggressive, sped-up approach is all Charles Kelley's doing. He even had the hospital form their own collections division."

"I've heard he's a mean son of a bitch," Liam agreed. "I steer clear. Do you remember Grady Quillen?"

"Yeah, I do," Brian said. "I'm surprised you brought him up, because he is the one who served me the papers for the hospital suit against me."

"That's why I mentioned him. I'd heard he worked as a process server after his retirement for the collections department here. I thought he might be someone for you to talk with for some advice."

"He gave me the name of a lawyer," he said. "He also told me how busy he is, meaning that MMH Inwood is suing a lot of people, so I'm not alone."

"I can second that. A neighbor of mine is also being sued."

"He said the same thing about one of his neighbors," Brian said. "MMH Inwood is a lot more predatory than I thought. Until this happened, I'd always considered it a valuable part of the community. Now I'm not so sure."

"How did you get here?"

"I came in an ambulance," Brian said.

"I could call the precinct and have a squad car come and drive you home," Liam offered.

"No need," he said. "It's a short walk. But thanks for offering."

After a final conversation about how much everyone at the precinct missed Deputy Inspector Conor Murphy, Brian said goodbye. He thanked Liam for coming to his rescue in Charles Kelley's office, admitting that he'd gone there in a fit of rage without giving it any thought.

As Brian emerged back out into the sunshine, he stopped for a moment to eye the gleaming black Maybach sedan again. Seeing as the luxury car was owned by someone involved with healthcare, it seemed immoral at best.

CHAPTER 16

August 31

I n a kind of trance, Brian headed home totally unaware of his surroundings. The impulsive, histrionic display in Kelley's office was so contrary to his usual style of careful planning and goal-oriented behavior. He knew that there was no way the episode could help rectify the situation in which he now found himself trapped. To make matters worse, calling Charles Kelley a new age robber baron was probably kowtowing to the man's monumental ego.

Turning onto Park Terrace East and starting up the hill, Brian slowed his pace and then stopped. In the middle of his brooding, he realized what had really propelled him into Kelley's office: It had been a way to avoid facing Juliette, Aimée, and Hannah or even thinking about telling them the horrible news. In many ways he was unconsciously denying Emma's death, and the act of telling the others, including Camila, would shatter that tenuous denial.

"Maybe they already called the hospital," Brian wondered out loud, but he knew that was wishful thinking.

The burden of the truth was most likely squarely on him. What he feared the most was telling Juliette. He couldn't even imagine what her reaction was going to be.

Taking a deep breath, Brian recommenced walking. He knew he was not as adept in the psychological arena as he was in the action realm, so for the next few minutes he tried not to think at all.

From the moment Brian entered the house he could tell that the news had not preceded him. He could hear the songful cartoon soundtrack of *Pinkalicious & Peterrific* coming from the kitchen, and Aimée and Hannah were in the living room quietly talking. Both adults immediately appeared in the foyer's archway as Brian removed his mask and shoes.

"How is Emma?" Aimée asked warily. Hannah was standing next to her, but slightly behind, with a look of agonizing worry on her face.

Once again Brian choked up as he had with Liam Byrne. It took him a minute to pull himself together. By then both women knew what was coming. "Emma didn't make it," Brian finally managed with difficulty.

Hannah let out a high-pitched but thankfully short-lived wail as her face contorted into an expression of horror. In contrast, Aimée responded by putting her arms around Brian and hugging him tightly. "I can't imagine what you are feeling. I'm so, so sorry, mon fils."

"Thank you," Brian choked. While Aimée held on to him, with a halting voice he recounted the details of what had happened. It was difficult to repeat, but he thought they deserved to know.

Finally, Aimée let go of Brian and exchanged a quick glance with Hannah, who had quieted down. "We have to tell Juliette," Aimée said, keeping her emotions in check.

Hannah nodded several times, wiping tears from her face. "Yes, that's the first thing that needs to be done, no question, and it should be Brian who does it."

"Bien sûr," Aimée added. "I agree completely."

"And a wake has to be planned and notices sent out," Hannah said. "There is a lot to do."

"I don't want a wake," Brian blurted. He was shocked that such a suggestion was Hannah's first reaction, but he knew he shouldn't have been. He was well aware that Hannah's method of dealing with any crisis was to suppress emotion with activity and planning. Emma had pointed it out on multiple occasions.

"But there has to be a wake!" Hannah countered in a manner that brooked no argument. "It's expected!" She was equally shocked at Brian's response, which was a sharp break from recognized and revered Irish tradition.

"Not here," Brian pleaded. "Not around Juliette. And I have to think about what I can afford. Plus, these are not normal times." As he spoke Brian realized he had no idea what Emma would have wanted. Despite the dangers they'd confronted as NYPD ESU officers, they'd never spoken with each other about their deaths and what their preferences might be.

"Well, there has to be a wake and a funeral mass even if it is limited because of the pandemic. And we can help with the expenses."

"Not here," Brian repeated, but realized this spur-of-the-moment response might seem selfish to Hannah and her family. He and Emma, although they'd grown up with a strong Irish connection to the Catholic faith, had drifted away from it during college. Neither had made a complete apostasy, but both felt the church was too ritualistic and out of touch with the times. As a consequence, they had not kept up with all the obligations on a regular basis, like going to mass and attending confession.

"That's fine," Hannah said with resignation. To her credit, she recovered quickly. "We can have the wake at our house. I can also make all the arrangements for the funeral mass at the Church of the Good Shepherd. Meanwhile you two and Camila can concentrate on Juliette. Is there a funeral home involved yet?"

"I called Riverside on Broadway," Brian said.

"A good choice," Hannah said. "I've worked with them before. They are very professional."

"That was my experience, too," Aimée said. "They were particularly helpful with Conor's funeral."

"I remember," Hannah recalled. "All right, I'm off. Good luck with Juliette." Without waiting for a response, she bent down and slipped on her shoes. She then put on her mask. "Let's be in touch," she added before leaving.

"Wow," Brian let out as he closed the front door behind Hannah. "She's really motivated."

"Hannah has been like that for as long as I've known her," Aimée said. "It's her defense mechanism. And I'm not surprised. After all, it is an Irish tradition with a death to channel emotion as much as possible into celebration rather than pure mourning. It's a tradition I've come to appreciate, especially after your father's passing."

"Yes, I remember you saying as much."

"Now it is time for the difficult part," Aimée said. "Are you ready to face your daughter?"

"Hardly," Brian admitted, his heart squeezing in his chest. "Do you really think I can do this?"

"Absolutely," Aimée reassured him. "It has to be you. Do you want a suggestion? I don't want to interfere, but as your mother I do have some advice."

"Please," Brian said, desperate for any guidance.

"This would be a good time to take advantage of some of the consoling power of faith," Aimée advised. "For the last year I've been taking Juliette to mass with me, which I've appreciated you and Emma allowing. She's absorbed a lot. Although she mostly enjoys the dressing-up part, she has been responsive to discussions about beliefs, especially when we talked about heaven and Grandpa Conor. I think it is a way of making death seem not so final, particularly in a child's mind."

"Okay, I guess I can do that," Brian said, thankful for any suggestions.

"I know you can," Aimée said while giving Brian's shoulder a reassuring squeeze.

Together, Brian and Aimée went into the kitchen. Juliette looked up at them briefly but then went back to watching her PBS cartoon. Brian motioned for Camila to step out into the hallway, while Aimée sat down with Juliette and watched TV.

Once out of the room, Brian told Camila the news about Emma.

"No, no!" Camila muffled her voice as she made the sign of the cross. "I'm so sorry, Brian."

"Thank you. I'm still in a kind of denial about it all, but I have to tell Juliette, as hard as it will be. How has she been doing after seeing the seizure?"

"Not so good," Camila said. "At first, I couldn't get her to talk about it. Then, when she did, she didn't say much and instead started complaining again about not feeling well."

"How so?"

"First she says she's not hungry and feels sick to her stomach," Camila began. "She won't eat anything no matter what I suggest. And she's complaining again she has a headache. But it can't be much of a headache because all she wants to do is watch TV, so I don't know what it is. In general, she's very cranky, which I suppose is entirely understandable."

"Has she said anything at all about what she saw?"

"No, not a word," Camila said. "And I didn't know whether to bring it up. I mean, it upset me. It was so violent."

"It's very disturbing," Brian agreed. "Especially the second time. All right, thank you. Either way, I have to tell her that her mother is gone and hope we can handle her reaction."

Despite all the hostage-negotiating seminars and discussions he'd had during his ESU training, Brian now felt totally unequipped to deal with his own four-year-old daughter. Nonetheless, he walked back into the kitchen and sat at the breakfast nook table across from his mother and Juliette. Unsure how to begin, he first reached out, picked up the remote off the table, and turned off the TV.

Juliette reacted instantly and angrily, reaching for the remote, but Brian extended it beyond her reach. "I need to talk with you, Juliette," he told her. "After that we can turn the TV back on."

Juliette looked at her father with obvious anger as if she knew what was coming, yet Brian persisted, trying to think of the best way to take his mother's suggestion. "Mommy was very sick, as you know," he began, "and she wasn't feeling better, but now she has gone to heaven and all her pain is gone. She's with Grandpa Conor, and they are very happy being together."

For a few seconds Brian closed his eyes, feeling monumentally unsuited for this discussion, saying things he didn't quite believe himself. And for a brief moment he wondered if Heather Williams and Charles Kelley ever thought that their behavior led to horrible situations like these, ones that should never have to happen. When he opened his eyes, Juliette was still staring at him as if digesting what Brian had said. Taking a deep breath, he continued: "So, Mommy will not be coming home. But I want you to know that I am here for you, as are your grandmas and Camila. We are all here for you."

Suddenly Juliette let out a tortured wail somewhat

akin to Hannah's, then scrambled out of her seat and leaped onto Brian's lap. With her arms around his neck and her legs around his midsection, she hugged him tightly and buried her face in his shirt. He could feel her sob. Brian hugged her back and exchanged a helpless glance with Aimée. He didn't know what to do or what else to say. But one thing he did know was that Juliette was his sole responsibility and his life's work from that moment on.

As suddenly as Juliette had begun crying, she stopped and disengaged herself from Brian's embrace. She regained her seat and spoke up for the first time: "When will Mommy come home from the hospital?"

"Honey, I told you she won't be coming home," Brian said. "She's with Jesus and Grandpa in heaven."

Instead of asking any more questions, Juliette lunged for the TV remote, and this time Brian let her have it. In the next instant the happy, melodious soundtrack of *Pinkalicious & Peterrific* filled the room, especially after Juliette raised the volume. Aimée stood up and tried to give Juliette a reassuring hug, but Juliette resisted, preferring to keep the TV in view.

"Your daddy is right." Aimée spoke loud enough to be heard over the TV. "We're all here for you, so you are safe even if your mommy had to go to heaven."

Camila then followed suit and got the same lack of response from Juliette. The three adults exchanged a glance and a shrug, communicating that there apparently wasn't anything else to do for the moment. Juliette had been told, even if she didn't want to believe it for the time being.

For several minutes Brian just stood there leaning against the sink, looking at his daughter and mother, and thinking about his mother-in-law's reaction while his mind flip-flopped between disjointed thoughts and emotions about Heather Williams, Charles Kelley, and Emma. Focusing on Emma, he found himself questioning if it could possibly be true that she was gone forever. Or equally as disturbing: Would she still be alive if he'd insisted somehow on her staying in the hospital? How responsible was he for having let it happen?

Brian felt a new wave of emotion well up inside of him, which he hardly thought would be appropriate to display in his daughter's presence. Pushing away from the kitchen counter in hopes of having a moment alone, he left the room and headed for the home office. For the time being he'd let Aimée and Camila bear the burden of comforting Juliette.

Seated at the large partner's desk positioned under a chandelier, Brian made it a point not to look across at Emma's empty seat. Instead, he woke up his sleeping monitor to go over finances in a vain attempt to rein in his emotions. With Emma gone, he'd need to seriously think about the viability of Personal Protection LLC and whether it would survive now without her input and partnership. Then, with surprise, he found himself wondering if he should investigate the possibility of trying to reverse his retirement and get his old NYPD ESU job back. Under his current circumstances the idea of a guaranteed salary, decent health benefits, and pension plan had enormous appeal.

In the middle of such thinking, the business landline started to ring. Hoping it meant someone was in need of security, Brian snatched up the phone. To his dismay it wasn't a prospective client, but rather a Premier Collections agent. With an irritatingly high-pitched voice, the individual launched into a rapid threatening tirade, saying that if Brian didn't immediately offer an acceptable plan for paying off his $189,375.86 debt, his credit rating was going to be trashed, making it impossible for him to get a credit card, any kind of loan, or a mortgage.

In his hyperemotional state, Brian lost control, telling the caller to go fuck himself. He then slammed the phone down with such force it caused a portion of the handset to pop off. For a split second Brian scanned the desk's surface for something else to destroy, but the urge quickly passed. Then the phone rang again. This time Brian didn't answer it. Knowing what he did about collection agencies, he was aware that he was destined to be pestered relentlessly. It was the name of the game.

Letting the phone ring, he pulled up his online banking account and looked at the balances. Things were hardly looking rosy, especially with the thought of an upcoming funeral. He really had no idea what kind of money would be involved, and he wondered selfishly how much his in-laws, the O'Briens, might be willing to shoulder following Hannah's offer. Unfortunately, he knew that he would soon be finding out answers to these questions. Finally, the phone stopped ringing, and except for the distant sounds of the PBS cartoon coming from the kitchen, the room returned to silence. The one thing the call did do was remind him that he was indeed being sued, meaning he needed to do something before his time limit to respond to the complaint ran out. The specter of losing the house loomed in the back of his mind. He could not let that happen for a number of reasons, chief of which was Juliette. Losing her mother was going to create a terrible insecurity, and losing her home on top and the familiarity of her room would just add immensely to the impact.

"All right, that's it," he said out loud. Pulling out his phone for a Google search, he typed in "Patrick McCarthy." He needed a lawyer, expense be damned, and with Grady recommending him, Patrick seemed like a good risk to take, especially with him being part of the community.

To his surprise, the lawyer answered on the second ring, making Brian wonder if that was a positive or a negative sign. He'd fully expected having to talk with either a secretary or leave a message. For a moment, Brian was caught off guard, but that changed as soon as he introduced himself.

"I know you," Patrick said. "Wasn't your father chief of police?"

"He was," Brian confirmed. "Commander of the 34th Precinct."

"I know your sister as well. We were in the same grade. What can I do for you?"

"Well, I'm being sued for almost two hundred thousand dollars by MMH Inwood," Brian said. He liked the sound of Patrick's voice, as it conveyed a sense of confidence.

"That, unfortunately, is a familiar story."

"Really?" Brian was still a bit surprised to hear that. "Have you handled many such cases?"

"Quite a few," Patrick said. "Especially lately with the pandemic. Have you been served?"

"Just this morning, by Grady Quillen."

"Then we have thirty days to respond," Patrick said. "When would you like to get together?"

"As soon as possible." Knowing himself as a man of action, Brian needed to be active to keep from being overwhelmed by Emma's passing and worry about losing the house.

"I could see you as early as tomorrow. Would that work for you?"

"Absolutely," Brian said. "The earlier the better."

"I could be here at the office at seven thirty. Is that too early for you?"

"That would be fine," Brian said. He thought the chances he'd be able to sleep very much that night were slim.

"I'll see you then," Patrick confirmed. "Bring your service papers, of course. And also a mask. I require it in my office."

"No problem," Brian said. He liked hearing that Patrick was sticking to appropriate Covid-19 pandemic rules.

"My office is at 5030 Broadway," Patrick said. "I don't have a secretary, so when you get here in the morning, call me, and I'll come down and let you in."

"I look forward to meeting you," Brian said before disconnecting.

CHAPTER 17

September 1

As he had expected, Brian found sleep almost impossible that night. Even with the sleep medication, which he felt guilty taking since it had been prescribed for Emma, he spent most of the night wandering the house with his mind in turmoil. On multiple occasions he found himself looking in on Juliette. Each time he found her asleep, holding on to Bunny and looking peaceful. He was impressed the child seemed to have weathered the news with more equanimity than he had anticipated, which relieved him to a degree. He gave full credit to the grandmothers, both of whom had spent the rest of the day and evening with her. They'd even taken her out for a walk in her beloved Isham Park and then on to the Church of the Good Shepherd to light a devotional candle for Emma. When Aimée had told Brian of the plan, he'd rolled his eyes at the idea of resorting to ritual with a four-year-old, yet the episode seemed to have soothed Juliette considerably, making him wonder if he should rethink the role of religion in his and Juliette's life. There was absolutely no doubt in his mind that what was holding him together at the moment was his responsibility to his daughter to make sure she could navigate this emotional sea of losing her mother.

By seven A.M., with Juliette and Camila still sleeping, Brian prepared to leave the house. He wrote a note for Camila and texted Aimée to let her know where he was. He then collected the papers Grady had served him from the home office.

One of the many beauties of living in Inwood was how close everything was. Because the neighborhood was only a little more than a square mile, with a third of it forest-covered parkland, everything was within walking distance, in particular the commercial establishments along Broadway. Brian's route took him down the West 215th Street double stairway, a unique Inwood landmark that played a fond role in his childhood.

When he reached Patrick McCarthy's building, which was one of the few multistoried modern commercial structures in Inwood, he followed Patrick's directions and called to be let in. As he did so, he briefly questioned what it might mean if the lawyer wasn't successful enough to have a secretary, but he let the thought go when he saw Patrick get off the elevator and approach. He was impressive-looking and younger than Brian expected. He was tall, maybe even close to Charles Kelley's height.

"Welcome," Patrick said as he opened the door. His voice in person was more confident sounding than it had been on the phone.

As Brian passed by the man on his way inside, he did feel an immediate if minor bond. Like him, Patrick had dark, almost black hair with blue eyes.

"I appreciate you being willing to come in person despite the pandemic," Patrick said as they walked back to the elevator. "I think it is important for us to literally see eye to eye if we are going to work together. Besides, I need the papers you were served, which I see you have brought." Brian handed them over as they got into the elevator.

As they rode up to the fourth floor, Patrick leafed through the papers while Brian gave a capsule history of Emma's illness, hospitalization, and then death the day before. That news took Patrick by surprise. "I'm so sorry," he said with real empathy. "You are being sued for several hundred thousand dollars and you've lost your wife. What a terrible combination."

"I lost my wife and my business partner," he added.

"I'm in awe that you are able to function so soon after your loss."

"I suppose I'm still in denial, if I'm being honest," Brian said. "I'm also a very active person. It's always been difficult for me to sit around under any circumstances."

Inside Patrick's office, which was singularly spartan, Brian sat in one of two metal folding chairs while Patrick lowered himself into in an aged desk chair behind a metal desk. The only other furniture was a small bookcase and a file cabinet. The décor was hardly suggestive of a lucrative practice. The only hint of it being the twenty-first century was an iMac, keyboard, and mouse on the desk.

"Well, I will answer the complaint, and we will get a court date," Patrick offered as he aligned the court papers by tapping them on the desk before carefully laying them down in front of himself. Looking directly at Brian, he said, "I have to be up front with you. We've got an uphill battle here."

"When Grady served me, and, by the way, he gave you a good recommendation, he said you had tried to help his neighbor Nolan O'Reilly, but that things hadn't worked out."

"That's an understatement, but we tried our best."

"That's not a very good advertisement," Brian said, hoping for some reassurance that his situation would be different.

"I can understand why you might feel that way. As I said, it is an uphill battle, and I'll tell you why. Judges are, more often than not, forced to rule in the hospital's favor because services have been rendered and everyone had been forced under duress of the admission process to sign a form that they will be responsible for the bill. Plus, the hospitals can charge whatever they damn well please without telling the patient or the family anything beforehand."

"I can attest to that," Brian said with a short, mirthless laugh. "But I would like to know if my case is significantly different than the O'Reillys', since there'd been a summary judgment involved in theirs."

"I'm sorry, but because of attorney–client confidentiality rules, I can't discuss the details of other cases. I hope you understand."

"I suppose," Brian said. He didn't think merely confirming a summary judgment would be a violation, but he let it go. "Have you had a lot of experience with this kind of case?"

"Tons of experience, unfortunately. I've got more than twenty open cases right now."

"Similar to mine?"

"Strikingly so," Patrick confirmed. "MMH Inwood has been suing many families for outstanding hospital bills, particularly since the Covid-19 pandemic began."

"Have you had some cases where the outcome is a bit better than the O'Reillys'? Grady told me they even lost their house."

"Absolutely," Patrick said. "Rest assured, I've had many with a significantly better outcome."

"Okay, that's encouraging. To be honest, my biggest concern is losing my house."

"Understandable," Patrick said with sympathy. "Are you up to date with your mortgage payments?"

"No," he admitted, feeling a jolt of fear. "Does that make a difference?"

"I'm afraid it does." Patrick raised his eyebrows. "With the New York State Homestead Act, a home is protected in a bankruptcy filing, but not if the home is in arrears on the mortgage."

"Shit," Brian responded. "It's only been a couple of months' lapse because of the pandemic."

"If you can possibly manage it, I'd strongly recommend bringing it up to date as soon as you can."

"The bank is aware why I've not paid," Brian said.

"I've certainly been in contact with them, and they actually encouraged it. My wife and I started a new security business at the worst possible time: the middle of December, just before the pandemic hit. We'd been trying to preserve our cash to hold the business together."

"I understand, but I'm sure the other side will try to exploit it. So, if you can, I'd bring it up to date."

They then spent a few minutes talking about Patrick's fees, which he agreed to put off after an initial, modest retainer of five hundred dollars. "Believe me, I can understand your situation," Patrick said. "We're all in it, thanks to this pandemic. You can pay me the balance when your company gets back to providing you with an income."

"That's very kind of you," Brian said, thankful and pleased. He felt strongly that such trust was yet another benefit of living in this community.

"Okay," Patrick said, placing both his hands flat on top of Brian's papers. "I'll take care of these with the court immediately. Meanwhile, I'll need to get the hospital bill. Have you been given one?"

Brian let out a short, disgusted laugh. "With effort I got one, but it's useless. The damn thing is in code. I can't make sense of nine-tenths of it."

"That leads me to another question. Have you considered retaining a medical billing advocate?"

"It's interesting that you ask. My mother asked the same question. I'd never even heard of a medical billing advocate."

"It is a sign of the times," Patrick said. "Many hospitals have become so rapacious because they are being driven by private equity people to maximize profit, and one way to camouflage it is to make the billing process as incomprehensible as possible."

"How might a billing advocate help my case?"

"He or she would go over your bill with a fine-toothed comb. They understand the confusing language and invariably find all sorts of mistakes and overcharges. Sometimes they alone can reduce the bill by half or more."

"Who would have thought it would come to this?" Brian said, throwing up his hands in amazement. "It's so damn ironic. Hospitals are supposed to save people, not cheat them."

"As I said, it is a sign of the times. The US Congress has been asleep at the wheel, allowing medical costs to go through the roof. And it's across the board: hospital prices, drug prices, or device prices like artificial joints— it's all the same."

"So you recommend I find an advocate?"

"Very strongly recommend it," Patrick said. "Even if it is yet another expense for you."

"Do you have anyone specific you recommend?"

"I do. There's one right here in this building who is excellent in my experience. She's helped me on a number of cases. Her name is Megan Doyle, and she also went to PS 98 like we did."

"Megan Doyle," Brian repeated. "She's actually the one my mother mentioned. She said she'd helped a neighbor."

"I'm not surprised. Megan has helped a lot of people."

"Do you have her contacts by chance?"

"I can do better than that," Patrick said. "I could give her a shout right here and now. It's better to start the process ASAP because she'd need to get a complete copy of your hospital record, and hospitals are not cooperative with billing advocates to say the least. In fact, they make it as difficult as possible, creating all sorts of hoops and delays that have to be navigated."

"I already have a hospital bill, which I could provide her," Brian offered.

"She'll get a better, significantly more complete one," Patrick said. "Mark my words. The bills a hospital gives to patients are never broken down like she'll demand. Should I call her? She'll need to see you to start the process."

"Do you think she'd see me now while I'm here?"

"I believe she will. This wouldn't be the first time she's helped a client of mine."

"Fine, give her a try," Brian said.

Using the speaker on his phone, Patrick made the call. In contrast to him, Megan Doyle had a secretary who put Patrick through directly to her. The call was friendly, curt, and decisive. Megan would squeeze him in between appointments, and told him he should come down directly after seeing Patrick.

After a short conversation involving another shared client, Patrick disconnected the call, then looked over at Brian. "You'll like her," he said. "She's very personable but very professional, and she's good at what she does."

"Even if my bill is reduced to half, I'm going to be

hard put to pay it off," Brian said warily. "But let me ask you something else. What about going after my supposed health insurance company called Peerless? They've turned down my claims, denying any fiscal responsibility despite all the premiums I paid. To me it's a fraud."

"I'll be happy to look into it, if you insist, but I can tell you up front that the chances it would be successful are minuscule. Short-term health insurance is a tolerated scam in my experience. They have spent millions in legal fees to protect themselves with their contracts. Did you read your policy?"

"No, I didn't," he admitted.

"That's what they count on," Patrick said. "They advertise themselves as being inexpensive, and they are. They love to take your premiums but are loath to pay out anything at all, and when they do, it is never even close to being adequate."

"Why is it tolerated?" Brian asked, genuinely confused.

"That's a question I can't answer," Patrick said with a shake of his head.

"I have one other issue that should be looked into. I think there's a chance my wife was discharged before it was safe and possibly because I wasn't paying the bill. I think that Charles Kelley, the hospital CEO, has created a very strongly profit-driven culture that's willing to put patients in danger."

Patrick's eyebrows raised. "Let me understand what you are implying. Do you think there might be negligence involved?"

"I do," Brian said. "If she had still been in the hospital under a seizure watch, she'd probably be alive today."

"Hmm. That could possibly put a different spin on the situation down the road," Patrick pondered. "At the same time, I wouldn't count on it influencing this current case. What I can do is run it by a malpractice attorney friend of mine, provided you give me the okay."

"Sure, if you think it is appropriate."

"I'll give it more thought," Patrick said. "Meanwhile, I'll start the process of getting you a court date." He stood up, and Brian did the same, interested to meet his very first medical billing advocate.

CHAPTER 18

September 1

Conveniently it took Brian mere minutes to go from Patrick McCarthy's office down to Megan Doyle's on the ground floor. But the change was substantial. In contrast to Patrick's space, there was a generous-sized waiting room and a receptionist, suggesting that Megan was doing significantly better financially than Patrick. Business for Megan was apparently brisk in spite of the pandemic, or maybe because of it.

To Brian, the elderly receptionist looked strikingly similar to the librarian of his middle school, and he was tempted to ask if she was related but couldn't remember the librarian's name. In keeping with the needs of the pandemic, a plexiglass shield had been added to the woman's desk. Combining that barrier with his mask, he had to speak up when he gave his name.

"Miss Doyle will see you as soon as she can between patients," the receptionist responded equally loudly. "Meanwhile, please fill out this form so we have all your contact information."

Armed with the form on a clipboard, Brian turned to look for the most appropriate spot to sit in the waiting area. Despite it being as early as it was, there were two people waiting who had chosen opposite corners of the room beneath the windows that looked out on Broadway. In keeping with social distancing requirements, Brian went to the other end of the room.

As he was filling out the form, he thought about the receptionist calling Megan's clients "patients." It struck him as mildly bizarre that Megan was considered an integral part of the medical community, suggesting that dealing with a ridiculous hospital bill was somehow akin to setting a broken bone.

As he finished with the form, a fourth person came into the waiting area. What caught Brian's attention was the woman's age. Although the man and the woman under the windows were somewhere near his mother's age of seventy, this newly arrived individual was closer to Brian's thirty-six. She was dressed in biking shorts and a bright pink jersey with white stripes. And similar to Brian, when she gave her name to the receptionist behind the plexiglass, she spoke up to make sure she was heard. Her name was Jeanne Juliette-Shaw. Then the receptionist told her the same thing she'd said to him, indicating she, too, was being squeezed in. The only difference was that she was not given a form to fill out, implying that she was an existing client.

Despite the circumstance of being in a medical billing advocate's office, his life in total disarray, and it being in the middle of a pandemic, Brian couldn't help but be intrigued with this stranger on three accounts. The first was the woman's youth, which suggested that similar to Brian, she shouldn't be struggling with a difficult hospital bill. Second was her obvious French accent. When she pronounced her given name, it was "jhân," not "jēēn," suggesting that she had grown up in France just like Aimée. And third was her family name: Juliette-Shaw, calling to mind his daughter's given name.

Jeanne retreated to the remaining corner of the room, relatively close to him although certainly more than the required six feet away. As she sat down, she nodded a greeting to Brian, who couldn't help but closely watch her despite recognizing he might be acting mildly impolite. She then took out her phone from a pocket on the back of her bike jersey and became engrossed.

"Excuse me," Brian said, unable to restrain himself. "I couldn't help but hear the first part of your hyphenated family name, Juliette. It's quite . . ." For a brief moment he didn't know what to say, as he had spoken impulsively and hadn't planned ahead. Finally, after an awkward pause, he added: "It's quite beautiful."

"Thank you," she said, but quickly reverted her attention back to her phone.

"It caught my attention because it's my four-year-old daughter's name," Brian added, in an attempt to initiate a conversation.

Jeanne looked up again. Because of her face mask, he couldn't be sure of her reaction, but there was a faint crinkle of the corners of her eyes at least suggesting a smile, but to his dismay she didn't speak, forcing Brian to stumble ahead: "The reason we chose the name is that it was my mother's maiden name. My mother grew up in France. She didn't come here to the United States until college age, actually to go to Barnard College, where she met my father, who was going to Columbia on a hockey scholarship and then had us kids."

Brian felt distinctly uncomfortable, which was why he'd carried on so long. Although social to a fault, he'd never been particularly comfortable talking with women he didn't know.

"Juliette is not that common as a surname," Jeanne said. "Even in France. Where in France did your mother come from?"

"Normandy," Brian said, relieved to be asked a question. "Near Bayeux."

"That's a very interesting part of France."

"Have you been there?"

"Of course. Everyone visits Bayeux because of the tapestries."

"I suppose you are right," he said. "Even I have seen the tapestries: several times, in fact. My mother took me and my brothers and sister to France every year to visit our French grandparents. To make it easier, she even got us all French passports so we could zip through immigration. My middle name is Yves, after my mother's dad." Brian didn't know why he felt pressured to keep speaking. Being a private person normally, it was unlike him to be so revealing about himself.

"You and your siblings were very lucky," Jeanne said.

"We were," Brian agreed. Then, in hopes of turning the conversation away from himself, he said: "You have a distinctive and charming accent. Are you French?"

"Yes and no," she said. "Like your mother, I grew up in France. I, too, came here to the USA to attend college but ended up staying and becoming a citizen. I consider myself American as well as French."

"As you should. Could you be related to my mother's family since, as you say, Juliette is not a common family name?"

"I doubt it," Jeanne said. "I grew up in a totally different area of France that's not that well known outside of the country. It's called the Camargue. It's way in the south, and all my relatives have lived there forever."

"You are right, I've never heard of the Camargue, but I'll ask my mother."

"She'll know of it; it's the Rhône River delta," Jeanne explained. "It's marshy and agricultural with more birds, cattle, and horses than people."

"I'll check it out with Google," he said. "I should introduce myself. My name is Brian Murphy."

"Nice to meet you, Brian," she said. "I'm Jeanne Juliette-Shaw."

"It's a pleasure to meet you, too. If you don't mind, let me ask you a question about Megan Doyle. Is this your first visit, like it is mine?"

"No, she's been working with me for a number of months. I'm just here to sign some final paperwork."

"Has she been helpful?"

"She's been most definitely helpful," Jeanne confirmed. "I just wish I had come to her sooner. I wasn't even aware such people existed."

"Nor was I, not until a few days ago."

"One of the main things I miss about France is the healthcare system," she said. "It is so, so much better. Here it can be a disaster, and I am living proof."

"So, I assume you had a large hospital bill, too?"

"Énorme," Jeanne said. "Huge."

"Were you sued as well?"

"Oh, yeah! Yes, I was sued."

"A local hospital?" Brian asked.

"Yes again. MMH Inwood."

"Did you not have insurance?" Brian asked.

"We had insurance, but it was a short-term policy and ultimately worthless," Jeanne said. "They didn't pay anything."

"Could it have been Peerless Health Insurance, by any chance?"

"How did you guess?" she said, eyebrows raised.

"Merely by your saying they didn't pay anything," he said with a scoff. "We had the same insurance, and they haven't paid a dime. I've learned it's their modus operandi, thanks to their CEO, Heather Williams."

"I've heard of her," Jeanne said. "She's popular with Wall Street."

"What excuse did Peerless give for not paying any of your bill, if you don't mind me asking?"

"They claimed my husband's heart attack was due to a preexisting condition," Jeanne began. "Somehow they found out he had gone to a doctor several years ago with chest pain. Even though the doctor at the time found nothing except mildly elevated cholesterol and blood pressure, the insurance company claimed his heart attack was due to a preexisting condition. Unfortunately, it held up in court. We were duped. We didn't know that short-term health insurance could do such a thing."

"That is criminal. I mean, almost everything can to some extent be considered a preexisting condition."

"I couldn't agree more," she said. "It is criminal."

"Did your husband at least do okay medically?"

"I wish," Jeanne said. "He died after multiple procedures, waiting for a heart transplant. It didn't happen. With lousy health insurance, which wasn't going to cover anything, and without adequate personal resources for the half-million-dollar procedure, the hospital dragged its feet. It became clear to us that the chances of him getting a heart were not good. He lived for a while with what's called a ventricular assist device, but it wasn't much of a life."

"I'm so sorry to hear that," Brian said, feeling self-conscious he'd asked. And then he surprised himself by saying with a catch in his voice: "I can certainly sympathize. I lost my wife, too, just yesterday."

"Oh, no!" Jeanne exclaimed. "What happened?"

"It was a viral disease called eastern equine encephalitis, or EEE for short, that she got from a mosquito. I think she'd been bitten while we were having a beach barbecue a few weeks ago."

"Good lord! So tragic. I've never heard of EEE."

"I hadn't, either," Brian said. "But it's a developing problem that I'm afraid we are all going to hear more and more about. The Asian tiger mosquitoes that carry it have spread all the way up to Canada from the tropics."

"Between that and coronavirus, it seems that viral diseases are becoming an existential threat. And you say your wife died just yesterday?"

He nodded.

"You poor man. How can you be out and about? I couldn't even leave home for weeks after my husband died."

Brian took several deep breaths, started to speak, and then had to pause again. Finally, he managed: "I'm still in the denial and anger stage, I suppose. But I had to get out, especially with MMH Inwood suing me and threatening my house. That's why I'm here to see Megan Doyle and a lawyer upstairs, hoping they can help."

"I assume you mean Patrick McCarthy. Wow! You are on a similar trajectory as I. If it is any consolation, I can at least assure you that they work well together."

"That's good to hear. Thank you."

"This kind of situation would never happen in France," she said. "It's enough to make me think seriously of moving back even though there is a lot to love about this country." Then, wrinkling her forehead, she added: "You said you have a daughter. How is she taking this tragedy?"

"Not well, I'm afraid. She's always been a mommy's girl. She's had a lot of trouble since my wife was hospitalized two weeks ago. Telling her yesterday that her mother died was possibly the most difficult thing I've done in my life."

"It's an awful experience for a child to lose a parent, particularly a mother, no offense to you as a father."

"No offense taken. I get it."

"Your biggest challenge will be to convince her you will be there for her, that she is safe. Fear of abandonment will be her biggest concern, which you'll need to address head-on."

"It sounds to me like you know more about this kind of situation than I. Have you had some professional mental health training? Or are you a parent yourself?"

"No, I'm not a parent," Jeanne said. "But I did study psychology at Fordham University, where I met my husband, probably similar to the way your mother met your father. I also took a master's degree in school psychology and was an elementary school psychologist for a few years. While in that position, I had to deal with several students who had lost parents."

"Well, that explains it," Brian said, impressed by her experience.

"You'll have to be prepared for a potentially wide range of symptoms on your daughter's behalf," she explained. "She could get psychosomatic symptoms, like gastrointestinal complaints. In the mental arena, she could exhibit practically no change to outright regression."

"What do you mean by 'regression'?"

"Reverting to an earlier age. For instance, she could stop talking, forget her potty training, or demand a bottle and refuse to eat solid food. There's no way to predict. You'll have to be prepared for whatever comes."

At that moment the door to the inner office opened, and a white-haired man appeared on crutches. He was immediately followed by a woman Brian assumed was Megan Doyle. Despite the mask covering half her face, she looked younger than he expected, quite a bit younger than Patrick McCarthy, more like a college-aged woman than a professional with graduate training. She was dressed in a blue blazer over blue jeans with a white, open-necked blouse. Her medium-length light brown hair was a forest of curls. But what he liked immediately was that she projected a sense of assurance and almost cheerleader exuberance as she greeted the two older clients who were waiting by the windows, saying she'd be with them shortly.

After handing off some papers to the receptionist and taking the clipboard that contained the form Brian had filled out, she also greeted Jeanne before calling out his name and waving for him to follow her back into her office.

"Good luck," Jeanne said as Brian got to his feet.

"Thanks," he said, taking a deep breath. "I'm going to need it."

CHAPTER 19

September 1

Like Megan's outer office, the inner one was a polar opposite of Patrick McCarthy's shabby domain. It was hardly posh, but the furniture was relatively new, indeterminately modern, and constructed of a blond wood with a Scandinavian simplicity. Besides the obligatory desk and chairs, there was a good-sized bookcase that Brian could see was nearly filled with myriad hospital billing manuals and coding texts, underlining his ignorance of the entire field, one he never even knew existed.

"Please," Megan said, pointing to one of the chairs that was a bit more than six feet away from her desk. She sat behind her desk and quickly scanned the form that Brian had filled out.

"Okay," she began cheerfully. "This preliminary meeting won't take but a few minutes, and it is mainly to get you to sign a patient advocacy authorization form, so we can get the ball rolling to get a complete copy of your hospital bill. It will also give us an opportunity to talk about my fees. I see you are being sued by MMH Inwood for nearly one hundred and ninety thousand dollars."

"It's going to go up," he warned. "There will be an additional charge for an ED visit yesterday." Brian then gave her a quick history of Emma's illness and her death the day before.

"I'm so sorry to hear you have lost your wife," Megan said with genuine empathy. Her shoulders visibly sagged.

"It's the worst part," Brian said. "But the financial impact is a real issue I still have to deal with. Do you think you can help me?"

"Absolutely, without a shred of doubt," Megan said, regaining her fervor. "I've yet to have a client whose bill I haven't significantly reduced. I can assure you that MMH Inwood pads their bills and makes billing errors with as much or more regularity than the other hospitals in the city, especially for the uninsured or poorly insured. By poorly insured I mean those people whose health insurance companies haven't negotiated significant deductions in the hospital's charge master price."

"I apologize, but what is the hospital's 'charge master'? Is it like a list of prices for their services? I've never seen that."

"Nor will you see it, even if you ask," Megan said. "It's not meant for the public to see. It's a list of artificially high prices for goods and services that merely serves as a starting point for negotiating deductions for the more powerful, meaning large, health insurance companies. These prices have nothing to do with cost plus profit, which is how prices are usually determined in a real market and how Medicare tries to determine how much it will pay. And to make matters worse, hospitals keep raising their charge master prices, particularly when a hospital chain buys a failing community hospital. It's all a big game as hospitals and health insurance both benefit the more money is thrown at healthcare. Unfortunately, it is people like you who suffer the most because of this stupid and enormously expensive game. You end up being charged the artificially high charge master price, which is much more than everyone else pays."

"Good grief. I knew none of this. I feel like a babe in the woods, for Christ's sake."

"Don't be hard on yourself. Most people have no idea of any of this unfortunate reality, and most people still labor under the delusion that all hospitals and health insurance companies exist to help them in their time of need."

"I'm afraid I fell into that group for sure."

"All right, enough of this grim reality," Megan said, regaining her enthusiasm. "As soon as you sign this patient privacy authorization form, I will start the uphill climb of getting a complete, fully itemized bill, which is never easy because they will try hard to keep it from me. But don't worry. I know all their tricks and all their delay tactics. Have you been dealing with anyone in particular in the hospital's billing office?"

"Yes," Brian said. "A Roger Dalton."

"Good. He's almost human." She laughed at her own

joke. "And I assume you are working with Patrick Mc-Carthy as well since he called me?"

"Yes, starting just today," Brian confirmed.

"Perfect!" Megan said. "We have a good working relationship. Do you have any questions for me?"

"I don't know enough to have any questions at the moment." He knew he'd probably have a dozen as soon as he walked out of the office.

"Let me give you a quick thumbnail sketch of what will most likely happen," she added. "Although I can't promise you anything, but by my past experience with MMH billing, I should be able to reduce your bill anywhere between twenty-five to ninety percent. I know that is an awfully large range, but that's been my experience. As soon as I get your completely itemized bill, I'll start to work. After this in-person meeting, we can work remotely for the most part. I assume you have a computer and internet."

"Yes, of course," he said. "Actually, I have thought of a question. You seem to be busy. Are there a lot of Inwood people in need of your services?"

"Too many. And the pandemic has made it worse with people losing their employment-based healthcare and either going it alone or resorting to short-term health policies like you did. It's another developing part of the Covid-19 American tragedy."

"What about your fees? How will I be paying you?"

"You can either pay by the hour or as a percentage of what I save you," Megan said. "It will be your choice, and you can decide at some later point. After I get a look at your hospital bill, I'll be able to give you a better idea of what my fees might be."

"Patrick offered to put off payment until after the pandemic eases up and my business picks up. Are you willing to offer that as well?"

"I am," Megan said. "I'm sorry to have to cut this short, but I need to get back to seeing my scheduled clients. But first, let's have you sign this patient privacy authorization form to get the ball rolling."

"Of course." He got to his feet and approached the corner of the desk where she had slid the papers that needed his signature.

With the papers signed and in hand, he followed Megan out into the waiting room. While she called one of the elderly clients, Brian went to the receptionist as he'd been instructed and handed over the signed form. As he was doing it and listening to her saying she would be in touch if anything more would be needed on his part, he was trying to work up the courage to re-engage Jeanne Juliette-Shaw. Luckily, he didn't have to improvise. To his relief, as soon as he was finished with the receptionist, Jeanne stood up and approached him. In her hand she was holding a business card.

"Excuse me, Brian," she began. "I am truly sorry about your wife, and I have been thinking more about your daughter. The experience I had as a school psychologist suggests it is not going to be easy for you or her. If I can be of help in some way, particularly if there are problems, I'd be happy to do so. I'm not working presently for a number of reasons, which I won't bore you with, so I would be available if you were so inclined. Of course, it would be entirely pro bono."

Brian was immediately overwhelmed by Jeanne's generosity and impressed with the force of her character. "That's incredibly kind of you," he stammered.

"I wanted to give you my number if you are interested," Jeanne said, extending the business card.

He took the card and tried to read it but with difficulty. His eyes had teared up at Jeanne's offer and her altruism threatened to dissolve the veil of denial he'd erected to keep his emotions in check. "I might very well call you," he stammered.

"I'm sorry if I'm upsetting you," Jeanne said. "But I would like to help if you think I could."

"You are not upsetting me," Brian struggled to say, even though he was lying. He focused on the business card to get himself under control. In bold letters it said: SHAW ALARMS followed by a Washington Heights address. Her title was vice president. There was an office telephone number, but it was crossed out, and below that was a mobile number.

"Whoa," Brian said, taking a deep breath to pull himself together. "All this time I didn't know I was speaking with a vice president!"

"Vice president of a bankrupt alarm company," Jeanne corrected with a laugh of dismissal. "Shaw Alarms was forced into bankruptcy after I tried to pay MMH Inwood what I owed, which was impossible, and then was sued by them."

"My God," he remarked as rising anger saved him from his mournful emotions. Jeanne's story was a stark reminder of how predatory MMH Inwood was and how perverse Peerless was to more people than just him. "MMH's suit caused your company to go under?"

"Yes, with a little help from the pandemic."

"Sounds like a perfect storm," Brian said. "A storm I'm caught in as well. My wife and I started a personal security company just as the pandemic was starting in Wuhan, China. There's been almost no work for us since it arrived here in the US."

"You'll notice on the card that the office landline phone number is crossed out," Jeanne remarked. "But the mobile number is still operative. So please call if you decide you'd like to get ahold of me for some professional advice regarding your daughter. Or yourself, for that matter. Having recently lost my spouse, I can imagine what you are going through."

"Do you live in Inwood?"

"I do. On Seaman Avenue. My unit overlooks Emerson Playground."

"That's one of my daughter's favorite spots," Brian said, managing a smile.

"I can understand why," Jeanne responded. "Where do you live?"

"West 217th Street."

"Nice! I'm familiar with the neighborhood. Do you by any chance live in one of those darling single-family homes?"

"I do, and I'd like to keep it from MMH Inwood's predatory hands," he said, his mood going dark and anxious again.

"Amen," Jeanne responded, giving him a sympathetic look.

CHAPTER 20

September 1

As Brian came in through the front door of his house, he had no idea what to expect. No one had texted him for the two-plus hours he'd been away. The first thing he noticed was the soundtrack from a PBS cartoon coming from the kitchen; it sounded like *Curious George*. Thankfully there was no arguing or crying. The second thing he heard was Aimée and Hannah talking in the living room. Aimée waved and beckoned him to come in.

"Did you have any luck?" she questioned.

"It depends on what you mean by luck," he said. "I did retain a lawyer. His name is Patrick McCarthy, he was in Erin's class in elementary school, and he seems competent enough although he looks younger than I expected."

"I'm sure he'll be good," Aimée reassured him. "It's a fine family. And his father is a lawyer, too."

"I also retained a medical billing advocate. It's Megan Doyle, the one you mentioned helped a neighbor. I have to say she seems very professional although she looks even younger than the lawyer. The important thing is that she's confident she can lower Emma's hospital bill significantly. It crossed my mind that she might even be a bit overconfident, but we'll see."

"I'm pleased to hear you've taken my advice. She certainly aided Alana Jenkins. But we want to warn you about Juliette. She's not doing so well."

"What's wrong?" After taking the sound of the cartoon coming from the kitchen as a modicum of promising news, this was not what he wanted to hear.

"She refuses to talk to either one of us."

Brian nodded while replaying in his mind Jeanne's warning about regression.

"And she won't eat," Aimée continued. "Camila has really risen to the task and bent over backward, even making her favorite breakfast of eggs, bacon, and toast strips with sugar. To give Camila a break, I sat with Juliette for a time, trying to get her to interact with me, but I had no luck. It's such a change from yesterday afternoon when we took her to the Church of the Good Shepherd, and she was acting herself. Now all she wants to do is watch cartoons, and she cries if anyone tries to interfere."

"That's not good," he said. "All right, I'll go in and see if I can turn things around."

"Before you do, how are you doing?" Aimée asked, catching Brian off guard.

As if his mindset were poised on a knife blade, as soon as Aimée asked her question, he felt a wave of emotion wash over him. She saw it and responded by standing up, coming over to him, and giving him a long hug. Brian didn't resist. When she finally let go, he wiped the corners of his eyes with the back of his hand. "Sorry," he managed.

"Nothing to be sorry about," Aimée insisted. She pulled him toward the couch where she'd been sitting. "Before you see to Juliette, join us for a moment. Hannah has some news she needs to share with you."

Lacking the strength to resist, Brian sat and sighed, sounding like a balloon losing its air. Hannah spoke up immediately. "I'm happy to say I've made a lot of progress," she began. She moved forward where she was sitting on the opposing couch. "I've been in touch with Riverside Funeral Home, and they have been most helpful. As soon as Emma is prepared, which I've been told will be in a few hours, they will bring her to our home for a proper wake, which will start this afternoon and continue overnight. Some family members and even neighbors have offered to help with food, drink, and other preparations like candles and flowers and arranging the house. How does all this sound to you?"

Hannah paused in her monologue and looked at him for some kind of response. Brian didn't know how he felt about all this traditional rigmarole but was unwilling to openly object even if he did. It was so apparent to him that Hannah was trying to come to terms with her daughter's death by attending to all the details. Once again, he wished he and Emma had discussed death in some form or fashion so he'd have some idea of what she would have wanted. If he had to guess, he thought she'd want her mother to decide if that could somehow be a help. With that in mind, all he did was nod.

"Okay," Hannah said, as if relieved by Brian's tacit agreement. "For tomorrow, I have arranged a funeral mass at the Church of the Good Shepherd, followed by interment at Woodlawn Cemetery. I hope you don't mind, but we have gone ahead and covered the expenses."

"That's very generous of you," he managed to say. He wasn't one who expected or generally accepted handouts, but this was an exceptional time, and he was grateful, considering the state of his finances.

"We're happy to help, knowing your security business is struggling," Hannah said, offering him a sympathetic look. "The one thing I'd like to ask you to do is to alert some of Emma's NYPD friends and colleagues about her passing even though attendance will be limited at both the wake and the funeral mass because of the pandemic."

"I can do that," Brian said. It also occurred to him that at the same time it might be an opportunity to at least float the idea of his returning to the NYPD with the ESU commander, Deputy Chief Michael Comstock. With Emma gone, he truly had no idea how much enthusiasm he still had about Personal Protection LLC, especially with the ongoing pandemic.

"Good!" Hannah voiced, slapping her knees with the palms of her hands before getting to her feet. "I'm sorry to have to leave you two to handle Juliette for the time being, but I have to get home to make sure everything goes smoothly. There's so much to do."

"We understand," Aimée said. "We'll see to Juliette, and thank you for bearing the burden of the wake and the funeral."

"It's the least I can do," Hannah said with a wave of dismissal. She turned around, hurried into the foyer for her shoes, and disappeared out the front door.

For a moment mother and son eyed each other.

"She's a whirlwind," he offered at last.

Aimée nodded. "She needs to be, and you are generous to allow it."

"I don't have the energy to interfere. Besides, I don't know what Emma would have wanted other than not wanting her mother to suffer."

"Je comprends," Aimée said. "Besides, your worry at the moment really has to be Juliette. My mothering instinct tells me she is going to need a lot of your attention. I'm more than willing to help, but I'm afraid the major burden will fall on you."

"My fathering instinct is giving me the same message," Brian agreed as he reached into his pants pocket and produced the card for the defunct business that Jeanne had given him. "To that end, I had an unexpected experience waiting to see Megan Doyle. Another of Ms. Doyle's clients came in, and I heard her give her name: Jeanne Juliette-Shaw." He handed the card to Aimée.

"Really?" she questioned. She looked at the business card and raised her eyebrows. "That's surprising. Juliette is not a common family name."

"That's exactly why I had the nerve to strike up a conversation," he said. "It turns out that she, like you,

grew up in France and, also like you, came to the United
States for college, Fordham University to be exact, and
met her husband-to-be."

"Une telle coïncidence," Aimée said. She handed the
business card back. "Mon Dieu! Did you ask where in
France she's from?"

"I did. She's from the Camargue."

"Fascinating, but I surely don't know any Juliette
families from the Camargue," Aimée said. "I'll have to
ask my mother. It's a unique part of France, rather
sparsely populated. I've never visited myself. What I do
remember about it is that they have a special breed of
horse called the Camargue, which has a unique light
gray, almost white coat."

Suddenly the sound of the cartoon emanating from
the kitchen stopped, yet there was no further sound from
Juliette. Brian tensed, and he and Aimée exchanged a
questioning glance as they listened for a moment.

"I wonder what that means?" he asked.

"I wonder the same. At least there's no complaint
from Juliette, so it can't be all that bad."

"I guess," Brian said as he visibly relaxed. "Anyway, to
get back to my story, I know it sounds odd under the
circumstances for me to have had a conversation with a
stranger while waiting to talk to a medical billing advocate, but our situations are surprisingly similar. Jeanne
also recently lost a spouse and was sued by MMH Inwood. But most interesting of all is that we talked briefly
about Juliette. She has a graduate degree in psychology,
had been a school psychologist, and had experience with

students who'd lost parents. She offered to give some advice, which is why she gave me the card with her mobile number. In fact, she even warned me that Juliette might regress and have psychosomatic symptoms."

"Sounds like she could really be useful," Aimée said. "Considering how Juliette has behaved this morning, I think some professional advice might be wise. Perhaps you should call her. My sense is that Juliette is going to need help, and your presence and attention are going to be crucial but might not be enough."

"You might be right," Brian said, getting to his feet and starting for the kitchen. Instead of following, Aimée headed toward the foyer. "Aren't you coming, too?" he asked.

"I think I should go and give Hannah a hand, and I think Juliette needs your undivided attention."

He nodded and continued into the kitchen. To his surprise Juliette wasn't there, just Camila rinsing the dishes and putting them in the dishwasher.

"Where's Juliette?" he asked.

"She's upstairs in her room," she said. "She suddenly said she wasn't feeling well and wanted to go to bed. To tell you the truth, although I wasn't happy to hear her say she wasn't feeling well, I was glad to hear her say something. It was the first time she has spoken since she woke up."

"That's not good," Brian said, recalling Jeanne's warning about regression.

"She did look a little flushed to me and I thought I saw her have a chill, so I took her temperature. It was 101."

"Uh-oh," Brian voiced. "Why would she have a fever?

But wait! Is 101 a fever for a four-year-old?" He knew temperatures varied considerably during the day, even in adults but more so in children.

"Interesting you asked," Camila said. "I questioned it myself, so I googled it. I got the impression that anything over 100.4 could be considered a fever, but it's sort of borderline. But combined with her saying she doesn't feel well the last few days, it makes me nervous."

Remembering also that Jeanne mentioned Juliette might develop psychosomatic symptoms, he wondered if that could include a fever. He truly didn't know, and despite his EMT medical knowledge, he'd not had much pediatrics experience. Although he was mildly reluctant to call Jeanne the same day he'd met her for fear of taking advantage of her generosity, he thought the potential fever issue serious enough to overcome his hesitation. Sitting down on the banquette, he took out his phone and Jeanne's old business card. After giving Camila a brief description of Jeanne's professional qualifications, he placed the call, hoping Jeanne wouldn't think he was being too pushy by calling so soon. It had to ring a number of times, and just when he thought her voicemail message was about to start, she answered. He could tell she was out of breath. After he gave his name, he asked if he was calling at an inopportune moment and if she was still at Megan Doyle's.

"Heavens no, on both accounts. I'm glad to hear from you. I'm on my bike in Inwood Hill Park not too far from the Indian Caves. It just took me a minute to get my phone out of my back pocket."

"I'm sorry to interrupt what must be a fun ride," Brian said. "But I have a specific question, if you have a moment. You mentioned that my daughter might have psychosomatic symptoms in response to my wife's death. Can a fever be a psychosomatic symptom?"

"Good question! If I remember correctly, fever can definitely be a psychosomatic symptom. But I think it has only been seen in children considerably older than your daughter. You said she is four, correct?"

"Yes, she's four, but also like you suggested, just today she seems to be behaving as if she is much younger. She's stopped talking for the most part."

"Oh, dear," Jeanne said. "That doesn't sound so good. Listen, I can stop by if you would like and see if I can talk with her. I'm generally pretty good with kids. If you are concerned about Covid, I can also reassure you that I had a test just last week that was negative, and I abide by the pandemic rules to the letter."

"I would appreciate that very much," Brian said, and gave his house number. He then added that he'd had a relatively recent negative test as well, and as a family they'd been careful about following all the recommended precautions.

"Sounds good! We should be okay in that regard, and I'm on my way."

After he disconnected the call, he sat at the banquette for a few minutes, thinking how lucky he'd been by striking up a conversation with Jeanne. Even though he'd been fully engaged in the process of raising Juliette, Emma had been most definitely in the driver's seat. Now on his own, he felt like a fish out of water. "Well, that couldn't have gone any better," he said to Camila, who had sat down across from him. "She's coming over."

"I hope she can help," she said.

"I'm going to go up to Juliette's room and see if she'll talk. Do you want to come with me, or do you need a break?"

"I'll come. There's nothing for me to do in the office."

On the way up the back stairs, Brian gave Camila a thumbnail sketch of meeting Jeanne similar to what he'd told his mother.

"What a lucky encounter," she said as they headed along the upstairs hallway and entered Juliette's room. "She could be a big help."

Still in her pajamas, Juliette was lying on her side on the bed, facing away. As Brian came around the end of her bed, he could see that her eyes were open and unblinking, yet she didn't move. She was also sucking her thumb, which she hadn't done for years. It seemed to him further evidence that she was regressing. Her other hand was clutching Bunny to her chest.

"Hello, Pumpkin," Brian said, using one of his many endearing nicknames for her. She didn't respond or even move. "Camila said you weren't feeling well. Can you tell me what's wrong? Do you have a sore throat or is your stomach upset?" There was no response. "Camila said you had a chill, is that right?" Still no response.

Brian put his palm on Juliette's forehead, and she felt warm to him. "How about coming back to the kitchen and we'll watch something, whatever you want? We'll watch it together. What do you think? Is that a good idea?" Juliette didn't move or answer. He looked back at Camila, who shrugged her shoulders as if to say "I told you so." Redirecting his attention back to Juliette, Brian said: "I want to take your temperature again. Should we do it here or in the kitchen?"

"I want my mommy," Juliette whispered just loud enough for him to hear, and it melted his heart.

"I know you do, Pumpkin," Brian whispered back. "I miss her, too, but Mommy is in heaven. I'm here and someone else is coming who wants to meet you. Are you okay with that?"

When Juliette didn't respond or move, he gave her shoulder a squeeze just to make contact. "Okay, I'll get the thermometer, and I'll be right back."

CHAPTER 21

September 1

Jeanne, Camila, and Brian stepped out of Juliette's room, and all three hesitated at the top of the main staircase. Both Brian and Camila had been impressed with the creative way that Jeanne had managed to interact with Juliette and gotten her to talk. What she'd done was first engage Bunny as if Bunny was the one suffering, telling Bunny that as a little girl, she had a very similar rabbit friend who was so important to her that she'd brought her to America. Jeanne had then asked Juliette if she could hold Bunny, and to Brian's and Camila's surprise, Juliette had handed her the floppy stuffed rabbit.

"Oh, poor Bunny," she had said, stroking its head. "No wonder she's not feeling well. She's missing one of her eyes."

"But she can see fine," Juliette responded. With that little exchange Jeanne had started a conversation and had been able to switch the topic to Juliette's symptoms. Within a relatively short time she was able to get the child to admit to a sore throat, a headache, and an upset stomach.

"You certainly have a way with children," Camila observed.

"Thank you," she said. "I had a lot of practice being a school psychologist."

"So, what do you think?" Brian asked.

"I do think Juliette is experiencing psychosomatic symptoms, but I'm a little concerned she might also actually be sick," Jeanne said. "The fever issue is what bothers me. You say you confirmed her temperature is elevated?"

"I did," he said. "I took it again just before you got here. It's 100.8, which I guess is just over borderline. She has a fever, but not much of one."

"Whether it's a fever is beyond my expertise. I'm hardly a doctor, but tell me this: Is there any chance she might have been exposed to the coronavirus? I hate to say it, but there is a very slight chance she could have Covid."

"Not while I've been with her," Brian said. "And not here in the house." He looked at Camila questioningly.

"Certainly not here in the house," Camila said. "We haven't had any visitors, aside from the medical personnel yesterday, and they were in full protective gear. And I can't imagine when she could have been exposed on the few times she and I have gone out since Emma was hospitalized. On those occasions we only went to Emerson Playground or Isham Park, and she didn't socialize and wore her mask. But you know, thinking about how she has been acting makes me think she hasn't been feeling well for some time."

"I agree," Brian said. "Ever since my wife got sick, and Juliette saw her have a seizure, she hasn't been herself."

"Well, if we have learned anything over the last eight months, coronavirus spreads remarkably easily in certain situations," Jeanne remarked. "My advice is that she should at least be seen by her pediatrician. Does she have one?"

"Of course," he said. "Dr. Rajiv Bhatt on Broadway. Let's go down to the office, and I'll give him a call."

Brian led while the others followed. As they filed in, he turned on the light.

"A nice touch," Jeanne said as she glanced around. "I haven't been in too many offices with a crystal chandelier."

"It was a formal dining room that my wife and I turned into an office for our security business," Brian explained as he gestured for Jeanne to take one of several side chairs.

"I'm going to get some coffee and then check on Juliette to make sure she is still sleeping," Camila said. "Does anyone want anything from the kitchen?"

"I'm good," Brian called out as he searched his contacts for Dr. Bhatt's office number.

"Thank you, but I'm fine, too," Jeanne said with a wave.

As the call went through, he looked over at his visitor, who was still dressed in her biking clothes. "You look like you are an avid biker," he said. "My wife and I were, too."

"It was the one sport my husband and I did together."

Brian raised his hand to indicate his call had connected. He listened but didn't speak, then quickly disconnected and put the phone down. "Busy," he said.

"Camila seems very committed to your daughter," Jeanne said.

"She is. Unbelievably so. I am so lucky to have her. We hired her because of her business background, but she ended up moving in with us because of the pandemic. Since then she's become family in a very real way. I truly don't know what I'd do if she were to decide to leave."

"I hope you aren't offended by my asking," she said, "and you don't have to answer if you don't want to, but I'm intrigued by you saying that you and your wife had a security business. What's your background to have that kind of expertise?"

"We were both New York City policemen," Brian explained. "But more importantly we both were graduates of the Emergency Service Unit Academy and then served as ESU officers for a combined total of ten years, which is an extraordinary amount of law enforcement experience between the two of us."

"Excuse my ignorance, but I'm not familiar with ESU," Jeanne said.

"It stands for Emergency Service Unit. It's like special forces with the military. Whenever the NYPD are confronted with someone dangling off a skyscraper or a bridge, an active shooter, a hostage situation, a mass casualty event like 9/11, or even serving a high-risk warrant, we were the ones who were called to take care of it."

"You mean you were a member of a SWAT team?"

"Special Weapons and Tactics was just one small aspect of our role," he said. "ESU training was really extensive and intense. We were cross-trained in multiple disciplines and immersed in SCUBA, negotiation tactics, jumping out of helicopters, EMT requirements, you name it. My wife, Emma, was one of very few women who took the training. It was very physical, to say the least."

"My word. It sounds to me like you are overtrained to do mere personal security."

"That was the idea. We thought we'd be in high demand with our backgrounds. It's just that the timing turned out to be problematic thanks to Covid-19." He raised his phone. "Let me try the pediatrician again."

Brian redialed and listened. He listened for longer than Jeanne expected without speaking and then let out a sigh of frustration before disconnecting. "Damn, he's on vacation!"

"Did the recording give the name and number of a covering doctor?"

"No," he said. "I'm not surprised. There aren't too many pediatricians in the immediate area. What's suggested in his outgoing message is for anything that can't wait until he gets back this coming Monday should be seen at the MMH Inwood Emergency Department. He's made arrangements that the MMH ED doctors have online access to his records if it's needed for the continuity of care."

"Might continuity of care be important in Juliette's case?" she asked.

"It could be," Brian said reluctantly. "I don't know for sure, but Juliette was a premature baby and spent her first couple of months in the Children's Hospital at Columbia-Presbyterian Hospital. That was where we originally met Dr. Bhatt."

"Okay, that solves it. Let's have her be seen at MMH Inwood. It might even be easier since they can go ahead and do a Covid-19 test straightaway."

"I don't know!" Brian said with a questioning expression. "In the middle of being in for nearly two hundred thousand dollars, the MMH Inwood ED might be the last place I want to take her. Hell, they might even refuse to see her for all I know."

"They aren't going to refuse to see her," Jeanne scoffed. "By law I don't think they can refuse."

"Maybe so, but they sure as hell might be less than accommodating or even rude to us."

"I can't imagine," Jeanne said. "The MMH Inwood might be predatory and overly profit centered, but I've come to understand there is a definite divide between their clinical side and their billing and collections shenanigans. Not once did I have the impression the doctors doing the day-to-day care had any idea of what was going on on the business side. Of course, whether they should have is an entirely different question."

"I disagree," he countered. "With my wife, it was the chief medical officer who saw fit to discharge her, and

I've been worried it might have been because the hospital wasn't being paid."

"Hmmm," she voiced. "You might be right. Do you know that the position of chief medical officer is a relatively new position in hospitals?"

"I didn't," Brian said.

"During my lawsuit and because of my budding interest in business issues when I changed from being a school psychologist to running an alarm company, I've spent many hours researching modern-day hospital business practices. It's eye-opening, to say the least, or maybe horrifying is a better term. One of the things I came to understand was that the chief medical officer, or CMO in hospital jargon, is really an administrator hired by the hospital CEO. Although originally trained as a doctor, the CMO usually has some subsequent business background like an MBA, so their main interests revolve more around hospital costs than clinical outcomes. Although it sounds similar, the chief medical officer isn't the same as chief of surgery or chief of internal medicine, whose orientation is just the opposite."

"I had no idea," Brian said. "I thought the CMO might have been a combined position representing both surgery and internal medicine and still more attuned to what's best for the patient."

"No, it's definitely administrative and mostly geared toward keeping costs down to maximize profits," Jeanne said. "I hope I'm not boring you with all this economic minutia."

"Quite the contrary, but you are making me more concerned my wife was discharged prematurely. I feel so naïve about this current medical world."

"You and a lot of other people. Unfortunately, it's all about money. The sheer amount of money involved in healthcare attracted private equity because of the sky-high potential profits. It's the private equity investors who have forced hospitals to hire a bevy of compensation consultants."

"What the hell are compensation consultants?"

"They are highly trained businesspeople whose sole goal is to maximize revenue," Jeanne explained. "They don't care if the company is a hospital or trucking firm. Their shenanigans and advice have contributed significantly to a major uptick in hospital prices and thereby profit."

"I thought a lot of hospitals were now struggling financially," he said, realizing he'd been getting mixed information from Roger Dalton.

"That's true," she said. "But that's just since the coronavirus has forced them to cut back on lucrative elective surgery like joint replacements. Otherwise, hospitals, particularly chain hospitals, have been virtual gold mines thanks in large part to their teams of compensation consultants. It's the community hospitals and rural hospitals, which are still primarily oriented toward patient care and the neighborhoods they serve, that are hurting. They are either going out of business or being snapped up by hospital chains backed by private equity, which quickly turn them into money-making machines. And it's happening across the country, thanks to all their compensation consultants and CEOs like Charles Kelley. Welcome to the twenty-first century."

"It all infuriates me," Brian snapped. "With what you are saying, I'm even more convinced my wife was discharged because of economics. What a disaster!"

"It's possible," Jeanne said. "I give you that. But the point I want to make is that the MMH Inwood CMO and the compensation consultants have nothing to do clinically with what happens on a day-to-day basis in the Emergency Department. No one there will have any idea you owe the hospital money or that the hospital is suing you. And to get back to Juliette, I really think she should be seen and seen at MMH with her medical records available if needed and get a Covid test. Actually, what I think will be more of a problem is that she's going to refuse to go, but I'll be happy to help convince her if you would like."

"I'm sure you are right; she won't want to go. She can be very willful. It's very generous of you to offer help, which I sincerely appreciate, but *why* are you, if I might ask without sounding ungrateful?"

"To be entirely honest, it's mostly because I feel for you having just lost your wife yesterday," Jeanne said. "I have a visceral idea of what you are going through because of my own recent grief. I don't know how you are coping as well as you are."

"Like I said in Megan's office, it's with a lot of denial, but I'm also one of those people who needs to be doing something, and Juliette needs me to support her and hold together what I can of our life."

"I understand," she said, getting to her feet. "Let's see if we can get her to cooperate without too much difficulty."

At that moment his cell phone rang. He answered as he got to his feet, motioning to Jeanne to hold on for a moment. It was Aimée calling from the O'Briens'.

"Emma's wake is about to start," Aimée said. "Hannah asked me to call because she wants to know when you and Juliette are going to come over? I know you sounded reluctant earlier, but she thinks it is important for Juliette to say goodbye to her mother and maybe leave something for her in the casket."

"A problem has arisen," Brian began, wincing at the whole idea of the wake, particularly in relation to his daughter. He had forgotten all about it with his rising concerns about his daughter's health status. "Juliette seems to have a fever and doesn't feel great, making us worry she might have coronavirus."

"Oh, no!" Aimée exclaimed. "Mon Dieu! What are you going to do? Are you going to have her tested?"

"Yes, I think we must, as it could have dire consequences if she's positive. We're going to take her to the MMH Inwood ED."

"You and Camila?"

"No, with Jeanne Juliette-Shaw, the woman I mentioned earlier," Brian said. "I called her because Juliette hasn't been talking, and Jeanne came over and has been very helpful. She was able to get Juliette to open up.

That's how we know Juliette's not feeling well, because up until then she wasn't talking. Luckily, she doesn't have any cough or breathing issues, but what can I say? We can't ignore it. I tried to call her pediatrician, but he's on vacation."

"Oh, goodness, mon fils," Aimée said empathetically. "I'll let Hannah know so she can perhaps hold things up. If Juliette is positive, we'll have to cancel the wake since we'll all have to quarantine. This could be a disaster on top of a disaster. Can you call me as soon as you know? Hannah's going to be really upset. All this planning activity is what's holding her together."

"Of course," Brian said, feeling a tinge guilty with his reservations about the wake, especially whether Juliette should be subjected to seeing her mother's body. He wasn't even sure how he felt about it himself.

As they headed for the stairs with Brian in the lead, Jeanne asked: "What was the name of the chief medical officer who encouraged your wife to be discharged before she probably should have been?"

"Dr. Kathrine Graham," he called over his shoulder.

"I thought so," she said irritably. "What a lousy ambassador for the medical profession! She was also the one I blame for MMH Inwood not being all that motivated to find a heart for my husband. Of course, the real fault really falls on Charles Kelley, who's responsible for the culture and hiring her. Doesn't it all irritate you to death when you think about it?"

Brian paused at the top of the stairs and waited for her. "It makes my blood boil," he admitted angrily as she gained the landing. "I even stormed into Kelley's office right after Emma died, and I would have done the same for Heather Williams's if it had been handy. But I can't think about this kind of stuff right now. I've got to concentrate on Juliette and finding a way out of this mess."

CHAPTER 22

September 1

Reaching into his pocket, Brian took out his phone and checked the time. "Shit," he whispered. "We've been here almost two hours." He was talking to Jeanne but didn't want Juliette to hear, which was unlikely because she had earbuds in and was watching cartoons on his laptop. The three of them were sitting relatively by themselves in the corner of the ED waiting room.

Getting Juliette to come to the hospital hadn't been easy. At first, she downright refused, but Jeanne used the same tactic she'd used to get Juliette to talk in the first place. She spoke extensively to Bunny, explaining to the toy why she had to go to the hospital for a Covid-19 test. Then when Bunny finally agreed, Juliette did the same. Camila drove them and also agreed to come and pick them up after Juliette had been seen.

"I'm starting to think they are definitely being passive-aggressive and making us wait," Brian said, still speaking softly. "I'm not as confident as you that there is the disconnect between the business side and the clinical side here in the ED. It doesn't seem that busy for us to have to wait almost two hours with a sick four-year-old."

"Let's avoid jumping to conclusions. They've been busy enough with the three ambulances that arrived since we got here. And the clerks and the triage nurse couldn't have been nicer. Plus, we have no idea what's going on back in the treatment rooms."

"I'm surprised that Juliette hasn't complained," Brian said, glancing over at his daughter.

"She's been an angel," Jeanne agreed. "Let's give the ED team the benefit of the doubt and hope she'll be seen shortly."

"I have another question for you as a school psychologist. When we were in my office, it was my mother who phoned. She was calling me to say that my wife's wake was about to begin and wanted to know when I would be bringing Juliette. I don't know how I feel about subjecting a four-year-old to her mother's wake. What's your opinion?"

"Probably like your mother, as an outsider of sorts I've developed a lot of respect for Irish funeral traditions, including wakes. There was a wake for my husband, and I was surprised by how many children showed up, including a nephew of ten and two nieces about Juliette's age."

"But it's her mother, not an aunt or uncle. I'm worried that forcing her to see the body will just add insult to injury. I mean, she already had to witness her having two seizures."

"My advice is to ask Juliette what she wants to do. Spell it out as an opportunity to say goodbye but remind her that her mother will not speak to her or even respond in any way at all. Just be totally up front and let her decide."

"Really?" he questioned skeptically. It seemed beyond him to turn such a decision over to a four-year-old.

"In my experience, children are capable of making a lot of decisions for themselves," Jeanne said. "More than a lot of people give them credit for. Anyway, that's my advice."

"Okay, thanks. I'll think about it."

"What about the viral illness your wife had? Is it at all contagious?"

"No, eastern equine encephalitis needs the mosquito vector," Brian said. "I've learned the mosquito has to bite an infected songbird, which is the normal host, and then bite a human or some other animal."

"Why is it called 'equine'?"

"It first showed up in horses."

"Thank God it at least doesn't spread like Covid-19," she said.

"You got that right," Brian said without a lot of enthusiasm. He had too many other things to worry about.

"It's terrifying to think you can get a fatal disease attending a summer barbecue. What's amazing to me is that I've never learned so much about viruses until this year."

"We healthy human beings have no real appreciation of how close we are to the precipice at any given time," he said. "It's especially disturbing when the institutions you count on to help when you need it, like hospitals and health insurance, can't be depended upon."

"It's a scary situation on so many levels."

"How much did MMH Inwood sue you for?" Brian said. "I hope you don't mind me asking."

"No, I don't mind at all," Jeanne reassured him. "It was a bit over four hundred thousand dollars."

"Yikes," Brian said. "How did your bill get that high?"

"It's easy," she said. "There were multiple admissions involved, several stays in the cardiac intensive care unit, and the surgery to implant the ventricular assist device. It adds up quickly, especially for people like you and me with lousy health insurance."

"That's what I've been learning," he said bitterly.

"The four hundred thousand–plus was before I got Megan Doyle involved. She's cut it down almost in half."

"That's encouraging."

"Yeah, but it's still about a quarter of a million dollars," Jeanne said. "That's enough to bankrupt most Americans except the top one percent. What excuse did Peerless give for not paying any of your hospital bill? It couldn't have been the preexisting excuse they used for us."

Brian gave a short, disgusted laugh. "No, they didn't claim Emma's problem was a preexisting condition. There were two parts to their strategy. The first part was the ED bill, which they said they weren't going to cover because Emma was ambulatory and should have gone to a GP who could have arranged admission. They said they

were trying to rein in the overuse of hospital Emergency
Department visits. It was just a bogus excuse, and they
invited me to sue, the bastards. With the hospital bill it
was a unique way of interpreting the deductible. I won't
bore you with the details. But even if they were going to
pay, it would have only been a thousand dollars a day,
which, when my wife and I were in the market to get
health insurance we could afford, we mistakenly thought
was a significant contribution. We had no idea how piti-
fully inadequate it is."

"We were duped in the same way."

"How long ago did your husband pass away?" Brian
asked. "If you'd rather not talk about it, I understand."

"It's all right. It was just a little over a year ago."

"Did MMH Inwood sue you right away like me?"

"No," Jeanne began. "Stupid me tried to pay them
the original amount. There was some cash in the business, so I gave them sixty-five thousand up front and
agreed to pay twenty thousand a month for two years. I'd
made several monthly payments, but then the pandemic
hit, and everything shut down, and the alarm business
mostly dried up. That's when they sued me."

"Did they have something to do with your company's
bankruptcy?"

"Of course," she said. "They also garnished any income I might have earned from the business if I'd tried
to keep it going. But to tell you the truth, with my husband's passing, I wasn't all that interested in running the
company even though I had learned a lot about alarm
technology and business in the three years I'd spent in-

volved. While he was alive it made sense because he was a techie, not a businessman, and he had been paying someone much too much to run the business side of the operation."

"I can understand. I'm already wondering if I have what it takes to try to make a go of Personal Protection LLC without my wife. I'm probably more like your husband, since Emma handled the business side along with Camila. I've already wondered if I should try to get my old position back with the NYPD ESU."

"I'm going to go back to school psychology as soon as the legal dust settles," Jeanne said. "The only reason I've held off is because I certainly don't want MMH Inwood garnishing my wages."

"I want to go home," Juliette said suddenly, taking out her earbuds.

"I'm sure you do, sweetie," Brian agreed. "I do, too. I think I'll see what is holding things up." As he started to get up, Jeanne reached out and gripped his arm.

"For what it's worth, I don't think you'll get any satisfaction making a fuss," she said. "And you could make things worse. Just a suggestion."

He hesitated, looking over at the information desk, which was always a beehive of activity. When they'd first arrived two hours earlier, a triage nurse had listened to their story about Juliette's symptoms, noted she was a patient of Dr. Rajiv Bhatt, whose records were available if needed since she had been a preemie, checked Juliette's vital signs, and told them they'd be seen shortly. That was the last contact they'd had without any apology or explanation. At the same time, he knew Jeanne was correct and that raising a ruckus could very well be counterproductive.

"I'll be a perfect gentleman," Brian promised. "I just need to make sure we haven't been forgotten somehow."

CHAPTER 23

September 1

"Juliette Murphy!" a nurse in gown and mask called out after emerging from the depths of the Emergency Department.

"God! It's about time," Brian mumbled as he got to his feet. It had been more than three hours that they had been waiting. Mercifully, Juliette had fallen asleep about a half hour earlier.

"It's been a long wait," Jeanne agreed. "But, again, try not to act angry, for Juliette's sake."

"It's going to be difficult for me not to point out that we've seen a number of people arrive, be seen, and leave while we've been sitting here with a sick four-year-old."

"I can't imagine you'll get any satisfaction if you act irritated," Jeanne said. "And try to remember that at least she's going to be seen, and you'll get the Covid-19 test out of the way."

"Okay, okay," he said, taking a deep breath to calm himself. "You are right. I'll try to be nice." He then reached down and picked Juliette up. "Come on, Pumpkin!" he urged. "We'll get you checked out and then get you home." She mumbled a brief complaint but fell back asleep almost immediately in Brian's arms with her head on his shoulder. While he reached for Bunny, he added to Jeanne: "No matter what you say, I'm convinced they've been keeping us waiting because of the outstanding bill I owe. I'm sorry, but it's the only explanation."

"You don't know that for sure," Jeanne said.

"I feel it."

"Feeling it and knowing it are two different things."

"Maybe," Brian said. "Can you get the rest of the stuff?"

"Leave it! I'll watch it. No worries."

"You're not coming with us?"

"I'm not family and with the pandemic rules, we're lucky they let me even in the waiting area. I'll be here when you're done. Good luck."

"You're probably right," he said. "Okay! We'll try to at least make this part quick."

With the sleeping Juliette in one arm and Bunny in the other, Brian walked the width of the waiting room and approached the nurse who'd called out Juliette's name. She was wearing a face shield as well as a mask.

"Well, well," the nurse said good-naturedly. "The sweetie seems to have fallen asleep. I think that is a good sign, maybe she's feeling better."

"We've been waiting more than three hours," he said, struggling to keep his voice neutral.

"Sorry about that. We've been busy as usual. My name is Olivia. Would you please follow me?"

Still carrying the sleeping Juliette and Bunny, Brian trailed the nurse back to a tiny ambulatory examination room with an exam table, a sink, two chairs, and a built-in desk with a monitor. Olivia patted the exam table, asked him to put Juliette down, and then washed her hands. At first Juliette resisted, but then became cooperative in the new surroundings when Olivia gave her a hemostat to hold. In a gentle and kind fashion, Olivia took Juliette's vital signs while keeping up a conversation about Bunny, which Juliette had taken from Brian.

"What's her temperature?" Brian asked.

"Ninety-eight point six," Olivia read off the number. "Nice and normal."

"Really?" he questioned. "Last time we took it at home it was almost 101. Are you sure of your reading?"

"I'll take it again," Olivia offered happily. She was using a thermal scanner. "Yup! Normal." Addressing Juliette, she asked: "And how do you feel now, love?"

"I want to go home," Juliette said.

"I'm sure you do," Olivia responded. She looked briefly at the tablet she was holding and then asked, "But what about your sore throat, and headache, and upset stomach?"

"I'm okay now," Juliette said.

"Are you sure?" Brian asked, butting in, shocked at the reversal of Juliette's complaints.

"Yes," Juliette insisted. "And Bunny feels better, too."

"I'm so glad," Olivia said. "Okay, Dr. Kramer will be in to see you, Miss Juliette, in just a few minutes. Is that okay?"

Juliette nodded, handing back the hemostat before Olivia left the room.

"Are you sure you don't have a sore throat any longer?" Brian asked, mystified.

Juliette nodded and then started to climb down from the exam table, but Brian stopped her and sat down next to her. Taking a cue from Jeanne, he talked more about her symptoms using Bunny as a go-between. She continued to be insistent that Bunny's throat, head, and stomach were fine.

It was almost twenty minutes before an extremely youthful Dr. Mercedes Kramer came swooping ebulliently into the tiny exam room along with Olivia. Now bored, Juliette answered all the doctor's rapid-fire questions with a curt no: no sore throat, no congestion, no headache, no coughing, no vomiting, and no generally feeling bad. Maintaining a happy chatter, Dr. Kramer quickly washed her hands and then rapidly but thoroughly examined the child, even allowing Juliette to listen to her own heart. When she was finished, she said: "Miss Juliette, I think you are in fine shape." She then gave Juliette a reassuring shoulder squeeze.

"Dr. Kramer, can I speak with you alone for a moment?" Brian said when the doctor turned to him, presumably to declare Juliette a picture of health.

"Of course," Dr. Kramer said, motioning for him to step out into the corridor.

"I thought it best to tell you that my daughter is under a lot of stress," Brian said, struggling to stay in control of his emotions, now heightened by the long wait to be seen and Juliette's disappearing symptoms. "Her mother died yesterday from EEE and my daughter happened to witness her suffering two grand mal convulsions, including the one yesterday that resulted in her death."

"Oh, what a terrible story," Dr. Kramer voiced with sympathy. "I'm so sorry for your loss. Was your wife seen here in our ED?"

"Yes," Brian said. "Yesterday. She was brought in by ALS ambulance."

"Oh, yes. I heard about that case. Such a tragedy for an otherwise healthy young woman. EEE is a bad disease, but it seems that your daughter is weathering your wife's passing rather well."

"Actually, she hasn't," he argued. "During the two weeks that my wife had been sick, my daughter had been struggling emotionally and behaviorally. Then it all came to a head yesterday when she was told her mother had died. She stopped communicating, and then today she had a chill, and when her temperature was taken, it was 101."

"She's afebrile now," Dr. Kramer stated.

"But her fever was real," Brian insisted. "I took it myself. It wasn't quite 101 but very close. I'm worried that she might be coming down with something, like Covid."

"Has she been exposed to someone with Covid?" Dr. Kramer asked. "Or has she been to any large functions or gatherings?"

"No, not at all."

"Have any of her friends or anyone in the family tested positive?"

"No, no one. And even when she was occasionally out, she didn't socialize, and she has been very good about wearing a mask. Or at least that is what I was told. But, still, her symptoms made us worry she might have the virus."

"She likely doesn't have Covid-19," Dr. Kramer said. "And she has plenty of reason to have significant psycho-somatic symptoms, including a slight elevation in body temperature. If someone has contracted Covid-19 and has begun to have symptoms, even mild symptoms, they don't just spontaneously recover in a matter of hours. Trust me!"

"How can you be sure about my daughter?" he questioned. "I'd like her to at least have a Covid-19 test and maybe some blood work just to be on the safe side."

"Mr. Murphy, your daughter is afebrile, currently has no symptoms, and has a completely negative physical exam. She doesn't need blood work or a Covid-19 test. Besides, we currently are swamped with Covid-19 tests for people with real indications and for those being admitted as inpatients."

"We've waited for more than three hours to be seen," Brian snapped. "The least you could do is indulge me."

"I'm sorry to hear you've had to wait," Dr. Kramer said, trying to remain calm. "We make an effort to see everyone in a timely fashion according to their need."

"I've heard that before, but it's not been that busy. Three hours is a long time to wait with a sick child."

"We try to triage as best as we can," Dr. Kramer said with growing irritation. "We need to give priority to the sickest patients."

"You're not hearing me. We've witnessed a number of people who walked in after us who didn't look or act sick, were seen, and walked out while we were ignored. I'll tell you what it makes me think. I think we have been forced to wait because I owe the hospital a ton of money for my wife's treatment. And now, also because of that, you are refusing to really look into my daughter's symptoms. You don't want to do any lab tests because you worry you won't get paid."

Clearly taking offense, Dr. Kramer said: "Mr. Murphy, we here in the ED have no idea of any patient's financial status vis-à-vis the hospital. We don't discriminate at all for any reason whatsoever except the degree of emergency involved. With an ambulatory patient, once they are signed in, we diagnose and we treat just as soon as we can. We order tests when we think they are called for. That's the long and short of it."

At that moment, Olivia stuck her head out from the examination room. "Sorry to interrupt, but Miss Juliette and Bunny very much want to go home."

"Mr. Murphy, I strongly recommend you listen to your daughter and go home. You both are under a lot of stress. I'm sorry for your loss." With that, Dr. Kramer turned on her heels and walked away.

Feeling newly annoyed at now being patronized, Brian stared after her, resisting going after her to get in the last word. Instead, he turned around and went into the examination room.

"Let's go, Pumpkin!" he said, reaching to pick Juliette and Bunny up into his arms.

CHAPTER 24

September 1

By the time Brian got out to Jeanne in the waiting area, he'd calmed down to a degree. What had helped was seeing that Juliette had been entertained while he was having words with Dr. Kramer. Once again Olivia had given her the hemostat to play with, and now Juliette was telling him she wanted to be a surgeon when she grew up.

"Well, what was found?" Jeanne asked, pocketing her phone. She stood up and picked up his laptop.

"Absolutely nothing," Brian answered, his frustration clearly showing. "They gave her a clean bill of health, and they refused to do any blood work or give her a Covid-19 test. We waited for three hours for nothing."

"What about her fever?"

"It was gone," Brian said. He sat Juliette down so he could get out his phone to call Camila. "I couldn't believe it. They took her temperature twice with a thermal scanner. Both times 98.6. I'm not sure they believed that it had been 101 earlier."

"Are you okay?"

"A little stressed," he admitted. "I was hoping that they would have been willing to be a bit more aggressive diagnostically."

As Brian made the call to arrange for them to be picked up, Jeanne asked Bunny how she felt about the examination. Juliette responded by talking about playing with the hemostat and explained how it functioned. As soon as he finished contacting Camila, all three walked out into the warm afternoon sunshine to stand at the turnout in front of the hospital. While they waited, Jeanne asked why the doctor didn't do a Covid-19 test at the very least.

"She didn't think it was necessary, especially with no history of exposure or symptoms," Brian explained irritably. "She told me that their testing was currently swamped with people with definite symptoms and those who were about to be admitted as inpatients."

"Isn't a temperature elevation, a sore throat, and a headache enough to qualify?"

"By the time Juliette was seen she didn't have any symptoms and had no fever," Brian said with obvious frustration. "I still tried to force the issue, but the doctor was adamant, saying that Covid-19 symptoms don't resolve over the course of a few hours, and for what it's worth, I'm sure she is right. As for Juliette's symptoms, the doctor attributed them to being psychosomatic."

"Even the fever?"

"Yeah, even the fever."

"Well, at least Juliette seemed to have enjoyed herself

and now wants to be a surgeon," Jeanne said, trying to look on the bright side.

"I wish I could say the same for myself," Brian said. "The doctor's attitude irked me, and I'm afraid I kind of provoked her by accusing the ED of purposefully making us wait."

"Uh-oh, I was afraid of that."

"I couldn't help myself," he confessed.

"Well, at least we know Juliette is okay," Jeanne offered. "Now I think you should call your mother and let her know so the wake can get underway."

"Oh, shit!" Brian whispered, gritting his teeth. "I was trying not to think about that. I still don't know how I feel about the whole wake idea. I'm not sure I can face it or want to subject Juliette to it."

"I know exactly what you mean. I felt the same reservation going to my husband's, Riley's, wake a year ago. But you know what? Ultimately, I was glad I was forced to participate, and it gave me an appreciation for the Irish funeral traditions as a celebration of a life rather than purely a mourning for a loss. On top of that, I actually became closer to my in-laws because of it."

"So you really changed your mind about your husband's wake after going?"

"Yes, I did," Jeanne said. "It definitely helped me deal with the whole situation. I truly was glad I was pressured to attend."

"All right, I'll take your word for it, but what about you-know-who?" He nodded down at Juliette, who was holding on to Brian's hand. "Do you really think I should ask her if she wants to go?"

"As I said, Riley had a young nephew and two young nieces, all of whom came to his wake. Two of them I think were four, same as your daughter. At the time, I was somewhat fearful of the effects on their young psyches, but they weathered it well and seemed to have been appreciative of being included. As I said, my advice is to ask her. Kids that age have some intuitive idea of what death means."

"Oh, boy," he muttered. He looked down at Juliette, who had let go of his hand to retrieve Bunny from the sidewalk. As she was wiping off the stuffed rabbit, Brian said, "Juliette, I have a question I need to ask you."

"You are going to do it here?" Jeanne asked with alarm. "Do you think this is the right place?"

"Why not? Suddenly I have the courage and need to get it out. Do you think asking her here is a mistake?"

"No, I guess not."

"Juliette, love," Brian continued while retaking her hand. "Yesterday we lost Mommy. She died and went to heaven, and today Grandma and Grandpa O'Brien are having a celebration of Mommy's life called a wake. Mommy's body will be there for people to see for the last time to say goodbye before she is buried."

"How can Mommy's body be at Grandma's if she went to heaven?" Juliette asked, looking up at him.

"Her spirit or soul went to heaven," Brian explained, exchanging a rapid glance with Jeanne for reassurance.

She nodded encouragement. "Her empty body is still here with us. But there is no life. She won't talk or move."

"Will she look icky?" Juliette asked, making a face.

"No, she will probably look beautiful just like always," Brian reassured her, struggling with his own emotions. "You can bring something to leave with Mommy's body if you would like to keep her company."

"Can I bring Bunny?"

"Of course you can bring Bunny," he said, taking a deep breath to keep himself under a semblance of equanimity. He glanced again at Jeanne and could tell she was having the same control issues. "I'm sure that Mommy's spirit will be very happy if you bring Bunny."

"I want to go and bring Bunny," Juliette insisted.

"Okay, perfect. You, Bunny, and I will all go together." He again looked over at Jeanne, who gave him a thumbs-up.

"I want you to come, too," Juliette said, looking up at Jeanne.

"Thank you, sweetheart," Jeanne said. She was touched and exchanged a quick, teary glance with Brian. "But I don't think that would be appropriate. The wake is for family, especially during the pandemic when the number of visitors will likely be limited. But if you'd like I'll come and visit you tomorrow, and you can tell me all about it."

"Okay," Juliette said agreeably as the Murphys' Subaru appeared, coming up the driveway onto the hospital grounds.

CHAPTER 25

September 1

The ride from MMH Inwood to the house took only a few minutes, but it was long enough for Brian to call Aimée and report that Juliette had been given a clean bill of health, providing a green light for Emma's wake. Aimée had been pleased on both accounts and promised to let Hannah know immediately. She then asked when Brian and Juliette would be arriving, and he said they'd come over within the hour.

Camila turned into the Murphy driveway and stopped alongside the house. After everyone got out, Camila and Juliette headed for the back door, which led directly into the kitchen. Jeanne held up, saying she'd get her bike from where she'd placed it back by the garage and head home. "I hope all goes well at the wake," she added. "And I hope it has the same effect on you my husband's had on me."

"I hope so, too. And I want to thank you sincerely for your help and generosity. You've been amazing with Juliette. Really! I can't thank you enough."

"It's been my pleasure," Jeanne said. "She's a darling little girl. And dealing with her has reminded me of what I missed about being a school psychologist. It's so much more rewarding than running a business. So, if you need more help with her, say, after the wake and funeral, I'm certainly available, and you have my number."

"As I said and I say again, I appreciate your generosity."

After Jeanne retrieved her bike Brian walked with her back out to the street.

"I'm sorry about the pavement around here," he said. "Be careful. They ground down the street in preparation to repave it, but when it's going to get done is anybody's guess. With all the utilities sticking up, it's treacherous."

"I'll be careful," Jeanne promised. "I'll walk the bike, until I think it's safe."

"Good idea. Thanks again for everything. Truly."

"You are welcome," Jeanne said, waving over her shoulder as she walked her bike down toward Park Terrace West. Brian watched her until she turned the corner.

Using the front door, he entered the house. He found Camila and Juliette upstairs in Juliette's room, trying to decide which of her many church dresses that Grandma Aimée had bought for her that she wanted to wear. While that was in process, Brian went into his closet, got out the only dark suit he owned, and put it on. He couldn't remember the last time he'd worn it. He then pushed around his unruly, relatively short hair with a hairbrush. Returning to Juliette's room, he saw that she had made up her mind about her outfit and was now almost ready. She looked precious in a pink dress with her golden hair braided and tied with a matching ribbon. On her feet were black patent-leather shoes. Whether such clothes were appropriate for a wake, he had no idea, but he didn't care. If that was what Juliette wanted to wear, it was fine with him. She was holding Bunny tightly, clutched against her chest.

As he was admiring his daughter, he felt his phone vibrate, indicating he'd gotten a text message. Taking it out, he saw it was from Roger Dalton, and opening the message, he read that Roger wanted him to call as soon as possible. Brian couldn't help but wonder what it might be about, knowing it couldn't be anything good. But then he thought that perhaps it had something to do with Patrick McCarthy or Megan Doyle and their need to obtain a full printout of the hospital record. But whatever it was, he decided to put it off until after the wake. He was already under enough stress despite everything that Jeanne had said and still had reservations about going, both for himself and Juliette. He also decided at some appropriate time in the future to let it be known that when his own time came, he'd prefer not to have his body go through all such rituals.

"How about you, Camila?" he said when Juliette was completely ready. "I apologize for not asking earlier whether you'd like to come with us, but you are welcome."

"No, thank you. I think a wake is for immediate family," Camila said, echoing Jeanne.

"You feel like family to me," Brian observed.

"Thank you for that, but others might not feel the

same. I prefer to stay here." She then pulled Brian to the side and said in a lowered voice, "With Jeanne gone, Juliette seems to be reverting back to her silent mode. She's hardly talking again."

"Oh, no," he said. "Good grief! That's not encouraging. What's your opinion? Should I rethink taking her to the wake?"

"No, I'm convinced she wants to go," Camila said. "She wouldn't have been so involved in picking out a dress and her hairstyle if she didn't. Just keep it in mind that the whole situation is extremely stressful for her."

"That's understandable," Brian said, thinking of his own ambivalence. "All right, let's get it over with."

As they exited the house, he complimented Juliette on how lovely she looked but got no response. Nor did she speak as they descended the steps in the front yard when he asked how she felt about going to the wake now that they were on their way. The only response he got was when he asked her if she had enjoyed meeting Jeanne. The answer was a simple *yes* without any elaboration.

The trip only took a few minutes, and the only minor problem was Juliette navigating the roughly striated street in her patent-leather shoes when they needed to cross to the other side. As they got closer to the O'Briens', which was also one of the very few single-family homes in Inwood, they could see about a dozen people standing in the small front yard and a few more on the front porch, all engaged in small group conversations and mostly maintaining a reasonable amount of social distancing. All were wearing masks, including the handful of children who were present. Many of the adults were holding cut-crystal glassware, which Brian assumed contained Jameson whiskey. Despite the masks, he recognized most people although there were a few he couldn't place. Over the years he'd met almost all of Emma's many relatives at various holiday gatherings. Emma had three older brothers with families, and Emma's mother and father had a total of five siblings altogether. Brian also recognized a few of his relatives on his father's side, including an uncle who was a retired NYPD officer. He didn't see any of his siblings, but assumed they'd merely not yet arrived. None of them were currently living in Inwood.

After coming through the front gate of the proverbial white picket fence and heading for the steps up to the front porch, Brian nodded to a number of people and he also thanked those who were close enough to voice their condolences, but he didn't stop. As he and Juliette gained the porch, Hannah appeared from within the house as if she had been watching for them.

"Welcome, you two," Hannah said with a kind of nervous energy. Then, taking Juliette's hand, she added: "Come, Juliette. Come and say a proper goodbye to your beautiful mother." She then scooped Juliette up in her arms and headed indoors. Brian was mildly taken aback by her fervor, but realized it made sense given that Emma had been the beloved baby as well as the only girl with three older brothers.

Suddenly bereft of his daughter, he was besieged by well-wishers. Brian thanked all and touched elbows with a number of others, all the while wondering what was happening with Juliette inside the house. As soon as he could, he excused himself and went inside.

In the foyer Brian noticed the mirror above the console table had been turned around. It was a tradition he'd seen before at Irish wakes he'd attended. Pausing, he glanced around the interior of the O'Briens' large house. In the background he could hear Celtic music playing softly, and a dozen-plus people were standing in small groups in the living and dining rooms conversing quietly.

In the dining room the table was heaped with food, mostly sandwiches. Brian's father-in-law, Ryan O'Brien, a large and considerably overweight man in his early sixties, was in the living room manning a makeshift bar on a bureau. To the right in a leaded-glass windowed alcove was the bier with a large, expensive-looking open coffin and a cascade of white flowers, mostly roses, which were emitting a pleasant aroma. From where he was standing he could see Emma's body outfitted in a white dress with her head and striking red hair resting against a white satin pillow. The image gave Brian a physical and emotional jolt, but he was distracted by the sight of Hannah standing next to the coffin, holding Juliette in her arms. It was obvious Hannah was talking but because of the distance compounded by the background music, he couldn't hear what was being said. Regardless, Juliette appeared frozen, staring at her mother with one hand around Hannah's neck and the other still clutching Bunny.

Moving closer in hopes of hearing what Hannah was saying, Brian's effort was thwarted by laughter coming from several male relatives grouped around Ryan. Just as he was getting close enough to hear, someone behind him called out his name. Turning, he saw his mother coming in his direction. She'd emerged from the kitchen, carrying a tray of additional sandwiches even though the dining table was already heaped with them.

Momentarily torn between his daughter and his mother, he turned toward his mother as she rapidly approached.

"Great to see you two," Aimée said. "How are you holding up, mon chéri?"

"Reasonably well," Brian answered. "I'm just concerned about Juliette."

"Have either of you eaten anything? We've got lots of food, with more coming."

"I'm not hungry," he said. The last thing he wanted to do was eat or drink.

"I'm glad you brought Juliette. I sensed you were reluctant. What changed your mind?"

"Jeanne Juliette-Shaw," Brian said. "The woman I told you about from Megan Doyle's office. She suggested I ask Juliette if she wanted to come, which I did, and Juliette agreed. It surprised me but maybe it shouldn't. Jeanne seems to really understand children."

"Well, I know how pleased Hannah is," Aimée said. "She's been beside herself waiting for you and Juliette to arrive."

At that moment Brian and Aimée watched as Hannah leaned forward, allowing Juliette to tuck Bunny in alongside Emma's right side at chest level. Then Juliette tentatively reached out with an extended index finger and touched Emma's firm and lifeless cheek. Almost immediately Juliette pulled her hand back as if she'd touched something scorchingly hot and let out a whimper loud enough for both Brian and Aimée to hear.

His heart skipped a beat, and he stepped forward just as Hannah turned around and faced into the room. Seeing her father, Juliette reached out with both hands. Feeling instantly protective, Brian gladly took hold of his daughter, who quickly buried her head in the crook of his neck and wrapped her arms tightly around his head.

"Juliette was very good and said goodbye to her mother," Hannah said. "And she gave her Bunny to keep her company. I'm very proud of her."

Feeling Juliette holding on to him with surprising force, Brian was immediately concerned that the experience hadn't been without some psychological pain, making him wonder if he'd made the wrong decision to bring her. It was yet another reminder that his life's work had totally devolved to her needs.

"Your cousins will be here shortly," Hannah told Juliette as she reached out and patted the child on the back. "Are you hungry? We have cake coming out soon."

Juliette didn't answer but rather gripped his neck with more intensity.

"I think I'll take her home," Brian decided on the spot. "My sense is that it has been a bit difficult for her."

"You should stay and have something to eat!" Hannah offered quickly. "We have a lot of food, including the cake I mentioned."

"I'm really not hungry. Thank you for all your efforts on Emma's behalf."

"You are welcome," Hannah said. "Will you be back? I'm sure there are lots of people who would like to offer you their condolences."

"Possibly," Brian answered, although he knew he didn't mean it. He'd had enough as well. His consuming love of his wife was for her essence or soul, certainly not for her eviscerated, empty body. He could appreciate that such funeral rituals were helpful for some people and served a social function, but not for him and maybe not for Juliette as well. Recalling the phrase "dust to dust" and its meaning from his catechism instruction as a child, he was developing a new regard for the benefits of cremation.

"Okay," Hannah said tensely. "Tomorrow the mass will be at ten at the Church of the Good Shepherd followed by the funeral. If you'd like to walk with us, you are more than welcome. We could come by and pick you up."

"Thank you," Brian said, not knowing how he felt about it. "I'll let you know."

Without putting Juliette down, he headed for the door. As he went, a number of people gestured toward him with their drinks as if making some kind of toast. He nodded in acknowledgment but didn't stop. Outside, as he crossed the porch, descended the front steps, and then walked the length of the walkway, other people did the same, but thankfully no one tried to stop him. It wasn't until they were on the street that Juliette indicated she wanted to be put down. After he had, he took her proffered hand, and they walked on in silence. At the halfway mark, he asked her if she was all right and if she was glad she'd said goodbye to her mother. When she didn't respond, he worried anew whether it had been a mistake to bring her to the wake, although at least he was glad he'd given her the opportunity to decide and hadn't forced her to go.

Sensing Juliette might have trouble coming to terms with the experience, Brian was glad that Jeanne had offered to help. He also found himself again wondering if the likes of Charles Kelley and Heather Williams had any conception of the real pain and consequences their selfish policies engendered in real families. It was enough to make him furious all over again.

CHAPTER 26

September 1

When Brian and Juliette came in through the front door, they were met by a concerned Camila.

"How did it go?" Camila asked. "You're back much earlier than I expected."

"Do you want to tell her?" Brian asked Juliette as they both took off their shoes and face masks. When she stayed silent, he added: "Juliette touched Mommy, and it upset her. Isn't that right, Pumpkin?"

Juliette made a beeline for the stairs, apparently retreating to the sanctuary of her room.

Brian and Camila watched her go. "In retrospect, I don't think her going to the wake was that great an idea," he said when the child was out of hearing range. "It wasn't a disaster, or at least I hope not, and it appeared she was doing reasonably well in her grandmother's arms until she touched Emma's face. I don't know if it was her decision to do it or if Hannah encouraged her, or even if it is important. One way or the other, it freaked her out. I'm not surprised. I wouldn't have wanted to do it myself. At any rate, I thought it best to bring her home right away."

"Oh, dear," Camila exclaimed, looking up the stairs. "I'll go up and help her out of her fancy dress and get her into something more comfortable. Then I'll see if she is hungry."

"Thank you," Brian said with a relieved sigh.

"What about you?" she questioned. "How are you holding up?"

"So-so," Brian said, holding his hand out and tilting it from side to side. "I'm finding the funeral rituals hard to get through. I didn't like them when my father died, and I like them even less in relation to Emma. For me, the grieving should be personal, not public."

"Are you going to go back to the wake?" Camila asked. "If you are, I'll keep Juliette occupied."

"I don't think so. I've also had enough public mourning for one day. I'll be in the office. I need to make a call."

Sitting at his desk, he found himself staring at Emma's empty work station. The sudden acknowledgment that she was gone for good swept over him, bringing an overwhelming sense of loss along with it. Luckily the emotions abated almost as quickly as they had emerged when he thought of Juliette suffering upstairs in her room. Her immediate needs trumped any thoughts of indulging his own emotions, and he had to concentrate on helping her come to terms with losing her mother at the tender age of four.

Yet looking at Emma's empty chair also reminded him

of the thoughts he'd had yesterday about Personal Protection LLC and whether he wanted to continue building the company in such a difficult time. With that issue in mind, Brian put off calling Roger Dalton, which was who he'd intended to call, and instead rang Deputy Chief Michael Comstock, the commanding officer of the NYPD ESU. Fully expecting to have to leave his name and number and get a call back, Brian was pleasantly surprised when he found himself talking with his former commanding officer. Although the deputy chief had not been happy losing two very popular and talented officers when he and Emma had retired, he now sounded very happy to hear from Brian.

"How are you and Emma and how is your security company navigating the pandemic?" Michael asked.

"I'm afraid I have bad news on both fronts," he said. "The company is doing very poorly at the moment. It might have been the worst possible time to start a security firm because of the pandemic. There's been almost no work. But worse still, Emma passed away just yesterday from a virus."

"Oh, no!" Michael said. "Oh, I'm so very sorry. That's terrible news. Was it Covid-19?"

"No, it wasn't," Brian said with a catch in his voice. "It was eastern equine encephalitis."

"Is that something like West Nile virus?"

"It's similar," Brian said. "It's a different virus, but it is also spread by mosquitoes. We think she got it when we had a beach barbecue on Cape Cod."

"Such a tragedy, such a loss! She was an exceptional

woman. When are the services scheduled, so we can send a delegation, myself included?"

"Services and funeral are tomorrow. Thank you for your offer to attend, but due to the pandemic, it's only going to involve immediate family."

"Understood," Michael said regretfully. "Well, you have my most sincere condolences to you and your whole family."

"Thank you, sir. There is something else I want to discuss with you. With my wife gone, I'm questioning my interest in continuing with our struggling company, especially with the pandemic and no end in sight. What I wanted to inquire is whether you might look kindly on me reversing my retirement and rejoining the ESU." Brian found himself superstitiously crossing his fingers, hoping for an affirmative reply even though he'd not yet completely given up on Personal Protection LLC.

"It depends on your level of commitment," Michael began. "With your indirect question, it sounds to me as if you haven't quite made up your mind, which is understandable since it's so soon after your wife's passing. Let me say this: With all your training, the city has a significant investment in you, and that's definitely to your advantage. But to give you a second chance here at the ESU, I'd want to be convinced you are one-hundred-percent committed to returning before I give the green light. To be perfectly honest, both your and your wife's sudden resignation had a negative effect on morale for a time since both of you were highly respected around here."

"I'm sorry," Brian said. "That certainly wasn't our intention."

"Here's what I recommend. When you are up to it, come out here to headquarters and meet with me and then spend some quality time participating in some of our activities. Because of the pandemic, there wasn't a new class of cadets this spring. Instead we've ramped up refresher and recertification activities for the entire ESU force, particularly in the TAC House and SCUBA unit. Does that sound appealing to you?"

"Very appealing," he agreed. "I'd love it and the sooner the better as far as I am concerned."

"Well, I'll leave that up to you and your family. I'm sure you need some time to adjust and mourn your wife."

"On the contrary," Brian said. "I need to keep busy. I would like nothing better than to get back into fighting shape and run recertification drills. It would actually help me cope."

"Okay, then," Michael said. "Without a new class of cadets, currently my calendar is flexible although all that will soon change. Next month there will be a new, small class despite the pandemic."

"Would as soon as tomorrow afternoon be possible for me to stop by and see you, say around three?" Brian asked. "I'd even like to participate in any drills if possible." The idea of experiencing simulated assaults in the TAC House had enormous appeal, as did any type of special weapons exercise. He had not practiced once with any firearm since December, not even with his omnipresent P365 Sig Sauer automatic, which he could currently feel pressing against the small of his back.

"I'm sure I can find the time. I'll also spread the word with the instructor team. It's good timing. I know there is going to be a sizable group in the TAC House tomorrow, including some officers from the A team. You can at least observe initially. I'm sure everyone will be delighted to see you."

"Likewise," Brian said. When he had been an ESU member back before his retirement, he'd often spend his days off at the ESU Academy at Floyd Bennett Field helping the instructors with the cadets and even participating, as it helped to hone his skills and maintain his recertification requirements.

"And if you change your mind tomorrow after the funeral I'll understand," Michael said. "Just let me know, and I can let the others know."

"Of course."

After appropriate goodbyes, Brian disconnected the call and stared ahead for a moment with unseeing eyes. The idea of intense physical activity gave him a modicum of relief from the emotional devastation of Emma's passing as well as his ongoing concern about Juliette's adjustment to losing her mother. Unfortunately, it didn't last, since the memory of needing to call Roger Dalton intervened.

With his phone still in his hand, he placed the call. As it went through, he again wondered if it was going to have something to do with Patrick McCarthy and Megan Doyle needing a full printout of the hospital bill. From what Megan had said, he expected the hospital to attempt to drag its feet.

"I thought you should know that the value of the suit brought against you by Premier Collections might soon be raised by $26,399.46," Roger stated as soon as he came on the call. "Unless, of course, something miraculous happens."

With some difficulty Brian held himself in check. He was offended by Roger's derisive attitude, and had he been there in his office, he might have been hard put not to intimidate the skinny bastard in some physical way. In Brian's mind he'd been fully exposed as the irritating front man for the profit-crazy Charles Kelley.

"Did you hear me?" Roger demanded when Brian didn't respond.

"I did, but I was waiting for you to tell me what this additional twenty-six-some-odd-thousand represents?"

"It's the latest ED charges for Emma Murphy," Roger said. "As if you couldn't guess."

"Is this for yesterday?" he asked with surprise, even disbelief, at the speed involved in the billing.

"Yes, it is for yesterday," Roger said. "Since you are already significantly delinquent, the hospital doesn't have high hopes for payment. What people like you don't understand is that our considerable expenses mount second by second, day by day, and we don't have the luxury of avoiding paying them as soon as they are due."

"Go ahead and submit the bill to Peerless," Brian ordered as he was about to discontinue the call. He was growing to seriously dislike the man. It was as if the bureaucrat was deriving sadistic pleasure out of pushing the knife MMH Inwood had sticking in him a little bit deeper.

"I already submitted it," Roger spat. "You and your health insurance deserve each other. They got back to me within the hour to inform me that once again they would not be covering."

"Wait just a second!" Brian exploded. "How could that possibly be? This was an emergency of the highest order. My wife didn't walk in on this occasion. She was carried in while being given CPR!"

"Peerless was given all the records including statements from the paramedics who responded to your 911 call," Roger said. "Why they have refused the claim, I have no idea, but you better look into it quickly and get their decision reversed or the amount of money involved in your lawsuit by Premier Collections will be amended upward."

"I will certainly find out." Brian felt a renewed burst of anger toward Peerless and Heather Williams's schemes, a resentment that was now equal to his hate of Charles Kelley and Roger Dalton. At the same time, the amount of money involved for a few hours in the emergency room seemed beyond the pale and equally as infuriating. Although he knew complaining about prices to Dalton was an exercise in futility, he couldn't help himself. "I'll certainly talk with Peerless, but how the hell could a couple of hours in your ED cost more than twenty-six thousand dollars? That's highway robbery, especially considering the outcome."

"I resent that," Roger snapped. "As I've said, over and over, running a trauma 1 ED twenty-four-seven is hugely expensive. Your wife used the facility and the high-tech equipment. She also required an entire team of highly trained people and equipment to carry on the CPR and do an emergency neurological assessment. Furthermore . . ."

Unable to listen to another word, Brian cut Roger off by disconnecting the call. He felt like a volcano ready to explode. Getting up from his desk, he quickly went down into the basement, where he and Emma had set up a small workout room with a stationary bike, a rack of free weights, and a flat-screen TV. Needing an outlet for his anger and frustration, he picked up two forty-five-pound hand weights and did a series of curls until he couldn't do any more. With a loud clank, he dropped them back into the rack.

Feeling a bit less out of control, he reclimbed the stairs and returned to the office. After sitting down and taking a deep breath, he placed a call to Ebony Wilson, which, as he anticipated, took some time to connect. The process required him to suffer again through several long, agonizing bouts of Muzak.

"Hello, this is Ebony Wilson, claims adjustment supervisor," she said with her honeyed voice when she finally came on the line. "And with whom do I have the pleasure of speaking?"

After Brian identified himself, he asked if she remembered him, resulting in a short laugh: "Of course I remember you! How could I not? You became the talk of

the company the way you waltzed in here despite all the
security our CEO demands. I have to say, you were extremely lucky you weren't arrested or even seriously
hurt."

"I'm not sure that would have been the outcome had
the situation escalated," Brian countered, indulging in a
bit of law enforcement patois. "But luckily that's water
over the dam. What I need to talk to you about is yet
another claim denial involving my wife, and I demand an
explanation."

"I'm sure there is one. I'll be happy to look into it.
Can you give me your policy number again, so I can
bring it up on my screen?"

After Brian did as he was told and after he had to suffer through yet another bout of Muzak, Ebony eventually returned on the line. "Okay, sorry for the wait. I
have the adjuster's report in front of me. I see the claim
again involved another ED visit for your wife, Emma
Murphy. I also see she is no longer with us. My sincerest
condolences."

"Thank you," he said, rolling his eyes at the irony of
someone from Peerless expressing condolences. "Last
time Peerless saw fit not to cover an ED visit was because
my wife had walked in during the afternoon. The explanation was that she didn't need the resources of a Trauma
1 ED just to be admitted to the hospital. On this occasion, as I'm sure you can plainly see, she was literally
carried in while undergoing CPR."

"Yes, I see that," Ebony agreed. "But I also see that
the CPR wasn't necessary."

"Come again?" Brian asked with astonishment.

"It appears that our adjusters went over this claim rather carefully from their extensive write-up," she said. "What they gathered from the paramedics' report was that the patient was already brain dead in the paramedics' judgment prior to even being put in the ambulance. In New York State, paramedics legally can determine death, meaning treatment efforts from then on were superfluous and Peerless is not fiscally responsible for them."

"That's crazy," Brian blurted. "The paramedics started the CPR in our home and continued it all the way to the hospital."

"That might have been the case, but they clearly thought the patient had suffered brain death from extended hypoxia. At least that's what was in the report. I can understand you might not like this decision, and the same recourses are open to you if you feel our adjusters are in error. You can request a review and/or you can seek legal advice. It's your right."

Unable to take any more of such self-serving malarkey, Brian disconnected the call. Feeling equally as upset as he did after speaking with Roger Dalton, he was about to return to the basement workout room for another bout with the barbells when Camila came in.

"I'm sorry to bother you," she said, unaware of Brian's state of mind, "but there's a new problem with Juliette."

Caught between two polar emotions of rage and solicitude, he let his head fall into his hands and for a moment he forcibly massaged his scalp while his brain tried to reboot itself.

"Are you okay?"

After gritting his teeth and then running his fingernails through his thick hair several times almost to the point of pain, he looked up at Camila. The whites of his eyes were bright red. "What's the problem?"

"She's crying and seems inconsolable. She wants Bunny back."

"Good God," Brian managed, unable to think of an easy solution.

"She's upstairs in her room and is really upset, and I don't know what to say to her."

"I'll handle it," Brian said. He stood up and headed for the stairs. Despite all his training both at the Police Academy and particularly at the ESU Academy about how to deal with psychological crises associated with hostage taking, suicide prevention, and talking down armed and desperate criminals, the thought of facing his bereaved daughter about her beloved stuffed rabbit seemed an impossible task. As he entered her room and looked down on her coiled up in a fetal position on her bed and sobbing, he felt totally inadequate. The rage he'd felt only moments before evaporated and was replaced completely by concern for his daughter.

Sitting on the edge of her bed, Brian stroked Juliette's back. "Camila says you miss Bunny and want her back. Is that right?"

If anything, she seemed to respond by crying with more intensity.

"We can get her back if that's what you want," he said. "Or we can pick out a new Bunny."

When there was still no response, Brian looked up at Camila standing in the doorway. She shrugged her shoulders, indicating she was at a loss.

"Okay," Brian said. "Let's see if we can find any wonderful rabbit toys to get for you so Mommy can have the company of Bunny like you wanted." He reached for Juliette's tablet and searched online for stuffed rabbits. He wasn't certain there would be any, but he was pleasantly surprised. There was page after page of all sorts of stuffed rabbits, some that looked like Bunny and some that were significantly more attractive, especially given Bunny's worse-for-wear condition. "Look at this," he continued. "There's lots and lots of options."

If anything, Juliette's tears only increased, and when Brian tried to put the tablet in her line of vision, she roughly pushed it away. It was clear she wasn't going to have anything to do with searching for a new Bunny, but Brian was mildly encouraged. She'd at least responded.

"Do you want to go back to Grandma's house and get Bunny?" he asked. He put down the tablet.

She shook her head no, which encouraged Brian even more. "If you stop crying and talk to me, we can figure this out," he said. "Do you want me to go back to Grandma's by myself?"

He waited for a few minutes and even repeated the question about him going back to the wake on his own and retrieving the rabbit. But Juliette didn't respond although the tears lessened. Continuing with the back stroking, Brian remained sitting on the edge of the bed for several more minutes before getting to his feet and approaching Camila.

"I'm as lost as you are," he said in a lowered voice. "I have no idea what to do. Do you think I should just go back to the wake and get the damn rabbit?"

"I'm not even sure that would have much of an effect. What about calling Jeanne? She's amazing with Juliette. Maybe she might have a suggestion?"

"Actually, that's probably the best idea."

Taking out his phone, he stepped out into the hallway and made the call, hoping for the best. It felt a little embarrassing calling a woman whom he'd just met for advice for the second time in one day. But he was desperate. He was relieved when she answered in a friendly fashion using his name, meaning she'd at least probably added his name and number to her contacts.

"I hope I'm not catching you back in Inwood Hill Park," he said, trying to be lighthearted despite the circumstances.

Jeanne laughed. "No, I'm home, but I must confess that I did go back and finish my ride when I left you. How did it go at the wake for you and your daughter?"

"It was a big stress for both of us," Brian said. "And indirectly that is why I am calling. You encouraged me to call if I needed help. Well, Juliette put Bunny in the casket to keep my wife's body company."

"Bless her soul," she said.

"Unfortunately, she has had a change of heart. At the moment she is crying her eyes out, wanting Bunny back.

To make matters worse, she's not talking again. I'm at a loss. Do you have any suggestions? I've offered to go back to the wake and get the damn thing, which I'm not excited about doing, but she won't acknowledge that will make her feel better."

"Oh, dear!" Jeanne voiced. Brian could hear her sigh. "Off the top of my head, I think your inclination is correct. I don't think you should go back and get the toy. She misses her mother and now misses Bunny, probably conflating the two. She might be somehow thinking that if she gets the rabbit back, she'll also get her mother back."

"I suppose that is possible. I'm also concerned that if she did get Bunny back, it would always remind her of seeing and touching her dead mother."

"Did Juliette touch her mother's body?"

"She touched her face. I don't know if she was encouraged or did it on her own. I was across the room when it happened, and her grandmother was holding her, letting her reach over into the coffin with the toy. I think it spooked her."

"I can well imagine. Would it be okay if I came over and tried to talk with her? I have an idea that might help."

"Oh, please do," Brian said gratefully. "Both Camila and I are at a complete loss of how to handle this. It's heartrending to see her suffer."

"I'll be over as soon as I can."

CHAPTER 27

September 1

It was just over forty minutes later that Brian heard the doorbell chime. He had been waiting impatiently, alternately sitting with Juliette and pacing in the living room.

"You are like the proverbial cavalry arriving at the last minute to save the day," he said, trying to make light of the situation as he welcomed Jeanne back. No longer in bike clothes, she was dressed in a white summer blouse and black shorts and carrying a shopping bag.

"I'm sorry if it took too long. I had to shower and get out of my bike gear."

"Not a problem now that you are here," Brian said. "But I have to admit, we've been eagerly awaiting your arrival. We're really at a loss." As she took off her mask, he noticed something he'd not noticed before. In contrast to his pale complexion, hers was almost as olive as Camila's. When he mentioned it as she removed her shoes, she explained that there was a bit of Algerian in her heritage and maybe even a bit of Moroccan even farther back.

"How is Miss Juliette doing?" Jeanne asked as they mounted the stairs.

"Not much change," Brian answered. "She stopped crying when we told her you were coming over to see her, but she's still not speaking. Camila and I have alternately stayed with her since you and I spoke on the phone."

"Sometimes that's all you can do in a situation like this," she said. "Patience is a virtue with children. Insecurity is going to be a challenge for her for a while, maybe for life."

As they entered Juliette's room, Camila stood up from the bed where she'd been sitting. She'd been reading to Juliette even though Juliette had remained unresponsive and curled up on her side. As Camila and Jeanne exchanged a verbal greeting, Juliette surprised everyone by rolling over on her back. She stared up at Jeanne.

"Hello, ma Juliette," she said, trying to sound upbeat while sitting down in the spot that Camila had just vacated. "I've heard that your visit to your grandma's was upsetting. Is that right?"

Juliette nodded.

"Seeing your mommy like that must have been scary," Jeanne said. "But at least you got to say goodbye."

Juliette nodded again.

"Did it feel strange when you touched her?" Jeanne asked.

With an added expression of distaste, Juliette said, "It was icky."

"I'm sure it was. You were brave. I understand that you did something very nice: You gave your mommy Bunny to keep her company."

"I want Bunny back," Juliette demanded with a defiant expression.

"I'm sure you want both your mother and Bunny back. But I have an idea of what might help, and it is here in this shopping bag." She raised the bag so Juliette could see it plainly. "Are you interested to see what it is?"

Juliette's expression softened. "Yes," she said.

Jeanne opened the bag, reached in, and pulled out another stuffed rabbit. It was about the same size as Bunny but a light gray instead of a light brown and less floppy except for the ears, which were longer. It was also in far better condition and had both of its eyes.

"This is Jeannot Lapin," Jeanne said, pronouncing the name in a distinctly French fashion. "I told you about her earlier. She's been my friend since I was about your age, but she would like to live with you if you will have her and treat her well."

To Brian's surprise and joy, Juliette reached for the stuffed toy, and when she had it in her hands, she examined it closely. When it apparently passed muster, she tried hugging it. She then looked up at Jeanne and once again nodded.

"She is a beautiful rabbit," Brian said to his daughter. "I think she is fantastic. Do you like her as much as I do?" When Juliette indicated she did, he asked: "What will her name be: Jeannot Lapin or Bunny 2?"

"Jeannot Lapin," Juliette declared, impressing everyone by imitating Jeanne's French pronunciation perfectly.

"Jeannot Lapin it is," Brian said with relief. "What about Bunny: Can she stay with Mommy?"

"Yes," Juliette answered without hesitation.

He exchanged a grateful glance with Jeanne, once again feeling thankful he'd had the serendipitous pleasure of meeting her in Megan Doyle's office. Even if Megan Doyle's efforts were to come to naught, Brian was certain he'd feel indebted just for the opportunity of meeting Jeanne and the help she was bringing to Juliette.

Camila, who had been watching from the doorway, now came into the room and added her appreciation. After giving the stuffed rabbit a long list of praises, she asked the rabbit if she was hungry. Juliette answered for her, saying that she was hungry for eggs and bacon.

"Then let's take her down to the kitchen and see that she gets fed," Camila said. "I'm hungry, too."

As Juliette and Camila filed out of the room, Brian turned to Jeanne. "Bravo," he said. "Once again, I can't thank you enough. You really are a child whisperer. Thank you so much for all your help and for parting with such a personal possession. Can I at least pay you something for it?"

With true mirth, she laughed. "I've gotten more than adequate compensation from that toy. I couldn't have imagined a better fate for it now. It was my mother who insisted I bring it here to the USA. I'm lucky I was able to find it after we talked. When I moved into my current, smaller apartment, I had to pack away a lot of my belongings."

"Regardless, giving it to Juliette is enormously generous. Frankly, had you suggested it on the phone, I probably wouldn't have thought it would work. I tried to get her excited about looking at stuffed rabbits online, and she was totally uninterested. Again, it's obvious you have a way with children."

"Thank you for the compliment," Jeanne said. "Maybe it's the child in me, but I do love interacting with young people. Obviously, that was why I ended up in school psychology, at least for a time. And I find Juliette darling. You are lucky to have her. I truly regret that Riley and I didn't have children. We shouldn't have put it off for the sake of the damn business."

"I can understand your feeling. In many ways Juliette is holding me together."

"I can see how committed you are," she agreed.

"I've had some more bad news about Peerless and MMH Inwood," Brian said. "It never stops. Can I bend your ear? I feel like complaining to someone."

"Of course."

"Let's go down to the living room and at least be comfortable."

As they descended the stairs, Jeanne said, "I think you are doing a marvelous job trying to deal with Juliette's grief, but what about yours? You've lost a wife and a life partner, after all."

"You are right. As I've said, it's mostly denial. It's also true that I haven't had time to really let it sink in."

"If it is anything like my experience, it's going to be tectonic when it hits."

"I can imagine. I guess I should be thankful for Juliette."

"That's my point exactly," Jeanne said. "But beware, it might be paralyzing."

In the living room they sat on opposing couches beneath the large, multipaned window looking out onto West 217th Street. Brian related the calls he'd had, first with Roger Dalton at MMH Inwood and then with Ebony Wilson.

"I can't believe Peerless," Jeanne exclaimed when he finished his rant. "They certainly have perfected the art of disclaiming responsibility, but they can't have just singled us out. They must do it to all their policy holders."

"I'm sure they do," Brian said. "It's no wonder they have the money to pay their CEO millions. It's a type of legalized fraud. Like last time, I was told I could request a review, which is guaranteed to be an exercise in futility, or I can sue. Proceeding with a lawsuit is probably equally as pointless as asking for a review. With their in-house attorneys, they have undoubtedly prepared for any and every eventuality. On top of that, suing is expensive, with no guarantees."

"Having grown up in France where this type of tolerated robbery involving healthcare would never happen, I have to wonder how has it come to be here in the United States that hospitals and health insurance companies operate with such impunity?"

"I think it has been a kind of accident of history," Brian said. "It certainly wasn't planned that healthcare got associated with employment here in the USA way back during World War II. And from my own experience, having relatively good health insurance from being a member of the NYPD made me indifferent to cost. I never cared or questioned. I guess it's a kind of moral hazard, and the consequences have been dramatic over the years. Can you ever imagine that a few hours in the emergency room for my wife would cost almost twenty-seven thousand dollars, only for her to end up dead? Beyond the emotional costs, that's akin to being forced to buy something like a car without knowing the price and being given a nonfunctioning wreck with no recourse."

"In France the government has tried to hold down costs, but it's not easy with what's going on here in the USA."

"France and the entire rest of the industrialized world as far as I know have tried to rein in healthcare costs," Brian said. "It's a uniquely American disaster, although what's happening here is putting pressure on prices elsewhere I'm afraid."

"I agree with you. It's American capitalism run amok with no moral balance in an industry that's supposed to be altruistic. Private equity shouldn't be allowed to interfere in healthcare."

"You're so right," he agreed with a shake of his head. "Talk about irony: It's a tragedy of personal greed trumping altruism."

"Exactly, and the final result is to cause suffering for people like us," Jeanne said. "It's infuriating, and Charles Kelley and Heather Williams are poster children for the whole damn situation."

"It's a wonder they can sleep at night."

"They must make it a point to avoid thinking about the lives they turn upside down. Unfortunately, I'm a prime example. Not only did I lose my husband, but in the course of my lawsuit and bankruptcy, I lost my business, most of my savings until Patrick and Megan put a stop to it, and then even my house."

"Don't tell me that," he pleaded. "You lost your house?"

"I'm afraid so," Jeanne confirmed. "It was partially my fault. While trying to pay off the hospital, I got behind on the mortgage, which exposed it to Kelley's pit bull lawyers."

"Yikes," Brian said. "At the moment that's my biggest worry, especially if it aggravates Juliette's sense of security. I'm behind on my mortgage payments as well."

"From my experience, I'd advise you to change that if you can."

"I know. Patrick McCarthy recommended the same thing. The trouble is, I need some income. As I said when we were in the hospital waiting for Juliette to be seen, I've been thinking of trying to get my old NYPD job back. I even called my commanding officer a little while ago and made plans to go out to the ESU Headquarters tomorrow after the funeral to talk to him about it."

"That sounds like a prudent plan to me, as this pandemic is not going away tomorrow."

"I have to do something," Brian said. "He suggested for me to join in on some of the training opportunities they've set up in lieu of having a new class of cadets. I'd like nothing better than to immerse myself in some simulation exercises, whether I end up back on the force or not. The mere physicality of it would be therapeutic. I haven't gotten any real exercise since I came back from Cape Cod, and I need to find a way to take my mind off of things."

"I think it's a wonderful idea," Jeanne said. "And to encourage it, I'd be happy to come over tomorrow and help with Juliette, provided you wouldn't mind."

"Mind?" Brian questioned with an exaggerated expression of surprise. "I'd love it. It would be a great relief. Leaving Camila to carry the burden of Juliette, especially if the funeral upsets her as much as the wake, was the only reservation I had. One thing I can say without exaggeration is that my daughter seems to truly adore you."

"Likewise," she said. "It will be a pleasure to spend time with her. But to get back to what we were talking about earlier, I find myself wondering if you and I are outliers, or if there are other people in this community who have suffered like we have at the hands of Charles Kelley and Heather Williams."

"That's a good question. If I had to guess, I'd say we're not alone by a long shot. Grady Quillen, the retired cop who served me, said he's been a busy bee for Premier Collections, especially of late. And Megan Doyle seems pretty booked, too."

"The more I think about it, the more curious I am," Jeanne pondered. "If there is a huge number, why hasn't it been the subject of some kind of exposé in the media so that Kelley and Williams could get the comeuppance they deserve?"

"That's maybe even a better question. Personally, I'd hate that kind of notoriety myself with my sad story in the tabloids, but you are right: It seems like perfect fodder for the likes of the *Post* or *Daily News*. Tearjerker stories about powerful elite ogres who are being paid millions to exploit the masses have a strong appeal for obvious reasons. Maybe it has something to do with patient–client privilege that makes the media hesitant."

"But they wouldn't have to use real names," Jeanne said. "I think it's curious. At least I'm curious. I'd like to find out how many people right here in Inwood have suffered like we have and learn their individual horror stories. The local hospital is supposed to help people and the community, not bankrupt everybody."

"It wouldn't be difficult to get a good idea of the numbers regarding MMH and Charles Kelley in terms of lawsuits," Brian said. "It would be more difficult to dig up much of anything about Peerless Health and Heather Williams."

"How so?"

"That kind of general information about lawsuits is available on the New York Civil Court's and the New York Supreme Court's websites. All you'd have to do is run a search using Premier Collections as the plaintiff."

"I didn't know such information was available. How about giving it a try?"

"Come on into the office! We'll use my computer."

A few minutes later, with Jeanne looking over his shoulder, he brought up the New York City Supreme Court website and typed in his search parameters. A millisecond later they were taken aback. Just since 2014 there had been many hundreds if not thousands of cases in Manhattan involving MMH Inwood and the significantly larger MMH Midtown. Scrolling forward, they also could see that there had been a significant uptick in activity since the beginning of the Covid-19 pandemic.

"My God!" Brian murmured. "Who would have guessed? And these are only cases involving more than twenty-five thousand dollars. If we look at the Civil Court for under twenty-five thousand there will probably be a lot more. It seems as if MMH and Premier Collections have sued a sizable portion of the entire metropolitan New York population."

"Let's look at the Civil Court website," Jeanne said.

A number of clicks later, they were again shocked by the numbers. "This is certainly eye-opening," Brian said. "The trouble is we can't use this resource to tease out the cases here in Inwood like you wanted. At least I can't do it. Maybe Patrick McCarthy might be able to. As a litigator, he has more options available to him for online data on these websites. What would also be interesting to know is how many of the cases are pending like mine and how many are closed."

"This is a bigger problem than I could have imagined." As if weighed down by this new information, Jeanne collapsed into one of the side chairs with her legs splayed out in front of her, her arms limp at her sides. "And to think the hospital prevails in most all the cases because the 'services have been rendered.' Those are the words Patrick McCarthy used to explain to me why I lost my case. People don't realize what they are signing when they go into the hospital."

"You've got that right," he said. "Especially when it involves an emergency situation. They're told 'sign here' to get their loved one treated, and they sign without reading anything. I did, too."

"People also count on their health insurance to take care of things and not only think about their profits."

"The whole situation is outrageous. It's also frustrating during these lawsuits that the court can't rule on the prices the hospital charge, no matter how ridiculous they are. It's got to be discouraging to be a judge."

"Plus, most hospitals won't tell you their charge master prices, which they've spent the last fifty years raising beyond any reason."

"Oh, yeah," Brian said with renewed disgust. "I forgot about the infamous charge master prices. How do you know about that?"

"I told you that when I got sued, I spent quite a lot of effort researching USA hospital business practices. What do you know about it?"

"Only what Megan Doyle happened to tell me during our brief meeting."

"It's a major part of the hospital scam," Jeanne said. "The only time patients can find out what things cost is after the services have been rendered, and they get the bill, and even then, they have to hire someone like Megan Doyle to figure it all out. It's absurd."

"I know how we could get at least a partial list of Inwood residents that MMH Inwood has sued or is in the process of suing," he said. "We could ask Grady Quillen, who served me. He wouldn't be restricted by any patient–client confidentiality issues as far as I know."

"Do you think he would give you that information?"

Brian shrugged. "I don't see why not. We've been acquaintances for years, and my father was his commanding officer. We could assure him we wouldn't give out our source, so his employer wouldn't find out. He already gave me one name: Nolan O'Reilly, whose story rivals ours, as he lost his son and his house in the process."

"If we could put together even a couple of dozen or so stories combined with the sheer number of court cases, we might be able to get either the *Post* or the *Daily News* interested enough to run an exposé." Abruptly she sat up straighter in her chair, her amber eyes sparkling. "And do you know what else we could do?"

"No, not really," he said, raising his eyebrows in curiosity.

"We could go to our city council member for the 10th District," Jeanne said excitedly. "I'm sure we could get him interested and involved. The more I think about all of this, the stranger it seems that it has been allowed to go on for so long."

"It's definitely an unconscionable problem," Brian agreed, but without the enthusiasm she was exhibiting. He was much too emotionally caught up in his own precarious situation, with his wife's funeral scheduled for the following day and Juliette's problematic behavior, to think about some kind of social movement, no matter how appropriate.

"Suddenly I feel a little like an Erin Brockovich," Jeanne said zealously. "Did you see that film with Julia Roberts?"

"I think so," he said, struggling to reboot his brain. "Yes, I saw it."

Suddenly Camila appeared in the archway leading out into the front hall. "I'm sorry to interrupt, but Juliette just threw up and now says she's feeling sick again."

"Oh, God! Where is she?" Brian asked nervously, getting to his feet.

"She's upstairs in her room," Camila said. "I think you'd better go and check on her."

CHAPTER 28

September 1

Disturbingly similar to a few hours earlier, Juliette was lying on her side, immobile, facing the wall with her legs drawn up. The only difference was now she was clutching Jeannot Lapin against her chest in a firm embrace.

"Camila says you're feeling bad again, Sweet Pea," Brian said as he sat down on the edge of the bed and stroked her back as he'd done earlier. Jeanne moved to stand at the foot of the bed. "Can you tell me what's wrong?"

Juliette didn't respond or move and Brian could see she had her eyes closed. He also noticed she wasn't sucking her thumb, which he thought was mildly encouraging.

"What about Jeannot Lapin?" he asked, imitating Jeanne's earlier way of getting Juliette to talk by addressing the rabbit. "She looks like she's not feeling so good, either."

"She is hot," Juliette said, turning her head and looking up at her father. "She's cold and then she's hot."

Brian reached out and pretended to feel the rabbit's forehead and then did the same with Juliette's. "You are right," he agreed. "Jeannot feels a little warm to me. Maybe we should take her temperature."

"Her name is Jeannot Lapin," Juliette corrected before rolling over onto her back.

"You're right," Brian said. "I stand corrected." He turned, looked up at Camila, and asked her if she'd bring the thermometer.

"Of course," Camila said and disappeared.

"Does Jeannot Lapin have a sore throat?" he asked, redirecting his attention to his daughter and continuing with the indirect questioning.

Juliette shook her head.

"How about a cough, or does she just feel sick? Does she think she might throw up again?"

Juliette shook her head for the second time.

"How about a headache?" Jeanne asked.

"Yes, she has a headache," Juliette said.

Brian and Jeanne exchanged a glance. Each shrugged their shoulders, not knowing what else to ask. Camila returned with the thermometer. Juliette allowed her to put it under her tongue before Camila stepped back out of Brian and Jeanne's way.

"How long after eating did Juliette throw up?" Brian asked Camila.

"It was while she was eating. By the time I had made the bacon and eggs, she didn't seem very hungry and ate very slowly. Then she threw up sitting at the table. It was all very sudden."

He nodded. "Maybe there was something wrong with the eggs."

"I don't think so," Camila said. "I had some myself and had no problem."

After waiting for the usual three minutes, Brian took the thermometer out of Juliette's mouth and then twirled it in his fingers, looking for the column of mercury. "100.8 again," he said when it flashed into view. "No wonder Jeannot Lapin feels hot."

Standing up, he motioned for Jeanne to step out of the room with him. Once in the hall he said: "It's certainly not a particularly worrisome fever, but I think it is a fever, nonetheless. What should we do? God! I wish that Dr. Bhatt wasn't on vacation. The last thing I want to do is go back to the MMH Inwood ED, not with the way we were treated earlier."

"I'm with you there," Jeanne said. "I don't think it will be necessary, but I do wish they had at least done a Covid test."

"The doctor was adamant it wasn't indicated, but who knows. I'm still irritated. I also wish they had done basic blood work just to be sure she wasn't coming down with something."

"I have to use the bathroom fast," Juliette said urgently to Camila from inside the room yet loud enough for Brian and Jeanne to hear. As they ducked back inside, they saw Juliette and Camila disappear into the bathroom and the door slam behind them.

"Uh-oh," Brian said. "Sounds like more stomach issues."

While they waited, he picked up Jeannot Lapin as a nervous gesture and gave it a close inspection. "This little rabbit has been a godsend. I've never been into stuffed animals, but this one is damn cute. Did you really have it since you were Juliette's age?"

"Just about," Jeanne said. "Maybe a year older."

"How did it stay so pristine?" Brian asked. "In comparison, Bunny looks like she'd been through a war."

"I don't know, to be truthful. I guess I've always been on the meticulous side."

Five minutes later Juliette and Camila emerged from the bathroom. Juliette made a beeline for Brian and rescued Jeannot Lapin. Then she climbed back up on the bed and rolled over on her side, assuming the same position she'd been in when Brian and Jeanne had arrived.

"A bit of diarrhea," Camila reported. "And some cramps, but I think she feels better now."

"Thank goodness," he said. He placed his palm on her forehead. "She seems to be about the same temperature as before." Juliette pushed his hand away.

"She said she wanted to sleep," Camila said.

"I think that's a great idea," Brian said. "Is that right, Pumpkin? You want to take a nap?"

Juliette nodded, and he could see she had her eyes closed. "Okay," he said. "Hopefully you'll feel back to normal when you wake up. We'll be downstairs if you need us, okay?" He straightened up and herded the others out of Juliette's room.

As they were descending the stairs, Jeanne asked if Brian might be willing to give Grady Quillen a call to see if he was comfortable giving the names of the Inwood families he'd served over the last year.

"I suppose, but to be honest, I'm not sure I have the stamina at the moment to pursue the kind of Erin Brockovich investigation you have in mind."

"Of course you don't," Jeanne reassured him. "As I said, I don't know how you are functioning as well as you are. But I have both the time and the inclination. If you can get me the names, I'll start the process and you can participate as much or as little as you'd like."

"All right," Brian said. It was the least he could do in the face of all the help and support Jeanne was so generously providing.

CHAPTER 29

September 2

As dawn's light slowly crept into the master bedroom preluding sunrise, Brian's eyes popped open. Other than his eyelids, he purposefully didn't move a muscle lest he disturb Juliette, who was sleeping on her side with her head on a pillow facing him. She was in Emma's place in the bed, and Jeannot Lapin was on its back between them with Juliette's arm thrown over the stuffed rabbit's midsection.

As far as sleep was concerned, the first part of Brian's night had not gone well. He'd had trouble going to sleep even though he was clearly exhausted from having slept so poorly the night before. He'd even dozed off in the kitchen while having something to eat with both Camila and Jeanne. They'd encouraged him to go to bed, which he did, but by the time he got upstairs, out of his clothes, and brushed his teeth, he no longer felt tired.

Finally, after ten o'clock, he'd broken down and tried one of Emma's Ambien tablets, which provided a few hours of sleep before he was awakened by the sound of his bedroom door creaking open. By reflex from his martial arts training, he'd tensed, ready to spring up and face any potential intruder, but it wasn't necessary. With the help of the half-light in the room coming in through the white, gauzy curtains from the streetlight outside the window, he recognized Juliette in her nightgown holding Jeannot Lapin. Brian had sat up and asked her if she was okay, and she'd answered by asking him if she could sleep with him.

"Absolutely, Sweet Pea," Brian had said immediately, throwing back the edge of the sheet. Juliette responded by jumping up onto the bed, scrunching down under the covers, and placing Jeannot Lapin between them. A moment later she'd melted his heart by saying: "I miss Mommy."

With some difficulty, Brian had told her that he understood and that he missed Mommy, too. With those few words spoken, Juliette had fallen asleep and eventually he had dozed off while hoping he could at least partially fill the void that Emma's passing had created.

As the intensity of the daylight gradually increased, Brian got a progressively better view of his angelic daughter's features, and he marveled at the sheer mystery and mind-boggling implausibility of the reproductive process. How could it have been possible for him and Emma to create such a perfect human being? But then in the middle of his appreciation, he noticed something disturbing. Juliette's forehead was covered with tiny, iridescent droplets of perspiration, and the discovery brought a pang of fear down his spine. With the pandemic threatening a fall surge, a prolonged fever was certainly not a welcome sign.

Being careful not to wake his daughter, Brian slipped out of the bed. As carefully as he could, he folded down the light cotton blanket, leaving only the sheet to cover her. He then turned down the air-conditioning a few degrees before he went to retrieve the thermometer in her bedroom. Although he hated to do it because she was sleeping soundly, when he got back he woke her by gently shaking her shoulder.

Juliette's response at being disturbed was to cry and then complain that she didn't feel well. He could see that the whites of her eyes were mildly suffused red.

"What's bothering you?" he asked. "Is your throat sore?"

Juliette nodded. "And I have a headache," she said, putting her hand momentarily on her forehead.

"I think you might have a fever." He felt her forehead with his hand, admitting to himself that she did feel warm. "We need to take your temperature."

Although she initially complained that she didn't want her temperature taken, she eventually succumbed to Brian's persistent urging. As they waited for the requisite three minutes, he stroked her head, marveling at the color of her hair and wondering where it had come from in either his or Emma's genealogy. Juliette kept her eyes closed the entire time.

When the time was up, Brian took out the thermometer. When he read it he caught his breath. It was 102.3!

Making an effort to camouflage his concern, he said: "Yes, you do have a fever. Do you feel warm?"

"No, I feel cold," she said, and ostensibly shivered.

Quickly, he replaced the blanket that he had earlier turned down. After he told her to stay in bed, he slipped on his robe and walked down the hall. When he reached Camila's room, he knocked softly. From inside he heard a muffled: "Just a minute." A moment later the door opened, and a sleepy Camila stood in the door frame, clutching her robe closed.

"Juliette has awakened with a temperature of over 102," Brian told her. "Sorry to wake you, but we need your help. As much as I hate doing it, I think she's got to be seen again at the ED, and I need you to drive us so I don't have to worry about parking."

"Oh, no! I'm sorry to hear," Camila said, now looking more alert. "She seemed fine yesterday after her upset stomach. Are there any other symptoms?"

"Yes, she again has a sore throat and headache. On the positive side, I don't think she has any digestive complaints, but I didn't specifically ask her."

"Do you want to go right away?"

"I do," Brian said. "I'd like to get in and out of the ED as quickly as possible. We're both expected to show up for Emma's funeral mass at ten and the sooner we get there the sooner we'll be seen."

"Let me throw on some clothes."

"Of course," he said. "I'll dress also and get Juliette's robe. At the moment she's in my room. She came in in the middle of the night feeling lonely and ended up staying with me."

"The poor dear. Okay, I'll be quick."

After returning to his room with Juliette's robe in hand, Brian approached the bed. Juliette appeared to have fallen back asleep, but her eyes opened the moment he sat down. "I was just talking with Camila," he said. "She's going to drive us back to the hospital so the doctors can take a look at you again."

"I don't want to go to the hospital."

"I'm afraid we have to go," Brian said, suppressing the urge to say he didn't want to go, either. He sat her up and helped her get her arms into her bathrobe. "We have to find out what's making you have a fever, so we can get you some medicine to make you and Jeannot Lapin feel better. I imagine she's not feeling so well, either."

While he ducked into the master bedroom's walk-in closet to dress, he found himself suddenly transfixed by the sight of the clothes hanging on Emma's side. At this moment, with no warning whatsoever, his glass house of denial spontaneously shattered, forcing him to acknowledge that his wife had died, that she was gone, that she wasn't coming back, and he was never again going to hear her crystalline voice or her infectious laughter or feel her touch or experience one of those marvelous episodes when they shared the very same thought at the same time. "Shit," he hissed through clenched teeth, quiet enough so Juliette couldn't hear. The existential question of why this terrible loss had happened to him leaped into the forefront of his mind, but he had no answer. All he knew was that this totally unexpected, unforeseen tragedy had happened because of a tiny mosquito.

Feeling suddenly drained of strength, Brian was forced to reach up and grab the hanger rod to keep himself upright. At the same time, he felt a rush of tears, and he let himself cry. But after a few quiet sobs, he regained his equilibrium. Remembering Juliette out in the room, he yanked himself back to reality. "Pull yourself together!" he commanded in a forced whisper, recognizing that Juliette's needs trumped feeling sorry for himself. She needed him to buck up, and with the kind of determination that had characterized his life to date, he rapidly put on the same dark suit he'd worn for his brief appearance at the wake. Not knowing how long he'd be in the emergency department, and certainly hoping it wouldn't be as long as the previous day, he wanted to be ready for the funeral mass at ten.

By the time they were in the Subaru heading for the hospital, it was going on eight o'clock. Hoping for the best but wanting to be ready for the worst, he again had his laptop with an attached DVD player and a selection of Juliette's particularly favorite movies in a backpack. He also knew there was internet in the ED, so they'd also be able to stream PBS cartoons or other movies if Juliette preferred. Also, at Camila's suggestion, he had some snacks if needed. All in all, he felt reasonably prepared provided they were treated fairly and didn't have to wait for three hours. As he had anticipated, Juliette was obviously not feeling well and had resisted going, but now that they were in the car, she acted resigned and silent.

"If you can give me a little warning, I can be back here, so you don't have to wait," Camila said as Brian and Juliette got out at the hospital. He gave a thumbs-up as he and Juliette donned their masks and headed for the door.

The ED waiting room was sparsely populated, which encouraged Brian. At the information desk there was no line, and Brian was able to check in straightaway with one of the clerks who recognized them from having been there the day before. The clerk then passed on the information to a triage nurse who seemed distracted as she read aloud the symptoms of a 102.2 fever, sore throat, and headache with an episode of vomiting and diarrhea the previous day. She then wordlessly took Juliette's temperature with a thermal scanner. Luckily Juliette was tolerant and silent through it all.

"What's the temperature?" he asked.

"100.8," the nurse replied.

"It was much higher less than an hour ago," Brian said. He was relieved to hear it had come down yet worried it might put them in a less urgent section on the patient list. "Maybe you could take it again, please, just to be sure."

Without comment, but with subtle signs of annoyance that were not lost on Brian, the nurse took the temperature again. "100.8," she voiced with a roll of her eyes as if retaking the temperature had been an imposition.

"Excuse me," he said. "Did my asking to retake my daughter's temperature provoke you in some way?"

"I've been here since eleven o'clock last night," the

nurse responded, ignoring Brian's question. "We'll be with you as soon as we can." She then walked off.

"Good grief," Brian let out under his breath. Already his interaction with the ED staff was only marginally acceptable in his opinion, making him worried whether the current visit might end up rivaling yesterday's fiasco.

Retreating to a relatively deserted corner of the waiting room, he and Juliette made themselves as comfortable as possible. Juliette wanted to lie down, and Brian allowed her to do so on a blanket he'd brought with them from the car. When he asked her if she wanted to watch something on the laptop, she said she wanted to sleep. As she settled in, he noticed that the perspiration that he'd seen earlier on her forehead had disappeared, making him more confident that the thermal scanner temperature the nurse had taken had been correct. It also made Brian wonder why, like yesterday, Juliette's symptoms had suddenly disappeared.

"What about your headache and a sore throat?" he asked her, but she chose not to answer and already had her eyes closed. Thankful she was being cooperative, he didn't press her. Instead he made himself as comfortable as he could, wondering how long they would have to wait. In the distance he heard the undulating sound of an approaching ambulance. As the siren progressively increased, he couldn't help but selfishly hope it wasn't some major trauma that would engulf the ED and extend the wait.

Trying to avoid revisiting the momentarily paralyzing episode he'd had in the closet, Brian kept his mind busy by mulling over the conversation he'd had the day before with Jeanne about how many other people in the community out of its sixty thousand residents had experienced the kind of tragedy that he and Jeanne had suffered. Although at the time he had thought that he didn't have the time or the fortitude to participate in any intensive investigation in the near term, Jeanne had asked him to call Grady Quillen and ask if he would provide a list of all the neighborhood people he'd served in the last year or so.

As Brian had expected, Grady had been more than happy to provide the information, especially after Brian had assured him that his being the source would never be revealed to anyone, especially Premier Collections. Grady had promised he'd print out a list and get it to Brian, and also mentioned something particularly disturbing. Nolan O'Reilly, the friend who'd lost his son and house, had just died by suicide. If nothing else, that terrible news was enough to galvanize him to join Jeanne's commitment to look into the problem as a neighborhood disaster.

The ambulance he had heard approaching arrived, and it was obvious that it involved a major problem as various ED personnel started scurrying about. For a second Brian wondered if Emma's arrival two days ago had caused the same stir, but he quickly pushed the thought out of his mind lest it lead to another emotional storm.

Over the next thirty to forty minutes, more ambulatory patients began arriving, forming a line with six-foot separations at the information desk. There were also several more ambulances. It was disturbingly obvious to Brian that the ED was becoming busier.

After an hour of waiting and with Juliette asleep, he got up when there happened to be no one in line for the information desk. Trying to keep himself calm but feeling progressively irritated that he and Juliette were being forced to wait as long as they had, especially since the time of Emma's funeral mass was rapidly approaching, Brian headed over to the clerk who had initially checked them in.

After taking a quick glance back at Juliette to make sure she was still asleep, Brian got the clerk's attention. "Excuse me," he said, trying to keep the frustration out of his voice. "My daughter and I have been waiting more than an hour for her to be seen. What's the holdup?"

A free triage nurse who'd overheard his question stepped closer and intervened. "What's the name?" she asked in a neutral tone.

Brian gave Juliette's full name, and the nurse consulted her tablet. "Okay, yes, I see your daughter's name," she said. "She's definitely in the queue. You'll just have to be patient. We have to deal with real emergencies first."

For several beats, he debated whether to respond to the implication that Juliette's fever of 102.2 with flu-like symptoms was not an emergency or whether to raise the issue about his seeing other patients come and go into the ED, but for the moment he held himself in check. He could hear Jeanne's words from yesterday warning him that raising a ruckus could make things worse. Biting his ongue, Brian headed back to his seat next to Juliette's sleeping form.

Thinking about Jeanne, he took out his cell phone and called her in an effort to keep himself under control. As the call went through, he worried again he was taking advantage of her and hoped she wouldn't mind hearing from him so soon. To his relief, any concerns were instantly dispelled by the alacrity with which she answered.

"Good morning!" she said brightly. "I'm so glad to hear from you. I've been wanting to call you but was worried it might be too early. Have you gotten the defendant list from Grady Quillen?"

"Wow! I'm impressed. You really are motivated about this."

"I suppose I am," Jeanne said. "Have you heard from him? Is that why you are calling?"

"I'm afraid I haven't gotten the list yet," he said. "No, that's not why I am calling. Unfortunately, I'm back in the ED. Juliette woke up this morning with a 102.2 fever."

"Oh, no!" Jeanne cried. "That's not what I wanted to hear. Does she have other symptoms or just a fever?"

"She has a sore throat and headache again," Brian said. "I was hoping that by getting here as early as we did, we'd be seen quickly. It didn't happen. We've been here for more than an hour already, and we haven't been called."

"Oh, God! How frustrating!" Jeanne said. "I'm sorry. How is Juliette behaving?"

"She's being an angel," Brian said. "She's sleeping.

I'm the one who might misbehave. I'm feeling paranoid again that we're being purposefully and passive-aggressively ignored."

"Is the ED particularly crowded?" Jeanne asked.

"It wasn't when we arrived," he said. "At least it didn't appear to be out here in the waiting room. Of course, I can't see when ambulances arrive, and I know at least one did. What bugs me is that just like yesterday people have walked in after we did and already have been seen, and it's getting more crowded now."

"Would you like me to come over and keep you company?"

"That's nice of you to offer," Brian responded. "But I'm hoping we'll be called soon, and I'm already feeling guilty about counting on you to come over later this afternoon to spend time with Juliette while I go out to the ESU Academy."

Before Jeanne could respond, Brian's phone vibrated in his hand, indicating he had a call coming in. It was Aimée. "I've got to go. My mother is trying to get through, and I'm sure it's about the funeral."

"No problem," Jeanne said. "I'm available if you need me."

He switched lines and greeted his mother.

"Why don't we all go to the funeral mass and burial together like Hannah suggested?" Aimée said with no preamble. "We could pick you and Juliette up on our way to the Church of the Good Shepherd. And tell Juliette that Grandma would love to see her in that new blue dress that—"

"There's a problem," Brian said, interrupting. "Juliette woke up with a high fever, and we are again back at the Emergency Department waiting to be seen."

"Mon Dieu! I'm sorry to hear," Aimée said. "How is she feeling now?"

"At the moment she's asleep," Brian answered. "Even that's not normal behavior for her." He didn't mention that the temperature was significantly lower now.

"Goodness gracious! This is not good news. What do you think; will you be able to make the church service?"

"It's totally dependent on when Juliette will be seen and then how she feels," he said. "I'm hoping she'll at least be seen soon, since we've already been here more than an hour."

"I certainly hope you and Juliette make it," Aimée said. "You'll be sorely missed, and I know Hannah will be beside herself if you don't. But will you come even if Juliette isn't up to it?"

"I'll try my best," Brian said, feeling a bit guilty that he wasn't being entirely up front. Not knowing how he felt about any of the funeral rites or how his wife might have felt, he wasn't as disappointed as he guessed his mother and Hannah would be if he and Juliette couldn't make the funeral mass or, perhaps, even the interment at the cemetery. Although he certainly wanted to honor his wife's memory and not offend anyone, so far the funeral rituals seemed to be more of a challenge to his emotional stability than a help. At the same time, he recognized the mass and the burial might be consoling on some level as a kind of closure and certainly not as upsetting as the wake. Brian desperately wanted himself and Juliette to remember Emma with the vitality that she embodied rather than as a cold, unresponsive shell staged with makeup to look as if she were merely sleeping.

"Well, I hope Juliette is seen soon," Aimée said.

Suddenly Juliette woke up as if from a bad dream and began crying.

"Uh-oh," he said. "I have to go. Juliette's awake and not happy."

"Okay, try to keep me informed, my dear," Aimée said and rang off.

"What's the matter, Pumpkin?" Brian asked soothingly as he pocketed his phone. Juliette was looking around, seemingly orienting herself.

"I'm hungry and I want to go home," she managed to say, choking back more tears.

"I'm glad you are hungry," Brian said as he got out the graham crackers and mentally thanked Camila for suggesting them. "But we have to stay until the doctor sees you and tells us why you have a fever. What about watching something fun?"

"I want to go home," Juliette repeated, obviously becoming more cranky.

"I do, too," he said. He got out the collection of DVDs he'd brought. Thankfully Juliette started pawing through them while munching on a cracker until she came across a *Pink Panther* DVD. Without saying anything, she handed it to Brian and with a sense of relief that she had found something, he set her up watching it.

With Juliette occupied, he sat back and tried to be

patient, but as time passed, he found himself getting progressively irritated. Finally, after a total of two hours, at which point he knew the funeral mass was probably beginning, he couldn't sit still any longer. After making sure that Juliette had significant time remaining on her current DVD, he walked back to the information desk.

On this occasion, Brian had to stand in line before getting to talk with one of the clerks, and it wasn't the woman whom he'd spoken to earlier. It was a youthful man with hair down to his shoulders.

"My daughter, Juliette Murphy, and I have been here for more than two hours," Brian snapped, tired of forcing himself to be polite. "I'm beginning to think we are being purposefully ignored. I want to be reassured that is not the case and find out when we will be seen."

The clerk treated him to an overtly questioning expression that was obvious even with his mask. After telling Brian to wait a minute, he got up and stepped over to speak with one of the free triage nurses. Brian watched them converse and had the impression the clerk was new to his job. After checking her tablet, it was the triage nurse who came back to speak with Brian.

"We're sorry you've had to wait, Mr. Murphy," she said consolingly and with respect. "We try our best to see everyone as quickly as we can, but with the Covid-19 pandemic, we've been stressed, as I'm sure you have heard."

"That I understand," Brian said, struggling to keep the anger out of his voice but not succeeding. He told her he'd seen people arrive after them and already be seen, and voiced concern that he was being treated differently because he had outstanding hospital bills.

"Oh, heavens, no!" she said. "I can assure you that we have no idea of your financial situation with the hospital. We see the sickest patients first. Some of those people you've seen most likely came in for something very easy to solve, like a prescription refill. We will get to your daughter as soon as we can."

Feeling frustrated and questioning that people might come into the ED just to get prescriptions refilled, he went back to Juliette and tried to rein in his growing anger. Despite what the triage nurse had said about the ED not being influenced by financial considerations, he still had his doubts. With Charles Kelley so focused on profits, such an orientation and culture had to trickle down into all corners of the hospital. He was sure of it.

It wasn't until three-quarters of an hour later that Juliette was called, and by then Brian was fit to be tied. To him, as angry as he was and for having been forced to miss his wife's funeral mass, there seemed to be no explanation other than that they were being overtly discriminated against.

To Juliette's chagrin the nurse who greeted them wasn't Olivia, but she quickly established herself as being equally as good with children. After leading them back to the same exam room they'd visited the day before, Nurse Jane pretended to take Jeannot Lapin's vital signs as she took Juliette's. And when Juliette asked for a hemostat to play with, Jane happily complied. She also acted impressed when Juliette demonstrated how well she could use the instrument by attaching it and releasing it at various locations on Jeannot Lapin.

"What's the temperature?" Brian asked after the nurse took it. He made a distinct effort to keep his voice from reflecting his irritation.

"98.2," Jane said happily. "Same with the rabbit."

With this surprising news and despite his annoyance, it was time for Brian to roll his eyes, feeling mildly embarrassed as well as exasperated that the main reason for coming to the ED had vanished just as it had the day before. Of course, he was pleased the fever was gone, but he was also perplexed. Had she really had a fever or could the thermometer at home be malfunctioning? But then he reminded himself of the perspiration on Juliette's forehead. That had been real, meaning something must have been wrong. Particularly because of his EMT training, he knew more than most people about symptoms and signs of disease, and a disappearing fever of 102.2 made no sense to him, nor did it make sense that Juliette's sore throat had vanished when Jane asked her about it. The only symptom that remained was the headache. When Jane asked Juliette where she felt the pain and whether it was localized, Juliette motioned all over her head.

With the vital signs retaken, Jane said that the doctor would be in to see Juliette in a few minutes and left. Yet it was more than a few minutes; it was twenty minutes, long enough for Juliette to start crying, saying she wanted to go home, and long enough to allow his befuddlement to morph back to anger. In his mind, having been forced to wait three hours, two days in a row, couldn't have been by chance. It had to be punitively deliberate, not to mention inconsiderate and unethical.

Suddenly there was a loud knock on the door and before Brian could respond, in walked an ebullient Dr. Robert Arnsdorf along with Jane. He was an athletic-looking physician, who Brian guessed was in his fifties, comparable in height with Brian but slenderer and with a bit of white hair protruding from beneath his surgical cap. A stethoscope was casually slung around his neck. Brian was relieved it wasn't Dr. Kramer.

"Ah, I see Miss Murphy is a little unhappy," Dr. Arnsdorf said friskily, seemingly for Juliette's benefit. "What's the problem today, my chickadee?" Without waiting for an answer, he looked down at his tablet and began reading.

In his agitated state Brian found the doctor's breezy attitude and seeming unpreparedness galling rather than playful and certainly not endearing. Juliette didn't buy it, either, and continued crying until Jane got her reinterested in playing with the hemostat.

"The problem is we've been waiting for over three hours," Brian blurted out.

"Sorry about that," Dr. Arnsdorf said simply. "Let me finish Dr. Kramer's note." After a moment he put the tablet down on the desk. "Okay, seems that we've had a repeat from yesterday: A phantom fever and sore throat along with a single episode of vomiting and diarrhea yesterday afternoon. Interesting."

"I hardly think 'interesting' is an appropriate description," Brian said.

"First, let me extend my sincere condolences about your wife," Dr. Arnsdorf said, continuing to ignore Brian's displeasure. "It's entirely understandable that there have been psychosomatic symptoms, including a fever. But, to be on the safe side, let's take a look." He nodded as if agreeing with himself. Then after a brief wash of his hands, he quickly examined Juliette, starting by first looking into her mouth, throat, nose, and ears. He then listened to her chest and let her listen to his. Finally, he palpated her abdomen while she was lying on her back, managing to get her relaxed enough to elicit a little laugh. Brian watched the rapid exam and stayed quiet throughout although he already was concerned that the doctor had a low index of suspicion.

"You are in perfect health," Dr. Arnsdorf declared to Juliette while playfully touching her on the tip of the nose with his index finger. He then turned to Brian. "I think she is fine, very healthy in fact. And I'm impressed with her size, having been a preemie. My guess is she's out there on the positive side of the bell curve development-wise for her age."

"What does her having been a preemie have to do with anything?" Brian asked. In his hypersensitive state, it seemed like a statement out of the blue, like trying to change the subject.

"Nothing, really," Dr. Arnsdorf said. "The doctor's note from yesterday noted Juliette was a tiny baby when she was born. We've seen a handful of Dr. Bhatt's patients over the last couple of days. He's a fine pediatrician. Did you meet him when he was a resident at Columbia-Presbyterian Children's Hospital?"

"Yes," Brian said. He relaxed a twinge, realizing he shouldn't fault doctors for being thorough even though Juliette's current situation had nothing to do with her spending the first month of her life in a NICU at Columbia. She'd been transferred there from MMH Inwood right after delivery.

"My advice if these phantom symptoms continue is to consider having her talk to a pediatric social worker," Dr. Arnsdorf said, picking up his tablet as if he was about to leave. "Also, perhaps you should make an appointment to see Dr. Bhatt when he comes back after his vacation."

"Wait a second," Brian began. "I'm not comfortable assuming her symptoms are psychosomatic. She hasn't been acting herself even before my wife's passing, and this morning she woke up with a real fever. She had perspiration covering her forehead. Especially with this pandemic still going on and a second wave expected, I at least want her to have a Covid test. I'd also like to see if her blood count is normal."

"I disagree," Dr. Arnsdorf countered. "I agree with Dr. Kramer. Your daughter also complained of a sore throat, but her throat looks perfectly normal. Likewise, her ears. And her temperature at the moment is actually low, not high."

"I want her to have some blood work," Brian demanded, losing patience. "And a Covid test at a minimum."

"The hospital is backed way up on its Covid testing,"

Dr. Arnsdorf said with exasperation. He'd been making an effort to placate Brian but was beginning to resent his insistence.

"There's something not right with my daughter. This is the second time in two days we've been here."

"Calm down, Mr. Murphy," Dr. Arnsdorf said, forcing himself to be calm as well. "We've been asked by our lab on a temporary basis only to do testing on patients with a strong indication, who have sustained symptoms, or have been exposed to someone with Covid-19, or are being admitted to the hospital. Your daughter doesn't fit in any of these categories. Covid-19 symptoms vary from patient to patient, but they don't come and go over a few hours in the same patient, not in our experience. As for doing a blood count or any other blood work, I don't see any rationale whatsoever. Subjecting a child to a phlebotomy, which can be a traumatic experience, shouldn't be done unless there is a strong indication."

"Does your reluctance to do the little I'm asking have anything to do with this hospital suing me for the bill to treat my late wife's EEE? Are you people all so damn worried I won't pay whatever outrageous price you've put on these tests?"

For a second Dr. Arnsdorf stared at Brian in shocked surprise. "Absolutely not!" he said, finding his voice. "That's an insult. You are one paranoid individual, Mr. Murphy."

"Of course I'm paranoid," he retorted. "It's hard not to be paranoid in this day and age dealing with healthcare. Don't tell me you aren't fully aware that your CEO is one hell-bent profit-motivated individual intent on keeping prices high and costs low to justify his multimillion-dollar salary."

"I'm a doctor!" Dr. Arnsdorf retorted. "I take care of people, not business."

"That's a cop-out if I ever heard one," Brian snapped. "Yes, you are a doctor, and MMH Inwood is a hospital, which is supposed to be your house and not Charles Kelley's gravy train."

"I've had enough of this conversation." Dr. Arnsdorf turned back to the sink and rewashed his hands before swiftly leaving the exam room.

Equally fed up and sensing he was getting nowhere, Brian turned to Juliette and scooped her up in his arms. He ignored Jane as she said goodbye to Juliette. On their way to the waiting room, Brian struggled to get out his phone, and while walking and carrying Juliette, he used Siri to call Camila.

"My, you have been there a long time," Camila said immediately as she came on the line.

"Don't remind me," Brian said. "Can you come and get us?"

"Of course! I'll be there shortly. How is Juliette doing?"

"She's doing fine," he said. "I'm the one who's struggling."

CHAPTER 30

September 2

Once Brian and Juliette were in the car, Camila briefly tried to get both to talk to find out what had happened, but it quickly became clear to her that neither was so inclined. With Juliette it was because she was busy getting the laptop out of the backpack to return to the DVD she'd been watching earlier. With Brian it was apparent from the outset that he was seriously irritated. In Camila's experience, he rarely got upset, but when he did, she'd learned it was best to let him mull over whatever was bothering him, which usually didn't take long. And true to form, by the time they drove out of the hospital grounds, he let out a protracted sigh and said with a shake of his head: "Well, that was another exercise in futility."

"I'm sorry to hear," Camila said. "What happened? What did they find?"

"Nothing," Brian answered with disgust. "But in their defense, by the time we were seen after another three-hour wait, once again her fever had vanished along with most of her symptoms. I think she still has a headache, but that's it, and apparently even the headache is better. It clearly hasn't hindered her from watching videos." He glanced over his shoulder to see if Juliette was back to watching, and she was. "The doctors are convinced it's all psychosomatic, fever included."

"I suppose that's possible," Camila said. "Did they do any tests this time to make certain?"

"None," Brian said. "That's what irked me. I tried to get them to do even a routine blood test, but no go with the excuse they're backed up with their Covid testing. It's all very suspicious to me. I'm worried that they didn't do any tests because they're afraid they are not going to get paid since I already owe them so damn much money."

"Do you really think that is a possibility?" Camila asked.

"I do," Brian said. "Having to wait to be seen more than three hours two days in a row and then refusing to do anything I asked speaks volumes. And this morning when we first arrived, the triage nurse acted put out when I asked her to repeat Juliette's temperature."

"Next week Dr. Bhatt will be back."

"Hallelujah," he said. "I can't wait."

"By the way, a Grady Quillen stopped by and left you a large manila envelope. He said that you would know what it was about. It's on your desk."

"I do," Brian said. "It's a list of people like me and Jeanne who he's served."

When they pulled into the driveway and stopped, Juliette said she was hungry.

"How about you, Brian?" Camila asked as they all got out of the car. "Want to join us?"

"You guys go ahead. I've got to call my mom. I'm afraid Juliette and I have missed at least the funeral mass."

"Oh, my goodness," Camila said. "That's right. I'll hurry with Juliette."

"Don't rush!" he said. "Let Juliette enjoy her belated breakfast. I'm delighted she's hungry, and to be truthful, I'm not sure what I want to do at this point."

Once in the house, Brian went to the office. He knew he had to contact his mother, but he hesitated. It was now 12:20 P.M., and he imagined the interment was in progress, meaning even if he tried to rush out to Wood-lawn Cemetery, he had probably missed the ceremony. He felt fairly guilty and worried that he'd let Hannah down, yet Juliette's well-being was far more important to him than his sense of responsibility to his in-laws. Besides, he had to admit that he felt relieved not to have witnessed the stark reality of putting Emma's body in the ground.

Instead of making a mad dash to the cemetery or even calling Aimée, he sat down at his desk and used a letter opener to get at the contents of the manila folder Grady had brought over. After he and Jeanne had seen on the internet the huge number of people the Manhattan Memorial Hospital had sued or was suing in the metropolitan area, he wasn't totally surprised the list comprised hundreds of Inwood residents whom Grady had served. Having spent his entire life in the neighborhood, Brian fully expected there would be a number of people he knew personally. Sure enough, just with a random glance, he found Donavan Bligh's name with an address on Indian Road, a ten-minute walk from where Brian was sitting. He knew the family because they had a son who'd been in his sister Erin's class at P.S. 98 like Patrick McCarthy.

Although Brian was now more interested to help Jeanne learn the gory details of a number of the cases to hopefully motivate the media and maybe even the local politicians to do something, he slipped Grady's list back into its envelope, and put it aside. He then got his phone out with the intention of calling Aimée, but still he hesitated. Instead of initiating the call, he put the phone down on the desk and stared at it. Not only did he feel guilty about missing the burial, but he also now worried about the possibility of his call coming at just the wrong time if the interment was still in progress. If that happened, he'd only be adding insult to injury. With that concern in mind, he wondered if he should wait just a little longer, or send her a text instead. He knew Aimée was expecting him to be in contact.

While Brian sat paralyzed by indecision, the phone suddenly rang with its raucous "old phone" ringtone, making him jump. In a kind of panic, he snapped it up to see who was calling. To his great irritation it was Roger Dalton. Recalling the anger the man's phone call had incited the previous day, he debated whether to answer. He was already in a foul mood, and Roger Dalton, as the embodiment of MMH Inwood's business tactics as well as Kelley's sidekick, was fast becoming for him a persona non grata. Yet rationality intervened, making Brian again question whether he might be calling concerning Megan Doyle's or Patrick McCarthy's need to get a complete printout of Emma's hospital bill. With that possibility in mind, he answered but quickly wished he hadn't.

"This is rapidly becoming a farce," Roger said without even identifying himself. "I don't know why I'm making the effort to call you other than feeling some sympathy for what's happening to your life. Another charge for which you are responsible was brought to my attention. Of course, I immediately sent it to Peerless Health, and in their usual rapid but disappointing way, they have refused any coverage. Ergo, if you don't get them to reverse yet another denial, it will be added to your growing delinquency. Can I expect you to look into this quickly and get back to me?"

For a moment Brian struggled to control an almost overwhelming vexation and didn't answer immediately, partially because Roger Dalton had at least expressed an ounce of empathy. "Is this new charge for my daughter's Emergency Department visit?"

"It is indeed," Roger said.

"You are not talking about today, are you?"

"No, yesterday," Roger said. "Did you return to the ED today?"

"Yes, I just got home. I was there all morning."

"Oh, dear," Roger said. "Well, that makes it more important to get in touch with your insurance company.

Because your account is flagged, I'll be hearing about a new charge probably this afternoon. Both these charges will be added to your default unless you would like to take care of these ED bills yourself. Is that a possibility?"

"How much is the charge?" he asked hesitantly. Since nothing had been done in the way of laboratory tests or imaging, he thought there was a possibility he could show some good faith, but it depended on the amount.

"Yesterday's charge is $1,776.55," Roger said. "We'd be happy to accept a check or credit card."

"Wait a second!" Brian blurted. "That's almost two thousand dollars! There must be some mistake. We had to wait for so long that my daughter's symptoms disappeared, so nothing was done: no tests, no nothing. That's impossible."

"Quite the contrary," Roger said. "The facility was used and the facility charge is a good portion of the bill. On top of that, your daughter was seen by a doctor, so there was a charge for that."

"I have never even heard of a facility charge," Brian said. "What the hell does that mean?"

"It means that everyone who is seen in the ED has to pay some costs involved in constructing and maintaining the whole facility and all its necessary equipment, including all the X-ray machines, MRIs, you name it."

"How much was the facility fee?" he asked.

"Let me check," Roger said. There was a brief pause before he added: "Eleven hundred dollars."

"Good God! I'm being charged eleven hundred dollars for merely walking into the ED."

"No, you are being charged eleven hundred dollars for your daughter to be seen, examined, and treated in a Trauma 1 facility."

Brian tried to rein in his outrage. Instead he harkened back to the lecture Megan had given him about hospital-inflated charge master prices used to negotiate with the larger health insurance companies, but which Medicare didn't pay. "If my daughter was on Medicare, how much would the facility fee be then?"

"That's proprietary information," Roger answered.

"Oh, come on, Roger," Brian said. "I'm sure I could call Medicare and they would tell me. You expressed some sympathy for what I'm going through. Help me out here, so I can begin to understand what I'm up against. How much would Medicare pay? I won't tell anyone you told me." Brian rolled his eyes at his own falsity.

"It is true Medicare could tell you," Roger admitted.

"There you go," he said. "Save me the effort."

"Somewhere in the three- to four-hundred-dollar range," Roger said. "It depends on what part of the ED was actually used."

"That's quite a difference," Brian responded, keeping his real thoughts to himself. "When we first met, you gave a lot of credit to Charles Kelley. Has he been involved with this facility charge situation?"

"Of course," Roger said. "It's a key element in his turning the hospital around financially."

"Interesting," Brian managed. Struggling to contain himself, he changed the subject. He knew it was a hopeless cause arguing about prices with the likes of Roger

Dalton or finding fault with his CEO and hero. "Did Peerless give you any reason for denying the claim for my daughter's ED visit?"

"No," Roger said. "They rarely do. That's for you to find out and try to rectify. What about this most recent ED bill? Do you want to use a credit card? I could take direct payment over the phone. It's your choice."

"I'll call Peerless," Brian said.

"Fine," Roger said with irritation. "You do that."

Without another word being spoken, he found that the call had been disconnected. Yesterday he'd hung up on Roger Dalton; today Roger Dalton had hung up on him.

With his own anger and resentment mounting, Brian subjected himself once again to the frustration of calling Ebony Wilson. As he waited through the required hold music, he tried to imagine what reason Peerless was going to give for denying Juliette's ED visit. He also marveled at what a nightmare American healthcare had become for himself, his family, and apparently for too many of his neighbors and friends. After this whole ordeal, he'd be happy to never have to speak with another healthcare representative again.

After more than a half hour, Ebony Wilson came on the line using her signature pleasant voice with its mildly southern accent.

"It's Brian Murphy again," he said in response to her initial scripted introduction. He then immediately rattled off his policy number without being asked and said he was again calling about a claim denial and wanted yet another explanation.

"Let me check for you," she said cheerfully. If she'd been offended by his abrupt disconnect the day before or his current supercilious attitude, she didn't let on. Brian assumed that she probably had to deal with a lot of angry people in her role as a claims adjustment supervisor of a company that made it a point to deny claims.

After less than five minutes of additional Muzak punishment she came back. "I see the latest claim was for Juliette Murphy at the MMH Inwood ED. Is this the claim you are inquiring about?"

"Yes," he said. "Why was this one rejected, or are all claims automatically rejected?"

"Our adjusters are experienced, hardworking, and very qualified professionals," Ebony said by rote, seemingly immune to Brian's brashness. She then went on to say: "This claim was denied for two reasons. The first was because of a preexisting condition, which your policy does not cover."

"What kind of preexisting condition?" he interjected with surprise.

"Serious prematurity," she said. "The attending physician had noted that the child had been born at thirty weeks, weighing only two-and-a-half pounds, which required more than a month in the neonatal intensive care unit."

"But that was four years ago," Brian sputtered. "After the first year she caught up size-wise, and she's been fine ever since."

"Prematurity has lots of potential complications down

the road, or so I've been told," Ebony said. "Do you want to hear the second reason?"

"I'm not so sure . . ."

"The visit was in the middle of the day at a Trauma 1 Emergency Department," she continued. "Your daughter should have been seen by her pediatrician or an urgent-care center."

"I called the pediatrician's office and was advised to take my daughter to the MMH Inwood ED," Brian argued. "I was following doctor's orders."

"We here at Peerless take our responsibility of reducing healthcare costs very seriously," Ebony said. "That means encouraging people to use lower-cost alternatives."

"I've heard this argument from you already," he snapped. He could feel his pulse pounding in his ears.

"Again, if you don't like our adjusters' decisions you have the right to resubmit the claim and request a review or . . ."

"Or I can sue," Brian said, filling in the rest.

"That is correct, and thank you for being a Peerless Health Insurance customer," Ebony finished, again by rote.

Without another word and infuriated by the call, he disconnected and, like yesterday, immediately charged down the cellar steps and hurried into the small basement workout room. Using the same forty-five-pound weights, he quickly exhausted himself. Brian had always been a physical and mildly self-righteous person whose first instinct when attacked or wronged was to strike out.

With his size, strength, and agility, he'd had to learn to suppress such urges, using sports as a release. When competitive athletics wasn't available, barbells or strenuous cardio activity would suffice.

Ten minutes later and feeling moderately under control, he returned upstairs and sat back down at his desk. Looking at the phone lying on the blotter, he again debated getting in touch with Aimée. He knew he should, but when he picked up the phone, he still didn't call his mother. Instead, he called Jeanne, more for moral support than anything else, although he planned on using the Grady material as an excuse.

Again the phone rang more times than he would have liked, and he felt guilty about calling her so much. As he was thinking about what voice message to leave and whether to leave any, she answered. It was clear she was out of breath.

"Am I catching you out on your bike again?" he asked, hearing what he thought was the sound of wind in the background.

"You are," Jeanne admitted. "Sorry. I had to get the phone out, this time from my backpack."

"No reason to apologize," Brian said. "I should be the one apologizing for interrupting your ride again. Are you back in the park?"

"I am, but now I'm riding along the Hudson River, and it's beautiful. I wanted to get out and get some exercise. What about Juliette? How is she? What did the doctor find this morning?"

"Once again they found nothing, and she's remarkably improved despite the 102.2 fever and multiple complaints when she woke up. And once again, they did absolutely nothing despite us again waiting more than three hours. I can't help but feel it was a deliberate slight, same as I did yesterday. Anyway, by the time she was seen, her fever was gone, same with her sore throat. I don't know about the headache. They said she was fine, thought her complaints were all psychosomatic, and recommended a social worker should her symptoms come back."

"Did they run any tests this time to be sure?"

"None, even though I made a big stink," Brian said. "No matter what I said, the doctor refused. I know you might think I'm being paranoid, but I really do think it is all about the money. I'm sorry, but having to wait more than three hours two days in a row and refusing to do any tests, even a simple blood test, has to be deliberate. It can't be a coincidence."

"There's no way to know," Jeanne said.

"True, but it's my gut feeling," Brian insisted. "The doctor tried to tell me some bull about him not knowing anything about the business side of the hospital, but he has to know. They all have to know. I wouldn't be surprised if the chief medical officer was on their backs all the time with the way that my hospital account manager carries on about the cost of running the Emergency Department. My guess is that Kelley is watching every penny they spend in the ED to make sure it's a money-making venture."

"You're probably right."

"Speaking of my hospital account manager, I had to have yet another phone conversation with him a little while ago that was as maddening as ever," Brian said. "Then of course I had to talk again to the Peerless claims adjustment supervisor, which was equally as infuriating. It never ends, but I'll tell you the gory details later."

"Oh, my," Jeanne said with sympathy. "What a day you are having."

"Well, at least Juliette's feeling better than when she awoke," Brian said. "She even said she was hungry when we got home."

"That's good to hear," she said. "I hate to ask, but what about the funeral services for your wife? Were they postponed?"

"I wish," he responded. "I'm afraid Juliette and I missed both the mass and the burial. We went to the hospital early enough that I thought we'd be back in plenty of time. It's unfortunate that didn't happen thanks to the damn ED, but what could I do? Juliette's fever of over 102 had to take precedence even though it spontaneously resolved. I know my mother will understand, and I just hope Emma's mother does, too."

"I'm so sorry," Jeanne said. "You poor man. You have so much on your plate."

"There is a bit of good news," Brian interjected to change the subject. "Grady delivered, as I was confident he would. I have his service list, and it's going to make our investigation easy now that we have hundreds of Inwood names and addresses."

"Terrific," Jeanne exclaimed. "I'm excited to get on

with that. The more I think about it, the more important I believe exposing all of this is. Someone has to do it."

"Are you still planning on coming over this afternoon to spend time with Juliette?"

"Absolutely! I'm looking forward to it," she said. "That's why I wanted to get some exercise in this morning. What about you? Are you still planning on visiting the ESU Academy?"

"I am," Brian admitted. "With all this extra stress, I'm looking forward to it even more. I'll be leaving soon for a three o'clock meeting, and hope I, too, can get in some exercise while I'm there. It would do wonders for my psyche."

"I have a confession to make," Jeanne said. "Last night I googled NYPD ESU, and I have to say, I was really impressed. Kudos to you and your wife. The training you guys went through is intense. I had no idea. You put your life on the line, literally. Have you really rappelled down skyscrapers and out of helicopters?"

"That and more," Brian answered with a bit of pride, although he was usually more self-effacing.

"I'm truly impressed," Jeanne said. "In French we say 'très impressionné.'"

He laughed in spite of himself. "Je me rappelle the expression."

"I'm not sure I'll see you before you leave," she said. "I've got to bike home and shower. But I'll see you when you get back. Try to enjoy yourself!"

"Merci beaucoup," Brian said. He then disconnected before bringing up Aimée's number.

CHAPTER 31

September 2

The mere act of driving out onto the Floyd Bennett Field in the southeastern part of Brooklyn was therapeutic for Brian. He'd not been there for almost a year and had forgotten the effect of the huge expanse of 1,300 acres of mostly grassland, pristine salt marshes, and five enormous, decaying runways all within the confines of New York City. He knew something of the history of the place, as did all ESU officers who spent eight months training at the school. It had been a commercial airport in its early life but then was taken over by the federal government in World War II to be used mostly as a Naval Air station and a Coast Guard facility. It was now primarily administered by the National Park Service. The NYPD had used a small portion of the eastern part of the field as far back as 1934 for an aviation unit, which was still the case. The Emergency Service Unit's headquarters and academy were also positioned there a bit later in four recycled Coast Guard buildings immediately adjacent to the aviation facility.

As he pulled up in front of the ramshackle admin and classroom building that served as the heart of the ESU complex, he had to smile at its appearance. When he'd been part of the unit, he'd been there so often that he never appreciated how decrepit the old buildings were. Perhaps when they had been built by the Coast Guard more than a half century earlier as hangars and barracks, they hadn't looked too bad, but they clearly had never been architectural exemplars. When compared to the new, multistory NYPD Academy in Queens, the ESU Academy looked like a forgotten afterthought despite its enormously important mission.

After opening the car's door, Brian hesitated as another part of his brain interrupted the pleasurable reveries he'd experienced driving onto the field. Like a sudden thunderstorm plunging a beautiful summer day into gloom, thoughts of Emma came back in a rush. It was here at the academy and in this very building that he'd first met her when she was a recruit and just starting her training. Brian could well remember the day because it had been one of his days off, and he had debated whether to go out to the academy to lend a hand with the new class of cadets. Little did he know that the day would change his life. He could vividly recall as if it were yesterday and from their first interaction how impressed he'd been with the way Emma stood out from her classmates. Her enthusiasm was palpable and sheer athleticism was obvious, especially as one of the very few females willing not only to take the physical punishment the training entailed but somehow enjoy it. It had been the same way he had reacted to the training when he'd been a recruit.

In an effort to regroup from a sudden paralyzing stab of grief, Brian reclosed the car door, shut his eyes, leaned his head against the steering wheel, and took a few deep breaths. It seemed so utterly impossible that Emma was gone. Despite the understanding both he and Emma shared as ESU officers that they were putting themselves at risk of death on a daily basis, they hadn't given the possibility much thought. With their youth and health, it seemed a theoretical problem that had been easy to ignore.

Before leaving home to head out to Floyd Bennett Field, he had finally forced himself to call his mother. During the call he'd learned that the burial had indeed taken place. He'd also learned that he and Juliette had been sorely missed at the interment, but everyone understood the reasons for his absence. Aimée told him that at the conclusion of the ceremonies, Hannah had suffered a major emotional breakdown now that all the funeral planning she'd busied herself with was over.

"God damn it!" Brian shouted in the confines of the car as he pounded the steering wheel with his fist to the point of pain. Luckily both withstood the abuse. For a fleeting moment he thought about dashing into the makeshift weight room set up in the larger, hangar-type building to his left to let off some steam. But the urge quickly passed when he diverted his thoughts to Juliette, his new raison d'être. In a minor panic, he struggled to get his phone out of his pocket to put in a call to Camila. He felt a sudden urge to make sure everything was okay even though he'd only been gone an hour. Juliette's fever of 102.2 that morning still plagued him despite its rapid resolution, especially since earlier he'd googled "psychosomatic fever" to learn that it was considered rare in children Juliette's age, especially as high as 102.

Camila answered on the first ring and relieved him by immediately reporting that Juliette had eaten a healthy meal and that Jeanne had arrived. She added that they were all busy playing an old board game that Juliette enjoyed called Dinosaur.

"I just arrived at the academy," Brian said. "I haven't yet gone inside but I'm about to. I just wanted to check in before I get involved in a training exercise."

"All is well here," Camila assured him. "Juliette is acting completely normal and seems happy, so relax and enjoy yourself. Everything is under control. By the way, a call came in about a possible security gig. I said that you would call them back. Are you up for that?"

"Of course," Brian said, trying to be positive, although if pressed he wasn't entirely sure he could handle a difficult job under the circumstances. "Was there a rush on the callback?"

"Heavens, no," Camila said. "It's a possible wedding, but it's not until December, and it didn't strike me as a definite. Do you want to speak with Jeanne?"

"Tell her I'll speak with her later," he said, checking the time. "I'm on the brink of being late for my meeting."

After a quick goodbye, Brian disconnected, turned the ringer off, and pocketed the phone. He then took a few more deep breaths. Hearing that Juliette was acting normal was reassuring, and he was confident Jeanne could help if need be. The sudden, paralyzing rush of grief reminded him he had a long way to go to deal with Emma's loss, but at the moment it was important for him to hold his own emotions in check as much as possible. Translated into the near term, that meant he needed some income and benefit security and rejoining the ESU, if they would have him, would accomplish both. With that in mind, he reopened the car door and got out.

As he walked toward the admin building door, he noted how quiet the entire, relatively large compound was. All he could hear were some seagulls in the distance. In normal non-pandemic times, the place would be hopping with thirty to fifty recruits in training, dispersed into smaller groups. Beyond the large hangar building and to the right of the huge ESU garage he could see the group of cars used for practicing with the "jaws of life" to rescue people after car wrecks. Beyond the car wrecks was an NYC subway car, which looked like a huge fish out of water in the middle of an old airport. It was used for tactical and rescue training, seeing as it was the ESU who was called to get people—or what was left of them—out from under subway trains when they jumped or were pushed. Brian could well remember training for all sorts of rescues, whether from the tops of bridges, the sides of skyscrapers, or underwater, and most all of it happened here at the ESU Headquarters.

The interior of the admin building reflected the exterior in all its ramshackle glory. The first person Brian encountered was Helen Gurly, a very capable African American woman who'd served the last four ESU commanding officers. When an ESU officer had an administration problem, they all knew Helen was the first person to go to.

"Well, well, what a sight for sore eyes," Helen said with her usual candor and humor. "The boss man is waiting on you, so go right on in!"

He thanked her and said that seeing her made him feel like coming home. She responded with a wave of dismissal, accompanied by a smile that he could detect despite her face mask.

Although the usual uniform for ESU personnel was dark blue for normal activities or black for tactical situations, Deputy Chief Michael Comstock always wore a bracingly white, impeccably ironed shirt with epaulettes and scalloped breast pocket flaps. He was a big man with a completely shaved head, hazel eyes, and a full rounded face with a ruddy complexion. Although certainly part of the brass, with his rank of deputy chief, he could compete physically with the rest of the ESU team and was respected for it. He was, in short, what a leader should be. His office and its furniture, like the entire building, looked worse for wear, but the ensemble had a homey touch with lots of family pictures alongside the compulsory head shots of the mayor and police commissioner.

As soon as Brian walked in, Michael put down his pen and stood up. With a smile he extended his elbow over his desk, so he and Brian could do the pandemic-inspired elbow-touch greeting. Michael laughed while he did it as a kind of acknowledgment that everybody was caught in the Covid-19 nightmare and had to make the best of it. He then pointed to a seat a good six feet in front of his desk.

"Let me again express my sincere condolences for your loss," Michael began. "It's a loss for all of us. Everyone I've told is heartbroken. She was, like yourself, well liked and respected around here."

"Thank you, sir," Brian said. "It's been a shock, as you can imagine. It might have been the very last thing I could have expected happening." He braced himself against tears, which he could feel coming on. He hadn't wanted to talk about Emma but knew it was inevitable.

"We and the rest of the staff are sorry we couldn't attend the burial today to pay our proper respects," Michael said.

"I appreciate that." Brian purposefully avoided saying he'd not been there, either, hoping to move the subject away from that day's events.

"After your call yesterday, I talked to a number of the staff," Michael continued. "I particularly made it a point to talk with your A team commander, Captain Deshawn Williams. I also talked with Sal Benfatti, our TAC House sergeant. I'm happy to report that the response was uniformly positive. Everyone would be thrilled to have you back on the force, Deshawn in particular. So, if you were at all concerned about how you would be received, I can tell you there would be no problem whatsoever."

"That's reassuring to hear," Brian said. He had hoped there wouldn't be any resentment, and it was reassuring to have it confirmed.

"But I have to emphasize again that your rejoining has to be a true commitment," Michael warned. "I don't want to put through the paperwork if there is going to be any waffling. You have to be sure. Are we clear on this?"

"Perfectly clear," Brian said. "My plan is to spend a week or two re-immersing myself here, running recertification drills and just getting back into physical shape. After that, I'm certain I'll be able to make an absolute commitment. I'd also like to spend some time at one of the shooting ranges. I didn't realize how much I'd miss the opportunity to practice and stay current. This has been the first year in the past decade I didn't attend the spring Sig Sauer course up in New Hampshire."

"I can appreciate what you are saying," Michael said, "which is why the ESU puts so much emphasis on re-training and recertification. No worries! I can arrange for you to have access to one of the shooting ranges. Do you have your NYPD ID?"

"Of course," Brian responded. He'd never been without his ID since joining the force more than a decade ago, even after his retirement.

"Where would you prefer? Camp Smith or Rodman's Neck in the Bronx?"

"Rodman's Neck," Brian answered without hesitation. "It's closer. I've got a four-year-old daughter who is having a difficult time with my wife's passing, and I'd like to stay closer to home, at least in the short run." Brian knew Rodman's Neck was less than a half-hour drive from Inwood.

"I understand," Michael said. "I'm sure she is suffering, the poor child. I'd forgotten about your daughter although I do remember the anguish you had when she was born and spent so long in the hospital. I trust that she's been healthy since."

"Very healthy, thank you," Brian said, reluctant to mention the recent health concerns.

"The reason I even suggested Camp Smith is that it has a considerably longer range, if that is something that interests you."

"Rodman's Neck has a three-hundred-yard rifle range," Brian said. "That's long enough for my purposes. Actually, at least initially, I'll probably only use the pistol range."

"I had an ulterior motive mentioning Camp Smith's longer range," Michael said. "I don't know if you've heard, but we are in the process of possibly replacing our Remington 700 sniper rifle, the old standby, with the newer Remington MSR. Since I recall you were quite extraordinary with the sniper rifle, I'm wondering if you would mind giving the new one a try and give us your impression. We're trying to figure out if the benefits justify the cost. The MSR is considerably more expensive."

"I'd be happy to give my opinion," Brian said eagerly. Playing a bit of an advisory role in the face of everything else that was going on had a lot of appeal. "Would you like me to check the rifle out sooner rather than later?"

"The sooner the better," Michael answered. "Today, in fact, if it is possible. I'm tasked to submit a report on it, and to that end, I've had a few people try it, and the response has been mixed. Of course, some people have trouble with change of any kind and are accordingly biased. I've tried it, but I was never that good with a sniper rifle. Your opinion would be helpful, having been one of our crack shots."

"I'll enjoy putting it through its paces at three hundred yards," Brian said. "And today will be fine. Will they have one out at Rodman's Neck for me to use?"

"I imagine they do, but I can do better than that. I'll sign one out to you, and you can take it with you to the range. Having it in your possession will give you a chance to make the customizing adjustments beforehand. I'll call Rodman's Neck while you are over at the TAC House. I assume that the TAC House was your plan for this afternoon?"

"It is," Brian responded. "Other than speaking with you, sir."

"Perfect," Michael said. "I'll sign you out a Remington MSR and call Rodman's Neck and make the arrangements. How many rounds of ammo would you like?"

"A couple of boxes should be enough. Can you also give me a couple of boxes of nine-millimeter for my Sig Sauer, so I can use one of the pistol ranges as well?"

"Not a problem," Michael answered. "But I'll give you three boxes for the MSR just to be sure. You can bring back what you don't use. Is there anything else you wanted to do here this afternoon besides the TAC House?"

"Yes, I'd like to meet up with Detective Jose Garcia. I assume he's still the SCUBA instructor."

"Oh, yes!" Michael confirmed. "He's not going anywhere. He's here for life."

Jose Garcia had been one of his favorite instructors. Jose had managed to turn the required SCUBA training Brian had to undergo from a dreaded experience into a joy. Although he was still certified, he hadn't made a refresher SCUBA dive in well over a year. Prior to his ESU training, Brian had never been that comfortable in the water. He'd always joked that it had taken life millions of years to get out of the water, and he didn't see any reason to reverse the trend. Now he loved it.

"Could you let him know I'll be stopping by after my session at the TAC House? I'd like him to pick me out some equipment so that I can do a recertification dive in the next couple of days."

"You got it," Michael said. "And when you are done with your rounds, stop back here. I'll have one of the Remington MSRs and the ammo available."

"Thank you, sir," he said. "I really appreciate your help and support." Being back at his former stomping grounds and with his former colleagues, he was already feeling more secure about the future.

CHAPTER 32

September 2

Just to the north of the ESU admin building was another sizable, nondescript commercial structure that looked equally as aged and dilapidated as the others. This building contained the TAC House, or Training Ammunition Combat edifice. As Brian approached, he again had to smile. On this occasion it wasn't because of its run-down appearance. It was because from the outside there was no hint whatsoever of what was inside.

Brian pushed through a battered outside door and stepped into a simulated night scene. What confronted him in the expansive, darkened, several-story interior was a worse-for-wear modular structure the size of a modest one-story house. It had no ceiling and could be configured in various ways to represent an entire apartment with an outer door, a kitchen, living room, bathrooms, and bedrooms, an office, or any indoor structure. It was used for adaptive urban, non-ballistic assault exercises in various lighting conditions and with various numbers of targets played by instructors positioned inside, sometimes armed with non-lethal weaponry. Several catwalks above were used by the instructors to watch the simulated assaults so they could comment and make recommendations.

In addition to the TAC House structure, Brian was also confronted in the half-light by a group of seven ESU officers heavily armed and outfitted in the usual ESU tactical gear with midnight-black uniforms and bullet-proof vests with multiple pockets for gear and ammunition. In addition, they were wearing helmets, gloves, eye protection, and balaclava face masks in anticipation of taking part in the next drill. Although Brian had no chance of identifying anyone in face masks and dim light, most of the officers recognized him and immediately crowded around to say hello and extend their sympathies about Emma's passing. One officer, Carlos Morales, who was a member of the A team and who Brian knew well, said he'd heard a rumor that Brian might be rejoining the ESU. All of them cheered as a group when Brian told them he was giving it serious thought.

"Do it, do it, do it!" rang out as a spontaneous chant from the group. Brian laughed, unsure of how to respond. Finding his voice, he admitted he was leaning toward rejoining but wanted to make sure it was the right decision for his daughter and career.

For Brian this was even more of a homecoming than seeing Helen Gurly in the admin building, and it soothed his soul. It made him remember how much he valued being a member of a group with a common interest, extending all the way back to grammar school when he first began participating in organized sports. Through high school and college, it had been the same, and it had been one of the reasons he'd gravitated toward law enforcement as a career. In many ways he'd not been entirely aware of how much he missed this type of camaraderie since his retirement.

Suddenly the animated conversation was interrupted by someone within the TAC House yelling "Police! Police!" followed by a series of non-lethal rounds being fired, indicating that the simulation drill that was in progress when Brian arrived had terminated in gunplay. The blanks were particularly loud in the confined spaces.

"That's it, guys," Carlos called out to the group. "We're on deck, front and center!" He then picked up a ballistic shield that he had leaning against his leg. He was going to be the lead man on the next assault simulation. Another officer picked up a Blackhawk Halligan bar used to breach the outer door. Every member of the assault group had a specific, planned role to play to maximize safety, which was key if it were a real-life situation.

"Where's the tactic sergeant?" Brian asked Carlos.

"He's up on the catwalk," Carlos said, pointing to the wooden stairs to Brian's right.

"Good luck," Brian said, making a halfhearted salute gesture. He then walked to the stairs and started up. At the top Brian could see down into the illuminated mock living room/kitchen below, which was empty for the moment. Raising his eyes, he searched the maze-like elevated walkways that created an opportunity for the instructors to closely follow the activity below during a simulated assault. Brian could make out Sergeant Sal Benfatti with two of his instructors at the far end over the bedroom area. The tactic sergeant was leaning over the railing while talking down to the assault team below. Brian assumed he was giving a mixture of both praise and criticism regarding the simulation.

By the time Brian made it over to where the group was standing, Sal had finished his analysis with the group below and was conferring with the two instructors by his side. Below, Brian could see the team that had just completed the drill along with several instructors who had been acting as the bad guys. Brian had the sense the drill had been a mock-up hostage situation.

"Ah, Brian Murphy," Sal said welcomingly, seeing Brian approach. They knew each other well, not only from Brian's cadet days, but also because Brian had frequently helped out and participated in TAC House activities. Sal introduced Brian to his two instructors, who'd come on board since Brian's retirement.

As expected, Brian initially had to weather a brief conversation with Sal about Emma, but they soon turned to discussing why Brian was there; namely, to participate in a number of assault simulations. "I hope you weren't counting on starting today," Sal said. "This next drill is our last."

"That's fine," Brian said. "With your permission, I'd like to come back in the next couple of days."

"Terrific! We'll look forward to it. We'd love to have you. Do you want to stay and watch the next drill with us?"

"Absolutely," Brian answered.

The group moved from over the bedroom area to over the living room/kitchen. On this occasion there were to be two armed suspects, one in the kitchen area behind an island and the other in the living room sitting on the couch. When all was ready, Sal initiated the assault with a remote device. In the next second the front door was quickly breached with the Halligan bar, and Carlos swooped into the room with his ballistic shield followed closely by his team, all yelling "Police! Police!" at the top of their lungs while executing a predetermined set of movements.

On this occasion, with the two suspects in the front area of the sham apartment, there was an immediate shootout. Since the two officers directly behind Carlos precisely followed their preordained ballet with one concentrating on the kitchen and the other on the living room area, they bested the suspects. Within seconds the drill was over to well-deserved acclaim.

Twenty minutes later Brian walked out of the TAC House building, feeling particularly good about the visit. Having watched the drill and having experienced the palpable esprit de corps of the people involved made him progressively confident that rejoining the ESU was the proper decision for him, especially when he compared it with some of the security gigs he'd done. A number of those jobs involved squiring around and kowtowing to the demands of entitled wealthy narcissists and their spoiled offspring. In many ways Brian was coming more and more to identify himself as a blue-collar kind of guy who liked to get his hands dirty. It almost seemed as if the NYPD ESU, with its constant action, was tailor-made for him.

Rounding the northern end of the admin building, Brian walked into the middle of a dozen ESU officers who'd just finished a recertification SCUBA dive and were busy rinsing their equipment. In a repeat of what had happened when Brian first entered the TAC House, there was a warm interaction with condolences about Emma and encouragement for Brian to rejoin the ranks.

Entering the largest of the four buildings that formed the ESU complex, Brian walked into the SCUBA section. Passing through the storage and maintenance area, he entered Detective Jose Garcia's cramped and rather messy office. The detective was at his desk with the guts of a regulator exposed, as he did most of the upkeep and repair work himself. Similar to Michael Comstock, Jose was a big, thickset man, and except for a significant difference in complexion, they could have been brothers, down to the shaved heads. The main difference was that Jose had an impressive number of tattoos covering his forearms from a stint in the US Navy directly out of high school.

Although Brian would have preferred not to talk again about Emma's passing, he knew he didn't have a choice. Emma was extraordinarily well liked both at the academy and in the unit, probably more than Brian because of his mild but recognized self-righteous streak on certain subjects, including extremists on both sides of the political divide. One of Emma's admirable qualities had been her acceptance of others.

"So, Michael says you are interested in doing a recertification dive with us," Jose said.

"I am," Brian confirmed. "It's not critical since I'm still certified, but I would enjoy it. It's your fault. You turned me from a committed terrestrial into an amphibian."

Jose laughed with true mirth. "You were a tough cookie to crack, but I was optimistic."

They then spent a few minutes reminiscing about some of the dives they'd done together, particularly one to retrieve the body of a suicide jumper in the East River, where the currents can be notorious.

"Well, then," Jose said when there was a pause in their reminiscing. He slapped his desk with the palms of both hands and stood up. "Let's get you ready for a dive by setting you up with a locker, a wet suit, whatever else you might want, including one of our newest regulators. You are going to love it."

Fifteen minutes later, with all the dive equipment set aside in a locker, Brian left the SCUBA area and walked the length of the large hangar-like building. He emerged back out in the sunshine on its west side, and from there it was a short route back to the admin building. As he neared it, he felt really good about his visit as well as progressively convinced that in the not-too-distant future he would be back to being an ESU officer.

"Deputy Chief Comstock had to leave for an impromptu meeting downtown with the police commissioner," Helen Gurly explained when Brian approached her desk. "But no worries. He had me make the arrangements with Rodman's Neck and all you have to do is show your ID at the gate and then meet up with Captain Ted Miller, one of the firearms and tactics instructors, at the gunsmith. He'll be expecting you, provided you get there before six. There's also a surprise for you waiting on the deputy chief's desk that I'm told you already know about."

"You are talking about the Remington?" Brian asked.

"None other. Have a good day, I'm outta here." With that, Helen grabbed her bag, said that it was a joy to see him again, and pushed past on her way out into the corridor.

Entering Michael's office, Brian saw a camouflaged rifle bag with a shoulder strap on the desk along with five boxes of ammunition: three in 7.62mm NATO caliber for the rifle and two in 9mm for his pistol. Unzipping the bag, he found himself admiring a particularly lethal-looking, light tan sniper rifle with a folding stock and a suppressor. What impressed him immediately was the amount of customizing adjustments available, and how intuitive they were to utilize. Within minutes he adapted the length between the stock and the trigger to his needs, as well as the height and position of the cheek piece and the position of the scope. As for the finer adjustments of the telescopic sight for parallax and minute of angle, he'd do that at the shooting range when he'd be able to experience how well engineered the firearm actually was in comparison with the older Remington 700. After refolding the stock, Brian returned the weapon to its bag and slung it over his shoulder. Picking up the boxes of ammunition, he headed back out to his Subaru.

As he climbed into the car, he felt pleased with his visit to ESU Headquarters and more inclined to believe that rejoining the NYPD would be a wise move for many reasons. What especially encouraged him was that Michael Comstock, the commanding officer, had ostensibly recovered from his pique about his and Emma's retirement and wanted him back on board.

CHAPTER 33

September 2

Ten minutes later Brian was heading north on the Belt Parkway with Jamaica Bay off to his right and sparkling in the summer sunlight. The traffic was moderate, but being late afternoon and rush hour, he knew that would significantly change despite the pandemic. As far as the timing was concerned, he thought it was a good time to visit the Rodman's Neck shooting range. As an active NYPD officer, he'd been there more times than he could count for various firearms classes and recertification exercises, which usually had been in the mornings when it was always crowded. There were seven shooting ranges, of which six were for pistols and one for rifles, and the complex was used by not only the NYPD, but also the FBI, NYC Correction, New York Fire Marshals, and even ICE.

As he drove, his thoughts drifted back to Juliette and how the day had begun, including the aggravating visit to the ED. After the disturbing call with Roger Dalton earlier and finding out the cost of yesterday's visit, he wondered what the charges were going to be for today. Reluctantly, he assumed it would be equally as outrageous considering what he now knew about hospital business practices.

Facing at least an hour of downtime before arrival at Rodman's Neck, Brian thought it a good opportunity to check in with Camila to give her an idea of when he'd be arriving home. He also considered broaching the idea that he was thinking of rejoining the NYPD, as such a move would impact her life, though he realized it wasn't the best time. As for Juliette, he was relatively confident she was doing okay following the positive news about her behavior he'd gotten earlier. Surely if anything significant had changed, Camila or Jeanne would have called or texted. For that reason, it was shocking when Camila started the conversation by saying that Juliette's fever had returned.

"Good grief!" Brian responded with alarm. He sat up straighter, gripping the steering wheel. This was not what he wanted to hear. "How high?"

"Not high," Camila responded. "Nothing like this morning. It was 100.5."

"What made you decide to take her temperature?" he asked. He relaxed slightly, settling back into his seat. He wasn't happy about the fever returning, and it brought back with a rush his frustration that he'd been unable to get the ED doctors to do any kind of testing, even a simple blood count. Although he was the first one to admit he wasn't a doctor or a psychologist, his daughter's on-again-off-again symptoms bothered him, and he had a reluctance to ascribe them to being psychosomatic at this point.

"She suddenly had a visible chill," Camila said. "Both Jeanne and I saw it. When we asked her about it, she said she wasn't feeling good and wanted to go up to her room. It came as a surprise because she'd eaten well and was clearly having fun playing Dinosaur."

"What about her headache?" Brian said. The headache seemed to be the one constant symptom.

"Yes, she still says she has a headache," Camila said, "but that's it: no other complaints like sore throat or upset stomach. I asked her specifically. As for the headache, I thought it had improved given the way she was interacting with us. She seemed to be her old self."

In the back of his mind, he wondered what should be done if a high fever returned, vowing that there was no way he'd take her back to MMH Inwood. Briefly he considered taking her to one of the neighborhood urgent-care centers, but he nixed the idea because they wouldn't be able to do a Covid test and have the results right away. Instead, if need be, he decided he'd drive her down to Columbia-Presbyterian in Washington Heights, thinking that was probably what he should have done originally. "I've finished my meeting at the ESU Headquarters," Brian said after a pause. "I'm on my way to the NYPD shooting range for an hour or so. But I could cancel and come directly back home if you think I should."

"Not for Juliette's sake, if that's your thought. While I was taking her temperature, she got very sleepy. She's up in her room resting. I've just checked on her. I think we should let her sleep."

"Okay, fair enough." Preoccupied with this surprise news about Juliette, Brian decided against bringing up the issue of his possible return to the police department. "Call or text if there is a change in her status, and I'll come back straightaway. What about Jeanne? Is she still there?"

"No, when Juliette went to sleep about a half hour ago, Jeanne left. She did take the papers that your friend Grady Quillen dropped off. I hope that was okay."

"That's fine," he assured her.

After ringing off with Camila, Brian considered contacting Jeanne to get her take on Juliette, but he held off, thinking it might be best to first check on Juliette himself when he got home. He worried he was taking too much advantage of her generosity by contacting her so often; plus, if this was a medical problem and not a psychological issue, he wasn't sure she could add much.

As he expected, traffic did slow up considerably approaching the Whitestone Bridge to cross the East River, but then it sped up again once he was on the other side. All in all, he turned in to Rodman's Neck peninsula just about an hour later. For the next quarter of a mile, after passing a broad field containing a baseball diamond and a number of warning signs about unauthorized entry, he drove through virginal forested land that was almost as unexpected within New York City as was the wide-open expanse of Floyd Bennett Field.

Ahead appeared a guard gate similar to those on military installations. He pulled to a stop. Lifting his mask up over his nose and mouth, he rolled down the window and presented his NYPD ID to the friendly uniformed NYPD officer. There was no problem thanks to Helen Gurly's efforts, and Brian was permitted to drive into the shooting range. Reminiscent of Floyd Bennett Field, it was composed of a motley group of buildings, some in better shape than others and some reflective of their military origins. Like Floyd Bennett Field, Rodman's Neck had a history that included use by the armed forces, this time both the army and navy, although the facility eventually had been given over to the NYPD. Besides the shooting ranges there were also outdoor TAC facilities and even a biohazard safety level 4 lab, and at the far end of the peninsula there was an isolated pit for detonating bombs and other explosive devices like confiscated fireworks.

As he expected, the expansive parking area was nearly empty this late in the afternoon, allowing him to park directly in front of the admin building. Although he'd been mildly concerned about finding Captain Ted Miller of the Firearms and Tactics Unit, it turned out to be extremely easy, as the man was expecting Brian and was waiting for him just inside the entrance door.

"You just made it under the wire," Ted said. He was a mildly overweight man with a salt-and-pepper crew cut whom Brian recognized from having dealt with him in the past. "There's been no one using the rifle range for more than an hour and Mark Bellows, the range master, has been eager to close up shop, so we best head there first and then use the pistol range after. Is that okay with you?"

"Fine with me," Brian answered, thankful for the man's assistance.

Once he had been supplied with the required eye and ear protective gear, they used Ted's vehicle to drive the mile or so out to the rifle range. It was hardly an impressive physical setup and the immediate area looked more like a partially deserted dump thanks to a handful of abandoned vehicles and storage containers sprinkled about. Brian had used the range in the past, so he wasn't surprised. The row of connected shooting positions was constructed of rough-hewn, unfinished lumber that had grayed over the years and, taken together, looked a little like the starting gate at a horse racetrack. Ahead stretched a grassy field of more than three hundred yards facing a dunelike hill.

Sergeant Mark Bellows was a beefy firearms and tactics officer who looked somewhat long in the tooth and ready for retirement. He was friendly enough but clearly eager to leave for the day. "What distance are you looking to use?" he asked in a tired voice.

"I'd like to use all three," Brian said. He knew the range was set up for one hundred, two hundred, and three hundred yards, so he wouldn't have to use a range finder.

"Okay," Mark said resignedly. "Pick any firing position that suits your fancy and let's do it. I've refreshed all the targets, so you are good to go. Just let me know when you are ready."

Brian didn't care which position he used and just picked one at random as Ted and Mark stood back and chatted together. After getting the rifle out of its bag, he unfolded the stock and placed the gun on its bipods, using the rifle bag under the stock for added stability. Once again, he appreciated the mere appearance of the gun as a stunningly formidable weapon, particularly with its perforated handguard and suppressor. The fact that he knew it was reportedly deadly accurate close to a mile added to his sense of awe.

Quickly Brian used the cloudless sky as a backdrop to adjust the ocular so that the crosshairs visible within the scope were clear. Then he adjusted the focus on the side of the scope for the target at one hundred yards, opened a box of ammunition, filled the rifle's magazine with ten cartridges, and inserted the magazine into the underside of the rifle.

"I'm ready," he called over his shoulder.

"Okay," Mark responded immediately. "Commence firing."

Using the bolt handle on the rifle, Brian loaded the first round into the barrel chamber. The ease and the feel of this action impressed him. There was no doubt in his mind that he was using a precision instrument. Totally relaxed, he sighted through the scope and saw the target clearly. Using a very steady pull on the trigger, Brian shot a round and immediately saw the hole appear in the target slightly lower than he anticipated. After a minor elevation adjustment of minute of angle, he shot another round, and on this occasion the hole appeared exactly where he intended: dead center. The sound and the feel of the weapon were outstanding, far better than what he remembered with the Remington 700. Then in rapid succession he fired eight more times, emptying the weapon.

After quickly refilling the magazine with ten more cartridges, he moved to the target positioned at two hundred yards. Repeating the process, he found he didn't have to change the minute of angle to achieve equivalent and impressive accuracy. Moving then out to the three-hundred-yard targets, he again repeated the process, shooting ten more rounds and finding that he did have to make a very slight adjustment as he'd done initially.

Knowing that the range master was impatient to leave and concerned about getting home himself after hearing about Juliette's latest fever, Brian checked the gun's breech to be absolutely sure it was empty, removed the magazine, and called over his shoulder that he was done.

"Cease fire," Mark called out as if there were other people firing besides him. Then he added: "Wow, that was quick. Are you sure you are finished?"

"I am." Brian stood up and started to repack the Remington MSR back into its shoulder bag. Under normal circumstances he would have enjoyed continuing to put the gun through its paces, but he felt guilty about not getting home earlier. And he felt that with the thirty rounds he did fire, he could give Deputy Chief Comstock a definite thumbs-up about the weapon. In his estimation it was clearly better than the older model, but whether it was worth the increased cost was another question entirely, especially since he didn't know the details.

"Would you like to go downrange and retrieve your targets?" Mark asked.

"No, thanks," Brian said. "I could see what I needed to see through the scope."

From the rifle range, Ted dropped Brian off at the pistol range, telling him that the range master was expecting him.

At the range, he wasn't alone despite the lateness of the afternoon, sharing the facility with a half dozen other NYPD officers. As a consequence, he couldn't be quite so efficient timewise, as safety protocols had to be scrupulously followed. Still, Brian managed to go through a full box of fifty cartridges in relatively rapid order. After forty minutes, he was already on his way back to his car, having left the protective equipment with the range master. Climbing in after putting the Remington in the back of the Subaru, he forwent the opportunity to have either gun serviced at the gunsmith, which he'd usually done in the past. Instead, to save time, he planned on cleaning the pistol himself later in his basement, and as for the rifle, it had been used so little he doubted it needed any attention whatsoever.

As soon as Brian could, he put in a call to Camila. Although he hadn't gotten any call or text from her, he was still uneasy about Juliette. He was relieved when Camila reported that all was quiet.

"Is she still sleeping?" he asked.

"Last time I looked, about a half hour ago," Camila

said. "I have a feeling she's down for the night as soundly as she is sleeping."

"I'm on my way now," Brian said. "I'll be home in twenty minutes, tops."

"There's no need to hurry."

"Okay, good," he said, feeling some relief. "In that case, how about I pick up some Mexican takeout from Tijuana Restaurant on my way home?"

"That's a good idea."

"Why don't you call and order for the three of us in case Juliette wakes up?"

"Okay," Camila said agreeably. "What should I order for you?"

"I don't care," Brian said. He actually wasn't particularly hungry although Mexican food sounded good. "Just double up whatever you want."

"When you called earlier, I forgot to tell you that your mother and your brothers and sister stopped by after the funeral," Camila said. "I told them where you were. I hope that was okay."

"Of course," he said through gritted teeth. Hearing that his family had come by fanned his guilty feelings about missing the funeral formalities. "They're probably at my mother's. I'll call them when I get back."

"There was also another request about a possible security gig," Camila said. "It's for another potential December wedding. The info is on your desk with the other one."

"Okay, thank you," Brian said. He thought it mildly ironic that just when he was seriously thinking about go-

ing back to the NYPD, there'd been two requests for
security work after it had been so quiet. He couldn't help
but superstitiously wonder if such a coincidence was a
kind of subliminal message that he shouldn't be so quick
to abandon Personal Protection LLC.

Traffic was heavy and the driving slow, even stop-
and-go in places. Still mystified by Juliette's recurrent
fever, he changed his mind and decided to call Jeanne
after all. Although earlier he'd worried about calling her
too much and planned on waiting until he was able to
check on Juliette himself, he still felt comfortable enough
to get her opinion and perhaps ameliorate some of his
anxiety that was mounting the longer it took to get
home.

"How was your visit to the ESU?" she asked the moment they were connected, dispensing with any traditional hellos. She sounded happy to be hearing from
him, which relieved him of his concerns of calling her
too frequently.

"The visit couldn't have gone better," he said. "The
best part is that it made me feel even more inclined to go
back to being a cop. At the same time, ironically enough,
there've been a couple inquiries about security gigs this
very afternoon to muddy the waters."

"Serious inquiries?" she asked.

"That I don't know until I call them back," Brian
said. "Both involve possible December weddings."

"I'm not sure if you should count on December weddings," Jeanne said. "Especially with the coronavirus
spike that's expected."

"You're probably right," he agreed.

"More to the point, it sounds as if your visit to the ESU was a good idea."

"It was a great idea," Brian agreed. "I even got a chance to visit the shooting range, which I enjoyed just as much. I hadn't been able to do that for almost a year."

"Good for you," Jeanne said.

"Now to a more important topic: Juliette. I was distressed, to say the least, when Camila told me that her fever had returned, and I wanted to get your take."

"I'm not completely convinced it was a fever even though she had an obvious chill," Jeanne said. "It was only a tad over a hundred: certainly nothing like the 102 you saw this morning. But I'll tell you what surprised me more than the possible fever was how quickly her mood changed. One minute she was enjoying herself immensely, even giggling because she was doing so well with the board game the three of us were playing. But then it was like a shadow came over her face, and she seemed miserable. She didn't want to finish the game even though she was clearly about to win fair and square."

"That is strange," Brian agreed. "It's not like her at all. She's a competitive little thing." He audibly sighed. "I can't help it, but I think she's fighting something off. Whether it's a cold or flu or what, I don't know. Luckily it's unlikely to be Covid, with the way the symptoms come and go, at least according to the MMH ED docs. But I wish they weren't so quick to label them psychosomatic. It irks me to death that they refuse to do any testing, even a simple blood test, much less a Covid test."

"Well, in their defense, she certainly has reasons to have a psychosomatic reaction," Jeanne said. "How is she doing now?"

"Camila just told me she's still sleeping soundly. I'm actually not home yet. I'm stuck in traffic, but I'll be home shortly, and I'll let you know what I think if you'd like."

"Please do," Jeanne said. "On another note, I've had a chance to look at the list that your friend Grady supplied. Although we suspected as much, I'm shocked at the number of Inwood residents MMH has sued. It's unconscionable. It's like they want to suck every last penny out of this neighborhood. I'm looking forward to hearing some of the actual stories and putting together a real exposé. This can't go on."

"I agree," Brian said, but he wasn't interested in getting into a protracted discussion about MMH at the moment, as caught up as he was with Juliette's ongoing problems. And then as traffic began to speed up and require more of his attention, he told Jeanne he'd call her back after he'd had an opportunity to check on her.

Unfortunately, after loosening up, the traffic again quickly bogged back down, with some of the worst congestion in Marble Hill, just across the Harlem River from Inwood. By the time he pulled up in front of the Tijuana Restaurant, the trip from Rodman's Neck had taken over an hour rather than the twenty minutes he'd expected. Less than ten minutes later, with their takeout dinner in hand, he pulled into his driveway.

"Is Juliette still sleeping?" Brian asked as he entered

the kitchen and put the sizable bag on the table. Camila had come into the kitchen when she heard his car arrive and was getting out the dishes and flatware.

"To be truthful, I haven't checked since you and I talked on the phone," Camila said. "I've been in the office again looking at our books." She grimaced. "I do hope one of these inquiries materializes into a gig. It's not a pretty picture if they don't."

"Tell me about it," Brian said sardonically. "And the books are going to look even worse when I catch up with the house mortgage, which I should have done today. The longer I wait, the more chance the house will be at risk with the MMH Inwood lawsuit."

"Both callback numbers are on your desk."

"Duly noted," Brian said without a lot of enthusiasm. After his conversation with Jeanne, he wasn't optimistic that either wedding would take place. Although he was beginning to feel guilty he'd not mentioned to Camila the possibility of his rejoining the NYPD, he was loath to bring up the issue before he was more certain of what he thought was best for him to do.

With Camila busy unpacking the food, he climbed the stairs to look in on Juliette. Soundlessly he pushed open the door. With the blackout curtains closed, the room was filled with a dim half-light, just adequate enough to see the outline of her sleeping form but no details. Moving closer, he silently bent over for a better view. Now he could make out that she was on her back with her slender arms out of the covers and her right hand clutching Jeannot Lapin to her chest. As his eyes adjusted to the near darkness, he could appreciate the cherubic features of her face. To Brian she looked like the most beautiful child in the world, suddenly reminding him of Emma's verbatim adoration of her that fateful afternoon in Wellfleet, Massachusetts.

The sudden remembrance of his wife's words caused him to catch his breath. It had been just over two weeks since their fateful barbecue, but it seemed like a lifetime with all that had happened. Pulling himself together with some difficulty, Brian went back to observing Juliette, noticing with relief that her breathing was gentle and rhythmic.

Just to be sure and being careful not to disturb her, he gently placed the palm of his hand against her forehead to feel if it was overly warm or moist with perspiration. To his relief, neither was the case. Removing his hand yet still bending over her, he felt almost intoxicated by parental love and so very thankful that he and Emma had had a child so soon in their relationship. Although Juliette was without a doubt her own person, Brian felt she embodied an essence of Emma that would live on.

Straightening up, Brian tiptoed out of the room, carefully closing the door behind him. Confident her temperature was normal and that she was sleeping soundly, he felt a definite sense of relief. As the foundation on which he intended to rebuild his life, her well-being was by far his primary concern. As long as she was okay, he felt empowered to face the current challenges of dealing with the impending MMH lawsuit, deciding between continuing with Personal Protection or rejoining the

NYPD, and otherwise surviving the ongoing coronavirus pandemic. On top of all that, he even felt that by combining efforts with Jeanne, the two of them could possibly do something about the toxic healthcare system that was responsible for her woes, his and Juliette's suffering, and probably Emma's death.

CHAPTER 34

September 3

Brian awakened from a vivid dream he was having about effortlessly running through a landscape sprinkled with abandoned vehicles that was visually reminiscent of Rodman's Neck shooting range. As he opened his eyes, he noticed the streetlight sifting through the white gauzy curtains. As he held his breath to figure out what might have roused him from his deep slumber, he heard a car's tires complain against the striated pavement. Glancing around the darkened room, he also noticed the curtains were rustling from a soft breeze, but he couldn't imagine that could have disturbed his sleep.

Turning over, he glanced at the bedside clock, noting that it was 3:25 A.M. Rolling back, he stared up at the ceiling and again listened as the sound of the car out in the street faded, wondering if another mosquito could have gotten inside. He strained his ears for the characteristic whine, but heard nothing. But then he became aware of a rhythmic, distant thumping that he seemed to feel rather than hear. For several minutes his mind tried to place the disturbance, wondering if something could be amiss with the refrigerator or the washing machine way down in the basement, thinking perhaps Camila couldn't sleep and decided to do a load of laundry.

Unable to come up with an explanation, Brian turned over onto his stomach, putting the pillow over his head in an attempt to go back to sleep before his mind latched on to one of the many problems that had been making sleep impossible lately. Yet despite the pillow, he could still feel the thumping even though it was nearly subliminal. Angrily throwing off the pillow, he sat up and as he became progressively more and more awake, the thumping sound suddenly sounded all too familiar.

"No!" Brian gasped as he leaped to his feet. Clad only in his Calvin Klein pajama bottoms, he rushed from the bedroom, and dashed down the hallway into Juliette's room. Snapping on the light, he was confronted by his worst nightmare. Juliette was in the throes of a seizure, her back arching and her head rhythmically banging against the headboard. The image was all too familiar.

Screaming Camila's name, he rushed to the bedside and pulled Juliette's convulsing body away from the head of the bed. Her face was scrunched into a grimace, but most worrisome of all, her lips were startlingly blue. Quickly he rolled her onto her side, and saliva spilled out onto the sheets from between her clenched teeth.

Camila appeared in the doorway in her pajamas. As she caught sight of Juliette, her face metamorphosed into an expression of horror. "Should I call 911?" she shouted through the hand covering her mouth.

"There's no time," Brian shouted back, understanding too well that by the color of her lips, she'd been seizing much too long. "You'll have to drive us to MMH Inwood."

As he tried to scoop up Juliette, which he found extraordinarily difficult with the strength of her contractions, Camila disappeared. When Brian finally got the child into his arms, he found it equally as hard to carry her through the doorway and particularly down the stairs. Running along the main hallway on the ground floor and into the kitchen, he was relieved to see that Camila had left the door ajar for him. Outside, she had also opened the rear door of the car, and she was now in the driver's seat with the engine running.

Ducking headfirst into the car while clutching Juliette against his chest, he managed to climb in and collapse back against the seat. Holding the bucking child as best he could, he reached out and pulled the door closed.

"Go, go!" he shouted, making sure Juliette's head couldn't hit any surfaces as Camila rapidly backed out of the driveway and accelerated up West 217th Street. Again, when Camila turned left onto Park Terrace East and then right onto West 218th Street, Brian had to use all his strength to keep himself upright and Juliette's head safe.

Although the ride was just minutes, with Camila merely slowing at red lights instead of stopping, the eight-minute journey seemed to take a lifetime as he held his seizing daughter against his body. "Please stop, please stop," Brian murmured over and over again until Camila pulled up to the emergency entrance with squealing tires.

Leaping out of the driver's seat, Camila ran around the car to help open the door for him. It again took all of his strength to exit the car with Juliette in his arms. He then ran for the entrance, impatiently waiting for the automatic sliding door to open enough to run inside.

Despite the hour, there were more than a dozen people in the waiting room. Without the slightest hesitation, Brian ran directly up to the counter. Immediately one of the triage nurses, upon seeing Juliette's convulsions, waved for him to follow her back into the treatment area. Within seconds she guided Brian at a run into one of the Trauma 1 rooms.

"Put her here on the table!" the nurse ordered, patting the location with a gloved hand.

Brian laid Juliette down on the sheet-covered exam table, holding on to her lest her convulsions caused her to fall off onto the floor. To his relief word must have spread quickly because other medical personnel flooded into the room and pressed in around the table. All were dressed in scrub clothing. One youthful woman quickly asked Brian how long Juliette had been seizing.

"I don't know," Brian cried. "I heard a kind of thumping from my bed for maybe five or ten minutes and couldn't figure out what it was. How long it had been going on before it woke me up, I have no idea. Then it took about ten minutes to get here. I'm afraid it's probably been going on at least thirty minutes, though probably more."

"Okay!" the woman said quickly, redirecting her attention to the medical people in the room. "We need an IV immediately or intraosseous access. Start oxygen and an oximeter! We'll need an ECG and glucose and let's get a body temperature, BP, and intubation setup. Draw up four milligrams of midazolam. Let's go!"

As a flurry of activity erupted around his daughter, a nurse pulled him back and away from the table. Brian resisted, not wanting to leave Juliette. "I've had EMT training," Brian said in his defense.

"That doesn't matter," the nurse said. She handed him a face mask. "You need to leave! And you have to check in properly and provide the patient's name."

"She's been seen here several times," Brian sputtered while putting on the face mask. "In fact, she was seen here less than twenty-four hours ago. Her name is Juliette Murphy. Just look it up on your tablet."

"You have to check in at the front desk today as well," the nurse said evenly, trying to calm him down.

"But why?" Brian demanded. He knew he was beside himself and not thinking clearly. "I'm telling you, she was just seen yesterday by Dr. Arnsdorf, and Dr. Kramer the day before. Really, look it up! You can get all you need to know and then some." As he spoke, he was trying to keep his eye on Juliette over the nurse's shoulder. There was a lot of frantic activity, which encouraged him and terrified him in equal measure.

"What was found on those two occasions?" the nurse asked.

"Nothing," Brian snapped. "Nothing was found and

nothing was done. Both times we were here for more than three hours, and they wouldn't even do a damn blood test. They insisted her symptoms were psychosomatic. Obviously, they weren't!" He noticed more medical personnel arriving, enhancing the sense of a developing crisis and magnifying his fears. More urgent orders were called out, including a call for anesthesia and neurology consults.

"Do I have to call security?" the nurse asked calmly but decisively. Gently she urged Brian to move toward the hallway.

Finally, sensing the inevitable, Brian allowed himself to be led from the trauma room and then out into the waiting area. His last image of Juliette was a gaggle of medical staff hovering over her convulsing body. A few minutes later he found himself waiting to talk to one of the intake clerks. As he was waiting, the nurse who had urged him out of the trauma room returned with a set of scrub pants, shirt, and slippers. Despite his state of anxiety and irritation, he thanked her and immediately put the outfit on over his pajama pants.

When he finally got to talk to a clerk, he felt stupid even bothering to list Peerless Health as his health insurance carrier, but he did anyway. With that out of the way, he found a seat and tried to calm himself. As he waited, time dragged. Each minute was emotionally exhausting, and he tried not to think about what was happening back in the treatment room.

A short time later he was shocked to see Camila walk into the waiting area and search for him. He stood up and waved. Once she saw him, she came over, carrying a shopping bag.

"How is she?" she asked when she got close, her face creased with worry.

"I haven't heard anything yet but hoping I will soon," Brian said. "I'm surprised to see you. I didn't expect for you to come back until I called."

"I didn't expect to come back, either," Camila said. "But when I got back to the house, I remembered that you were in your pajama bottoms. So I got a pair of jeans, a shirt, socks, and shoes out of your room." She held up the shopping bag. "But I see they have supplied you with some hospital clothes, so maybe you don't want them. I can take them back."

"You're so kind," he said, moved by her thoughtfulness. "Thank you, but these scrubs will do, and I don't want to go through the angst of finding a place to change."

"Understandable," Camila said. Then, reaching into her pocket she added: "Oh, also, I brought your phone from your bedside table. I know I'd feel naked without mine."

"That I can use," Brian said. He took the phone and turned it on. "Again, thank you for your kindness. I don't know what Juliette and I would do without you. Truly." Despite the fear of not knowing what was currently happening with his daughter, he marveled at the luck of having teamed up with Camila. He truly felt she'd become like family given the way she clicked with Juliette, especially with all the crises they had gone through lately.

"It's been a mutual win-win," Camila said. "Do you need me to stay and keep you company? If so, there's a problem with the car. It's right out front in a no-parking zone."

"No, I'm okay," he said. "I'll call you when we are ready to come home."

"Do you expect Juliette will have to stay in the hospital?"

"I have no clue," Brian answered. He was trying not to think about the immediate future. "But given how serious it looked, I imagine so."

"It's probably best. I'll be waiting for your call."

Brian watched Camila as she walked back to the exit, wondering if he should have encouraged her to stay, given how unhinged he felt. As she waited for the sliding glass door to open, she turned and waved to him. Camila's question of whether Juliette would need to stay in the hospital was unsettling, to say the least. Since Juliette had never had a seizure and since Emma's EEE started with a seizure, the implications were now suddenly obvious to him. He had thought it was just a flu, but Juliette could have contracted the same horrible illness at the same fateful barbecue two weeks earlier.

With shaking fingers, he used his phone to pull up the Wikipedia article he'd found about eastern equine encephalitis back when Emma had been diagnosed. Scrolling to find out about the length of the incubation period, he felt his stomach sink when he learned that it could take between four and ten days for symptoms to appear, which is a rather large variation. From his EMT training, he knew that such an interval was based on statistics, meaning for some cases it could take less and in others more.

Still holding his phone but now staring straight ahead with unseeing eyes, Brian suddenly reluctantly acknowledged there was a very good chance that Juliette had been suffering from EEE the whole time, especially when he thought back to her multiple flu-like complaints over the previous ten days or so. Emma's illness had had a faster trajectory, but started out like the flu.

"God damn it," he murmured through clenched teeth. This sudden very real possibility not only terrified him, but it also made him wonder why it hadn't been considered by the doctors who had seen Juliette, especially since they knew Emma had died of EEE right here in their hospital.

Going back to his phone, Brian quickly searched to find out whether there was a blood test for EEE. Finding out there was only fanned the growing antipathy he had for MMH Inwood. Not only had the powers that be made him and Juliette wait more than three hours on each of their two visits, but they had refused to do any testing even though it could have been key to properly diagnosing and treating her.

Forcing himself to go back to the EEE Wikipedia article, Brian reluctantly reread with growing horror that a large portion of those patients suffering encephalitis as evidenced by a seizure or other serious neurological symptoms ended up with severe intellectual impairment, personality disorders, significant paralysis, and cranial nerve disfunction.

Suddenly he stood up with the urge to run back to the treatment room where Juliette was to shout out that she could very well have EEE. But he held up, realizing that making the diagnosis at that moment was secondary to getting her seizure under control. Not only could the interruption do more harm than good, it might get him thrown out of the ED, and he needed to be there for Juliette when things settled down. As difficult as it was, Brian held himself in check. He also faulted himself for not thinking about EEE when Juliette first complained she wasn't feeling well and for not specifically demanding the test. Had he insisted, it would have been more difficult for the two doctors to fall back on assuming all of Juliette's complaints were psychosomatic.

Instead of running back to the treatment room, he nervously paced back and forth. Sitting still and waiting was driving him crazy. A few people eyed him warily, but he didn't care.

The siren of an approaching ambulance caught his attention as it got louder and louder before trailing off upon arrival outside. A few minutes later there was evidence of a flurry of activity back in the ED's treatment area, but it soon passed.

Twenty minutes later and unable to stand the wait any longer, Brian hurried back to the information desk. Forced by security to wait his turn, he demanded to know how his daughter was doing and if the seizure had been controlled.

"What's the name?" a bleary-eyed clerk who was nearing the end of his shift asked in a tired voice.

"Juliette Murphy," Brian practically shouted angrily.

The clerk rolled his eyes at his tone before spending what seemed like an excessive amount of time on his monitor. Just before Brian was about to boil over, the clerk said, "There doesn't seem to be any information yet, but I'm sure the doctors will be out to talk with you soon. Next!" He tilted his head to the side to get the attention of the person behind Brian.

Hardly satisfied, Brian returned to his seat, beside himself with anxiety. Out of desperation, he took out his phone. He needed to talk to someone and for a few moments debated whom to call. It wasn't an easy decision, since it was now five in the morning. He thought first of Camila since she'd been already disturbed by the situation, but he hesitated, thinking she might have gone back to sleep and that she'd already helped enormously. He thought about his mother but was afraid she might make things worse by being more anxious than he. He thought about some of his ESU buddies, particularly those who worked the graveyard shift, but he nixed the idea, as he'd not spoken to them in months and they might be in the middle of a call. He then thought about Jeanne, whom he knew would probably be the best choice considering her background with children, yet he wavered.

Despite all his reservations about taking advantage of her and as a sign of his desperation, he impulsively called, especially because she was the only one who could truly sympathize with his problems from her own experience. While the connection went through, he winced at disturbing her sleep, and he struggled to think of what to say. After the fourth ring, he seriously considered disconnecting, but then she answered.

"Uh-oh," she said sleepily, the moment she answered. "This can't be good news."

"I'm sorry to disturb you—" Brian began.

"Don't be silly," Jeanne interrupted, already sounding more awake. "What's up? Did Juliette's fever spike again?"

"Worse than that," he admitted. "She's had a seizure in her sleep, a bad one. I don't even know how long she'd been seizing when the noise woke me up, but it might have been for a while."

"Mon Dieu! Where are you?"

"I'm afraid I'm back at the MMH Inwood ED," Brian said. "My least favorite place."

"How is she?"

"I haven't heard," Brian said, running a hand nervously through his hair. "We've been here about an hour. They haven't told me anything. They haven't even told me they've stopped the seizure. Nothing!"

"You poor man," Jeanne said with true empathy in her voice. "Would you like me to come and join you to keep you company?"

"Thank you for offering," he said. "That's a lot to ask, and besides, I imagine I'll be hearing shortly that she'll be admitted. I just needed to talk to someone. I'm sorry I woke you."

"Don't be silly," Jeanne chided. "I'm glad you called. And I'm going to come join you whether you want me to or not. Case closed."

"Are you sure?" Brian asked. He wasn't the kind of

person who normally asked for favors, and he considered self-sufficiency a virtue, but even he recognized he was particularly vulnerable at the moment. Besides, he didn't have the mental strength to talk her out of it.

"I'll be there in fifteen to twenty minutes," Jeanne said definitively.

With a bit of surprise, Brian found that she had hung up on him. Slowly he pocketed his phone, then bent over and cradled his head in his hands. He'd never felt quite so weak in his life, and as a consequence found himself praying, not in the way he'd learned as a child, but more as an attempt to bargain with a God he wasn't sure he believed in. He promised that he could learn to accept losing his wife and soul mate, but only if his daughter made it out of this unscathed.

Sudden yelling interrupted his thoughts, and he straightened up. The disturbance was coming from an obviously inebriated individual who'd stumbled into emergency with his business attire askew. Uniformed hospital security personnel responded immediately by emerging from their windowed enclave overlooking the ED entrance and the waiting room. The man was efficiently corralled and escorted to a separate section of the ED. After that, an expectant peace returned.

Brian tried to go back to his bargaining, but he found he couldn't after the drunken disruption. His growing worry about Juliette's condition was crowding out the possibility of any other thoughts. Twenty minutes later, Jeanne dashed into the waiting area, searching for Brian. He stood up and waved. The moment she spotted him, she hurried over. Despite the social distancing protocols and their short friendship, they embraced, holding on to each other to the point that Brian began to feel self-conscious.

"Sorry," he managed as he released her.

"No need to apologize," Jeanne said as they both sat down. "Have you heard anything?"

"Nothing at all," he responded. "I don't know why they're keeping me in the dark like this. It's torture. They could have at least come out and told me the seizure's been controlled but that they want to do X, Y, and Z. Hell, I'd understand. I'm all for testing. For all I know, they're doing an MRI or some other test that takes a long time. I just wish they'd let me know."

"We should hear soon," Jeanne said, trying to be encouraging.

"With her having a seizure like this, I'm concerned she got infected with EEE just like Emma, even on that same night. I read someplace that mosquitoes prefer female hosts."

"You're joking," Jeanne said.

"No, I'm serious. It's true. Female mosquitoes, which are the ones that bite, prefer human female type O blood. If Juliette does have EEE, it would explain all the complaints she's had over the last week or so, including the fever. What irks me to death is that when we brought her in here, not once, but twice, they never thought of testing her for it."

"That does seem surprising in retrospect," Jeanne admitted.

"It's more than surprising," Brian said. "To me it smacks of malpractice, especially when there's a good chance they didn't do any testing because I owe them so damn much money and they were afraid they'd not get paid. And that's on top of treating us like second-class citizens, making us wait for so long."

"Maybe it's best if we talk about something else while we wait," Jeanne said, seeing Brian's face flush and sensing his anxiety.

"As if I can think of anything else."

"How about talking about our upcoming investigation," Jeanne said. "I spent some time looking at your friend Grady's list. I counted the cases and there are almost five hundred Inwood families that have been sued or are being sued. Can you imagine?"

"Now I can. I used to think we as a community were lucky to have MMH here, but not any longer."

"It should be an asset," Jeanne said, "and it could be again."

"Maybe if . . ." he started. He wasn't so sure, not with Kelley and company in charge, but he didn't finish his thought. At that moment, both he and Jeanne saw two doctors emerge from back in the treatment area and head in their direction. They were both dressed in scrubs, although the male doctor was wearing a long white coat. As they got closer, Brian recognized the woman despite her mask. She was the one who'd called out orders back in the Trauma 1 room. Both had grave looks on their faces.

A new burst of worry propelled him to his feet, and

Jeanne followed suit as the two physicians halted about six feet away from them. The male doctor, with a name tag that said DR. ANISH SINGH, CHIEF OF EMERGENCY MEDICINE, spoke with a lilting subcontinent-Asian accent. He identified himself and asked if Brian was the father of Juliette Murphy.

"I am," Brian managed as his pulse raced. He could feel Jeanne clutch his arm.

Dr. Singh cleared his throat, obviously uncomfortable. "I'm very sorry to have to report that despite our efforts, your daughter didn't make it. We tried—"

With lightning speed and before the doctor could finish his sentence, Brian lunged forward, grabbed a handful of Dr. Singh's scrub shirt and coat from the front of his chest, and practically lifted the slightly built doctor off his feet. He yanked the man's masked face within inches of his own, all the while yelling over and over: "No! No! No!"

Jeanne tried to pull Brian's arm away without success. She was shocked by the suddenness of the assault and overwhelmed by his strength. Several security guards burst out of their windowed alcove and came running over. Everyone in the waiting room, clerks and patients alike, stopped whatever they were doing and stared at the sudden ruckus like a freeze frame in a movie.

"You people let her die!" Brian snarled through clenched teeth behind his face mask. "You could have made the diagnosis yesterday, but no, you didn't, you wouldn't! All because of money."

The two security men arrived, and they, too, tried to

break Brian's iron grip on Dr. Singh's clothing, but it wasn't until he let go that they succeeded. "Easy now!" one of the guards said.

While Dr. Singh calmly rearranged his shirt and jacket, he told the security guards that he was fine and that they should back off. Reluctantly, they let go of Brian, who was continuing to eye Dr. Singh with barely controlled fury. Jeanne regrasped his arm, although she, too, was aghast at the news and had trouble finding her voice.

"We tried very hard to save your daughter," Dr. Singh said. "I don't know what you are implying about money, but I can assure you that concerns about cost do not influence one iota of what we do with patients here in the Emergency Department, and they certainly didn't in regard to your daughter. We pulled out all the stops."

"I don't believe you," Brian snapped, causing the two guards to step forward once more.

Dr. Singh motioned for the guards to stand down. "You don't believe in the last hour we tried everything possible for your daughter? Is that what you are saying?"

"She was seen here yesterday and the day before," Brian blurted. "No diagnostics were done. Nothing, and it was probably because the hospital believes I owe hundreds of thousands of dollars. It should have been determined that she possibly had EEE like her mother, who died from it days before right here in this Emergency Department. And if that had happened like it should have, we would have known there was a risk for seizures. But no! Charles Kelley and his profit culture reigns supreme and no testing was done on either occasion."

"We have no idea of who owes the hospital money," Dr. Singh said. "I can assure you of that. We take all comers and treat them equivalently. As for a missed diagnosis, that concerns me, and I have already planned to look into it. Meanwhile I have to ask . . . do you want to view your daughter's body?"

Brian felt the strength suddenly drain out of his body. The instantaneous rage that had overwhelmed him moments earlier was replaced by a paralyzing sense of loss. There was no way that the daughter who'd become the bedrock of his life and lifeline of his emotions with Emma's passing could be taken from him, too.

"What do you think?" Jeanne asked softly. "Do you want to see her?"

"I don't know," he said weakly. "I don't know if I can take it, but I suppose I should."

"Do you want me to come with you?"

It took Brian a moment to decide. "Yes," he said at last. "I would appreciate it. Thank you."

With Jeanne holding on to his limp arm, they followed the doctor back into the treatment area and finally into the trauma room. A clean white sheet had been draped over the treatment table, covering Juliette's small body.

Dr. Singh stepped up to the table and grasped the edge of the sheet. He then looked over at Brian and Jeanne. "I want to warn you that by medical examiner rules, we don't remove various equipment like endotracheal tubes and intravenous devices until the body has been cleared by an authorized medical examiner investigator."

Neither Brian nor Jeanne responded audibly, but both nodded that they understood.

Respectfully, Dr. Singh slowly pulled down the sheet, progressively exposing Juliette's pale, fragile body down to the navel. As the doctor had warned, an endotracheal tube distorted her mouth. Intravenous lines ran into both arms, and ECG leads were still attached to her chest. For both Brian and Jeanne, it was a jarring, horrifying sight.

"Did she have EEE like my wife?" Brian asked, averting his eyes.

"The neurology consult believes she did," Dr. Singh said with regret. "To be sure we'll have to wait for the blood test to confirm it."

"Why bother?" he responded bitterly. "Isn't it a bit too late?"

"Yes, I believe it is too late," Dr. Singh said as he bowed his head. "I will leave you two. No rush. Stay as long as you would like." He turned around and walked out into the corridor.

Brian and Jeanne looked at each other, standing alone among all the high-tech equipment of the Trauma 1 room. His eyes brimmed with tears he'd been fighting. "I don't know why I didn't think of EEE, either," he managed between gasps. "I should have." He picked up the edge of the sheet and pulled it back over Juliette's body, unable to grasp how he had also been so mentally blind.

With tears running down her own face, Jeanne enveloped Brian with both arms and for several minutes they hugged in silence. "It's not your fault. You're not the doctor."

"I suppose," he said listlessly.

"You were correct about what you said to the doctor," Jeanne insisted. "Ultimately it is Charles Kelley's fault."

"Charles Kelley and Heather Williams," Brian added. "I'd be hard put to say who was more responsible."

Still holding on to each other for mutual support, they headed for the door leading out into the hallway, wondering where they could possibly go from here.

BOOK 3

CHAPTER 35

September 3

What are you going to do with her things?" Jeanne asked. She and Brian were standing at the open door of Juliette's bedroom, looking in at the disheveled bed. Jeannot Lapin was in a heap on the floor after apparently being batted off the bed during Juliette's seizure. Jeanne had been surprised when Brian suggested they make the visit the moment they had entered the house.

Without answering, Brian stepped into the room, picked up the stuffed rabbit, and then returned out into the hallway. As he did so, he closed the door behind him. "I'm not going to do anything with her things," he said. "At least not now. Maybe sometime in the future."

"Are you sure that is wise?" Jeanne said. "I could at least pack everything for you to get it out of sight. I'm afraid it is going to be painful keeping them around."

"That's generous of you," Brian said. "There's no need. I'm just going to leave the door closed, but I wanted to return Jeannot Lapin. I know it means something to you, otherwise you wouldn't still have had it." He held out the plush toy.

Jeanne took the rabbit and hesitated before responding. The day had been extremely painful for her, and she could only imagine how traumatic it had been for Brian. She'd grown fond of Juliette in the few days that she had known her, and realized it was perhaps that Juliette represented the daughter she'd wanted but never had. And now Jeannot Lapin would always be associated in her mind as Juliette's friend and not hers. "I appreciate the gesture," she said at length. "I hope you understand, but I'd prefer to let Jeannot Lapin remain with Juliette." She reached out and grasped the doorknob to Juliette's room, looking up at Brian but not yet opening the door. "Do you mind?"

"Of course not."

Leaving the door ajar for moment, Jeanne went into Juliette's room. After straightening the covers, she carefully placed Jeannot Lapin on the bed. Once back in the hall, she closed the door behind her.

"I'm sorry to have caught you up in all this," Brian said as they descended the stairs.

"Don't be. The best way to stop feeling sorry for oneself is to start feeling sorry for someone else. Losing a spouse is a terrible experience, I can attest to that. But losing a child is far worse. Would you like me to leave or do you want to talk or maybe sit in silence?"

"I'm not sure," Brian admitted. "But I don't want you to leave. That's for certain. I think I'd like to talk."

"Where should we sit?"

Brian shrugged. He was taking everything moment by moment. "I guess in the office."

As they entered, Jeanne noticed the bulky, strange-looking shoulder bag on Emma's desk. She couldn't make out what it was, partially because of the dimness in the room. The only windows of the former dining room were high and made of leaded glass. Most of the light was coming in through the archway leading into the living room. Preferring semidarkness, Brian had not switched on the chandelier.

"It's a rifle bag," Brian said as he noticed Jeanne peering at it. He threw himself heavily into his desk chair and groaned. On the day Emma died, he thought he had experienced the worst moment of his life, but the pain he was experiencing with Juliette gone was unparalleled.

"It looks odd," Jeanne said, bending over and looking at it closer. One end came to a protruding cylinder about the size and shape of the business end of a duster. "It doesn't look long enough to hold a rifle."

"It's a special rifle," Brian said. "It's a sniper weapon, meaning it is very, very accurate. In order to make it easier to transport, the stock folds against the barrel."

"My goodness," Jeanne exclaimed. "What they won't think of next." She sat in one of the several side chairs and, like Brian, groaned as she settled in.

Both Brian and Jeanne were physically and emotionally exhausted. Starting at 3:25 A.M. for Brian and 4:45 A.M. for Jeanne, it had been a long day—what felt like the longest day of his life.

The most emotionally difficult part had been in the

ED waiting to get the required paperwork done right after they had viewed the body. All at once, there had been a flood of emergency cases arriving by ambulance, including several early morning automobile accidents that had taken the attention of most of the doctors, nurses, and even clerks. To complicate the situation, just before ten o'clock Aimée and Hannah had arrived, both in a panic. From a call to Camila, Aimée had learned Juliette had had a bad seizure during the night and was in the ED. Aimée in turn had called Hannah and both had come directly to the hospital without phoning ahead. When they arrived, it fell to Brian to tell them that Juliette had passed, which put them both into a hysterical condition. As a result, Brian had to spend considerable effort to calm both of them, rather than come to terms with his own deeply broken state.

Luckily for Brian, Hannah eventually took control. Although she had been depressed since Emma's burial, this new tragedy caused her to regain composure, and she again accepted the burden of planning the next few days. At first Brian expressed some reluctance to go along with the full funeral procedure again after the experience of Emma's passing, but his reservations were immediately dismissed by Hannah and Aimée. Ultimately, he yielded to their wishes both because objecting would have taken too much energy, which he didn't have, and because he thought it would be selfish to deny them fulfilling what they thought was their responsibility. It was painfully obvious to Brian that they both were hurting and it was also apparent to him that the planning process was helping them deal with the horror of losing a beloved granddaughter.

Once the paperwork and other formalities had been done at the ED and the body was released, it was off to Riverside Funeral Home. Both Brian and Jeanne followed along but didn't say much nor were their opinions actively sought. In some regards it had surprised them that neither Aimée nor Hannah objected to or even questioned Jeanne's presence, since neither had met her before now.

From the funeral home it was on to the O'Briens', so Brian could tell Emma's father that one of his granddaughters had passed away and that there was to be another wake in their home. Why it had to be him rather than Hannah, Brian didn't question, but since Ryan was going to be paying, as Hannah had offered and as he'd done for Emma, Brian felt obligated to deliver the horrible news. It was only after that visit that Brian and Jeanne were able to excuse themselves and walk home to Brian's house. It felt like the calm after a wildly destructive storm.

"What would you like to talk about?" Jeanne asked after a few minutes of silence.

"I don't know," Brian admitted. "It's hard to concentrate. My mind and emotions are going a mile a minute."

"I'll tell you what I'd like to talk about," Jeanne declared. "I want to talk about feeling pissed that MMH Inwood and Peerless Health have essentially killed both our spouses and your beautiful child. Just sitting with you in the ED brought back the entire saga of my husband's torture and death like it was yesterday. There were more times than I'd like to count that we were forced to wait in that same waiting room while he suffered and ultimately died."

"We have a right to be enraged," Brian agreed. "In fact, I've never felt this deeply furious before. Well, that's not really true. I felt this way the day Emma died, but it's worse today. There was an ounce of doubt about whether the hospital was responsible for Emma's death, but there's none in respect to what happened today. They should have diagnosed Juliette and the fact that they didn't or wouldn't infuriates me. Psychosomatic? Please!" Brian's eyes darted around the room as if he was looking for something to destroy. "I want to break something. Anything."

"I know how you must be feeling," Jeanne agreed. "I can remember when Riley died, I had the same inclinations, and I'm embarrassed to say I did break some dishes. But it certainly didn't solve anything. Let's funnel this rage we're feeling into exposing this disaster by using the list your friend has provided us. The fact that there are almost five hundred cases possibly just like ours in Inwood shocks me. What does that mean for the entire city, or the entire country for that matter? This surely can't be an isolated phenomenon."

Listening to Jeanne had Brian trying to focus his anger. What she was saying was undoubtedly true, and the details of the one case that Grady Quillen had mentioned to him involving Nolan O'Reilly sounded as heartrending as his own.

"I think this could be a true media event," Jeanne continued passionately. "Especially if they question how the hell it has come to this in the richest country in the world. There's no doubt in my mind that the finger will ultimately point at the profit motive of private equity."

"And Charles Kelley and Heather Williams are certainly poster children for that culture," Brian added.

"What shocks me is that none of the politicians are focusing on this," Jeanne said. "There's lots of talk about healthcare in general, but not specifics about what the situation is doing to individual people like us and how Kelley and Williams and people like them can get away with what they are doing."

"My guess is that it's all about money, appropriately enough," Brian said. "I've heard in the past that the healthcare industry, mostly hospitals, health insurance, and drug companies, spend millions on lobbying to maintain the status quo. They like their profits and don't want change. It means giving big bucks to politicians on both sides of the aisle."

"Like how much? I'm sure that doesn't happen in France."

"Let's check it out," Brian said, eager to do something, anything. He turned on his monitor. After typing into Google, "how much per year does the healthcare industry spend on lobbying," he hit enter. In a millisecond the results flashed onto the screen. "Here it is! My God! Five hundred and ninety-four million dollars in 2019! That's more than one and a half million dollars a day. That's absurd."

"It's more than absurd," Jeanne said. "It's crazy. As I said, that would never happen in France, or anyplace in Europe for that matter. No wonder it's come to this point. Why is this bribing allowed? I mean, they maybe call it lobbying but surely in this instance it's pure bribery."

"As I recall, it has something to do with 'free speech,' which I personally think is ludicrous," Brian said. "It got turned into a constitutional issue. Whether we uncover five hundred stories as sad and tragic as ours, I can't imagine it would be enough to change this entrenched system, mostly because of the wildly extravagant lobbying but also because of the news cycle. It could be a big story and most likely would be, but then twenty-four hours later, it would be on to something else."

"Maybe we could dribble the stories out over time," Jeanne suggested.

"I don't think that would work, either," Brian said with some discouragement. "A handful of sad stories might get on page one the first day, but then subsequent ones would quickly get relegated to less prominent positions. It's the way the media works. A scoop on day one is often yesterday's lunch on day two."

"Does that mean you are giving up on the cases Grady Quillen gave us?" Jeanne asked, sensing Brian's pessimism.

"Not necessarily. But what we have to do is think up a way to give the story staying power, so that it evolves over time and maintains public interest."

For several minutes neither Brian nor Jeanne spoke as

they pondered. The news cycle was short, particularly in this day and age with the internet supplying instantaneous information 24/7. They stared at each other expectantly, hoping the other would come up with an idea, something to assuage their anger and sadness yet have enough staying power to effect change. But neither spoke until after a kind of visual pas de deux that involved their eyes drifting in tandem over to the bag on Emma's desk before coming back to stare at each other. Later they would question whose eyes strayed first, but they couldn't decide. It was as if the idea germinated in both of them simultaneously.

"You said the sniper rifle is very, very accurate," Jeanne said, breaking the silence. "What does that mean in terms of distance?"

"More than a half mile for most of them," Briand found himself responding.

"How about this one?" Jeanne said, nodding toward the rifle bag. "Does it have a specific name?"

"It's called a Remington MSR. And it is particularly accurate out to nearly a mile."

"Hmm," Jeanne thought out loud. "Call me crazy and desperate, but I'm starting to think of a story that would have real staying power and one that the media would devour as rightful revenge. Everyone loves a good revenge story, after all."

"If you are thinking what I think you might be thinking, I have to confess it crossed my mind, too. Especially when I was using the rifle yesterday at the shooting range."

"How easy would it be, if I may ask? I assume you have some idea, as a security expert."

"Very easy, would be my guess," Brian said. "And that's even with them wasting significant money on personal protection. I've seen Kelley's and Williams's day security people, and none of them impressed me. As kind of a joke, I even offered my services to Heather Williams."

Emotionally wrought, Jeanne and Brian stared at each other with unblinking eyes. "I can't believe myself, yet there is something utterly satisfying about the idea," Jeanne said after a few moments of silence.

"I know precisely what you mean," Brian said. "It's crazy on one hand but gratifying on another. It brings to mind the moment I learned about the Hammurabi code, or 'an eye for an eye,' back when I was in the fourth grade. It made sense to me then, even more than what I was learning in catechism on Sundays about turning the other cheek. And it certainly makes sense to me now."

"Is this something we could do together?" Jeanne asked with a gleam in her eye.

Brian looked at Jeanne askance, trying to gauge her mindset. "Are you offering?" he asked after a pause.

"I suppose I am," Jeanne said. "I mean, if you went ahead and did something on your own, by our even discussing it as we're apparently doing, I'm technically already a coconspirator."

"Well, I suppose we could do it together," Brian said, warming to the idea. There was no doubt that while dealing with his anger after Emma had died, he'd thought about getting rid of both Charles Kelley and Heather Williams, yet he'd dismissed the idea as a passing retribution fantasy even though he'd spent considerable time mulling it over. And now with Juliette's death, it had resurfaced but had been relegated to the back of his mind as repressed anger, waiting to be brought forward as Jeanne's comments were now doing. "There's no doubt it would be far easier as a team approach, especially if it involved dealing with an alarm system, since I trust you are up on all the latest technology." One of his fantasies had involved breaking into the executives' homes and confronting them directly.

"Unless something earth-shaking has appeared over the last year, I'm up to speed," Jeanne said. "Since it's obvious you've thought about this, what would hypothetically be the most efficient way to accomplish it?"

"Through very careful planning and preparation," Brian said firmly. "Both killings would have to happen the same evening or night, one after the other, for it to work. If there was a delay on the second one, even of only a day or so, that individual's security people might be on guard, making it more difficult. That's number one. Number two: We'd have to keep from being detained. Otherwise, we wouldn't be able to feed the media, and the search for us would be a big part of the ongoing story. That's what will keep it on page one for as long as we are at large. And three: We'd have to present a manifesto to various outlets of exactly why the assassinations were done to raise the story above and beyond the pure eye-for-an-eye, tooth-for-a-tooth revenge aspect. I'd like every hospital and health insurance CEO to live in fear that they could be next unless there is significant change to the system."

"How would we avoid being arrested?" Jeanne asked. "Surely your NYPD colleagues would figure out the whodunit rather quickly, particularly with a manifesto, and be after us, especially if we were continuing to try to feed the media."

"We'd avoid arrest by not being found," Brian said simply. "That's why our planning will have to include a sanctuary: someplace where it will be hard for them to find us, and when they do, their hands are tied."

"Like what kind of sanctuary? I don't understand."

"The same night that the killings are done or at least by the next morning, we'd have to leave the country. Probably the best place to go would be Cuba. It's close, easy to get there, and there are quite a few US fugitives living on the island whom the Cuban government refuses to extradite. Cuba loves giving the middle finger to the US government. Hell, we might even be considered heroes since we'd be able to give them the ability to prove that their healthcare system is a lot more equitable than ours, which it is, by the way."

"Wow, you have been thinking a lot about this," Jeanne said, clearly impressed by Brian's thoroughness.

"I confess I've spent many sleepless, angry hours pondering the idea," Brian admitted. "Just not all that seriously, I suppose. But I can tell you that with Juliette's assing and in my current state of mind, it doesn't sound so preposterous anymore. They ruined my life for their own personal gain, and they should suffer. I know that is not very Christian, but that's how I feel."

"Let me ask you this," Jeanne said. "If and when you have one of these lowlifes in your sights, could you actually pull the trigger? As much as I would ultimately like them to be gone, I'm not sure I could do it."

"That's a good question," Brian answered. "But I don't think I'd hesitate. In the line of duty, regrettably enough, I've had to make that decision in milliseconds when confronted by bad guys. I didn't hesitate then and each of those perps was responsible for one or two deaths. I'm certain that Charles Kelley and Heather Williams are in another league in causing deaths above and beyond our spouses and my child. On top of that, they've ruined the lives of countless others. So no, I don't imagine I would hesitate for a moment, especially if it might serve to expose and change the whole hideous system."

"Do you know anybody in Cuba?" Jeanne asked. She felt her pulse quicken. In her mind the discussion had definitely moved from the purely hypothetical to the possible.

"Not personally," Brian said. "But I know Camila has some extended family in Cuba who I imagine would be willing to help us if she were to ask. Obviously, I wouldn't even broach the issue with her until we were there. No one can know what we are planning, and I mean no one. Not even family."

"This is beginning to sound serious," Jeanne said.

"Am I right or are you still fantasizing out loud? B₌ honest."

"I'm not sure," Brian admitted. "But the more I think about it, the more serious I become."

"Which means you would be willing to give up your life here in the United States?"

"I've already lost what I valued most, my wife and my child."

"What about this house?"

"I'll deed it to Camila," Brian said. "If I hang around here, there's a good chance the hospital would get to repossess it through the courts. Without Emma and Juliette, it doesn't mean anything to me, and Camila deserves it. If she owns it, the hospital can't touch it."

Jeanne took a deep breath to organize her thoughts. The extent of Brian's planning had left her mind in disarray. She'd had her own fantasies about revenge, but over the year since Riley's passing, they'd faded. Suddenly, with Juliette's death, they were back with a vengeance. Just like Brian, she felt strongly that Charles Kelley and Heather Williams had ruined her life as she knew it, taking away her spouse, her savings, and her most recent livelihood all because of their insatiable personal greed. But when she thought about everything Brian had just said, her only hesitations were about Cuba. She'd been to the Caribbean with her husband on several occasions, and it had been pleasant enough for a week, but ultimately boring. The idea of spending the rest of her life there was daunting.

"I have another idea about a sanctuary," Jeanne said suddenly. "Are you open to hearing it or are you set on Cuba?"

"Of course I'm open to hear," Brian said. "Fire away."

"When we first met, I believe you told me your mother had gotten you a French passport when you were a child. Do I remember correctly, or have I dreamed that up?"

Instead of answering, Brian leaned over and opened the middle drawer of his desk. Reaching in and rustling through the contents, he extracted a burgundy-colored pamphlet and plopped it on the desktop. The front of the passport was embossed with gold lettering and an impressive seal. "Voilà," he said.

"Parfait! That means you are a French citizen."

"So?" Brian questioned. "You're not thinking we can sanctuary in France, are you?"

"Yes, I am," Jeanne insisted. "I assume you recall the saga about the film director Roman Polanski."

"Vaguely," Brian said. "I'm not much of a film buff, and I don't think I could name any of the films he directed. Why do you ask?"

"Do you recall that he's a fugitive from US criminal justice?"

"Now that you mention it, I do. What's the point?"

"The point is that France doesn't extradite its citizens to the US," Jeanne continued. "And Roman Polanski is living proof. He fled the US awaiting sentencing on five criminal charges, including rape."

"Interesting," Brian admitted. He immediately warmed to the idea of finding sanctuary in France. It would be immeasurably more rewarding on just about every conceivable level than being restricted to Cuba, especially a Cuban prison, which wasn't out of the question.

"I'm not a lawyer," Jeanne continued, "and we coulc still eventually be subject to arrest and prosecution, but it would be in France, not here in the US. In France I'm certain public opinion would be far more kindly in our favor. French people will be outraged at our stories. I certainly would have been."

"We'd still need to hide out, at least in the short run and maybe for a month," Brian countered. "How would that work?"

"We could hide out in Camargue," Jeanne suggested. "It's really off the beaten path, and my family has several isolated, deserted farmhouses that were acquired with large tracts of grazing land. One of them I remember isn't that far from one of the towns, called Saintes-Maries-de-la-Mer, which is close to the sea. It's actually very beautiful in its own fashion. Do you like to ride horses?"

Brian laughed in spite of himself. It suddenly seemed vaguely humorous under the circumstances to be asked if he liked to ride horses as part of a plan to off two healthcare executives. "That's something I haven't done much of," he admitted. "But I suppose I could learn to like it."

"My family has a lot of horses," Jeanne said. "It's the main way to get around in Camargue. I started riding when I was five or six. Regardless, I think France is our best bet. When the authorities investigate, it's going to lead to you, not me, for multiple reasons. First, your dis- appearance is going to ring all sorts of alarm bells, espe- cially given that you've just lost a wife and a child. And you have the skills and means. My medical horror story is old and won't draw any more attention than any of the other almost five hundred cases. And right now, since I'm not working and have lost my business, I could leave tomorrow, and no one would notice or care, except maybe for a few friends and Riley's family. But that will be easy to take care of, as I can just say that I've had enough of America, and I'm returning to my home country, case closed.

"So here's what I propose. On the evening or night in question we make separate air arrangements, so we're not associated, and we fly separate routes to some major European city, like Frankfurt or Madrid or Rome, just not France. I rent a car and pick you up, which ends your tracking, meaning Interpol won't have much to go on. And then we drive to Camargue. Until they find you, which isn't likely as long as we're discreet, I doubt I'll even be a suspected accomplice."

For a moment Brian was dumbfounded as he went over the details of what Jeanne had proposed. It was brilliant, and he couldn't help but be impressed. He'd been mulling over hypothetical thoughts like this for days, namely, how to keep the media enthralled enough to have a major impact on the healthcare system. But Jeanne had come up with a terrific plan of escape and sanctuary in minutes. "That's a great idea," he admitted once he found his voice. "It's perfect. Let's start planning and see how we feel. I imagine the planning process alone will be therapeutic for me."

"For me, too," Jeanne agreed, sitting back in her chair. "Where do we start?"

CHAPTER 36

September 3

Turning left off Broadway, Brian drove up the long driveway leading to MMH Inwood. He and Jeanne were in the Subaru. He had merely told Camila he was going out for a drive, which she had accepted without question. In many respects she was as devastated as Brian over Juliette's death and had been trying to help Aimée and Hannah with the plans for the wake.

"You know what a Maybach looks like, don't you?" Brian asked as they crested the small hill and the whole hospital and the modest, outside parking area came into view. When she had asked him how they would start, he'd told her that they had to find out where each target lived by following them home. They had flipped a coin to see who would be first, and Charles Kelley had won.

"I suppose," Jeanne said, but in truth she wasn't certain. She wasn't a car person. For her they generally all looked the same except that some were larger than others.

"Nope, it's not here," Brian said. To find Kelley's

Maybach, he had assumed they'd have to drive to the East Side, where MMH Midtown was located. Yet on the slight chance the CEO might have been on one of his relatively infrequent visits to Inwood, Brian thought the ten minutes it would take to check was worth it. Discovering he wasn't there didn't faze Brian, and he used the hospital turnaround to head back down to Broadway.

"How long do you estimate the planning stage will take?" Jeanne asked as they headed south on the Henry Hudson Parkway running alongside the Hudson River. "Now that we have officially started, I'm eager to get this done."

"It all depends on what we find," Brian said. "I'm relatively confident they live in the ritzy metropolitan areas of either Long Island, New Jersey, or southern Connecticut. And, frankly, the ritzier the better, where homes are widely separated from each other with expansive lawns and private outdoor sports facilities, like swimming pools and tennis courts. That's what I'm counting on. It would also be nice if their homes weren't too far apart to make logistics easier, especially since we're obligated to do both in the same night. But we'll have to take what we get."

"At least we have the rifle," Jeanne said. "That's the key piece of equipment, but I suppose you could always get one."

"It would not be hard," Brian agreed. "Whatever we do need, I'm sure I can get now that I've got access to ESU Headquarters. For instance, if we end up having to break and enter, they've certainly got all the assault tools we'd need. I'll feel guilty about taking advantage of Deputy Chief Comstock's hospitality, but this is important. Honestly, giving up the camaraderie of the ESU might be the only thing besides my family that I will miss after all this is said and done."

"What do you think the chances are that we'll have to do a home invasion?" she asked.

"No way to guess. As I said, it will depend on what their living arrangements are. But if we do, that's where your role will be key. Tell me this: If we do have to go into one or both homes, do you have the equipment you might need or will you have to obtain it?"

"I won't need much," Jeanne reassured him. "I already have a powerful eight-watt handheld radio that should do just fine."

"Really?" Brian questioned. "That's all? These people are pulling down multimillion-dollar salaries. They've surely been talked into expensive, elaborate alarm systems."

"No doubt, but expense aside, they all use the same technology, transmitting wirelessly to their base station or receiver. All I'd have to do is figure out the frequency and then swamp it."

"I don't understand, but I'm going to trust that you do," Brian said.

"I do," Jeanne affirmed.

Within just a few minutes they were able to cross Central Park, and ten minutes later had reached Manhattan Memorial Hospital on Park Avenue. To Brian's relief, it was obvious that Charles Kelley was still on-site, which he admitted had been a minor concern. His Maybach was parked in a no-parking zone right in front of the hospital's main entrance where patients were either dropped off or picked up, the same way it had been at MMH Inwood the day Emma had died. As an added confirmation, the same overweight chauffeur-cum-bodyguard was leaning up against the vehicle's passenger-side fender. As Brian cruised by, he could see that the man was smoking just like he'd been doing on their first interaction, looking as cocky as ever.

"That's encouraging." He pointed out the car. "There's Kelley's Maybach."

"Where?" Jeanne asked, turning around to look behind. There were cars all over the place, most double-parked with their hazard lights on.

"It's the limo right smack-dab in front of the hospital where there's supposed to be no waiting," Brian said. "You didn't see it? It's the only Maybach."

"The cars all look the same to me," she said as she continued scanning the area. "Oh, now I see it. The one with the chauffeur."

"Yes, that's it." He continued up Park Avenue for several blocks before making a U-turn. After passing the hospital again while heading in the opposite direction, he made yet another U-turn. A block away from the Maybach, he pulled over to the curb at a fire hydrant and turned off the Subaru's motor. "Now we wait."

Jeanne used her phone to check the time. "It's perfect timing," she pointed out. "It's after five, when executives begin to head home to their mansions."

He nodded. "Have you ever seen Charles Kelley?" he asked.

"Not that I know of," Jeanne said.

"He's got some height," Brian recalled, the man's image seared in his memory. "Sandy-colored hair and very tall. He'll stand out when he appears."

"I suppose this is a good car to follow someone without them knowing," she said.

"It's perfect," Brian agreed. "Completely nondescript."

"Do you think they'll figure out they are being followed?"

"It depends on the level of professionalism of the driver," he said. "Kelley's chauffeur, who is probably doubling as a bodyguard, didn't impress me, which will lessen his index of suspicion. A true professional has to think that at every minute the worst can happen. I imagine for us, if there is to be a problem, it will be when we get off the main roads, especially if Kelley lives in a particularly isolated area. The key thing is always to have a few cars between you and your mark if possible."

"That makes sense."

Timing turned out to be near perfect, and they didn't have long to wait for Kelley to appear. The chauffeur, whom they could see over the roofs of the intervening cars, suddenly stiffened, adjusted his hat—which had been tilted back on his head—and threw away his cigarette. In the next instant they got a very brief view of the tall, sandy-haired Kelley as he emerged from the hospital and in a blink of an eye disappeared from view, presumably ducking down into his limo. Brian responded by starting the car, saying, "Here we go."

He pulled out into the traffic but slowed as he neared MMH Midtown, to the chagrin of the yellow cab behind him. In a fit of displeasure and horn blowing, the cab pulled out from behind Brian and passed him, briefly slowing down as he came abreast to give Brian the finger before speeding off. The reason Brian was slowing was to make sure Kelley's car pulled away from the curb before the Subaru arrived at the hospital entrance.

"We've got to stay close until we're relatively sure where Kelley is heading," Brian said.

"I understand." Jeanne nodded her head.

Once the Maybach was clearly traveling north, Brian picked up speed to catch up. After going four or five blocks he added: "I guess we can eliminate South Jersey because they would have gone in the opposite direction toward the Lincoln Tunnel."

Jeanne didn't answer. She was holding on as best she could. To stay close to Kelley's car, Brian was driving aggressively.

It wasn't until they crossed over the Robert F. Kennedy Bridge and connected with the Long Island Expressway that he was reasonably sure where they were going. At each major freeway intersection, Brian had rapidly closed the gap between the Subaru and Kelley's Maybach to a single car, but then had dropped back again when it was apparent Kelley was not turning.

"So, we're heading to Long Island," Brian announced, ostensibly relaxing and allowing as many as four cars between them. Jeanne eased up on the death grip she had on the passenger handle on the Subaru's dash.

Forty minutes later they turned off the Long Island Expressway onto Community Drive. It was an area he was familiar with to an extent, having assisted the Great Neck Police Department on occasion.

"Now I have a more specific idea of where we are going," Brian said. "I'd guess Kings Point. It's certainly appropriately ritzy. Now it gets touchy. We're going to have to close the gap."

Luckily there was still considerable traffic, but it dwindled the farther out on the peninsula they drove. By the time they got to Shore Drive in Kings Point, the Subaru and the Maybach were alone. Since the road was relatively straight, Brian let a considerable distance intervene, and slowed when he saw the Maybach's brake lights go on before it turned off the road into a gated driveway. By the time Brian and Jeanne arrived, the wrought-iron gate was closing. He slowed to a crawl and stopped briefly. Looking through the gate, they could see a massive, relatively new, faux-Mediterranean home.

"It looks like an impregnable oasis," she commented.

Around the property was a reinforced concrete wall at least eight feet high whose top was embedded with shards of glass. Above the wall were coils of razor wire. "Appropriately enough, it looks more like a prison from out here than a home," Brian scoffed. "But I doubt it is as impregnable as it looks. The name of the road is encouraging."

"How so?" Jeanne asked.

"I'll show you in a second," he said. "Now that we have the address, let's check it out with Google Maps' satellite view."

After driving ahead for a hundred yards, they pulled over to the side of the road. Most of the homes were hidden behind high walls, fences, or vegetation. Brian got out his phone and used Google Maps to bring up the area on his screen. Jeanne leaned over so she could see as well.

"As I remembered, Shore Drive is literally a road along the shore, bordering Long Island Sound," he said while he zoomed in on the image of Kings Point, New York. He then pointed off to the right out of the car window. "All these houses along this side of the road are shore-front."

"Got it."

Returning his attention to the phone, Brian zoomed in more and used his finger to point. "And here's Kelley's house. Do you see it?"

"In all its glory. Rather large, I'd say."

"It is, and quite impressive. It's also encouraging for our purposes. It's got a swimming pool, a guesthouse-cum-garage, and a tennis court with what appears to be a basketball hoop. Obviously, Mr. Kelley thinks of himself as quite an athlete. And look at the size of the pier with a cabana at the end. Pretty fancy."

"But the wall?" Jeanne questioned. "Isn't that a major problem if we're thinking of using a sniper rifle?"

"That might be true if we were looking to shoot from the landside of the property," Brian said. "But from the waterside you can see it's a different story, which is why

I'm pleased that Kelley's property is waterfront. See how the wall ends at the water's edge? It's typical for security-minded people to spend lots of effort on the landside but nothing from the seaside. They don't want to block their view, which is entirely understandable. It's why they paid such a premium for the lot."

While they were concentrating on Brian's phone, they weren't aware of the car pulling up behind them until the police cruiser's emergency light penetrated into the Subaru's interior.

"Oh, shit," Brian murmured, glancing in the side mirror.

She turned to look out the back window at the police car. "What's the matter?" she asked nervously. "Is this going to be a problem?"

"Not in the short run," he reassured her. "But if it gets recorded, it's got me situated near the MMH CEO's house."

"Do you care?"

"Not necessarily, I'd just prefer it didn't happen." Brian got out the car's registration, his driver's license, and his NYPD ID in anticipation of the officer's arrival.

A few minutes ticked by. "What do you think he's doing?" Jeanne asked, continuing to peer out the back window.

"I'm sure he's calling his dispatcher," he said. "The Kings Point PD is a modest organization. I'm sure he's solo, and you're supposed to let dispatch know what you're up to."

A few minutes later the uniformed police officer got

out of his cruiser, put on his peaked cap, adjusted his gear belt, then walked up to the Subaru. Brian lowered the window as he came closer.

"Afternoon," the policeman said. He was an older gentleman with white hair and fleshy jowls. "May I see your license and registration, please?"

"Of course," Brian replied pleasantly. He handed them out the window, being sure to keep the NYPD ID on top, which the policeman immediately noticed.

"Hmm," he said. "Retired NYPD?"

"Yup," Brian affirmed. "Retired from the ESU not quite ten months ago to start a private security firm."

"Interesting," the policeman said. "Excuse me, but I'll be right back."

"What's he doing now?" Jeanne fretted as she watched the policeman climb back into his vehicle.

"Just checking if it all matches up," Brian said knowingly. "He's being appropriately careful."

A few minutes later the policeman got out of his car and returned to the Subaru. He handed back Brian's license, registration, and ID. "Sorry to bother you people," he said. "But the homeowners out here are sensitive about strange cars, particularly strange parked cars. They call us all the time. Are you lost? Do you need any directions?"

"We're fine," Brian reassured him. "Thank you, Officer. Just making our way home."

"Okay. Have a nice evening," the policeman said.

Brian returned the documents to their proper locations, pocketed his phone, and put the Subaru in gear. "I didn't see that coming, but it is a good lesson. You have to expect the unexpected in what we are doing. Regardless, I'd say we've made significant progress. Next up is finding out where Heather Williams lives. Once we have that, we can get down to business."

"How about we do it tomorrow?" she said.

"I'm with you," he said. "I need this. It will keep me from the reality of what happened this morning."

CHAPTER 37

September 11

As there was no place to pull over at the bed-and-breakfast Jeanne had found on Seaman Avenue just down the street from her former apartment, Brian had to double-park. In Inwood, as in the rest of Manhattan, double- and even sometimes triple-parking was a way of life. With his hazard lights on, he used his phone to text her that he was outside waiting.

It had been just a little more than a week since he and Jeanne had followed Charles Kelley's Maybach out to his fancy estate in Kings Point, and it had been an enormously busy time for both. They had continued their extensive and meticulous planning with progressive zeal and, in the process, became only more committed to exacting revenge on both Charles Kelley and Heather Williams. From a practical standpoint he attributed their efforts as the chief reason he'd been able to get through the immediate aftermath of Juliette's death. Had it not been for the considerable concentration that the planning involved, he doubted he would have been able to

emotionally weather the wake, the funeral, and the interment. Even so, it hadn't been easy by any stretch of the
imagination. During his appearance at the wake, he tried
his best not to look at Juliette's body, which he was
mostly successful at doing, and at the burial he kept his
eyes closed during the ceremony and spent the time going over in his mind all the contingencies he could imagine for the plan.

After Brian had left the wake at around two P.M., he'd
gotten in his car and picked up Jeanne from her apartment on Seaman Avenue. She had not attended the wake
since they had decided it best if they were no longer seen
together by his family and Camila, so she'd be less likely
to be implicated when all hell broke loose. By three they
had been parked by a fire hydrant on Sixth Avenue in
view of the building where Peerless Health had its home
office. As a reward for their patience, they'd seen Heather
Williams emerge at four P.M. sharp with her entourage
and climb into a waiting Mercedes.

As they'd started the following process, mimicking
what they'd done with Kelley, they'd made a wager on
where they might be going, with Brian favoring Green-
wich, Connecticut, because of Heather Williams's apparent love of horses, and Jeanne favoring the fancy areas of
New Jersey for the same reason. Both had turned out to
be wrong. When they found themselves again heading
out to Long Island, they started to entertain the hope
that the two like-minded executives lived in the same
very wealthy town, which would make things a lot easier.
But that had not turned out to be the case, as they'd sped

past both turnoffs from the Long Island Expressway that led out to Kings Point.

Instead, the Mercedes had left the expressway and then headed north on the way out to the second north-facing Long Island peninsula. It had turned out that Heather Williams lived in Sands Point, essentially across the Manhasset Bay from Charles Kelley's house, reminding Brian of the fictitious East Egg and West Egg of F. Scott Fitzgerald's novel *The Great Gatsby*. As such, it was just as convenient as if they lived in the same town and maybe more so because Heather Williams's house was also waterfront property. The difference was that Heather's mansion was on a significantly larger plot of land that included a stable and a fenced-in paddock, which they had been able to discover by looking at satellite maps. Neither could be seen from the road. Like Kelley's house, the property had a wireless controlled gate, a surrounding wall, a swimming pool, and a lengthy pier.

Brian's phone chimed, indicating he'd gotten a text message. When he checked it, he saw that Jeanne was on her way down. Accordingly, he got out of the car and opened up the back. The rear seats were down to provide more storage space, and a blanket covered what was there. Brian pulled the blanket aside for Jeanne's things. Already present was his luggage, the rifle bag with the Remington MSR, assault tools he'd borrowed from the ESU Academy, night-vision goggles, a ketamine dart pistol, rope, a window anchor for rapid escape, his P365 Sig Sauer fitted with a different barrel and a suppressor, and a few other sundries he thought he might need. In his luggage was his French passport and as much cash as he could amass without causing undue alarm. For clothes he was wearing his black ESU tactical uniform but stripped of any markings.

As he waited, Brian called on all his extensive experience as an ESU officer about to initiate a dangerous mission to keep his emotions in check. He knew all too well how important it was to maintain a clear mind so as not to make inadvertent, silly mistakes. Part of it was to control his breathing and even heart rate, but most important was to keep his attention homed in on the details of the plan.

Jeanne appeared at the heavy glass art nouveau door to the six-story apartment building that housed the bed-and-breakfast she had booked when she moved out of her rented apartment, having given away what furniture and household equipment she had. Seeing she was struggling with a large shoulder bag, a roll-on suitcase, and another sizable valise, he rushed to help. As he had requested, she, too, was dressed in dark clothing.

"Let me help," Brian offered after pulling the glass entrance door completely open. He took the valise, which was a good deal heavier than he anticipated. "What's in this?" he questioned with a quizzical chuckle.

"Books I can't live without," she answered with a laugh of her own, though he could tell by her movements that she was on edge more than he.

They got Jeanne's things into the back of the car, and Brian replaced the blanket that served as a tarp. They were planning on leaving the car for a number of hours and didn't want to invite a break-in. Luckily it would be in a safe, supervised place.

A few minutes later they were heading north on Broadway en route to City Island, New York, part of the Bronx. Six days earlier they'd rented a black inflatable Zodiac boat with a forty-horsepower outboard motor, a mooring slip, and fishing gear from Butler Marine.

"I can't believe we're really doing this," Jeanne admitted, trying to get herself to relax now that they were underway. "Is this really happening after all this planning and preparation?"

"I hope so," he said, also coming to terms with the fact that his life as he knew it was about to be over.

"Are you as angry now as you were the day Juliette died?"

"Even more so," Brian said. "The more we learned about the lifestyle of these extortionists, the more outraged I've become. I've lost everything I love and cherish while they wallow around in their swimming pools. And to add insult to injury, MMH is still dragging its feet after all that has happened just to provide Megan Doyle with a full copy of the hospital bill."

"I feel the same way," Jeanne agreed.

"Of course, things can still go awry despite our planning," Brian cautioned. "There could be unexpected glitches, but everything is looking good, including the weather. Luckily both Kelley and Williams are such creatures of habit, which makes it possible for everything to fall into place."

The first thing that they had done after discovering

where the two executives lived was to rent the Zodiac
boat on City Island, a mere two miles across the Long
Island Sound from both locations. They'd then spent the
next four days supposedly fishing in and around Manhasset Bay armed with a pair of powerful binoculars. Since
they weren't using any bait, they didn't have to deal with
actually catching any fish. Instead, they were able to
study both mansions, noting, as Brian had suspected,
that there were no walls or fences on the waterside of
either property. Despite constantly moving from place to
place to avoid being at all suspicious, they'd quickly
learned that both executives adhered to predictable
workday schedules upon their arrivals at home.

Although Heather Williams lived a bit farther from
Manhattan than Charles Kelley, she was the first to arrive
home, at five o'clock. When she got there, the first evidence was several dark-suited men who walked the
grounds, even checking inside the substantial sailing
yacht tied to the long, massive pier. A few minutes after
they left the scene, she appeared in a riding outfit along
with several beagles. With the dogs frolicking along beside her, she walked across the paddock to her nearby
stable, where she was greeted by a stable hand. A half
hour or so later she reappeared mounted on a horse. For
the next hour, she exercised the horse in the paddock at
varying speeds, even doing a few jumps. An hour later
she was in the pool, swimming laps. Having watched this
program over a few days, they understood it as her daily
warm-weather routine while in residence in her Sands
Point mansion. Online, Jeanne had learned that she

spent July and August at her house in the Hamptons with her horses, often playing polo at the Meadowbrook Polo Club. All in all, from Brian's perspective, he was encouraged that both the riding and the swimming would offer multiple opportunities for a sniper shot.

Charles Kelley's routine was somewhat similar, although on arrival he did a cursory property check himself, accompanied by his liveried driver. A half hour later they both re-emerged onto the terrace, one from within the house and the other from around the side, both dressed in T-shirts, shorts, and high-top sneakers. Since the driver didn't come from inside the house, Brian assumed he lived on the premises but in the guesthouse. He recognized that the driver's presence would need to be taken into consideration if a home invasion became necessary.

After reappearing in athletic gear, both Charles and his driver proceeded to the tennis court. They didn't play tennis but rather played one-on-one basketball, during which Charles invariably prevailed by a wide margin. In contrast to Heather Williams's solitary riding routine and its favorability for a sniper shot, Charles Kelley's basketball playing was not ideal, not only because he wasn't alone, but because the court was surrounded by a metal chain-link fence. As Brian explained to Jeanne, trying to target through the fence could be a problem, since there was a substantial probability that a bullet would be deflected, potentially wounding the target instead of killing him.

The most disappointing aspect of Charles Kelley's routine, as they observed on the first day, was that after his basketball triumph, he didn't swim solitary laps like

Heather Williams in his Olympic-sized pool as they had hoped. But it was a good thing they had been patient and stayed while the sun set because Charles had eventually reappeared. To their surprise he suddenly emerged out of a Moorish arched door onto a second-floor balcony, and what surprised them even more was that he was naked save for a towel casually thrown over his shoulder. Later, thanks to the floor plans they had obtained online from the Kings Point Building and Assessor's Office, they learned that the door led out from a master bedroom/bath complex. While they watched him on that first occasion and on subsequent evenings, Charles Kelley always took lengthy outdoor showers. Thanks to his significantly above-average height, he was visible from mid-thorax to the crown of his head the entire time—a perfect setup for a sniper shot.

"I hope you remembered your French passport," Jeanne said half in jest and half to break the tense silence as they turned onto the Cross County Parkway, heading east. In contrast to his practiced calmness, she was a ball of nerves.

"I remembered mine," Brian said. "I hope you brought yours, too."

"No problem for me. I'm bringing everything I still own. You are the one leaving an entire house full of furniture, an extended family, all your personal stuff, and a lifetime behind."

It was true. The last few days had been hectic for him, trying to get everything done, including signing the new deed to transfer the house to Camila and sign over the

car as well. Luckily Patrick McCarthy had been willing
to help, since he wrongly assumed it was merely a private
deal that Brian had arranged with Camila to keep the
house from the hands of MMH Inwood via their subsid-
iary Premier Collections.

With the major assets out of the way, Brian then tried
to decide what to bring with him as souvenirs of his past
life. Ultimately, he settled on just taking some clothes
and nothing else. The mere process of trying to decide
on more personal things had evoked too much pain and
even more anger in him. The only thing he was going to
miss was his family and some of his NYPD buddies,
though he was confident he'd be seeing them sometime
in the future.

The plan that they had settled on, provided things went
as they envisioned that day, was for him to take Jeanne
directly to JFK Airport, where she was scheduled to take
one of the last flights of the night heading to Europe. It
was a Turkish Airlines flight to London. From there she
was scheduled to go on to Frankfurt, Germany, where she
would pick up a rental car. Brian was to go from dropping
Jeanne off at JFK to Floyd Bennett Field in order to return
the Remington plus the equipment he'd borrowed from
the ESU Academy. He was then to drive out to Newark
Airport where he was scheduled to take a morning Delta
flight to London. From there he was to also connect to
Frankfurt, where he and Jeanne would meet up and drive
to the South of France.

Ten minutes later they were heading south on the
Hutchinson River Parkway, and Jeanne again broke the

silence. "What do you think are the chances we'll need to break into one or both houses?"

"I'm counting on the chances being relatively small," Brian said. "Both Kelley and Williams strike me as mildly obsessive-compulsive creatures of habit, as we've observed. If there is to be a break-in, it will be at Charles Kelley's and only if he fails to follow his normal outdoor shower routine. You've remembered your handheld two-way radio, right?"

"Of course." She patted the shoulder bag on her lap. "And one for you, too, so that we can communicate if need be."

"Good idea," he said.

One of the first things they'd done after determining where each executive lived was to go by the homes the following morning so that Jeanne could figure out the frequencies of their respective wireless security systems. She'd done it with her laptop when the outer gates had opened and closed for a delivery. She had explained that by dialing in the frequency on her radio, she would be able to swamp the respective systems, making it possible if need be for her and Brian to walk in their front doors without being detected and deal with any indoor motion detectors. She reminded him that the key thing that she'd have to remember was to let her radio stop transmitting for a second or two every so often to keep the central alarm system from recognizing it was being artificially overwhelmed. Brian wasn't sure he understood, but was confident that she knew what she was doing.

"I know it sounds silly considering what we are planning to do," Jeanne said, speaking up yet again after a few more miles of silence. Although he was pensive under the circumstances, as accustomed as he was to anticipating action and controlling his emotions, she had a nervous urge to talk. "But I'm glad we learned that both of them had been recently divorced."

"I know what you mean," Brian agreed.

During their intense, weeklong investigation of Heather Williams's and Charles Kelley's habits, they had learned a number of unexpected things, some of which were encouraging for what they were planning to do. They discovered that prior to the coronavirus pandemic both executives had undergone messy and rather public divorces, during which custody of the involved children had been awarded to the respective former spouses, none of which surprised them. This information bolstered the impression Brian and Jeanne had that Heather and Charles were grossly egotistical, greedy, unempathetic, narcissistic people, and accordingly bad parents.

A few minutes later they drove across City Island Bridge and turned onto City Island Avenue, a straight-shot street that ran due south the entire length of City Island. It was now slow going because of traffic, both vehicular and pedestrian, made worse by numerous double-parked cars and a series of traffic lights.

"I like this neighborhood," Jeanne commented as they passed numerous hole-in-the-wall restaurants, all of which had expanded their outdoor dining onto the sidewalk and into the street due to the pandemic restricting their indoor seating. "It feels authentic and reminds me of parts of the Jersey Shore, with a kind of run-down but charming honky-tonk feel." The architecture ran from ramshackle modern to bastardized Victorian.

Brian was preoccupied and didn't answer. At this point of the journey, it was taking longer than he'd planned, as they had never driven the length of City Island Avenue in the afternoon. It was now almost four-thirty, and he wanted to be in position at least by five, when Heather Williams would arrive home. The plan was to wait until after the security people had done their daily sweep of the grounds before he would take up his intended position within a group of dark green Adirondack chairs grouped at the end of Heather Williams's pier. His intention was to shoot supine, using the chairs as cover. Jeanne was to remain in the Zodiac beneath the pier alongside the sailing yacht to be prepared for a fast getaway if it was necessary. A similar strategy was to be used at Charles Kelley's, only there Brian was going to take advantage of being able to shoot from within the cabana, which offered significantly more cover.

"Jesus Christ!" Brian complained, losing a bit of his composure as they were forced to wait behind a pickup truck double-parked outside of the Original Crab Shanty. There was no break in the line of cars coming from the opposite direction.

"Are you getting nervous?" Jeanne asked, glancing in his direction.

"Only time-wise," Brian admitted. "I hope we haven't planned this too tightly."

Finally, there was a break in the incessant oncoming

traffic, allowing Brian to skirt the truck blocking the road. He quickly accelerated but then immediately had to stop for a traffic light that inconveniently turned red.

"I think we are good," she reassured him. "We're almost there."

Jeanne was correct, and they were able to pull into Butler Marine just a few minutes later. It was on the opposite, east side of the street such that the marina faced out toward Hart Island. Traversing the parking lot, he drove as close as he could to the base of the dock, which was home to the slip where their Zodiac slowly bobbed. Once there he quickly did a three-point turn and backed up as close as he could.

"Okay," Brian said, jumping out of the car. "Let's get her loaded up quickly. No turning back now." They gave each other a look of agreement.

Along with some of the fishing gear and several canoe paddles, Brian gingerly picked up the bag containing the Remington MSR and slung it over his shoulder. Jeanne gathered up the rest of the fishing gear, and the two of them walked out to the boat without attracting any undue attention from the half dozen or so people attending to their boats farther out on the dock. While Jeanne climbed on board to stow everything and make ready, he went back to the car to get the equipment he'd borrowed from the ESU if a home invasion became necessary, including the ketamine dart pistol. The dart gun was in case they had to deal with Charles Kelley's two pit bulls, which they had learned about during their extensive reconnaissance.

With everything shipshape in the Zodiac and the outboard idling, Brian went back to the Subaru, pulled the blanket back over their luggage, and moved the car to park as close as possible to the marina's office. He thought that would be the safest place in the lot because the office was open until eleven P.M. with people coming and going. At that point of the venture, a theft of their luggage would be an unqualified disaster.

"Are you happy time-wise now?" Jeanne questioned nervously once they were underway and heading out through the marina's rather elaborate dock system. Following the rules, he had the boat going at a very slow speed to avoid any wake.

"We're good," Brian said, knowing that the distance between the marina and Heather Williams's pier was just a little more than two miles. Since there was little wind and no waves or chop, crossing the Sound into Manhasset Bay would only take five to ten minutes.

Once out in the open water, Brian pushed the boat's throttle forward and let the forty-horsepower engine do its thing. With the resultant noise and stiff breeze, conversation was near impossible. Instead of trying to converse, they both mused privately about what the next few hours would bring. At the same time, they couldn't help but appreciate the near-perfect late summer day and the salty smell of the sea. And once they cleared the southern tip of City Island and were in open water, they could admire the impressively jagged skyline of Manhattan along the horizon off to their right. Had the circumstances been different, they might have even enjoyed themselves.

Entering the mouth of Manhasset Bay, he cut back on the throttle, and the boat rapidly slowed and settled into the water. There were a few fishermen in view, and the last thing that Brian wanted to do was draw attention to themselves by potentially irritating anyone. Several hundred yards out from the tip of Heather Williams's pier, Brian turned off the engine completely. He handed one of the fishing rods to Jeanne and picked one up himself. They both dropped their weighted lines into the water on opposite sides of the boat and pretended to be fishing.

Thanks to the prevailing westerly breeze, they were drifting directly toward their ultimate target. About a hundred yards away from the pier, he tossed out the anchor and the boat's westward drift slowed dramatically. It was now five o'clock. Pretty much on schedule, the security people appeared, meaning Heather had arrived at home, and Brian and Jeanne watched as they followed their established routine of inspecting the grounds, the pool house, and the sailboat. As he watched one of them board the vessel, he wondered if there'd been a problem in the past with the yacht, perhaps a homeless person taking up residence or something of that nature to explain its invariable inclusion in their rounds.

Most important, they never gave any heed to Brian and Jeanne while doing their security check. If they were at all concerned about a couple of people fishing a hundred yards or so off the end of the pier, they didn't let on. Brian was mildly surprised but gave them the benefit of the doubt since they weren't the only fishermen in the area. Once the security men were on their way off the pier, essentially finishing their inspection, he quickly pulled the anchor. In response, the boat's westward drift recommenced.

By the time Heather appeared from inside the house decked out in her riding gear, which comprised a tattersall vest, a black velveteen riding helmet, and a pair of white, form-fitting riding breeches, Brian and Jeanne were close enough to the pier for the deck to restrict their view. Depending on the tide, the pier could be as much as seven feet off the surface of the water, but at the moment it was about six. Although they couldn't see the beagles, they could hear them in their excitement as Heather followed her normal routine, heading for the stable.

As close as they were to the pier and wanting to avoid being seen by neighbors, Brian and Jeanne snatched up the paddles and quickly moved the Zodiac under the pier's expanded T-shaped end. Shaded from the sun, it was like entering a forest of pressure-treated pilings with the deck above serving as the forest's canopy. Speaking curtly in hushed tones and using mostly gestures, Brian directed Jeanne to help turn the Zodiac around and then hold it in position facing out into the bay in case a fast escape was necessary. As they had earlier decided, Jeanne would be staying in the boat.

With care, he then removed the Remington from its protective cover. Before he'd left home, he'd readjusted its telescopic sight from its three-hundred-yard setting back to the hundred-yard setting, which was the distance Brian estimated from the end of the pier to the waterside edge of the paddock. All he had to do to the gun was unfold the stock and secure it since he'd already made all the other adjustments prior to his visit to Rodman's Neck. He then handed the readied rifle to Jeanne while he climbed out of the boat and moved around to the outside of the ladder. When he was in position, she handed him the rifle.

"Bonne chance," she whispered, giving his arm a squeeze.

After flashing Jeanne a thumbs-up, Brian carefully made his way up the perfectly vertical ladder. While holding the rifle in his left hand, it was a difficult process and would have been far easier if the gun had a shoulder strap. It required hugging the ladder with his body and sliding his right hand up its side between each step.

Finally gaining the deck, he immediately crouched down among the gaggle of Adirondack chairs while he slowly and silently rearranged them to form an outward-facing U. He made sure there was ample space for him to lie supine in the middle. After being in the relative darkness beneath the deck, he now had to squint against the bright, late afternoon sunlight. Once he was happy with the chair placement, he lay down, facing in toward land. Carefully he advanced the barrel of the rifle beneath the chair that formed the base of the U and set it on its bi-pod. After making himself comfortable, he leaned against the cheek-rest and sighted through the telescopic sight. Using the bolt action, he loaded a shell into the firing chamber.

Since Heather Williams had yet to appear from inside

the stable, Brian used the time to scan around the swimming pool with the aid of the telescopic sight. If a paddock shot proved unacceptable for some unexpected reason, he wanted to have a plan for the pool. While he was so occupied, he saw Heather appear out of his left eye already mounted and coming toward him. Quickly he moved the gun to bring her image into the telescopic field. As was her normal routine, she started out at a walk coming toward him and moving clockwise around the paddock. Later she would trot, and canter, and even gallop. Since this walking entailed the least up-and-down movement, Brian was eager to make the shot quickly. As for the velveteen riding helmet, he was mildly concerned about what it might do to the bullet. Instead of taking any risk for a deflection, he decided to target just below the helmet from the rear, aiming for the brain stem. As he waited, she reached the curve and began turning to her right. The dogs at this point were considerably out in front of her in their eagerness.

With some difficulty but benefitting from experience, he maintained his breathing at a calm pace although he was conscious his pulse had quickened. All of their planning came down to mere moments. Without moving any other muscle in his relaxed body, he slipped his right index finger within the trigger guard and gently connected with the trigger. Through the telescopic sight, he followed Heather Williams's progress on the turn as well as her methodical up-and-down movement. Soon he was observing her profile, and then as she began to turn away, he increased the pressure on the trigger while lin-

ing up the crosshairs on the base of the woman's skull.
At just the right moment, he made the shot. With the
suppressor there was just a thumping hiss with the recoil.
By reflex he used the bolt to rapidly eject the used car-
tridge and reload. But a second shot wasn't necessary.
Heather Williams fell off the horse with such suddenness
the horse didn't interrupt its walking even though it was
now riderless.

A quick check of Heather's body with the telescopic
sight confirmed no movement whatsoever. Knowing he
had no time to lose, Brian pulled the rifle back from
beneath the Adirondack chair and pocketed the empty
casing. He quickly scampered over to the ladder and in a
repeat of how he'd climbed up, he descended. A moment
later he handed off the rifle to Jeanne.

"How did it go?" she asked in a forceful whisper.

He flashed another thumbs-up as he boarded the Zodiac. Quickly he started the outboard engine, put the
boat in gear, and steered out from under the deck. After
going some fifty feet, both he and Jeanne looked back.
The horse and the dogs could be seen at the far end of
the paddock, where the horse had stopped to eat the
grass. Heather Williams in her tattersall vest and white
breeches was still in the exact position she'd been when
she'd tumbled to the ground.

It was Jeanne's turn to give Brian a thumbs-up as he
increased the speed to a no-wake fast walk. It wasn't until they were a good three or four hundred yards away
that Brian slowed even more so they could talk without
shouting. Several boats passed them, heading into

Manhasset Bay from the Long Island Sound, one with a water skier.

"It went perfectly, without a hitch," he assured her. He looked back yet again to the Williams mansion, this time using binoculars. The scene hadn't changed. The horse and dogs were still at the far end of the paddock, and Heather Williams's body was at the near end. It still had not been discovered, although it was only a matter of time. "I've never done anything like that. It was so quick, and so different from the messy shootings I've been involved with in the line of duty. I don't know how to feel, except relieved that one nasty, greedy narcissist is gone."

"Which is a tribute to the love you had for your wife and child," Jeanne said. "I exhaled, too, when I heard the gun, which, by the way, I barely heard."

"That's thanks to the suppressor," Brian said. "It definitely bought us some needed time."

"I suppose I shouldn't be saying this," Jeanne said. "But it's rewarding that so far everything is going so well. The world is already a better place without her."

"It's thanks to our careful planning. One down and one to go. Let's hope the Charles Kelley portion goes as smoothly. I'd really like to avoid having to do a break-in. With the sniper rifle there are infinitely fewer chances of complications and collateral damage."

Following her suggestion, they went back to using the fishing rods by putting them in holders mounted in the stern, pretending they were trolling as they slowly motored across Manhasset Bay on their way to Charles Kelley's. They were not in a hurry now that they were at least a half mile away from Heather Williams's and with a significant number of other boaters in the area, taking advantage of the beautiful weather. They also preferred not to arrive at Kelley's mansion too soon, as he wouldn't appear on his outdoor shower balcony until it was near sunset or soon thereafter. At that moment it was just a little after six and almost a full hour before they needed to be in position.

"Are your parents excited about your homecoming?" Brian asked, eager for conversation to avoid any nerves setting in. He knew that Jeanne had only recently informed her parents, in case a glitch in the planning process made it necessary to put off the operation.

"You have no idea," she said. "They're ecstatic, figuring I was a lost cause. They are already busy setting up that farmhouse I mentioned."

"When will you tell them about me?" Brian asked. He'd spent his life constantly and comfortably ensconced in various groups like athletic teams, which was part of the reason he'd joined the NYPD originally right out of college. It was going to take time to adjust to feeling both rootless, solitary, and totally dependent on others.

"As the saying goes, 'we'll cross that bridge when we come to it,'" Jeanne answered. "I'm not at all concerned."

When they were a hundred yards or so off of Charles Kelley's pier, Brian cut the outboard engine and again tossed out the anchor. This side of the bay was shallower, and the anchor immediately took hold. With fishing poles in hand again, they passed the binoculars back and forth.

"It's encouraging to see he's humiliating his driver/bodyguard again," Jeanne commented when it was her turn to survey the scene.

"I agree. It means he's following his normal routine. Fingers crossed that he keeps it up, especially by taking his nightly outdoor shower."

"I'm not worried," she said.

"Lucky you," Brian responded teasingly.

At a little after seven, they made their move. Following the successful playbook they'd used at Heather Williams's, they paddled in under the end of Charles Kelley's pier, positioned the Zodiac for a fast exit if necessary, and Brian used the ladder to get up to the deck. He then entered the cabana, which afforded considerably more concealment than the group of Adirondack chairs on Heather's pier. Conveniently the cabana had a window-like opening facing inland with louvered shutters and a table that Brian turned lengthwise to serve as a perfect placement for the Remington on its bipod. Cracking open one of the shutters while sitting in a chair, he sighted through the telescopic sight. The waterside view of the Spanish-themed house was par excellence, even better than he'd had at Heather Williams's, which had proven to be so efficacious.

The problem, however, was that after waiting some time, there was no Charles Kelley in sight. Although he and his driver/bodyguard had long since stopped their basketball, Kelley had not appeared, even after the sun set. Just when Brian was beginning to despair and had begun reluctantly thinking about the timing of a break-in, which he assumed would have to be after full darkness, the light in the master bedroom flicked on.

Trying to be optimistic, Brian leaned his head against the cheek-rest and sighted through the scope. His view of the second-story outdoor shower couldn't have been better, and he estimated that the distance was very similar to what it had been when he shot Heather Williams, namely a hundred yards or so. Using the bolt action, he put a shell into the firing chamber and slipped his index finger inside the trigger guard, hoping for the best.

Slowly the minutes ticked by, but still no Charles Kelley. Normally steady under stress, Brian could feel the trickle of perspiration on his forehead as well as his pulse significantly quicken. Still, with self-control, he kept his breathing slow and steady.

Then suddenly the Moorish arched door swung open, and Charles Kelley appeared towel in hand rather than over his shoulder. Even from a hundred-plus yards and sitting inside the cabana, Brian could hear the intermittent strains of some rock music emanating from within the house, causing Charles to bob and weave to the beat. With such erratic movement, Brian bided his time, watching through the scope as Charles turned on the shower and adjusted the temperature. Finally, when all was to his liking, Charles stepped into the enclosure, shut the door, and put his head directly under the torrent.

Since he was visible from mid-thorax up and facing away, it was a perfect setup for another brain stem shot.

With careful precision, Brian placed the crosshairs directly at the base of the man's skull, and hesitated for a moment, thinking of Emma and Juliette. The subsequent wave of emotions urged him to press against the trigger.

The rifle made the same thumping whoosh as it had when he'd shot Heather Williams. By force of habit and reflex, Brian used the bolt to eject the empty shell and load another bullet. But again, a second shot was not necessary. As with Heather, Charles instantly fell, disappearing from view behind the shower door. Brian could clearly see a large circular bloodstain centering on a sizable crater in the tiled wall. There was little doubt that the armor-piercing bullet had completely traversed Charles's head to exit out the forehead.

He pocketed the rifle's magazine and removed the bullet from the firing chamber. He took a deep breath before standing up and retracing his steps to the ladder. A moment later he started down.

"Well, how did it go?" Jeanne questioned in a whisper, yet loud enough to be heard over the lapping of the water against the pier's piling. She took the rifle so he could climb aboard the Zodiac.

"Again, it couldn't have been better," Brian managed. "They're gone. It's over. Emma, Juliette, and Riley and countless others have been avenged and maybe, just maybe, we've started the ball rolling to change a sick healthcare system."

"That's the hope," Jeanne said. "Now I think we'd better get out of here."

"Right you are," Brian managed, starting the motor.

Five minutes later he gave the Zodiac's engine full throttle and brought it up to planing speed as they rounded the tip of Kings Point and headed due west. A mile and a half ahead they could see the twinkling lights of City Island. Although the sun had long since set, the sky was still a light silver-gray, and Brian turned on the boat's running lights even though they'd be back at Butler Marine well before total darkness.

With the sound of the outboard, speech was near impossible. Both Brian and Jeanne were isolated in their thoughts, but he didn't mind, as it gave him time to recover. With the stiff sea breeze in his face, he felt a strong sense of peace despite having little idea what the next chapter of his life was to be.

EPILOGUE

October 18

Similar to what he had been doing for more than a month, Brian tried to imitate the ease with which Jeanne mounted her horse. As per usual, it didn't quite work, as the horse moved just as he was throwing his leg over the animal's back. Getting himself up off the ground and readying himself for another try, he was prepared to blame the horse if Jeanne said anything derogatory, but she didn't. Although he didn't fall on his next attempt, it was hardly an impressive mounting, and he could hear her giggle as he settled into the saddle.

Prepared on their white Camargue horses, they started off just after four P.M. on a lazy Sunday afternoon. Their goal was the Mediterranean coast, which lay about nine miles due south. This was to be their first visit to the beach since their arrival in Camargue five weeks earlier. It had been Jeanne's idea to go for a seaside picnic as a change of scene. She'd been eager to show the coastline to him, as it had been one of her favorite destinations when she was a teenager.

The Camargue had turned out to be as interesting for Brian as Jeanne had suggested it would be. He had no idea such a wild, mostly uninhabited place existed in France where there were many more horses, cattle, and sheep than human beings. Those parts of northern France where he'd visited as a boy along with his siblings had every square inch taken up by old stone walls, carefully planted hedges, paved roads, planted fields, and venerable buildings, all evidence that the area had been occupied and altered by humans for untold centuries. In sharp contrast, Camargue was more than three hundred square miles of open space with a flat horizon that seemed to go on forever. One-third of it was lakes, brine lagoons, and marshland. Often the only signs of human interference in the natural order were some cultivated agricultural fields in the northern part, a number of man-made canals that were straighter than natural waterways, and a lot of dikes to keep certain areas dry in times of rising waters. The rare homes were simple, quaint, white stucco structures with picturesque water-reed roofs, exactly like the one that Jeanne and Brian had been occupying since their arrival.

The night of the shooting had gone exceptionally smoothly, which they had attributed to a combination of their extensive planning and the rigid schedules of both Charles Kelley and Heather Williams. On top of that was good luck—a lot of good luck. By the time they'd returned to Butler Marine that night, gotten their deposit back for the Zodiac and fishing gear, and picked up the Subaru, it still wasn't quite seven-thirty. With such efficiency, they had time to spare, giving them an opportunity to stop for food on City Island, which they ate while driving out to Floyd Bennett Field in Brooklyn to return all the borrowed ESU equipment. The original plan was for Brian to make the visit himself after dropping Jeanne off at JFK Airport, but with so much time on their hands, she had preferred to stay with him to limit how long she'd have to cool her heels in the terminal.

Even returning the equipment took less time than planned. Probably because of the pandemic, there were only two duty officers at the ESU Academy, neither of whom Brian knew. Usually there were always a number of ESU officers hanging out instead of cruising the city awaiting action. What took the most time was Brian's decision to write a thank-you note to Deputy Chief Comstock for offering him the chance to rejoin the ESU. In the note he explained that Juliette's sudden and unexpected death had caused him to change his plans, and he wouldn't be rejoining. As a postscript, Brian said that he thought the Remington MSR was a superb piece of engineering and that it should be considered as part of the NYPD's armory, the cost notwithstanding. He left the rifle on Michael's desk with the note on top.

Then after dropping Jeanne off at JFK, Brian had so much free time that he decided to drive home to leave the car in the driveway, blow off some steam for a few hours in the workout room, and then use a ride-share to get out to Newark around 6:30 A.M. Originally, he had planned to leave the car at the airport and call Camila to retrieve it.

"Come on, slowpoke," she teased as she interrupted his reverie by suddenly turning her horse off the dirt trail to begin galloping across a wet, marshy field and putting a huge flock of greater flamingoes to flight in the process. Another thing he had learned about the Camargue was that it's the home to more waterbirds than he'd seen anywhere else in his life.

Brian urged his horse to follow, but the animal wasn't so eager to pick up the pace, and he wasn't sure how to make him change his mind. Finally, he was able to get the horse to canter but not gallop. Ahead, Jeanne had pulled up to wait for him. For several weeks both of them had been riding with the *gardians*, otherwise known as the Camargue cowboys. The *gardians* had begun a roundup of the semi-feral cattle that lived on Jeanne's parents' land. As a consequence, he was learning to ride, and he was also recalling his French.

All in all, Brian was slowly becoming comfortable with his new life, had begun to relax to a degree, and felt extraordinarily lucky that he'd met Jeanne. Otherwise, he might have ended up in Cuba for whatever that might have meant. When the two of them had first arrived in Arles, the major French city just north of the Camargue, after their drive from Frankfurt, Brian had no idea of what the near future would bring. Although he'd worried about his acceptance by her parents, it turned out to not be a problem. They had driven north to Arles to pick up Jeanne when she returned the rental car. If they had been surprised by his presence or the fact that Jeanne had driven all the way from Frankfurt rather than flying into France itself, they didn't let on. She had explained that they were so surprised and pleased by her unexpected return to live in France that they weren't about to question any of the details, including what the relationship was between her and Brian, at least in the near term.

"You have to move your body more forward if you want your horse to gallop," Jeanne reminded Brian as he reached her. "And don't be afraid to use your legs, that's the key."

"You make it look so easy," he complained.

On the opposite side of the expansive marshy field, they picked up another trail heading south, lined on both sides by tamarisk and white poplar trees. Jeanne explained that it was a more direct route to the sea, which she'd forgotten about.

As they walked southward, Brian went back to his musings. So far, the fallout from Heather Williams's and Charles Kelley's deaths had exceeded expectations. The following day it was front-page news, with wild speculations regarding the perpetrators. Some journalists, particularly those on Fox News, indulged in creative conspiracy theories involving homegrown far-left terrorists, citing the victims' wealth and standing in the financial world. On the second day the killings had moved to a back section, but on the third day, thanks to the manifesto Brian and Jeanne had sent to the *New York Times* about the two executives and the role that private equity and the profit motive were playing in healthcare, along with the complete list of the residents of Inwood that the Manhattan Memorial Hospital was suing for extravagant bills, the story moved back to the front page. Healthcare, its costs and payment arrangements, plus the fact that US legislators had been asleep at the wheel while the system got out of hand, were becoming a progressively bigger story, to which the killings of Charles Kelley and Heather Williams were adding a real immediacy.

Although the media response so far was better than he'd hoped, there was one issue that confounded Brian: how long it was taking for him to become more than a person of interest. His only explanation was that the detectives of the NYPD weren't approaching the case with their usual gusto, perhaps because of his many friends, particularly in the ESU. What he did know was that his sudden disappearance combined with his enormous debt to MMH had raised appropriate suspicions and that he'd been tracked to Frankfurt and Interpol was supposedly looking for him. But that was it. According to the papers, his parents and siblings had all been interviewed, but Brian had made sure that they knew absolutely nothing. He imagined they must have felt confused and devastated by his sudden disappearance, but he knew it was for the best.

And now Brian was actually looking forward to being exposed. He wanted the story of Emma's and Juliette's avoidable deaths to be revealed, as it would put a shockingly human touch to the generalizations put forth in the manifesto. His current pleasant interlude in Camargue was just a precursor of what was to come when he'd be formally charged, and his extradition requested. Only then would the whole US healthcare mess become an international story of shame about capitalism run amuck with real victims.

"Well, what do you think?" Jeanne asked when they

finally arrived at the seacoast. They had pulled to a stop at the edge of a vast, totally empty, sandy beach that stretched out in both directions. Huge cumulus clouds were arranged along the horizon with the late-afternoon sun tinting them gold, and a mild onshore breeze caressed their faces.

"It's gorgeous," Brian observed. Despite there being only small dunes at the beach's edge, the scene and time of day reminded him of the fateful afternoon two months earlier on Cape Cod. With some effort he pushed the recollection out of his mind, as he didn't want to think of the disastrous consequences set in motion on that August day. "Where are all the people?" he asked, to stay in the present.

Jeanne laughed instead of answering, and with a toss of her head, she gave free rein to her horse, which was eager to gallop in the wash of the waves. Brian attempted to follow by rising up in his stirrups, leaning forward, and using his legs as she had explained to him earlier. To his surprise and glee, the horse obeyed on this occasion. A moment later he was racing behind Jeanne, holding on for dear life while scrunching his eyes against the salt spray that her horse was kicking up.

The sense of freedom was exhilarating and for a few minutes he reveled in the ability to think of absolutely nothing. Unfortunately, it came to an abrupt end when Jeanne pulled back on her reins and Brian followed suit. For a few minutes they walked the horses, allowing the animals to catch their breaths.

"Let's stop here," she said, pointing to a copse of gnarled tamarisk trees at the back of the beach. They dismounted and let the horses forage for what they could find in the beachgrass and wild alfalfa behind the narrow dunes.

Surprising Brian, Jeanne pulled a blanket out of her backpack along with some local cheese, bread, and a split of white wine. "Surprise," she exclaimed with an impish smile. "A little treat for us."

He spread the blanket while Jeanne opened the wine. A moment later they were sitting down, savoring the seascape and the wine. But their cheer and good spirits didn't last. Within minutes Brian realized they weren't alone. Over the sound of the breaking waves and despite the onshore breeze, he heard the characteristic whine of mosquitoes, and a second later several landed on his bare arms intent on a blood meal. With a sense of panic he recognized the characteristic markings: black bodies with white polka dots and white ringlets on their legs. There was no doubt in his mind—they were the dreaded Asian tiger mosquitoes.

"Oh, my God!" Brian shouted. He leaped to his feet while feverishly fanning away the cloud of insects now circling his head. "We're being attacked."

Taken aback, Jeanne said: "It's just mosquitoes. Camargue is known for them."

"These aren't 'just' mosquitoes," Brian cried. "They're Asian tiger mosquitoes. We have to get the hell out of here!"

Sensing his desperation and urgency, she rapidly gathered the food, the wine, and the glasses. Brian snatched up the blanket. They then ran back through the dunes to fetch the horses.

A short time later as they were cantering back along

the water's edge to the spot where they'd arrived at the beach, Jeanne called over to Brian, who was riding abreast: "It just occurred to me why you are so upset. The day we met you told me about Asian tiger mosquitoes and your barbecue."

He nodded before yelling back: "The bastards carry the virus that killed Emma and Juliette as well as a bunch of other deadly diseases. I didn't know they were in France, too."

"I didn't know, either," Jeanne said with worry. "But we don't have eastern equine encephalitis here. At least I've never heard of it."

"You can't be sure in this day and age," Brian countered. "Just two months ago, I didn't know we had EEE in the United States. And now with climate change and the way the world is interconnected, it could be anywhere, just like the Asian tiger mosquitoes. As the Covid-19 pandemic has shown, we're in an existential war with viruses, and I'm afraid we're at a distinct disadvantage."

"What are you talking about?" she questioned. "What kind of disadvantage?"

"Viruses have been around adapting and evolving for more than a billion years before we humans ever appeared on the scene. Biologically speaking, that is one hell of a head start, so only God knows who is going to prevail."

"You're scaring me," Jeanne said, casting a troubled look in Brian's direction.

"We all should be scared. A competitive viral challenge is one we humans have to face."

ACKNOWLEDGMENTS

Viral could not have been written without the support and help of several family members and friends willing to read early drafts and offer helpful comments and suggestions. Thank you! However, there are two people I want to specifically acknowledge, as they were instrumental in acquainting me with the highly selective New York City Police Department's ESU, or Emergency Service Unit, and with the impressive amount of training required to become a member. Although these two individuals bear no responsibility for any descriptive mistakes I may have made in the novel, their input was critical, particularly by allowing me to visit and observe the ESU Academy in action. In alphabetical order . . .

Tom Janow, retired NYPD Detective First Grade and now a Critical Care Paramedic

David Reilly, NYPD Emergency Service Unit Lieutenant

ANNOTATED BIBLIOGRAPHY

The goal of the novel *Viral* is to entertain and utilize the fact that most people are riveted by dramas and movies of "justified" revenge despite the moral dictum that "two wrongs do not make a right." But the larger goal is an attempt to use fiction as a method to awaken the general public's indignation about the sorry state of American healthcare, which is all too often not providing the help and support expected, and even destroying some people's lives in the process. The reason is simple: American healthcare has mushroomed into an economic behemoth, where clever financial types can enjoy ever-increasing profits for themselves and for the funds they manage. *Viral* might be the first novel to specifically address this issue, but there have been a number of terrific nonfiction treatises that have sought the same objective. For those readers who would like to look into the problem in greater depth, I recommend the following books, all of which are wonderfully readable and disturbingly enlightening:

Brill, Steven. *America's Bitter Pill: Money, Politics, Backroom Deals, and the Fight to Fix Our Broken Healthcare System*. New York: Random House, 2015.

Makary, Marty, MD. *The Price We Pay: What Broke American Health Care—and How to Fix It*. New York: Bloomsbury Publishing, 2019.

Rosenthal, Elisabeth. *An American Sickness: How Healthcare Became Big Business and How You Can Take It Back*. New York: Penguin Press, 2017.

With crazy work schedules and looming family pressures, the last thing colleagues-turned-spouses Dr. Laurie Montgomery and Dr. Jack Stapleton need is a murder. But when Laurie's med school friend Dr. Sue Passero dies in the hospital parking garage, Laurie insists on an autopsy and asks Jack to take on the case.

What starts out as a forensic inquiry into Sue's tragic passing turns into a dangerous cat-and-mouse chase between Jack and a troubled killer—a sociopathic, narcissistic medical provider who, if Jack isn't careful, might just administer another lethal blow.

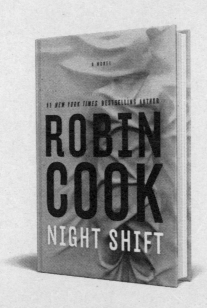

PROLOGUE

Dr. Susan Passero, an internist at the Manhattan Memorial Hospital, known colloquially as the MMH, ushered her forty-first and final patient of the day, Florence Williams, out of the examination room. It was nearly 6:00 P.M. She said a warm goodbye and encouraged Florence to keep up the good work adhering to her rather complicated medication schedule. Returning to the room, Sue took a deep breath, readjusted her Covid-19 face mask, and sat back down at the computer terminal to finish the required entry. Like most doctors, she despised being so chained to the demands of the electronic health record, because of the interference it invariably caused between herself and her patients, yet she knew that modern medicine demanded it. When she was finished and had dutifully checked all the required boxes, she washed her hands for the thousandth time that day, pocketed her stethoscope, and headed out into the clinic proper.

As per usual, she was the last doctor to finish seeing scheduled patients, so the clinic was all but empty. At the far end of the waiting room, the housekeeping crew was already starting the necessary daily cleaning. Sue, on a first name basis with most of the crew members, waved to them, and they waved back. It had been a normal, busy Monday, and Mondays were always the busiest day of the week, since on top of the scheduled visits, a number of the patients who'd come into the emergency department over the weekend invariably needed follow-up.

Sue Passero was a big-boned, athletic, African American woman whose physique still reflected her accomplishments in the collegiate sports of soccer, basketball, and softball. Mindful of her appearance, she was dressed in a silk dress under her white doctor's coat and wore her hair in a contemporary short, spiky style. As an outgoing person, she was friendly to everyone at the hospital. Despite being a board-certified internist with subspecialty training in cardiology, she was never tempted to assume a "holier than thou" attitude with the other hospital employees, like some narcissistic doctors she knew. The reason was simple. Out of necessity through high school, college, and even medical school, she'd worked just about every low-level academic medical center job, including cleaning monkey cages. The result was that she sincerely appreciated everyone's input. At the same time, she was demanding. No matter what someone's work entailed, they had to give 100 percent, which was the way she had always approached her duties, including as a doctor.

"All done!" Sue called out to Virginia Davenport after leaning into the scheduling secretaries' office. Like Sue, Virginia was always the last clinic secretary to leave for the day. In her role as the most senior clinic employee, she took her job seriously, which was why she and Sue clicked and worked as a well-oiled machine.

"Here's your patient schedule for tomorrow," Virginia said leaping up and handing Sue a printout. Virginia was a tall, slender woman with an oval face framed by tight, blonde curls and punctuated with dark eyes and very white teeth.

"Thank you, girl," Sue said, taking the paper like a handoff to a relay-race sprinter as she moved along the hallway. Now that she was done with seeing patients, she wanted to wrap up the day, get in her car, and head home to New Jersey. As she hustled down to her tiny office, she glanced at the schedule. It looked like any other day of late, with thirty patients scheduled, although that would invariably balloon up.

"I also printed that article about the medical serial killer that you asked me to," Virginia said, running to keep up with Sue. "Plus, here are your phone calls that came in while you were seeing your patients and need a response."

Without slowing, Sue took article and the phone messages, glancing at the article. It was a *New York Times* piece from October about a Texas nurse who had been found guilty of killing four postoperative patients by injecting air into their arteries. Entering her office, Sue slipped behind her desk and sat down. "You are a dear," she said, looking up at Virginia, who had followed her. This final interaction between them was part of their daily routine before Sue's departure. "Did you happen to read the article?"

"I did," Virginia said. "It would be hard not to after seeing the title. It's horrific that there are people capable of that kind of behavior, especially in the medical profession."

"What scares me about this particular case is that the nurse's motivation was to keep certain patients in the intensive care unit so he could get more work hours. Can you believe it? I mean, it's a new one for me. I can sort of understand in a sick way the so-called 'mercy killers,' who mistakenly profess to be saving people from pain and suffering. I can even intellectually understand the scarier 'hero' syndrome, misguided sociopaths trying to burnish their image by putting patients in jeopardy to get credit for supposedly saving them." As she was speaking, Sue pulled open one of the desk's deep side drawers and extracted a large blue folder closed with an elastic. Opening it, she slipped in the article to join other similar ones.

"It's a terrifying thought, no matter what the motivation," Virginia said. "The hospital is supposed to save people, not kill them. I tell you, the world seems to be getting more and more crazy."

"Any of these calls demand immediate attention?" Sue asked, holding up the list of names and phone numbers. "Or can I call from my car on my way home?"

"Nothing earth shattering," Virginia assured her.

Although not trained in health care per se, but rather psychology and social work, Virginia had learned over the ten years she'd worked in the internal medicine clinic to recognize true medical emergencies. From experience, Sue had learned to trust her. "Has the MMH ever had a mercy killer?"

"Interesting you should ask. I'm afraid the answer is yes. About fifteen years ago, my friend Laurie . . ."

"Dr. Laurie Montgomery?" Virginia questioned. Virginia knew Laurie from having set up numerous lunches and even an occasional dinner date for her and Sue. She was aware the two women were old friends from their college days and had even gone to medical school together.

"None other," Sue said. "Laurie, in her inimitable style as a medical examiner extraordinaire, outed a nurse here who was being paid by a shady organization working for a health insurance company to kill postoperative patients who carried bad genes."

"Why?"

"To save the insurance company money. With their genetic baggage, the involved patients were destined to need lots of expensive healthcare."

"Oh my goodness," Virginia said, covering her mouth with her hand in dismay. "That's awful. That's worse than the Texas nurse. How many MMH patients were involved?"

"A half a dozen or so," Sue said. "I don't remember exactly. It was bad, and I've tried to forget the details but not the lesson. It was an awful reminder of how much business interests have taken over medicine. Especially with private equity trying to eke out every last penny of compensation."

"That's unfortunately true," Virginia said. "And mentioning business interests reminds me that you have a hospital Compliance Committee meeting tomorrow at noon!"

"Thank you. I appreciate the reminder, and if that's it, I'm out of here." Sue slapped the surface of her desk, stood up, and pulled off her long white coat. The fact that she had another committee meeting didn't surprise her. As a particularly dedicated member of the MMH staff, she felt it was her duty to volunteer for multiple committees. Currently she was an active member of the Mortality and Morbidity Committee, the Infection Control Committee, and the Compliance Committee. On top of that, she was actively vying for a seat on the Hospital Board. Luckily, Virginia was willing to assist with all this added work.

"You are all caught up," Virginia assured her, heading for the doorway. "Drive carefully on your way home. See you in the morning."

"Same to you on the subway." Sue pulled on her winter coat hanging on the back of the door. Picking up her phone, purse, and the list of patients she needed to contact, she followed Virginia out into the hall, where they parted ways. Sue was intent on getting out of the highrise garage before the rush of cars coming in for the night shift starting at 7:00. Although most of the employees came by mass transit, enough private vehicles were involved that it could be a minor traffic jam.

The route required taking the pedestrian bridge from the outpatient building to the main building and from there a second pedestrian bridge to the garage. Although a few of the night shift personnel were arriving, as well as some visitors, it was not nearly as busy as it would get between 6:30 and 7:00. Sue found her car where it had been parked that morning by the valet service in the doctor's section, which was already mostly empty, as was usually the case. As she approached her beloved BMW with its heavily tinted windows, she reached into her coat pocket and fondled the electronic key fob, pressing the door unlock button. The car responded by turning on its interior lights as well as its outside lights.

Sue opened the driver's side door and tossed her purse onto the passenger seat before slipping in behind the wheel. Leaning forward, she reached for the starter button, but her hand never made it. To her shock and horror, a cloth hood was thrown over her head and pulled down around her shoulders. As she reached up to tear the hood away, an arm came around her throat, yanking her back against the head rest with such force that her back arched away from the seat. Letting go of the hood, she tried to pull the arm away using both her hands while crying out in utter terror. Unfortunately, her voice was muffled due both to the hood and the compression on her neck. In the next instant, she felt a stabbing pain in her right thigh.

Gritting her teeth, Sue managed to pull away the arm encircling her head enough to take a breath. But then a second arm came to the aid of the first, dislodging one of her hands and repinning her head back against the headrest and restricting her airway.

Out of sheer desperation, Sue bit down on the arm through the cloth hood. She was rewarded by a loud curse from her attacker, but she was not released. If anything, the compression of her neck and the hyperextension of her back increased. As forcefully as she could, she tried to dig the nails of her left hand into the restraining arm, but as she struggled to do so, she suddenly became aware that she was losing strength. It was as if the muscles in her arms and neck were becoming unresponsive. At first, she thought it might be a kind of fatigue from making a superhuman effort, but it relentlessly progressed. Rapidly her hands literally lost their grip on the arm encircling her neck. Then, even more frightening, she found herself struggling to breathe.

Marshaling her last ounce of strength, Sue tried once more to cry out, but no sound escaped her lips, and with an agonizing roar in her ears, she lost consciousness . . .

CHAPTER 1

Tuesday, December 7, 6:45 A.M.

Without making it obvious, Dr. Jack Stapleton put muscle into the mild hill climb on West Drive in Central Park where it bordered the reservoir. It had given him a bit of satisfaction to overtake and pass a small, tight covey of younger, serious bicyclists on their imported road bikes, all of them clad in skintight, fancy bike duds printed with all sorts of European product endorsements and wearing clip-in, expensive bike shoes. He, of course, was on his relatively new US-made Trek bike that was every bit as fancy as the others, but his dress was far different. Instead of pricey bike clothes, he was wearing his usual brown, wide-wale corduroy jacket, blue jeans, and an indigo chambray shirt with a dark green knit tie. Instead of bike shoes, he had on Nike kicks. His only concessions to the 45-degree weather were gloves and a scarf.

As he had done practically every morning since he had arrived in New York City to begin his new life and second medical career as a New York City medical examiner at the Office of the Chief Medical Examiner, or OCME, Jack was using his bike for the commute from his home on the Upper West Side to the Lower East Side. It was a far different mode of transportation than he'd used when he was a conservative midwestern ophthalmologist quite a few years previously. Back then he'd driven a Mercedes to his office every day, attired in a glen-plaid suit with carefully polished shoes.

The current pace setter of the group of well-heeled cyclists responded just as Jack envisioned. It would have been demoralizing to have a middle-aged, possibly blue-collar individual pass them, so he stood up and began a chase. There was no way for the cyclist to know that Jack probably rode his bike more often than they did. Nor did they have any idea that Jack also played demanding street basketball practically on a daily basis, weather permitting, and was accordingly in tip-top physical shape. The rest of the cyclists followed the lead of the pace setter, standing up and pumping furiously.

Meanwhile, remaining seated, Jack increased his own effort such that his lead slightly increased despite the more obvious efforts of the pursuing bicyclists. Several minutes later, as Jack crested the hill and began his descent, he stopped pedaling and allowed himself to coast, which permitted the clot of pursuers to finally catch and overtake him to regain their sportive dignity.

Under more normal circumstances, Jack would have continued the impromptu race all the way to the south end of the park, where he'd exit on his way to the OCME. But on this particular morning, his attention switched from aggravating the "serious" cyclists to musing about the Brooks School he was passing to his right on Central Park West. It was where his son, JJ, was enrolled in the fifth grade. As if it were yesterday and with understandable chagrin, Jack could remember his disastrous visit there two years previously when Laurie, his wife, asked him to go to talk to the school authorities in her stead about their concern that JJ needed to take Adderall for ADHD after JJ had gotten into a few tussles on the playground.

What made Jack an inappropriate substitute for Laurie was that he was absolutely convinced there was nothing atypical about JJ. He was simply a child with an XY chromosome pair and a lot of energy. Combining that reality with Jack's belief that there had to be some kind of conspiracy between the pharmaceutical and education industries, both of which seemed to be overly eager to start kids on what was essentially speed, Jack had unfortunately made sure that the Brooks School knew exactly how strongly he felt. He had succeeded only in alienating the school authorities, who threatened to expel JJ. Ultimately, Jack had agreed, along with Laurie's insistence, to have JJ at least evaluated by a psychiatrist, who seemed to agree with the diagnosis, but luckily by that time it no longer mattered. The evaluation process had taken long enough that it was apparent to all that JJ was not having any more playground shenanigans. The school's insistence on medication fell by the wayside—that is, until the previous week, when JJ had started another fight during recess.

Suddenly the whole issue had resurfaced, and it was the reason Jack was now on his way to the OCME so early in the morning. The night before, Jack had been harangued by both Laurie and Laurie's mother, Dorothy, who were again championing the use of ADHD medication. Awakening way before the alarm and not wishing to be again subjected to more pressure before rethinking all the pros and the cons of the situation, Jack had decided to leave the apartment before anyone else was awake.

Jack's normal route would have taken him to the southeastern corner of Central Park, but because of the dramatic uptick in bicycle use in Manhattan due to a combination of frustratingly heavy vehicular traffic, the Covid-19 pandemic, and e-bikes, a major proliferation of bike lanes had been created. The result was that Jack's commute was significantly faster and safer, though Laurie doubted the latter. Now Jack exited the park in the southwest corner onto Columbus Circle. From there he used the dedicated bike lane to head south on Broadway and Seventh Avenue all the way to 30th Street. Conveniently, 30th Street also had a bike lane, although it wasn't as safe, since it was merely painted on the pavement alongside the parked cars. Jack's destination was at the corner of 30th Street and First Avenue, where the old OCME building stood, which still housed the autopsy suite.

As Jack rounded Columbus Circle and started down Broadway, his thoughts went back to Dorothy's position, and he realized she evoked serious ambivalence in his thinking. In relation to his daughter, Emma, who had been diagnosed several years previously with autism, Dorothy had played a significantly positive role. She had taken it upon herself to organize and then manage the complicated interviewing, selecting, and scheduling of the behavioral therapists, speech therapists, and physical therapists who were responsible for Emma's impressive progress. But even Emma's improvement was not without some controversy. It had gotten to the point where Jack was inclined to enroll Emma in a specialized school for children on the autism spectrum that was close to the Brooks School. But Dorothy disagreed and so far had convinced Laurie to her point of view in favor of keeping Emma home under her current regimen.

Worse than the mild disagreement over Emma's situation was Dorothy's continued anti-vaccine stance, since she still insisted that it had been Emma's infant MMR vaccine that had caused Emma's autism, even though the possibility had been scientifically proven not to be the case. Worse still, her anti-vaccine feelings extended to the Covid-19 vaccine, and no matter what Jack or Laurie said, Dorothy refused the jab. Making her intransience that much worse was the fact that Dorothy had all but moved in with them, taking over the second guest room right after her husband, Laurie's stern cardiac-surgeon father, had passed away three months previously.

On several occasions, Jack had tried to broach the issue of establishing some appropriate time frame for Dorothy to move back to her spacious Park Avenue co-op, but Laurie wouldn't hear of it. It was her belief that

Emma was benefiting greatly from having her grandmother constantly around and that Dorothy was still much too fragile to move back to an empty apartment.

All in all, Jack was feeling a bit like the odd man out, especially with Laurie acting more and more like the "chief" both at the OCME and at home. Not wanting to force the issue and possibly cause a major dislocation in the fragile home environment, Jack looked to work to occupy his mind and emotions. As he'd done in the past, he needed to scare up some kind of difficult case to monopolize his thoughts. It had worked in the past: Investigating a chiropractic death had helped him deal with JJ's diagnosis of neuroblastoma when the boy was an infant. One of the definite benefits of being a medical examiner was that every day was different and there was always the possibility of confronting a perplexing circumstance. He and Laurie certainly had proved that over the years.

After crossing First Avenue at the corner of 30th Street, Jack rode down along the old OCME building that had long ago outlasted its usefulness. When it had been built more than a half century previously, it had been state of the art. Now it was hardly that. A new autopsy building with offices for the medical examiners and the toxicology department was sorely needed. It was to be built near the new high-rise OCME building four blocks to the south but had been held up by budgetary problems. Currently it was one of Laurie Montgomery's main objectives in her role as the Chief Medical Examiner of the City of New York, and she was counting on the new mayor, soon to be sworn in, to give it the green light.

Turning in at the receiving bay where bodies arrived and departed, Jack rode between the parked Sprinter M. E. vans. Hoisting his bike onto his shoulder, he climbed the side stairs up to the platform. Then, walking the bike, he passed the security office and waved to the guards who were busy in the process of changing shifts. Jack did the same passing the mortuary techs' office. Off to the left where the Hart Island coffins for unclaimed bodies were stored, Jack secured his bike with a cable lock to a standpipe, along with his helmet. He was the only one who used a bike to commute to work and there was no official bike stand. Nearby was the darkened isolated autopsy room for decomposing bodies.

Eager to see what the night had brought in terms of new cases, Jack climbed the stairs one floor, passed through the Sudden Infant Death Syndrome room, and entered part of the ID area where the day began for OCME. It was a little after 7:00 in the morning, and he was keyed up to see what kind of mayhem awaited him and his colleagues after a weekend in a city of almost nine million people.

ROBIN COOK

"Master of the medical thriller."
—*The New York Times*

Praise for the Dune novels of
Brian Herbert and Kevin J. Anderson

"*Dune: House Atreides* is a terrific prequel, but it's also a first-rate adventure on its own. Frank Herbert would surely be delighted and proud of this continuation of his vision."
—Dean Koontz

"Congratulations to Herbert and Anderson for transporting us back to this richly excavated world. . . . A spicy melange treat for both new and long-time fans of the series."
—Billy Dee Williams (*Star Wars* and *Lady Sings the Blues*)

"[Fans] rejoice in this chance to return to one of science fiction's most appealing futures."
—*The New York Times Book Review*

"Brian Herbert and Kevin J. Anderson succeed in weaving their own intricate saga. *Dune: House Atreides* does its predecessors justice."
—*USA Today*

"[The authors] have brought this classic saga back to an exciting and dynamic life."
—*The Denver Post*

"Every bit as complex and compelling as the original Dune novels."
—*St. Petersburg Times*

"A spirited and entertain
here comes from watc
threads that will conver
—*The P*

"The attendant excitement and myriad revelations not only make this novel a terrific read in its own right, but will inspire readers to turn, or return, to its great predecessor."
—*Publishers Weekly* (starred review)

"Exploring the world of Duke Leto Atreides and Baron Vladimir Harkonnen should fascinate most of *Dune*'s vast fandom. . . . Herbert *pere* would be proud."
—*Booklist*

DUNE: HOUSE HARKONNEN

DUNE
HOUSE HARKONNEN

BRIAN
HERBERT

AND

KEVIN J.
ANDERSON

NEW YORK

Dune: House Harkonnen is a work of fiction.
Names, characters, places, and incidents either are products
of the authors' imagination or are used fictitiously.
Any resemblance to actual persons, living or dead,
events, or locales is entirely coincidental.

2020 Del Rey Mass Market Edition

Copyright © 2000 by Herbert Limited Partnership
Maps copyright © 1999 by David Cain

Published in the United States by Del Rey,
an imprint of Random House, a division of
Penguin Random House LLC, New York.

DEL REY is a registered trademark and the CIRCLE colophon is a
trademark of Penguin Random House LLC.

Originally published in hardcover in the United States by Bantam,
an imprint of Random House, a division of
Penguin Random House LLC, in 2000.

ISBN 978-0-593-15961-3
Ebook ISBN 978-0-553-89783-8

Printed in the United States of America

randomhousebooks.com

Book design by Edwin Vazquez

3 4 5 6 7 8 9

Del Rey mass market edition: November 2020

ACKNOWLEDGMENTS

Jan Herbert, with appreciation for her unflagging devotion and constant creative support.

Penny Merritt, for helping manage the literary legacy of her father, Frank Herbert.

Rebecca Moesta Anderson's tireless support and enthusiasm for this project, her ideas, imagination, and sharp eyes truly enhanced this project.

Robert Gottlieb and Matt Bialer of the William Morris Agency, Mary Alice Kier and Anna Cottle of Cine/Lit Representation—all of whom never wavered in their faith and dedication, seeing the potential of the entire project.

Irwyn Applebaum and Nita Taublib at Bantam Books gave their support and attention to such an enormous undertaking.

Pat LoBrutto's excitement and dedication to this project— from the very start—helped to keep us on track. He made us consider possibilities and plot threads that made *Dune: House Harkonnen* even stronger and more complex.

Picking up the editorial reins, Anne Lesley Groell and Mike Shohl offered excellent advice and suggestions, even at the eleventh hour.

Our U.K. editor, Carolyn Caughey, for continuing to find things that everyone else missed, and for her suggestions on details, large and small.

Anne Gregory, for editorial work on an export edition of *Dune: House Atreides* that occurred too late to list her in the credits.

As always, Catherine Sidor at WordFire, Inc., worked tirelessly to transcribe dozens of microcassettes and type many hundreds of pages to keep up with our manic work pace. Her assistance in all steps of this project has helped to keep us sane, and she even fools other people into thinking we're organized.

Diane E. Jones and Diane Davis Herdt worked hard as test readers and guinea pigs, giving us honest reactions and suggesting additional scenes that helped make this a stronger book.

The Herbert Limited Partnership, including Ron Merritt, David Merritt, Byron Merritt, Julie Herbert, Robert Merritt, Kimberly Herbert, Margaux Herbert, and Theresa Shackelford, all of whom have provided us with their enthusiastic support, entrusting us with the continuation of Frank Herbert's magnificent vision.

Beverly Herbert, for almost four decades of support and devotion to her husband, Frank Herbert.

And, most of all, thanks to Frank Herbert, whose genius created such a wondrous universe for all of us to explore.

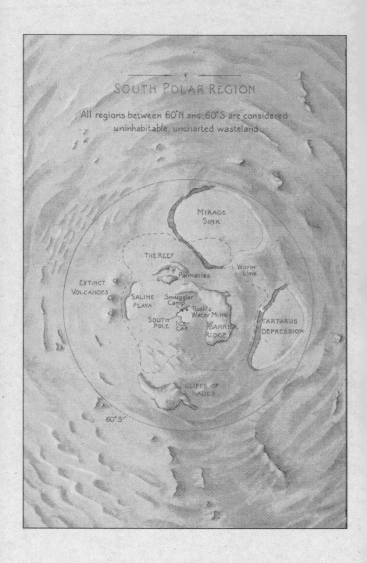

SOUTH POLAR REGION

All regions between 60°N and 60°S are considered
uninhabitable, uncharted wasteland

MIRAGE
SINK

THE REEF

Palmaries

WORM
LINE

EXTINCT
VOLCANOES

SALINE
PLAYA

SMUGGLER
CAMP

Tuck's
Water Mine

SOUTH
POLE

ICE
CAP

BARRIER
RIDGE

TARTARUS
DEPRESSION

CLIFFS OF
HADES

60°S

CALADAN

= GRASSY PLAINS
= FORESTS
= FUNDI RICE LOWLANDS
= SEAWEED

Armada Bluff

ELECRAN ISLANDS

EASTERN CONTINENT

Sistersin
Isolation

WINE REGION

SOUTHERN CONTINENT

Atreides Landing
(Spaceport)

Cidrit Town

Paradan Melon Farms

Wingboat Factories

SERENA'S NECKLACE

Sea Creature Processing Islands

WESTERN CONTINENT

River Gorges

Agamemnon Canyon

Sihaya Ridge Training Facilities

Paradan Melon Farms

Cala City
(Castle Caladan, Spaceport)

CORAL REEFS
(Coral Gem Beds)

Lake Argent

Horizo

CORAL REEFS
(Coral Gem Beds)

Underwater Park

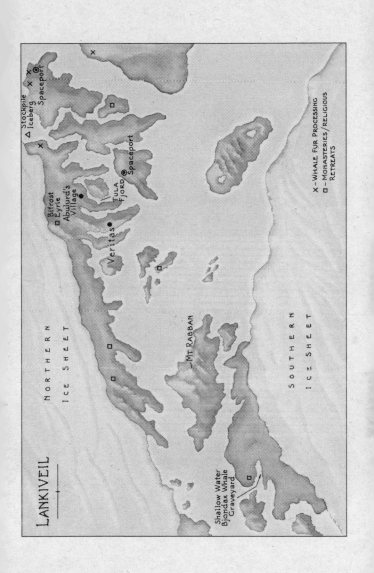

LANKIVEIL

NORTHERN
ICE SHEET

△ Stockpile
Iceberg
◉ Spaceport

× ×
× ×

×

□

□ Bifrost
Eyrie
Abulurd's
Village

Tula
Fjord ◉ Spaceport

● Veritas

□

□

× — WHALE FUR PROCESSING

□ — MONASTERIES/RELIGIOUS
RETREATS

MT RABBAN

SOUTHERN
ICE SHEET

□

Shallow Water
Bjondax Whale
Graveyard

DUNE: HOUSE HARKONNEN

Discovery is dangerous . . . but so is life. A man unwilling to take risks is doomed never to learn, never to grow, never to live.

—PLANETOLOGIST PARDOT KYNES,
An Arrakis Primer, written for his son Liet

WHEN THE SANDSTORM CAME HOWLING UP FROM THE SOUTH, PARDOT Kynes was more interested in taking meteorological readings than in seeking safety. His son Liet—only twelve years old, but raised in the harsh ways of the desert—ran an appraising eye over the ancient weather pod they had found in the abandoned botanical testing station. He was not confident the machine would function at all.

Then Liet gazed back across the sea of dunes toward the approaching tempest. "The wind of the demon in the open desert. *Hulasikali Wala*." Almost instinctively, he checked his stillsuit fittings.

"Coriolis storm," Kynes corrected, using a scientific term instead of the Fremen one his son had selected. "Winds across the open flatlands are amplified by the planet's revolutionary motion. Gusts can reach speeds up to seven hundred kilometers per hour."

As his father talked, the young man busied himself sealing the egg-shaped weather pod, checking the vent closures, the heavy doorway hatch, the stored emergency supplies. He ignored their signal generator and distress beacon; the static from the sandstorm would rip any transmissions to electromagnetic shreds.

In pampered societies Liet would have been considered just a boy, but life among the hard-edged Fremen had given him a tightly coiled adulthood that few others achieved even at twice his age. He was better equipped to handle an emergency than his father.

The elder Kynes scratched his sandy-gray beard. "A good storm like this can stretch across four degrees of latitude." He powered up the dim screens of the pod's analytical devices. "It lifts particles to an altitude of two thousand meters and suspends them in the atmosphere, so that long after the storm passes, dust continues to fall from the sky."

Liet gave the hatch lock a final tug, satisfied that it would hold against the storm. "The Fremen call that El-Sayal, the 'rain of sand.'"

"One day when you become Planetologist, you'll need to use more technical language," Pardot Kynes said in a professorial tone. "I still send the Emperor occasional reports, though not as often as I should. I doubt he ever reads them." He tapped one of the instruments. "Ah, I believe the atmospheric front is almost upon us."

Liet removed a porthole cover to see the oncoming wall of white, tan, and static. "A Planetologist must use his *eyes*, as well as scientific language. Just look out the window, Father."

Kynes grinned at his son. "It's time to raise the pod." Operating long-dormant controls, he managed to get the dual bank of suspensor engines functioning. The pod tugged against gravity, heaving itself off the ground.

The mouth of the storm lunged toward them, and Liet closed the cover plate, hoping the ancient meteorological apparatus would hold together. He trusted his father's intuition to a certain extent, but not his practicality.

The egg-shaped pod rose smoothly on suspensors, buffeted by precursor breezes. "Ah, there we are," Kynes said. "Now our work begins—"

The storm hit them like a blunt club, and vaulted them high into the maelstrom.

DAYS EARLIER, ON a trip into the deep desert, Pardot Kynes and his son had discovered the familiar markings of a botanical testing station, abandoned thousands of years before. Fremen had ransacked most of the research outposts, scavenging valuable items, but this isolated station in an armpit of rock had gone undiscovered until Kynes spotted the signs.

He and Liet had cracked open the dust-encrusted hatch to peer inside like ghouls about to enter a crypt. They were forced to wait in the hot sun for atmospheric exchange to clear out the deadly stale air. Pardot Kynes paced in the loose sand, holding his breath and poking his head into the darkness, waiting until they could enter and investigate.

These botanical testing stations had been built in the golden age of the old Empire. Back then, Kynes knew, this desert planet had been nothing special, with no resources of note, no reason to colonize. When the Zensunni Wanderers had come here after generations of slavery, they'd hoped to build a world where they could be free.

But that had been before the discovery of the spice melange, the precious substance found nowhere else in the universe. And then everything had changed.

Kynes no longer referred to this world as Arrakis, the name listed in Imperial records, but instead used the Fremen name: *Dune*. Though he was, by nature, Fremen, he remained a servant of the Padishah Emperors. Elrood IX had assigned him to unravel the mystery of the spice: where it came from, how it was formed, where it could be found. For thirteen years Kynes had lived with the desert dwellers; he had taken a Fremen wife, and he'd raised a half-Fremen son to follow in his footsteps, to become the next Planetologist on Dune.

Kynes's enthusiasm for this planet had never dimmed. He thrilled at the chance to learn something new, even if he had to thrust himself into the middle of a storm. . . .

THE POD'S ANCIENT suspensors hummed against the Coriolis howl like a nest of angry wasps. The meteorological vessel bounced on swirling currents of air, a steel-walled balloon. Wind-borne dust scoured the hull.

"This reminds me of the aurora storms I saw on Salusa Secundus," Kynes mused. "Amazing things—very colorful and very dangerous. The hammer-wind can come up from out of nowhere and crush you flat. You wouldn't want to be caught outside."

"I don't want to be outside in this one, either," Liet said.

Stressed inward, one of the side plates buckled; air stole through the breach with a thin shriek. Liet lurched across the deck toward the leak. He'd kept the repair kit and foam sealant close at hand, certain the decrepit pod would rupture. "We are held in the hand of God, and could be crushed at any moment."

"That's what your mother would say," the Planetologist said without looking up from the skeins of information pouring through the recording apparatus into an old datapack. "Look, a gust clocked at *eight* hundred kilometers per hour!" His voice carried no fear, only excitement. "What a monster storm!"

Liet looked up from the stone-hard sealant he had slathered over the thin crack. The squealing sound of leaking air faded, replaced by a muffled hurricane din. "If we were outside, this wind would scour the flesh off our bones."

Kynes pursed his lips. "Quite likely true, but you must learn to express yourself objectively and quantitatively. 'Scour the flesh off our bones' is not a phrasing one would include in a report to the Emperor."

The battering wind, the scraping sand, and the roar of the storm reached a crescendo; then, with a burst of pressure inside the survey pod, it all broke into a bubble of silence. Liet blinked, swallowing hard to clear his ears and throat. Intense quiet throbbed in his skull. Through the hull of the creaking vessel, he could still hear Coriolis winds like whispered voices in a nightmare.

"We're in the eye." Glowing with delight, Pardot Kynes stepped away from his instruments. "A sietch at the center of the storm, a refuge where you would least expect it."

Blue static discharges crackled around them, sand and dust rubbing together to generate electromagnetic fields. "I would prefer to be back in the sietch right now," Liet admitted.

The meteorological pod drifted along in the eye, safe and silent after the intense battering of the storm wall. Confined together in the small vessel, the two had a chance to talk, as father and son.

But they didn't. . . .

Ten minutes later they struck the opposite sandstorm wall, thrown back into the insane flow with a glancing blow of the dust-thick winds. Liet stumbled and held on; his father managed to maintain his footing. The vessel's hull vibrated and rattled.

Kynes looked at his controls, at the floor, and then at his son. "I'm not sure what to do about this. The suspensors are"— with a lurch, they began to plunge, as if their safety rope had been severed—"failing."

Liet held himself against an eerie weightlessness as the crippled pod dropped toward the ground, which lay obscured by dusty murk. As they tumbled in the air, the Planetologist continued to work the controls.

The haphazard suspensors sputtered and caught again just before impact. The force from the Holtzman field generator cushioned them enough to absorb the worst of the crash. Then the storm pod slammed into the churned sand, and the

Coriolis winds roared overhead like a spice harvester trampling a kangaroo mouse under its treads. A deluge of dust poured down, released from the sky.

Bruised but otherwise unharmed, Pardot and Liet Kynes picked themselves up and stared at each other in the afterglow of adrenaline. The storm headed up and over them, leaving the pod behind. . . .

AFTER WORKING A sandsnork out through the clogged vent opening, Liet pumped fresh air into the stale confinement. When he pried open the heavy hatch, a stream of sand fell into the interior, but Liet used a static-foam binder to pack the walls. Using a scoop from his Fremkit as well as his bare hands, he set to work digging them out.

Pardot Kynes had complete confidence in his son's abilities to rescue them, so he worked in dimness to collate his new weather readings into a single old-style datapack.

Blinking as he pushed himself into the open air like an infant emerging from a womb, Liet stared at the storm-scoured landscape. The desert was reborn: Dunes moved along like a marching herd; familiar landmarks changed; footprints, tents, even small villages erased. The entire basin looked fresh and clean and new.

Covered with pale dust, he scrambled up to more stable sand, where he saw the depression that hid the buried pod. When they'd crashed, the vessel had slammed a crater into the wind-stirred desert surface, just before the passing storm dumped a blanket of sand on top of them.

With Fremen instincts and an inborn sense of direction, Liet was able to determine their approximate position, not far from the South False Wall. He recognized the rock forms, the cliff bands, the peaks and rilles. If the winds had blown them a kilometer farther, the pod would have crashed into the blister-

ing mountains . . . an ignominious end for the great Planetologist, whom the Fremen revered as their *Umma*, their prophet.

Liet called down into the hole that marked the buried vessel. "Father, I believe there's a sietch in the nearby cliffs. If we
go there, the Fremen can help us dig out the pod."

"Good idea," Kynes answered, his voice muffled. "Go
check to make sure. I'll stay here and work. I've . . . got an
idea."

With a sigh, the young man walked across the sand toward
the jutting elbows of ocher rock. His steps were without
rhythm, so as not to attract one of the great worms: step,
drag, pause . . . drag, pause, step-step . . . drag, step, pause,
step. . . .

Liet's comrades at Red Wall Sietch, especially his blood-
brother Warrick, envied him for all the time he spent with the
Planetologist. Umma Kynes had brought a vision of paradise
to the desert people—they believed his dream of reawakening
Dune, and followed the man.

Without the knowledge of the Harkonnen overlords—
who were only on Arrakis to mine the spice, and viewed people only as a resource to be squeezed—Kynes oversaw armies
of secret, devoted workers who planted grasses to anchor the
mobile dunes; these Fremen established groves of cacti and
hardy scrub bushes in sheltered canyons, watered by dew-
precipitators. In the unexplored south polar regions, they had
planted palmaries, which had gained a foothold and now
flourished. A lush demonstration project at Plaster Basin produced flowers, fresh fruit, and dwarf trees.

Still, though the Planetologist could orchestrate grandiose,
world-spanning plans, Liet did not trust his father's common
sense enough to leave him alone for long.

The young man went along the ridge until he found subtle
blaze marks on the rocks, a jumbled path no outsider would
notice, messages in the placement of off-colored stones that

promised food and shelter, under the respected *al'amyah* Travelers' Benediction rules.

With the aid of strong Fremen in the sietch, they could excavate the weather pod and drag it to a hiding place where it would be salvaged or repaired; within an hour, the Fremen would remove all traces and let the desert fall back into brooding silence.

But when he looked back at the crash site, Liet was alarmed to see the battered vessel moving and lurching, already protruding a third of the way out of the sand. With a deep-throated hum, the pod heaved and strained, like a beast of burden caught in a Bela Tegeusan quagmire. But the pulsing suspensors had only enough strength to wrench the vessel upward a few centimeters at a time.

Liet froze when he realized what his father was doing. *Suspensors. Out in the open desert!*

He ran, tripping and stumbling, an avalanche of powder sand following his footsteps. "Father, stop. Turn them off!" He shouted so loudly that his throat grew raw. With dread in the pit of his stomach, he gazed across the golden ocean of dunes, toward the hellish pit of the faraway Cielago Depression. He scanned for a telltale ripple, the disturbance indicating deep movement. . . .

"Father, come out of there." He skidded to a stop in front of the open hatch as the pod continued to shift back and forth, straining. The suspensor fields thrummed. Grabbing the edge of the door frame, Liet swung himself through the hatch and dropped inside the weather pod, startling Kynes.

The Planetologist grinned at his son. "It's some sort of automated system—I don't know what controls I bumped into, but this pod just might lift itself out in less than an hour." He turned back to his instruments. "It gave me time to collate all our new data into a single storage—"

Liet grabbed his father by the shoulder and pulled him

from the controls. He slammed his hands down on the emergency cutoff switch, and the suspensors faded. Confused, Kynes tried to protest, but his son urged him toward the open hatch. "Get out, now! Run as fast as you can toward the rocks."

"But—"

Liet's nostrils flared in angry exasperation. "Suspensors operate on a Holtzman field, just like shields. You know what happens when you activate a personal shield out in the open sand?"

"The suspensors are working again?" Kynes blinked, then his eyes lit up as he understood. "Ah! A worm comes."

"A worm *always* comes. Now run!"

The elder Kynes staggered out of the hatch and dropped to the sand. He recovered his balance and oriented himself in the glaring sun. Seeing the cliff line Liet had indicated, a kilometer away, he trudged off in a jerky, mismatched walk, stepping, sliding, pausing, hopping forward in a complicated dance. The young Fremen dropped out of the hatch and followed along, as they made their way toward the safety of rocks.

Before long, they heard a hissing, rolling sound from behind. Liet glanced over his shoulder, then pushed his father over a dune crest. "Faster. I don't know how much time we'll have." They increased their pace. Pardot stumbled, got back up.

Ripples arrowed across the sands directly toward the half-buried pod. Toward *them*. Dunes lurched, rolled, then flattened with the inexorable tunneling of a deep worm rising to the surface.

"Run with your very soul!" They sprinted toward the cliffs, crossed a dune crest, slid down, then surged forward again, the soft sand pulling at their feet. Liet's spirits rose when he saw the safety of rocks less than a hundred meters away.

The hissing grew louder as the giant worm picked up speed. The ground beneath their boots trembled.

Finally, Kynes reached the first boulders and clutched them

like an anchor, panting and wheezing. Liet pushed him farther, though, onto the slopes, to be sure the monster could not rise from the sand and strike them.

Moments later, sitting on a ledge, wordless as they sucked hot air through their nostrils to catch their breath, Pardot Kynes and his son stared back to watch a churning whirlpool form around the half-buried weather pod. In the loosening powder, as the viscosity of the stirred sand changed, the pod shifted and began to sink.

The heart of the whirlpool rose up in a cavernous scooped mouth. The desert monster swallowed the offending vessel along with tons of sand, forcing all the debris down into a gullet lined with crystal teeth. The worm sank back into the arid depths, and Liet watched the ripples of its passage, slower now, returning into the empty basin. . . .

In the pounding silence that followed, Pardot Kynes did not look exhilarated from his near brush with death. Instead, he appeared dejected. "We lost all that data." The Planetologist heaved a deep breath. "I could have used our readings to understand those storms better."

Liet reached inside a front pocket of his stillsuit and held up the old-style datapack he had snatched from the pod's instrument panel. "Even while watching out for our lives—I can still pay attention to research."

Kynes beamed with fatherly pride.

Under the desert sun, they hiked up the rugged path to the safety of the sietch.

Behold, O Man, you can create life. You can destroy life. But, lo, you have no choice but to experience life. And therein lies both your greatest strength and your greatest weakness.

—Orange Catholic Bible,
Book of Kimla Septima, 5:3

ON OIL-SOAKED GIEDI PRIME, THE WORK CREW LEFT THE FIELDS AT THE END of a typically interminable day. Encrusted with perspiration and dirt, the workers slogged from trench-lined plots under a lowering red sun, making their way back home.

In their midst, Gurney Halleck, his blond hair a sweaty tangle, clapped his hands rhythmically. It was the only way he could keep going, his way of resisting the oppression of Harkonnen overlords, who for the moment were not within earshot. He made up a work song with nonsense lyrics, trying to get his companions to join in, or at least to mumble along with the chorus.

We toil all day, the Harkonnen way,
Hour after hour, we long for a shower,
Just workin' and workin' and workin' . . .

The people trudged along silently. Too tired after eleven hours in the rocky fields, they hardly gave the would-be troubadour a notice. With a resigned sigh, Gurney finally gave up his efforts, though he maintained his wry smile. "We are indeed miserable, my friends, but we don't have to be dismal about it."

Ahead lay a low village of prefabricated buildings—a settle-

ment called Dmitri in honor of the previous Harkonnen patri-
arch, the father of Baron Vladimir. After the Baron had taken
control of House Harkonnen decades ago, he'd scrutinized
the maps of Giedi Prime, renaming land features to his own
tastes. In the process he had added a melodramatic flair to the
stark formations: Isle of Sorrows, Perdition Shallows, Cliff of
Death. . . .

No doubt a few generations hence, someone else would
rename the landmarks all over again.

Such concerns were beyond Gurney Halleck. Though
poorly educated, he did know the Imperium was vast, with a
million planets and decillions of people . . . but it wasn't likely
he'd travel even as far as Harko City, the densely packed,
smoky metropolis that shed a perpetual ruddy glow on the
northern horizon.

Gurney studied the crew around him, the people he saw
every day. Eyes downcast, they marched like machines back to
their squalid homes, so sullen that he had to laugh aloud. "Get
some soup in your bellies, and I'll expect you to start singing
tonight. Doesn't the O. C. Bible say, 'Make cheer from your
own heart, for the sun rises and sets according to your perspective on the universe'?"

A few workers mumbled with faint enthusiasm; it was better than nothing. At least he had managed to cheer them up
some. With a life so dreary, any spot of color was worth the
effort.

Gurney was twenty-one, his skin already rough and leathery from working in the fields since the age of eight. By habit,
his bright blue eyes drank in every detail . . . though the village of Dmitri and the desolate fields gave him little to look at.
With an angular jaw, a too-round nose, and flat features, he
already looked like an old farmer and would no doubt marry
one of the washed-out, tired-looking girls from the village.

Gurney had spent the day up to his armpits in a trench,
wielding a spade to throw out piles of stony earth. After so

many years of tilling the same ground, the villagers had to dig deep in order to find nutrients in the soil. The Baron certainly didn't waste solaris on fertilizers—not for *these people*.

During their centuries of stewardship on Giedi Prime, the Harkonnens had made a habit of wringing the land for all it was worth. It was their right—no, their *duty*—to exploit this world, and then move the villages to new land and new pickings. One day when Giedi Prime was a barren shell, the leader of House Harkonnen would undoubtedly request a different fief, a new reward for serving the Padishah Emperors. There were, after all, many worlds to choose from in the Imperium.

But galactic politics were of no interest to Gurney. His goals were limited to enjoying the upcoming evening, sharing a bit of entertainment and relaxation down at the meeting place. Tomorrow would be another day of back-breaking work.

Only stringy, starchy krall tubers grew profitably in these fields; though most of the crop was exported as animal feed, the bland tubers were nutritious enough to keep people working. Gurney ate them every day, as did everyone else. *Poor soil leads to poor taste*.

His parents and coworkers were full of proverbs, many from the Orange Catholic Bible; Gurney memorized them all and often set them to tunes. Music was the one treasure he was allowed to have, and he shared it freely.

The workers spread out to their separate but identical dwellings, defective prefabricated units House Harkonnen had bought at discount and dumped there. Gurney gazed ahead to where he lived with his parents and his younger sister, Bheth.

His home had a brighter touch than the others. Old, rusted cookpots held dirt in which colorful flowers grew: maroon, blue, and yellow pansies, a shock of daisies, even sophisticated-looking calla lilies. Most houses had small vegetable gardens where the people grew plants, herbs, vegetables—though any produce that looked too appetizing might be confiscated and eaten by roving Harkonnen patrols.

The day was warm and the air smoky, but the windows of his home were open. Gurney could hear Bheth's sweet voice in a lilting melody. In his mind's eye he saw her long, straw-colored hair; he thought of it as "flaxen"—a word from Old Terran poems he had memorized—though he had never seen homespun flax. Only seventeen, Bheth had fine features and a sweet personality that had not yet been crushed by a lifetime of work.

Gurney used the outside faucet to splash the gray, caked dirt from his face, arms, and hands. He held his head under the cold water, soaking his snarled blond hair, then used blunt fingers to maul it into some semblance of order. He shook his head and strode inside, kissing Bheth on the cheek while dripping cold water on her. She squealed and backed away, then returned to her cooking chores.

Their father had already collapsed in a chair. Their mother bent over huge wooden bins outside the back door, preparing krall tubers for market; when she noticed Gurney was home, she dried her hands and came inside to help Bheth serve. Standing at the table, his mother read several verses from a tattered old O. C. Bible in a deeply reverent voice (her goal was to read the entire mammoth tome to her children before she died), and then they sat down to eat. He and his sister talked while sipping a soup of stringy vegetables, seasoned only with salt and a few sprigs of dried herbs. During the meal, Gurney's parents spoke little, usually in monosyllables.

Finishing, he carried his dishes to the basin, where he scrubbed them and left them to drip dry for the next day. With wet hands he clapped his father on the shoulder. "Are you going to join me at the tavern? It's fellowship night."

The older man shook his head. "I'd rather sleep. Sometimes your songs just make me feel too tired."

Gurney shrugged. "Get your rest then." In his small room,

he opened the rickety wardrobe and took out his most prized possession: an old baliset, designed as a nine-stringed instrument, though Gurney had learned to play with only seven, since two strings were broken and he had no replacements.

He had found the discarded instrument, damaged and useless, but after working on it patiently for six months . . . sanding, lacquering, shaping parts . . . the baliset made the sweetest music he'd ever heard, albeit without a full tonal range. Gurney spent hours in the night strumming the strings, spinning the counterbalance wheel. He taught himself to play tunes he had heard, or composed new ones.

As darkness enclosed the village, his mother sagged into a chair. She placed the precious Bible in her lap, comforted more by its weight than its words. "Don't be late," she said in a dry, empty voice.

"I won't." Gurney wondered if she would notice if he stayed out all night. "I'll need my strength to tackle those trenches tomorrow." He raised a well-muscled arm, feigning enthusiasm for the tasks all of them knew would never end. He made his way across the packed-dirt streets down to the tavern.

In the wake of a deadly fever several years ago, four of the prefab structures had been left empty. The villagers had moved the buildings together, knocked down the connecting walls, and fashioned themselves a large community house. Although this wasn't exactly against the numerous Harkonnen restrictions, the local enforcers had frowned at such a display of initiative. But the tavern remained.

Gurney joined the small crowd of men who had already gathered for the fellowship down at the tavern. Some brought their wives. One man already lay slumped across the table, more exhausted than drunk, his flagon of watery beer only half-consumed. Gurney crept up behind him, held out his baliset, and strummed a jangling chord that startled the man to full wakefulness.

"Here's a new one, friends. Not exactly a hymn that your mothers remember, but I'll teach it to you." He gave them a wry grin. "Then you'll all sing along with me, and probably ruin the tune." None of them were very good singers, but the songs were entertaining, and it brought a measure of brightness to their lives.

With full energy, he tacked sardonic words onto a familiar melody:

O Giedi Prime!
Thy shades of black are beyond compare,
From obsidian plains to oily seas,
To the darkest nights in the Emperor's Eye.

Come ye from far and wide
To see what we hide in our hearts and minds,
To share our bounty
And lift a pickax or two . . .
Making it all lovelier than before.

O Giedi Prime!
Thy shades of black are beyond compare,
From obsidian plains to oily seas,
To the darkest nights in the Emperor's Eye.

When Gurney finished the song, he wore a grin on his plain, blocky face and bowed to imagined applause. One of the men called out hoarsely, "Watch yourself, Gurney Halleck. If the Harkonnens hear your sweet voice, they'll haul you off to Harko for sure—so you can sing for the Baron himself."

Gurney made a rude noise. "The Baron has no ear for music, especially not lovely songs like mine." This brought a round of laughter. He picked up a mug of the sour beer and chugged it down.

Then the door burst open and Bheth ran in, her flaxen hair loose, her face flushed. "Patrol coming! We saw the suspensor lights. They've got a prisoner transport and a dozen guards."

The men sat up with a jolt. Two ran for the doors, but the others remained frozen in place, already looking caught and defeated.

Gurney strummed a soothing note on his baliset. "Be calm, my friends. Are we doing anything illegal? 'The guilty both know and show their crimes.' We are merely enjoying fellowship. The Harkonnens can't arrest us for that. In fact, we're demonstrating how much we like our conditions, how happy we are to work for the Baron and his minions. Right, mates?"

A somber grumbling was all the agreement he managed to elicit. Gurney set aside his baliset and went to the trapezoidal window of the communal hall just as a prisoner transport pulled up in the center of the village. Several human forms could be seen in shadow behind the transport's plaz windows, evidence that the Harkonnens had been busy arresting people—all women, it appeared. Though he patted his sister's hand and maintained his good humor for the benefit of the others, Gurney knew the troopers needed few excuses to take more captives.

Brilliant spotlights targeted the village. Dark armored forms rushed up the packed-dirt streets, pounding on houses. Then the door to the communal building was shouldered open with a loud crash.

Six men strode inside. Gurney recognized Captain Kryubi of the baronial guard, the man in charge of House Harkonnen security. "Stand still for inspection," Kryubi ordered. A shard of mustache bristled on his lip. His face was narrow and his cheeks looked sunken, as if he clenched his jaw too often.

Gurney remained by the window. "We've done nothing wrong here, Captain. We follow Harkonnen rules. We do our work."

Kryubi looked over at him. "And who appointed you the leader of this village?"

Gurney did not think fast enough to keep his sarcasm in check. "And who gave *you* orders to harass innocent villagers? You'll make us incapable of doing our tasks tomorrow."

His companions in the tavern were horrified at his impudence. Bheth clutched Gurney's hand, trying to keep her brother quiet. The Harkonnen guards made threatening gestures with their weapons.

Gurney jerked his chin to indicate the prisoner escort vehicle outside the window. "What did those people do? What crimes worthy of arrest?"

"No crimes are necessary," Kryubi said, coolly unafraid of the truth.

Gurney took a step forward, but three guards grasped his arms and threw him heavily to the floor. He knew the Baron often recruited guards from the farming villages. The new thugs—rescued from bleak lives and given new uniforms, weapons, lodgings, and women—often became scornful of their previous lives and proved crueler than off-world professionals. Gurney hoped he would recognize a man from a neighboring village, so he could spit in his eye. His head struck the hard floor, but he sprang back to his feet.

Bheth moved quickly to her brother's side. "Don't provoke them anymore."

It was the worst thing she could have done. Kryubi pointed at her. "All right, take that one, too."

Bheth's narrow face paled when two of the three guards grabbed her by her thin arms. She struggled as they hauled her to the still-open door. Gurney cast his baliset aside and lunged forward, but the remaining guard produced his weapon and brought the butt down hard across the young man's forehead and nose.

Gurney staggered, then threw himself forward again,

swinging balled fists like mallets. "Leave her alone!" He knocked one of the guards down and tore the second one away from his sister. She screamed as the three converged upon Gurney, pummeling him, slamming their weapons so brutally into him that his ribs cracked; his nose was already bloodied.

"Help me!" Gurney shouted to the saucer-eyed villagers. "We outnumber the bastards."

No one came to his aid.

He flailed and punched, but went down in a flurry of kicking boots and pounding weapons. Struggling to lift his head, he saw Kryubi watching as his men pulled Bheth toward the door. Gurney pushed, trying to throw off the heavy men who held him down.

Between the gauntleted arms and padded legs, he saw the villagers frozen in their seats, like sheep. They watched him with stricken expressions, but remained as motionless as stones in a castle keep. "Help me, damn you!"

One guard punched him in the solar plexus, making him gasp and retch. Gurney's voice was gone, his breath fading. Black spots danced in front of his eyes. Finally, the guards withdrew.

He propped himself on an elbow just in time to see Bheth's despairing face as the Harkonnen men dragged her into the night.

Enraged and frustrated, he swayed back to his feet, fighting to remain conscious. He heard the prison transport power up in the square outside. Haloed by a glow of illumination against the windows of the tavern, it roared off toward another village to pick up more captives.

Gurney blinked at the other men through swollen eyes. *Strangers*. He coughed and spat blood, then wiped it from his lips. Finally, when he could wheeze, he said, "You bastards just sat there. You didn't lift a finger to help." Brushing himself off, he glared at the villagers. "How can you let them do this to us? *They took my sister!*"

But they were no better than sheep, and never had been. He should have expected nothing different now.

With utter contempt, he spat blood and saliva on the floor, then staggered toward the door and out.

Secrets are an important aspect of power. The effective leader spreads them in order to keep men in line.

—PRINCE RAPHAEL CORRINO,
Discourses on Leadership in a Galactic Imperium,
Twelfth Edition

THE FERRET-FACED MAN STOOD LIKE A SPYING CROW ON THE SECOND level of the Residency at Arrakeen. He gazed down into the spacious atrium. "You are certain they know about our little soiree, hmmm-ah?" His lips were cracked from the dry air; they had been that way for years. "All the invitations personally delivered? All the populace notified?"

Count Hasimir Fenring leaned toward the slender, loose-chinned chief of his guard force, Geraldo Willowbrook, who stood beside him. The scarlet-and-gold-uniformed man nodded, squinted in the bright light that streamed through prismatic, shield-reinforced windows. "It will be a grand celebration for your anniversary here, sir. Already beggars are massing at the front gate."

"Hmm-m-ah, good, very good. My wife will be pleased."

On the main floor below, a chef carried a silver coffee service toward the kitchen. Cooking odors drifted upward, exotic soups and sauces prepared for the evening's extravagant festivities, broiled brochettes of meat from animals that had never lived on Arrakis.

Fenring gripped a carved ironwood banister. An arched Gothic ceiling rose two stories overhead, with elacca wood crossbeams and plaz skylights. Though muscular, he was not a large man, and found himself dwarfed by the immensity of this house. He'd commissioned the ceiling himself, and another in the Dining Hall. The new east wing was his concept as well, with its elegant guest rooms and opulent private pools.

In his decade as Imperial Observer on the desert planet, he had generated a constant buzz of construction around him. Following his exile from Shaddam's court on Kaitain, he'd had to make his mark somehow.

From the botanical conservatory under construction near the private chambers he shared with Lady Margot, he heard the hum of power tools along with the chants of day-labor crews. They cut keyhole-arched doorways, set dry fountains into alcoves, adorned walls with colorful geometric mosaics. For luck, one of the hinges supporting a heavy ornamental door had been symbolically shaped as the hand of Fatimah, beloved daughter of an ancient prophet of Old Terra.

Fenring was about to dismiss Willowbrook when a resounding crash made the upper floor shudder. The two men ran down the curving hallway, past bookcases. From rooms and lift tubes, curious household servants poked their heads into the corridor.

The oval conservatory door stood open, revealing a mass of tangled metal and plaz. One of the workers shouted for medics over the din of screaming. A fully laden suspensor scaffold had collapsed; Fenring vowed to personally administer the appropriate punishment, once an investigation had pointed fingers at the likely scapegoats.

Shouldering his way into the room, Fenring looked up. Through the open metal framing of the arched roof, he saw a lemon-yellow sky. Only a few of the filter-glass windows had been installed; others now lay shattered in the tangle of scaffolding. He spoke in a tone of disgust. "Unfortunate timing, hmmmm? I was going to take our guests on a tour tonight."

"Yes, most unfortunate, Count Fenring, sir." Willowbrook

watched while household workers began digging in the rubble to reach the injured.

House medics in khaki uniforms hurried past him into the ruined area. One tended a bloody-faced man who had just been pulled from the debris, while two men helped remove a heavy sheet of plaz from additional victims. The job superintendent had been crushed by the fallen scaffold. *Stupid fellow*, Fenring thought. *But lucky, considering what I'd have done to him for this mess*.

Fenring glanced at his wristchron. Two more hours until the guests arrived. He motioned to Willowbrook. "Wrap it up here. I don't want any noise coming from this area during the party. That would provide entirely the wrong message, hmmm? Lady Margot and I have laid out the evening's festivities most carefully, down to the last detail."

Willowbrook scowled, but obviously thought better of showing defiance. "It will be done, sir. In less than an hour."

Fenring simmered. In reality he cared nothing for exotic plants, and initially had agreed to this expensive remodeling only as a concession to his Bene Gesserit wife, the Lady Margot. Although she'd requested only a modest airlocked room with plants inside, Fenring—ever ambitious—had expanded it to something far more impressive. He conceived plans to collect rare flora from all over the Imperium.

If ever the conservatory could be finished . . .

Composing himself, he greeted Margot in the vaulted entry just as she returned from the labyrinthine souk markets in town. A willowy blonde with gray-green eyes, perfect figure, and impeccable features, she stood nearly a head taller than he. She wore an aba robe tailored to show off her figure, the black fabric speckled with dust from the streets.

"Did they have Ecazi turnips, my dear?" The Count stared hungrily at two heavy packages wrapped in thick brown spice paper carried by male servants. Having heard of a merchant's arrival by Heighliner that afternoon, Margot had hurried into

Arrakeen to purchase the scarce vegetables. He tried to peek under the paper wrappings, but she playfully slapped his hand away.

"Is everything ready here, my dear?"

"Mmm-m-m, it's all going smoothly," he said. "We can't tour your new conservatory tonight, though. It's too messy up there for our dinner guests."

WAITING TO GREET the important guests as they arrived at sunset, Lady Margot Fenring stood in the mansion's atrium, adorned on its wood-paneled lower level with portraits of Padishah Emperors extending back to the legendary General Faykan Corrin, who had fought in the Butlerian Jihad, and the enlightened ruler Crown Prince Raphael Corrino, as well as "the Hunter" Fondil III, and his son, Elrood IX.

In the center of the atrium, a golden statue showed the current Emperor Shaddam IV in full Sardaukar regalia with a ceremonial sword raised high. It was one of many expensive works the Emperor had commissioned in the first decade of his reign. Around the Residency and grounds were numerous additional examples, gifts from her husband's boyhood friend. Although the two men had quarreled at the time of Shaddam's ascension to the throne, they had gradually grown closer again.

Through the dust-sealed double doors streamed elegantly dressed ladies, accompanied by men in ravenlike post-Butlerian tuxedos and military uniforms of varying colors. Margot herself wore a floor-length gown of silk taffeta with emerald shimmer-sequins on the bodice.

As a uniformed crier announced her guests, Margot greeted them. They filed past into the Grand Hall, where she heard much laughter, conversation, and clinking of glasses. Entertainers from House Jongleur performed tricks and sang witty songs to celebrate the Fenrings' ten years on Arrakis.

Her husband strutted down the grand staircase from the second floor. Count Fenring wore a dark blue retrotuxedo with a crimson royal sash across the chest, personally tailored for him on Bifkar. She bent to allow the shorter man to kiss her on the lips. "Now go in and welcome our guests, dear, before the Baron dominates every conversation."

With a light step, Fenring avoided an intent, frumpy-looking Duchess from one of the Corrino subplanets; the Duchess passed a remote-cast poison snooper over her wine-glass before drinking, then slipped the device unobtrusively into a pocket of her ball gown.

Margot watched her husband as he went to the fireplace to talk with Baron Harkonnen, current holder of the siridar-fief of Arrakis and its rich spice monopoly. The light of a blazing fire enhanced by hearth prisms gave the Baron's puffy features an eerie cast. He wasn't looking at all well.

In the years she and Fenring had been stationed there, the Baron had invited them to dine at his Keep or attend gladiatorial events featuring slaves from Giedi Prime. He was a dangerous man who thought too much of himself. Now, the Baron leaned on a gilded walking stick whose head had been designed to resemble the mouth of a great sandworm of Arrakis.

Margot had seen the Baron's health decline dramatically over the past decade; he suffered from a mysterious muscular and neurological malady that had caused him to gain weight. From her Bene Gesserit Sisters she knew the reason for his physical discomfiture, how it had been inflicted upon him when he'd raped Reverend Mother Gaius Helen Mohiam. The Baron, however, had never learned the cause of his distress.

Mohiam herself, another carefully selected guest for this event, passed into Margot's line of sight. The gray-haired Reverend Mother wore a formal aba robe with a diamond-crusted collar. She smiled a tight-lipped greeting. With a subtle flicker of fingers, she sent a message and a question. "What news for Mother Superior Harishka? Give details. I must report to her."

Margot's fingers responded: "Progress on the Missionaria Protectiva matter. Only rumors, nothing confirmed. Missing Sisters not yet located. Long time. They may all be dead."

Mohiam did not look pleased. She herself had once worked with the Missionaria Protectiva, an invaluable Bene Gesserit division that sowed infectious superstitions on far-flung worlds. Mohiam had spent decades here in her younger years, posing as a town woman, disseminating information, enhancing superstitions that might benefit the Sisterhood. Mohiam herself had never been able to infiltrate the closed Fremen society, but over the centuries, many other Sisters had gone into the deep desert to mingle with the Fremen—and had disappeared.

Since she was on Arrakis as the Count's consort, Margot had been asked to confirm the Missionaria's subtle work. Thus far she'd heard unconfirmed reports of Reverend Mothers who had joined the Fremen and gone underground, as well as rumors of Bene Gesserit—like religious rituals among the tribes. One isolated sietch supposedly had a holy woman; dusty travelers were overheard in a town coffee tent speaking of a messiah legend clearly inspired by the Panoplia Propheticus . . . but none of this information came directly from the Fremen themselves. The desert people, like their planet, seemed impenetrable.

Maybe the Fremen murdered the Bene Gesserit women outright and stole the water from their bodies.

"Those others have been swallowed up by the sands." Margot's fingers flickered.

"Nevertheless, find them." With a nod that ended the silent conversation, Mohiam glided across the room toward a side doorway.

"Rondo Tuek," the crier announced, "the water merchant."

Turning, Margot saw a broad-faced but wiry man stride across the foyer with an odd, rolling gait. He had tufts of rusty-gray hair at the sides of his head, thinning strands on his pate, and widely separated gray eyes. She reached out to greet him. "Ah, yes—the smuggler."

Tuek's flat cheeks darkened, then a broad smile cracked his squarish face. He wagged a finger at her, in the manner of a teacher to a student. "I am a water supplier who works hard to excavate moisture from the dirty ice caps."

"Without the industriousness of your family, I'm sure the Imperium would collapse."

"My Lady is too kind." Tuek bowed and entered the Grand Hall.

Outside the Residency, poor beggars had gathered, hoping for a rare show of graciousness from the Count. Other spectators had come to watch the beggars, and gaze longingly up at the ornate facade of the mansion. Water-sellers in brightly dyed traditional garb jingled their bells and called out an eerie cry of "Soo-Soo Sook!" Guards—borrowed from the Harkonnen troops and obliged to wear Imperial uniforms for the event—stood by the doorways, keeping out undesirables and clearing the way for the invited. It was a circus.

When the last of the expected guests arrived, Margot glanced at an antique chrono set into the wall, adorned with mechanical figures and delicate chimes. They were nearly half an hour late. She hurried to her husband's side and whispered in his ear. He dispatched a messenger to the Jongleurs, and they fell silent—a signal familiar to the guests.

"May I have your attention please, hmmm?" Fenring shouted. Pompously dressed footmen appeared to escort the attendees. "We will reconvene in the Dining Hall." According to tradition, Count and Countess Fenring trailed behind the last of their guests.

On either side of the wide doorway to the Dining Hall stood laving basins of gold-embedded tile, decorated with intricate mosaics containing the crests of House Corrino and House Harkonnen, in accordance with political necessity. The crest denoting the previous governors of Arrakis, House Richese, had been painstakingly chiseled out to be replaced with a blue Harkonnen griffin. The guests paused at the basins, dipped their hands into the water, and slopped some onto the floor. After drying their hands, they flung towels into a growing puddle.

Baron Harkonnen had suggested this custom to show that a planetary governor cared nothing for water shortages. It was an optimistic flaunting of wealth. Fenring had liked the sound of that, and the procedure had been instituted—with a benevolent twist, however: Lady Margot saw a way to help the beggars, in a largely symbolic way. With her husband's grudging concurrence, she let it be known that at the conclusion of each banquet, beggars were welcome to gather outside the mansion and receive any water that could be squeezed from the soiled towels.

Her hands tingling and damp, Margot entered the long hall with her husband. Antique tapestries adorned the walls. Free-floating glowglobes wandered around the room, all set at the same height above the floor, all tuned to the yellow band. Over the polished wooden table hung a chandelier of glittering blue-green Hagal quartz, with a sensitive poison snooper concealed in the upper reaches of the chain.

A small army of footmen held chairs for the diners, and draped a napkin over each guest's lap. Someone stumbled and knocked a crystal centerpiece to the floor, where it shattered. Servants hurried to clean it up and replace it. Everyone else pretended not to notice.

Margot, seated at the foot of the long table, nodded graciously to Planetologist Pardot Kynes and his twelve-year-old son, who took their assigned seats on either side of her. She'd been surprised when the rarely seen desert man accepted her invitation, and she hoped to learn how many of the rumors about him were true. In her experience, dinner parties were notorious for small talk and insincerity, though certain things did not escape the attention of an astute Bene Gesserit observer. She watched the lean man carefully, noting a repair patch on the gray collar of his dress tunic, and the strong line of his sandy-bearded jaw.

Two places down from her, Reverend Mother Mohiam slid into a chair. Hasimir Fenring took his seat at the head of the table, with Baron Harkonnen on his right. Knowing how the Baron and Mohiam loathed one another, Margot had seated them far apart.

At a snap of Fenring's fingers, servants bearing platters of exotic morsels emerged from side doorways. They worked their way around the table, identifying the fare and serving sample portions from the plates.

"Thank you for inviting us, Lady Fenring," Kynes's son said, looking at Margot. The Planetologist had introduced the young man as Weichih, a name that meant "beloved." She could see a resemblance to the father, but while the older Kynes had a dreaminess in his eyes, this Weichih bore a hardness caused by growing up on Arrakis.

She smiled at him. "One of our chefs is a city Fremen who has prepared a sietch specialty for the banquet, spice cakes with honey and sesame."

"Fremen cuisine is Imperial class now?" Pardot Kynes inquired with a wry smile. He looked as if he'd never thought of food as anything more than sustenance, and considered formal dining to be a distraction from other work.

"Cuisine is a matter of . . . taste." She selected her words diplomatically. Her eyes twinkled.

"I take that as a no," he said.

Tall, off-world servingwomen moved from place to place with narrow-necked bottles of blue melange-laced wine. To the amazement of the locals, plates of whole fish appeared, surrounded by gaping Buzzell mussels. Even the wealthiest inhabitants of Arrakeen rarely sampled seafood.

"Ah!" Fenring said with delight from the other end of the table, as a servant lifted a cover from a tray. "I shall relish these

Ecazi turnips, hmmmm. Thank you, my dear." The servant ladled dark sauce onto the vegetables.

"No expense is too great for our honored guests," Margot said.

"Let me tell you why those vegetables are so expensive," a diplomat from Ecaz groused, commanding everyone's attention. Bindikk Narvi was a small man with a deep, thundering voice. "Crop sabotage has drastically reduced our supply for the entire Imperium. We've named this new scourge the 'Grumman blight.'"

He glared across the table at the Ambassador from Grumman, a huge heavy-drinking man with creased, dark skin. "We have also discovered biological sabotage in our fogtree forests on the continent of Elacca." All of the Imperium prized Ecazi fogtree sculptures, which were made by directing growth through the power of human thought.

Despite his bulk, the Moritani man—Lupino Ord—spoke in a squeaky voice. "Once again the Ecazis fake a shortage to drive prices up. An ancient trick that has been around since your thieving ancestors were driven from Old Terra in disgrace."

"That isn't what happened at all—"

"Gentlemen, please," Fenring said. The Grummans had always been a very volatile people, ready to fly into a vengeful frenzy at the slightest perceived insult. Fenring found it all rather thin-skinned and boring. He looked at his wife. "Did we make a mistake in the seating arrangement, my dear, hmmm?"

"Or perhaps in the guest list," she quipped.

Polite, embarrassed laughter bubbled around the table. The quarreling men grew quiet, though they glared at one another.

"So nice to see that our eminent Planetologist has brought along his fine young son," Baron Harkonnen said in an oily tone. "Quite a handsome lad. You have the distinction of being the youngest dinner guest."

"I am honored to be here," the boy replied, "among such esteemed company."

"Being groomed to succeed your father, I hear," the Baron continued. Margot detected carefully hidden sarcasm in the basso voice. "I don't know what we'd do without a Planetologist." In truth, Kynes was rarely seen in the city, and almost never submitted the required reports to the Emperor, not that Shaddam noticed or cared. Margot had gleaned from her husband that the Emperor was occupied with other—as yet unrevealed—matters.

The young man's intent eyes brightened. He raised a water flagon. "May I propose a toast to our host and hostess?" Pardot Kynes blinked at his son's boldness, as if surprised that the social nicety had not occurred to him first.

"An excellent suggestion," the Baron gushed. Margot recognized a slackness in his speech from consuming too much melange wine.

The twelve-year-old spoke in a firm voice, before taking a sip. "May the wealth you display for us here, with all this food and abundance of water, be merely a pale reflection of the riches in your hearts."

The assembled guests endorsed the blessing, and Margot detected a flicker of greed in their eyes. The Planetologist fidgeted and finally spoke what was on his mind, as the clinking of glasses diminished. "Count Fenring, I understand you have an elaborate wet-planet conservatory under construction here. I would be very interested in seeing it." Margot suddenly understood why Kynes had accepted the invitation, the reason he had come in from the desert. Dressed in his plain but serviceable tunic and breeches, covered by a sandy-brown cloak, the man resembled a dirty Fremen more than an Imperial servant.

"You have learned our little secret, hmmm-ah?" With obvious discomfort, Fenring pursed his lips. "I had intended to show it to my guests this evening, but sadly certain . . . hmmm-ahh, *delays* have made that impossible. Some other time, perhaps."

"By keeping a private conservatory, do you not flaunt things that the people of Arrakis cannot have?" young Weichih asked.

"*Yet*," Pardot Kynes said under his breath.

Margot heard it. *Interesting.* She saw that it would be a mistake to underestimate this rugged man, or even his son. "Surely it is an admirable goal to collect plants from all over the Imperium?" she suggested, patiently. "I see it as a display of riches the universe has to *offer*, rather than a reminder of what the people *lack*."

In a low but firm tone, Pardot Kynes admonished the young man, "We did not come here to force our views on others."

"On the contrary, please be so good as to explain your views," Margot urged, trying to ignore insulting looks still being exchanged across the table by the Ecazi and Grumman ambassadors. "We won't take offense, I promise you."

"Yes," said a Carthag weapons-importer from halfway down the table. His fingers were so laden with jeweled rings he could barely lift his hands. "Explain how Fremen think. We all want to know that!"

Kynes nodded slowly. "I have lived with them for many years. To begin an understanding of the Fremen, realize that survival is their mind-set. They waste nothing. Everything is salvaged, reused."

"Down to the last drop of water," Fenring said. "Even the water in dead bodies, hmmmm?"

Kynes looked at his son, then back at Margot. "And your private conservatory will require a great deal of that precious water to maintain."

"Ahh, but as Imperial Observer here, I can do anything I please with natural resources," Fenring pointed out. "I consider my wife's conservatory a worthwhile expenditure."

"Your rights are not in doubt," Kynes said, his tone as steady as the Shield Wall. "And I am the Planetologist for Emperor Shaddam, as I was for Elrood IX before him. We are each bound to our duties, Count Fenring. You will hear no speeches from me about ecological issues. I merely answered your Lady's question."

"Well, then, Planetologist, tell us something we don't know about Arrakis," the Baron said, gazing down the table. "You've certainly been here long enough. More of my men die here than in any other Harkonnen holding. The Guild can't even put enough functional weather satellites in orbit to provide reliable surveillance and make predictions. It is most frustrating."

"And, thanks to the spice, Arrakis is also most profitable," Margot said. "Especially for you, dear Baron."

"This planet defies understanding," Kynes said. "And it will take more than my brief lifetime to determine what is going on here. This much I know: We must learn how to live with the desert, rather than against it."

"Do the Fremen hate us?" Duchess Caula, an Imperial cousin, asked. She held a forkful of brandy-seasoned sweetbreads halfway to her mouth.

"They are insular, and distrust anyone who is non-Fremen. But they are honest, direct people with a code of honor that no one at this table—not even myself—fully understands."

With an elegant lift of her eyebrows Margot asked the next question, watching carefully for his reaction. "Is it true what we've heard, that you've become one of them yourself, Planetologist?"

"I remain an Imperial servant, my Lady, though there is much to be learned from the Fremen."

Murmurs rose from different seats, accompanied by louder pockets of discussion while the first dessert course arrived.

"Our Emperor still has no heir," Lupino Ord, the Grumman ambassador, commented. The big man's voice was a lilting shrill. He'd been drinking steadily. "Only two daughters, Irulan and Chalice. Not that women aren't valuable . . ." He looked around mischievously with his coal-black eyes, catching the disapproving gazes of several ladies at the table. "But without a male heir, House Corrino must step aside in favor of another Great House."

"If he lives as long as Elrood, our Emperor might have a century left in him," Margot pointed out. "Perhaps you haven't heard that Lady Anirul is with child again?"

"My duties sometimes keep me out of the mainstream of news," Ord admitted. He lifted his wineglass. "Let us hope the next one is a boy."

"Hear, hear!" several diners called out.

But the Ecazi diplomat, Bindikk Narvi, made an obscene hand gesture. Margot had heard about the long-standing animosity between the Archduke Armand Ecaz and Viscount Moritani of Grumman, but hadn't realized how serious it had grown. She wished she hadn't seated the two rivals so close to one another.

Ord grabbed a thin-necked bottle and poured more blue wine for himself before a servant could do it for him. "Count Fenring, you have many works of art featuring our Emperor—paintings, statues, plaques bearing his likeness. Is Shaddam funneling too much money into such self-serving commissions? They have sprouted up all over the Imperium."

"And someone keeps defacing them or knocking them down," the Carthag weapons-importer said with a snort.

Thinking of the Planetologist and his son next to her, Margot selected a sweet melange cake from the dessert tray. Perhaps the guests had not heard the *other* rumors, that those benevolent gifts of artwork contained surveillance devices to monitor activities around the Imperium. Such as the plaque on the wall right behind Ord.

"Shaddam desires to make his mark as our ruler, hmmm?" Fenring commented. "I have known him for many years. He wishes to separate himself from the policies of his father, who served for so interminably long."

"Perhaps, but he's neglecting the training of actual Sardaukar troops, while allowing the ranks of his generals . . . What are they called?"

"Bursegs," someone said.

"Yes, while allowing the ranks of his Bursegs to increase, with exorbitant pensions and other benefits. Morale among the Sardaukar must be ebbing, as they are called upon to do more with fewer and fewer resources."

Margot noticed her husband had grown dangerously quiet. Having narrowed his large eyes to slits, he was staring at the foolish drunk.

A woman whispered something to the Grumman ambassador. He ran a finger over the lip of his wineglass. "Oh yes, I apologize for stating the obvious to someone who knows our Emperor so well."

"You're an idiot, Ord," Narvi thundered, as if he'd been waiting for any chance to shout an insult.

"And you're a fool and a dead man." The Grumman ambassador stood up, knocking his chair over behind him. He moved too swiftly, too accurately. Had his drunkenness all been an act, an excuse, just to provoke the man?

Lupino Ord drew a gleaming cutterdisk pistol and, with ear-piercing reports, fired it repeatedly at his adversary. Had he planned this, provoking his Ecazi rival? Cutterdisks tore Narvi's face and chest apart, killing him long before the poisons on the razor edges could have any effect.

Diners cried out and scattered in all directions. Footmen grabbed the reeling ambassador and wrestled the expended weapon from him. Margot sat frozen in place, more astonished than terrified. *What have I missed? How deep does this animosity between Ecaz and House Moritani go?*

"Lock him in one of the underground tunnels," Fenring commanded. "Station a guard at all times."

"But I have diplomatic immunity!" Ord protested, his voice squeakier now. "You don't dare hold me."

"Never assume what I might dare." The Count glanced at the shocked faces around him. "I could simply allow my other guests to punish you, thus exercising their own . . . *immunity*, hmmm?" Fenring waved an arm, and the sputtering man was taken away until protected passage back to Grumman could be arranged.

Medics hurried in, the same ones Fenring had seen earlier at the conservatory disaster. Clearly, they could do nothing for the mutilated Ecazi ambassador.

Quite a body count around here today, Fenring mused. *And I didn't kill any of them.*

"Hmmm-ah," he said to his wife, who stood by him. "I fear this will become an . . . incident. Archduke Ecaz is bound to issue a formal complaint, and there's no telling how Viscount Moritani will respond."

He commanded the footmen to remove Narvi's body from the hall. Many of the guests had scattered to other rooms of the mansion. "Shall we call people back?" He squeezed his wife's hand. "I hate to see the evening end like this. Maybe we could bring in the Jongleurs, have them tell amusing stories."

Baron Harkonnen came up beside them, leaning on his wormhead cane. "This is your jurisdiction, Count Fenring, not mine. You send a report to the Emperor."

"I'll take care of it," Fenring said, tersely. "I'm journeying to Kaitain on another matter, and I will provide Shaddam with the necessary details. And the proper excuses."

In the days of Old Terra there were experts in poisons, deviously clever persons who dealt in what were known as "the powders of inheritance."

—Filmbook excerpt,
Royal Library of Kaitain

GRINNING WITH PRIDE, COURT CHAMBERLAIN BEELY RIDONDO MARCHED through the doorway. "Your Imperial Majesty, you have another new daughter. Your wife has just delivered a fine and healthy girl."

Instead of rejoicing, Emperor Shaddam IV cursed under his breath and sent the man away. *That makes three! What use is another daughter to me?*

He was in a foul mood, worse than any since the struggles to remove his decrepit father from the Golden Lion Throne. At a brisk pace Shaddam entered his private study, passing beneath an ancient plaque that read, "Law is the ultimate science"—some nonsense from Crown Prince Raphael Corrino, a man who'd never even bothered to wear the Imperial crown. He sealed the door behind him and thumped his angular frame into the textured, high-backed suspensor chair at his desk.

A man of middle height, Shaddam had a loosely muscled body and an aquiline nose. His long nails were carefully manicured, his pomaded red hair combed straight back. He wore a gray Sardaukar-style uniform with epaulets and silver-and-gold trim, but the military trappings no longer comforted him as they once had.

In addition to the birth of yet another daughter, he had much on his mind. Recently, at a gala concert in one of the inverted-pyramid stadiums on Harmonthep, someone had released a giant inflated effigy of Shaddam IV. Obscenely insulting, the gaudy caricature made him look like a buffoon. The inflatable construction had drifted over the vast laughing crowds until the Harmonthep dragoon guards had shot it down in flaming tatters—and any fool could see the symbolism in *that* act! Despite the most rigorous crackdown and interrogation, even Sardaukar investigators were not able to determine who'd been responsible for creating or releasing the effigy.

In another incident, hundred-meter-high letters had been scrawled across the granite wall of Monument Canyon on Canidar II: "Shaddam, does your crown rest comfortably on your pointy head?" In scattered worlds across the Imperium, dozens of his new commemorative statues had been defaced. Nobody had ever seen the perpetrators.

Someone hated him enough to do this. *Someone.* The question kept gnawing at his Imperial heart, along with other worries . . . including an impending visit from Hasimir Fenring to report on the secret synthetic spice experiments being conducted by the Tleilaxu.

Project Amal.

Initiated during his father's reign, this research was known to only a few. Perhaps the most closely guarded secret in the Imperium, Project Amal could, if successful, give House Corrino a reliable, artificial source of melange, the most precious substance in the universe. But the damned Tleilaxu experiments were taking years too long, and the situation upset him more and more with each passing month.

And now . . . a third cursed *daughter*! He didn't know when—or if—he would bother to gaze upon this useless new girl-child.

Shaddam's gaze moved along the paneled wall, to a bookcase that contained a stand-up holophoto of Anirul in her wedding gown, shelved next to a thick reference volume of great historical disasters. She had large doe eyes—hazel in some light, darker at other times—that concealed something. He should have noticed before.

It was the third time this Bene Gesserit "of Hidden Rank" had failed to produce the required male heir, and Shaddam had made no contingency plans for such an eventuality. His face grew hot. He could always impregnate a few concubines and hope for a son, but while legally married to Anirul, he would face tremendous political difficulties if he attempted to declare a bastard his heir for the Imperial throne.

He could also kill Anirul and take another wife—his father had done that enough times—but such a course of action would risk the wrath of the Bene Gesserit Sisterhood. Everything could be solved if Anirul would just give him a son, a healthy male child he could call his heir.

All these months of waiting, and now this . . .

He'd heard that the witches could actually choose the gender of their children, through manipulations in body chemistry; these daughters could be no accident. He'd been deceived by the Bene Gesserit power brokers who had foisted Anirul on him. How dare they do that to the Emperor of a Million Worlds? What was Anirul's true purpose in his royal household? Was she gathering blackmail information to use against him? Should he send her away?

He tapped a stylus on his blood-grained elacca wood desk, stared at an image of his paternal grandfather, Fondil III. Commonly known as "the Hunter" for his propensity to attack every vestige of rebellion, Fondil had been no less feared in his own household. Though the old man had died long before Shaddam's birth, he knew something of the Hunter's moods and methods. Had Fondil been faced with an arrogant wife, he would have found a way to rid himself of her. . . .

Shaddam pressed a button on his desk, and his personal Chamberlain reentered the study. Ridondo bowed, showing the gleaming top of his high forehead. "Sire?"

"I wish to see Anirul now. *Here.*"

"The Lady is in bed, Sire."

"Don't make me repeat my order."

Without another word, Ridondo faded into the woodwork, disappearing through the side door with long, spidery movements.

Moments later a pale and overly perfumed lady-in-waiting arrived. In a shaky voice, she said, "My Emperor, the Lady Anirul wishes me to convey that she is weakened from the birth of your child. She begs your indulgence in permitting her to remain in bed. Might it be possible for you to consider coming to visit her and the baby?"

"I see. She begs my indulgence? I am not interested in seeing another useless daughter, or in hearing further excuses. This is a command from your Emperor: Anirul is to come *here now.* She is to do it alone, without the aid of any servant or mechanical device. *Is that understood?*"

With any luck, she would drop dead along the way.

Terrified, the lady-in-waiting bowed. "As you wish, Sire."

Presently, a gray-skinned Anirul stood in the doorway of his private study, holding tight to the fluted support column. She wore a wrinkled scarlet-and-gold robe that did not entirely conceal the nightclothes underneath. Though swaying on her feet, she held her head high.

"What do you have to say for yourself?" he demanded.

"I've just had a difficult childbirth, and I'm quite weak."

"Excuses, excuses. You are intelligent enough to figure out what I mean. You've been clever enough to fool me all these years."

"*Fool* you?" She blinked her doe eyes at him as if he were out of his mind. "Forgive me, Majesty, but I am tired. Why must you be so cruel, calling me here like this and refusing to see our daughter?"

His lips were colorless, as if the blood had drained from them. His eyes were flat pools. "Because you could give me a male heir, but refuse to do so."

"There is no truth in that, Majesty, only rumors." It required all of her Bene Gesserit training to remain standing.

"I listen to intelligence reports, not rumors." The Emperor peered at her through one open eye, as if he could see her in more minute detail that way. "Do you wish to die, Anirul?"

It occurred to Anirul that he might kill her after all. *There is certainly no love between us, but would he dare risk the Sisterhood's ire by disposing of me?* At the time of his ascension to the throne, Shaddam had agreed to marry her because he'd needed the strength of a Bene Gesserit alliance in the uneasy political climate. Now, after a dozen years, Shaddam felt too confident in his position. "Everyone dies," she said.

"But not the way I could arrange for you."

Anirul tried not to show emotion and reminded herself that she was not alone, that within her psyche were the collective memories of the multitudes of Bene Gesserit who had come before her and remained in Other Memory. Her voice was utterly calm. "We are not the complex, devious witches we're made out to be." This was not true, of course, though she knew Shaddam couldn't possibly have more than suspicions to the contrary.

His demeanor didn't soften. "What's more important to you . . . your Sisters or me?"

She shook her head in dismay. "You have no right to ask me such a thing. I've never given you any reason to feel I've been less than faithful to the crown."

Lifting her head proudly, Anirul reminded herself of her position in the long history of the Sisterhood. She would never admit to him that she had orders from the Bene Gesserit hierarchy never to give birth to a Corrino son. The wisdom of her Sisters echoed through her mind. *Love weakens. It is dangerous, for it clouds reason and diverts us from our duties. It is an aberration, a disgrace, an unforgivable infraction. We cannot love.*

Anirul tried to divert Shaddam's anger. "Accept your daughter, Sire, for she can be used to cement important political alliances. We should discuss her name. What do you think of Wensicia?"

With sudden alarm she became aware of warm moisture on her inner thighs. Blood? Had the stitches broken? Red droplets were falling onto the carpet.

Anirul saw him peering down at her feet. New rage consumed the Emperor's features. "That carpet has been in my family for centuries!"

Don't show weakness. He's an animal . . . will attack weakness and back down from strength. She turned slowly, allowing several more drops to fall, then staggered away. "Given the history of House Corrino, I am certain that blood has been spilled on it before."

It is said that there is nothing firm, nothing balanced, nothing durable in all the universe—that nothing remains in its original state, that each day, each hour, each moment, there is change.

—Panoplia Propheticus of the Bene Gesserit

ON THE RUGGED SHORE BENEATH CASTLE CALADAN, A LONE FIGURE STOOD at the end of a long dock, profiled against the sea and the newly risen sun. He had a narrow, olive-skinned face with a high-bridged nose, giving him the look of a hawk.

Out on the water, a fleet of fishing coracles was just departing, trailing wakes behind them. Men in heavy sweaters, coats, and knit hats scrambled about on the cluttered decks, preparing their gear for the day. In the village downshore, wisps of smoke rose above the chimneys. Locals called it "old town," the site of the original settlement centuries before the elegant capital city and spaceport were built on the plain behind the Castle.

Duke Leto Atreides, dressed casually in blue fishing dungarees and a white tunic with a red hawk crest, took a deep breath of invigorating salt air. Though he was master of House Atreides, representing Caladan to the Landsraad and the Emperor, Leto liked to rise early with the fishermen, many of whom he knew on a first-name basis. Sometimes they invited the Duke to their homes, and despite the objections of his Security Commander, Thufir Hawat, who trusted no one, he occasionally joined them for a fine meal of cioppino.

The salt wind picked up, whipping the sea into dancing whitecaps. He wished he could accompany the men, but his responsibilities were too great here. And there were matters of importance beyond his world as well; he owed allegiance to the Imperium as well as the people he ruled, and he found himself thrust into the middle of great things.

The shocking murder of an Ecazi diplomat by a Grumman ambassador was no small matter, even on distant Arrakis, but Viscount Moritani didn't seem to care about public opinion. Already the Great Houses were calling for Imperial intervention in order to avoid a larger conflict. The day before, Leto had sent his own message to the Landsraad Council on Kaitain, volunteering his services as a mediator.

He was only twenty-six years old, but a veteran of a decade at the helm of a Great House. He attributed his success to the fact that he had never lost touch with his roots. For that, he could thank his late father, Paulus. Ostensibly, the Old Duke had been an unpretentious man who mixed with his people, just as Duke Leto did now. But his father must have known—though he'd never admitted it to Leto—that this was also a good political tactic, one that endeared the Duke to his people. The requirements of the office made for a complex mixture; sometimes Leto couldn't tell where his personal and official personas began and left off.

Shortly after being thrust into his responsibilities, Leto Atreides had stunned the Landsraad with his dramatic Trial by Forfeiture, a bold gamble to escape being framed for an attack on two Tleilaxu ships inside a Guild Heighliner. Leto's gambit had impressed many of the Great Houses, and he'd even received a congratulatory letter from Hundro Moritani, the puckish and unlikeable Viscount of Grumman, who often refused to cooperate—or even participate—in matters of the Imperium. The Viscount said he admired Leto's "brash flouting of the rules," proving that "leadership is made by strong men with strong convictions, not clerks who study commas on lawslates." Leto wasn't entirely sure that Moritani believed in his innocence; instead, he thought the Viscount simply enjoyed seeing Duke Atreides get away unpunished, against such insurmountable odds.

On the other side of the dispute, Leto had a connection to House Ecaz as well. The Old Duke, his father, had been one of the great heroes in the Ecazi Revolt, battling beside Dominic Vernius to overthrow violent secessionists and defend the Landsraad-sanctioned rulers of the forested world. Paulus Atreides himself had stood beside the grateful young Archduke Armand Ecaz during the victory ceremony that restored him to the Mahogany Throne. Somewhere among the Old Duke's possessions lay the Chain of Bravery that Armand Ecaz had placed around Paulus's thick neck. And the lawyers who had represented Leto during his Landsraad trial had come from the Ecazi region of Elacca.

Since he was respected by both parties in the feud, Leto thought he might make them see a way to peace. Politics! His father had always taught him to be careful to consider the whole picture, from the tiniest to the largest elements.

From his tunic pocket Leto brought out a voicescriber and dictated a letter to his cousin, Shaddam IV, congratulating him on the joyous birth of another child. The message would be sent by official Courier on the next Guild Heighliner departing for Kaitain.

When Leto could no longer hear the putt-putting of the fishing boats, he hiked up the steep zigzag path that led to the top of the cliff.

HE SHARED A breakfast in the courtyard with twenty-year-old Duncan Idaho. The round-faced young man wore a green-and-black Atreides trooper uniform. His wiry dark hair had been cropped short, out of his eyes for vigorous weapons training. Thufir Hawat had spent a lot of time with him, proclaiming him to be a particularly skilled student. But Duncan had already reached the limits of what the warrior Mentat could teach him.

As a boy, he had escaped from Harkonnen bondage to Castle Caladan, where he'd thrown himself upon the mercy of the Old Duke. As he grew up, Duncan remained one of the most loyal members of the Atreides household, and certainly the best weapons trainee. Longtime military allies of House Atreides, the Swordmasters of Ginaz had recently granted Duncan Idaho admission into their renowned academy.

"I will be sorry to see you go, Duncan," Leto told him. "Eight years is a long time. . . ."

Duncan sat straight, showing no fear. "But when I return, my Duke, I will be better able to serve you in all ways. I'll still be young, and no one will dare threaten you."

"Oh, they'll still threaten me, Duncan. Make no mistake about that."

The young man paused before giving him a thin, hard smile. "Then *they* will be making the mistake. Not me." He lifted a slice of paradan melon to his mouth, took a bite of the yellow fruit, and wiped away the salty juice that ran down his chin. "I am going to miss these melons. Barracks food can't compare." He cut his portion into smaller sections.

Bougainvillea vines trailed up the stone walls around them, but it was still winter and the plants were flowerless. With unseasonable warmth and predictions of an early spring, though, buds had already begun to appear on trees. Leto gave a contented sigh. "I've seen no more beautiful place in all the vast reaches of the Imperium than Caladan in the spring."

"Certainly, Giedi Prime can't compare." Duncan raised his guard, uneasy to see how relaxed and content Leto appeared. "We must remain constantly on the alert, my Duke, not permitting the slightest weakness. Never forget the ancient feud between Atreides and Harkonnen."

"Now you sound like Thufir." Leto scooped up a sweet

mouthful of his pundi rice pudding. "I'm sure there is no finer man than you in the service of the Atreides, Duncan. But I fear we may be creating a monster in sending you away for eight years of training. What will you be when you return?"

Pride infused the young man's deeply set blue-green eyes. "I will be a Swordmaster of the Ginaz."

For a long moment, Leto thought of the extreme dangers at the school. Nearly a third of all students died during training. Duncan had laughed off the statistics, saying he had already survived far worse odds against the Harkonnens. And he was right.

"I know you will succeed," Leto said. He felt a thickness in his throat, a deep sadness at letting Duncan go. "But you must never forget compassion. No matter what you learn, don't come back here with the attitude that you're better than other men."

"I won't, my Duke."

Leto reached under the table and brought out a long, thin parcel and passed it across the table. "This is why I asked you to join me for breakfast."

Surprised, Duncan opened it and removed an ornately carved ceremonial sword. He gripped the inlaid rope pattern of the pommel. "The Old Duke's sword! You're lending it to me?"

"*Giving* it to you, my friend. Remember when I found you in the weapons hall, just after my father died in the bullring? You had taken this sword from the display rack. It was nearly as tall as you were then, but now you've grown into it."

Duncan could find no words to thank him.

Leto looked the young man up and down, appraising him. "I believe if my father had lived to see the man you've become, he might have given it to you himself. You're grown now, Duncan Idaho—worthy of a Duke's sword."

"Good morning," a cheerful voice said. Prince Rhombur Vernius sauntered into the courtyard, still bleary-eyed but dressed. The fire-jewel ring on his right hand gleamed in stray sunlight. His sister Kailea walked beside him, her coppery hair held back by a golden clasp. Rhombur glanced from the sword to the tears brimming in Duncan's eyes. "What's going on here?"

"Giving Duncan a going-away present."

Rhombur whistled. "Pretty fancy for a stableboy."

"Perhaps the gift is too much," Duncan said, looking at Duke Leto. He stared at the sword, then glared at Rhombur. "I'll never work in the stables again, though, Prince Vernius. The next time you see me I'll be a Swordmaster."

"The sword is yours, Duncan," Leto said in his firmest tone, one he had copied from his father. "There will be no further discussion of the matter."

"As you wish, my Duke." Duncan bowed. "I beg to be excused, to prepare for my trip." The young man strode across the courtyard.

Rhombur and Kailea sat at the table, where their breakfast plates had been set up. Kailea smiled at Leto, but not in her customary warm fashion. For years, the pair had been tiptoeing around romantic involvement, with the Duke unwilling to get any closer because of political concerns, his need to wed the daughter of a powerful Great House. His reasons were strictly those his father had drilled into him, a Duke's responsibility to the people of Caladan. Only once had Leto and Kailea held hands; he had never even kissed her.

Lowering her voice, Kailea said, "Your father's sword, Leto? Was that really necessary? It's so valuable."

"But only an object, Kailea. It means more to Duncan than to me. I don't need a sword to retain fond memories of my father." Then Leto noted the blond stubble on his friend's face, which made Rhombur look more like a fisherman than a Prince. "When was the last time you shaved?"

"Vermilion hells! What difference does it make how I look?" He took a drink of cidrit juice, puckered his lips at the tartness. "It's not as if I have anything *important* to do."

Kailea, eating quickly and quietly, studied her brother. She had penetrating green eyes; her catlike mouth was turned down in disapproval.

As Leto looked across the table at Rhombur, he noted that his friend's face still retained a childlike roundness, but the brown eyes were no longer bright. Instead they revealed deep sadness over the loss of his home, the murder of his mother, the disappearance of his father. Now only he and his sister remained of their once-great family.

"Makes no difference, I suppose," Leto said. "We have no affairs of state to conduct today, no trips to glorious Kaitain. In fact, you may as well stop bathing altogether." Leto stirred his bowl of pundi rice pudding, then his voice became uncharacteristically sharp. "Nonetheless, you remain a member of my court—and one of my most trusted advisors. By now, I'd hoped you might develop a plan to regain your lost holdings and position."

As a constant reminder of the glory days of Ix, when House Vernius had ruled the machine world before the Tleilaxu takeover, Rhombur still wore the purple-and-copper helix on the collar of every shirt. Leto noted that the shirt Rhombur wore was badly wrinkled and needed to be washed.

"Leto, if I had any idea what to *do*, I would jump on the next Heighliner and try." He looked flustered. "The Tleilaxu have sealed Ix behind impenetrable barricades. Do you want Thufir Hawat to send in more spies? The first three never found their way underground to the cavern city, and the last two vanished without a trace." He tapped his fingers together. "I just have to hope the loyal Ixians are fighting from within and will soon overthrow the invaders. I expect everything will turn out all right."

"My friend, the optimist," Leto said.

Kailea scowled at her breakfast and finally spoke up. "It's been a dozen years, Rhombur. How long does it take for everything to magically fix itself?"

Uncomfortable, her brother tried to change the subject. "Have you heard that Shaddam's wife just gave birth to their third daughter?"

Kailea snorted. "Knowing Shaddam, I'll bet he's none too pleased that it wasn't a male heir."

Leto refused to accept such negative thoughts. "He's probably ecstatic, Kailea. Besides, his wife still has many childbearing years left." He turned to Rhombur. "Which makes me think, old friend—*you* should take a wife."

"To keep me clean and make sure I shave?"

"To begin your House again, perhaps. To continue the Vernius bloodline with an heir in exile."

Kailea almost said something, seemed to have second thoughts. She finished a melon, nibbled on a piece of toast. Presently she rose and excused herself from the table.

During the long silence, tears glistened on the lower lids of the Ixian Prince's eyes, then rolled down his cheeks. Embarrassed, he wiped them away. "Yes. I've been thinking about that myself. How did you know?"

"You've told me so more than once, after we've shared two or three bottles of wine."

"The whole thing is a crazy idea. My House is dead, and Ix is in the hands of fanatics."

"So, start a new House Minor on Caladan, a new family trade. We could look over the list of industries and see what's needed. Kailea has plenty of business sense. I'll provide the resources you need to get established."

Rhombur allowed himself a bittersweet laugh. "My fortunes will always remain closely allied with yours, Duke Leto Atreides. No, I'd better remain here to watch your backside, making sure you don't give the whole Castle away."

Leto nodded without smiling, and they clasped hands in the half handshake of the Imperium.

Nature commits no errors; right and wrong are human categories.

—PARDOT KYNES,
Arrakis Lectures

MONOTONOUS DAYS. THE THREE-MAN HARKONNEN PATROL CRUISED OVER the golden swells of dunes along a thousand-kilometer flight path. In the unrelenting desert landscape, even a puff of dust caused excitement.

The troopers flew their armored ornithopter in a long circle, skirting mountains, then curving south over great pans and flatlands. Glossu Rabban, the Baron's nephew and temporary governor of Arrakis, had ordered them to fly regularly, to be *seen*—to show the squalid settlements that Harkonnens were watching. Always.

Kiel, the sidegunner, considered the assignment a license to hunt any Fremen found wandering near legitimate spice-harvesting operations. What made those dirty wanderers think they could trespass on Harkonnen lands without permission from the district office in Carthag? But few Fremen were ever caught abroad in daylight, and the task had grown dull.

Garan flew the 'thopter, rising up and dipping down to catch thermals, as if operating an amusement ride. He maintained a stoic expression, though occasionally a grin stole across his lips as the craft bucked and jostled in rough air. As they completed their fifth day on patrol, he continued to mark discrepancies on topographical maps, muttering in disgust each time he found another mistake. These were the worst charts he had ever used.

In the back passenger compartment sat Josten, recently transferred from Giedi Prime. Accustomed to industrial facilities, gray skies, and dirty buildings, Josten gazed out over the sandy wastelands, studying hypnotic dune patterns. He spotted the knot of dust off to the south, deep in the open Funeral Plain. "What's that? Spice-harvesting operation?"

"Not a chance," the sidegunner Kiel said. "Harvesters shoot a plume like a cone into the air, straight and thin."

"Too low for a dust devil. Too small." With a shrug, Garan jerked the 'thopter controls and soared toward the low, reddish-brown cloud. "Let's take a look." After so many tedious days, they would have gone out of their way to investigate a large rock sticking out of the sand. . . .

When they reached the site, they found no tracks, no machinery, no sign of human presence—and yet acres of desert looked devastated. A mottled rust color stained the sands a darker ocher, as if blood from a wound had dried in the hot sun.

"Looks like somebody dropped a bomb here," Kiel said.

"Could be the aftermath of a spice blow," Garan suggested. "I'll set down for a closer look."

As the 'thopter settled on the churned sands, Kiel popped open the hatch. The temperature-controlled atmosphere hissed out, replaced by a wave of heat. He coughed dust.

Garan leaned over from the cockpit and sniffed hard. "Smell it." The odor of burned cinnamon struck his nostrils. "Spice blow for sure."

Josten squeezed past Kiel and dropped onto the soft ground. Amazed, he bent down, picked up a handful of ocher sand and touched it to his lips. "Can we scoop up some fresh spice and take it back? Must be worth a fortune."

Kiel had been thinking the same thing, but now he turned

to the newcomer with scorn. "We don't have the processing equipment. You need to separate it from the sand, and you can't do that with your fingers."

Garan spoke in a quieter, but firmer voice. "If you went back to Carthag and tried to sell raw product to a street vendor, you'd be hauled in front of Governor Rabban—or worse yet, have to explain to Count Fenring how some of the Emperor's spice ended up in a patrolman's pockets."

As the troopers tromped out to the ragged pit at the center of the dissipating dust cloud, Josten glanced around. "Is it safe for us to be here? Don't the big worms go to spice?"

"Afraid, kid?" Kiel asked.

"Let's throw him to a worm if we see one," Garan suggested. "It'll give us time to get away."

Kiel saw movement in the sandy excavation, shapes squirming, buried *things* that tunneled and burrowed, like maggots in rotten meat. Josten opened his mouth to say something, then clamped it shut again.

A whiplike creature emerged from the sand, two meters long with fleshy segmented skin. It was the size of a large snake, its mouth an open circle glittering with needle-sharp teeth that lined its throat.

"A sandworm!" Josten said.

"Only a runt," Kiel scoffed.

"Newborn—do you think?" Garan asked.

The worm waved its eyeless head from side to side. Other slithering creatures, a nest of them, squirmed about as if they'd been spawned in the explosion.

"Where in the hells did they come from?" Kiel asked.

"Wasn't in my briefing," Garan said.

"Can we . . . catch one?" Josten asked.

Kiel stopped himself from making a rude rejoinder, realizing that the young recruit did have a good idea. "Come on!" He charged forward into the churned sand.

The worm sensed the movement and reared back, uncertain whether to attack or flee. Then it arced like a sea serpent and plunged into the sand, wriggling and burrowing.

Josten sprinted ahead and dove facefirst to grasp the segmented body three-quarters of the way to its end. "It's so strong!" Following him, the sidegunner jumped down and grabbed the thrashing tail.

The worm tried to tug away, but Garan reached the front, where he dug into the sand and grabbed behind its head with a stranglehold. All three troopers wrestled and pulled. The small worm thrashed like an eel on an electric plate.

Other sandworms on the far side of the pit rose like a strange forest of periscopes sprouting from the sea of dunes, round mouths like black Os turned toward the men. For an icy moment, Kiel feared they might attack like a swarm of marrow leeches, but the immature worms darted away and disappeared underground.

Garan and Kiel hauled their captive out of the sand and dragged it toward the ornithopter. As a Harkonnen patrol, they had all the equipment necessary to arrest criminals, including old-fashioned devices for trussing a captive like a herd animal. "Josten, go get the binding cords in our apprehension kit," the pilot said.

The new recruit came running back with the cords, fashioning a loop which he slipped over the worm's head and cinched tight. Garan released his hold on the rubbery skin and grabbed the rope, tugging while Josten slipped a second cord lower on the body.

"What are we going to do with it?" Josten asked.

Once, early in his assignment on Arrakis, Kiel had joined Rabban on an abortive worm hunt. They had taken a Fremen guide, well-armed troops, even a Planetologist. Using the Fremen guide as bait, they had lured one of the enormous sandworms and killed it with explosives. But before Rabban could take his trophy, the beast had *dissolved*, sloughing into amoeba-creatures that fell to the sand, leaving nothing but a cartilaginous skeleton and loose crystal teeth. Rabban had been furious.

Kiel's stomach knotted. The Baron's nephew might consider it an insult that three simple patrolmen could capture a worm, when he'd been unable to do so himself. "We'd better drown it."

"Drown it?" Josten said. "What for? And why would I want to waste my water ration to do that?"

Garan stopped as if struck by a thunderbolt. "I've heard the Fremen do it. If you drown a baby worm, they say it spits out some kind of poison. It's very rare."

Kiel nodded. "Oh, yeah. The crazy desert people use it in their religious rituals. It sends everybody into frenzied, wild orgies, and a lot of them die."

"But . . . we've only got two literjons of water in the compartment," Josten said, still nervous.

"Then we only use one. I know where we can refill it, anyway." The pilot and his sidegunner exchanged glances. They had patrolled together long enough that they'd both thought of the same thing.

As if understanding its fate, the worm bucked and thrashed even more, but it was already growing weaker.

"Once we get the drug," Kiel said, "let's have some fun."

AT NIGHT, WITH the patrol 'thopter running in stealth mode, they flew over the razor-edged mountains, approaching from behind a ridge and landing on a rough mesa above the squalid village of Bilar Camp. The villagers lived in hollowed-out caves and aboveground structures that extended out to the flats. Windmills generated power; supply bins glittered with tiny lights that attracted a few moths and the bats that fed on them.

Unlike the reclusive Fremen, these villagers were slightly more civilized but also more downtrodden: men who worked as desert guides and joined spice-harvesting crews. They had forgotten how to survive on their world without becoming parasites upon the planetary governors.

On an earlier patrol, Kiel and Garan had discovered a camouflaged cistern on the mesa, a treasure trove of water. Kiel didn't know where the villagers had gotten so much moisture; most likely, they had committed fraud, inflating their census numbers so that Harkonnen generosity provided more than they deserved.

The people of Bilar Camp covered the cistern with rock so that it looked like a natural protrusion, but the villagers placed no guards around their illegal stockpile. For some reason desert culture forbade thievery even more than murder; they trusted the safety of their possessions from bandits or thieves of the night.

Of course, the Harkonnen troopers had no intention of *stealing* the water—that is, no more than enough for their own needs.

Dutifully, Josten trotted along with their sloshing container, which held the thick, noxious substance exuded by the drowned worm after it had stopped thrashing and bucking inside the container. Awed and nervous about what they'd done, they'd dumped the flaccid carcass near the perimeter of the spice blow and then taken off with the drug. Kiel had been concerned that the toxic exhalation from the worm might eat its way through the literjon.

Garan operated the Bilar cistern's cleverly concealed spigot and refilled one of their empty containers. No sense in letting all the water go to waste just for a practical joke on the villagers. Next, Kiel took the container of worm bile and upended it into the cistern. The villagers would certainly have a surprise next time they all drank from their illegal water hoard. "Serves them right."

"Do you know what this drug will do to them?" Josten asked.

Garan shook his head. "I've heard plenty of crazy stories."

"Maybe we should make the kid try it first," the side-gunner said.

Josten backed away, raising his hands. Garan looked at the contaminated cistern again. "I bet they tear off their clothes and dance naked in the streets, squawking like dinfowl."

"Let's stay here and watch the fun for ourselves," Kiel said.

Garan frowned. "Do *you* want to be the one to explain to Rabban why we're late returning from patrol?"

"Let's go," Kiel answered quickly.

As the worm-poison infused the cistern, the Harkonnen troopers hurried back to their ornithopter, reluctantly content to let the villagers discover the prank for themselves.

Before us, all methods of learning were tainted by instinct. Before us, instinct-ridden researchers possessed a limited attention span—often no longer than a single lifetime. Projects stretching across fifty or more generations never occurred to them. The concept of total muscle/nerve training had not entered their awareness. We learned how to learn.

—Bene Gesserit Azhar Book

IS THIS TRULY A SPECIAL CHILD? THE REVEREND MOTHER GAIUS HELEN MO-hiam watched the perfectly proportioned girl perform *prana-bindu* muscular-nervature exercises on the hardwood floor of the Mother School's training module.

Recently returned from the abortive banquet on Arrakis, Mohiam tried to look at her student with impartiality, suppressing the truth. *Jessica. My own daughter . . .* The girl must never know her heritage, must never suspect. Even on the secret Bene Gesserit breeding charts, Mohiam was not identified by her Sisterhood-adopted name, but by her birth name of "Tanidia Nerus."

Twelve-year-old Jessica stood poised, arms at her sides, trying to relax herself, trying to arrest the movement of every muscle in her body. Gripping an imaginary blade in her right hand, she stared straight ahead at a chimerical opponent. She summoned untapped depths of inner peace and concentration.

But Mohiam's sharp eye noted the barely discernible twitches in Jessica's calf muscles, around her neck, over one eyebrow. This one would need more practice in order to perfect the techniques, but the child had made excellent progress and showed great promise. Jessica was blessed with a supreme patience, an ability to calm herself and listen to what she was told.

So focused, this one . . . so full of potential. As she was bred to be.

Jessica feinted to the left, floated, whirled—then stiffened to become a sudden statue again. Her eyes, while looking at Mohiam, did not see her taskmistress and mentor.

The stern Reverend Mother entered the training module, stared into the girl's clear green eyes, and saw an emptiness there, like the gaze of a corpse. Jessica was gone, lost among her nerve and muscle fibers.

Mohiam dampened a finger and placed it in front of the girl's nose. She felt only the faintest stirring of air. The budding breasts on the slender torso barely moved. Jessica was close to a complete *bindu* suspension . . . but not quite.

Much hard work remains.

In the Sisterhood, only total perfection was good enough. As Jessica's instructor, Mohiam would go over the ancient routines again and again, reviewing the steps that must be followed.

The Reverend Mother pulled back, studying Jessica but not rousing her. In the girl's oval face, she tried to identify her own features, or those of the father, Baron Vladimir Harkonnen: The long neck and small nose reflected Mohiam's genetics, but the widow's peak at the hairline, the wide mouth, generous lips, and clear skin derived from the Baron . . . back when he'd been healthy and attractive. Jessica's widely set green eyes and hair the color of polished bronze came from more distant latencies.

If you only knew. Mohiam recalled what she'd been told of the Bene Gesserit plan. Jessica's own daughter, when grown to womanhood, was destined to give birth to the Kwisatz Haderach—the culmination of millennia of careful breeding. Mohiam looked into the girl's face, searching for any twitch, any hint of grand historical import. *You are not ready to discover this yet.*

Jessica began to speak, mouthing word-shapes as she recited a mantra as ancient as the Bene Gesserit School itself: "Each attacker is a feather drifting on an infinite path. As the feather approaches, it is diverted and removed. My response is a puff of air that blows the feather away."

Mohiam stepped back as her daughter snapped into a blur of motion, attempting to float through reflex moves. But Jessica still struggled to *force* her muscles to flow silently and smoothly, when she should have *allowed* them to do so.

The girl's movements were better than before, more focused and precise. Jessica's recent progress had been impressive, as if she'd experienced a mind-clarifying epiphany that lifted her to the next level. However, Mohiam still detected too much youthful energy and unharnessed intensity.

This girl was the product of a vicious rape by Baron Harkonnen, after the Sisterhood had blackmailed him into providing them with a daughter. Mohiam had exacted her revenge during the sexual attack, controlling her internal body chemistry in the Bene Gesserit way, inflicting him with a painful, debilitating disease. Such a delightfully slow torture. As his ailment progressed, the Baron had relied on a cane for the past Standard Year. At the Fenrings' banquet, she'd been sorely tempted to tell the gross man what she'd done to him.

But if Mohiam *had* told him, there would have been another act of violence in the Dining Hall of the Residency at Arrakeen, far worse than the squabble between the Ecazi and Grumman ambassadors. She might even have found it necessary to kill the Baron with her deadly fighting skills. Jessica herself, despite her limited training, could have dispatched the man—her own father—quickly and easily.

Hearing a whir of machinery, Mohiam watched a life-size doll emerge from the floor. The next phase of the routine. In a blur the girl whirled and decapitated it with a single slashing kick.

"More finesse. The killing touch must be delicate, precise."

"Yes, Reverend Mother."

"Still, I am proud of what you have accomplished." Mohiam spoke in an uncharacteristically gentle tone, one that her superiors would not condone, had they heard it. Love, in any form, was prohibited.

"The Sisterhood has great plans for you, Jessica."

"Xuttuh" is a word that means many things. Every Bene Tleilax knows it was the name of the first Master. But just as that man was more than a mere mortal, so there are depths and complexities in the appellation. Depending upon tone and vocal inflection, "Xuttuh" can mean "hello" or "blessings be upon you." Or it can constitute a prayer encompassed in a single word, as a devotee prepares to die for the Great Belief. For such reasons, we have chosen this as our new name for the conquered planet formerly known as Ix.

—Tleilaxu Training Disk

A CONTINGENCY PLAN IS ONLY AS GOOD AS THE MIND THAT DEVISES IT.

Deep in the labyrinthine research pavilion, Hidar Fen Ajidica understood that maxim only too well. One day, the Emperor's man would attempt to kill him; therefore, careful defensive preparations were necessary.

"This way, please, Count Fenring," Ajidica said in his most pleasant voice while thinking, *Unclean powindah.* He glanced peripherally at the man. *I should slay you now!*

But the Master Researcher could not accomplish this safely, and might never have the proper opportunity. Even if he did succeed, the Emperor would send in his investigators and even more Sardaukar troops to interfere with the delicate work.

"It is good to hear that you are finally making progress on Project Amal. Elrood IX did commission it over a dozen years ago, hmmmm?" Fenring strolled along a featureless corridor in the underground city. He wore a scarlet Imperial jacket and tight-fitting gold trousers. His dark hair was razor-cut, sticking out in patches to emphasize his overlarge head. "We have been extremely patient."

Ajidica wore a white lab coat with ample pockets. Chemical odors clung to the fabric, his hair, his corpselike gray skin. "I warned all of you in the beginning that it could take many years to develop a completed product. A dozen years is a mere eyeblink to develop a substance the Imperium has wanted for centuries upon centuries." His nostrils narrowed as he forced a thin smile.

"Nevertheless, I am pleased to report that our modified axlotl tanks have now been grown, that preliminary experiments have been conducted, and the data analyzed. Based on this, we have discarded unworkable solutions, thus narrowing down the remaining possibilities."

"The Emperor is not interested in 'narrowed possibilities,' Master Researcher, but in *results*." Fenring's voice was frozen acid. "Your expenses have been immense, even after we financed your takeover of Ixian facilities."

"Our records would stand up to any audit, Count Fenring," Ajidica said. He knew full well that Fenring could never allow a Guild Banker to look at the expenditures; the Spacing Guild, more than any other entity, must not suspect the aim of this project. "All funds have been properly applied. All spice stockpiles are accounted for, exactly according to our original agreement."

"Your agreement was with Elrood, little man, not with Shaddam, hmmmm? The Emperor can stop your experiments at any moment."

Like all Tleilaxu, Ajidica was accustomed to being insulted and provoked by fools; he refused to take offense. "An interesting threat, Count Fenring, considering that *you* personally initiated the contact between my people and Elrood. We have recordings, back on the Tleilaxu homeworlds."

Fenring bristled, and pushed ahead, deeper into the research pavilion. "Just by observing you, Master Researcher, I have learned something," he said in an oily voice. "You have developed a phobia of being underground, hmmm? The fear came upon you recently, a sudden onslaught."

"Nonsense." Despite his denial, sweat broke out on Ajidica's forehead.

"Ah, but I detect something mendacious in your voice and expression. You take medication for the condition . . . a bottle of pills in the right pocket of your jacket. I see the bulge."

Trying to conceal his rage, Ajidica stammered, "I am in perfect health."

"Hm-m-m-ah, I would say that your continued health depends upon how well things are going here. The sooner you complete Project Amal, the sooner you will be able to breathe fresh air again back on beautiful Tleilax. When was the last time you were there?"

"A long time ago," Ajidica admitted. "You cannot know what it looks like. No *powin*"—he caught himself—"no outsider has ever been permitted beyond the spaceport."

Fenring simply answered with a maddening, too-knowing smile. "Just show me what you have done here, so that I can report to Shaddam."

At a doorway Ajidica raised his arm to block Fenring's passage. The Tleilaxu closed his eyes and reverently kissed the door. The brief ritual deactivated the deadly security systems, and the door melted into narrow cracks in the wall.

"You may enter safely now." Ajidica stepped aside to let Fenring cross into a white smoothplaz room, where the Master Researcher had set up a number of demonstrations to show the progress of the experiments. In the center of the enormous oval room sat a high-resolution microscope, a metal rack containing laboratory bottles and vials, and a red table holding a dome-shaped object. Ajidica saw intense interest in Fenring's overlarge eyes as he approached the demonstration area. "Don't touch anything, please."

Subtle treacheries hung thick in the air, and this Imperial *powindah* would never see or comprehend them until it was too late. Ajidica intended to solve the riddle of the artificial spice, then escape with the sacred axlotl tanks to a safe planet in the farthest reaches of the Imperium. He had made a number of clever arrangements without revealing his identity, using promises and bribes, transferring funds . . . all without the knowledge of his superiors on the Bene Tleilax homeworlds. He was alone in this.

He had decided that there were heretics among his own people, followers who had adopted their identity as downtrodden scapegoats so well that they had forgotten the heart of the Great Belief. It was like a Face Dancer who had disguised himself so well, he had forgotten who he truly was. If Ajidica meekly allowed such people access to his great discovery of amal, they would surrender the one thing that would gain them the supremacy they deserved.

Ajidica planned to continue in his role, until he was ready. And then he could take the artificial spice, control it himself, and help his people and their mission . . . whether they wanted him to or not.

Count Fenring murmured as he leaned close to the domeshape on the table. "Most intriguing. Something is inside, I presume, hmmm-ah?"

"Something is inside of everything," Ajidica replied.

He smiled inwardly as he imagined a glut of artificial spice flowing into the interplanetary marketplace, wreaking economic havoc within CHOAM and the Landsraad. Like a tiny leak in a dam, a bit of inexpensive melange would ultimately become a raging torrent to turn the Imperium upside down. If played right, Ajidica would be the kingpin of the new economic and political order—not to serve himself, of course, but to serve God.

The magic of our God is our salvation.

Ajidica smiled at Count Fenring, revealing sharp teeth. "Rest assured, Count Fenring, our goals in this matter are mutual."

In time, wealthy beyond imagining, Ajidica would develop tests to determine loyalty to his new regime, and he would begin assimilating the Bene Tleilax. Though it was too dangerous to bring them into his scheme now, he had several candidates in mind. With proper military support—perhaps even converts among the Sardaukar stationed here?—he might even set up headquarters in the lovely capital city of Bandalong. . . .

Fenring continued to snoop at the demonstration equipment. "Have you ever heard the saying 'Trust but verify'? It's from Old Terra. You'd be surprised at the little tidbits I pick up. My Bene Gesserit wife collects objects, knickknacks and the like. I collect pieces of information."

The Tleilaxu's narrow face twisted into a frown. "I see." He needed to finish this annoying inspection as quickly as possible. "If you will look over here, please." Ajidica removed an opaque plaz vial from the rack and lifted the lid, letting out a strong odor reminiscent of raw ginger, bergamot, and clove. He passed the container to Fenring, who peered at a thick, orangish substance.

"Not quite melange," Ajidica said, "though chemically it has many spice precursors." He poured the syrup on a scanning plate, inserted it into the microscope reader, then beckoned Fenring to look through the eyepiece. The Count saw elongated molecules connected to one another like the strands of a cable.

"An unusual protein chain," the Master Researcher said. "We are close to a breakthrough."

"How close?"

"The Tleilaxu also have sayings, Count Fenring: 'The closer one gets to a goal, the farther off it appears to be.' In matters of scientific research, time has a way of stretching. Only God possesses intimate knowledge of the future. The breakthrough could occur in a matter of days, or years."

"Double-talk," Fenring muttered. He fell silent when Ajidica pressed a button at the base of the dome.

The foggy surface of the plaz cleared, revealing sand on the bottom of the container. The Tleilaxu researcher pressed another button, filling the interior with a fine dust. The sand moved, a tiny mound in motion that surfaced, like a fish emerging from murky water. A worm-shape the size of a small snake, it was a little over half a meter in length, with tiny crystal teeth.

"Sandworm, immature form," Ajidica said, "nineteen days· from Arrakis. We don't expect it to survive much longer."

From the top of the dome, a box dropped to the sand on a hidden suspensor, then opened to reveal more of the glistening orange gelatin. "Amal 1522.16," Ajidica said. "One of our many variations—the best we've developed so far."

Fenring watched as the mouth of the immature worm quested left and right, revealing glimmering thorns far back in its gullet. The creature slithered toward the orange substance, then stopped in confusion and didn't touch it. Presently it turned and burrowed back into the sand.

"What is the relationship between the sandworms and the spice?" Fenring asked.

"If we knew that, we would have the puzzle solved. If I were to put real spice in that enclosure, the worm would consume it in a primal frenzy. Still, though the worm can identify the difference, at least it did approach the sample. We tempted the beast, but did not satisfy it."

"Nor did your little demonstration satisfy me. I am told that there continues to be an Ixian underground movement, causing difficulties. Shaddam is concerned about interference with his most important plan."

"A few rebels, Count Fenring—inadequately funded, with limited resources. Nothing to worry about." Ajidica rubbed his hands together.

"But they have sabotaged your communications systems and destroyed a number of facilities, hmmm?"

"The death throes of House Vernius, no more. It has been well over a decade, and soon it will die down. They cannot get near this research pavilion."

"Well, your security worries are over, Master Researcher.

The Emperor has agreed to dispatch two additional legions of Sardaukar, as peacekeepers, led by Bashar Cando Garon, one of our best."

A look of alarm and surprise came over the diminutive Tleilaxu. His pinched face reddened. "But that isn't necessary, sir. The half legion already in place is more than sufficient."

"The Emperor does not agree. These troops will emphasize the importance of your experiments to him. Shaddam will do anything to protect the amal program, but his patience has run out." The Count's eyes narrowed. "You should think of this as good news."

"Why is that? I do not understand."

"Because the Emperor has not yet ordered your execution."

A center for the coordination of rebellion can be mobile; it does not need to be a permanent place where people meet.

—CAMMAR PILRU,
Ixian Ambassador in Exile
Treatise on the Downfall of Unjust Governments

THE TLEILAXU INVADERS HAD INSTITUTED A BRUTAL CURFEW FOR ANYONE not assigned to the late work shift. For C'tair Pilru, slipping away to attend the hushed rebellion meetings was just another way to thumb his nose at their restrictions.

At the freedom fighters' irregular, carefully guarded gatherings, C'tair could finally remove his masks and disguises. He became the person he once had been, the person he remained inside.

Knowing he'd be killed if caught, the short, dark-haired man approached the meeting place. He clung to oily night shadows between blocky buildings on the cavern floor, making no sound. The Tleilaxu had restored the projected sky on the cavern ceiling, but they had reconfigured the sparkle of stars to show the constellations over their own homeworlds. Here on Ix, even the heavens were wrong.

This was not the glorious place it should be, but a hellish prison beneath the surface of the planet. *We will change all that. Someday.*

During more than a decade of repression, black marketeers and revolutionaries had built their secret network. The scattered resistance groups interacted to exchange supplies, equipment, and information. But each gathering made C'tair nervous. If they were caught together, the fledgling rebellion could be snuffed out in a few moments of lasgun fire.

When possible, he preferred to work alone—as he had always done. Trusting no one, he never divulged details of his surreptitious life, not even to other rebels. He'd made private contacts with rare off-worlders at the port-of-entry canyon—openings and landing pads in the sheer cliff wall where carefully guarded ships hauled Tleilaxu products to waiting Heighliners in orbit.

The Imperium required vital items of Ixian technology, which were now manufactured under Tleilaxu control. The invaders needed the profits to finance their own work, and they could not risk outside scrutiny. Although they could not seal Ix completely away from the rest of the Imperium, the Tleilaxu used the services of very few outsiders.

Sometimes, under the direst of circumstances and at great risk to himself, C'tair could bribe one of the transport laborers to skim a shipment or snag a vital component. Other black marketeers had their own contacts, but they refused to share that information with each other. It was safer that way.

Now, slipping through the claustrophobic night, he passed an abandoned manufactory, turned onto an even darker street, and picked up his pace. The meeting was about to begin. Perhaps tonight . . .

Though it seemed hopeless, C'tair continued to find ways to strike against the Tleilaxu slave masters, and other rebels did the same. Infuriated that they could not capture any saboteurs, the masters made "examples" out of hapless suboids. After torture and mutilation, the scapegoat would be hurled off the Grand Palais balcony to the distant cavern floor, where great Heighliners had once been built. Every expression on the victim's face, every dripping wound, was projected on the holo-sky, while recorders transmitted his wails and screams.

But the Tleilaxu understood little of the Ixian psyche. Their brutality only caused greater unrest and more incidents of violent rebellion. Over the years, C'tair could see the Tleilaxu being worn down, despite efforts to crush the resistance with shape-shifting Face Dancer infiltrators and surveillance pods. The freedom fighters continued the struggle.

Those few rebels with access to uncensored outside news reported on the activities in the Imperium. From them, C'tair learned of impassioned speeches before the Landsraad made by his father, the exiled Ixian Ambassador—little more than futile gestures. Earl Dominic Vernius, who'd been overthrown and gone renegade, had vanished completely, and his heir, Prince Rhombur, lived in exile on Caladan, without a military force and without Landsraad support.

The rebels could not count on rescue from the outside. *Victory must come from inside. From Ix.*

He rounded another corner, and in a narrow alleyway stepped onto a metal grating. Narrowing his dark eyes, C'tair looked from side to side, always expecting someone to spring out of the shadows. His demeanor was furtive and quick, drastically different from the cowed and cooperative routine he followed in public.

He gave the password, and the grate lowered, taking him beneath the street. He hurried down a dark corridor.

During the day shift, C'tair wore a gray work smock. He had learned how to mimic the simple, lackluster suboids over the years: He walked with a stooped gait, eyes dull with disinterest. He had fifteen identity cards, and no one bothered to study faces in the shifting masses of laborers. It was easy to become invisible.

The rebels had developed their own identity checks. They posted concealed guards outside the abandoned facility under infrared glowglobes. Transeyes and sonic detectors provided a further bubble of protection—none of which would help if the freedom fighters were discovered.

On this level, the guards were visible. When C'tair mumbled his password response, they waved him inside. Too easily.

He had to tolerate these people and their inept security games in order to acquire the equipment he needed, but he didn't have to feel comfortable about it.

C'tair scanned the meeting site—at least *that* had been carefully selected. This closed-down facility had once assembled combat meks to train fighters against a spectrum of tactics or weapons. But the Tleilaxu overlords had unilaterally determined that such "self-aware" machines violated the strictures of the Butlerian Jihad. Though all thinking machines had been obliterated ten thousand years before, severe prohibitions were still in effect and emotions ran high. This place and others like it had been abandoned after the revolt on Ix, production lines left to fall into disrepair. Some equipment had been cannibalized for other uses, the rest turned into scrap.

Other pursuits preoccupied the Tleilaxu. *Secret work*, a vast project staffed only by their own people. No one, not even members of C'tair's resistance group, had been able to determine what the overlords had in mind.

Inside the echoing facility, flinty-eyed resistance fighters spoke in whispers. There would be no formal agenda, no leader, no speech. C'tair smelled their nervous sweat, heard odd inflections in the low voices. No matter how many security precautions they took, how many escape plans they devised, it was still dangerous to have so many gathered in one place. C'tair always kept his eyes open, aware of the nearest exit.

He had business to conduct. He'd brought a disguised satchel containing the most vital items he had hoarded. He needed to trade with other scavengers to find components for his innovative but problematic transmitter, the rogo. The prototype allowed him to communicate through foldspace with his twin brother D'murr, a Guild Navigator. But C'tair rarely succeeded in establishing contact, either because his twin had mutated so far from human . . . or because the transmitter itself was falling apart.

On a dusty metal table, he brought out weapons components, power sources, communications devices, and scanning
equipment—items that would have led to his immediate execution if any Tleilaxu had stopped to ask his business. But
C'tair armed himself well, and he had killed the gnomish men
before.

C'tair displayed his wares. He searched the faces of the rebels, the crude disguises and intentional dirt smudges, until he
spotted a woman with large eyes, prominent cheekbones, and
a narrow chin. Her hair had been raggedly chopped in an effort to destroy any hint of beauty. He knew her as Miral
Alechem, though that might not have been her real name.

In her face, C'tair saw echoes of Kailea Vernius, the pretty
daughter of Earl Vernius. He and his twin brother had both
fancied Kailea, flirted with her . . . back when they'd thought
nothing would ever change. Now Kailea was exiled on Caladan, and D'murr was a Guild Navigator. The twins' mother,
a Guild banker, had been killed during the takeover of Ix. And
C'tair himself lived like a furtive rat, flitting from hideout to
hideout. . . .

"I found the crystalpak you requested," he said to Miral.

She withdrew a wrapped item from a sack at her waist.
"I've got the module rods you needed, calibrated precisely . . .
I hope. I had no way of checking."

C'tair took the packet, feeling no need to inspect the merchandise. "I can do it myself." He handed Miral the crystalpak,
but did not ask what she had in mind for it. Everyone present
searched for ways to strike against the Tleilaxu. Nothing else
mattered. As he exchanged a nervous glance with her, he
wondered if she might be thinking the same thing he was,
that under different circumstances they might have had a personal relationship. But he couldn't allow her that close to him.
Not anyone. It would weaken him and divert his resolve. He
had to remain focused, for the sake of the Ixian cause.

One of the door guards hissed an alarm, and everyone fell

into fearful silence, ducking low. The muted glowglobes dimmed. C'tair held his breath.

A humming sound passed overhead as a surveillance pod cruised above the abandoned buildings, trying to pick up unauthorized vibrations or movements. Shadows smothered the hiding rebels. C'tair mentally reviewed the location of every possible escape from this facility, in case he needed to duck out into the blinding darkness.

But the humming device cruised onward down the length of the city grotto. Shortly afterward, the nervous rebels stood again and began muttering to themselves, wiping sweat off their faces, laughing nervously.

Spooked, C'tair decided not to remain any longer. He memorized the coordinates for the group's next gathering, packed up his remaining equipment, and looked around, scanning the faces once more, marking them in his mind. If they were caught, he might never see these people again.

He nodded a final time at Miral Alechem, then slipped off into the Ixian night, flitting under artificial stars. He had already made up his mind where he would spend the remainder of the sleep shift . . . and which identity he would choose for the following day.

It is said that the Fremen has no conscience, having lost it in a burning desire for revenge. This is foolish. Only the rawest primitive and the sociopath have no conscience. The Fremen possesses a highly evolved worldview centered on the welfare of his people. His sense of belonging to the community is almost stronger than his sense of self. It is only to outsiders that these desert dwellers seem brutish . . . just as outsiders appear to them.

—PARDOT KYNES,
The People of Arrakis

"LUXURY IS FOR THE NOBLE-BORN, LIET," PARDOT KYNES SAID AS THE groundcar trundled across the uneven ground. Here, in privacy, he could use his son's secret sietch name, rather than *Weichih*, the name reserved for outsiders. "On this planet you must instantly become aware of your own surroundings, and remain alert at all times. If you fail to learn this lesson, you won't live long."

As Kynes operated the simple controls, he gestured toward the buttery morning light that melted across the stark dunes. "There are rewards here, too. I grew up on Salusa Secundus, and even that broken and wounded place had its beauty . . . though nothing to match the *purity* of Dune." Kynes exhaled a long breath between his hard, chapped lips.

Liet continued to stare out the scratched windowplaz. Unlike his father, who reeled off whatever random thoughts occurred to him, making pronouncements that the Fremen heeded as if they were weighty spiritual matters, Liet preferred silence. He narrowed his eyes to study the landscape, searching for any small thing out of its place. Always alert.

On such a harsh planet, one had to develop stored perceptions, each of them linked to every moment of survival. Though his father was much older, Liet wasn't certain the Planetologist understood as much as he himself did. The mind of Pardot Kynes contained powerful concepts, but the older man experienced them only as esoteric data. He didn't understand the desert in his heart or in his soul. . . .

For years, Kynes had lived among the Fremen. It was said that Emperor Shaddam IV had little interest in his activities, and since Kynes asked for no funding and few supplies, they left him alone. With each passing year he slipped farther from attention. Shaddam and his advisors had stopped expecting any grand revelations from the Planetologist's periodic reports.

This suited Pardot Kynes, and his son as well.

In his wanderings, Kynes often made trips to outlying villages where the people of the pan and graben scratched out squalid lives. True Fremen rarely mixed with the townspeople, and viewed them with veiled contempt for being too soft, too civilized. Liet would never have lived in those pathetic settlements for all the Solaris in the Imperium. But still, Pardot visited them.

Eschewing roads and commonly traveled paths, they rode in the groundcar, checking meteorological stations and collecting data, though Pardot's troops of devoted Fremen would gladly have done this menial work for their "Umma."

Liet-Kynes's features echoed many of his father's, though with a leaner face and the closely set eyes of his Fremen mother. He had pale hair, and his chin was still smooth, though later he would likely grow a beard similar to the great Planetologist's. Liet's eyes had the deep blue of spice addiction, since every meal and breath of sietch air was laced with melange.

Liet heard a sharp intake of breath from his father as they passed the jagged elbow of a canyon where camouflaged catchtraps directed moisture to plantings of rabbitbush and poverty grasses. "See? It's taking on a life of its own. We'll 'cycle' the planet through prairie phase into forest over several generations. The sand has a high salt content, indicating old oceans, and the spice itself is alkaline." He chuckled. "People in the Imperium would be horrified that we'd use spice by-products for something as menial as fertilizer." He smiled at his son. "But we know the value of such things, eh? If we break down the spice, we can set up protein digestion. Even now, if we flew high enough, we could spot patches of green where matted plant growth holds the dune faces in place."

The young man sighed. His father was a great man with magnificent dreams for Dune—and yet Kynes was so focused on one thing that he failed to see the universe around him. Liet knew that if any Harkonnen patrols found the plantings, they would destroy them and punish the Fremen.

Though only twelve, Liet went out on razzia raids with his Fremen brothers and had already killed Harkonnens. For more than a year, he and his friends—led by the brash Stilgar—had struck targets that others refused to consider. Only a week before, Liet's companions had blown up a dozen patrol 'thopters at a supply post. Unfortunately, the Harkonnen troops had taken their revenge against poor villagers, seeing no difference between settled folk and the will-o'-the-sand Fremen.

He hadn't told his father about his guerrilla activities, since the elder Kynes wouldn't understand the necessity. Premeditated violence, for whatever reason, was a foreign concept to the Planetologist. But Liet would do what needed to be done.

Now, the groundcar approached a village tucked into the rocky foothills; it was called Bilar Camp on their terrain maps. Pardot continued to talk about melange and its peculiar properties. "They found spice too soon on Arrakis. It deflected scientific inquiry. It was so useful right from the outset that no one bothered to probe its mysteries."

Liet turned to look at him. "I thought that was why you were assigned here in the first place—to understand the spice."

"Yes . . . but we have more important work to do. I still report back to the Imperium often enough to convince them I'm working at my job . . . though not very successfully."

Talking about the first time he'd been to this region, he drove toward a cluster of dirty buildings the color of sand and dust.

The groundcar jounced over a rough rock, but Liet ignored it and stared ahead at the village, squinting in the harsh light of the desert morning. The morning air held the fragility of fine crystal. "Something's wrong," he said, interrupting his father.

Kynes continued talking for a few seconds and then brought the vehicle to a stop. "What's that?"

"Something is wrong." Liet pointed ahead at the village.

Kynes shaded his eyes against the glare. "I don't see anything."

"Still . . . let us proceed with caution."

IN THE CENTER of the village, they encountered a festival of horrors.

The surviving victims wandered about as if insane, shrieking and snarling like animals. The noise was horrific, as was the smell. They had ripped hair out of their heads in bloody clumps. Some used long fingernails to claw the eyes out of their faces, then held the scooped eyeballs in their palms; blind, they staggered against the tan walls of dwellings, leaving wet crimson smears.

"By Shai-Hulud!" Liet whispered under his breath, while his father let out a louder curse in common Imperial Galach.

One man with torn eye sockets like bloody extra mouths above his cheekbones collided with a crawling woman; both victims flew into a rage and ripped at each other's skin with bare hands, biting and spitting and screaming. There were muddy spots on the street, overturned containers of water.

Many bodies lay sprawled on the ground like squashed insects, arms and legs stiffened at odd angles. Some buildings were locked and shuttered, barricaded against the crazed wretches outside who pounded on the walls, wailing wordlessly to get in. On an upper floor Liet saw a woman's terrified face at the dust-streaked windowplaz. Others hid, somehow unaffected by the murderous insanity.

"We must help these people, Father." Liet leaped out of the sealed groundcar before his father had brought it to a complete stop. "Bring your weapons. We may need to defend ourselves."

They carried old maula pistols as well as knives. His father, though a scientist at heart, was also a good fighter—a skill he reserved for defending his vision for Arrakis. The legend was told of how he had slain several Harkonnen bravos who'd been attempting to kill three young Fremen. Those rescued Fremen were now his most loyal lieutenants, Stilgar, Turok, and Ommun. But Pardot Kynes had never fought against anything like this. . . .

The maddened villagers noticed them and moaned. They began to move forward.

"Don't kill them unless you must," Kynes said, amazed at how quickly his son had armed himself with a crysknife and maula pistol. "Watch yourself."

Liet ventured into the street. What struck him first was the terrible stink, as if the foul breath of a dying leper had been captured in a bottle and slowly released.

Staring in disbelief, Pardot stepped farther from the groundcar. He saw no lasgun burn marks in the village, no chip scars from projectile weapons, nothing that would have indicated an overt Harkonnen attack. Was it a disease? If so, it might be contagious. If a plague or some kind of communicable insanity was at work here, he could not let the Fremen take these bodies for the deathstills.

Liet moved forward. "Fremen would attribute this to demons."

Two of the bloody-faced victims let out demonic shrieks and rushed toward them, their fingers outstretched like eagle claws, their mouths open like bottomless pits. Liet pointed the maula pistol, uttered a quick prayer, then fired twice. The perfect shots hit each of the attackers in the chest, and they fell dead.

Liet bowed. "Forgive me, Shai-Hulud."

Pardot watched him. *I have tried to teach my son many things, but at least he has learned compassion. All other information can be learned from filmbooks . . . but not compassion. This was born into him.*

The young man bent over the two bodies, studied them closely, pushing back his superstitious fear. "I do not think it's a disease." He looked back at Pardot. "I've assisted the sietch healers, as you know, and . . ." His voice trailed off.

"What, then?"

"I believe they've been poisoned."

One by one, the tortured villagers wandering the dusty streets fell onto their backs in screaming convulsions, until only three remained alive. Liet moved quickly with the crysknife and dispatched the last victims painlessly and efficiently. No tribe or village would ever accept them again, no matter how much they recovered, for fear that they had been corrupted by demons; even their water would be considered tainted.

Liet found it odd how easily he had taken command in front of his father. He gestured toward two of the sealed buildings. "Convince the people inside those barred dwellings that we mean them no harm. We must discover what happened here." His voice became low and icy. "And we must learn who is to blame."

Pardot Kynes moved to the dusty building. Fingernail scratches and bloody handprints marked the mud-brick walls and pitted metal doors where crazed victims had tried to pound their way in. He swallowed hard and prepared to make his case, to convince the terrified survivors that their ordeal was over. He turned back to his son. "Where will you be, Liet?"

The young man looked at an overturned water container. He knew of only one way the poison could affect so many people at once. "Checking the water supply."

His face etched in concern, Pardot nodded.

Liet studied the terrain around the village, saw a faint trail leading up the side of the overhanging mesa. Moving with the speed of a sun-warmed lizard, he scurried up the mountain path and reached the cistern. The evidence of its location had been cleverly disguised, though the villagers had made many errors. Even a clumsy Harkonnen patrol could have discovered the illegal reservoir. He studied the area quickly, noting patterns in the sand.

Smelling a harsh alkaloid bitterness near the upper opening of the cistern, he tried to place the odor. He'd experienced it rarely, and only during great sietch celebrations. *The Water of Life!* The Fremen consumed such a substance only after a Sayyadina had converted the exhalation of a drowned worm, using her own body chemistry as a catalyst to create a tolerable drug that sent the sietch into an ecstatic frenzy. Unconverted, the substance was a ferocious toxin.

The villagers in Bilar Camp had drunk pure Water of Life, before it was transformed. Someone had done this intentionally . . . poisoning them.

Then he saw the marks of ornithopter pads in the soft soil atop the plateau. *It had to be a Harkonnen 'thopter.* One of the regular patrols . . . a practical joke?

Frowning grimly, Liet descended to the devastated village, where his father had succeeded in bringing out the survivors who had barricaded themselves within their dwellings. Through luck, these people had not drunk the poisoned water. Now they fell to their knees in the streets, surrounded by the awful carnage. Their keening cries of grief drifted like the thin wails of ghosts along a sheer cliffside.

Harkonnens did this.

Pardot Kynes moved about doing what he could to comfort them, but from the quizzical expressions on the villagers' faces, Liet knew his father was probably saying the wrong things, expressing his sympathy in abstract concepts that they had no ability to understand.

Liet moved down the slope, and already plans were forming in his mind. As soon as they returned to the sietch, he would meet with Stilgar and his commando squad.

And they would plan their retaliation against the Harkonnens.

An empire built on power cannot attract the affections and loyalty that men bestow willingly on a regime of ideas and beauty. Adorn your Grand Empire with beauty, with culture.

—From a speech by CROWN PRINCE RAPHAEL CORRINO
L'Institut de Kaitain Archives

THE YEARS HAD BEEN UNKIND TO BARON VLADIMIR HARKONNEN.

In a rage, he swiped his wormhead walking stick across the counter in his therapy room. Jars of ointments, salves, pills, and hypo-injectors crashed to the tile floor. "Nothing works!" Each day, he felt worse, looked more revolting. In the mirror he saw a puffy, red-faced caricature of his Adonis-self, hardly recognizable as the person he had once been.

"I look like a tumor, not a man."

With darting movements, Piter de Vries stepped into the room, ready to offer assistance. The Baron struck at him with the heavy cane, but the Mentat sidestepped the blow with the grace of a cobra.

"Get out of my sight, Piter." The Baron reeled, trying to catch his balance. "Or this time I really will think of a way to kill you."

"Whatever my Baron wishes," de Vries said in a too-silken voice. He bowed and retreated to the door.

The Baron held affection for few people, but he appreciated the devious workings of the twisted Mentat's mind, his convoluted plans, his long-term thinking . . . regardless of his obnoxious familiarity and lack of respect.

"Wait, Piter. I need your Mentat brain." He lumbered forward, leaning on the walking stick. "It's the same old question. Find out why my body is degenerating, or I will dispatch you to the deepest slave pit."

The whip-thin man waited for the Baron to catch up with him. "I shall do my best, Baron. I know full well what happened to all of your doctors."

"Incompetents," he growled. "None of them knew anything."

Formerly healthy and full of tremendous energy, the Baron suffered from a debilitating disease whose manifestations disgusted and frightened him. He had gained an enormous amount of weight. Exercise did not help, nor did medical scans or even exploratory surgeries. For years he had tried every healing procedure and bizarre experimental treatment— all to no avail.

For their failures, a score of House doctors had received torturous deaths at the hands of Piter de Vries, often through imaginative application of their own instruments. As a result, no high-level medical practitioners remained on Giedi Prime—or at least none were visible; those who had not been executed had gone into hiding or fled to other worlds.

More annoyingly, servants had begun disappearing, too— and not always because the Baron had ordered them killed. They had fled outside the Castle Keep into Harko City, vanishing into the ranks of uncounted and unheeded laborers. As he ventured out into the streets accompanied by his guard captain Kryubi, the Baron found himself constantly looking for people who even *resembled* the servants who had abandoned him. Wherever he went, he left a trail of bodies. The killings brought him little pleasure, though; he would rather have had an *answer*.

De Vries accompanied the Baron as he hobbled into the corridor; his walking stick clicked along the floor. Soon, the big man thought, he would have to wear a suspensor mechanism to remove the burden from his aching joints.

A team of workmen froze as the two approached. The

Baron noted that they were repairing wall damage he had caused in a rage the day before. Each of them bowed as the Baron clicked past and breathed audible sighs of relief when they saw him disappear around a corner.

When he and de Vries reached a cerulean-curtained drawing room, the Baron lowered himself onto a black sligskin settee. "Sit beside me, Piter." The Mentat's inky eyes darted around, like those of a trapped animal, but the Baron snorted with impatience. "I probably won't kill you today, provided you give me good advice."

The Mentat maintained his casual demeanor, revealing none of his private thoughts. "Advising you is the sole purpose of my existence, my Baron." He remained aloof, even arrogant, because he knew it would be far too costly for House Harkonnen to replace him, though the Bene Tleilax could always grow another Mentat from the same genetic stock. In fact, they probably already had replacements, just waiting.

The Baron drummed his fingers on the arm of the settee. "True enough, but you don't always give the advice I need." Looking closely at de Vries, he added, "You are a very ugly man, Piter. Even with my disease, I'm still prettier than you."

The Mentat's salamander tongue darted over lips stained crimson by sapho juice. "But my sweet Baron, you always liked to look at me."

The Baron's face hardened, and he leaned close to the tall, thin man. "Enough relying on amateurs. I want you to obtain a Suk doctor for me."

Surprised, de Vries drew a quick breath. "But you have insisted that we maintain complete secrecy about the nature of your condition. A Suk must report all activities to his Inner Circle—and send them the bulk of his fee."

Vladimir Harkonnen had led members of the Landsraad to believe he'd grown corpulent through his own excesses—which was an acceptable reason to him, one that did not imply weakness. And, given the Baron's tastes, it was a lie easy to believe. He did not wish to become a pitiable laughingstock among the other nobles. A great Baron should not suffer from a simple, embarrassing *disease*.

"Just find a way to do it. Don't go through regular channels. If a Suk can cure me, then I'll have nothing to hide."

SEVERAL DAYS LATER, Piter de Vries learned that a talented if somewhat narcissistic Suk doctor had been stationed on Richese, an ally of the Harkonnens. The wheels in the Mentat's mind began to turn. In the past, House Richese had aided Harkonnen-inspired plots, including the assassination of Duke Paulus Atreides in the bullring, but the allies often disagreed on priorities. For this most sensitive of all matters, de Vries invited the Richesian Premier, Ein Calimar, to visit the Baron's Keep on Giedi Prime, to discuss "a mutually profitable enterprise."

An older, meticulously dressed man who retained his youthful athleticism, Calimar had dark skin and a wide nose with wire-rimmed eyeglasses perched on it. He arrived at the Harko City Spaceport wearing a white suit with gold lapels. Four guards in blue Harkonnen livery escorted him into the Baron's private quarters.

Once he stepped inside the private chambers, the Premier's nose twitched at an odor, which did not escape his host's bemused notice. The nude body of a young boy hung in a closet only two meters away; the Baron had intentionally left the door open a crack. The corpse's putrid odor mixed and interlocked with older ones that had permeated the rooms to such a degree that even strong perfumes did not conceal them.

"Please sit." The Baron pointed to a couch where faint bloodstains could still be seen. He had prepared this entire meeting with subliminal threats and unpleasantness, just to set the Richesian leader on edge.

Calimar hesitated—a moment that delighted the Baron—

hen accepted the seat, but declined an offer of kirana brandy, though his host took a snifter for himself. The Baron slumped into a bobbing suspensor chair. Behind him stood his fidgety personal Mentat, who stated why House Harkonnen had requested the meeting.

Surprised, Calimar shook his head. "You wish to rent my Suk doctor?" His nose continued to twitch, and his gaze searched the room for a source of the odor, settling on the closet door. He adjusted his golden spectacles. "I'm sorry, but I am unable to comply. A personal Suk physician is a responsibility and an obligation . . . not to mention an enormous expense."

The Baron pouted. "I have tried other doctors, and I would prefer to keep this matter private. I cannot simply advertise for one of the arrogant professionals. Your Suk doctor, though, would be bound by his oath of confidentiality, and no one needs to know he left your service for a brief period." He heard the whining tone in his own voice. "Come, come, where is your compassion?"

Calimar looked away from the dark closet. "Compassion? An interesting comment from you, Baron. Your House hasn't bothered to help us with *our* problem, despite our entreaties over the last five years."

The Baron leaned forward. His wormhead walking stick lay across his lap, its tip filled with serpent-venom darts pointed toward the white-suited man. Tempting, so tempting. "Perhaps we could come to an understanding." He looked questioningly at his Mentat for an explanation.

De Vries said, "In a word, he means *money*, my Baron. The Richesian economy is floundering."

"As our ambassador has explained repeatedly to your emissaries," Calimar added. "Since my House lost control of the spice operations on Arrakis—you replaced us, don't forget—we have attempted to rebuild our economic foundation." The Premier held his chin high, pretending that he still had some pride left. "Initially, the downfall of Ix was a boon to us, removing competition. However, our finances remain somewhat . . . strained."

The Baron's spider-black eyes flashed, relishing Calimar's embarrassment. House Richese, manufacturers of exotic weaponry and complex machines, experts in miniaturization and Richesian mirrors, had made initial market-share gains against rival Ixian companies during the upheavals on Ix.

"Five years ago the Tleilaxu began shipping Ixian products again," de Vries said with cold logic. "You are already losing whatever gains you made in the past ten years. Sales of Richesian products have fallen off severely with the renewed availability of Ixian technology."

Calimar kept his voice steady. "So you see, we must have resources to enhance our efforts and invest in new facilities."

"Richese, Tleilax, Ix . . . we try not to interfere in squabbles between other Houses." The Baron sighed. "I wish there could just be peace throughout the Landsraad."

Anger seeped into the Premier's features. "This is more than a *squabble*, Baron. This is about *survival*. Many of my agents are missing on Ix and presumed dead. It disgusts me even to consider what the Tleilaxu may use their body parts for." He adjusted his spectacles; perspiration glistened on his forehead. "Besides, the Bene Tleilax are not a House of any sort. The Landsraad would never accept them."

"A mere technicality."

"We arrive at an impasse then," Calimar announced, making as if to rise. He looked once more at the ominous closet door. "I did not believe you'd be willing to meet our stiff price, regardless of how excellent our Suk doctor is."

"Wait, wait—" The Baron held up a hand. "Trade agreements and military pacts are one thing. Friendship is another. You and your House have been our loyal ally in the past. Perhaps I didn't fully understand the scope of your problem before."

Calimar tilted his head back, gazed down the bridge of his nose at the Baron. "The scope of our problem consists of many zeros and no decimal points."

Set in folds of fat, his black eyes took on a crafty gaze. "If you send me your Suk doctor, Premier, we shall rethink the situation. I'm sure you will be most pleased to hear the financial details of our offer. Consider it a down payment."

Calimar refused to move. "I would like to hear the offer now, please."

Seeing the stony expression on the Premier's face, the Baron nodded. "Piter, tell him our proposal."

De Vries quoted a high price for the rental of the Suk, payable in melange. No matter how much this Suk doctor cost, House Harkonnen could squeeze out the extra income by liquidating some of their hidden, illegal spice stockpiles, or by tightening production on Arrakis.

Calimar pretended to consider the offer, but the Baron knew the man had no choice but to accept. "The Suk will be sent to you immediately. This doctor, Wellington Yueh, has been working on cyborg studies, developing a machine-human interface to restore lost limbs through artificial means, an alternative to having the Tleilaxu grow replacements in their axlotl tanks."

"'Thou shalt not make a machine in the likeness of a human mind,'" de Vries quoted—the primary commandment arising out of the Butlerian Jihad.

Calimar stiffened. "Our patent lawyers have gone over this in detail, and there is no violation whatsoever."

"Well, I don't care what his specialty is," the Baron said impatiently. "All Suk doctors have broad reservoirs of knowledge upon which they can draw. You understand that this must be kept in strict confidence?"

"That is not a matter of concern. The Suk Inner Circle has held embarrassing medical information on every family in the Landsraad for generations. You need not worry."

"I am more worried that *your* people will talk. Do I have your promise that you will not divulge any details of our bargain? It could prove just as embarrassing to *you*." The Baron's dark eyes seemed to sink deeper into his puffy face.

A stiff nod from the Premier. "I am pleased to be of assistance, Baron. I have had the rare privilege of closely observing this Dr. Yueh. Allow me to assure you that he is most impressive indeed."

Military victories are meaningless unless they reflect the wishes of the populace. An Emperor exists only to clarify those wishes. He executes the popular will, or his time is short.

—Principium,
Imperial Leadership Academy

BENEATH A BLACK SECURITY HOOD, THE EMPEROR SAT IN HIS ELABORATE suspensor chair as he received information from the ridulian report crystal. After delivering the encrypted summary, Hasimir Fenring stood beside him while words streamed through Shaddam's mind.

The Emperor did not like the news.

At the conclusion of the progress summary, Fenring cleared his throat. "Hidar Fen Ajidica conceals much from us, Sire. If he were not vitally important to Project Amal, I would *terminate* him, hmmmm?"

The Emperor swung the security hood from his head, removed the glittering crystal from its receptacle. Adjusting his eyes to the bright morning sunshine that passed through a skylight in his private tower quarters, he peered at Fenring. The other man lounged at the Emperor's desk of golden chusuk wood inlaid with milky soostones, as if he owned it.

"I see," Shaddam mused. "The little gnome isn't pleased to receive two more legions of Sardaukar. Commander Garon will put pressure on him to perform, and he feels the vise tightening around him."

Fenring got up to pace in front of a window that overlooked a profusion of orange and lavender blossoms in a rooftop garden. He picked at something lodged beneath one of his fingernails and flicked it away. "Don't we all, hmmm?"

Shaddam noticed that the Count's gaze had strayed to the holophotos of his three young daughters that Anirul had mounted on the wall—annoying reminders that he still had no male heir. Irulan was four years old, Chalice a year and a half, and baby Wensicia barely two months. Pointedly, he switched off the images and turned to his friend.

"You're my eyes in the desert, Hasimir. It disturbs me that the Tleilaxu have been smuggling infant sandworms from Arrakis. I thought it couldn't be done."

Fenring shrugged. "What could it possibly matter if they took a small worm or two? The creatures die soon after they leave the desert, despite every effort to care for them."

"Perhaps the ecosystem should not be disturbed." The Emperor's scarlet-and-gold tunic trailed over the edge of the suspensor chair onto the floor. He nibbled on a morsel of crimson fruit from a bowl beside him. "In his last report, our desert Planetologist claims that reductions in particular species could have devastating consequences on food chains. He says there are prices to be paid by future generations for the mistakes of today."

Fenring made a dismissive gesture. "You shouldn't bother yourself with his reports. If you brought me back from exile, Sire, I could remove such worries from your mind. I'd do your thinking for you, hmmm-ah?"

"Your assignment as Imperial Observer is hardly exile. You are a Count, and you are my Spice Minister." Distracted, Shaddam thought about ordering something to drink, perhaps with music, exotic dancers, even a military parade outside. He had only to command it. But such things did not interest him at the moment. "Do you desire an additional title, Hasimir?"

Averting his overlarge eyes, Fenring said, "That would only call more attention to me. Already it is difficult to conceal from the Guild how often I journey to Xuttuh. Besides, trivial titles mean nothing to me."

The Emperor tossed the pit of his fruit into the bowl, frowning. Next time he would order the preparers to cut out the seeds before serving them. "Is 'Padishah Emperor' a trivial title?"

At the sound of three beeps, the men looked up at the ceiling, from which a clearplaz tube spiraled down to a receptacle on the Emperor's chusuk wood desk. An urgent message cylinder streaked through the tube and thunked into place. Fenring retrieved the cylinder, cut off a Courier's seal, and removed two sheets of rolled *instroy* paper, which he passed to the Emperor, restraining himself from examining them first. Shaddam unrolled them, scanned the pages with an expression of growing distress.

"Hmmmm?" Fenring asked, in his impatient manner.

"Another formal letter of complaint from Archduke Ecaz, and a declaration of kanly against House Moritani on Grumman. Most serious, indeed." He wiped red juice from his fingertips onto his scarlet robe, then read further. His face flushed. "Wait a minute. Duke Leto Atreides has already offered his services to the Landsraad as a mediator, but the Ecazis are taking the matter into their own hands."

"Interesting," the Count said.

Angrily, Shaddam thrust the letter into Fenring's hands. "Duke Leto found out before I did? How is this possible? I'm the Emperor!"

"Sire, the flare-up is not surprising, considering the disgraceful behavior at my formal banquet." Seeing the blank look, he continued. "The Grumman ambassador assassinating his rival right at the dinner table? You remember my report? It came to you months ago, hmmmm?"

As Shaddam struggled to put the pieces together in his mind, he waved dismissively at a blackplaz shelf beside his desk. "Maybe it's over there. I haven't read them all."

Fenring's dark eyes flashed with annoyance. "You have time to read esoteric reports from a Planetologist, but not from me? You would have been prepared for this feud if you'd paid attention to my communiqué. I warned you the Grummans are dangerous and bear watching."

"I see. Just tell me what the report says, Hasimir. I'm a busy man."

Fenring recounted how he'd had to release the arrogant Lupino Ord, owing to diplomatic immunity. With a sigh, the Emperor summoned attendants and called an emergency meeting of his advisors.

IN THE CONFERENCE room adjoining Shaddam's Imperial office, a team of Mentat legal advisors, Landsraad spokesmen, and Guild observers reviewed the technicalities of kanly, the careful ballet of warfare designed to harm only actual combatants, with minimal collateral damage to civilians.

The Great Convention prohibited the use of atomic and biological weapons and required that disputing Houses fight a controlled feud through accepted direct and indirect methods. For millennia, the rigid rules had formed the framework of the Imperium. Advisors recounted the background of the current conflict, how Ecaz had accused Moritani of biological sabotage in their delicate fogtree forests, how the Grumman ambassador had murdered his Ecazi counterpart at Fenring's banquet, how Archduke Ecaz had formally declared kanly against Viscount Moritani.

"Another item of note," said the Imperial Trade Chief, waving one knobby finger like a rapier in the air, "I have learned that an entire shipment of commemorative coins—minted, if you recall, Sire, to celebrate your tenth anniversary on the Golden Lion Throne—has been stolen in an audacious raid on a commercial frigate. By self-styled space pirates, if reports are to be believed."

Shaddam glowered, impatient. "How is a petty theft relevant to the situation here?"

"That shipment was bound for Ecaz, Sire."

Fenring perked up. "Hmmmm, was anything else stolen? War matériel, weapons of any kind?"

The Trade Chief checked his notes. "No—the so-called raiders commandeered *only* the Imperial commemorative coins, leaving other valuables behind." He lowered his voice and mumbled, as if to himself, "However, since we used inferior materials in minting those coins, the financial losses are not significant. . . ."

"I recommend that we dispatch Imperial Observers to Ecaz and to Grumman," Court Chamberlain Ridondo said, "in order to enforce the forms. House Moritani has been known to . . . ah, stretch their interpretation of formal rules." Ridondo was a skeletally gaunt man with yellowish skin and a slippery way of accomplishing tasks while allowing Shaddam to take the credit; he had fared well in his position as Chamberlain.

Before Ridondo's suggestion could be discussed, though, another message cylinder thumped into the receptacle beside the Emperor's chair. After scanning the message, Shaddam slammed it onto the conference table. "Viscount Hundro Moritani has responded to the diplomatic insult by carpet-bombing the Ecazi Palace and its surrounding peninsula! The Mahogany Throne is physically destroyed. A hundred thousand noncombatants dead, and several forests are on fire. Archduke Ecaz barely escaped with his three daughters." He squinted down at the curling *instroy* paper again, then looked quickly at Fenring but refused to ask for advice.

"He disregarded the strictures of kanly?" the Trade Chief said in shock. "How can they do that?"

The sallow skin on Chamberlain Ridondo's towering forehead wrinkled with concern. "Viscount Moritani does not have the honor of his grandfather, who was a friend of the Hunter. What is to be done with wild dogs such as these?"

"Grumman has always hated being part of the Imperium, Sire," Fenring pointed out. "They constantly seek opportunities to spit in our faces."

The discussion around the table took on a more frenetic tone. As Shaddam listened to the talk, trying to look regal, he reflected on how different it was to be Emperor from how he'd imagined. Reality was exceedingly complicated, with too many competing forces.

He recalled playing war games with young Hasimir, and realized how much he missed his boyhood friend's companionship and advice. But an Emperor could not reverse important decisions lightly—Fenring would remain in his Arrakis assignment and in the allied duty of overseeing the artificial spice program. It was better if spies believed the stories of friction between them, though perhaps Shaddam could schedule more frequent visits with his childhood companion. . . .

"The forms must be obeyed, Sire," Ridondo said. "Law and tradition bind the Imperium. We cannot allow one noble house to ignore the strictures as they choose. Clearly, Moritani sees you as weak and unwilling to intervene in this squabble. He's taunting you."

The Imperium will not slip through my fingers, Shaddam vowed. He decided to set an example. "Let it be known throughout the Imperium that a legion of Sardaukar troops is to be stationed on Grumman for a period of two years. We'll put a leash on this Viscount." He turned to the Spacing Guild observer at the far end of the table. "Furthermore, I want the Guild to levy a heavy tariff on all goods delivered to and from Grumman. Such income to be used for reparations to Ecaz."

The Guild representative sat in silence for a long, cold moment, as if pondering the "decision," which was in reality only a request. The Guild was beyond the control of the Padishah Emperor. Finally, he nodded. "It will be done."

One of the court Mentats sat rigidly in his chair. "They will appeal, Sire."

Shaddam sniffed. "If Moritani has a case, let him make it."

Fenring tapped his fingers on the table, considering consequences. Shaddam had already dispatched two legions of
Sardaukar to oversee the Tleilaxu on Ix, and now he was sending more to Grumman. In other trouble spots around the Imperium he had increased the visible presence of his crack
military troops, hoping to smother any thoughts of rebellion.
He had increased the ranks of the Bursegs throughout the
military, adding more mid-level commanders to be dispatched
with troops, as needed.

Even so, small and annoying instances of sabotage or defacement continued to occur in random places, such as the
theft of commemorative coins bound for Ecaz, the balloon
effigy of Shaddam floating over the Harmonthep stadium, the
insulting words painted on the cliffs of Monument Canyon. . . .

As a result, the loyal Sardaukar were spread too thinly, and
because of the costly Project Amal, the Imperial treasury had
insufficient funds to train and supply new troops. Thus, the
military reserves were being depleted, and Fenring saw troubled times ahead. As House Moritani's actions proved, some
forces in the Landsraad sensed weakness, smelled blood. . . .

Fenring considered reminding Shaddam of all this, but instead he held his own counsel as the meeting continued. His
old friend seemed to think he could handle things without
him—so let the man prove it.

The Emperor would get himself deeper and deeper into
trouble, and finally he would have to call his exiled "Spice Minister" back to Kaitain. When that occurred, Fenring would
make him grovel . . . before finally assenting.

Organizational structure is crucial to the success of a movement. It is, as well, a prime target for attack.

—CAMMAR PILRU,
Ixian Ambassador in Exile
Treatise on the Downfall of Unjust Governments

BEFORE THE NEXT MEETING OF THE RESISTANCE GROUP, C'TAIR DISGUISED himself as an introverted suboid worker. Under the guise, he spent days of reconnaissance in the underground warrens where the rebels planned to gather.

Interspersed with islands of stalactite buildings, the holo-projected sky looked wrong, mimicking light from a sun that did not belong to Ix. C'tair's arms ached from placing heavy crates on self-motivated pallets that delivered supplies, equipment, and raw materials into the sealed-off research pavilion.

The invaders had commandeered a cluster of industrial facilities and modified the construction, building over rooftops and connecting side passages. Under House Vernius, the facilities had been masterfully designed to be both beautiful and functional. Now they resembled rodent nests, all sloping barricades and armored gables that shimmered beneath defensive fields. Their covered windows looked like blind eyes.

What are the Tleilaxu doing in there?

C'tair wore drab clothes, let his face hang slack and his eyes grow dull. He focused on the tedious monotony of his tasks. When dust or dirt smudged his cheeks, when grease smeared his fingers, he did nothing to clean himself, just plodded like clockwork.

Although the Tleilaxu did not consider suboids worthy of

ttention, the invaders had rallied these workers during their takeover of Ix. Despite promises of better conditions and better treatment, the Tleilaxu had ground the suboids under their heels, far more than their experiences under Dominic Vernius.

When he was off shift, C'tair lived in a rock-walled chamber within the suboid warrens. The workers had little social life, did not speak much to each other. Few noticed the newcomer or asked his name; none of them made overtures of friendship. He felt more invisible there than when he had hidden in a shielded chamber for months during the initial revolt.

C'tair preferred invisibility. He could accomplish more that way.

Slipping off by himself, he evaluated the secret meeting place beforehand. He took bootleg equipment into the empty supply chamber to scan for surveillance instruments. He did not dare underestimate the Tleilaxu—especially since two more legions of Imperial Sardaukar had been stationed here to keep even tighter control.

He stood in the center of the chamber and turned in a slow circle, concerned about the five tunnels leading into the chamber. *Too many entrances, too many spots for an ambush.* He pondered for a moment, then smiled as an idea occurred to him.

The following afternoon he stole a small holoprojector, with which he imaged comparable featureless rock. Moving silently, he set up the projector inside one of the openings and switched it on. A false barrier of rock now blocked one of the tunnels, a perfect illusion.

C'tair had lived with suspicion and fear for so long that he never expected his plans to go well. But that didn't mean he stopped hoping. . . .

THE FREEDOM FIGHTERS arrived one by one as the appointed time approached. No one risked traveling with any other rebel;

each wore a disguise, each came prepared with an excuse for his business down in the suboid tunnels.

C'tair arrived late—safely late. The furtive resistance fighters exchanged vital equipment and discussed plans in harsh whispers. No one had an overall strategy. Some of their schemes were so impossible C'tair had to force himself not to laugh, while others seemed like suggestions he might want to imitate.

He needed more crystalline rods for his rogo transmitter. After each attempt to communicate with his distant Navigator brother, the crystals splintered and cracked, leaving him with pounding headaches.

The last time he'd tried the rogo, C'tair had been unable to contact D'murr, sensing his twin's presence and a few staticky thoughts but without linking up. Afterward, lying awake for hours in his darkened chamber, C'tair felt lost and depressed, entirely alone. He realized just how much he had counted on his brother's well-being, and on hearing that others from Ix had escaped and survived.

At times, C'tair wondered exactly what he had accomplished in all his years of struggle. He wanted to do more, wanted to strike forcefully against the Tleilaxu—but what could he do? He stared at the gathered rebels, people who talked a great deal but accomplished little. He watched their faces, noting greed in the black marketeers and ferretlike nervousness in others. C'tair wondered if *these* were truly the allies he needed. Somehow he doubted it.

Miral Alechem was also there, bartering furiously for more components to add to her mysterious plan. She seemed different from the others, willing to take necessary action.

Unobtrusively, he worked his way over to Miral and caught the gaze of her large, wary eyes. "I've studied the components you buy"—he nodded toward the few items she held in her hands—"and I can't fathom your plan. I might . . . I might be able to help. I've done a good deal of tinkering myself."

She took a half step back, like a suspicious rabbit, trying to read the meaning behind his words. Finally, she spoke through pale lips, but her mouth remained drawn. "I have an . . . idea. I need to search—"

Before she could continue, C'tair heard a movement in the tunnels, footsteps that were at first faint and then louder. The lookout guards shouted. One ducked inside the room as projectile gunfire rang out.

"We're betrayed!" shouted one of the rebels.

In the confusion, C'tair saw Sardaukar soldiers and Tleilaxu warriors converging from the four exits, blocking the tunnels. They fired into the gathered resistance fighters as if it were a shooting gallery.

Screams, smoke, and blood filled the air. Sardaukar hurried in with hand weapons drawn; some used only their fists and fingers to kill. C'tair waited for the smoke to thicken, for the rebels to fly into a greater frenzy—and then lunged forward.

Seeing no escape, Miral crouched low. C'tair grabbed her by the shoulders. She began to fight him, thrashing as if he were her enemy, but C'tair pushed her backward toward the solid rock wall.

She fell directly through. He plunged after her into the holo-covered opening. He felt a twinge of guilt for not shouting to the others, but if all the rebels disappeared through the same escape hatch, the Sardaukar would be upon them in moments.

Miral looked around in confusion. C'tair grabbed her arm and dragged her along. "I planned for an escape ahead of time. A hologram." They began sprinting through the tunnel.

Miral stumbled beside him. "Our group is dead."

"It was never *my* group," C'tair said, panting. "They're amateurs."

She looked at him as they ran, her dark eyes boring into his. "We must separate."

He nodded, then both took divergent tunnels.

Far behind him, he heard the Sardaukar cry out as they discovered the disguised opening. C'tair ran faster, taking a left tunnel, then an uphill branch, doubling back to a different grotto. Finally, he reached a lift tube that would take him out into the immense cavern.

Like a suboid going to work on the late shift, he fumbled for one of his identity cards and swiped it through a reader. The lift tube whisked him toward the stalactite buildings that had once been inhabited by bureaucrats and nobles who served House Vernius.

Within the ceiling levels, he raced across connecting walkways, slipped between buildings, and looked down at the glittering lights of corrupted manufactories. Finally, inside the crustal levels of what had once been the Grand Palais, he made his way to the shielded bolt-hole he had abandoned long ago.

He slipped to the chamber and locked it. He hadn't found it necessary to hide there for a long time—but tonight he'd come closer to capture than ever before. In the silent darkness, C'tair rolled onto the musty-smelling cot that had been his bed for so many tense evenings. Panting, he stared at the low ceiling, black above him. His heart pounded. He could not relax.

He imagined seeing stars above his room, a blizzard of tiny lights that showered across the open night sky on Ix's pristine surface. As his thoughts traveled out into the sprawling expanse of the galaxy, he envisioned D'murr flying his Guild ship . . . safely away from here.

C'tair had to contact him soon.

The universe is our picture. Only the immature imagine the cosmos to be what they think it is.

—SIGAN VISEE,
First Head Instructor,
Guild Navigator School

D'MURR, A VOICE SAID IN THE BACK OF HIS AWARENESS. *D'MURR* . . .

Within the sealed navigation chamber atop his Heighliner, D'murr swam in spice gas, kicking his webbed feet. Orange eddies swirled around him. In his navigation trance, all star systems and planets were a grand tapestry, and he could travel along any thread he chose. He derived supreme pleasure from entering the womb of the universe and conquering its mysteries.

It was so peaceful in deep, open space. The brightness of suns came and went . . . a vast, eternal night dotted with tiny points of illumination.

D'murr performed the higher-order mental calculations required to foresee a safe course through any star system. He guided the immense ship through the limitless void. He could encompass the reaches of the universe and transport passengers and freight to any place he desired. He saw the future and conformed to it.

Because of the outstanding abilities he had demonstrated, D'murr was among only a few mutated humans who had risen through the Navigators' ranks so swiftly. *Human*. The word was little more than a lingering memory for him.

His emotions—strange detritus from his original physical form—swung him in a way he had not expected. In the seventeen Standard Years he'd spent growing up on Ix with his twin brother, C'tair, he had not possessed the time, wisdom, or desire to understand what it meant to be *human*.

And for the past dozen years, admittedly by his own choice, he'd been removed from that dubious reality and vaulted into another existence, part dream, part nightmare. Certainly his new appearance could frighten any man who was unprepared for the sight.

But the advantages, the reasons he had joined the Guild in the first place, more than compensated for that. He experienced cosmic beauty unknown to other life-forms: What they could only imagine, he actually *knew*.

Why had the Spacing Guild accepted him at all? Very few outsiders were admitted to the elite corps; the Guild favored their own Navigator candidates—those born in space to Guild employees and loyalists, some of whom had never walked upon solid ground.

Am I only an experiment, a freak among freaks? Sometimes, with all the contemplative time on a great voyage, D'murr's mind wandered. *Am I being tested at this very moment by some means that can scan my aberrant thoughts?* Whenever the wild awareness of his previous human self came over him, D'murr felt as if he were standing on the edge of a precipice, deciding whether or not to leap into the void. *The Guild is always watching.*

While floating in the navigation chamber, he journeyed among the remnants of his emotions. An unusual sense of melancholy enveloped him. He had sacrificed so much to become what he was. He could never land on any planet unless he emerged in a wheeled and enclosed tank of spice gas. . . .

He concentrated hard, drove his thoughts back into line. If he allowed the human self to become too strong, D'murr might send the Heighliner reeling off course.

"D'murr," the nagging voice said again, like the throbbing pain of a mounting headache. "D'murr . . ."

He ignored it. He tried to convince himself that such thoughts and regrets must be common for Navigators, that others experienced them as often as he did. But why hadn't the instructors warned him?

I am strong. I can overcome this.

On a routine flight to the Bene Gesserit world of Wallach IX, he piloted one of the last Heighliners constructed by Ixians, before the Tleilaxu took over and reverted to an earlier, less efficient design. Mentally he reviewed the passenger list, seeing the words imaged on the walls of his navigation tank.

A Duke was aboard—Leto Atreides. And his friend Rhombur Vernius, exiled heir to the lost fortunes of Ix. Familiar faces and memories . . .

A lifetime ago, D'murr had been introduced to young Leto in the Grand Palais. Navigators overheard snippets of Imperial news and could eavesdrop on business conducted over the communication channels, but they paid little attention to petty matters. This Duke had won a Trial by Forfeiture, a monumental act that had granted him respect throughout the Imperium.

Why would Duke Leto be going to Wallach IX? And why did he bring the Ixian refugee?

The distant, crackling voice cut in again: "D'murr . . . answer me . . ."

With sudden clarity he realized it was a manifestation of his former life. Loyal, kind C'tair attempting to stay in touch, though for months D'murr had been unable to reply. Perhaps it was a distortion caused by the continuing evolution of his brain, widening the gulf between himself and his brother.

The atrophied vocal cords of a Navigator could still utter words, but the mouth was primarily used to consume more and more melange. The mind-expansion of the spice trance pushed away D'murr's former life and contacts. He could no longer experience love, except as a flickering memory. He could never again touch a human being. . . .

With one of his stubby webbed hands he withdrew a concentrated melange pill from a container and popped it into his tiny mouth, increasing the flow of spice through his system. His mind floated a little, but not enough to dull the pain of the past, and of the attempted mental contact. This time his emotions were too strong to overcome.

His brother finally stopped calling to him, but he would return soon. He always did.

Now, the only sound D'murr heard was the steady hiss of gas entering the chamber. *Melange, melange.* It continued to pour into him, filling his senses completely. He had no individuality left, could barely tolerate speaking to his own brother anymore.

He could only listen, and remember. . . .

War is a form of organic behavior. The army is a means of survival for the all-male group. The all-female group, on the other hand, is traditionally religion-oriented. They are the keepers of sacred mysteries.

—Bene Gesserit Teaching

AFTER DESCENDING FROM THE ORBITING HEIGHLINER AND PASSING through the intricate atmospheric defensive systems, Duke Leto Atreides and Rhombur Vernius were met in the Mother School's spaceport by a contingent of three black-robed women.

Wallach IX's blue-white sun was not visible from the ground. A bone-chilling breeze whipped into the open-air portico where the group stood. Leto felt it through his clothing and could see white feathers of breath curl from his exhalations. At his side, Rhombur pulled the collar of his jacket tight.

The leader of the escort committee introduced herself as Mother Superior Harishka—an honor Leto had not expected. *What have I ever done to warrant such attention?* When he'd been imprisoned on Kaitain, awaiting his Trial by Forfeiture, the Bene Gesserit had secretly offered him assistance, but had never explained their reasons. *The Bene Gesserit do nothing without a clear purpose.*

Old but energetic, Harishka had dark almond eyes and a direct manner of speaking. "Prince Rhombur Vernius." She bowed to the round-faced young man, who swept his purple-and-copper cape in a dashing gesture of his own. "It is a pity what happened to your Great House, a terrible pity. Even the Sisterhood finds the Bene Tleilax . . . incomprehensible."

"Thank you, but uh, I am certain everything will work out. Just the other day our Ambassador in Exile submitted another petition to the Landsraad Council." He smiled with forced optimism. "I seek no sympathy."

"You seek only a concubine, correct?" The old woman turned to lead the way out of the portico and onto the grounds of the Mother School complex. "We welcome the opportunity to place one of our Sisters in Castle Caladan. I am sure she will benefit you, and the Atreides."

They followed a cobblestone pathway between interlinked stucco buildings with terra-cotta roof tiles, arranged like the scales on a reef lizard. In a flower-filled courtyard, they paused at a stylized black quartz statue of a woman kneeling. "The founder of our ancient School," Harishka said, "Raquella Berto-Anirul. By manipulating her own body chemistry, Raquella survived what would have been a lethal poisoning."

Rhombur bent to read the brass plaque. "It says that all written and pictorial records of this woman were lost long ago when invaders set fire to the library building and destroyed the original statue. Uh, how do you know what she looked like?"

With a wrinkled smile, Harishka said cryptically, "Why, because we are witches." Without another word, the robed old woman led the way down a short stairway and through a humid greenhouse where Acolytes and Sisters tended exotic plants and herbs. Perhaps medicines, perhaps even poisons.

The Mother School was a place of legend and mythology seen by few men, and Leto had been astonished at the warm acceptance that his brash request had received. He had asked the Bene Gesserit to select a talented, intelligent mate for Rhombur, and his tousle-haired friend had agreed to go "shopping."

At a brisk pace Harishka crossed a grassy field where women in short, lightweight robes performed impossible stretching exercises to a vocal cadence called out by a wrinkled, stooped old woman who matched them, move for move. Leto found their bodily control astonishing.

When they finally entered a large stucco building with dark timbered beams and highly polished wooden floors, Leto was glad to be out of the sharp wind. The building had a dusty chalkboard smell from old plaster walls. The foyer opened into a practice hall, where a dozen young women in white robes stood motionless in the center, as erect as soldiers waiting for inspection. Their hoods were thrown back over their shoulders.

Mother Superior stopped in front of the acolytes. The two Reverend Mothers accompanying her went to stand behind the young women. "Who here seeks a concubine?" Harishka inquired. It was a traditional question, part of the ritual.

Rhombur stepped forward. "I do—uh, Prince Rhombur, firstborn son and heir of House Vernius. Or perhaps I seek even a wife." He glanced over at Leto and lowered his voice. "Since my House is renegade, I don't have to play silly political games. Unlike some people I know."

Leto flushed, remembering the lessons his father had taught him. *Find love wherever you like, but never marry for love. Your title belongs to House Atreides—use it to strike the best possible bargain.*

He had recently traveled to forested Ecaz to meet with Archduke Armand in his provisional capital after the Moritani carpet-bombing of his ancestral château. Under the Emperor's crackdown, sending a legion of Sardaukar to Grumman to keep the fuming Viscount at bay, open hostilities between the two Houses had stopped, at least for the moment.

Archduke Armand Ecaz had requested an investigation team to study the alleged sabotage of the famous Ecazi fogtree forests and other crops, but Shaddam had refused. "Let sleeping dogs lie" had been his official Imperial response. And he expected the problem to end there.

Recognizing Leto's diligent attempts to calm the still-uneasy tensions, the Archduke had informally mentioned that his eldest daughter, Sanyá, might be a marriageable prospect for House Atreides. Upon hearing the suggestion, Leto had considered the assets of House Ecaz, their commercial, political, and military power, and how they might complement the resources of Caladan. He had not even looked at the girl in question. *Study the political advantages of a marriage alliance.* His father would have been pleased. . . .

Now, Mother Superior said, "These young women are well trained in the myriad ways of pleasing nobility. All have been chosen according to your profile, Prince."

Rhombur approached the line of women and looked closely at each of their faces. Blondes, brunettes, redheads, some with skin as pale as milk, some as sleek and dark as ebony. All were beautiful, all intelligent . . . and all studied him with poise and anticipation.

Knowing his friend as he did, Leto was not surprised to see Rhombur pause in front of a rather plain-looking girl with wide-set sepia eyes and mousy brown hair cut as short as a man's. She met Rhombur's appraisal without looking away, without feigning a demure reaction as some of the others had done. Leto noted the faintest smile curving her lips upward.

"Her name is Tessia," the Mother Superior said. "A very intelligent, talented young woman. She can recite the ancient classics perfectly, and plays several musical instruments."

Rhombur tilted her chin up, looked into her dark brown eyes. "But can you laugh at a joke? And tell an even better one in return?"

"Clever wordplay, my Lord?" Tessia answered. "Do you prefer a distressingly bad pun, or a joke so bawdy it'll make your cheeks burn?"

Rhombur guffawed with delight. "This one!" As he touched Tessia's arm, she stepped out of line and walked with him for the first time. Leto was pleased to see his friend so happy, but his heart was heavy as well, considering his own lack of a relationship. Rhombur often did things on impulse, but had the fortitude to make them turn out right.

"Come here, children," Harishka said in a solemn tone. "Stand before me and bow your heads." They did so, holding hands.

With a paternal frown, Leto stepped forward to straighten Rhombur's collar and brushed an offending wrinkle from his shoulder pad. The Ixian Prince flushed, then mumbled his thanks.

Harishka continued, "May you both lead long, productive lives and enjoy each other's honorable company. You are now bound. If, in years to come, you should choose to marry and seal the bond beyond concubinage, you have the blessings of the Bene Gesserit. If you are not satisfied with Tessia, she may return here to the Mother School."

Leto was surprised to witness so many ceremonial trappings in what was, fundamentally, a business agreement. By Courier from Caladan, he had already agreed upon a range of prices. Still, Mother Superior's words imbued the relationship with some structure and established a foundation for good things to come.

"Prince Rhombur, this is a special woman, trained in ways that may surprise you. Heed her advice, for Tessia is wise beyond her years." Mother Superior stepped back.

Tessia leaned forward to whisper in Rhombur's ear, and the exiled Prince laughed. Looking at his friend, he said, "Tessia has an interesting idea. Leto, why don't you select a concubine for yourself? There's plenty to choose from." He gestured toward the other Acolytes. "That way you won't have to keep making eyes at my sister!"

Leto blushed furiously. His long-standing attraction to Kailea must be obvious, though he had taken steps over the years to conceal it. He had refused to take her to his bed, torn as he was by the demands of ducal duty and the admonitions of his father.

"I've had other lovers, Rhombur. You know that. City and village girls find their Duke attractive enough. There's no shame in it—and I can maintain my honor with your sister."

Rhombur rolled his eyes. "So, some fisherman's daughter from the docks is good enough for you, but my sister isn't?"

"That's not it at all. I do this out of respect for House Vernius, and for you."

Harishka broke in, "I am afraid the women we have brought here are not suitable for Duke Atreides. These have been selected for compatibility with Prince Rhombur." Her prunish lips smiled. "Nonetheless, other arrangements might be made. . . ." She glanced up at an interior balcony, as if someone were watching them in concealment from above.

"I am not here for a concubine," Leto said gruffly.

"Uh, he's the independent sort," Rhombur said to Mother Superior, then raised his eyebrows at Tessia. "What are we to do with him?"

"He knows what he wants, but does not know to admit it to himself," Tessia said with a clever smile. "A bad habit for a Duke."

Rhombur patted Leto on the back. "See, she's already giving good advice. Why don't you just take Kailea as your concubine and be done with it, Leto? I'm growing tired of your schoolboy angst. It's certainly within your rights and, uh, we, both know it's the best she can aspire to be."

With an uneasy laugh, Leto dismissed the idea, though he had considered it many times. He had been hesitant to approach Kailea with such a suggestion. What might her reaction be? Would she demand to be more than a concubine? That was impossible.

Still, Rhombur's sister understood political realities. Before the Ixian tragedy, the daughter of Earl Vernius would have been an acceptable match for a Duke (perhaps that's what old Paulus had had in mind). But now, as head of House Atreides, Leto could never marry into a family that no longer held any Imperial title or fief.

What is this Love that so many speak of with such apparent familiarity? Do they truly comprehend how unattainable it is? Are there not as many definitions of Love as there are stars in the universe?

—The Bene Gesserit Question Book

FROM AN INTERIOR BALCONY OVERLOOKING THE WAITING ACOLYTES, twelve-year-old Jessica watched the concubine-selection process with intent eyes and sharp curiosity. Standing beside the girl, Reverend Mother Mohiam had instructed her to observe, so Jessica drank in every detail with practiced Bene Gesserit scrutiny.

What does the teacher want me to see?

On the polished hardwood floor, Mother Superior stood talking with the young nobleman and his newly selected concubine, Tessia al-Reill. Jessica had not predicted that choice; several of the other Acolytes were more beautiful, more shapely, more glamorous . . . but Jessica did not know the Prince or his personality, was not familiar with his tastes.

Did beauty intimidate him, an indication of low self-esteem? Perchance the Acolyte Tessia reminded him of someone else he had known? Or maybe he was simply attracted to her for some difficult-to-define reason . . . her smile, her eyes, her laugh.

"Never try to understand love," Mohiam cautioned in a directed-whisper, sensing the girl's thoughts. "Simply work to understand its effects in lesser people."

Below, one of the other Reverend Mothers brought a document on a writing board and handed it to the Prince for his signature. His companion, a black-haired, hawk-featured nobleman, peered over his shoulder to review the fine print. Jessica could not make out their spoken words, but she was familiar with the ancient Ritual of Duty.

The dark-haired Duke reached forward to fix his companion's collar. She found the gesture oddly endearing, and she smiled.

"Will I be presented to a nobleman one day, Reverend Mother?" she whispered. No one had ever explained what Jessica's purpose in the Bene Gesserit might be, and it was a constant source of curiosity to her—one that often irritated Mohiam.

The Reverend Mother formed a scowl on her plain, aging face, as Jessica had suspected she would. "When the time is right, you will know, child. Wisdom is understanding when to ask questions."

Jessica had heard this admonition before. "Yes, Reverend Mother. Impatience is a weakness."

The Bene Gesserit had many such sayings, all of which Jessica had committed to memory. She sighed in exasperation, then controlled the reaction, hoping her teacher had not seen. The Sisterhood obviously had some plan for her—why wouldn't they reveal her future? Most other Acolytes had some idea of their predetermined paths, but Jessica saw only a blank wall ahead of her, with no writing on it.

I am being groomed for something. Prepared for an important assignment. Why had her teacher brought her to this balcony, at this precise moment? There was no accident in this, no coincidence; the Bene Gesserit planned everything, thought everything through with utmost care.

"There is hope for you yet, child," Mohiam murmured. "I instructed you to observe—but you are intent on the wrong person. Not the man with Tessia. Watch the other one, watch them both, watch how they interact with each other. Tell me what you see."

From her high vantage, Jessica studied the men. She breathed deeply, let her muscles relax. Her thoughts, like minerals suspended in a glass of water, clarified.

"Both men are nobles, but not blood kin, judging from differences in their dress, mannerisms, and expressions." She did not take her eyes from them. "They have been close friends for many years. They depend on one another. The black-haired one is concerned for his friend's welfare."

"And?" Jessica heard excitement and anticipation in her teacher's voice, though she could not imagine why. The Reverend Mother's eyes were riveted on the second nobleman.

"I can tell by his bearing and interaction that the dark-haired one is a leader and takes his responsibilities seriously. He has power, but does not wallow in it. He is probably a better ruler than he gives himself credit for." She watched his movement, the flush of his skin, the way he looked at the other Acolytes and then forced himself to turn away. "He is also lonely."

"Excellent." Mohiam beamed down at her pupil, but her eyes narrowed. "That man is Duke Leto Atreides—and you are destined for him, Jessica. One day you will be the mother of his children."

Though Jessica knew she should take this news impassively, as a duty she must perform for the Sisterhood, she suddenly found a need to calm her hammering heart.

At that moment Duke Leto glanced up at Jessica, as if sensing her presence in the balcony shadows—and their gazes met. She saw a fire in his gray eyes, a strength and wisdom beyond his years, the result of bearing difficult burdens. She felt herself drawn to him.

But she resisted. Instincts . . . automatic reactions, responses . . . *I am not an animal*. She rejected other emotions, as Mohiam had taught her for years.

Jessica's previous questions vanished, and for the moment she formed no new ones. A deep, calming breath brought her to a state of serenity. For whatever reasons, she liked the look of this Duke . . . but her duty was to the Sisterhood. She would wait to learn what lay in store for her, and she would do whatever was necessary.

Impatience is a weakness.

Inwardly, Mohiam smiled. Knowing the genetic threads she'd been ordered to weave, the Reverend Mother had staged this brief but distant encounter between Jessica and Duke Atreides. Jessica was the culmination of many generations of careful breeding to create the Kwisatz Haderach.

The mistress of the program, Kwisatz Mother Anirul, wife of Emperor Shaddam, claimed that the highest likelihood of success would occur if a Harkonnen daughter of the current generation produced an Atreides daughter. Jessica's secret father was Baron Harkonnen . . . and when she was ready she would be joined with Duke Leto Atreides.

Mohiam found it supremely ironic that these mortal enemies—House Harkonnen and House Atreides—were destined to form such an incredibly important union, one that neither House would ever suspect . . . or condone.

She could hardly restrain her excitement at the prospect: Thanks to Jessica, the Sisterhood was only two generations away from its ultimate goal.

When you ask a question, do you truly want to know the answer, or are you merely flaunting your power?

—DMITRI HARKONNEN,
Notes to My Sons

BARON HARKONNEN HAD TO PAY FOR THE SUK DOCTOR TWICE.

He'd thought his massive payment to Richesian Premier Calimar would be sufficient to obtain the services of Dr. Wellington Yueh for as long as would be required to diagnose and treat his debilitating illness. Yueh, though, refused to cooperate.

The sallow Suk doctor was totally absorbed in himself and his technical research on the orbiting laboratory moon of Korona. He showed not the slightest respect or fear when the Baron's name was mentioned. "I may work for the Richesians," he said in a firm, humorless voice, "but I do not *belong* to them."

Piter de Vries, sent to Richese to work out the confidential details for the Baron, studied the doctor's aged, wooden features, the oblivious stubbornness. They stood together in a small laboratory office on the artificial research station, a grand satellite that shone in the Richesian sky. Despite the emphatic request of Premier Calimar, narrow-faced Yueh, with long drooping mustaches and a rope of black hair gathered into a silver Suk ring, declined to go to Giedi Prime. *Self-confident arrogance*, de Vries thought. *That can be used against him.*

"You, sir, are a Mentat, accustomed to selling your thoughts and intelligence to any patron." Yueh drew his lips together and studied de Vries as if he were performing an autopsy . . . or wanted to. "I, on the other hand, am a member of the Suk Inner Circle, graduate of full Imperial Conditioning." He tapped the diamond tattoo on his wrinkled forehead. "I cannot be bought, sold, or rented out. You have no hold over me. Now, please allow me to return to my important work." He gave a minimal bow before taking his leave to continue research in the Richesian laboratories.

That man has never been put in his place, never been hurt . . . never been broken. Piter de Vries considered it a challenge.

IN THE GOVERNMENTAL buildings of Triad Center, Richesian Premier Calimar's apologies and posturing meant nothing to de Vries. However, he could easily make use of the man's authorization to pass through the security gates and guards, to return to the Korona satellite research station. With no choice in the matter, the Mentat went to Dr. Yueh's sterile medical laboratory. Alone, this time.

Time to renegotiate for the Baron. He did not dare return to Giedi Prime without a fully cooperative Suk doctor.

He moved with mincing steps into a metal-walled room filled with machinery, cables, and preserved body parts in tanks—a mixture of the best Richesian electromechanical technology, Suk surgical equipment, and biological specimens from other animals. The smells of lubricants, rot, chemicals, burned flesh, and burning circuits hung heavy in the cold room, even as the station's air-recyclers attempted to scrub the contaminants. Several tables contained sinks, metal and plaz piping, snaking cables, dispensing machines. Rising above the dissection areas, shimmering holo blue-prints portrayed human limbs as organic machines.

As the Mentat gazed across the laboratory, Yueh's head suddenly appeared on the other side of one of the counters—

lean and grease-smeared, with facial bones so prominent they seemed to be made of metal.

"Please don't disturb me further, Mentat," he said in an abrupt voice, preempting conversation. He didn't even ask how de Vries had found his way back to the restricted Korona moon. The diamond tattoo of Imperial Conditioning glistened on his forehead, buried under a smear of dark lubricant from a careless wipe of his hand. "I am very busy."

"Still, Doctor, I must speak with you. My Baron commands it."

Yueh narrowed his eyes, as if imagining how some of his prototype cyborg parts might fit on the Mentat. "I am not interested in your Baron's medical condition. It is not my area of expertise." He looked at the laboratory racks and tables filled with experimental prosthetics, as if the answer should be obvious. Yueh remained maddeningly aloof, as if he couldn't be touched or corrupted by anything.

De Vries approached to within garroting distance of the shorter man, talking all the while. No doubt he would face serious punishment if he was forced to kill this annoying doctor. "My Baron used to be healthy, trim, proud of his physique. Through no change in diet or exercise, he has nearly doubled his body weight in ten years. He suffers from a gradual deterioration of muscular functions and bloating."

Yueh frowned, but his gaze turned back to the Mentat's. De Vries caught the flicker of expression and lowered his voice, ready to pounce. "Do those symptoms sound familiar to you, Doctor? Something you've seen elsewhere?"

Now Yueh became calculating. He shifted so that racks of test apparatus separated him from the twisted Mentat. A long glass tube continued to bubble and stink on the far side of the chamber. "No Suk doctor gives free advice, Mentat. My expenses here are exorbitant, my research vital."

De Vries chuckled as his enhanced mind spun through possibilities. "And are you so engrossed in your tinkering, Doctor, hat you've failed to notice that your patron, House Richese, is nearly bankrupt? Baron Harkonnen's payment could guarantee your funding for many years."

The twisted Mentat reached abruptly into his jacket pocket, causing Yueh to flinch, fearing a silent weapon. Instead de Vries brought out a flat black panel with touch pads. The holoprojection of an old-style sea chest appeared, made entirely of gold with precious-gem studs inlaid on its top and sides in the patterns of blue Harkonnen griffins. "After you diagnose my Baron, you could continue your research however you see fit."

Intrigued, Yueh reached out, so that his hand and forearm passed through the image. With a synthetic squeal, the lid of the holo-image opened to reveal an empty interior. "We will fill this with whatever you please. Melange, soostones, blue obsidian, opafire jewels, Hagal quartz . . . blackmail images. Everyone knows that a Suk doctor can be bought."

"Then go buy yourself one. Make it a matter of public record."

"We prefer a more, ah, confidential arrangement, as Premier Calimar promised."

The sallow old doctor pursed his dark lips again, deep in thought. Yueh's entire world seemed focused on a small bubble around him, as if no one else existed, no one else mattered. "I cannot provide long-term care, but I could perhaps diagnose the disease."

De Vries shrugged his bony shoulders. "The Baron doesn't want you any longer than necessary."

Staring at the sheer amount of wealth the Mentat was promising him, Yueh imagined how much more productive his work would be here on Korona, given adequate funding. Still, he hesitated. "I have other responsibilities. I have been assigned here by the Suk College for this specific purpose. Cyborg prostheses will be a valuable market for Richese, and us, once proven."

With a sigh of resignation, de Vries pressed a key on the pad, and the treasure chest became noticeably larger.

Yueh stroked his mustaches. "It might be possible for me to travel between Richese and Giedi Prime—under an assumed identity, of course. I could study your Baron, then return here to continue my work."

"An interesting idea," the Mentat said. "So you accept our terms?"

"I agree to examine the patient. And I shall consider what to put in the treasure chest you offer." Yueh pointed toward a nearby counter. "Now hand me that measuring scope. Since you interrupted, you can help me with constructing a proto-type body core."

TWO DAYS LATER on Giedi Prime, adjusting to the industrial air and the heavier gravity, Yueh examined the Baron in the infir-mary of Harkonnen Keep. All doors closed, all windows cov-ered, all servants sent away. Piter de Vries watched through his peephole, grinning.

Yueh discarded the medical files the Baron's doctors had compiled over the years, documenting the progress of the dis-ease. "Foolish amateurs. I am not interested in them, or their test results." Opening his diagnostic kit, the doctor withdrew his own set of scanners, complex mechanisms that only a highly trained Suk could decipher. "Remove your clothing, please."

"Do you want to play?" The Baron tried to retain his dig-nity, his command of the situation.

"No."

The Baron distracted himself from the uncomfortable probings and proddings as he considered ways to kill this pompous Suk if he, too, failed to discover the cause of the disease. He drummed his fingertips on the examining table. "None of my physicians could suggest any effective course of treatment. Given the choice of a clean mind or a clean body, I had to take my pick."

Ignoring the basso voice, Yueh donned a pair of goggles with green lenses. "Suggesting that you strive for both is too much to ask?" He initialized the power pack and scanning routines, then peered at the gross, naked form of his patient. The Baron lay on his belly on the examination couch. He muttered constantly, complaining about pains and discomforts.

Yueh spent several minutes examining the Baron's skin, his internal organs, his orifices, until a string of subtle clues began to fit together in his mind. Finally, the delicate Suk scanner detected a vector path.

"Your condition appears to be sexually generated. Are you able to use this penis?" Yueh said without the slightest trace of humor. He might have been giving a stock quote.

"*Use* it?" The Baron gave a rude snort. "Hells and damnations, it's still the best part of me."

"Ironic." Yueh used a scalpel to scrape a sample from the foreskin, and the Baron yelped in surprise. "I need to run an analysis." The doctor didn't give the slightest hint of an apology.

With the slender blade Yueh smeared the fragment of skin onto a thin slide and inserted it into a slot in the front underside of his goggles. Using finger controls, he rotated the specimen in front of his eyes, under varying illuminations. The goggle plaz changed color from green to scarlet to lavender. Then he sent the sample through a multistage chemical analysis.

"Was that necessary?" the Baron growled.

"It is only the beginning." Yueh then removed more instruments—many of them sharp—from his kit. The Baron would have been intrigued, if he'd been able to use the tools on someone else. "I must perform many tests."

———

AFTER SLIPPING INTO a robe, Baron Harkonnen sat back, gray-skinned and sweaty, sore in a thousand places that had not hurt before. Several times he'd wanted to kill this arrogant Suk doctor—but he didn't dare interfere with the protracted diagnosis. The other physicians had been helpless and stupid; now he would endure whatever was necessary in order to obtain his answer. The Baron hoped the treatment and eventual cure would be less aggressive, less painful than Yueh's original analysis. He poured from a decanter of kirana brandy and gulped down a mouthful.

"I have reduced the spectrum of possibilities, Baron," Yueh said, pursing his lips. "Your ailment belongs to a category of rare diseases, narrowly defined, specifically targeted. I can collect another full set of samples, if you would like me to triple-verify the diagnosis?"

"That will *not* be necessary." The Baron sat up, gripping his walking stick in case he needed to hit someone with it. "What have you found?"

Yueh droned on, "The transmission vector is obvious, via heterosexual intercourse. You were infected by one of your female lovers."

The Baron's momentary elation at finally finding an answer washed away in confusion. "I have no female lovers. Women disgust me."

"Yes, I see." Yueh had heard many patients deny the obvious. "The symptoms are so subtly general that I am not surprised less-competent doctors missed it. Even Suk teaching did not initially include a mention of it, and I learned of such intriguing diseases through my wife, Wanna. She is a Bene Gesserit, and the Sisterhood occasionally makes use of these disease organisms—"

The Baron lunged into a sitting position on the edge of the examination couch. A firestorm crossed his jowly face. "Those damnable witches!"

"Ah, so now you remember," Yueh said with smug satisfaction. "When did the contacts occur?"

Hesitation, then: "More than a dozen years ago."

Yueh stroked his long mustaches. "My Wanna tells me that a Bene Gesserit Reverend Mother is capable of altering her internal chemistry to hold diseases latent in her own body."

"The bitch!" the Baron roared. "She infected me."

The doctor did not seem interested in the injustice or the indignity. "More than just passively infected—such a pathogen is released by force of will. This was not an accident, Baron."

In his mind's eye the Baron envisioned horse-faced Mohiam, the sneering, disrespectful manner with which she had looked at him during the Fenrings' banquet. She had *known*, known all along—had been watching his body transform itself into this loathsome, corpulent lump.

And she had been the cause of it all.

Yueh closed up his goggles and slipped them back into his diagnostic kit. "Our bargain is concluded, and I will take my leave now. I have much research to complete on Richese."

"You agreed to treat me." The Baron lost his balance as he tried to surge to his feet. He collapsed back onto the groaning examination couch.

"I agreed to *examine* you, and no more, Baron. No Suk can do anything for your condition. There is no known treatment, no cure, though I am sure we'll eventually study it at the Suk College."

The Baron clenched his walking stick, finally standing. Seething, he thought about the venom-drenched darts hidden in its tip.

But he also understood the political consequences of killing a Suk doctor, if word ever got out. The Suk School had powerful contacts in the Imperium; it might not be worth the pleasure. Besides, he had murdered enough doctors already . . . at least he finally had an answer.

And a legitimate target for his revenge. He knew who had done this to him.

"I'm afraid you must ask the Bene Gesserit, Baron."

Without another word, Dr. Wellington Yueh hurried out of Harkonnen Keep and fled from Giedi Prime aboard the next Heighliner, glad that he would never have to deal with the Baron again.

Some lies are easier to believe than the truth.

—Orange Catholic Bible

EVEN SURROUNDED BY OTHER VILLAGERS, GURNEY HALLECT FELT COM-
pletely alone. He stared into the watery beer. The brew was
weak and sour, though if he drank enough of it, the pain in his
body and in his heart grew numb. But in the end he was left
with only a throbbing hangover and no hope of finding his
sister.

In the five months since Captain Kryubi and the Harkonnen patrol had taken her, Gurney's cracked ribs, bruises, and
cuts had healed. "Flexible bones," he told himself, a bitter
joke.

The day after Bheth's abduction, he'd been back in the
fields, slowly and painfully digging trenches and planting the
despised krall tubers. The other villagers, looking sidelong at
him, had continued to work, pretending nothing had happened. They knew that if productivity declined, the Harkonnens would come back and punish them even more. Gurney
learned that other daughters had been taken as well, but the
parents involved never spoke of it outside their families.

Back at the tavern, Gurney rarely sang anymore. Though
he carried his old baliset with him, the strings remained silent,
and music refused to issue from his lips. He drank his bitter
ale and sat sullenly, listening to the tired conversations of his
mates. The men repeated complaints about work, about the

weather, about uninteresting spouses. Gurney turned a deaf ear on all of it.

Though sickened to imagine what Bheth might be enduring, he hoped she was still alive. . . . She was probably locked inside a Harkonnen pleasure house, trained to perform unspeakable acts. And if she resisted or failed to meet expectations, she would be killed. As the patrol sweep had proved, Harkonnens could always find other candidates for their stinking brothels.

At home, his parents had blocked their own daughter from memory; without Gurney's painstaking attention, they would have let Bheth's garden die. His parents had even performed a mock funeral and recited verses from the battered Orange Catholic Bible. For a while, Gurney's mother lit a candle and stared at the flickering flame, her lips moving in a silent prayer. They cut calla lilies and daisies—Bheth's favorite flowers—and laid out a bouquet to honor her memory.

Then all of it ceased, and they moved on with their dreary lives without mention of her, as if she had never existed.

But Gurney never gave up.

"Don't you care?" he bellowed one night into his father's seamed face. "How can you let them do this to Bheth?"

"I didn't *let* them do anything." The older man seemed to stare right through his son, as if he were made of dirty glass. "There's nothing any of us can do—and if you keep trying to fight against the Harkonnens, they will pay you back in blood."

Gurney stormed out to sulk in the tavern, but the villagers there offered no more help. Night after night, he grew disgusted with them. The months passed in a blur.

Sloshing his ale, Gurney suddenly sat up at his table and realized what he was becoming. He saw his blunt face in the mirror each morning with a gradual awareness that he had stopped being *himself*. He, Gurney Halleck—good-natured, full of music and bluster—had tried to reawaken the life in these people. But instead he'd been transformed into one of *them*. Though barely in his twenties, he already looked like his aging father.

The drone of humorless conversation continued, and Gurney looked at the smooth prefab walls, the streaked window plates. This monotonous routine had not varied for generations. His hand clenched around the flagon, and he took stock of his own talents and abilities. He couldn't fight the Harkonnens with brute strength or weapons, but he had another idea. He could strike back at the Baron and his followers in a more insidious way.

Feeling renewed energy, he grinned. "I've got a tune for you, mates—the likes of which you've never heard before."

The men smiled uneasily. Gurney held the baliset, strummed its strings as brusquely as if he were peeling coarse vegetables, and sang out in a loud, blustery voice:

> *We work in the fields, we work in the towns,*
> *and this is our lot in life.*
> *For the rivers are wide, and the valleys are low,*
> *and the Baron—he is fat.*
>
> *We live with no joy, we die without grief,*
> *and this is our lot in life.*
> *For the mountains are high, and the oceans are deep,*
> *and the Baron—he is fat.*
>
> *Our sisters are stolen, our sons are crushed,*
> *our parents forget, and our neighbors pretend—*
> *and this is our lot in life!*
> *For our labor is hard, and our rest is short,*
> *while the Baron grows fat from us.*

As the stanzas continued the listeners' eyes widened in horror. "Stop this, Halleck!" one man said, rising from his seat.

"Why, Perd?" Gurney said with a sneer. "Do you love the

Baron so much? I hear he enjoys bringing strong young men like you into his pleasure chambers."

Bravely, Gurney sang another insulting song, and another, until finally he felt liberated. These tunes gave him a freedom he'd never before imagined. The onlookers were disturbed and uneasy. Many got up to leave as he continued to sing, but Gurney would not be swayed. He stayed until long after midnight.

When finally he walked home that night, Gurney Halleck had a spring in his step. He had struck back at his tormentors, though they would never know it.

He wouldn't get enough sleep going to bed at this hour, and work would begin early in the morning. But that didn't bother him—he felt recharged. Gurney returned to the darkened house where his parents had long since retired. He set the baliset in his personal wardrobe, lay back on his pallet, and dozed off with a smile on his lips.

LESS THAN TWO weeks later, a silent Harkonnen patrol entered the village of Dmitri. It was three hours before dawn.

Armed guards battered in the door of the prefab dwelling, though the Hallecks never kept it locked. The uniformed men lit blazing glowglobes as they marched in, knocking furniture aside, smashing crockery. They uprooted all the flowers Bheth had planted in old pots outside the front door. They tore down the curtains that covered the small windows.

Gurney's mother screamed and huddled far back on the bed. His father lurched up, went to the door of their chamber, and saw the troopers. Instead of defending his home, he backed away and slammed the bedroom door, as if that could protect him.

But the guards were only interested in Gurney. They dragged the young man from his bed, and he came out flailing wildly with his fists. The men found his resistance amusing, and flung him facedown on the fireplace hearth; Gurney chipped a tooth and scraped his chin. He tried to get back to his hands and knees, but two Harkonnens kicked him in the ribs.

After ransacking a small closet, one blond soldier came out with the nicked and patched baliset. He tossed it on the floor, and Kryubi made sure Gurney's face was turned toward the instrument. As the Harkonnens pressed their victim's cheek against the hearth bricks, the guard captain stomped on the baliset with a booted foot, breaking its spine. The strings twanged in a discordant jangle.

Gurney moaned, feeling a greater pain from that than from the blows he had received. All the work he had put into restoring the instrument, all the pleasure it had given him. "Bastards!" he spat, which earned him another pummeling.

He made a concentrated effort to see their faces, recognized a square-featured, brown-haired ditch-digger he'd known from a nearby village, now resplendent in his new uniform with the low-rank insignia of an Immenbrech. He saw another guard with a bulbous nose and a harelip, a man he was sure had been "recruited" from Dmitri five years before. But their faces showed no recognition, no sympathy. They were the Baron's men now, and would never do anything to risk being sent back to their former lives.

Seeing that Gurney recognized them, the guards dragged him outside and beat him with redoubled enthusiasm.

During the attack, Kryubi stood tall, sad, and appraising. He ran a finger along his shred of mustache. The guard captain watched in grim silence as his men punched and kicked and beat Gurney, drawing energy from their victim's refusal to cry out as often as they would have liked. They finally stepped back to catch their breath.

And brought out the sticks . . .

At last, when Gurney could no longer move because his bones were broken, his muscles battered, and his flesh covered with clotting blood, the Harkonnens withdrew. Under the harsh glare of clustered glowglobes, he lay bleeding and moaning.

Kryubi held up his hand and signaled the men to return to their craft. They took all the glowglobes but one, which shed a single flickering light upon the mangled man.

Kryubi stared at him with apparent concern, then knelt close by. He spoke quiet words meant only for Gurney. Even through the pain-fogged clamor in his skull, Gurney found it strange. He had expected the Harkonnen guard captain to crow his triumph so that all the villagers could hear. Instead, Kryubi seemed more disappointed than smug. "Any other man would have given up long ago. Most men would have been more intelligent. You brought this on yourself, Gurney Halleck."

The captain shook his head. "Why did you force me to do this? Why did you insist on bringing wrath down upon yourself? I've saved your life this time. Barely. But if you defy the Harkonnens again, we may have to kill you." He shrugged. "Or perhaps just kill your family and maim you instead. One of my men has a certain talent for gouging out eyes with his fingers."

Gurney tried to speak several times around broken, blood-thick lips. "Bastards," he finally managed. "Where's my sister?"

"Your sister is not of concern right now. She is gone. Stay here and forget about her. Do your work. We each have our job to do for the Baron, and if you fail in yours"—Kryubi's nostrils flared—"then I must do mine. If you speak out against the Baron, if you insult him, if you ridicule him to incite discontent, I will have to act. You're smart enough to know that."

With an angry grunt, Gurney shook his head. Only his anger sustained him. Every drop of his blood that spattered the ground he swore to repay with Harkonnen blood. With his dying breath he would discover what had happened to his ister—and if by some miracle Bheth remained alive, he would rescue her.

Kryubi turned toward the troop transport, where the guards had already seated themselves. "Don't make me come back." He looked over his shoulder at Gurney and added a very odd word. *"Please."*

Gurney lay still, wondering how long it would take for his parents to venture out and see whether he lived or not. He watched through blurred vision and pain-smeared eyes as the transport lifted off and left the village. He wondered if any other lights would come on, if any villagers would come out and help him, now that the Harkonnens were gone.

But the dwellings in Dmitri remained dark. Everyone pretended not to have seen or heard.

The strictest limits are self-imposed.

—FRIEDRE GINAZ,
Philosophy of the Swordmaster

WHEN DUNCAN IDAHO ARRIVED AT GINAZ, HE BELIEVED HE NEEDED NOTHING more than the Old Duke's prized sword to become a great warrior. His head full of romantic expectations, he envisioned the swashbuckling life he would lead, the marvelous fighting techniques he would learn. He was only twenty, and looked forward to a golden future.

Reality was quite different.

The Ginaz School was an archipelago of habitable islands scattered like bread crumbs across turquoise water. On each island, different Masters taught students their particular techniques that ranged from shield-fighting, military tactics, and combat skills to politics and philosophy. Over the course of his eight-year training ordeal, Duncan would move from one environment to the next and learn from the best fighters in the Imperium.

If he survived.

The school's main island served as the spaceport and administration center, surrounded by reefs that blocked waves from the choppy water. Tall clustered buildings reminded Duncan of the bristles on a spiny rat, like the one he'd kept as a pet inside the Harkonnen prison fortress.

Revered throughout the Imperium, the Swordmasters of Ginaz had built many of their primary structures as museums and memorials, rather than classrooms. This reflected the supreme confidence they felt in their personal fighting abilities, a self-assurance that bordered on hubris. Politically neutral, they served their art and allowed its practitioners to make their own choices regarding the Imperium. Contributing to the mythology, the academy's graduates had included the leaders of many Great Houses in the Landsraad. Master Jongleurs were commissioned to compose songs and commentary about the great deeds of the legendary heroes of Ginaz.

The central skyscraper, where Duncan would endure his final testing years hence, held the tomb of Jool-Noret, founder of the Ginaz School. Noret's sarcophagus lay in open view— surrounded by clear armor-plaz and a Holtzman-generated shield—yet only the "worthy" were allowed to see it.

Duncan vowed that he would prove himself worthy. . . .

He was met at the spaceport by a slender, bald woman wearing a black martial-arts *gi*. Brisk and businesslike, she introduced herself as Karsty Toper. "I have been assigned to take your possessions." She extended her hand for his rucksack and the long bundle containing the Old Duke's sword.

He clutched the blade protectively. "If you give me your personal guarantee that these items will be safe."

Her forehead furrowed, wrinkling her shaved head. "We value honor more than any other House in the Landsraad." Her hand remained extended, unwavering.

"Not more than the Atreides," Duncan said, still refusing to relinquish the blade.

Karsty Toper frowned as she considered. "Not more, perhaps. But we are comparable."

Duncan handed her the packages, and she directed him to a long-distance shuttle 'thopter. "Go there. You will be taken to your first island. Do what you are told without complaining, and learn from everything." She tucked the sword bundle and his rucksack under her arms. "We will hold these for you until it is time."

Without seeing the Ginaz city or the school administration tower, Duncan was flown far across the deep sea to a low, lush island like a lily pad that barely lifted itself out of the water. Jungles were dense and huts were few. The three uniformed crewmen dropped him on the beach and departed without answering any of his questions. Duncan stood all alone, listening to the rush of ocean against the island shore, reminded of Caladan.

He had to believe this was some sort of test.

A deeply tanned man with frizzy white hair and thin, sinewy limbs strode out to meet him, parting palm fronds. He wore a sleeveless black tunic belted at the waist. The man's expression appeared stony as he squinted into the light glaring off the beach.

"I am Duncan Idaho. Are you my first instructor, sir?"

"Instructor?" The man scowled. "Yes, rat, and my name is Jamo Reed—but prisoners don't use names here, because everyone knows his place. Do your work, and don't cause any trouble. If the others can't keep you in line, then *I* will."

Prisoners? "I'm sorry, Master Reed, but I'm here for Swordmaster training—"

Reed laughed. "Swordmaster? That's rich!"

Without giving him any time to settle, the man assigned Duncan to a rugged work crew with dark-skinned Ginaz natives. Duncan communicated by rough hand signals, since none of the natives spoke Imperial Galach.

For several hot and sweaty days, the men dug channels and wells to improve the water system for an inland village. The air was so thick with humidity and biting gnats that Duncan could barely breathe. As evening approached and the gnats dissipated, the jungle swarmed with mosquitoes and black flies, and Duncan's skin was covered with swollen bites. He had to drink copious amounts of water just to replace what he sweated out.

As Duncan labored to move heavy stones by hand, the sun

warmed the rippling muscles of his bare back. Workmaster Reed watched from the shade of a mango tree, arms folded across his chest, a studded whip gripped in one hand. He never said a word about Swordmaster training. Duncan voiced no complaints, demanded no answers. He had expected Ginaz to be . . . unexpected.

This has to be some kind of test.

Before attaining his ninth birthday, he'd suffered cruel tortures at the hands of the Harkonnens. He had watched Glossu Rabban murder his parents. Even as a boy, he had killed hunters in Forest Guard Preserve, and he'd finally escaped to Caladan only to see his mentor, Duke Paulus Atreides, slain in the bullring. Now, after a decade of service to House Atreides, he chose to view each day's effort as a training exercise, toughening himself for future battles. He *would* become a Swordmaster of Ginaz. . . .

A month later, another 'thopter unceremoniously dropped off a red-haired, pale-skinned young man. The newcomer looked out of place on the beach, upset and confused—just as Duncan must have appeared at his own arrival. Before anyone could speak to the redhead, though, Master Reed sent the work crews to hack at the dense undergrowth with dull machetes; the jungle seemed to grow back as fast as they could cut it down. Perhaps that was the point of sending convicts here, a perpetual but pointless errand, like the myth of Sisyphus he'd heard during his studies with the Atreides.

Duncan didn't see the redhead again until two nights later, when he tried to fall asleep in his own primitive palm-frond hut. In a shelter on the other side of the shoreline encampment, the newcomer lay moaning with a horrible sunburn. Duncan crept out to help him under the starlight of Ginaz, rubbing a creamy salve on the worst blisters, as he had seen the natives do.

The redhead hissed at the pain, bit back an outcry. He finally spoke in Galach, startling Duncan. "Thank you, whoever you are." Then he lay back and closed his eyes. "Damned poor way to run a school, wouldn't you say? What am I doing here?"

The young man, Hiih Resser, came from one of the Houses Minor on Grumman. As part of a family tradition, every other generation selected a candidate to be trained on Ginaz, but during his generation he was the only one available. "I was considered a poor choice, a cruel joke to send here, and my father is convinced I'm going to fail." Resser winced as he sat up, feeling his raw, blistered skin. "Everyone tends to underestimate me."

Neither of them knew how to explain his situation, stuck on an island populated by convicts. "It'll toughen us up at least," Duncan said.

The next day, when Jamo Reed saw them talking with each other, he scratched his frizzy white hair, scowled, then assigned them to different work details on opposite sides of the island.

Duncan did not see Resser again for quite a while. . . .

As months passed with no further information, no structured exercises, Duncan began to grow angry, resenting the wasted time when he could have been serving House Atreides. How was he ever going to become a Swordmaster at this rate?

One dawn as he lay in his hut, instead of the expected call from Workmaster Reed, Duncan heard a rhythmic beating of 'thopter wings, and his heart leaped. Racing outside, he saw a craft landing on the wide, wet beach just within the line of breakers. Wind from the articulated wings blew the leaf fronds like fans.

A slender, bald form in a black *gi* climbed out and spoke with Jamo Reed. The sinewy workmaster grinned and extended a warm handshake; Duncan had never noticed that Reed's teeth were so white. Karsty Toper stepped aside, letting her eyes rove across the curious prisoners who had emerged from their huts.

Workmaster Reed turned back to the convicts standing beside their ramshackle huts. "Duncan Idaho! Come over here, rat." Duncan ran across the rocky beach toward the 'thopter. When he got closer to the flying machine, he could see redheaded Hiih Resser already sitting inside the cockpit. He pressed a freckled, smiling face against the curved windowplaz.

The woman bowed her shaved head to him, then ran her eyes up and down his body like a scanner. She turned to Reed and spoke in Galach. "Success, Master Reed?"

The workmaster shrugged his whipcord shoulders, and his moist eyes suddenly filled with expression. "The other prisoners didn't try to kill him. He didn't get himself in trouble. And we worked some of the fat and weakness out of him."

"Is this part of my training?" Duncan asked. "A labor crew to toughen me up?"

The bald woman placed her hands on her narrow hips. "This was a genuine prison crew, Idaho. These men are murderers and thieves, assigned here for the rest of their lives."

"And you sent me here? With them?"

Jamo Reed came forward and gave him a surprising hug. "Yes, rat, and you survived. As did Hiih Resser." He gave Duncan a paternal pounding on the back. "I'm proud of you."

Embarrassed and confused, Duncan mustered a disbelieving snort. "I lived through worse prisons when I was an eight-year-old boy."

"And you will face worse from this day forward." In a nononsense tone, Karsty Toper explained, "This was a test of character and obedience—and patience. A Swordmaster must have the patience to study an opponent, to implement a plan, to ambush the enemy."

"But a real Swordmaster usually has more information about his situation," Duncan said.

"Now we have seen what you can do with yourself, rat." Reed wiped a tear from his own cheek. "Don't let me down—I expect to see you on your final day of testing."

"Eight years from now," Duncan said.

Toper directed him toward the still-fluttering 'thopter; he was delighted to see that she had brought the Old Duke's sword back to him. The bald woman had to raise her voice to be heard over the loud hum of the aircraft's engines as she applied thrust. "Now it is time to begin your real training."

Special knowledge can be a terrible disadvantage if it leads you too far along a path that you cannot explain anymore.

—Mentat Admonition

IN A MEDITATION ALCOVE IN THE DARKEST BASEMENT OF HARKONNEN KEEP, Piter de Vries could not hear the screech of amputation saws or the screams of torture victims from an open doorway just down the hall. His Mentat concentration was focused too intensely on other, more important matters.

Numerous harsh drugs enhanced his thinking process.

Sitting with his eyes closed, he pondered the clockwork of the Imperium, how the cogs meshed and slipped and ground together. The Great and Minor Houses of the Landsraad, the Spacing Guild, the Bene Gesserit, and the commercial trading conglomerate CHOAM were the key cogs. And all depended upon one thing.

Melange, the spice.

House Harkonnen reaped huge profits from its spice monopoly. When they'd learned of the secret "Project Amal" years ago, the Baron had needed little coaxing to realize how he would suffer financial ruin if a cheap melange substitute were ever developed—one that made Arrakis worthless.

The Emperor (or, more likely, Fenring) had hidden the artificial spice scheme well. He'd buried the vastly expensive project in the vagaries of the Imperial budget—imposed higher taxes here, trumped-up fines there, called in long-standing debts, sold valuable properties. But Piter de Vries knew where to look. Consequences, plans, preparations, third- and fourth-order ripples that could not remain invisible. Only a Mentat could follow them all, and the indications pointed to a long-term project that would bring about the economic ruin of House Harkonnen.

The Baron, however, would not go quietly. He had even attempted to start a war between the Bene Tleilax and House Atreides in order to destroy the "Amal" work . . . but that plan had failed, thanks to the damnable Duke Leto.

Since then, infiltrating spies onto the planet formerly known as Ix had proved predictably difficult, and his Mentat projections gave him no reason to believe the Tleilaxu had ceased their experiments. Indeed, since the Emperor was sending two more legions of "peacekeeper" Sardaukar to Ix, the research might finally be reaching a head.

Or Shaddam might be reaching the limits of his patience.

Now, in his Mentat trance, de Vries did not move a muscle, other than his eyes. A tray of mind-enhancing drugs hung around his neck, a slowly spinning platform like a table center-piece. A yellow carrion fly landed on his nose, but he didn't see it, didn't feel it. The insect crawled onto his lower lip and kissed the spilled, bitter sapho juice there.

De Vries studied the rotating smorgasbord of drugs, and with a flick of his eyes stopped the turntable. The tray tilted, pouring a vial of tikopia syrup into his mouth . . . and with it the hapless fly, followed by a capsule of melange concentrate. The Mentat bit down on the spice capsule and swallowed, tasting an explosion of sweet-burning cassia essence. Then he summoned a second capsule, more melange than he had ever consumed in one sitting. But he needed the clarity now.

A torture victim in a distant cell howled, babbling a confession. But de Vries noticed nothing. Impervious to distractions, he plunged deeper into his own mind. *Deeper.* He felt his awareness opening, an unfolding of time like the spreading petals of a flower. He flowed along a continuum, each part accessible to his brain. He saw his exact place in it.

In his mind's eye, one of several possible futures became clear, an extraordinary Mentat projection based upon an avalanche of information and intuition, enhanced by massive melange consumption. The vision was a series of painful film-book images, visual spikes driven into his eyes. He saw the Tleilaxu Master Researcher proudly holding a vial of synthetic spice, and laughing as he consumed it for himself. Success!

A blur. He saw the Harkonnens on Arrakis, packing up, leaving all their spice production behind. Troops of armed Sardaukar guards marched blurred figures to an Imperial transport, taking them away from holdings on the desert world. He saw the Harkonnen blue-griffin banner taken down from the fortress in Carthag and the Residency at Arrakeen.

And replaced with the green-and-black of *House Atreides!*

A strangled noise came from his throat, and his Mentat mind sifted through the prescient images, forced them into a pattern, and tried to translate what he had seen.

The Harkonnens will lose their spice monopoly. But not necessarily because of the amal being developed by the Tleilaxu in collusion with the Emperor.

How, then?

As the drugs' multitentacled hold tightened, smothering him, his mind streaked down one avenue of synapses after another. Each time, he found nothing, only dead ends. He circled around and tried again, but reached the same conclusion.

How will it happen?

Heavy consumption of mixed drugs was not an approved method of stimulating mind powers; but he wasn't a normal Mentat, a gifted person accepted into the School and trained in the arcane methods of data-sorting and analysis. Piter de Vries was a "twisted" Mentat—grown in a Tleilaxu axlotl tank from the cells of a dead Mentat and trained by others who had broken from the Mentat School. After dispensing their warped training, the Tleilaxu retained no control over their Mentats, though de Vries had no doubt that they had another fully grown ghola, genetically identical to him, just waiting in case Baron Harkonnen happened to lose patience with him one too many times.

The Tleilaxu "twisting" produced an enrichment that could be obtained in no other way. It gave de Vries greater capabilities, far beyond what normal Mentats could attain. But it also made him unpredictable and dangerous, potentially beyond control.

For decades the Bene Tleilax had experimented with drug combinations on their Mentats; in his formative years, de Vries had been one of their subjects. The effects had been unpredictable and inconclusive, resulting in alterations—improvements, he hoped—to his brain.

Ever since he'd been sold to House Harkonnen, de Vries had performed his own tests, refining his body, tuning it to the condition *he* wanted. With just the right mixture of chemicals he had achieved a high degree of mental clarity for faster processing of data.

Why will House Harkonnen lose the spice monopoly? And when?

It seemed wise to suggest to the Baron that he reinforce his operations, double-check the secret melange stockpiles hidden on Lankiveil and elsewhere. *We must protect ourselves from this disaster.*

His heavy eyelids flickered, lifted. Bright particles of light swam into his eyes; with difficulty, he focused his vision. He heard squealing. Past the half-closed door, two uniformed men wheeled a squeaky gurney, on top of which lay a misshapen lump that had once been a human form.

Why will House Harkonnen lose its spice monopoly? Sadly, he realized the drugs he had administered were wearing off, dissipated in the effort to unravel the troubled prescient vision. *Why?* He needed to take this to an even deeper level. *I must learn the answer!*

In a frenzy he detached the drug tray from his neck, dumping juice and capsules on the floor. Falling to his knees, he gathered all the pills he could find and swallowed them. Like an animal, he lapped up spilled sapho juice, before he huddled in a jittering heap on the cold floor. *Why?*

When a pleasurable feeling came over him, he lay back on the sticky, wet surface, staring at the ceiling. His involuntary body functions slowed, giving him the outward appearance of death. But his mind was racing, its electrochemical activity increasing, neurons sorting signals, processing, searching . . . electrical impulses leaping synaptic gaps, faster and faster.

Why? Why?

His cognitive pathways fired in all directions, crossed, sizzled; potassium and sodium ions collided with other radicals in his brain cells. The internal mechanisms broke down, no longer able to handle the fire-hose flow of data. He was on the brink of vaulting into mental chaos and slipping into a coma.

Instead, his marvelous Mentat mind went into survival mode, shutting down functions, limiting the damage. . . .

PITER DE VRIES awoke in a pool of spilled drug residue. His nostrils, mouth, and throat burned.

At the Mentat's side, the Baron paced back and forth, scolding him like a child. "Look at the mess you've made, Piter. All that wasted melange, and I almost had to purchase a new Mentat from the Tleilaxu. Don't ever be so thoughtless and wasteful again!"

De Vries struggled to sit up, wanting to tell the Baron about his vision, the destruction of House Harkonnen. "I . . . I have seen . . ." But he could not get the words out. It would take a long time before he was able to string sentences together coherently.

Worse yet—even with his desperate overdose, he still did not have an answer for the Baron.

Too much knowledge never makes for simple decisions.

—CROWN PRINCE RAPHAEL CORRINO,
Discourses on Leadership

WITHIN THE ICE-CHOKED ARCTIC CIRCLE OF LANKIVEIL, COMMERCIAL whale fur boats were like cities on the water, enormous processing plants that lumbered across the steel-gray waters for months before returning to spaceport docks to disgorge their cargo.

Abulurd Harkonnen, the Baron's younger half-brother, preferred smaller vessels with native crews. To them, whale hunting was a challenge and an art, rather than an industry.

Biting wind blew his ash-blond hair around his ears and shoulders as he squinted pale-eyed into the distance. The sky was a soup of dirty clouds, but he'd grown accustomed to the climate. Despite the glamorous and expensive Harkonnen palaces on other planetary holdings, Abulurd had chosen this frigid, mountainous world to call home.

He had been out on the sea for a week now, cheerfully attempting to assist the swarthy crew, though his appearance was far different from that of the Lankiveil natives. His hands were sore and covered with blisters that sooner or later would turn to calluses. The Buddislamic whalers seemed bemused that their planetary governor wanted to come out and work, but they knew his eccentricities. Abulurd had never been one for pomp and ceremony, for abusing his power, or showing off his riches.

In the deep northern seas, Bjondax fur whales swam in herds like aquatic bison. Golden-furred beasts were common; those with exotic leopard spots were much rarer. Standing next to rattling prayer wheels and streamers, lookouts on observation platforms scanned the ice-thick sea with binoculars, searching for lone whales. Off-shift whalers took turns praying. These native hunters were selective of the beasts they killed, choosing only those with the best coats that would bring in the highest prices.

Abulurd smelled the salt air and the omnipresent tang of impending sleet. He waited for the action to begin, for a fast hunt when the captain and his first mate would bellow orders, treating Abulurd as just another crewman. For now, he had nothing to do but wait and think about home. . . .

At night, when the whaling boat rocked and swayed, accompanied by the patter and thump of ice chunks bumping against the reinforced hull, Abulurd would sing or play a local betting game that involved stacked beads. He would recite required sutras with the gruff, deeply religious crew.

Glowing heaters inside the boat cabins could not match the roaring fireplaces in his bustling main lodge on Tula Fjord or his romantic private dacha at the mouth of the fjord. Although he enjoyed the whale hunt, Abulurd already missed his quiet and strong wife. He and Emmi Rabban-Harkonnen had been married for decades, and the separation of days would only make their reunion sweeter.

Emmi had noble blood, but from a diminished Minor House. Four generations ago, before the alliance with House Harkonnen, Lankiveil had been the fief of an unimportant family, House Rabban, which had devoted itself to religious pursuits. They built monasteries and seminary retreats in the rugged mountains, instead of exploiting the resources of their world.

Long ago, after the death of his father, Dmitri, Abulurd had taken Emmi with him to spend seven unpleasant years on Arrakis. His elder half-brother Vladimir had consolidated all the power of House Harkonnen in his iron fist, but their father' will had given control of spice operations to Abulurd, the kind and bookish son. Abulurd understood the importance of the position, how much wealth melange brought to his family, though he never grasped the nuances and political complexities of the desert world.

Abulurd had been forced to leave Arrakis in supposed disgrace. But no matter what they said, he *preferred* to live on Lankiveil with manageable responsibilities, among people he understood. He felt sorry for those being trampled by the Baron's overzealous efforts on the desert planet, but Abulurd vowed to do his best here, though he had not yet bothered to reclaim his rightful title of subdistrict governor. The tedious politics seemed like such a waste of human effort.

He and Emmi had only one son, thirty-four-year-old Glossu Rabban, who, according to Lankiveil tradition, was given the distaff name from his mother's bloodline. Unfortunately, their son had a coarse personality and took after his uncle more than his own parents. Although Abulurd and Emmi had always wanted more children, the Harkonnen bloodline had never been particularly fecund. . . .

"Albino!" shouted the lookout, a sharp-eyed boy whose dark hair hung in a thick braid kinked over his warm parka. "White fur swimming alone—twenty degrees to port."

The vessel became a hive of activity. Neuro-harpooners grabbed their weapons while the captain increased the engine speed. Men scrambled up deck ladders, shading their eyes and staring into water laden with icebergs that looked like buoyant white molars. It had been a full day since the last chase, so the decks were clean, the processing bins open and prepped, the men anxious.

Abulurd waited his turn to peer through a set of binoculars, staring across the whitecaps. He saw flashes that might have been an albino whale, but were instead just chunks of drifting ice. Finally, he spotted the creature as it breached, a creamy arc of white fur. It was young. Albinos, the rarest of the breed, were ostracized from the pod, cut loose and left without the support of the swimming herd. Rarely did they survive to full adulthood.

The men bent to their weapons as the vessel bore down upon its prey. Prayer wheels continued to spin and clack in the breeze. The captain leaned out from the bridge deck and shouted in a voice resonant enough to break solid ice. "If we get this one undamaged, we'll have enough shares to go home."

Abulurd loved to see the sheer joy and exhilaration on their faces. He felt the thrill himself, his heart pounding to keep the blood moving in this intense cold. He never took a share of the whaling profits, since he had no use for additional money, but allowed the men to divide it among themselves.

The albino beast, sensing pursuit, swam faster, heading toward an archipelago of icebergs. The captain increased the throbbing engines, churning a wake behind them. If the Bjondax whale dove, they would lose it.

Fur whales spent months at a time beneath the heavy ice sheets. There, in dark waters fed by volcanic vents full of nutrients and warmth, the whales devoured swarms of krill, spores, and Lankiveil's rich plankton that did not require direct sunlight for photosynthesis.

With a loud *pop*, one of the long-range rifles planted a pulse-tag on the white whale's back. In response to the prick, the albino dove. The crewman working the controls sent a jolt of electricity through the pulse-tag, which made the whale breach again.

The boat came about, grinding the starboard side against an iceberg, but the reinforced hull held as the captain closed the gap. Two master harpooners, moving with forced calm and precision, got into separate pursuit boats, sleek craft with narrow prows and ice-cutting keels. The men strapped themselves in, sealed the clear protective canopy over them, and dropped the craft into the icy water.

The pursuit boats bounced across the choppy water, striking chunks of ice but closing on the target. The main boat circled, approaching from the opposite direction. Each of the master harpooners crossed in front of the albino whale, popping the canopy enclosures and standing up in their compartments. With perfect balance, they hurled long stun-staves into the whale, delivering a blast of numbing energy.

The whale rolled and came toward the whaling boat. The master harpooners pursued, but by now the main boat was close enough and four other harpooners leaned over the deck. Like a well-practiced Roman legion hurling javelins, they pitched stun-staves with enough force to render the whale unconscious. The two pursuit craft approached the furred hulk and, working as a team, the master harpooners delivered the coup de grâce.

Later, as the pursuit craft were winched up to the boat, furriers and skinners strapped on spiked footwear and rappelled down the vessel sides to the floating carcass.

Abulurd had seen whales taken many times before, but he had an aversion to the actual butchering process, so he crossed to the starboard deck and stared northward at the mountain ranges of icebergs. Their rugged shapes reminded him of the steep rocks that formed the fjord walls near where he lived.

The whaling vessel had reached the far northern limit of even the native hunting waters. CHOAM whaling crews never ventured into these high latitudes, since their enormous vessels could not navigate the treacherous waters.

Alone at the bow, Abulurd enjoyed the prismatic purity of arctic ice, a crystal glow that enhanced the shrouded sunlight. He heard the grind of colliding icebergs and stared, not realizing what his peripheral vision registered. Something gnawed at his subconscious until finally his gaze centered on one of the monoliths of ice, a squarish mountain that appeared fractionally grayer than the others. It reflected less light.

He squinted, then retrieved a pair of binoculars left lying on the deck. Abulurd listened to the wet sounds behind him, the men shouting as they cut their prize into pieces ready to take home. He focused the oil lenses and stared at the floating iceberg.

Glad to have a distraction from the bloody work, Abulurd spent long minutes scrutinizing fragments that had been hacked out of the ice. The shards were too precise, too exact to have broken free from the glacial shelf and drifted about, battering and scraping other icebergs.

Then, at water level, he saw something that looked suspiciously like a *door*.

He marched up to the bridge deck. "You'll be at work here for another hour, won't you, Captain?"

The big-shouldered man nodded. "Aye. Then we go home tonight. Do you want to get down into the wet work?"

Abulurd drew himself up, queasy at the prospect of being smothered in whale blood. "No . . . actually, I'd like to borrow one of the small boats to go explore . . . something I found on an iceberg." Normally, he would have asked for an escort, but the whalers were all occupied with the butchery. Even in these cold, uncharted seas, Abulurd would be glad to be away from the smell of death.

The captain raised his bushy eyebrows. Abulurd could tell the gruff man wanted to express his skepticism, but he maintained his silence. His broad, flat face carried only respect for the planetary governor.

Abulurd Harkonnen knew how to handle a boat himself—often taking one into the fjords and exploring the coastline—so he declined the offer of other whalers to accompany him. Alone, he cruised away at a slow speed, watching out for dangerous ice. Behind him, the butchering continued, filling the iron-scented air with a richer smell of blood and entrails.

Twice as he piloted his boat through the maze of floating mountains, Abulurd lost sight of his target, but eventually he found it again. Hidden among the drifting icebergs, this one chunk seemed not to have moved. He wondered if it was anchored in place.

He brought the small boat up against the rugged side, then momentum-locked it to the ice. A feeling of unreality and displacement shrouded this strange monolith. As he gingerly stepped out of the boat and onto the nearest flat white surface, he realized just how exotic this object was.

The ice was not cold.

Abulurd bent to touch what appeared to be milky shards of ice. He rapped with his knuckles: The substance was some kind of polymer crystal, a translucent solid that had the appearance of ice—almost. He stomped hard, and the iceberg echoed beneath him. Very odd indeed.

He rounded a jagged corner to the place where he'd seen a geometrically even line of cracks, a parallelogram that might have been an access hatch. He stared at it until he found an indentation, an access panel that appeared to have been damaged, perhaps in a collision with a real iceberg. He found an activation button, and the trapezoidal covering slid aside.

He gasped as a strong cinnamon scent wafted out, a pungent odor that he recognized instantly. He had smelled enough of it during his time on Arrakis. Melange.

He breathed deeply just to make sure, then ventured into the eerie corridors. The floors were smooth, as if worn down by many feet. A secret base? A command post? A hidden archive?

He discovered room upon room filled with nullentropy containers, sealed bins that bore the pale blue griffin of House Harkonnen. A stockpile of spice put here by his own family—and no one had told him of it. A grid map showed how far the storehouse extended beneath the water. Here on Lankiveil, under Abulurd's own nose, the Baron had secreted a huge illegal hoard!

Such an amount of spice could have purchased this entire planetary system many times over. Abulurd's mind reeled, unable to comprehend the treasure he had stumbled upon. He needed to think. He needed to talk to Emmi. With her quiet wisdom, she would give him the advice he needed. Together they would decide what to do.

Though he considered the whaling crew to be honest, wholesome men, such a stockpile would tempt even the best of them. Abulurd left in a hurry, sealed the door behind him, and scrambled aboard his boat.

Upon returning to the whaling ship, he made sure to mark the coordinates carefully in his mind. When the captain asked if he had found anything, Abulurd shook his head and retreated into his private cabin. He didn't trust himself to control his expressions around the other men. It would be a long voyage home until he could get back to his wife. Oh, how he missed her, how he needed her wisdom.

BEFORE LEAVING THE dock at Tula Fjord, the captain presented the fur whale's liver to Abulurd as his reward, though it was worth little compared to the share of the albino's fur he had given to each of the crewmen.

When he and Emmi dined together at the main lodge for the first time in a week, Abulurd was distracted and fidgeting, waiting for the chef to finish her grand workings.

The steaming, savory whale liver came out on two gilded silver platters, surrounded by mounds of salted stringreens with a side dish of smoked oyster nuts. The long formal dining table could accommodate up to thirty guests, but Abulurd and Emmi sat next to each other near one end, serving themselves from the platters.

Emmi had a pleasant, wide Lankiveil face and a squarish chin that was not glamorous or beautiful—but Abulurd adored it anyway. Her hair was the truest color of black and hung straight, cut horizontally just below her shoulders. Her round eyes were the rich brown of polished jasper.

Often, Abulurd and his wife would eat with the others in the communal dining hall, joining in the conversations. But since Abulurd had just returned from a long whaling journey, everyone in the household knew the two wanted to talk quietly. Abulurd had no qualms about telling his wife the great secret he had discovered in the icy sea.

Emmi was silent, but deep. She thought before she spoke, and didn't talk unless she had something to say. Now she listened to her husband and did not interrupt him. When Abulurd finished his tale, Emmi sat in silence, thinking about what he had said. He waited long enough for her to consider a few possibilities, then said to her, "What shall we do, Emmi?"

"All that wealth must have been stolen from the Emperor's share. It's probably been there for years." She nodded to reinforce her own convictions. "You don't want to dirty your hands with it."

"But my own half-brother has deceived me."

"He must have plans for it. He didn't tell you because he knew you'd feel honor-bound to report it."

Abulurd chewed a mouthful of the tart stringreens and swallowed, washing it down with a Caladan blanc. With the smallest hints, Emmi could always tell exactly what he was thinking. "But I *do* feel honor-bound to report it."

She considered for a moment, then said, "If you call attention to this stockpile, I can think of many ways it could harm us, harm the people of Lankiveil, or harm your own family. I wish you had never found it."

He looked into her jasper-brown eyes to see if any glimmer of temptation had crossed them, but he saw only concern and caution there. "Perhaps Vladimir is avoiding taxes or just embezzling to fill the coffers of House Harkonnen," she ventured, her expression turning hard. "But he is still your brother. If you report him to the Emperor, you could bring disaster upon your House."

Abulurd realized another consequence and groaned. "If the Baron is imprisoned, then I would have to control all of the Harkonnen holdings. Assuming we keep the Arrakis fief, I'd have to go back there, or else live on Giedi Prime." Miserably, he took another drink of the wine. "I couldn't stomach either option, Emmi. I like it here."

Emmi reached over to touch his hand. She stroked it, and he raised her hand to his lips, kissing her fingers. "Then we've come to our decision," she said. "We know the spice is there . . . but we'll just leave it be."

The desert is a surgeon cutting away the skin to expose what is underneath.

—Fremen Saying

AS THE MOON ROSE COPPER-RED OVER THE DESERT HORIZON, LIET-KYNES and seven Fremen departed the rocks and made their way out to the soft curving dunes where they could be easily seen. One by one the men made the sign of the fist, in accordance with Fremen tradition at the sign of First Moon.

"Prepare yourselves," Stilgar said moments later, his narrow face like a desert hawk's in the moonlight. His pupils had dilated, making his solid blue eyes look black. He wrapped his desert camouflage around him, as did the other, older guerrillas. "It is said that when one waits for vengeance, time passes slowly but sweetly."

Liet-Kynes nodded. He was dressed to look like a weak, water-fat village boy, but his eyes were as hard as Velan steel. Beside him, his sietch-mate and blood-brother Warrick, a slightly taller lad, nodded as well. This night, the two would pretend to be helpless children caught out in the open . . . irresistible targets for the anticipated Harkonnen patrol.

"We do what must be done, Stil." Liet clapped a hand on Warrick's padded shoulder. These twelve-year-olds had already blooded more than a hundred Harkonnens apiece, and would have stopped keeping count, except for their friendly rivalry with each other. "I trust my brother with my life."

Warrick covered Liet's hand with his own. "Liet would be afraid to die without me at his side."

"With or without you, Warrick, I don't plan to die this night," Liet said, which elicited a deep laugh from his companion. "I plan to exact revenge."

After the orgy of poisoned death had fallen upon Bilar Camp, Fremen rage had spread from sietch to sietch like water soaking into sand. From the 'thopter markings found near the hidden cistern, they knew who was responsible. *All Harkonnens must pay.*

Around Carthag and Arsunt, word was passed to timid-looking workers and dusty servants who had been placed inside Harkonnen strongholds. Some of the infiltrators scrubbed the floors of troop barracks using dry rags and abrasives. Others posed as water-sellers supplying the occupation force.

As the tale of the poisoned village passed from one Harkonnen soldier to another in progressively exaggerated anecdotes, the Fremen informants noted who derived the greatest pleasure from the news. They studied the crew assignments and route logs of Harkonnen patrols. Before long, they had learned exactly which Harkonnen troopers were responsible. And where they could be found. . . .

With a high-pitched squeak and a dancing blur of gossamer wings, a tiny distrans bat swooped from observation outcroppings in the mountains behind them. When Stilgar held up a hand, the bat landed on his forearm, primly folding its wings and waiting for a reward.

Stilgar drew a tiny drop of water from the sipping tube at his throat and let the moisture fall into the bat's open mouth. Then he brought forth a thin cylinder and placed it to his ear, listening as the bat emitted complex, wavering squeaks. Stilgar tapped the bat on its head, then flung it into the night air again, like a falconer releasing his bird.

He turned back to his expectant troop, a predatory smile

on his moon-shadowed face. "Their ornithopter has been seen over the ridge. The Harkonnens fly a predictable path as they scan the desert. But they have been on patrol for so long, they are complacent. They do not see their own patterns."

"Tonight, they fly into a web of death," Warrick said from the dune top, lifting his fist in a very unboylike gesture.

The Fremen checked their weapons, loosed crysknives in sheaths at their sides, tested the strength of garroting cords. With swishing robes, they erased all marks of their passage, leaving the two young men alone.

Stilgar looked up at the night sky, and a muscle on his jaw flickered. "This I learned from Umma Kynes. When we were cataloging lichens, we saw a rock lizard that seemed to vanish before our eyes. Kynes said to me, 'I give you the chameleon, whose ability to match itself with its background tells you all you need to know about the roots of ecology and the foundations of personal identity.'" Stilgar looked gravely at his men, and his expression faltered. "I don't know exactly what he meant . . . but now we must all become chameleons of the desert."

Wearing light-colored clothes, Liet stepped up the slip-face of the dune, leaving deliberate, painfully apparent footprints. Warrick followed just as clumsily, while the other Fremen spread out on the flat sand. After pulling out breathing tubes and covering their faces with loose hoods, they flailed their arms in a blur of motion. Powdery sand engulfed them, and then they lay still.

Liet and Warrick ran about, smoothing wrinkles on the surface and leaving nothing but their own footprints. They finished just as the patrol 'thopter whirred over the line of rocks, flashing red lights.

The two white-clad Fremen froze out in the open, their bright clothes unmistakable against the pale, moonlit sand. No true Fremen would ever be caught in such a show of clumsiness . . . but the Harkonnens didn't know that. They would not suspect.

As soon as the 'thopter came into view, Liet made an exaggerated gesture of alarm. "Come on, Warrick. Let's make a good show of it." The two ran away pell-mell, as if in a panic.

Predictably, the 'thopter circled to intercept them. A powerful spotlight flooded down, then a laughing sidegunner leaned out of the 'thopter. He fired his lasgun twice, sketching a line of melted glass upon the sand surface.

Liet and Warrick tumbled down the steep side of a dune. The gunner fired three more blasts, missing them each time.

The 'thopter landed on the broad surface of a nearby dune . . . close to where Stilgar and his men had buried themselves. Liet and Warrick flashed each other a smile, and prepared for the second part of the game.

SIDEGUNNER KIEL SHOULDERED his still-hot lasgun rifle and popped open the door. "Let's go hunt some Fremen." He jumped onto the sand as soon as Garan had landed the patrol craft.

Behind them, the fresh-faced recruit Josten fumbled for his own weapon. "It would be easier just to shoot them from above."

"What kind of sport would that be?" Garan asked in his gruff voice.

"Or is it just that you don't want blood on your new uniform, kid?" Kiel called over his shoulder. They stood beside the armored craft looking across the moonlit dunes, where the two scrawny nomads stumbled away—as if they had any hope of escape once a Harkonnen trooper decided to target them.

Garan grabbed his weapon, and the three of them strode across the sands. The two Fremen youths scuttled like beetles, but the threat of the troops might cause them to turn around and surrender . . . or better yet, fight like cornered rats.

"I've heard stories about these Fremen." Josten panted as he kept up with the two older men. "Their children are said to be killers, and their women will torture you in ways that even Piter de Vries couldn't imagine."

Kiel gave a rude snort of laughter. "We've got lasguns, Josten. What are they going to do—throw rocks at us?"

"Some of them carry maula pistols."

Garan looked back at the young recruit, then gave a shrug. "Why don't you go back to the 'thopter and get our stunner, then? We can use a wide field if things get bad."

"Yeah," Kiel said, "that way we can make this last longer." The two white-clad Fremen continued to flounder across the sand, and the Harkonnen troopers closed the distance with purposeful strides.

Glad for the opportunity to be away from the fight, Josten sprinted over the dune toward the waiting 'thopter. From the dune top, he looked back at his companions, then rushed to the darkened craft. As he ducked inside, he encountered a man clad in desert tans, hands flicking across the controls with the speed of a snake on a hot plate.

"Hey, what are you—" Josten cried.

In the cabin light he saw that the figure had a narrow leathery face. The eyes captivated him, blue-within-blue with the sharp intensity of a man accustomed to killing. Before Josten could react, his arm was grabbed with a grip as strong as an eagle's talon, and he was dragged deeper into the cockpit. The Fremen's other hand flashed, and he saw a curved, milky-blue knife strike up. A bright icicle of pain slashed into his throat, all the way back to his spine—then the knife was gone before even a droplet of blood could cling to its surface.

Like a scorpion that had just unleashed its sting, the Fremen backed up. Josten fell forward, already feeling red death spreading from his throat. He tried to say something, to ask a question that seemed all-important to him, but his words only came out as a gurgle. The Fremen snatched something from his stillsuit and pressed it against the young man's throat, an absorbent cloth that drank his blood as it spilled.

Was the desert man saving him? A bandage? A flash of hope rose in Josten's mind. Had it all been a mistake? Was this gaunt native trying to make amends?

But Josten's blood pumped out too quickly and forcefully for any medical help. As his life faded, he realized that the absorbent pack had never been meant as a wound dressing, but simply to capture every droplet of blood for its moisture. . . .

WHEN KIEL CAME within firing distance of the two Fremen youths, Garan looked back into the moonlight. "I thought I heard something from the 'thopter."

"Probably Josten tripping on his own feet," the side-gunner said, not lowering his weapon.

The trapped Fremen staggered to a halt across a shallow pan of soft sand. They crouched and pulled out small, clumsy-looking knives.

Kiel laughed out loud. "What do you mean to do with those? Pick your teeth?"

"I'll pick the teeth from your dead body," one of the boys shouted. "Got any old-fashioned gold molars we can sell in Arrakeen?"

Garan chortled and looked at his companion. "This is going to be fun." Moving in lockstep, the troopers marched into the flat sandy area.

As they closed to within five meters, the sand around them erupted. Human forms popped out of the dust, covered with grit—tan human silhouettes, like animated corpses boiling up from a graveyard.

Garan let out a useless warning cry, and Kiel fired once with his lasgun, injuring one of the men in the shoulder. Then the dusty forms surged forward. Clustering around the pilot, they pressed in so close that he couldn't bring his lasgun to bear. They attacked him like blood-lice on an open wound.

As they drove Garan to his knees, he cried out like an old woman. The Fremen restrained him so that he could do little more than breathe and blink his eyes. And scream.

One of the white-clad "victims" hurried forward. The young man—Liet-Kynes—held out the small knife that Garan and Kiel had snickered at just moments ago. The youth darted downward, jabbing with the tip of the blade—but with precise control, as gentle as a kiss—to gouge out both of Garan's eyes, transforming his sockets into red Oedipal stains.

Stilgar barked out a command, "Bind him and keep him. We shall bring this one back to Red Wall Sietch alive, and let the women take care of him in their own way."

Garan screamed again. . . .

When the Fremen rushed forward to attack Kiel, the side-gunner responded by swinging his weapon like a club. As clawing hands grabbed for it, he surprised them by releasing the lasrifle. The Fremen who clutched the gun fell backward, caught off-balance by the unexpected action.

Then Kiel began to run. Fighting would do him no good. They had already taken Garan, and he assumed Josten was dead back at the 'thopter. So he left the Fremen, running as he had never run before. He sprinted across the night sands away from the rocks, away from the 'thopter . . . and out into the open desert. The Fremen might be able to catch him, but he would give them a run for it.

Panting, leaving his companions behind, Kiel raced across the dunes with no plan and no thought other than to flee farther and farther away. . . .

"WE'VE CAPTURED THE 'thopter intact, Stil," Warrick said, flushed with adrenaline and quite proud of himself. The commando eader nodded grimly. Umma Kynes would be exceedingly pleased at the news. He could always use a 'thopter for his agricultural inspections, and he didn't need to know where it came from.

Liet looked down at the blinded captive, whose gouged eye sockets had been covered by a cloth. "I saw what the Harkonnens did to Bilar Camp with my own eyes . . . the poisoned cistern, the tainted water." The other body had already been packed in the rear of the patrol 'thopter to be taken to the deathstills. "This doesn't pay back a tenth part of the suffering."

Going to his blood-brother's side, Warrick made a face of disgust. "Such is my scorn that I don't even want to take their water for our tribe."

Stilgar glowered at him as if he had spoken sacrilege. "You would prefer to let them mummify in the sands, to let their water go wasted into the air? It would be an insult to Shai-Hulud."

Warrick bowed his head. "It was only my anger speaking, Stil. I did not mean it."

Stilgar looked up at the ruddy rising moon. The entire ambush had lasted less than an hour. "We shall perform the ritual of *tal hai* so that their souls will never rest. They will be damned to walk the desert for all eternity." Then his voice became harsh and fearful. "But we must take extra care to cover our tracks, so that we do not lead their ghosts back to our sietch."

The Fremen muttered as fear dampened their vengeful pleasure. Stilgar intoned the ancient chant, while others drew designs in the sand, labyrinthine power-shapes that would bind the spirits of the cursed men to the dunes forever.

Out across the moonlit sands they could still see the clumsily running figure of the remaining trooper. "That one is our offering to Shai-Hulud," Stilgar said, finishing his chant. The *tal hai* curse was complete. "The world will be at balance, and the desert will be pleased."

"He's chugging like a broken crawler." Liet stood next to Stilgar, drawing himself up though he was still small compared to the commando leader. "It won't be long now."

They gathered their supplies. As many as possible piled into the patrol 'thopter, while the remaining Fremen slipped back across the sands. They used a well-practiced random gait so that their footsteps made no sound that was not natural to the desert.

The Harkonnen sidegunner continued to flee in a blind panic. By now, he might be entertaining a hope of escape, though the direction of his flight across the ocean of dunes would take him nowhere.

Within minutes, a worm came for him.

The purpose of argument is to change the nature of truth.

—Bene Gesserit Precept

IN ALL HIS DEVIOUS DEALINGS, BARON VLADIMIR HARKONNEN HAD NEVER before felt such loathing for anyone.

How could the Bene Gesserit bitch do this to me?

One smoky morning on Giedi Prime, he entered the exercise room of his Keep, locked the doors, and left orders not to be disturbed. Unable to use the weights or pulley equipment because of his increasing bulk, he sat on a floor mat and tried to perform simple leg lifts. Once, he had been perfection in human form—now he could barely raise each leg. Disgust enveloped him.

For two months, ever since hearing Dr. Yueh's diagnosis, he'd wanted to rip out Mohiam's internal organs one by one. Then, keeping her awake, jolted with life-support systems, he would do interesting things while she watched . . . burn her liver, make the witch-bitch eat her spleen, strangle her with her own entrails.

Now he understood Mohiam's smug expression at the Fenring banquet.

She did this to me!

He looked at himself in a floor-length mirror and recoiled. His face was puffy and swollen, slig-ugly. Reaching up with his heavy arms, he yanked the plaz mirror off the wall and slammed it to the floor, twisting the unbreakable material out of shape so that his reflection became even more distorted.

It was understandable that Mohiam might resent the rape, he supposed. But the witch had blackmailed him into the sexual act in the first place, demanding that he provide the damnable Sisterhood with a Harkonnen daughter—twice! It wasn't fair. *He* was the victim here.

The Baron simmered and stewed and raged. He didn't dare let any of his rivals in the Landsraad learn of the cause; it was the difference between strength and weakness. If they continued to believe he had grown bloated and corpulent because of excess, through his own overindulgences to flaunt his success, he could retain his power. If, however, they learned he had been inflicted with a disgusting disease by a woman who had forced him to have sex with her . . . The Baron could not abide that.

Yes, hearing Mohiam's screams would be a tasty revenge, but no more than a morsel, not sufficient for a man of his stature. She was only a repulsive appendage of the Bene Gesserit order itself. The witches considered themselves so superior, able to crush anyone—even the head of House Harkonnen. They must be punished, as a matter of family pride, a matter of asserting power and status in the name of the entire Landsraad.

Besides, he would enjoy it.

But if he acted precipitously, he would never wring a cure from them. The Suk doctor had claimed there was no known treatment for the disease, that it was in the hands of the Bene Gesserit. The Sisterhood had done this to the Baron, and only they could restore his once-beautiful body.

Damn them!

He needed to turn the tables, get into their diabolical minds and discover what lurked there. He would find a way to blackmail *them*. He would strip away their funereal black robes (figuratively) and leave them to stand naked, awaiting his judgment.

He threw the bent mirror across the tile floor, where it skidded and slammed into an exercise machine. Without his walking stick, he lost his balance, slipped, and tumbled back to the mat.

It was all too much to bear. . . .

After composing himself, the Baron hobbled into his cluttered workroom and summoned Piter de Vries. His voice boomed through the corridors, and servants dashed about, looking for the Mentat.

For a full month de Vries had been recovering from his foolish spice overdose. The idiot claimed to have seen a vision of House Harkonnen's downfall, but he'd been unable to offer any useful information as to how the Baron could combat such a dismal future.

Now the Mentat could make up for his failure by devising a strike against the Bene Gesserit. Every time de Vries pushed the Baron too far, annoying him to the point of impending execution, he managed to prove himself indispensable again.

How do I hurt the witches? How do I cripple them, make them squirm?

Still waiting, the Baron looked out of the Keep, studying Harko City, with its oil-streaked buildings and hardly a tree in sight. Usually he liked this view, but now it added to his despondency. He chewed the inside of his mouth, felt the tears of self-pity recede.

I will crush the Sisterhood!

These women were not stupid. Far from it. With their breeding programs and their political machinations, they had bred intelligence into their own ranks. To improve on this even more, they had wanted his superior Harkonnen genes as part of their order. Oh, how he hated them!

A careful plan would be required . . . tricks within tricks . . .

"My Lord Baron," Piter de Vries said, arriving silently. His voice rose from his throat like a viper slithering out of a pit.

In the corridor outside, the Baron heard loud voices and a

clattering of metal. Something thudded against a wall, and furniture crashed. He turned from the window to see his burly nephew stride through the doorway, right behind the Mentat. Even with normal footsteps, Glossu Rabban seemed to stomp across the floor. "I'm here, Uncle."

"Obviously. Now leave us. I called Piter, not you." Normally Rabban spent his time on Arrakis carrying out the Baron's wishes, but whenever he returned to Giedi Prime he wanted to participate in every meeting, every discussion.

The Baron took a deep breath, reconsidered. "On second thought, you may as well stay, Rabban. I need to tell you about this anyway." After all, this brute was his heir-presumptive, the best hope for the future of House Harkonnen. Better than soft-headed Abulurd, Rabban's father. How different they were, though each man had serious shortcomings.

Like a pathetic puppy, his nephew smiled, happy to be included. "Tell me what, Uncle?"

"That I'm going to have you put to death."

Rabban's pale blue eyes dulled for a moment, then he brightened. "No you aren't."

"How can you be so sure?" The Baron glowered, while the Mentat's darting eyes watched the interplay.

Rabban responded promptly. "Because if you were really going to put me to death, you wouldn't warn me first."

A smile stole across the Baron's plump face. "Perhaps you aren't a total fool after all."

Accepting the compliment, Rabban slumped into a chairdog, squirming until the creature molded to his form. De Vries remained standing, observing, waiting.

The Baron reiterated the details of the disease Mohiam had inflicted upon him—and his need for revenge against the Bene Gesserit. "We must come up with a way to get even with them. I want a plan, a delicious plan that will return the . . . favor . . . for us."

De Vries stood with his effeminate features slack, his eyes

unfocused. In Mentat mode, he rolled pattern-searches through his mind at hyperspeed. His tongue darted over his red-stained lips.

Rabban kicked the chairdog with his heel, adjusting to a different position. "Why not a full-scale military assault on Wallach IX? We can destroy every building on the planet."

De Vries twitched, and for a fraction of a second he seemed to glance at Rabban, but it was so quick that the Baron wasn't certain if it had occurred at all. He couldn't stand the notion of his nephew's primitive thoughts contaminating the finely tuned thinking processes of his valuable Mentat.

"Like a Salusan bull at a dinner party, you mean?" the Baron said. "No, we require something with more finesse. Look up the definition in a dictionary slate if the concept is unfamiliar to you."

Rather than being offended, Rabban leaned forward on the chairdog, narrowing his eyes. "We . . . have the no-ship."

Startled, the Baron turned to look at him. Just when he thought the clod was too dull-witted even to join the House Guard, Rabban surprised him with an unexpected insight.

They had dared use the experimental invisible ship only once, to destroy Tleilaxu vessels and frame the hapless young Duke Atreides. Because Rabban had murdered the eccentric Richesian inventor, they had no way of duplicating the technology. Even so, it was a weapon whose existence no one suspected, not even the witches.

"Perhaps . . . unless Piter has a different idea."

"I do, my Baron." De Vries's eyelids flickered, and the eyes came into focus. "Mentat summation," he said, in a voice that was more stilted than his normally smooth tone. "I have found a useful loophole in the Law of the Imperium. Something most intriguing, my Baron." Like a lawtech he quoted it word for word, then recommended a plan.

For a moment all of the Baron's bodily aches and pains vanished in euphoria. He turned to his nephew. "Now do you see the potential, Rabban? I would rather be known for finesse than brute force."

Grudgingly, Rabban nodded. "I still think we should take the no-ship. Just in case." He himself had piloted the invisible warcraft and launched the attack that should have triggered a full-scale Atreides-Tleilaxu war.

Not wanting to let the Mentat grow too smug, the Baron agreed. "It never hurts to have a backup plan."

THE PREPARATIONS WERE swift and complete. Captain Kryubi insisted that his men follow Piter de Vries's instructions to the letter. Rabban marched through the hangars and barracks like a warlord, maintaining an appropriate level of tension among the troops.

Guild transport had already been summoned, while a Harkonnen frigate was stripped and loaded with more than its normal complement of men and weapons, along with the ultrasecret ship that had been used only once, a full decade earlier.

From a military standpoint the invisibility technology was a potential boon unlike any other in recorded history. Theoretically, it would let the Harkonnens deliver crushing blows to their enemies without being detected in any way. Imagine what Viscount Moritani of Grumman would pay for such an advantage.

The unseen warcraft had functioned effectively on its maiden voyage, but further plans had been delayed while technicians repaired mechanical bugs that cropped up afterward. While most of the problems were minor, some—involving the no-field generator itself—proved more stubborn. And the Richesian inventor was no longer alive to offer assistance. Nevertheless, the ship had performed well enough in recent tests, though the quavery-voiced mechanics warned that it might not be entirely battleworthy. . . .

One of the slowest-moving cargo workers had had to be crushed gradually in a steam-press to give sufficient incentive to his peers so that they would not miss the scheduled departure time. The Baron was in a hurry.

THE FULLY LOADED frigate went into geostationary orbit over Wallach IX, directly above the Mother School complex. Standing on the bridge of the frigate with Piter de Vries and Glossu Rabban, the Baron transmitted no signal to the Bene Gesserit headquarters. He didn't have to.

"State your business," a female voice demanded over the comsystem, stiff and unwelcoming. Did he detect an undertone of surprise?

De Vries replied formally, "His Excellency the Baron Vladimir Harkonnen of Giedi Prime wishes to speak with your Mother Superior on a private channel."

"Not possible. No prior arrangements have been made."

The Baron leaned forward and boomed into the comsystem, "You have five minutes to establish a confidential connection with your Mother Superior, or I will communicate on an open line. That could prove, ah . . . embarrassing."

The pause was longer this time. Moments before the deadline, a different, rasping voice came over the speaker. "I am Mother Superior Harishka. We are on my personal comlink."

"Good, then listen carefully." The Baron smiled.

De Vries recited the case. "The articles of the Great Convention are most explicit regarding certain serious crimes, Mother Superior. These laws were established in the wake of the horrors committed by thinking machines on humanity. One of the ultimate crimes is the use of atomics against human beings. Another is aggression by biological warfare."

"Yes, yes. I am not a military historian, but I can get someone to quote the exact phrasing, if you wish. Does your Mentat not take care of such bureaucratic details, Baron? I don't see what this has to do with us. Would you like me to tell you a bedtime story as well?"

Her sarcasm could only mean she had begun to grow nervous. "'The forms must be obeyed,'" the Baron quoted. "The punishment for a violation of these laws is immediate annihilation of the perpetrators at the hands of the Landsraad. Every Great House has sworn to deliver an overwhelming combined force against the offending party." He paused, and his words became more menacing. "The forms have not been obeyed, have they, Mother Superior?"

Piter de Vries and Rabban looked at each other, both grinning.

The Baron continued. "House Harkonnen is prepared to bring a formal complaint before the Emperor and the Landsraad, charging the Bene Gesserit with the illegal use of biological weapons against a Great House."

"You speak nonsense. The Bene Gesserit have no aspirations of military power." She sounded entirely baffled. Was it possible she did not know?

"Know this, Mother Superior—We have incontrovertible evidence that your Reverend Mother Gaius Helen Mohiam intentionally inflicted a biological scourge upon my person while I was providing a service demanded by the Sisterhood. Ask the bitch yourself, if your underlings keep such information from you."

The Baron did not mention that the Sisterhood had blackmailed him with information about illegal spice-stockpiling activities. He was ready for that subject if it surfaced again, since all of his melange hoards had been moved to remote regions of distant Harkonnen worlds, where they would never be discovered.

Contented, the Baron sat back, listening to the deep silence. He imagined the appalled horror on the old Mother Superior's face. He twisted the knife deeper. "If you doubt our interpretation, read the wording of the Great Convention again and see if you care to risk it in open Landsraad court. Bear in mind, too, that the instrument of your attack—Reverend Mother Mohiam—was delivered to me on a Guild ship. When the Guild discovers that, they will not be pleased." He tapped his fingertips on a console. "Even if your Sisterhood is not demolished, you will receive severe sanctions from the Imperium, heavy fines, even banishment."

Finally, in a voice that almost managed to cover how the threat had shaken her, Harishka said, "You exaggerate your case, Baron, but I wish to be open-minded. What is it you want from us?"

He could feel her squirm. "I will take a shuttle down to the surface and meet with you privately. Send up a pilot to shepherd us through your planetary defense systems." He did not bother to point out his arrangements to transmit the evidence and accusations directly to Kaitain, should anything happen to them on this journey. The Mother Superior would already know.

"Certainly, Baron, but you will realize soon, this is all a terrible misunderstanding."

"Just produce Mohiam at the meeting. And be prepared to provide me with an effective treatment and cure—or else you and your Sisterhood have no hope of surviving this debacle."

The ancient Mother Superior remained unimpressed. "How large is your entourage?"

"Tell her we have a whole army," Rabban whispered to his uncle.

The Baron shoved him away. "Myself and six men."

"Your request for a meeting is granted."

When the link was shut down, Rabban asked, "Can I go, Uncle?"

"Do you remember what I said to you about finesse?"

"I looked up the word and all of its definitions, as you commanded."

"Stay here and think about it while I confer with the witch mother."

Angrily, Rabban stomped away.

An hour later a Bene Gesserit lighter docked with the Harkonnen frigate. A narrow-faced young woman with wavy chestnut hair stepped onto the entry dock. She wore a slick black uniform. "I am Sister Cristane. I will guide you to the surface." Her eyes glittered. "Mother Superior awaits."

The Baron marched forward with six hand-picked, armed soldiers. Piter de Vries spoke in a low voice that the witch could not hear. "Never underestimate the Bene Gesserit, my Baron."

With a grunt the Baron strode past his Mentat and boarded the lighter. "Not to worry, Piter. They're under our thumb now."

Religion is the emulation of the adult by the child. Religion is the encystment of past beliefs: mythology, which is guesswork, the hidden assumptions of trust in the universe, those pronouncements which men have made in search of personal power . . . all mingled with shreds of enlightenment. And always the ultimate unspoken commandment is "Thou shalt not question!" But we do anyway. We break that commandment as a matter of course. The work to which we have set ourselves is the liberating of the imagination, the harnessing of imagination to humankind's deepest sense of creativity.

—Credo of the Bene Gesserit Sisterhood

A BEAUTIFUL WOMAN CONFINED TO A DESOLATE WORLD, LADY MARGOT Fenring did not complain about the starkness, miserable heat, or lack of amenities in the dusty garrison town. Arrakeen was situated on a hard salt pan, with the inhospitable desert stretching off to the south and higher elevations, including the rugged Shield Wall, rising to the northwest. Since it was a few kilometers beyond the uncertain wormline, the settlement had never been attacked by one of the great sandworms, but this was still a subject of occasional concern. What if something changed? Life on the desert planet was never entirely secure.

Margot thought of the Sisters who had been lost there while working for the Missionaria Protectiva. Long ago, they had gone off into the desert, following the orders of Mother Superior—never to be seen again.

Arrakeen was immersed in the rhythms of the desert . . . the dryness and the premium put on water, the ferocious storms that blew in like great winds across a vast sea, the legends of danger and survival. Margot felt great serenity and spirituality here. It was a haven where she could contemplate nature, philosophy, and religion far from the inane bustle of the Imperial Court. She had time to do things in this place, time to discover herself.

What had those lost women found?

In the lemon glow of dawn, she stood on a second-floor balcony of the Residency. Fine dust and grit filtered the rising sun and gave the landscape a new look, leaving deep shadows where creatures concealed themselves. She watched a desert hawk fly toward the sun-drenched horizon, flapping its wings with slow power. The sunrise was like an oil painting by one of the great masters, a wash of pastels that sharply defined the rooftops of the town and the Shield Wall.

Somewhere out there, in countless sietches nestled in the rocky wasteland, dwelled the elusive Fremen. *They* had the answers she needed, the essential information Mother Superior Harishka had pressed her to obtain. Had the desert nomads listened to the teachings of the Missionaria Protectiva, or had they simply killed the messengers and stolen their water?

Behind her, the recently completed conservatory had been sealed with an airlock that opened only for her. Count Fenring, still asleep in their bedroom, had helped her to obtain some of the most exotic plants in the Imperium. But they were for her eyes alone.

Lately, she'd heard rumors of a Fremen dream for a green Arrakis—typical Edenic myths of the type often spread by the Missionaria Protectiva. That could have been an indication of the missing Sisters. It was not unusual, however, for a struggling people in a harsh environment to develop their own dreams of paradise, even without Bene Gesserit prompting. It would have been interesting to discuss the stories with Planetologist Kynes, perhaps ask him who the Fremen's mysterious "Umma" might be. She could not imagine how all this might be connected.

The desert hawk rose on thermals and soared.

Still standing at the balcony window, Margot took a sip of melange tea from a small cup; the soothing glow of its spicy essence filled her mouth. Though she had lived on Arrakis for a dozen years, she consumed spice only in moderation, careful not to become addicted enough that her eye color altered. In the mornings, though, melange enhanced her ability to perceive the natural beauty of Arrakis. She'd heard it said that melange never tasted the same twice, that it was like life, changing each time one partook of it. . . .

Change was an essential concept here, a key to understanding the Fremen. Superficially, Arrakis appeared always the same, a wasteland stretching into the unending distance, and into infinite time. But the desert was so much more than that. Margot's Fremen housekeeper, the Shadout Mapes, had suggested as much one day. "Arrakis is not what it seems, my Lady." Tantalizing words.

Some said the Fremen were strange, suspicious, and smelly. Outsiders spoke with a critical eye and sharp tongue, with no compassion or any attempt to understand the indigenous population. Margot, though, viewed the Fremen oddness as intriguing. She wanted to learn about their fiercely independent ways, to understand how they thought, and how they survived here. If she got to know them better, she could perform her job more effectively.

She could learn the answers she needed.

Studying the Fremen who worked in the mansion, Margot recognized barely discernible identifiers in body language, vocal inflection, odor. If the Fremen had anything to say, and if they thought you deserved to hear it, they would tell you. Otherwise, they went about their chores diligently, with heads bowed, disappearing into the tapestry of their society afterward like grains of sand in the desert.

In her search for answers, Margot had considered stating her questions outright, demanding any information about the missing Sisters, hoping the household servants would take her request out into the desert. But she knew the Fremen would simply vanish, refusing to be coerced.

Perhaps she should expose her own vulnerabilities to gain their trust. The Fremen would be shocked at first, then confused . . . and possibly even willing to cooperate with her.

My only duty is to the Sisterhood. I am a loyal Bene Gesserit.

But how to communicate without being obvious, without raising suspicions? She considered writing a note and leaving it in a place where it was sure to be found. The Fremen were always listening, always gathering information in their furtive ways.

No, Margot would have to be subtle, and also treat them with respect. She would have to tantalize them.

Then she remembered an odd practice that came to her through centuries of Other Memory . . . or was it just a bit of trivia she had read while studying on Wallach IX? No matter. On Old Terra, in an honor-based society known as Japan, there had been a tradition of hiring ninja assassins, quiet yet effective, in order to dodge legal entanglements. When a person wished to engage the services of the shadowy killers, he would go to a designated wall, face it, and whisper the name of the target and the fee offered. Though never seen, the ninja were always listening, and a contract was made.

Here in the Residency, the Fremen, too, were always listening.

Margot tossed her blonde hair over her shoulder, loosened her cool slikweave garment, and stepped into the hall outside of her offices. In the immense mansion, even in the cool early morning, people moved about, cleaning, dusting, polishing.

Margot stood in the central atrium and looked up toward the high-arched ceiling. She spoke in a soft, directed voice, knowing that the architecture of the old Residency created a whisper gallery. Some would hear her, in random places. She didn't know who, nor did she look to identify them.

"The Bene Gesserit Sisters, whom I represent here, hold the utmost respect and admiration for Fremen ways. And I, personally, am interested in your affairs." She waited for the faint echoes to die away. "If anyone could hear me, perhaps I have information to share about the *Lisan al-Gaib*—information you do not know at this time."

The *Lisan al-Gaib*, or "Voice from the Outer World," was a Fremen myth concerning a messianic figure, a prophet who bore striking parallels with the Sisterhood's own plans. Obviously, some prior representative of the Missionaria Protectiva had planted the legend as a precursor to the arrival of the Bene Gesserit's Kwisatz Haderach. Such preparation had been done on countless worlds in the Imperium; her comments were sure to spark Fremen interest.

She saw a flitting shadow, a drab robe, leathery skin.

Later that day, upon observing the Fremen employees moving about their household tasks, Margot thought they stared at her with a different kind of intensity, assessing her rather than just averting their blue-within-blue eyes.

Now, she began to wait, with the supreme patience of a Bene Gesserit.

THE NEXT ISLAND OF THE GINAZ SCHOOL WAS THE REMNANT OF AN AN-
cient volcano, a bleak scab raised out of the water and left to
dry in the tropical sun. The settlement inside the bowl of the
dry crater looked like another penal colony.

Duncan stood in formation on the stony exercise field with
a hundred and ten other young men, including the redheaded
Grumman trainee Hiih Resser. Of the original hundred and
fifty, thirty-nine had not completed their initial testing.

The curly black hair on Duncan's head had been shaved,
and he wore the loose black *gi* of the school. Each student carried whatever weapon he'd brought to Ginaz, and Duncan
had the Old Duke's sword—but he would learn to rely above
all on his own abilities and reactions, not a talisman that reminded him of home. The young man felt comfortable now,
and strong, and ready. He was eager to begin his training, at
long last.

Inside the crater compound, the junior training master
identified himself as Jeh-Wu. He was a muscular man with a
rounded nose, and a weak chin that gave him the appearance
of an iguana. His long dark hair was kinked into snake-like
dreadlocks. "The Pledge," he said. "In unison, please!"

"To the memory of the Swordmasters," Duncan and the
other students intoned, "in heart, soul, and mind, we do

pledge ourselves without condition, in the name of Jool-Noret. Honor is the core of our being."

A moment of silence ensued as they contemplated the great man who had established the principles upon which Ginaz was founded, whose sacred remains could still be viewed in the tall administration building on the main school island.

As they stood at attention, the new instructor strolled up and down each row, inspecting the candidates. Jeh-Wu thrust his head forward, paused in front of Duncan. "Produce your weapon." He spoke Ginazee, with the words translated into Galach by a thin purple collar that circled his neck.

Duncan did as he was told, handing over the Old Duke's sword hilt first. Jeh-Wu's eyebrows arched beneath massed dreadlocks that hung like a thundercloud on his head. "Fine blade. Marvelous metallurgy. Pure Damasteel." He flexed the blade expertly, bent it back, then released it to snap into position with a *thrummm* like a struck tuning fork.

"Each newly forged Damasteel blade is said to be quenched in the body of a slave." Jeh-Wu paused; his dreadlocks looked like serpents ready to strike. "Are you thickheaded enough to believe crap like that, Idaho?"

"That depends on whether or not it's true, sir."

The dour training master finally gave a thin smile, but did not answer Duncan. "I understand this is the blade of Duke Paulus Atreides?" He narrowed his eyes and spoke in a warmer voice. "See that you are worthy of it." He slipped it back into Duncan's scabbard.

"You will learn to fight with other weapons until you are ready for this one. Go to the armory and pick up a heavy broadsword, then don a full set of body armor—antique medieval plate." Now Jeh-Wu's smile seemed more sinister on his iguana-like face. "You'll need it for this afternoon's lesson. I intend to make an example of you."

———

ON THE PUMICE-AND-GRAVEL field in the crater, with forbidding crags all around him, Duncan Idaho clanked forward in full plate armor. The hauberk blocked his peripheral vision, forcing him to stare straight ahead through the slit. The metal pressed down on him, falling as if it weighed hundreds of pounds. Over his chain-mail shirt he wore shoulder plates, gorget, breastplate, greaves, cuirass, and tasset. He carried an enormous two-handed broadsword.

"Stand over there." Jeh-Wu pointed to a packed gravel area. "Consider how you intend to fight in that suit. It is not an easy task."

Before long, the island sun turned his outfit into a claustrophobic oven. Already sweating, Duncan struggled to stride across the uneven ground. He could barely bend his arms and legs.

None of the other students wore similar armor, but Duncan did not feel fortunate. "I'd rather be wearing a personal shield," he said, his voice muffled in the echoing helmet.

"Raise your weapon," the junior training master ordered.

Like a shackled prisoner, Duncan clumsily lifted the broadsword. With a conscious effort, he bent his stiff gauntlets into place around the hilt.

"Remember, Duncan Idaho, you have the best armor . . . supposedly the greatest advantage. Now, defend yourself."

He heard a shout from beyond his constricted range of vision, and suddenly he was surrounded by other students. They pummeled him with conventional swords, clanging against the steel plate. It sounded like a brutal hailstorm on a thin metal roof.

Duncan swiveled and struck out with his blade, but he moved too slowly. A pommel bashed his helmet, making his ears buzz. Although he swung again, he could barely see his opponents through the slit in his helmet, and they easily sidestepped the blow. Another blade rang against his shoulder plate. He fell to his knees, struggled to stand.

"Well, fight back, Idaho," Jeh-Wu said, raising his eyebrows in impatience. "Don't just stand there."

Duncan was reluctant to harm the other students with his huge broadsword, but none of his flat-bladed blows even touched a target. The students returned to pound him again. Sweat poured down his skin, and black spots danced in front of his eyes. The air inside his helmet grew stifling.

I can fight better than this!

Duncan responded with more energy, and the students dodged his thrusts and swings, but the heavy plate armor denied him free movement. In his ears, the roar of his breathing, the pounding of his heart was deafening.

The attack went on and on until he finally collapsed on the uneven gravel. The training master came forward and tore off the heavy helmet so that Duncan blinked in a blaze of sunlight. He gasped, shaking salty sweat out of his eyes. The heavy suit pinned him to the ground like a giant's foot.

Jeh-Wu stood over him. "You had the best armor of all of us, Duncan Idaho. You also had the largest sword." The training master looked down at his helpless form and waited for him to consider. "And yet you failed utterly. Would you care to explain why?"

Duncan remained silent; he didn't make any excuses for the abuse and embarrassment he had suffered during the exercise. It was clear there were hardships in life that a man had to face and overcome. He would accept adversity and use it to grow stronger. Life was not always fair.

Jeh-Wu turned to the other students. "Tell me the lesson here."

A short, dark-skinned trainee from the artificial world of Al-Dhanab barked out immediately, "Perfect defenses are not always an advantage. Complete protection can become a hindrance, for it limits you in other ways."

"Good." Jeh-Wu ran a finger along a scar on his chin. "Else?"

"Freedom of movement is a better defense than cumbersome armor," said Hiih Resser. "The hawk is safer from attack than the turtle."

Duncan forced himself to sit up, and slid the heavy broadsword aside in disgust. His voice was hoarse. "And the largest weapon is not always the deadliest."

The training master looked down at him, dreadlocks drooping, and gave him a genuine smile. "Excellent, Idaho. You may yet learn something here."

Learn to recognize the future the way a Steersman identifies guiding stars and corrects the course of his vessel. Learn from the past; never use it as an anchor.

—SIGAN VISEE,
First Head Instructor,
Guild Navigator School

DEEP BENEATH THE CITY GROTTOES ON IX, THE HOT SUBTERRANEAN TUN-
nels were illuminated red and orange. Generations ago, Ixian architects had drilled field-lined pits into the molten mantle of the planet, bottomless shafts that served as hungry mouths for industrial waste. The thick air smelled of acrid chemicals and sulfur.

Suboid workers sweated through twelve-hour shifts beside automated conveyors that dumped debris over the lip into the brimstone fires. Robed Tleilaxu guards stood perspiring, bored and inattentive. Dull-faced laborers tended the convey-ors, removing items of value, gleaning bits of precious metal, wires, and components from wreckage torn out of scrapped factories.

On the job, C'tair Pilru stole what he could.

Unnoticed on the line, the young man was able to snag sev-eral valuable crystals, tiny power sources, even a microsensor grid. After the Sardaukar raid on the freedom fighters two months earlier, he no longer had a network to supply him with the technological items he needed. He was all alone in his battle now, but he refused to concede defeat.

For two months he'd lived in paranoia. Though he still had a few peripheral contacts in the port-of-entry grottoes and the resource-processing docks, all the rebels C'tair knew, all the black marketeers he'd dealt with, had been slaughtered.

He kept a desperately low profile, avoiding his previous haunts, afraid that one of the captured and interrogated rebels had provided some clue to his identity. Out of contact with even Miral Alechem, he went deeper underground, literally, than he had ever gone before, working on a labor gang in the refuse-disposal shafts.

Beside him, one of the disposal workers fidgeted too much, glanced around too often. The man sensed intelligence in C'tair, though the dark-haired man studiously avoided him. He made no eye contact, did not initiate conversation, though his work partner clearly wanted to make a connection. C'tair suspected the man was another refugee pretending to be much less than he actually was. But C'tair could afford to trust no one.

He maintained his dull demeanor, pondering a shift in jobs. A curious work partner could be dangerous, perhaps even a Face Dancer mimic. C'tair might need to flee before anyone closed in on him. The Tleilaxu had systematically wiped out the Ixian middle class as well as the nobles, and would not rest until they had ground even the dust under their boot heels.

Accompanied by a Master, robed guards approached them one afternoon in the middle of a shift. With hair hanging limp in front of his fatigued eyes, C'tair was drenched in sweat. His curious work mate stiffened, then concentrated furiously on the task at hand.

C'tair felt cold and sick. If the Tleilaxu had come for him, if they knew who he was, they would torture him for days before executing him. He tensed his muscles, ready to fight. Perhaps he could throw several of them down into the one-way magma pit before he himself was killed.

Instead, the guards stepped up to the fidgety man beside C'tair. Leading them, a Tleilaxu Master rubbed his spidery fingers together and smiled. He had a long nose and a narrow chin; his grayish skin looked as if it had been leached of all life. "You, Citizen—suboid . . . or whatever you are. We have discovered your true identity."

The man looked up quickly, glanced over at C'tair as if beseeching him for help, but C'tair studiously averted his gaze.

"There's no longer any need to hide," the Master continued in a syrupy voice. "We've found records. We know that you were actually an accountant, one of those who kept inventories of Ixian-manufactured items."

The guard clapped a hand on the man's shoulders. The worker squirmed, panicked. All pretense slid away.

The Tleilaxu Master stepped closer, more paternal than threatening. "You misjudge us, Citizen. We have expended a great deal of effort to track you down because we have need of your services. We Bene Tleilax, your new masters, require intelligent workers to assist us in our government headquarters. We could use someone with your mathematical expertise."

The Master gestured around the hot, stinking chamber. The clatter of the automated conveyor rolled on, dumping rocks and twisted scraps of metal over the lip into the blazing pit. "This work is far beneath your skills. Come with us, and we will give you something much more interesting and worthwhile to do."

With a thin smile of hope, the man nodded faintly. "I'm very good at accounting. I could help you. I could be very valuable. You have to run this like a business, you know."

C'tair wanted to scream a warning. How could the man be so stupid? If he'd survived for a dozen years under Tleilaxu oppression, how could he not be aware of such an obvious trick?

"There, there," the Master said. "We'll have a council meeting, and you can tell us all your ideas."

The guard looked sharply at C'tair, and the Ixian's heart froze again. "Is our business of concern to you, Citizen?"

C'tair made every effort to keep his face slack, not to show fear in his eyes, to keep his voice slow and dull. "Now there'll be more work for me." He looked forlornly at the assembly line.

"Then work harder."

The guard and the Tleilaxu Master took their captive away. C'tair went back to his labors, staring at the debris, picking over every item before it toppled into the long shaft. . . .

Two days later, C'tair and his work shift were ordered to gather out on the floor of the main grotto so they could watch the execution of the accountant "spy."

WHEN HE ACCIDENTALLY stumbled upon Miral Alechem during his monotonous daily routine, C'tair covered his surprise well.

He had changed jobs again, nervous by the arrest of the hidden accountant. He never used the same identity card more than two days in a row. He moved from assignment to assignment, enduring a few curious looks, but Ixian workers knew better than to question. Any stranger could well be a Face Dancer who had infiltrated work gangs in an attempt to pick up talk of unrest or secret sabotage plans.

C'tair had to bide his time and make new plans. He frequented different food stations, standing in long lines where bland cooked fare was distributed to the workers.

The Tleilaxu had put their biological technology to work, creating unrecognizable food in hidden vats. They grew vegetables and roots by splitting cells so that the plants produced only shapeless tumors of edible material. Eating became a process rather than a pleasurable activity, as much a chore as the routine tasks during a shift.

C'tair remembered times he had spent in the Grand Palais with his father, the Ambassador to Kaitain, and his mother, an important Guild Bank representative. They had sampled out-world delicacies, the finest appetizers and salads, the best imported wines. Such memories seemed like fantasies now. He could not recall what any of that food had tasted like.

He straggled at the end of the line so that he did not have to fight the press of other workers. When he received his helping from the server, he noticed the large dark eyes, raggedly cropped hair, and narrow but attractive face of Miral Alechem.

Their gazes locked and recognition flashed between them, but both knew enough not to speak. C'tair glanced behind him toward the seating areas, and Miral raised her spoon. "Sit at that table, worker. It's just come free."

Without questioning, C'tair sat at the indicated place and began eating. He concentrated on his meal, chewing slowly to give her all the time she needed.

Before long, the line ended and the food shift was over. Finally, Miral came over, bearing her own food tray. She sat down, stared at her bowl, and began eating. Although C'tair did not look directly at her, they soon began a mumbled conversation, moving their lips as little as possible.

"I work at this food distribution line," Miral said. "I've been afraid to change assignments because it might draw attention to me."

"I have lots of identity cards," C'tair said. He had never given her his correct name, and he was going to leave it that way.

"We are the only two left," Miral said. "Of the whole group."

"There will be others. I've still got a few contacts. For now, I'm working alone."

"Can't accomplish much that way."

"Can't accomplish anything at all if I'm dead." When she slurped her food and didn't answer, he continued, "I've been fighting alone for twelve years."

"And you haven't accomplished enough."

"It will never be enough until the Tleilaxu are gone and Ix has been returned to our people." He clamped his lips together, afraid he had spoken too vehemently. He took two slow mouthfuls from his bowl. "You never told me what you were working on, those technological items you were scavenging. Do you have a plan?"

After glancing at him, Miral quickly tore her glance away. "I'm building a detection device. I need to find out what the Tleilaxu are doing in that research pavilion they keep so carefully guarded."

"It's scan-shielded," C'tair mumbled. "I've already tried."

"That is why I need a new device. I think . . . I think that facility is the reason behind their entire takeover."

C'tair was startled. "What do you mean?"

"Have you noticed that the Tleilaxu experiments have entered a new phase? Something very dark and unpleasant is happening."

C'tair paused with the spoon halfway to his mouth, looked over at her, and glanced down at his nearly empty bowl. He would need to eat more slowly if he wished to finish this conversation without anyone noticing.

"Our women have been disappearing," Miral said with a slash of anger in the back of her voice. "Young women, fertile and healthy. I've watched them vanish from the work rolls."

C'tair had not remained in one place long enough to notice details like that. He swallowed hard. "Are they abducted for Tleilaxu harems? But why would they take 'unclean' *Ixian* women?"

Supposedly, no outsider had ever seen a Tleilaxu female; he'd heard that the Bene Tleilax guarded their women zealously, protecting them from the contamination and perversions of the Imperium. Maybe Tleilaxu women were kept hidden because they were as gnome-ugly as the men.

Could it just be a coincidence that the missing females were all healthy and of childbearing age? Such women would make the best concubines . . . but the mean-spirited Tleilaxu did not seem the type who would indulge in extravagant sexual pleasures.

"I think the answer has something to do with what's going on in that shielded pavilion," Miral suggested.

C'tair set his spoon down. He only had one bite left in his bowl. "I know this much: The invaders came here with a terrible purpose, not just to take over our facilities or conquer this world. They have another agenda. If they simply wanted to take over Ix for their own profit, they would not have dismantled so many factories. They would never have ceased production of the new-design Heighliners, reactive fighting meks, and other products that brought a fortune to House Vernius."

With a nod, she said, "I agree. They intend to accomplish something else—and they're doing it behind shields and closed doors. Perhaps I'll learn what it is." Miral finished her meal and stood up. "If I do, I'll let you know."

After she left, C'tair felt a glimmer of hope again for the first time in many months. At least he wasn't the only one fighting the Tleilaxu. If one other person was involved in the effort, others must be forming pockets of resistance as well, here and there. But he hadn't heard of anything happening, not for months.

His hopes sagged. He couldn't stand the thought of waiting for the right opportunity, day after day, week after week. Perhaps he'd been thinking too small. Yes, he needed to change tactics and contact someone outside for assistance. He would have to reach *off-world*, no matter what the risk might be. He needed to search for powerful allies to help him overthrow the Tleilaxu.

And he knew of one person who had far more at stake than he did.

The Unknown surrounds us at any given moment. That is where we seek knowledge.

—MOTHER SUPERIOR RAQUELLA BERTO-ANIRUL
Oratory Against Fear

IN THE ORNATE MUMMER'S PORTICO OF THE IMPERIAL PALACE, LADY ANirul Corrino stood with a delegation from Shaddam's Court. Each person was dressed in extravagant finery, some ridiculously gaudy, as they awaited the arrival of yet another dignitary. It was a daily routine, but this guest was different. . . .

Count Hasimir Fenring had always been dangerous.

She squinted into Kaitain's ever-flawless morning sunlight, watched trained hummingbirds flit over flowers. From orbit, the vigilant weather-control satellites manipulated the flow of warm and cool air masses to maintain an optimal climate around the Palace. Against her cheeks Anirul felt the delicate kiss of a warm breeze, just the right accent on a perfect day.

Perfect . . . except for the arrival of Count Fenring. Though he had married a Bene Gesserit equally as shrewd as himself, Fenring still made Anirul's skin crawl; a disturbing aura of shed blood surrounded him. As the Kwisatz Mother, Anirul knew every detail of the Bene Gesserit breeding scheme, knew that this man had himself been bred as a potential Kwisatz Haderach in one of the offshoots of the program—but he'd been found lacking and was instead a biological dead end.

But Fenring possessed an extraordinarily sharp mind and dangerous ambitions. Though he spent most of his time in Arrakeen as the Imperial Spice Minister, he kept his boyhood

riend Shaddam under his thumb. Anirul resented this influ-
nce, which even *she*, as the Emperor's wife, did not have.

With a pompous clatter, an open coach drawn by two
olden Harmonthep lions approached the palace gates.
Juards waved the Count in, and the carriage rounded the cir-
ular drive in a commotion of wheels and enormous alloy-
hoed paws. Footmen stepped forward to open the carriage's
nameled door. Anirul waited with her retinue, smiling like a
tatue.

Fenring stepped down to the slate of the portico. He had
lecked himself out for the reception in a black frock coat and
op hat, a crimson-and-gold sash, and gaudy badges of office.
Because the Emperor admired regal trappings, it amused the
Count to play along.

He removed his hat and bowed, then looked up at her with
large, glittering eyes. "My Lady Anirul, so nice to see you,
hmmmm?"

"Count Fenring," she said with a simple bow and a pleasant
smile. "Welcome back to Kaitain."

Without a further word or modicum of civility, he put his
top hat back on his misshapen head and walked past her on his
way to an immediate audience with the Emperor. She followed him at a distance, flanked by the other peacock members of the Court.

Fenring's access to Shaddam was direct, and it seemed obvious to Anirul that he cared little for the fact that she disliked
him; nor did he question why she had formed such an opinion. He had no knowledge of his failed place in the breeding
scheme, or the potential he had missed.

Working with Sister Margot Rashino-Zea, whom he'd later
married, Fenring had assisted in arranging Shaddam's marriage to a Bene Gesserit of Hidden Rank—Lady Anirul herself. At the time, the new Emperor had needed to secure a
subtle but powerful alliance in the uneasy transition after the
death of old Elrood.

Foolishly, Shaddam failed to see his precarious position even now. The flare-up with Grumman was only one manifestation of unrest throughout the realm, as were the constant gestures of defiance, vandalism, and defacings of Corrino monuments. The people no longer feared or even respected him.

It disturbed Anirul that the Emperor thought he no longer required Bene Gesserit influence, and rarely consulted his ancient Truthsayer, the Reverend Mother Lobia. He had also grown more annoyed with Anirul for producing no sons, pursuant to her secret orders from the Sisterhood.

Empires rise and fall, Anirul thought, *but the Bene Gesserit remain.*

As she followed Fenring, she watched his athletic steps as he made his way toward her husband's throne room. Neither Shaddam nor Fenring understood all the subtleties and behind-the-scenes activities that glued the Imperium together. The Bene Gesserit excelled in the arena of history, where the glitter and pomp of ceremony had no importance. Compared with Kwisatz Mother Anirul, both the Padishah Emperor and Hasimir Fenring were rank amateurs—and didn't even know it.

Inwardly she smiled, sharing her amusement with the crowded Sisters in Other Memory, her constant companions from thousands of past lives. The millennia-long breeding program would culminate soon in the birth of a male Bene Gesserit of extraordinary powers. It would happen in two generations . . . if all plans came to fruition.

Here, while masquerading as a devoted wife to the Emperor, Anirul pulled all the strings, controlled every effort. She commanded Mohiam back on Wallach IX, who worked with her secret daughter by Baron Harkonnen. She watched the other Sisters as they laid plans within plans to connect Jessica with House Atreides. . . .

Ahead of her, Fenring moved confidently, knowing his way around the city-sized Imperial Palace better than any man, better even than Emperor Shaddam himself. He crossed a magnificent jewel-tiled entry and stepped into the Imperial Audience Chamber. The immense room contained some of the most priceless art treasures in a million worlds, but he had seen them all before. Without a backward glance, he tossed his hat to a footman and strode across the polished stone floor toward the throne. It was a long walk.

Anirul hovered next to one of the massive support columns. Courtiers flitted about in self-important business, entering private gossip stations. She skirted priceless statuaries as she made her way toward an acoustically superior alcove where she often stood within easy listening distance.

On the translucent blue-green Golden Lion Throne sat the Padishah Emperor Shaddam IV, the eighty-first Corrino to rule the Imperium. He wore layers of military-style clothing, accented by jangling medals and badges and ribbons. Weighed down by the trappings of rank, he could barely move.

His withered Truthsayer, Lobia, stood in an alcove off to one side of the crystal throne. Lobia was the third leg of Shaddam's advisory tripod, which included the high-browed Court Chamberlain Ridondo and Hasimir Fenring (though, since the Count's well-publicized banishment, the Emperor rarely consulted him in public).

Shaddam refused to notice his wife. Fifteen Bene Gesserit Sisters stationed in the Palace were like shadows flitting silently between rooms . . . there, but not there. As he *intended* them to be. Their loyalty to Shaddam was unquestioned, especially after his marriage to Anirul. Some served as ladies-in-waiting, while others cared for the royal daughters Irulan, Chalice, and Wensicia, and would tutor them one day.

The ferretlike Imperial Observer bobbed along a river of red carpeting, and then up the wide, shallow steps of the dais to the base of the throne. Shaddam leaned forward on his perch while Fenring came to a stop, bowed deeply, and looked up with a smile twitching his lips.

Even Anirul didn't know why the Count had rushed here from Arrakis.

But the Emperor did not look pleased. "As my servant, Hasimir, I expect you to keep me advised about events in your purview. Your latest report is incomplete."

"Hmmm-ahh, my apologies if Your Highness feels I have omitted something of importance." Fenring spoke quickly as his mind raced through possibilities, trying to guess the reason for Shaddam's ire. "I do not wish to trouble you with trivialities that are best handled by myself." His eyes flicked from side to side, calculating. "Ahhh, what concerns you, Sire?"

"Word has reached me that the Harkonnens are suffering heavy losses of men and equipment on Arrakis through guerrilla activities. Spice production has begun to fall off again, and I have been troubled by numerous complaints from the Spacing Guild. How much of this is true?"

"Hmmm-ah, my Emperor, the Harkonnens whine too much. Perhaps it is a ploy to raise the price of melange on the open market, or to justify a request for lower Imperial tariffs? How has the Baron explained it?"

"I could not ask him," Shaddam said, springing his trap. "According to reports from a Heighliner that just arrived, he has gone to Wallach IX with a fully armed frigate. What is that all about?"

Alarmed, Fenring raised his eyebrows, then rubbed his long nose. "The Bene Gesserit Mother School? I, hmmm, to be honest I was not aware of that. The Baron doesn't seem the sort who would consult with the Sisterhood."

Equally astonished, Anirul leaned forward at her listening post. Why would Baron Harkonnen possibly go to Wallach IX?

Certainly not to obtain advisors, for he had made no secret of his dislike for the Sisterhood after they'd forced him to provide a healthy daughter for the breeding program. Why then would he bring a military ship? She calmed her racing pulse. This didn't sound good.

The Emperor snorted. "Not much of an Observer, are you, Hasimir? Why, too, has there been a bizarre defacement of my most expensive statue in Arsunt? That's right in your backyard."

Fenring blinked his large, dark eyes. "I was not aware of any vandalism in Arsunt, Sire. When did it happen?"

"Someone took the liberty of adding anatomically correct genitalia to the front of my Imperial likeness—but because the perpetrator made the size of the organ so *small*, no one even saw it until recently."

Fenring had trouble stifling a laugh. "That is most, hmmm, unfortunate, Sire."

"I don't find it so amusing, especially when added to other outrages and insults. This has been going on for years. *Who is doing it?*"

Abruptly, Shaddam stood from his throne and brushed a hand down the front of his uniform, jangling the medals and badges. "Come to my private den, Hasimir. We must discuss this in greater detail."

When he raised his head in a haughty *Imperial* gesture, Fenring reacted too smoothly. Anirul realized that, although the affronts Shaddam mentioned had been real enough, the discussion had merely been a ploy to bring the Count here for another purpose. Something they would not discuss in front of others.

Men are so clumsy when they try to keep secrets.

While she would have found those secrets interesting enough, Anirul was much more concerned and alarmed about what the Baron intended at Wallach IX. She and the Truthsayer Lobia, on opposite sides of the Imperial throne, communicated by discreet hand signs.

A message would be dispatched to the Mother School immediately. Crafty old Harishka would have ample opportunity to plan an appropriate response.

Thinking, and the methods by which thoughts are communicated, inevitably create a system permeated by illusions.

—Zensunni Teaching

AS THE ARROGANT-LOOKING WITCH CRISTANE GUIDED BARON HARKONNEN through the maze of shadowy passageways, his walking stick clicked like gunshots on the cold flagstone floor. With his six guards behind him, he hobbled forward, trying to keep up.

"Your Mother Superior has no choice but to listen," the Baron said in a strident voice. *"If I don't get the cure I need, the Emperor will learn of the Sisterhood's crimes!"* Cristane ignored him; she tossed her short, chestnut hair and never looked back.

It was a damp night on Wallach IX, the outside silence broken only by cold breezes. Yellow globes illuminated the corridors of the complex of school buildings. No Sisters stirred, and only shadows moved. The Baron felt as if he were walking into a tomb—which it *would* be if he ever brought his case before the Landsraad. Breaking the Great Convention was the most serious offense the witches could commit. He held all the cards.

Haloed by pulsing light from poorly tuned glowglobes, Cristane marched ahead until she seemed to fade from view. The young witch glanced back, but did not wait for him. When one of the guards tried to assist the Baron, he responded by shoving the arm away and continuing on his own, as best he could manage. A shiver ran up his spine, as if someone had whispered a curse in his ear.

The Bene Gesserit had hidden fighting skills, and there must be swarms of them in this lair. What if the Mother Superior didn't care about his accusations? What if the old hag thought he was bluffing? Even his armed Harkonnen troopers could do nothing to keep the witches from killing him in their own nest, should they choose to attack.

But the Baron knew they dared not act against him.

Where are all the witches hiding? Then he grinned. *They must be afraid of me.*

With an angry huff, the Baron reviewed the demands he would make, three simple concessions and he would not file formal charges in the Landsraad: a cure for his disease, delivering Gaius Helen Mohiam to him intact and ready for utter humiliation . . . and the return of the two daughters he'd been coerced into fathering. The Baron was curious about how his offspring fit into the witches' plans, but he supposed he could back off on that demand, if necessary. He didn't really want a couple of female brats anyway, but it gave him negotiating room.

Sister Cristane moved ahead, while the guards hung back to match the Baron's painful, plodding pace. She turned a corner into shadows ahead of him. The pulsing glowglobes seemed too yellow, too filled with static. They began to give him a headache, and he wasn't seeing clearly.

When the Baron's entourage turned the corner, they saw only an empty hall. Cristane was gone.

The cool stone walls echoed with the disconcerted gasps of the Harkonnen escort. A weak breeze, like cadaverous breath, oozed across the air and stole under the Baron's clothing. Involuntarily, he shivered. He heard a faint whisper, like scuttling rodent feet, but saw no movement.

"Run ahead and check it out!" He nudged the squad leader in the side. "Where did she go?"

One of the troopers unshouldered his lasrifle and ran along the glowglobe-illuminated corridor. Moments later he shouted back, "Nothing here, my Lord Baron." His voice had an eerie, hollow quality, as if this place sucked sound and light from the air. "No one in sight anywhere."

The Baron waited, his senses alert. Cold sweat trickled down his back, and he narrowed his spider-black eyes, more in consternation than in terror. "Check all passageways and rooms in the vicinity, and report back to me." The Baron looked down the corridor, refusing to step deeper into the trap. "And don't be so edgy that you shoot each other."

His men disappeared from view, and he no longer heard their shouts or footsteps, either. This place felt like a mausoleum. And damned cold. He hobbled into an alcove and stood silently with his back to a wall, ready to protect himself. He unholstered a personal flèchette pistol, checked its charge of poisoned needles . . . and held his breath.

A glowglobe flickered over his head, dimmed. Hypnotic.

With a sound of running boots, one of his men reappeared, short of breath. "Please come with me, my Lord Baron. You need to see this."

Unsettled, the man led the way down a short set of stairs and past a library where filmbooks were still playing, their whispering voices droning into empty air, with no listeners. Cushion indentations remained on some of the chairs, where patrons had sat only moments ago. Everyone had disappeared without bothering to shut off the programs. The muffled speakers sounded like the voices of fading ghosts.

The Baron's distress grew as he hobbled from room to room with the troopers, then finally from building to building. They found no one, not even when his men used primitive life-tracer scanners. Where were the witches? In catacombs? Where had his escort Cristane gone?

Anger made the Baron's cheeks hot. How could he present his demands to the witch mother if he couldn't find her? Was

Harishka trying to buy time? By avoiding the confrontation, she had short-circuited his revenge. Did she think he would just go away?

He hated to feel helpless. Swinging his walking stick, the Baron smashed the nearest library reader, then flailed about, breaking everything he could find. With glee, the guards set about overturning tables, knocking down shelves, tossing heavy volumes through glass windows.

It accomplished nothing. "Enough," he said, then led the way down the corridor again.

Presently he stood in a large office; gold lettering on the door marked it as the workroom of the Mother Superior. The dark, highly polished desk was clear of objects, no files or records anywhere; its chair sat at an angle, as if pushed back abruptly. On a ceramic dish, incense still burned, imparting a faint odor of cloves. He knocked it onto the floor in a flurry of aromatic ash.

Damned witches. The Baron shivered. He and his men backed out of the room.

Outside again, he became disoriented, a disconcertingly alien feeling of being lost. Neither he nor his guards could agree upon the correct route back to the shuttle. The Baron strode across an outdoor park and into a passageway that skirted a large stucco-and-timber building where lights burned inside.

In the grand dining hall, hundreds of still-steaming meals rested on long plank tables, benches arranged neatly in place. No other people were in the room. *No one.*

With his finger, one of the troopers nudged a chunk of meat in a bowl of stew. "Don't touch that," the Baron barked. "Could be subdermal poison." It would be just the sort of thing the witches would try. The trooper recoiled.

The squad leader's pale-eyed gaze darted around; his uniform was damp with perspiration. "They must have been here only minutes ago. You can still smell the food."

The Baron cursed and swung his wormhead cane across the table, knocking plates, cups, and food to the floor. The clatter echoed off the walls and ceiling of the hall. But there was no other sound.

His men used detection equipment to check under the floors, in the walls and ceilings, sweeping in all directions without success.

"Check the calibration on those life-tracers. The witches are here somewhere, damn them!"

As he watched his men work feverishly, the Baron fumed. His skin crawled. He thought he heard a faint, smothered laugh, but it vanished into the haunted silence.

"Do you want us to torch this place, my Baron?" the squad leader asked, eager for the conflagration.

He imagined the entire Mother School in flames, the convoluted wisdom and history and breeding records consumed in an inferno. Perhaps the black-clad witches would be trapped inside their hidden bolt-holes and roasted alive. *That would be worth seeing*.

But he shook his head, angry at the answer forced upon him. Until the witches gave him the cure he desperately needed, Baron Harkonnen dared not strike against the Bene Gesserit.

Afterward, however . . . he would make up for lost time.

There is no reality—only our own order imposed on everything.

—Basic Bene Gesserit Dictum

FOR JESSICA IT WAS LIKE A CHILD'S GAME . . . EXCEPT THIS ONE WAS deadly serious.

Rustling like bats, hundreds of Sisters filled the dining hall, amused to watch the Baron's antics, dodging him as if it were a game of invisible tag. Some crouched under tables; Jessica and Mohiam pressed against the wall. All the women were in silent breathing mode, concentrating on the illusion. No one spoke.

They were in plain sight, but the befuddled Harkonnens could neither see nor sense them. The Baron saw only what the Bene Gesserit wanted him to see.

On top of the head table stood the dark, aged Mother Superior, smiling like a schoolgirl in the middle of a prank. Harishka folded rail-thin arms across her chest as the pursuers grew more and more frustrated and noticeably agitated.

A trooper passed only centimeters in front of Jessica. He waved a life-tracer, nearly striking her face. But the guard saw nothing but false readings. On the dial of the scanner, data blinked and flared as the soldier moved past Jessica—though to him nothing registered on the gauge. Devices could not easily be fooled . . . but men were different.

Life is an illusion, to be tailored to our needs, she thought, quoting a lesson she had learned from her teacher Mohiam. Every

Acolyte knew how to trick the eye, the most vulnerable of human senses. The Sisters made barely audible sounds, dampened their slight movements.

Knowing the swaggering Baron was on his way, Mother Superior had summoned the Sisters into the great dining hall. "Baron Harkonnen believes he is in control," she had said in her crackling voice. "He thinks to intimidate us, but we must remove his strength, make him feel impotent."

"We are also buying time for ourselves to consider this matter . . . and giving the Baron time to make his own mistakes. Harkonnens are not known for their patience."

Across the room, the clumsy Baron nearly brushed against Sister Cristane, who slid smoothly away.

"What the hells was that?" He whirled, sensing the movement of air, a brief scent of fabric. "I heard something rustle, like a robe." The guards raised their weapons, but saw no targets. The heavyset man shuddered.

Jessica exchanged a smile with her teacher. The Reverend Mother's normally flat eyes danced with glee. From her high table, Mother Superior stared down at the flustered men like a bird of prey.

In preparation for the mass hypnosis that now smothered the Baron and his men, Sister Cristane had allowed herself to be visible to them, so she could lead them into the web. But gradually the guide had faded from view as the Sisters concentrated, focusing their efforts on these pliable victims.

The Baron hobbled closer, his face a mask of unbridled fury. Jessica had the opportunity to trip him, but chose not to.

Mohiam moved to glide beside him, said something faint and eerie. "You shall *fear*, Baron." In a directed-whisper that carried only to the fat man's ears, this man she despised so much, Mohiam created a barely discernible susurration that twisted words from the Litany Against Fear into something altogether different:

"You shall fear. Fear is the mind-killer. Fear is the little-death that brings total obliteration." She walked around him, spoke to the back of his head. "You cannot face your fear. It will pass inside you and infect you."

He thrashed with his hand, as if to bat away a bothersome insect. His expression looked troubled. "When we look upon the path of your fear, there will be nothing left of you." Smoothly, Mohiam slipped away from him. "Only the Sisterhood will remain."

The Baron stopped dead in his tracks, his face pale, his jowls twitching. His black eyes glanced to the left, where Mohiam had been standing only seconds before. He swung his cane in that direction, so hard that he lost his balance and fell to the floor.

"Get me out of here!" he bellowed to his guards.

Two troopers rushed to help him to his feet. The squad leader guided them to the main doors and out into the passageway, while the remaining guards continued to search for targets, swinging the snub noses of their lasrifles back and forth.

At the threshold, the Baron hesitated. "Damned witches." He looked around. "Which way back?"

"To the right, my Lord Baron," the squad leader said in a firm voice. Unknown to him, Cristane hovered invisibly at his side, whispering directions in his ear. Upon reaching the shuttle, they would find it already set on automatic pilot, ready to take the Baron back through the planet's complex defenses to their frigate in orbit.

Unsuccessful, frustrated, helpless. The Baron was not accustomed to such feelings. "They wouldn't dare harm me," he muttered.

Nearby, several Sisters snickered.

As the Harkonnens fled like gaze hounds with their tails between their legs, ghostly laughter from the dining hall followed them.

Immobility is often mistaken for peace.

—EMPEROR ELROOD CORRINO IX

WITH GOOD HUMOR, RHOMBUR'S NEW CONCUBINE TESSIA ACCOMPANIED him around the grounds of Castle Caladan. It amused her that the exiled Prince seemed more like an excited, clumsy child than the heir to a renegade House. It was a sunny morning, with lacy clouds drifting high overhead.

"It is hard to get to know you, when you fawn upon me so, my Prince." They walked together along a terraced hillside path.

He clearly felt out of his league. "Uh, first you've got to call me Rhombur."

She raised her eyebrows, and her sepia eyes sparkled. "I suppose that is a start."

He flushed deeply as they continued to walk. "You must have smitten me, Tessia." He plucked a field daisy from a spray of flowers on a grassy embankment and extended it to her. "Since I'm the son of a great Earl, I suppose I shouldn't allow that, should I?"

Tessia accepted the offering and spun the flower coyly in front of her plain but intelligent-looking face. She peeked around the petals at him; her expression grew warm and understanding. "There are some advantages to living in exile, I suppose. Nobody notices who you're smitten with."

Then she pointed a stern finger at him. "Though I would

respect you more if you did something to counteract the dishonor that's fallen on your family. Simply being an optimist hasn't achieved anything for years, has it? Trusting that everything will turn out right, thinking that you can do nothing more than sit here and complain? Talking is no substitute for *doing*."

Surprised by the remark, Rhombur spluttered his response. "But I've, uh, requested that Ambassador Pilru file petition after petition. Won't my oppressed people try to overthrow the invaders, waiting for me to return? I expect to march back and reclaim my family name . . . anytime now."

"If you sit safely here and wait for your people to do your work for you, then you do not deserve to rule such a populace. Have you learned nothing from Leto Atreides?" Tessia put her hands on her slender hips. "If you ever intend to be an Earl, Rhombur, you must follow your passions. *And* get better intelligence reports."

He felt decidedly uncomfortable, stung by the truth in her words, but at a loss. "How, Tessia? I have no army. Emperor Shaddam refuses to intervene . . . and the Landsraad, too. I was only granted limited amnesty when my family went renegade. Uh, what else can I do?"

Determined, she grasped his elbow as they continued their brisk walk. "If you permit me, perhaps I might make suggestions. They teach us many subjects on Wallach IX, including politics, psychology, strategy facilitation. . . . Never forget that I am a Bene Gesserit, not a serving wench. I am intelligent and well educated, and I see many things that you do not."

Rhombur stumbled along with her, trying to regain his mental balance. Suspicious, he said, "Is this something the Sisterhood put you up to? Were you assigned as my concubine just to help me get Ix back?"

"No, my Prince. I won't pretend, though, that the Bene Gesserit wouldn't prefer to have a stable House Vernius back in power. Dealing with the Bene Tleilax is far more difficult . . .

and confusing." Tessia ran her fingers through her close-cropped brown hair, making it look as mussed as the Prince's perpetual tangles. "For myself, I would rather be the concubine of a Great Earl within the fabled Grand Palais on Ix, than of an exiled Prince who lives off the good graces of a generous Duke."

He swallowed hard, then plucked another field daisy and sniffed it himself. "I would rather be that person, too, Tessia."

LOOKING DOWN FROM a Castle balcony, Leto watched Rhombur and Tessia stroll hand in hand across a field of wildflowers swaying in the ocean breeze. Leto felt a heavy ache in his heart, a warm envy toward his friend; the Ixian Prince seemed to be walking on air, as if he had forgotten all about the troubles on his overthrown homeworld.

He smelled Kailea's perfume behind him, a sweet, flowery scent reminiscent of hyacinth and lily of the valley, but he hadn't heard her approach. He looked back at her, and wondered how long she had been standing there, watching him stare down at the inseparable lovers.

"She's good for him," Kailea said. "I never had much fondness for the Bene Gesserit before this, but Tessia is an exception."

Leto chuckled. "He does seem quite taken with her. A testament to Sisterhood seduction training."

Kailea cocked her head; she wore a jewel-studded comb in her hair, and had taken particular care to apply the most flattering touch of makeup. He had always found her beautiful, but at this moment she seemed . . . aglow.

"It takes more than dueling practice, parades, and fishing trips to make my brother happy . . . or any man." Kailea stepped out onto the sunlit balcony with Leto, and he became uncomfortably aware of how alone they were.

Back before the fall of Ix, when she had been the daughter

of a powerful Great House, Kailea Vernius had seemed a perfect match for Leto. Given time, in the normal course of events, Old Duke Paulus and Earl Dominic Vernius probably would have arranged a marriage.

But things were much different now. . . .

He could not afford to become entangled with a young woman from a renegade House, a person who—in theory—carried a death sentence if she ever tried to become involved in Imperial politics. As a noble daughter, Kailea could never become just a casual lover, like a girl from the village below Castle Caladan.

But he couldn't deny his feelings.

And wasn't a Duke entitled to take a concubine if he wished? There was no shame in it for Kailea, either, especially with her lack of prospects.

"Well, Leto—what are you waiting for?" She stepped close to him, so that one of her breasts grazed his arm. Her perfume made him dizzy with pheromones. "You are the Duke. You can have anything you desire." Kailea drew out the last word.

"And what makes you think there's anything I . . . desire?" To his own ears, his voice sounded strangely hollow.

Raising her eyebrows, she gave him a coy smile. "Surely you are accustomed to making difficult decisions by now?"

He hesitated, frozen. *Indeed*, he thought, *what am I waiting for?*

They both moved at the same time, and he took her warmly into his arms with a long-held sigh of relief and growing passion.

FROM THE TIME Leto was young, he remembered watching his father spend sunny days in the courtyard of Castle Caladan, where he would listen to the petitions, concerns, and well-wishes of the people. Old Paulus's bearish, bearded father had

called it "going about the business of being a Duke." Leto carried on the tradition.

A line of people trudged up the steep path to the open
gates, to participate in an archaic system in which the Duke
settled disputes. Though efficient legal systems existed in all
the large cities, Leto did this for the opportunity to maintain
contact with his people. He liked to respond personally to
their complaints and suggestions. He found it better than any
number of surveys, opinion polls, and reports from supposed
experts.

As he sat under the warm morning sun, he listened to one
person after another as the line shuffled forward. An old
woman, whose husband had gone to sea in a storm and never
returned, asked that he be declared dead, and went on to request Leto's blessing and dispensation to marry her husband's
brother. The young Duke told her to wait a month on both
accounts, after which he would approve her petition.

A ten-year-old boy wanted to show Leto a sea hawk he had
raised from the time it was a chick. The large red-crested bird
clutched the boy's leather-cuffed wrist, then flew up into the
open air of the courtyard, circled (much to the terror of the
sparrows nesting in the eaves), and came back to the boy when
he whistled. . . .

Leto loved to focus his attentions on personal details here
at home, where he could actually see how his decisions mattered to the lives of his people. The immense Imperium, supposedly spanning "a million worlds," seemed too abstract, too
vast to *matter* much here. Still, the bloody conflicts on other
worlds—such as between Ecaz and Grumman, or the ages-old
animosity between House Atreides and House Harkonnen—
affected their own populations in as personal a way as anything he saw here.

Leto had long been eligible for marriage—very eligible, in
fact—and other Landsraad members wanted to enter into an
alliance with House Atreides and mingle bloodlines. Would it

be one of the daughters of Armand Ecaz, or would some other family make him a better offer? He had to play the dynastic game his father had taught him.

For years now he'd longed for Kailea Vernius, but her family had fallen, her House gone renegade. A Duke of House Atreides could never marry such a woman. It would be political suicide. Still, that did not make Kailea any less beautiful, or desirable.

Rhombur, happy with Tessia, had suggested that Leto take Kailea as his ducal concubine. For Kailea there would certainly be no shame in becoming the chosen lover of a Duke. In fact, it would secure her precarious position here on Caladan, where she lived under a provisional amnesty, with no guarantees. . . .

Next, a balding man with squinting eyes opened a smelly basket. A pair of House Guards closed in on him, but moved back when he lifted out a warm, reeking fish that must have been dead for days. Flies buzzed around it. When Leto frowned, wondering what insult this could be, the fisherman blanched, suddenly realizing the impression he had made. "Oh no, no, m'Lord Duke! This ain't an offerin'. No—look, ye. This fish has *sores*. All my catch in the southern sea had sores." Indeed, the belly of the fish was rough and leprous. "The seakelp rafts out there are dyin' and they stink to the heavens. Somethin's wrong, and I thought ye should know 'bout it."

Leto looked over at Thufir Hawat, calling on the old warrior to use his Mentat skills. "A plankton bloom, Thufir?"

Hawat scowled, his mind racing, and then he nodded. "Likely killed off the seaweed, which is now rotting. Spreading disease among the fish."

Leto looked at the fisherman, who hurriedly covered his basket and held it behind his back to keep the smell far away from the Duke's chair. "Thank you, sir, for bringing this to our attention. We'll have to burn the dead kelp islands, maybe add some nutrients to the water to restore a proper plankton-and-algae balance."

"Sorry about the stink, m'Lord Duke." The fisherman fidgeted. One of Leto's guards took the basket and, holding it at arm's length, carried it outside the gates, where the sea breezes would absorb the odor.

"Without you, I might not have learned about the problem for weeks. You have our gratitude." Despite Caladan's excellent satellites and weather stations, Leto often learned information—more accurately and swiftly—through the people rather than these mechanisms.

The next woman wanted to give him her prize chicken. Then two men were disputing the boundaries of pundi rice fields and dickering over the value of an orchard lost by flood when a crumbling dike spilled water into the lowlands. An old lady presented Leto with a thick sweater she had knitted herself. Next, a proud father wanted Leto to touch the forehead of his newborn daughter. . . .

The business of being a Duke.

TESSIA EAVESDROPPED OUTSIDE the sitting area of the Castle apartment she shared with Rhombur, while Leto and the Prince discussed Imperial politics: the embarrassing vandalism of Corrino monuments, the declining health of Baron Harkonnen, the escalating and unpleasant conflict between Moritani and Ecaz (even with Sardaukar peacekeeping troops in place on Grumman), and the continued efforts of Leto's diplomatic corps to interject a note of reason to the situation.

The conversation eventually turned to the tragedies that had befallen House Vernius, how long it had been since the overthrow of Ix. Expressing resentment for this had become routine for Rhombur, though he never found the courage to take the next step toward reclaiming his birthright. Safe and content on Caladan, he had given up hoping for revenge . . . or at least had put it off for another, undetermined day.

By now, Tessia had had enough.

While still at the Mother School, she'd read thick files on House Vernius. Her knowledge of the history and politics of technology was a common interest with Rhombur. Even knowing all the Sisterhood's plans within plans, she felt as if she'd been made for him—and therefore obligated to nudge him into action. She hated to see him . . . *stuck*.

Wearing a floor-length black-and-yellow caliccee dress, Tessia placed a silver tray with flagons of dark beer on the table between the men. She spoke up, surprising them with her interruption. "I've already promised you my help, Rhombur. Unless you intend to do something about the injustice to your House, don't complain about it for another decade." Raising her chin arrogantly, Tessia spun about. "I, for one, don't want to hear it."

Leto saw the flash in her intense, wide-set eyes. In astonishment, he watched her leave the room with only a faint rustle of her dress. "Well, Rhombur, I expected a Bene Gesserit to be more . . . circumspect. Is she always so blunt?"

Rhombur looked stunned. He picked up his beer and swallowed a gulp. "How, in only a few weeks, did Tessia figure out exactly what I needed to hear?" A fire burned in his eyes, as if the concubine had merely provided the spark for the tinder that had been piling up inside him for so long. "Maybe you've been too kind all these years, Leto. Making me overly comfortable while my father stays in hiding, while my people remain enslaved." He blinked. "It's *not* going to turn out for the best all by itself, is it?"

Leto stared at him for a long moment. "No, my friend. No, it isn't."

Rhombur could not ask Leto to send massive forces on his behalf, because that would invite open warfare between House Atreides and the Bene Tleilax. Leto had already risked everything to prevent that from happening. Right now, he was just a piece of flotsam, without a purpose.

The Prince's face darkened with determination. "Maybe I ought to make a grand gesture, return to my homeworld, take a formal diplomatic frigate with a full escort—uh, I could rent one, I suppose—and land in the port-of-entry canyon on Ix. I'd publicly reclaim my name, demand that the Tleilaxu renounce their illegal seizure of our planet." He huffed. "What do you think they'd say to that?"

"Don't be foolish, Rhombur." Leto shook his head, wondering if his friend was serious or not. "They'd take you prisoner and perform medical experiments on your body. You'd end up in a dozen pieces and a dozen different axlotl tanks."

"Vermilion hells, Leto—what else am I going to do?" Distracted and disturbed, the Prince stood up. "If you will excuse me? I need to think." He trudged up a low riser to his private bedchamber and shut the door. Leto stared after his friend for a long moment, sipping his drink, before returning to his private study and the piled inventory documents awaiting his inspection and signature. . . .

Watching from an upstairs balcony, Tessia flitted down the winding stairs and slid open the bedroom door. Inside, she found Rhombur on the bed, staring at a picture of his parents on the wall. Kailea had painted it herself, longing for the days in the Grand Palais. In the picture, Dominic and Shando Vernius were dressed in full regalia, the bald Earl in a white uniform with purple-and-copper Ixian helixes adorning the collar, and she in a billowing lavender merh-silk gown.

Tessia massaged his shoulders. "It was wrong of me to embarrass you in front of the Duke. I'm sorry."

He saw the tenderness and compassion in her sepia gaze. "Why apologize? You're right, Tessia, though it's difficult for me to admit it. Maybe I'm ashamed. I *should* have done something to avenge my parents."

"To avenge all of your people—and to free them." She heaved an exasperated sigh. "Rhombur, my true Prince, do you want to be passive, defeated, and complacent . . . or triumphant? I'm trying to help you."

Rhombur felt her surprisingly strong hands working expertly at his knotted muscles, loosening them, warming them. Her touch was like a soothing drug, and he was tempted to sleep so that he could forget his troubles.

He shook his head. "I gave up without a fight, didn't I?"

The concubine's fingers worked down his spine to the small of his back, arousing him. "That doesn't mean you can't fight again."

WITH A DEEPLY puzzled expression, Kailea Vernius brought a shiny black packet to her brother. "It has our family crest on it, Rhombur. Just came from a Courier in Cala City."

His sister had green eyes and copper-dark hair held back by glazed-shell combs. Her face had grown into the lush beauty of womanhood with the soft edges of youth; she reminded Rhombur of their mother Shando, who had once been a concubine of Emperor Elrood's.

Perplexed, the Prince gazed at the helix on the package, but saw no other markings. Dressed in common, comfortable clothes, Tessia came up behind Rhombur while he used a small fishing knife to cut open the parcel. His brow wrinkled as he brought out a sheet of ridulian paper with lines, triangles, and dots on it. Then he caught his breath.

"It looks like a sub rosa message, an Ixian battle code written in a geometrical cipher."

Kailea pursed her lips. "Father taught me the complexities of business, but little of military matters. I didn't think I needed them."

"Can you decode it, my Prince?" Tessia asked in a voice that made Rhombur wonder if his Bene Gesserit concubine also had special translation skills.

He scratched his tousled blond hair, then reached for a notepad. "Uh, let me see. My tutor used to beat the codes into my head, but it's been years since I've thought about them." Rhombur sat cross-legged on the floor, then began scribbling the Galach alphabet in a scrambled order he'd memorized. He scratched out lines and recopied the pattern more carefully. With old memories coming back to him, he stared at the paper and his pulse quickened. Someone with inside knowledge had undoubtedly prepared this. But who?

Next Rhombur took a ruler and, measuring carefully, made a new sheet into a grid. Across the top, he wrote the scrambled alphabet, one letter inside each square, then added a pattern of coding dots. Placing the mysterious message next to his decryption sheet, he lined up dots with letters, then transcribed one word at a time. "Vermilion hells!"

Prince Rhombur Vernius, Rightful Earl of Ix: The Tleilaxu usurpers torture or execute our people for perceived infractions, then use the corpses for horrible experiments. Our young women are stolen in the darkness. Our industries remain overrun by invaders.

There is no justice for Ix—only memories, hopes, and slavery. We long for the day when House Vernius can crush the invaders and once again free us. With all due respect, we request your assistance. Please help us.

The note was signed by C'tair Pilru of the Freedom Fighters of Ix.

Rhombur leaped to his feet and hugged his sister. "It's the Ambassador's son—Kailea, do you remember?"

Eyes lit with half-forgotten happiness, she remembered how the dark-haired twins had flirted with her. "Nice-looking young man. His brother became a Guild Navigator, didn't he?"

Rhombur grew silent. For years he'd known such things were happening on his world, but he'd avoided thinking about it, hoping the problems would go away. How could he contact the rebels on Ix? As an exiled Prince without a House, how could he address the tragedy? He hadn't been willing to consider all the possibilities.

"Mark my words," Rhombur vowed. "I'm going to do something about this. My people have waited too long."

He pulled back from his sister, and his gaze moved around to Tessia, who stood watching him. "I'd like to help," she said. "You know that."

Rhombur drew his concubine and his sister to him in a great bear hug. Finally, he had a sense of purpose.

To learn about this universe, one must embark on a course of discovery where real dangers exist. Education cannot impart this discovery; it is not a thing to be taught and used or put away. It has no goals. In our universe, we consider goals to be end products, and they are deadly if one becomes fixated on them.

—FRIEDRE GINAZ,
Philosophy of the Swordmaster

TRANSPORT ORNITHOPTERS CARRIED THE GINAZ STUDENTS IN GROUPS, descending as they flew along the edge of a forbidding new island, beside black-lava cliffs worn slick over the centuries by cascading waterfalls. The mound of sharp rock rose out of the water like a rotten tooth, without jungles, without greenery, without apparent habitation. Surrounded by deep, treacherous water, the mountainous island—nameless, except for its military designation—lay at the eastern end of the archipelago.

"Ah look, another tropical paradise," Hiih Resser said, in a dry tone. Peering through one of the small portholes, crowded beside his classmates, Duncan Idaho knew this place would only hold new ordeals for all of them.

But he was ready.

The 'thopter gained altitude and flew up the windward side to the curving mouth of a steep crater. Smoke and ash still coughed out of vents, adding a heavy, hot pall to the humid air. The pilot circled around so they all could identify a single shining 'thopter landed on the crater rim; the small craft would be used in some part of their training, no doubt. Duncan could not guess what might be in store for them.

The 'thopter cruised to the base of the volcano, where jutting elbows of cracked reefs and steaming fumaroles formed their camp. Colorful self-erecting tents dotted flat surfaces of the lava rock, encircling a larger compound. No amenities whatsoever. When they landed, many of the students rushed out to choose their tents, but Duncan could not see how any one was preferable to another.

The tall Swordmaster waiting for them had leathery skin, a mane of thick gray hair that hung to the middle of his back, and haunting eyes set deeply into bony sockets. With a twinge of awe, Duncan recognized the legendary warrior, Mord Cour. As a child on Hagal, Cour had been the sole survivor of his massacred mining village; he'd lived as a feral boy in the forested cliffs, taught himself to fight, then infiltrated the bandit gang that had destroyed his village. After gaining their trust, he single-handedly slew the leader and all the bandits, then marched off to join the Emperor's Sardaukar. He had served as Elrood's personal Swordmaster for years before retiring to the academy on Ginaz.

After making them recite the Swordmaster's Pledge in unison, the legendary warrior said, "I have killed more people than any of you pups have ever met. Pray that you do not become one of them. If you learn from me, then I will have no excuse to slay you."

"I don't need any incentive to learn from *him*," Resser said to Duncan out of the corner of his mouth. The old man heard the muttered words and snapped his glance over to the red-headed student. In the back of the group, Trin Kronos, one of the other Grumman trainees (though much less friendly), snickered, then silenced himself.

As Mord Cour held Resser with his piercing gaze, waiting, Duncan cleared his throat and took one step forward. "Swordmaster Cour, he said that none of us needs an incentive to learn from a great man like you, sir." He gripped the hilt of the Old Duke's sword.

"No one requires an excuse to learn from a great man." Cour swiveled around to look at all the students. "You know why you are here? *Here*, on Ginaz, I mean?"

"Because this is where Jool-Noret started everything," the dark-skinned trainee from Al-Dhanab said promptly.

"Jool-Noret didn't do anything," Cour said, shocking them all. "He was a tremendous Swordmaster, skilled in ninety-three fighting methods. He knew about weapons, shields, tactics, and hand-to-hand combat. A dozen other skilled fighters followed him like disciples, begging Noret to teach them advanced skills, but the great fighter always refused, always put it off with the promise he would train them when the time was right. *And he never did!*

"One night a meteor struck the ocean offshore and sent a wave crashing into the island where Jool-Noret lived. The water flattened his hut and killed him in his sleep. It was all his followers could do to recover his body, that mummified relic they'll be proud to show you back on the administration island."

"But, sir, if Jool-Noret taught nothing, why was the Ginaz School founded in his name?" Resser said.

"Because his disciples vowed not to make the same mistake. Remembering all the skills they'd wanted to learn from Noret, they formed an academy where they could teach the best candidates all the fighting techniques they might require." The ash-choked breezes ruffled his hair. "So, are you all ready to learn how to become Swordmasters?"

The students answered with a resounding "Yes!"

Cour shook his long gray mane and smiled. The gusts of ocean wind sounded like sharp fingernails scraping the lava cliffs. "Good. We will begin with two weeks of studying poetry."

IN THE MINIMAL shelter of their colorful tents, the trainees slept on the rocks—cold during the night, baking hot during the day. Gray clouds of spewed ash blocked the sun. They sat without chairs, ate dried and salted food, drank tepid water that had been stored in old casks. Everything had an aftertaste of sulfur.

No one complained about the hardships. By then, Swordmaster trainees knew better.

In the rough environment, they learned about metaphors and verse. Even on ancient Terra, honor-bound samurai warriors had valued their prowess in composing haikus as much as they valued their skill with a blade.

When Mord Cour stood on a rock beside a steaming hot spring and recited ancient epics, the passion in his voice stirred the students' hearts. Finally, when the old man saw that he had made them all teary-eyed, he smiled and clapped his hands. Jumping down from the rock, Cour announced, "Success. Good, now it is time to learn fighting."

CLAD IN FLEXALLOY chain mail, Duncan rode astride an enormous armored turtle that kept snapping at its reins and its rider. Lashed into his saddle, legs spread to encompass the broad, plated shell, he balanced a wooden pike with a blunted metal tip. He held the shaft over one wrist and stared across at the three similarly armed opponents.

The fighting turtles were hatched from stolen eggs and raised in cove pens. The sluggish behemoths reminded Duncan of when he'd had to fight while wearing thick plate armor. But their horned jaws could slam shut like blast doors and, when they had a mind to, the turtles could lurch forward with hellish speed. Duncan could see from chipped and broken plates on the shells that these beasts were veterans of more combat than he had ever seen.

Duncan rapped his lance on the turtle's thick shell, thumping like a drummer. His beast stomped forward toward Hiih Resser's mount, thrashing its monstrous head from side to side and snapping at anything in reach.

"I'm coming to unseat you, Resser!" But Duncan's turtle chose that moment to stop, and no amount of urging could get it to move again. The other turtles wouldn't cooperate, either.

The turtle-joust was the ninth fighting event in a decathlon the students had to pass before they were admitted to the next level of the class. Through five grueling days breathing ash-thick air, Duncan had never placed lower than third—in swim-fighting, long-jumping, crossbows, slingshots, javelins, aerobic weightlifting, knife throwing, and tunnel-crawling. Throughout, standing on his high rock, Mord Cour had watched the proceedings.

Resser, who had become Duncan's friend and rival, also achieved a respectable score. The other Grumman students formed a clique of their own, clustering around the bullyish leader Trin Kronos, who seemed immensely full of himself and his heritage (though his demonstrated fighting abilities did not set him much apart from the others). Kronos crowed about his proud life serving House Moritani, but Resser rarely talked about his home or family. He was more interested in squeezing every bit of ability from Ginaz.

Each night, deep into the hours of darkness, Duncan and Resser would set to work in the base-tent library with a pile of filmbooks. Ginaz students were expected to learn military history, battle strategies, and personal fighting techniques. Mord Cour had also impressed upon them the study of ethics, litera-ture, philosophy, and meditation . . . all the things he had not been able to learn as a feral boy in the forested cliffs of Hagal.

In evening sessions with the Swordmasters, Duncan Idaho had memorized the Great Convention, whose rules for armed conflict formed the basis of Imperial civilization following the Butlerian Jihad. Out of such moral and ethical thinking, Ginaz had formulated the Code of the Warrior.

Now, while struggling to control his curmudgeonly turtle,

Duncan rubbed his red eyes and coughed. His nostrils burned from the ash in the air and his throat felt scratchy. Around him, the ocean roared against the rocks; fumaroles hissed and spat rotten-egg stink into the air.

After constant, ineffective prodding, Resser's turtle finally lunged forward, and the redhead had all he could do to remain seated and keep his blunted lance pointed in the right direction. Soon all the turtles began to move, lumbering together in a slow-motion frenzy.

Duncan dodged simultaneous pike thrusts from Resser and the second opponent, and struck out at the third with the butt of his own weapon. The blunt end of the lance bashed the student squarely on the chest armor, sending him sprawling. The downed trainee landed heavily on the rough ground, then rolled out of the way to avoid the snapping turtles.

Duncan flattened himself against the shell of his mount, evading another thrust from Resser. Then Duncan's turtle halted in its tracks to defecate—which took a long time.

Glancing around, helpless in his saddle, Duncan saw the remaining mounted adversary go after Resser, who defended himself admirably. While his turtle completed its business, Duncan waited for precisely the right moment, positioning himself to one side on the hard shell, as near to the combatants as he could get. Just as Resser countered with his own weapon and knocked down the other combatant, he raised his lance in a show of triumph—as Duncan knew he would. At that very moment, Duncan reached over and slammed his pike into the redhead's side, tumbling Resser off the turtle. Only Duncan Idaho remained, the victor.

He dismounted, then helped Resser climb to his feet and brushed sand from his chest and legs. A moment later Duncan's turtle finally began to move, lumbering about in search of something to eat.

———

"YOUR BODY IS your greatest weapon," Mord Cour said. "Before you can be trusted with a sword in battle, you must learn to trust your body."

"But Master, you taught us the *mind* is our greatest weapon," Duncan interrupted.

"Body and mind are one," Cour responded, his voice as sharp as his blade. "What is one without the other? The mind controls the body, the body controls the mind." He strutted along the rugged beach, sharp rocks crunching under his callused feet. "Strip off your clothes, all of you— down to your shorts! Take off your shoes. Leave all weapons on the ground."

Without questioning orders, the students peeled off their clothing. Gray ash continued to fall around them, and brimstone gases sighed up from fumaroles like hell's breath.

"After this final test, you can all be quit of me, and of this island." Mord Cour pursed his lips in a stern expression. "Your next destination has a few more flowers and amenities." Some of the students gave a ragged cheer, tinged with uneasiness about the ordeal they were soon to face.

"Since all of you passed a 'thopter-pilot competency test before coming to Ginaz, I'll keep my explanation brief." Cour gestured up the steep slope to the high crater lip, surrounded in hazy gray murk. "A craft awaits you on top. You saw it on your way in. The first to reach it can fly away to your clean and comfortable new barracks. Coordinates are already locked into the piloting console. The rest of you . . . will walk back down the mountain and camp here on the rocks again, without tents and without food." He narrowed the eyes on his ancient face. "Now, go!"

The students raced forward, using their energy reserves to get a head start. Although Duncan wasn't the fastest student off the mark, he chose his route more carefully. Steep cliff bands blocked some paths halfway up the sheer cone, while other couloirs tapered off to dead ends before reaching the top. Some gullies looked tempting, but thin streams and waterfalls promised a slippery, uncertain ascent. Upon seeing the 'thopter high up on the crater rim during their initial approach, he'd studied the slope with avid interest, preparing himself. Now he drew upon everything he had observed. And he started up.

As the terrain steepened, Duncan gained on those ahead of him, skillfully choosing gullies or couloirs, scrambling up rugged, knobby conglomerate rock while others got sidetracked into easy-looking gravel chutes that crumbled beneath their feet and sent them tumbling back down. He ran along connecting ridges and rounded shoulders that did not lead directly to the top but provided easier ground and permitted a faster ascent.

Years ago, when he'd raced for survival in the rugged Forest Guard Preserve on Giedi Prime, Rabban had tried to hunt him down. By comparison, this was easy.

The rough lava rock was sharp beneath Duncan's bare feet, but he had an advantage over most of his fellow students: calluses developed by years of walking without shoes on the beaches of Caladan.

He skirted a hot spring and climbed a fissure that gave him precarious hand- and footholds. He had to wedge himself into the crack, searching for protrusions and crannies he could use to haul himself up another body length. Some of the rotten rock broke loose and tumbled.

Elsewhere, he had no doubt that Trin Kronos and some of the other self-centered candidates would be doing their best to sabotage the competition, rather than focusing on increasing their own pace.

By sunset he reached the lip of the volcano—the first in his class. He had run without resting, climbed dangerous scree slopes, chosen his route carefully but without hesitation. With other competitors not far behind him, coming up all sides of the cone, he leaped over a steam vent and ran for the waiting ornithopter.

As soon as he spotted the craft, he looked over his shoulder to see Hiih Resser stumble up close behind him. The redhead's skin was scratched and covered with ash. "Hey, Duncan!" The air was thick with fumes and dust belched out from the crater. The volcano rumbled.

Close to victory, Duncan put on a burst of speed, closing the distance to the 'thopter. Resser, seeing he had no chance of winning, dropped back, panting, and gracefully acknowledged his friend's victory.

At the crater's far rim, Trin Kronos pulled himself up from an alternate route, his face flushed and angry at seeing Duncan so close to the waiting 'thopter. When he saw Resser, his fellow Grumman student, stagger to a breathless halt and concede, Kronos looked even more furious. Though they came from the same world, Kronos often went out of his way to express scorn for Resser, to humiliate the redhead and make his life miserable.

In this class, it was survival of the fittest, and many of the students had developed an intense dislike for each other. Just watching the way Kronos harassed his fellow Grumman trainee, Duncan had formed a harsh opinion of the spoiled son of a nobleman. Once Duncan flew off in the 'thopter, Kronos would probably wait for his Grumman friends, and they would pummel Resser to vent their own frustrations.

As Duncan placed one foot in the empty craft, he reached a decision. "Hiih Resser! If you can get here before I strap in and take off, I'm sure the 'thopter will carry two of us."

Farther away, Trin Kronos put on a burst of speed.

Duncan snapped on his safety harness, touched the retractor bar to shorten the wings for jet-boost takeoff, while Resser stared in disbelief. "Come on!"

Grinning, the redhead found new energy. He sprinted forward as Duncan slid the starter switch into position. In his years of service to the Duke, he'd been taught to fly by some of the best pilots in the Imperium. Now he went through the motions smoothly.

Railing against Duncan's decision to break the rules, Kronos raced forward, his feet kicking up broken rock. The 'thopter's instrument panel flashed on. An illuminated orange box told Duncan the jetpods were armed, and he heard the low, powerful hiss of the turbines.

Resser leaped onto the 'thopter skids just as Duncan raised the vehicle with the jet assists. Panting, the redhead grabbed the edge of the cockpit door and held on. He gulped in lungfuls of air.

Seeing he would never make it to the vessel, Trin Kronos stooped to snatch up a jagged, fist-sized lava rock and threw it, striking Resser's exposed hip.

Duncan depressed a glowing action-sequence button, and the wings snapped up and down, climbing high above the lava cap of the volcano. The jetpods kicked in, and the wings went into lift attitude. He let up on the power. Resser hauled himself all the way inside in a tangle of arms and legs. Wheezing and out of breath, he wedged himself into the meager open space beside Duncan in the cockpit and began to laugh.

The wind of the ornithopter's beating wings blasted the disappointed Kronos. Left behind, the young man hurled another rock, which bounced harmlessly off the plaz window-shield.

Duncan waved cheerfully and tossed Kronos a handlight from the 'thopter's supply kit. The Grumman caught it, expressing no gratitude for the assistance in the growing dark. Far behind him, the other students, fatigued and aching, would return to camp on foot to spend a miserable, cold night out in the open.

Duncan boosted power, extended the wings to their fullest setting. The sun sank below the horizon, leaving a red-orange glow across the water. Darkness began to fall like a heavy curtain over the string of islands to the west.

"Why did you do that for me?" Resser asked, wiping sweat off his brow. "This was supposed to be a solo test. The Swordmasters certainly didn't teach us to help each other."

"No," Duncan said with a smile. "It's something I learned from the Atreides."

He adjusted the instrument panel illumination to a lambent glow, and flew by starlight to the coordinates of their next island.

Never underestimate the power of the human mind to believe what it wants to believe, no matter the conflicting evidence.

—CAEDMON ERB,
Politics and Reality

IN AN EFFORT TO UNDERSTAND HOW THE SISTERHOOD HAD SHORT-circuited his demands, the Baron and Piter de Vries huddled in the metal-walled conference room of the Harkonnen military frigate. The ship orbited Wallach IX, weapons ready . . . but with no target. For two days, hourly comlink messages had been sent to the Bene Gesserit, without any response.

For once the Mentat had no answers as to where or how the witches had hidden; no probabilities, projections, or summations. He had failed. The Baron, who accepted no excuses for failure (and de Vries *had* failed him), was prepared to kill someone in a most unpleasant manner.

Feeling like an outsider, a brooding Glossu Rabban sat to one side watching them, wishing he could offer some insight. "They're witches after all, aren't they?" he finally said, but no one seemed interested in the comment. No one ever listened to his ideas.

Disgusted, Rabban left the conference room, knowing his uncle was glad to see him go. Why were they even *discussing* the situation? Rabban couldn't tolerate sitting around, getting nowhere. It made them all appear weak.

As the Baron's heir-presumptive, Rabban thought he had done well for House Harkonnen. He'd overseen spice operations on Arrakis, had even launched the first surreptitious strike in what should have been an all-out Atreides-Tleilaxu war. Time and time again he had proven himself, but the Baron always treated him as if he were slow-witted, even calling him "a muscle-minded tank brain" to his face.

If they had let me go down to the witches' school, I could have smelled them out.

Rabban knew exactly what needed to be done. He also knew better than to ask permission. The Baron would only say no . . . and the Baron would be wrong to deny him. Rabban would solve the problem himself and claim his reward. At long last his uncle would see his capability.

In heavy black boots, the burly man strode through the frigate corridors, intent on his mission. Around him the armed ship droned along in the silent embrace of gravity. He heard snatches of conversation as he passed cabins and duty stations. Men in blue uniforms hurried by, performing their duties, always deferential to him.

When he gave his command, the men dropped their tasks and hurried to slide open a bulkhead wall. Rabban stood with his hands on his hips, satisfied to gaze upon the hidden chamber that held a sleek, highly polished vessel, a one-man war-craft.

The experimental no-ship.

He had flown the invisible fighter inside a Guild Heighliner more than a decade ago, and the ship had performed its duty impeccably . . . completely silent and unseen. His pilotry had been flawless, though the scheme had ultimately failed. Too much planning had been the fatal error before. And Leto Atreides—damn him—had refused to behave as expected.

This time, though, Rabban's plan would be simple and direct. The ship and its contents were invisible. He could go anywhere, observe anything—and no one would suspect. He would spy on what the witches were up to, and then he could wipe out the entire Mother School if he wished.

He engaged the whisper-quiet engines of the attack craft,

and it dropped through the bottom of the orbiting frigate. With increasing anticipation, Rabban activated the no-field generator—and the ship vanished in open space.

During his descent toward the planet, all ship's systems functioned properly. The glitches from recent test flights had been repaired. High over a range of grass-covered hills, he banked toward the stucco and sienna-roofed buildings of the Mother School. So, the witches thought they could just disappear when the Baron demanded an audience? Were they snickering at their own cleverness? Now, the witches refused to answer repeated demands for a conference. How long did they imagine they could avoid the issue?

Touching a sensor button, Rabban armed the weapons. A massive, unexpected strike would engulf libraries and rectories and museums in flames, leveling them all to rubble.

That'll get their attention.

He wondered if the Baron had even discovered his departure yet.

As the silent craft swooped toward the school complex, he saw shifting crowds of women outside the clustered buildings, foolishly confident that they no longer needed to hide. The witches thought they could thumb their noses at House Harkonnen.

Rabban cruised lower. His weapons system grew hot; targeting screens glowed. Before he wrecked the main buildings, perhaps he would pick off a few of the vulturelike females one at a time, just for sport. With his silent and unseen ship, it would seem like a fiery finger of God striking them down for their arrogance. The no-ship came into range.

Suddenly the witches all looked up at him.

He felt something press against his mind. As he watched, the women shimmered and vanished. Then his vision blurred, and he felt his head throbbing . . . *hurting*. He pushed a hand against his temple, trying to focus. But the pressure within his skull increased like a bull elephant rampaging against his forehead.

Below, the images shimmered. The crowds of Bene Gesserit flickered into view again, then dissolved into afterimages. The buildings, the landmarks, the planetary surface, all wavered. Rabban could barely see the controls.

Disoriented, his head splitting with agony, Rabban grasped the piloting console. The no-ship squirmed like a living thing beneath him, and the vessel went into a spin. Rabban let out a gargling, befuddled cry, not even realizing his danger until crash-foam and restraint webbing slammed around him.

The no-ship caromed into an apple orchard, ripping a long brown furrow across the ground, then tumbled over onto its back. After a groaning pause, the ruined craft skidded down an embankment and into a shallow creek.

The mangled engines caught fire, and greasy blue smoke filled the cockpit. Rabban heard the hiss of fire-suppression systems as he clawed himself free of the foam and protective restraints.

Choking on bitter smoke, blinking acid tears from his eyes, Rabban activated an escape hatch in the belly of the ship and crawled from the wreckage. He tumbled off the hot, slippery metal and landed on his hands and knees in the steaming water of the creek. Befuddled, he shook his head. Looking back at the no-ship, he saw that its hull flickered in and out of visibility.

Behind him, women swarmed down the embankment, like black-robed locusts. . . .

WHEN BARON HARKONNEN received the unexpected comlink message from Mother Superior Harishka, he wanted to strangle her. For days, his shouts and threats had gone unanswered. Now, though, as he paced the floor of the frigate's command bridge, the old crone initiated contact herself. She appeared on the oval system screen.

"I'm sorry I wasn't available when you visited, Baron, and I apologize that our comsystems were down. I know that you have something to discuss with me." Her tone was maddeningly pleasant. "But I wonder if you might like to have your nephew returned first?"

Seeing her thin lips smile beneath those evil almond eyes, he knew his corpulent face must reflect his utter confusion. He spun to look at his troop captain, then at Piter de Vries. "Where is Rabban?" Both men shook their heads, as surprised as he was. "Bring me Rabban!"

Mother Superior gestured, and a few Sisters brought the burly man into view on the screen. Despite bloody scrapes and gashes on his face, Rabban appeared defiant. One of his arms hung limp at his side; his trousers were ripped at the knees, revealing jagged wounds beneath.

The Baron cursed under his breath. *What has that idiot done now?*

"He suffered some sort of mechanical malfunction in his vessel. Was he coming to visit us, I wonder? Perhaps to spy . . . or even to attack?" Next, a video image of the wrecked no-ship appeared on the screen, still smoldering at the edge of a ruined orchard. "He was flying a most interesting craft. Note how it phases in and out of view. Some sort of a damaged invisibility mechanism? Most ingenious."

The Baron's eyes nearly bulged out of his head. *Gods below, we've lost the no-ship, too!* Not only had his stupid nephew been caught by the Sisterhood, he had let the no-ship—the Harkonnens' most powerful secret weapon—fall into the hands of the witches.

Moving silently, Piter de Vries whispered in his ear, trying to calm him. "Take slow, deep breaths, my Baron. Would you like me to continue negotiations with the Mother Superior?"

With a supreme effort, the Baron composed himself, then

stepped away and turned back to the screen. He would deal with Rabban later. "My nephew is a complete dolt. He did not have my permission to take the ship."

"A convenient explanation."

"I assure you he will be severely punished for his brash actions. Of course we will also pay for any damages he caused to your school." He grimaced, chagrined at how easily he had conceded defeat.

"A few apple trees. No reason to file a claim . . . or report to the Landsraad—if you cooperate."

"Cooperate!" His nostrils flared, and he reeled backward, nearly losing his balance. *He* had evidence against *them*. "And would your report include a summary of how your Reverend Mother unleashed a biological weapon upon my person, in violation of the Great Convention?"

"Actually, our report would include a bit of speculation," Harishka said with a vise-tight smile. "You may recall an interesting incident a few years back when two Tleilaxu vessels were mysteriously fired upon inside a Guild Heighliner. Duke Leto Atreides was accused of the atrocity, but denied the charges—which seemed preposterous at the time, since no other ship was nearby. No *visible* ship, at least. We have confirmed that there was also a Harkonnen frigate in the vicinity, en route to Emperor Shaddam's coronation."

The Baron forced himself to remain motionless. "You have no proof."

"We have the *ship*, Baron." The image of the flickering wreckage appeared on the screen again. "Any competent court would come to the same conclusion. The Tleilaxu and the Atreides will be most interested in this development. Not to mention the Spacing Guild."

Piter de Vries looked from the Baron to the comscreen, wheels turning in his intricate mind, but he could find no acceptable solution.

"You're talking yourself into a death sentence, witch," the

Baron said in a low growl. "We have proof that the Bene Gesserit unleashed a harmful biological agent. One word from me, and—"

"And we have proof of something else, don't we?" Harishka said. "What do you think, Baron—do two proofs cancel each other out? Or is our proof far more interesting?"

"Provide me with the cure for my disease, and I'll consider withdrawing my accusations."

On the screen Harishka looked at him wryly. "My dear Baron, there is no cure. The Bene Gesserit use permanent measures. Nothing can be reversed." She seemed mockingly sympathetic. "On the other hand, if you keep our secrets, we will keep yours. And you may have your troublesome nephew back—before we do anything else that might be *irreversible*."

De Vries interrupted, knowing the Baron was about to explode. "In addition, we insist on the return of our crashed vessel." They could not allow the Sisterhood access to the no-field technology, though the Harkonnens themselves did not understand it.

"Impossible. No civilized person would want to see such an attack craft repaired. For the sake of the Imperium, we must take steps to arrest the development of this deadly technology."

"We have other ships!" the Baron said.

"She is a Truthsayer, my Baron," de Vries whispered. The old Bene Gesserit looked at them deprecatingly while the Baron sweated for a better response.

"What will you do with the wreckage?" The Baron clenched his fists together so hard that his knuckles cracked.

"Why . . . make it disappear, of course."

WHEN RABBAN RETURNED, the Baron gave him a cane thrashing and locked him in his stateroom for the duration of the trip back to Giedi Prime. Despite all his foolish impulsiveness, the

burly man remained the heir-presumptive of House Harkonnen.

For now.

The Baron paced the floor and pounded on the walls, trying to imagine the worst punishment he could inflict upon his
nephew, an appropriate penalty for the incredible damage
Rabban's clumsy attack had caused. Finally, it came to him,
and he smiled tightly.

Immediately upon returning home, Glossu Rabban was
sent to the remote planet of Lankiveil, where he would live
with his weakling father Abulurd.

It is the Atreides way to be examples of honor for our children, so that they may be the same for their own progeny.

—DUKE LETO ATREIDES,
First Speech to the Caladan Assembly

EIGHTEEN MONTHS HAD PASSED.

A full moon bathed Castle Caladan in silver, casting shadows of the turrets along the edge of the cliff that over-looked a troubled sea. From his discreet vantage in the ornamental garden, Thufir Hawat saw Duke Leto and Kailea Vernius strolling along the verge of the precipice, star-crossed lovers.

She had been his official, but unbound, concubine for more than a year, and sometimes the two enjoyed quiet, romantic moments like this one. Leto was in no hurry to accept any of the numerous offers of marriage alliances that came to him from other Houses of the Landsraad.

Hawat's constant surveillance irritated the Duke, who demanded some measure of privacy. But as Security Commander of House Atreides, the Mentat did not care. Leto had a troubling tendency to place himself in vulnerable positions, to be too trusting of the people around him. Hawat would rather incur his Duke's disfavor by being too attentive than allow a fatal mistake to slip past his scrutiny. Duke Paulus had died in the bullring because Hawat hadn't watched closely enough. He vowed never to make such an error again.

As Leto and Kailea walked in the chill night, Hawat worried that the trail was too narrow, too close to a deadly drop into the rocky surf. Leto refused to permit guardrails. He wanted the path exactly as his father had left it, since the Old Duke had also walked along the headlands, pondering problems of state. It was a matter of tradition, and the Atreides were brave men.

Hawat scanned the darkness with infrared glasses, saw no movement in the shadows other than his own troopers stationed on the trail and along the base of the rock face. With a tiny blacklight he signaled two of the men to take different positions.

He had to be constantly on the alert.

Leto held Kailea's hand and looked at her delicate features and her dark copper hair blowing in the night breeze. Her coat collar was turned up around her slender neck. As stunningly beautiful as any lady of the Imperium, Rhombur's sister carried herself like an Empress. But Leto could never marry her. He must remain true to traditions, as his father had done, and his grandfather before that. The course of honor . . . and political expediency.

However, no one, not even the ghost of Paulus Atreides, could argue against such a union if the fortunes of House Vernius were ever restored. For months, with Leto's wholehearted support, Rhombur had secretly been sending modest funds and other resources to C'tair Pilru and the Freedom Fighters of Ix through surreptitious channels, and he had received bits of information in return, schedules, surveillance images. Now that he had taken some action at last, Rhombur seemed more vital and alive than he'd been in a long time.

Pausing at the top of the trail that led down to the beach, Leto smiled, knowing Hawat was somewhere nearby, as always. He turned to the woman beside him. "Caladan has been my home since childhood, Kailea, and to me it is always beautiful. But I can see you're not really happy here." A nightgull flew up into the air, startling them with its thin screams.

"It's not your fault, Leto. You've already done so much for

my brother and me." Kailea didn't look at him. "This just isn't . . . where I had imagined I would be."

Knowing her dreams, he said, "I wish I could take you to Kaitain more often, so that you might enjoy the Imperial Court. I've seen how you light up at gala events. You're so radiant that it makes me sad having to bring you back to Caladan. It isn't glamorous here, not the life you were accustomed to." The words were an apology for all the things he could not offer her—the luxury, the prestige, the legitimacy of belonging to a Great House again. He wondered if she understood the sense of duty that bound him.

Kailea's soft voice sounded uncertain; she had seemed nervous all afternoon. She paused on the path. "Ix is gone, Leto, and all the glamour with it. I have accepted that." They turned to gaze in silence upon the night-black ocean before she spoke again. "Rhombur's rebels can never overthrow the Tleilaxu, can they?"

"We know too little about what's really going on there. Reports are scattered. You think he's better off not trying?" Leto looked hard at her with his smoke-gray eyes, trying to understand her anxiety. "Miracles can happen."

She seized the opening she had been waiting for. "Miracles, yes. And now I have one to tell you, my Duke." He looked at her with a blank expression. Kailea's lips curved in a complex smile. "I am going to have your child."

Stunned, he froze in place. Far out at sea, a pod of murmons sang a deep song as a counterpoint to throbbing sonic buoys that marked the treacherous reefs. Then, slowly leaning down, Leto kissed Kailea, felt the familiar moistness of her mouth.

"Are you pleased?" She sounded very fragile. "I didn't try to conceive. It just happened."

He stepped away from Kailea, held her at arm's length so he could study her face. "Of course!" He touched her stomach gently. "I've imagined having a son."

"Perhaps now would be a good time for me to consider obtaining another lady-in-waiting?" Kailea asked, anxiously. "I'll need assistance in preparing for childbirth—not to mention help with the baby when it is born."

He hugged her with strong arms. "If you want another lady-in-waiting, then you shall have her." Thufir Hawat would check out any candidates for the Atreides household with his usual thoroughness. "I'll get you ten if you wish!"

"Thank you, Leto." She stood on her toes to kiss his cheek. "But one should be sufficient."

DUST AND HEAT hung over everything. Hoping that the dry climate might help his condition, Baron Harkonnen spent more time on Arrakis. But he still felt miserable.

In his Carthag workroom, the Baron reviewed spice-harvesting reports, trying to concoct new ways to conceal earnings from the Emperor, from CHOAM, from the Spacing Guild. Owing to his increasing bulk, the desk had been customized with a cutout to accommodate his belly. His flaccid arms rested on the gritty desktop.

A year and a half ago, the Bene Gesserit had brought him to an impasse, with threats and counterthreats, blackmail in both directions. Rabban had lost their no-ship. He and the witches had remained at a safe but uneasy distance from each other.

Still, the wounds rankled, and he grew weaker—and fatter—every day.

His scientists had been trying to build another no-ship, without the assistance of the Richesian genius Chobyn, whom Rabban had slain. The Baron saw red every time he thought of his nephew's numerous blunders.

Plans and holorecordings of the original construction process had been flawed, or so the Baron's scientists claimed. As a result, their first new prototype had crashed into the obsidian slopes of Mount Ebony, killing the entire crew. *Serves them right*.

The Baron wondered if he would prefer a sudden death like that to torturous debilitation and decay. He had poured an enormous amount of solaris into a state-of-the-art medical research facility on Giedi Prime, with the grudging, part-time assistance of the Richesian Suk doctor Wellington Yueh, who was still more interested in his cyborg research than in finding ways to help the suffering Baron. The Richesian Premier still hadn't sent him a bill for the services, but the Baron didn't care.

Despite all this effort, there had been no results, and continued threats didn't seem to help. For the Baron, the simple act of walking, which he'd once done so effortlessly and with such grace, was now a major task. Soon the wormhead cane would not be enough.

"I have news of an interesting development, my Baron," Piter de Vries said, gliding into the dusty Carthag offices.

He frowned at the interruption. The gaunt Mentat, wearing a pale blue robe, hid his sapho-stained smile. "The concubine of Duke Leto Atreides has sent inquiries to the Imperial Court, seeking the services of a personal lady-in-waiting. I came to inform you as soon as I was able. However, because of the urgency involved, I . . . took the liberty of setting a plan in motion."

The Baron raised his eyebrows. "Oh? And what is this interesting plan that you felt needed no approval from me?"

"There is a certain matron living in the household of Suuwok Hesban, the son of Elrood's former Court Chamberlain Aken Hesban. For some time now, she has provided us with excellent information on the Hesban family. At my instigation, this matron, Chiara Rash-Olin, has let it be known that she is interested in the Atreides position, and is to be interviewed on Caladan."

"Inside the Atreides household?" the fat man said. He saw a

rafty smile form on the slender Mentat's face, which mir-
ored the Baron's own delight. "That provides some . . . inter-
sting opportunities."

KAILEA WAITED IN the lobby of the Cala Municipal Spaceport,
pacing a floor of embedded seashells and limestone fossils. Behind her stood dashing Captain Swain Goire, whom Leto had
assigned as her personal bodyguard. The guard's dark hair and
lean features reminded her of Leto's own.

She was early for the arriving shuttle and its passenger
from Kaitain. She had already met Chiara, interviewing the
matronly woman here on Caladan. The new lady-in-waiting
came with impeccable references, had even worked for the
family of Emperor Elrood's personal Chamberlain. She was
able to tell endless stories about the splendid court life on Kaitain. Kailea had accepted her immediately.

Why an intelligent old woman would ever want to leave
the Imperial capital for the comparative backwater of Caladan, she could not understand. "Oh, but I love the sea. And
I love the peace," Chiara had answered. "When you get older,
lovely child, you may feel the same way."

Kailea doubted that, but could hardly contain her excitement at the good fortune in finding this woman. She had
waited anxiously while Thufir Hawat inspected Chiara Rash-
Olin's past, questioned her about previous years of service.
Even the old Mentat had been unable to find fault with her
background.

As her pregnancy progressed, Kailea had counted the days
until Chiara began to fulfill her duties. On the day of the
scheduled arrival, Leto was holding court in Castle Caladan,
listening to the complaints and disputes of his people, but Kailea had departed early for the nearby airfield, which was dotted with skyclippers, 'thopters, and other aircraft.

With barely restrained anticipation, Kailea studied the

large spaceport building, marking details she hadn't noticed before. The original bulbous shape had been modified with interior moldings, modern windows, and decorations. But it still looked old and quaint, unlike the marvelous architecture of Kaitain.

She heard an atmospheric *thump*, felt it even through the floor. A streak of blue-orange light broke through the cloud cover from the supersonic descent of the bullet-shaped lighter. The small vessel slowed abruptly on high-powered suspensors, then came to a gentle perch on the field. Shields pulsed, flicked off.

"Precisely on time," Swain Goire said beside her. The handsome captain stood straight and tall, like a hero from a film-book. "The Guild prides itself on punctuality."

"Not soon enough for me." Kailea hurried forward to meet the disembarking passengers.

Chiara chose not to dress the part of a servant. Over her plump form she wore a traveling suit of comfortable zeetwill, and her iron-gray hair was coiffed into an elegant swirl, capped with a jeweled beret. Her pink cheeks glowed.

"What a pleasure to see you again, dear," Chiara purred. She breathed deeply of the moist, salty air. Behind her trailed eight suspensor-borne trunks, bulging at their clasps.

With a glance at Kailea's barely rounded belly and then into her green eyes, she commented, "It must be a routine pregnancy so far. You're looking well, my dear. A little peaked, perhaps, but I have remedies for that."

Kailea beamed. At last she had an intelligent companion, someone with Imperial sophistication to help her with the troubling details—household matters and business decisions required by her demanding, though loving, Duke.

Walking beside the old lady-in-waiting, Kailea asked the foremost question on her mind. "What's the latest from the Imperial Court?"

"Oh, my dear! There is so much to tell you."

It is true that one may become rich through practicing evil, but the power of Truth and Justice is that they endure . . . and that a man can say of them, "They are a heritage from my father."

—Fifth Dynasty (Old Terra) calendar
The Wisdom of Ptahhotep

AS FAR AS RABBAN WAS CONCERNED, HIS UNCLE COULD NOT HAVE CON-ceived a more cruel punishment for the no-ship debacle. At least Arrakis was warm and had clear skies, and Giedi Prime offered all the comforts of civilization.

Lankiveil was just . . . miserable.

Time dragged at such a pace that Rabban found himself appreciating the geriatric benefits of melange. He would have to live longer than a normal life span just to make up for all this abysmally wasted time. . . .

He had absolutely no interest in the isolated monastic fortresses deep in the mountains. Likewise, he refused to go to the villages that dotted the convoluted fjords: They held nothing but smelly fishermen, native hunters, and a few vegetable growers who found fertile land in the cracks of the steep black mountains.

Rabban spent most of his time on the largest island in the north, close to the glacial ice sheet and far from the swimming lanes of the Bjondax fur whales. It was not civilization by any standard, but at least it had factories, processing plants, and a spaceport to send loads of whale fur to orbit. There, he could be with people who understood that resources and raw materials existed for the benefit of whatever House owned them.

He lived in CHOAM company barracks and commandeered several large rooms for himself. Though he occasionally gambled with the other contract workers, he spent most of his time brooding and thinking of ways to change his life as soon as he returned to Giedi Prime. On other occasions, Rabban used an inkvine whip he had acquired from a Harkonnen employee, and occupied himself by thrashing the twisted black strands at rocks, ice chunks, or sluggish ra-seals sunning themselves on the metal piers. But that, too, grew boring.

For most of his two-year sentence, he stayed away from Abulurd and Emmi Rabban-Harkonnen, hoping they would never learn of his exile. Finally, when Rabban could hide his presence no longer, his father traveled up to the CHOAM processing centers, ostensibly on an inspection tour.

Abulurd met his son in the barracks building with an optimistic expression on his hangdog face as if he expected some kind of teary-eyed reunion. He embraced his only son, and Rabban broke away quickly.

Glossu Rabban, with square shoulders and a blocky face, heavy lips and a widow's peak, took after his mother more than his father, who had thin arms, bony elbows, and big knuckles. Abulurd's ash-blond hair looked old and dirty, and his face was weathered from being outside too much.

The only way Rabban got his father to leave, after hours of inane jabbering, was to promise that he would indeed come down to Tula Fjord and stay with his parents. A week later, he arrived at the main lodge, smelling the sour air, feeling the clamminess sink into his bones. Enduring their coddling, Rabban swallowed his disgust and counted the days until he could meet the Heighliner that would take him home.

In the lodge they ate elaborate meals of smoked fish, boiled clabsters, seafood paella, snow mussels and clams, pickled squid, and salted *ruh*-caviar, accompanied by the bitter, stringy vegetables that survived in Lankiveil's poor soil. The fishwife, a broad-faced woman with red hands and massive arms,

cooked one dish after another, proudly serving each one to
Rabban. She had known him as a child, had tried to spoil him,
and now she did everything but pinch his cheeks. Rabban
hated her for it.

He couldn't seem to get the foul tastes out of his mouth, or
the odors from his fingers or clothes. Only pungent wood-
smoke from the great fireplaces managed to relieve his anguished nose. His father found it quaint to use real fire instead
of thermal heaters or radiant globes. . . .

One night, bored and brooding, Rabban latched upon an
idea, his first imaginative spark in two years. The Bjondax
whales were docile and easily killed—and Rabban felt he could
interest wealthy nobles from Great and Minor Houses in coming to Lankiveil. He remembered how much joy he had taken
in hunting feral children at Forest Guard Preserve, how thrilled
he had been to kill a great sandworm on Arrakis. Perhaps he
could start a new whale-hunting industry, pursuing the enormous aquatic beasts for sport. It would add profit to the Harkonnen treasury and turn Lankiveil into something better
than the primitive hellhole it was now.

Even the Baron would be pleased.

Two nights before he was due to depart for home, he suggested the idea to his parents. Like an ideal family, they sat
together at table eating another meal from the sea. Abulurd
and Emmi kept looking at each other with pathetic sighs of
contentment. His ebony-eyed mother didn't speak much, but
she provided unwavering support to her husband. They
touched affectionately, brushed a hand from one shoulder to
an elbow.

"I plan to bring some big-game hunters to Lankiveil." Rabban sipped a watery glass of sweet mountain wine. "We'll
track down the fur whales—your native fishermen can act as
guides. Many people in the Landsraad would pay handsomely
for such a trophy. It'll be a boon to all of us."

Emmi blinked and looked over to see Abulurd's mouth

drop open in shock. She let him say what they were both thinking. "That would be impossible, son."

Rabban flinched at the offhand way this weakling called him *son*. Abulurd explained, "All you've seen are the processing docks up in the north, the final step in the whale fur business. But hunting proper specimens is a delicate task, done with care and training. I've been on the boats many times, and believe me, it's not a lighthearted task! Killing Bjondax whales was never meant for . . . sport."

Rabban's thick lips twisted. "And why not? If you're the planetary governor here, you're supposed to understand economics."

His mother shook her head. "Your father understands this planet better than you do. We just can't allow it." She seemed surrounded by an impenetrable veil of self-assurance, as if nothing could shake her.

Rabban simmered in his chair, more disgusted than angry. These people had no right to forbid him anything. He was the nephew of Baron Vladimir Harkonnen, the heir-apparent of a Great House. Abulurd had already proven he couldn't handle the responsibility. No one would listen to a failure's complaints.

Rabban pushed himself away from the table and stalked off to his suite. There, in a bowl made from an abalone shell, the house servants had arranged clumps of sweet-smelling lichens peeled from tree bark, a typical Lankiveil bouquet. With a swat, Rabban knocked it aside, shattering the shell on the weathered-plank floor.

THE ABRASIVE SOUNDS of Bjondax whale songs awoke him from a restless sleep. Outside the window in the deep channel, the whales hooted and honked in an atonal sound that made Rabban's skull resonate.

The night before, his father had smiled wistfully, listening to the beasts. He'd stood with his son out on the split-log balcony, which was slick from an ever-clinging mist. Gesturing out to the narrow fjords where dark shapes swam, Abulurd said, "Mating songs. They're in love."

Rabban wanted to kill something.

Fresh from hearing his father's refusal, he couldn't imagine how he shared a heritage from such people. He'd spent too long enduring the annoyances of this world; he'd tolerated the smothering attentions of his mother and father; he'd despised how they had thrown away the grandeur they could have achieved, and then allowed themselves to be *content* here.

Rabban's blood began to boil.

Knowing he could never sleep with the whale racket outside, he dressed and plodded down into the quiet great room. Orange embers in the cavernous fireplace lit the room as if the hearth were filled with lava. A few servants should be up, some cleaners in the back rooms, a cook in the kitchen preparing for the day ahead. Abulurd never posted guards.

Instead, the inhabitants of the main lodge slept with the quiet snores of the unambitious. Rabban hated it all.

He gathered a warm garment, even deigned to take mittens, and crept outside. He trudged down rugged steps to the waterline, the docks, and the fishing shed. The cold condensed a frost from the mist in the air.

Inside the dank and reeking shed, he found what he wanted: worn, jag-tipped vibro-spears for hunting fish. Certainly sufficient to kill a few fur whales. He could have brought along heavier weaponry, but that would have taken away all the sport.

Drifting in the placid fjord, Bjondax whales crooned in unison; their songs resonated like belches from the cliff walls. Gloomy clouds muffled the starlight, but an eerie illumination shone down so that Rabban could see what he was doing.

He untied one of the medium-sized boats from the dock—small enough that he could handle it by himself, yet with a thick hull and sufficient mass to withstand being bumped by lovesick fur whales. He cast off and powered up the humming motor, easing into the deep channel where the beasts splashed and played, singing foolishly to each other. The sleek forms drifted through the water, surfacing, bellowing with their vibrating vocal membranes.

Grasping the controls with a mittened hand, he guided his boat into deeper waters and approached the pod of whales. They swam about, undisturbed by his presence. Some even playfully collided with his craft.

He looked into the dark water to see the adults spotted like leopards—some with mottled patches, others a creamy gold. Numerous smaller calves accompanied them. Did the animals bring their children with them when they came to the fjords to spawn? Rabban snorted, then hefted the handful of jagged vibro-spears.

He stopped the engine and drifted, poised as the Bjondax beasts went about their antics, oblivious to danger. The monsters fell silent, apparently taking notice of his boat, then began hooting and burbling again. *Stupid animals!*

Rabban threw the first of many vibro-spears, a rapid sequence of powerful thrusts. Once the slaughter began, the whale song rapidly changed its tone.

THROWING ON THICK robes and slippers to cover themselves, Abulurd and Emmi raced toward the docks. Confused servants turned on the lights in the main lodge, and glowglobes shone into the darkness, startling shadows away.

The soothing whale songs had turned into a raucous cacophony of animal screams. Emmi gripped her husband's arm, helping him retain his balance as he stumbled down the stairs to the shore, trying to see out into the darkness, but the house lights behind them were too bright. They discerned only shadows, thrashing whales . . . and something else. Finally, they activated the glowbeacon at the end of the dock, which sprayed illumination across the fjord.

Emmi let out a dismayed sound, like grief being swallowed whole. Behind them, servants clattered down the steep staircase, some carrying sticks or crude weapons, not knowing whether they might be called upon to defend the main lodge.

A powerboat approached across the waters, its engine humming as it dragged a heavy load toward the dock. When Emmi nudged him, Abulurd ventured out onto the boards to make out who might be at the helm of the vessel. He did not want to admit what in his heart he already knew.

The voice of Glossu Rabban called out, "Throw me that rope so I can tie up here." Then he came into the light. He was sweating from exertion in the cold and had taken off his jacket. Blood covered his arms, his chest, his face.

"I've killed eight of them, I think. Got two of the smaller fur whales tied up here, but I'll need help retrieving the other carcasses. Do you skin them right at the dock, or take them to some kind of facility?"

Abulurd could only stare in paralyzed shock. The rope fell like a strangled snake from his grasp. Leaning over the edge of the boat, Rabban grabbed the rope and looped it around a dock cleat himself.

"You . . . killed them?" Abulurd said. "You murdered them all?"

He looked down to see the floating corpses of two Bjondax calves, their fur matted and soaked with blood oozing from numerous stab wounds. Their pelts were torn. Their eyes stared sightlessly like plates from the water.

"Of course I killed them." Rabban's heavy brow furrowed. "That's the idea when you go hunting." He stepped from the swaying boat and stood on the dock as if he expected to be congratulated for what he had done.

Abulurd clenched and unclenched his fists as an unaccustomed sensation of outrage and disgust burned within him.

All his life he had squelched it, but perhaps he did have the legendary Harkonnen temper.

From years of experience he knew that Bjondax whale-trapping needed to be done at certain times and locations, or else the great herds would shun a place. Rabban had never bothered to learn the basics of the whale fur business, had practiced none of the techniques, barely knew how to command a boat.

"You've slaughtered them in their mating grounds, you *idiot!*" Abulurd cried, and a look of insulted shock splashed across Rabban's face. His father had never spoken to him like this before.

"For generations they have been coming to Tula Fjord to raise their young and to mate before returning to the deep arctic seas. But they have a long memory, a generational memory. Once blood has tainted the water, they will avoid the place for as long as the memory lasts."

Abulurd's face turned blotchy with horror and frustration. His own son had effectively cursed these breeding grounds, spilling so much blood into the fjord that no Bjondax whale would return there for decades.

Rabban looked down at his prizes floating dead beside the boat, then scanned back across the fjord waters, ignoring what his father had just said. "Is anyone going to help me, or do I have to get the rest of them myself?"

Abulurd slapped him hard across the face—then stared in horror and disbelief at his hand, amazed that he had struck his son.

Rabban glowered at him. With only a little more provocation, he would kill everyone who stood there.

His father continued in a forlorn voice. "The whales won't come back here to spawn. Don't you understand? All of these villages in the fjord, all of the people who live here, depend on the fur trade. Without the whales, these villages will die. All the buildings up and down the waterline will be abandoned.

The villages will become ghost towns overnight. *The whales won't come back.*"

Rabban just shook his head, unwilling to understand the severity of the situation. "Why do you care about these people so much?" He looked at the servants behind his parents, the men and women who'd been born on Lankiveil with no noble blood and no prospects: just villagers, just workers. "They're nothing special. You rule them. If times are hard, they'll put up with it. That's the fact of their lives."

Emmi glared at him, finally displaying the powerful emotions she kept inside. "How dare you speak like that? It's been hard to forgive you for many things, Glossu—but this is the worst."

Still, Rabban exhibited no shame. "How can you both be so blind and foolish? Don't you have any conception of who you are? Of who I am? *We are House Harkonnen!*" he roared, then lowered his voice again. "I'm ashamed to be your son."

He strode past them without another word and went to the main lodge, where he cleaned himself and packed his few things, then left. Another day remained before he had permission from the Baron to leave the planet. He would spend the time out at the spaceport.

He couldn't wait to be back at a place where life made sense to him again.

A man who persists in stalking game in a place where there is none may wait forever without finding any success. Persistence in search is not enough.

—Zensunni Wisdom of the Wanderings

FOR FOUR YEARS, GURNEY HALLECK UNCOVERED NO CLUES ABOUT HIS SISter's whereabouts, but he never abandoned hope.

His parents refused to speak Bheth's name anymore. In their quiet, colorless evenings they continued to study the Orange Catholic Bible, reassuring themselves by finding quotes that affirmed their lot in life. . . .

Gurney was left alone with his grief.

On the night of his beating, with no help from the Dmitri villagers, his parents had finally dragged Gurney's broken and bruised body back inside the prefab dwelling. They owned few medical supplies, but a hardscrabble life had taught them the rudiments of first aid. His mother put him on the bed and nursed him as best she could, while his father stood by the curtains, sullenly waiting for the Harkonnens to return.

Now, four years later, the scars from that night gave Gurney a rougher profile than he'd had before; his ruddy face carried an unsettled look. When he moved, he felt sharp aches deep in his bones. As soon as he was able, he'd crawled out of bed and gone back to work. Doing his share. The villagers accepted his presence without comment, not even showing how relieved they were to have his assistance to help fill their quotas.

Gurney Halleck knew he no longer belonged with them.

He no longer took pleasure in his evenings down at the tavern, so he remained at home. After months of painstaking effort, Gurney managed to reassemble his baliset enough to make music, though its range was more limited and the tone remained distorted. Captain Kryubi's words had burned into his brain, but he refused to stop composing his songs or singing them in his own room, where other people could pretend not to hear them. The bitter satire had dried from his lyrics, however; now the songs were focused on remembrances of Bheth.

His parents were so pale and washed-out that he couldn't call to mind an image of them, though they sat in the next room. Yet even after so many years, he still recalled every line of his sister's face, every graceful nuance of her gestures, her flaxen hair, her expressions, her gentle smile.

He planted more flowers outside, tending the calla lilies and daisies. He wanted to keep the plants alive, to keep Bheth's memory clear and bright. As he worked, he hummed her favorite songs—and it felt as if she were there with him. He even imagined that they might be thinking of each other at the same time.

If she was still alive. . . .

Late one night, Gurney heard movement outside his window, saw a shadowy shape creeping through the darkness. He thought he was dreaming until he heard a louder rustle, a sharp intake of breath. He sat up quickly, heard something scurry away.

A flower lay on his windowsill, a fresh-cut calla lily like a totem, a clear message. Its creamy bowl of petals held down a scrap of paper.

Gurney grabbed the lily, outraged that someone would taunt him with Bheth's favorite flower. But as he smelled the heady scent of the blossom, he scanned the note. It was half a page long, written in rushed yet feminine handwriting. He read it so quickly he gathered only the gist of the message.

The first few words were: "Tell Mother and Father I am alive!"

Clutching the scrap, Gurney flung himself over the sill of the open window and sprinted barefoot through the dirt streets. He glanced from side to side until he saw a shadow dart between two buildings. The figure hurried on its way to the main road, which led to a transit substation and then on into Harko City.

Gurney did not call out. That would only make the stranger put on speed. He bounded along with a rolling gait, ignoring twinges of pain in his patchwork-healed body. *Bheth was still alive!* His feet scraped on the rough, dry ground.

The stranger left the village behind, striking out for the fringe fields; Gurney guessed he had a small private vehicle parked out by the crop patches. When the man turned and saw the vague silhouette sprinting toward him, he bolted.

Already panting, Gurney rushed forward. "Wait! I just want to talk to you."

The man didn't stop. In the moonlight, he saw booted feet and relatively nice clothes . . . not a farmer by any means. Gurney had lived a hard life that kept his body tuned like a clock spring, and he quickly closed the distance. The stranger stumbled on the uneven ground, giving Gurney just enough time to bend over and ram into him like a charging D-wolf taking down prey.

The man sprawled in the dust. He scrambled up again, lurching off into the fields, but Gurney tackled him. They rolled over the edge into a two-meter-deep trench where the villagers had planted stunted krall tubers.

Gurney grabbed the front of the man's fine shirt and shoved him up into a half-sitting position against the dirt wall of the trench. Rocks, gravel, and dust pattered all around them.

"Who are you? Have you seen my sister? Is she all right?"

Gurney shone his chrono-light on the man's face. Pale, widely set eyes, darting around. Smooth features.

The man spat dirt from his teeth and tried to struggle. His hair was neatly cut. His clothes were far more expensive than anything Gurney had ever seen.

"Where is she?" Gurney pressed his face close and held out the note as if it were accusatory evidence. "Where did this come from? What did she say to you? How did you know about the lily?"

The man sniffled, then pulled one of his arms free to rub a sore ankle. "I . . . I am the Harkonnen census taker for this district. I travel from village to village. It's my job to account for all the people who serve the Baron." He swallowed hard.

Gurney tightened his hold on the shirt.

"I see many people. I—" He coughed nervously. "I saw your sister. She was in a pleasure house near one of the military garrisons. She paid me money she'd managed to scrape together over the years."

Gurney took deep breaths, focused on every word.

"I told her my rounds would take me to Dmitri village. She gave me all her solaris and wrote that note. She told me what to do, and I did it." He slapped Gurney's hand away and sat up indignantly. "Why did you attack me? I brought you news of your sister."

Gurney growled at him. "I want to know more. How can I find her?"

The man shook his head. "She only paid me to smuggle this note out. I did it at great risk to my life—and now you're going to get me caught. I can't do anything more for you, or for her."

Gurney's hands moved up to the man's throat. "Yes, you can. Tell me which pleasure house, which military garrison. Would you rather risk the Harkonnens finding out . . . or have me kill you now?" He squeezed the man's larynx for good measure. "Tell me!"

In four years, this was the first word Gurney had received, and he couldn't let the opportunity slip away. But Bheth was alive. His heart swelled with the knowledge.

The census taker retched. "A garrison over by Mount Ebony and Lake Vladimir. The Harkonnens have slave pits and obsidian mines nearby. Soldiers keep watch over the prisoners. The pleasure house . . ." He swallowed hard, afraid to reveal the information. "The pleasure house serves all the soldiers. Your sister works there."

Trembling, Gurney tried to think how he might get across the continent. He possessed little knowledge of geography, but he could discover more. He stared up at the shadowy moon as it dipped behind the smoky clouds, already developing an ill-conceived plan to free Bheth.

Gurney nodded and let his hands fall to his sides. The census taker scrambled out of the trench and ran across the fields in a limping, cockeyed gait from his twisted ankle, kicking up dust and dirt. He headed toward a shelter of scrub brush, where he must have left a vehicle.

Numb and exhausted, Gurney slumped against the trench wall. He drew a deep breath, tasted determination. He didn't care that the man escaped.

At long last, he had a clue to his sister's whereabouts.

The effective ruler punishes opposition while rewarding assistance; he shifts his forces in random fashion; he conceals major elements of his power; he sets up a rhythm of counter movement that keeps opponents off balance.

—WESTHEIMER ATREIDES,
Elements of Leadership

AFTER LETO BECAME A FATHER, TIME SEEMED TO PASS EVEN FASTER.

Dressed in toy armor and carrying a laminated-paper shield, the small boy toddled forward, attacked the stuffed Salusan bull ferociously with his feathered *vara* lance, then retreated. Victor, the Duke's two-year-old son, wore a green-bordered cap with a red Atreides crest.

On his knees and laughing, Leto pulled the spiny-headed toy bull from side to side, so that the black-haired boy, still moving with baby clumsiness, had no easy target. "Do as I showed you, Victor." He tried to cover his grin with an expression of deadly seriousness. "Be careful with the *vara*." He lifted his arms and demonstrated. "Hold it like this, and thrust sideways into the monster's brain."

Dutifully, the boy tried again, barely able to lift the scaled-down weapon. The *vara*'s blunted tip bounced off the stuffed head, close to the white chalkite mark Leto had placed there.

"Much better!" He shoved the toy bull aside, gathered the boy in his arms, and lifted him high overhead. Victor giggled when Leto tickled his rib cage.

"Again?" Kailea said in a disapproving tone. "Leto, what are you doing?" She stood at the doorway with her lady-in-waiting, Chiara. "Don't raise him to enjoy that nonsense. You want him to die like his grandfather?"

With a hardened expression, Leto turned to his concubine. "The bull wasn't responsible, Kailea. It was drugged by traitors." The Duke didn't mention the secret he harbored, that Leto's own mother had been implicated in the plot, and Leto had exiled Lady Helena to live in a primitive retreat with the Sisters in Isolation.

Kailea looked at him, still not convinced. He tried to sound more reasonable. "My father believed the beasts were noble and magnificent. To defeat one in the ring takes great skill, and honor."

"Still . . . is this appropriate for our son?" Kailea glanced at Chiara, as if seeking support from the matronly woman. "He's only two years old."

Leto tousled the boy's hair. "It is never too early to learn fighting skills—even Thufir approves. My father never coddled me, and I won't spoil Victor, either."

"I'm sure you know best," she said with a sigh of resignation, but the agitated look in her eyes said otherwise. "After all, you're the Duke."

"It's time for Victor's tutoring session, dear." Chiara glanced at her jeweled wristchron, an antique Richesian bauble she had brought from Kaitain.

With a disappointed expression, Victor looked up at the looming figure of his father. "Go along now." Leto patted him on the back. "A Duke has to learn many things, and not all of them are as much fun as this."

The lad stood stubbornly for a moment, then trudged on short legs across the room. With a grandmotherly smile, Chiara picked him up and carried him away to a private tutoring room in the north wing of the Castle. Swain Goire, the guard assigned to watch over Victor, followed the lady-in-waiting. Kailea remained in the playroom while Leto propped the stuffed bull against a wall, wiped his own neck with a towel, and drank from a mug of cool water.

"Why does my brother always confide in you before he

says anything to me?" He could see she was upset and uncertain. "Is it true he and that woman are talking about getting married?"

"Not seriously—I think it was just something he spouted off the top of his head. You know how long it takes Rhombur to do anything. Someday, maybe."

With a look of disapproval, she pressed her lips together. "But she's just a . . . a Bene Gesserit. No noble blood at all."

"A Bene Gesserit woman was good enough for my cousin the Emperor." Leto did not mention the pain in his own heart. "It's his decision, Kailea. They certainly seem to love each other." He and Kailea had begun to drift apart as soon as his son was born. Or perhaps it had started as soon as Chiara had arrived with all her gossip and grand stories about the Imperial Court.

"Love? Oh, is that the only ingredient necessary for marriage?" Her face darkened. "What would your father, the great Duke Paulus Atreides, say to such hypocrisy?"

Trying to remain calm, he crossed to the playroom door and pulled it shut so that no one could hear. "You know why I can't take you as my wife." He remembered the terrible fights of his own parents behind the thick doors of their bedroom suite. He didn't want that to happen to him and Kailea.

Her delicate beauty was masked with displeasure. Kailea tossed her head, making curls of coppery hair bounce between her shoulder blades. "Our son should be Duke Atreides one day. I hoped you might change your mind once you got to know him."

"It's all about politics, Kailea." Leto flushed. "I love Victor very much. But I am the Duke of a Great House. I must think of House Atreides first."

At meetings of the Landsraad Council, other Houses paraded their eligible daughters before Leto, hoping to entice him. House Atreides was neither the richest nor the most powerful family, but Leto was well liked and respected, especially after his bravery during the Trial by Forfeiture. He was proud of what he had achieved on Caladan . . . and wished Kailea could appreciate him more for it.

"And Victor remains a bastard."

"Kailea—"

"Sometimes I hate your father because of the foolish ideas he pounded into your head. Since I can offer you no political alliances, and since I have no dowry, no *position*, I am not acceptable as a wife. But because you're a Duke, you can command me to your bed whenever you please."

Stung to hear how she had phrased her displeasure, he could imagine what Chiara must be saying to Kailea in the privacy of her own chambers. There could be no other explanation. Leto didn't particularly like the off-world woman, but to dismiss the lady-in-waiting might burn his few remaining bridges to Kailea. The two women put on airs together, enjoyed playing at highbrow conversations, imitating Imperial styles.

He stared out the streaked windowplaz, thinking of how happy he and Kailea had been only a few years earlier. "I don't deserve that, not after my family has done everything in its power for you and your brother."

"Oh, thank you, so much. It hasn't hurt your image either, has it? Help the poor refugees from Ix so that your beloved people can see what a benevolent ruler you are. Noble Duke Atreides. But those of us closer to you know you're only a man, not the legend you try to make yourself into. You're not *really* the hero of the common people, as you imagine yourself to be. If you were, you would agree—"

"Enough! Rhombur has every right to marry Tessia if he likes. *If* that's what he decides. House Vernius is destroyed, and there will be no political marriages for him."

"Unless his rebels win on Ix," she countered. "Leto, tell me the truth—do you secretly hope his freedom fighters *don't* succeed, so you will always have an excuse for not marrying me?"

Leto was appalled. "Of course not!" Apparently thinking she'd won, Kailea left the room.

In solitude, he considered how she had changed. For years he'd been smitten with her, long before taking her as his concubine. He had brought her close to him, though not as close as she wanted to be. At first she'd been helpful and supportive, but her ambitions had grown too great, and she had complicated his life immeasurably. Too often recently, he had seen her primping in front of the mirror, styling herself as a queen—but that was something she could never be. He couldn't change who she was.

But the joy he drew from his son outweighed all other problems. He loved the boy with an intensity that surprised even him. He wanted only the best for Victor, for him to grow up to be a fine, honorable man, in the Atreides fashion. Even though he could not officially name the child his ducal heir, Leto intended to give him every benefit, every advantage. One day, Victor would understand the things his mother did not.

AS THE BOY sat at a tutoring machine, playing shape-recognition games and color identifiers, Kailea and Chiara talked in low tones. Victor pushed buttons rapidly, achieving high scores for his age.

"My Lady, we must figure a way around the Duke. He is a stubborn man and intends to form a marriage alliance with a powerful family. Archduke Ecaz is after him, I hear, offering one of his daughters. I suspect Leto's purported diplomatic efforts in the Moritani-Ecazi conflict are a smoke screen to hide his true intentions."

Kailea's eyelids narrowed to slits as she considered this. "Leto is traveling to Grumman next week to talk with Viscount Moritani. They have no eligible daughters."

"He *says* he's going there, dear. But space is vast, and if Leto takes a detour, how would you ever know? After all my years at the Imperial Court, I understand these things only too well. If Leto produces an official heir, he'll sweep your Victor under the rug as nothing more than a bastard son . . . ruining your own position."

Kailea hung her head. "I said everything you told me to, Chiara, but I wonder if I'm pushing him too hard. . . ." Now, where Leto couldn't see her, she allowed her uncertainty and fear to show. "I'm so frustrated. There doesn't seem to be anything I can do. He and I were close before, but it's all gone so wrong. I had hoped that bearing his son would bring us together."

Chiara pursed her wrinkled lips. "Ah, dear, in ancient times such children were known as 'human mortar' to keep a family whole."

Kailea shook her head. "Instead, Victor has only exposed the problem for all to see. There are times when I think Leto hates me."

"Something can still be worked out, if you just trust me, my Lady." Chiara placed a reassuring hand on the young woman's shoulder. "Start by talking with your brother. Ask Rhombur to see what he can do." Her voice was sweet and reasonable. "The Duke always listens to him."

Kailea brightened. "That might work. It couldn't hurt to try."

SHE SPOKE WITH Rhombur in his Castle suite. He puttered around in the kitchen with Tessia, helping her prepare a salad of local vegetables. With a maddening, bemused smile on his face, Rhombur listened attentively while slicing a purple sea cabbage on a cutting board.

He didn't seem to grasp the seriousness of his sister's situation. "You have no right to complain about anything, Kailea. Leto has treated us royally—uh, especially you."

She let out an exasperated snort. "How can you say that?

've got more at stake, now that I have Victor." She was caught between flying into a rage or crumpling into despair.

Tessia blinked her sepia eyes. "Rhombur, the best hope for both of you is to overthrow the Tleilaxu. Once you restore House Vernius, all of your other problems become irrelevant."

Rhombur leaned over to kiss his concubine on the forehead. "Yes, my love—don't you think I'm trying? We've been secretly sending C'tair money for years, but I still don't know how well the rebels are doing. Hawat sent in another spy, and the man disappeared. Ix is a tough nut to crack, as we designed it to be."

Both Tessia and Kailea surprised each other by responding in unison. "You need to try harder."

The Universe operates on a basic principle of economics: everything has its cost. We pay to create our future, we pay for the mistakes of the past. We pay for every change we make . . . and we pay just as dearly if we refuse to change.

—Guild Bank Annals,
Philosophical Register

IT WAS SAID AMONG THE FREMEN THAT SHAI-HULUD WAS TO BE RE-spected, and feared. But even before the age of sixteen, Liet-Kynes had ridden worms many times.

On their first journey to the southern polar regions, he and his blood-brother Warrick had summoned one worm after another, riding them to exhaustion. Then they would plant a thumper, ready their Maker hooks, and call the next one. All Fremen were counting on them.

For hours without end, the two young men huddled in still-suits under hooded robes, enduring the heat of day under a dust-blue sky. They listened to the sand roaring beneath them, blazing with friction from the worm's passage.

Ranging far from the sixty-degree cartographical line of inhabited regions, they crossed the Great Flat and the open ergs, forded trackless seas of sand, reached the equator itself, and continued south toward the forbidden palmaries near the moist antarctic cap. Those plantings had been established and nurtured by Pardot Kynes as part of his great dream for re-awakening Dune.

Liet's gaze scanned the immensity. Winter winds blew the surface of the Great Flat as smooth as a tabletop. *This is surely the horizon of eternity.* He studied the austere landforms, the subtle gradations, and rock outcroppings. His father had lectured him about the desert for as long as his young mind had understood language. The Planetologist had called it a landscape beyond pity, without pause . . . no hesitation in it at all.

As dusk fell on the sixth day of their journey, their worm exhibited signs of agitation and fatigue, enough that it was willing to dive beneath the abrasive sand, even with its sensitive leading ring segments held open by hooks. Liet signaled to Warrick, pointing toward a low reef of rock and its sheltered crannies. "We can spend the night there."

Warrick used his goad sticks to turn the worm closer, then they released their hooks and made ready to dismount. Since Liet had summoned this particular behemoth, he gestured for his friend to run down the rough, segmented hide. "First on, last off," Liet said.

Warrick scrambled down to the sand wake where he could leap off the tail. He disengaged the airpack-assisted cargo cases filled with raw melange essence and guided them beyond the monster's reach. Warrick leaped off and made his way to a dune top. There, he stood motionless, thinking like the sand, as still as the desert.

Liet let the worm burrow itself into the ground and jumped away at the last moment, slogging through slumping powder sand, as if it were a swamp. His father loved to tell stories about miasmic marshes on Bela Tegeuse and Salusa Secundus, but Liet doubted those other worlds contained a fraction of the charm or vigor of Arrakis. . . .

As the son of the Umma Kynes, Liet benefited from certain advantages and opportunities. While he reveled in this important journey down to the antarctic, he knew his birthright did nothing to increase his chances of success. All young Fremen men were given such responsibilities.

The Spacing Guild required its regular spice bribe.

For a king's ransom in spice essence, Guild satellites would turn a blind eye toward the secret terraforming activities, would ignore Fremen movements. The Harkonnens could not understand why it was so difficult to get weather projections and detailed cartographic analyses, but the Guild always made excuses . . . because the Fremen never failed to pay their fee.

When Liet and Warrick found a sheltered corner of the lava reef on which to pitch their stilltent, Liet brought out the honeyed spice cakes his mother had made. The two young men sat in the comfort of long companionship, commenting on young Fremen women from the sietches they had visited.

Over the years, the blood-brothers had done many brave things—as well as many foolish things. Some had turned into disasters, some near escapes, but Liet and Warrick had survived them all. Both had taken numerous Harkonnen trophies, receiving scars in the process.

Far into the night they laughed about how they had sabotaged Harkonnen 'thopters, how they had broken into a rich merchant's warehouse and stolen precious delicacies (which had tasted awful), how they had chased a mirage across the open pan in search of an elusive white salt playa, so they could make a wish.

Content at last, the two went to sleep under the double moonlight, ready to awaken shortly before dawn. They had several days left to journey.

PAST THE SOUTHERN wormline, where moisture in the soil and large rocky inclusions made it impossible for sandworms to travel, Liet-Kynes and Warrick marched forward on foot. Following their instinctive sense of direction, they made their way through canyons and cold plains. In rocky gorges with tall conglomerate walls, they saw ancient, dry riverbeds. Their sensitive Fremen noses could detect an increased dampness in the frigid air.

The two young men spent a night at Ten Tribes Sietch, where solar mirrors melted the permafrost in the ground, adding enough free water for carefully tended plants to grow. Orchards had been planted there, along with dwarf palm trees.

Warrick stood with a broad grin on his face. He removed the stillsuit plugs from his nostrils and sucked in a breath of naked air. "Just smell the plants, Liet! The very air is alive." He lowered his voice and looked solemnly at his friend. "Your father is a great man."

The caretakers had a haunted yet ecstatic look on their faces, filled with religious fervor at seeing their efforts bear fruit. To them, Umma Kynes's dream was not just an abstract concept, but a genuine future to behold.

The Fremen there revered the son of the Planetologist. Some came forward to touch his arm and stillsuit, feeling that this brought them closer to the prophet himself. "And the desert shall rejoice, and blossom as the rose," one old man cried out, quoting from the Zensunni Wisdom of the Wanderings.

The others began a ritual chant. "What is more precious than the seed?"

"This water with which the seed germinates."

"What is more precious than the rock?"

"The fertile soil it covers."

The people continued in a similar fashion, but their adoration made Liet uncomfortable. He and Warrick decided to depart as soon as the requirements of hospitality had been met, after they had shared coffee with the Naib and slept well in the cold night.

The people of Ten Tribes Sietch gave them warm clothing, which they had not needed until now. Then Liet and Warrick set off again with their valuable burden of concentrated spice.

WHEN THE TWO young men reached the fabled fortress of the water merchant Rondo Tuek, the structure looked more like a dirty industrial warehouse than a fabulous palace set among glistening mountains of white ice. The building was square, connected by many pipes and trenches. Chewing machinery had eaten through the iron-hard soil to secure sparse frost buried in the dirt, leaving behind ugly mounds of debris.

Any pristine snow had long since been buried in layers of thick dust and blown pebbles, cemented together by frozen water. Extracting moisture was a simple operation—digging massive quantities of soil and cooking out the locked water vapor.

Liet broke off a chunk of the frozen ground and licked it, tasting salt as well as ice mingled with the grit. He knew the water was there, but it seemed as inaccessible to him as if it were on a far-off planet. They moved toward the big facility with their bobbing cases of distilled spice.

The structure was made of pseudocrete blocks fashioned out of debris from the ice-extraction process. The fortresslike walls were blank and undecorated, studded with windows and augmented by mirrors and power collectors that drank in the low-angled sunlight. Frost-extraction ovens emitted brown exhaust plumes, showering the air with cracked dust and grit.

Rondo Tuek owned an opulent mansion in Carthag, but it was said that the water merchant rarely visited his spectacular city dwelling. Tuek had made a tidy profit by mining the water in the south and marketing it to the northern cities and the villages of the sinks and pans.

However, the southern hemisphere's terrible weather, especially the unpredictable sandstorms, wrecked one shipment in four, and Tuek constantly had to purchase new machinery and hire new crews. Luckily for him, a cargo of antarctic water brought in enough profit to offset the losses. Few entrepreneurs were willing to take such risks, but Tuek had hidden connections with the smugglers, the Guild, and the Fremen. It was widely rumored, in fact, that the water operation was only a front, a legitimate business that concealed his real moneymaking enterprise: acting as an intermediary with smugglers.

Side by side, Warrick and Liet marched past the loud machinery and busy off-worlders to the entrance gates. Mainly, Tuek used mercenary laborers who never ventured north to spend time in the arid reality of Dune. The water merchant preferred it that way, since such men were better able to keep secrets.

Though Liet was smaller in stature than Warrick, he drew himself up and stepped forward to take the lead. A man in work overalls and insulated gloves trudged past them toward the work site, looking sidelong at the two.

Liet stopped him. "We are a delegation from the Fremen, here to see Rondo Tuek. I am Liet-Kynes, son of Pardot Kynes, and this is Warrick—"

The worker brusquely gestured behind him. "He's inside somewhere. Go find him yourself." Then he strode toward one of the growling pieces of machinery that gnawed the dirt-encrusted ice-rock.

Rebuffed, Liet looked at his friend. Warrick grinned and clapped him on the back. "We don't have time for formalities, anyway. Let us go find Tuek."

They ventured into the cavernous building, trying to look as if they belonged there. The air was chill, though heater-globes hummed against the walls and corners. Liet obtained vague directions from other workers, who gestured down one hall and then the next—until finally the two were totally lost in a maze of inventory offices, control terminals, and storage rooms.

A short, broad-shouldered man marched out, swinging both of his arms. "It's not hard to notice two Fremen in here," he said. "I'm Rondo Tuek. Come with me to my private chamber." The squat man cast a glance over his shoulder. "And bring your supplies. Don't leave that cargo lying around."

Liet had seen the man only briefly, years ago, at the Fenrings' banquet in the Residency at Arrakeen. Tuek had wide-set gray eyes, flat cheekbones, and almost no chin, making his face a perfect square. His rust-colored hair was thinning on top, but stood out in feathery brushes at his temples. An odd-looking man with an awkward gait, he was the antithesis of the flowing grace common to Fremen.

Tuek scuttled ahead. Liet and Warrick dragged the airpack-assisted containers behind them, hurrying to keep up. Everything in the place seemed drab and plain, a disappointment to Liet. Even in the most squalid sietch, the Fremen laid down colorful rugs and hangings, or carved decorative figures out of sandstone. Ceilings were etched with geometrical patterns, sometimes inlaid with mosaics.

Tuek led them to a broad wall as blank as any of the others. He looked from side to side to make sure his workers had cleared out of the area, then placed his palmprint against a reader. The lock hissed open to reveal a warm chamber filled with more opulence than Liet had ever imagined possible.

Crystal flasks of expensive kirana brandy and Caladan wines stood in alcoves. A jeweled chandelier shone faceted light against crimson curtains that gave the walls a muted softness, as comfortable as a womb.

"Ah, now we see the water merchant's hidden treasures," Warrick said.

The chairs were huge and plush. Entertainment holos lay stacked on a polished-slate table. Speckled mirrors on the ceiling reflected light from glowing Corinthian columns made of opalesque Hagal alabaster, lit from within by molecular fires.

"The Guild brings few comforts to Arrakis. Fine items are not appreciated by the Harkonnens, and few others can afford them." Tuek shrugged his broad shoulders. "And no one wants to transport them through the hells of the southern hemisphere just to reach my factory."

He raised his feathery eyebrows. "But because of my agree-nent with your people"—he pushed a control to seal the doors behind him—"the Guild sends occasional ships into direct polar orbit. Lighters come down with any supplies I request." He patted the heavy cargo containers that Warrick had brought. "In exchange for your monthly spice . . . payment."

"We call it a spice bribe," Liet said.

Tuek did not seem offended. "Semantics, my boy. The pure melange essence your Fremen take from the deep desert is more valuable than any scrapings the Harkonnen teams manage to find in the north. The Guild keeps these shipments for their own use, but who can understand what the Navigators get out of it?" He shrugged his rolling shoulders again.

He tapped his fingers against a pad on the slate table. "I am noting that we've received your payment for this month. I have instructed my quartermaster to provide you with sufficient supplies for your return journey before you depart."

Liet hadn't expected many pleasantries from Tuek, and he accepted the terse, businesslike manner. He didn't want to stay there any longer, though city folk or villagers might have lingered to admire the exotic trappings and lavish appointments. Liet had not been born to such fine things.

Like his father, he would rather spend his day out in the desert, where he belonged.

IF THEY PUSHED hard, Liet guessed they could make Ten Tribes Sietch by nightfall. He longed for the heat of the sun so he could flex his numb hands.

But it was the cold that impressed Warrick. He stood with his arms spread wide, his desert boots planted on the ground. "Have you ever felt such a thing, Liet?" He rubbed his cheek. "My flesh feels brittle." He drew in a deep breath, glanced down at his boots. "And you can sense the water. It's here, but . . . trapped."

He looked at the brown mountains of dust-encrusted glaciers. Warrick was impulsive and curious, and he called for his friend to wait. "We've completed our duty, Liet. Let us not be in such a hurry to return."

Liet stopped. "What do you have in mind?"

"We are here, in the legendary ice mountains. We've seen the palmaries and the plantings your father began. I want to explore for a day, feel solid ice beneath my feet. Climbing those stairstep glaciers would be equivalent to ascending mountains of gold."

"You won't be able to see raw ice. The moisture is all frozen into the dust and dirt." But seeing the eager expression on his friend's face, Liet's impatience melted away. "It is as you say, Warrick. Why should we be in such a hurry?" For the sixteen-year-olds, this could be a grander—and safer—adventure than their razzias against Harkonnen strongholds. "Let us go climb glaciers."

They hiked off under the perpetual dim daylight of the southern pole. The tundra had an austere beauty, particularly to someone accustomed to the reality of deserts.

As they left Tuek's industrial excavations behind, the plume of spewed dust and debris cast a brown haze over the horizon. Liet and Warrick climbed higher, chipping away rocks and finding a film of ice. They sucked on broken shards of the frozen ground, tasting bitter alkaline chemicals, spitting out the dirt and sand.

Warrick ran ahead, delighting in the freedom. As Fremen, they had been trained all their lives never to let down their guard—but Harkonnen hunters would not come to the southern pole. Here, they were probably safe. Probably.

Liet continued to scan the ground and the looming malleable cliffs that towered in great jumbles of frozen brown dirt. He bent to examine a scuff mark, a partial indentation. "Warrick, look at this."

They studied a single footprint pressed into spongy earth

that had softened during the height of a warm season. Upon closer inspection, they found subtle marks where other tracks had been carefully and intentionally obliterated.

"Who has been here?"

Warrick looked at him, and added, "And why are they hiding? We're far from Tuek's water factory."

Liet sniffed the air, squinted at the cliffs and rock formations, and saw a glint of frost through the low-hanging blanket of cold. "Maybe they are explorers, heading toward the pole to find cleaner ice to excavate."

"If that's the case, why bother covering their tracks?"

Liet looked in the direction the track pointed, up a rugged cliff face dripping with dusty mud frozen into free-form shapes. Attuned to the details of his environment, he stared and *stared*, studying every shadow, every crevice. "Something doesn't look right."

His awareness heightened, alarms went off in his body, and he gestured for Warrick to be still. Sensing no other sound or motion, the two crept forward. Since childhood, Liet and Warrick had known how to move without sound or trace across the desert.

Liet still could not determine what exactly struck him as out of place, yet as they approached, the sense of wrongness increased. Though the cold numbed their delicate senses, they moved ahead with the utmost care. Picking their path up stairsteps of frost-hardened dust, they saw what to Fremen eyes was obviously a trail.

People had moved along here up the slope.

The two young men tried to make themselves invisible against the cliff, thinking like part of the landscape, moving like natural components. Halfway up the slope, Liet noticed a faint discoloration in the wall, a patch too even, too artificial. The camouflage had been done well, but with a few clumsy mistakes.

It was a hidden door large enough for spacecraft. A secret storehouse for Rondo Tuek? Another Guild operation, or a smuggler's hideout?

Liet stood motionless. Before he could say anything, other patches opened beside the path, pieces of rock and ice so carefully camouflaged that even he hadn't noticed them. Four rough-looking men lunged out. They were muscular and wore casual uniforms cobbled together from several sources. And they held weapons.

"You move well and quietly, lads," one of the men said. He was tall and muscular, with bright eyes and a gleaming bald head. His mustache was dark and striking across his upper lip and down to his chin. "But you've forgotten that here in the cold, one can see *steam* from your breath. Didn't think of that, did you?"

A pair of grizzled men gestured with their weapons for the captives to enter the mountain tunnels. Warrick placed his hand on the crysknife hilt at his waist and looked over at his companion. They would be willing to die back-to-back if need be.

But Liet shook his head. These men wore no Harkonnen colors. In some places the insignia had been torn from armbands and shoulder pads. *They must be smugglers*.

The bald man glanced at one of his lieutenants. "We obviously have some fine-tuning to do with our camouflage."

"Are we your prisoners?" Liet asked, looking meaningfully at the guns.

"I want to learn what we did wrong that you could spot our hideout so easily." The muscular bald man lowered his weapon. "My name is Dominic Vernius—and you are my guests . . . for now."

The increasing variety and abundance of life itself vastly multiplies the number of niches available for life. The resulting system is a web of makers and users, eaters and eaten, collaborators and competitors.

—PARDOT KYNES,
Report to Emperor Shaddam IV

FOR ALL HIS WILES AND SCHEMES, EVEN WITH ALL THE BLOOD ON HIS hands, Hasimir Fenring could be so *wonderful* to her. Lady Margot missed him. He was away, having gone with Baron Harkonnen deep into the desert to inspect spice harvester sites after receiving an angry message from Shaddam about a shortfall in melange production.

With cold adherence to his clear-cut goals, her husband had committed numerous atrocities in the Emperor's name, and she suspected he'd had a hand in the mysterious death of Elrood IX. But her Bene Gesserit upbringing had taught her to value results and consequences. Hasimir Fenring knew how to get what he wanted, and Margot adored him for it.

She sighed each time she entered the lush wet-planet conservatory her husband had commissioned for her. Dressed in a comfortable yet stunning glitterslick housedress that changed color for each hour of the day, Margot pressed her hand against the palm-lock of the moisture-sealed door. As she stepped through the ornate mosaic arch into the verdant chamber, she breathed deeply of the rich air. Automatically, soothing music began to play, with baliset and piano.

The walls radiated yellow afternoon sunlight, where panes of filter glass converted the white sun of Arrakis to a color reminiscent of Kaitain days. Thick leaves waved in forced-air circulation like the banners of cheering citizens. Over the past four years, the plants in this chamber had flourished beyond her wildest expectations.

On a world where every drop of moisture was precious and beggars wandered the streets asking for water squeezings, where colorfully costumed water-sellers jingled their bells and charged exorbitant prices for just a sip, her private retreat was an extravagant waste. *And worth every drop*. As her husband always said, the Imperial Spice Minister could afford it.

Deep in her past, among the echoes of ancient lives still available to her, Margot remembered a sheltered wife in a strict Islamic household, a woman named Fatimah after the only daughter of Mohammed. Her husband had been wealthy enough to care for three wives, keeping them inside his house, giving each one a courtyard of her own. After her marriage ceremony, Fatimah had never gone outside the home again, nor had the other wives. Her entire world was contained within the lush courtyard, with its plants and flowers, and an open sky above. The trickling water in its central fountain provided a musical accompaniment to her stringed instruments. Sometimes butterflies or hummingbirds would drop down to feast on the nectar. . . .

Now, countless generations later, on a planet orbiting a sun farther away than that ancient woman could ever have imagined, Margot Fenring found herself in a similar place, sheltered and beautiful and full of plants.

A clockwork servok with long arms of pipe and hose misted the air, spraying the pruned trees, ferns, and flowers. The cool moistness chilled Margot's skin, and she breathed it into her lungs. Such luxury, after so many long years! She lifted a wet fan leaf, thrust her fingers into the loamy soil at the plant's base. No sign of the juice-sucking aphid mutants this plant had carried when it arrived from its tropical homeworld of Ginaz.

As she examined the roots, the voice of Reverend Mother

Biana whispered to her from Other Memory. The long-dead Sister, who had been groundskeeper at the Mother School two centuries earlier, counseled Margot in the gentle ways of horticultural science. The music—Biana's favorite song, a haunting troubadour melody from Jongleur—had sparked the inner ghost.

Even without Biana's memory-assistance, Margot prided herself on her knowledge of plants. Specimens from all over the Imperium flourished in the conservatory; she thought of them as the children she could not have with her genetic eunuch husband. She enjoyed watching the plants grow and mature on such a hostile world.

Her husband was also good at surviving hostile situations. She stroked a long, silken leaf. *I will protect you.*

Margot lost track of time, forgetting even to emerge for her meals. A Bene Gesserit Sister could fast for a week, if necessary. She was alone with her plants and her thoughts and the Other Memory of long-dead Sisters.

Contented, she sat on a bench by a fluted fountain at the center of the room. She placed a rootbound philarose on the bench beside her, and closed her eyes, resting, meditating. . . .

By the time she returned to herself, the sun had gone down in a blaze on the horizon, casting long shadows from rock escarpments to the west. Interior lights had turned on in the conservatory. Wonderfully rested, she carried the philarose to the potting bench and removed the plant from the container it had outgrown. She hummed the Jongleur tune to herself as she packed dirt around the roots in a new pot, completely at peace.

Turning around, Margot was startled to see a leathery-skinned man less than two meters away. He stared at her with deep blue eyes . . . something oddly familiar about him. He wore a jubba cloak, hood thrown back. *A Fremen!*

How had the man gotten in, despite all of the conservatory's stringent security measures and alarms, despite the palm lock keyed to her hand alone? Even with her enhanced Bene Gesserit senses, she had not heard him approach.

The philarose pot fell from her hands with a crash, and she dropped smoothly into a Bene Gesserit fighting stance, her body loose and poised, her trained muscles ready to deliver toe-pointed kicks that could disembowel an opponent.

"We have heard of your weirding way of battle," the man said without moving. "But you are trained never to employ it precipitously."

Wary, Margot took a slow, cold breath. How could he possibly know this?

"We received your message. You wished to speak with the Fremen."

Finally, she placed the man. She had seen him in Rutii, an outlying village during one of her tours. He was a self-styled priest of the desert, who administered blessings to the people. Margot recalled the priest's discomfort when he'd noticed her watching him, how he had stopped his activities and had gone away. . . .

She heard a rustling in the shrubbery. A shrunken woman stepped into view, also Fremen, also familiar. It was the Shad-out Mapes, the housekeeper, prematurely graying and wrinkled from the sun and wind of the desert. Mapes, too, had eschewed her customary household attire and instead wore a drab traveling cloak for a desert journey.

Mapes said, in a throaty voice, "Much water is wasted here, my Lady. You flaunt the richness of other worlds. This is not the Fremen way."

"I am not Fremen," Margot responded sharply, not yet ready to strike out with the paralyzing command of Bene Gesserit Voice. She had deadly weapons at her disposal that were unimagined by these primitives. "What do you want with me?"

"You have seen me before," the man said.

"You are a priest."

"I am an Acolyte, one of the Sayyadina's assistants," he answered without taking a step closer.

Sayyadina, Margot thought. Her pulse quickened. That was a title she'd heard before, signifying a woman who seemed eerily like a Reverend Mother. Such a name was taught by the Missionaria Protectiva.

Suddenly all became clear. But she had spoken her request to the Fremen so long ago, she had given up hope. "You heard my communication, my whispered message."

The priest lowered his head. "You say that you have information about the *Lisan al-Gaib*." The appellation was pronounced with a deep resonance and respect.

"And so I do. I must speak with your Reverend Mother." Calmly, stalling for time to settle her thoughts, Margot scooped up the plant she had dropped. Leaving the pot's shards and dirt on the floor, she placed the philarose into a fresh container, hoping it would survive.

"Sayyadina of another world, you must come with us," Mapes said.

Margot brushed dirt from her hands. Though she allowed no flicker of emotion on her face, her heart pounded with anticipation. Perhaps, finally, she would have hard information to report to Mother Superior Harishka. Maybe she would learn what had happened to the missing Sisters who, a century ago, had vanished into the deserts of Arrakis.

She followed the two Fremen out into the night.

To know what one ought *to do is not enough.*

—PRINCE RHOMBUR VERNIUS

THE WAVES PLAYED A SLOW LULLABY BENEATH THE WICKER-WOOD CORA-
cle, fostering a false sense of peace over troubled thoughts.

Duke Leto reached over the side and grabbed a floating
sphere in the thick mesh of leaves drifting along with them.
He drew out a jeweled knife from its golden sheath at his side
and cut the ripe paradan melon from its underwater plant
structure. "Here, Rhombur, have a melon."

He blinked in surprise. "Uh, isn't that the Emperor's knife?
The one Shaddam gave to you after the Trial by Forfeiture?"

Leto shrugged. "I prefer practicality over showiness. I'm
sure my cousin won't mind."

Rhombur took the dripping melon and turned it in his hands,
inspecting the rough husk in the hazy sunshine. "Kailea would
be horrified, you know. She'd rather you placed the Emperor's
knife on a suspensor plaque inside an ornamental shield."

"Well, she doesn't go out fishing with me much."

When Rhombur made no move to shuck the melon, Leto
took it back, used the tip of Shaddam's jeweled blade to peel
off the tough covering, then cracked the rind. "At least this
won't burst into flames if you let it sit out in the sun," Leto
chided, remembering the coral-gem debacle that had destroyed one of his favorite boats and stranded the two young
men on a distant reef.

"Not funny," Rhombur said, for he had been to blame.

Leto held up the knife, watching how the light glinted on the edge. "You know, I wore this as part of my formal uniform when I went to meet with Viscount Moritani. I think it got his attention."

"He's a hard man to impress," Rhombur said. "The Emperor has finally withdrawn his Sardaukar, and everything's quiet. Uh, do you think the Moritani-Ecazi feud is over now?"

"No, I don't think it is. The entire time I was on Grumman, I felt my nerves tingling. I think the Viscount is just biding his time."

"And you've put yourself in the middle of it." With his own knife, Rhombur cut away a section of the melon and took a bite. He winced, spat it over the side. "Still a little sour."

Leto laughed at his facial expression, then grabbed a small towel from a cubby. Wiping his hands and the ceremonial knife, he stepped inside the cabin, out of the bright sun, and started the engines. "At least all my duties aren't so unpleasant. We'd better get moving down to the delta. I promised I'd be at the barge port by noon to greet the first loads of this season's pundi rice harvest."

"Ah, the perils and demands of leadership," Rhombur said, following him down into the cabin. "Look in the coolpack—I brought along a surprise for you. You know that dark beer you like so much?"

"You don't mean the *Harkonnen* ale?"

"You'll have to drink it out here, where no one can see us. Got it from a smuggler. Without using your name, of course."

"Rhombur Vernius of Ix, I am shocked to find you consorting with smugglers and black marketeers."

"How else do you think I manage to infiltrate supplies to the rebels on Ix? I haven't been terribly effective so far, but I have indeed contacted some highly unsavory folk." He unsealed the coolpack and rummaged around for the unlabeled bottles. "And a few of them have proven, uh, quite resourceful."

The Duke guided the coracle into the current, following the lush shoreline. Thufir Hawat would probably lecture him for going so far without an Atreides honor guard. "I guess I could drink a bottle or two, then. As long as there's no Harkonnen profit in it."

Rhombur removed two containers from the coolpack and squeezed the tops to extrude spice-straws. "None whatsoever. Apparently, it was stolen during a raid on the brewery. A power outage caused a stir in the bottling plant, and, uh, somehow a pair of small Giedi cattle got loose inside the factory. There was substantial confusion, and a great deal of lost beer. A tragic waste. So many smashed bottles it would have been impossible to account for them all."

Standing at the coracle's engine controls, Leto sniffed at the dark liquid, stopped himself from taking a gulp. "How do we know it isn't tainted? I'm not in the habit of carrying a poison snooper onboard my own boat."

"This batch was bottled for the Baron himself. One look at his fat body, and you can well imagine how much of the stuff he must consume."

"Well, if it's good enough for Baron Harkonnen—*salud*." Leto took a sip of the bitter porter, filtered through melange crystals to enhance its flavor.

Slipping onto the bench behind Leto, Rhombur watched the Duke take them around a rocky point and then head toward a broad delta where barges laden with pundi rice converged. The Ixian Prince didn't sip from his beer yet. "This is a bribe," he admitted. "I need a favor. In fact, how about two favors?"

The Duke chuckled. "For *one* bottle of beer?"

"Uh, there's more in the coolpack. Look, I just want to be up-front with you. Leto, I consider you my closest friend. Even if you say no, I'll understand."

"You'll still be my friend if I say no to both favors?" Leto continued drinking through the straw.

Rhombur slid his bottle around on the table in front of him, from hand to hand. "I want to do something more significant for Ix, something more serious."

"You need more money? How else can I help?"

"Not money, well, not exactly. I've been sending C'tair Pilru funding and encouragement ever since he contacted me four years ago." He looked up, his forehead furrowed. "Word has reached me that the freedom fighters have been decimated, with only a few survivors. I think it's worse than even he lets on. It's time for me to stop playing around." Rhombur's eyes hardened, taking on a look Leto had last seen on Dominic Vernius during the revolt. "Let's give them some serious firepower so they can make a difference."

Leto took another long sip of beer. "I'll do anything within reason to help you regain your birthright, and I've always made that clear to you. What exactly do you have in mind?"

"I'd like to send explosives, some of the plaz-wafers in your armory. They're small and lightweight, so they're easily concealed and shipped."

"How many wafers?"

Rhombur didn't hesitate. "A thousand."

Leto whistled. "That'll cause a lot of destruction."

"Uh, that's the *point*, Leto."

He continued to steer the boat over a choppy intersection of currents toward the mouth of the river. Up ahead they could see the pilot boats and colorful seakites flown over the barge docks. "And how do you propose to get supplies onto Ix? Can your smuggler friends get the shipment to where C'tair can intercept it?"

"The Tleilaxu took control sixteen years ago. They're making regular shipments again, using their own transports and special Guild dispensations. They've had to loosen restrictions because they depend on outside suppliers for raw materials and special items. All the ships land on the rock shelves along the port-of-entry canyon. The hollowed-out grottoes there are big enough to accommodate warehouse frigates, and the tunnels intersect with the underground cities. Some of the frigate captains served under my father a long time ago, and they have, uh, offered to help."

Leto thought of the Earl of Ix, bald and boisterous, who had fought beside Paulus Atreides in the Ecazi Revolt. Based on his father's reputation as a war hero, Rhombur probably had more secret allies than even he realized.

"We can make special marked containers and get the word to C'tair. I think . . . I think we can pass all of the appropriate checkpoints." Suddenly angry, he pounded his fist on the wooden bench beside him. "Vermilion hells, Leto, I've got to *do* something! I haven't been able to set foot on my own home planet for nearly half my life!"

"If it were anyone else asking me this . . ." Leto caught himself, and said, "Possibly—so long as you conceal the involvement of House Atreides." He sighed. "Before I decide, what's the second favor?"

Now the Prince seemed truly nervous. "I've pondered how I should ask this, yet I couldn't come up with the right words. Everything seemed, uh, false and manipulative . . . but I need to tell you." He took a deep breath. "It's about my sister."

Leto, about to open a second beer, stopped short. His face darkened. "Some things are private matters, even from you, Rhombur."

The Prince gave him a commiserating smile. Since he had taken a Bene Gesserit as his concubine and fast friend, he had grown wiser. "The two of you have gotten off track, through no one's fault. It just happened. I know you still care deeply for Kailea—and don't try to deny it. She's done a lot for House Atreides, helping with the accounts and commercial matters. My father always said she had the best instinct for business in our family."

With a sad shake of his head, Leto said, "She used to be full of good advice. But since Chiara came, she's demanded more and more trappings and fineries. Even when I give them to her, Kailea seems dissatisfied. She's . . . she's not the same woman I fell in love with."

Rhombur drank from his own beer, smacked his lips at the bitterness. "Maybe that's because you've stopped giving her a chance, stopped letting her use her business skills. Put her in charge of one of your industries—paradan melons, pundi rice, coral gems—and watch the production increase. I can't imagine how far she might have gone if, uh, the revolt hadn't happened on Ix."

Leto pushed his bottle aside. "Did she put you up to this?"

"Leto, my sister is a rare woman. I'm asking this as your friend, and as her brother." Rhombur passed a hand through his tousled blond hair. "Give Kailea the opportunity to be more than a concubine."

Gazing at the exiled Prince, Leto became as cold and stiff as a statue. "So you want me to marry her?" Rhombur had never used their friendship to force an issue, and Leto had never dreamed he could deny his friend anything. But this . . .

Biting his lower lip, Rhombur nodded. "Yes, uh, I suppose that's what I'm asking."

They both remained silent for a long, long moment as the coracle swayed. A huge barge lumbered across the delta toward the docks.

Leto's thoughts churned, and he finally reached a difficult decision. He drew a deep breath, flaring his nostrils. "I'll say yes to one of your favors—but you must choose which one."

Rhombur swallowed hard, noted the anguished expression on Leto's face. After a long moment he looked away. When he squared his shoulders, Leto was uneasy about what he would say. He had put everything on the line.

Finally, the exiled Prince of Ix answered in a wavering voice, "Then I choose the future of my people. You have taught me the importance of this. I need those explosives. I just hope C'tair Pilru can put them to good use."

He leaned forward and took a long drink of the smuggled Harkonnen beer, then reached out to clasp Leto's forearm.

"If there's one thing I've learned from the Atreides, it's to put the people foremost, and personal wishes second. Kailea will just have to understand that."

The Duke took their coracle around sandbars into the river channel, toward the mounded barges bedecked with green ribbons fluttering in the breezes. People were gathered at the docks, loading sack after sack of Caladan's primary grain export. Wagons rolled up along the riverbank, while low-riding boats drifted in from flooded fields. Someone shot homemade fireworks into the air, which banged and sizzled with color in the cloudy skies.

Leto brought their boat up against the main docks near a fully loaded barge preparing to launch. A large ornamental podium, surrounded by green-and-white streamers, waited for him.

Pushing his difficult discussion with Rhombur to the back of his mind, Leto put on a noble face and enjoyed the festivities. It was one of his traditional duties as Duke Atreides.

Facts mean nothing when they are preempted by appearances.
Do not underestimate the power of impression over reality.

—CROWN PRINCE RAPHAEL CORRINO,
The Rudiments of Power

BARON HARKONNEN HOBBLED TO THE HIGHEST TOWER BALCONY OF THE family Keep overlooking the morass of Harko City. He leaned on his sandworm-head cane—and hated it.

Without the cane, though, he couldn't move.

Damn the witches and what they've done to me! He had never ceased brooding on how he might get his revenge, but since both the Sisterhood and House Harkonnen held mutual blackmail information, neither could move openly against the other.

I must find a more subtle way.

"Piter de Vries!" he bellowed to anyone who could hear him. "Send in my Mentat!"

De Vries lurked near him at all times, hovering there, spying and scheming. The Baron needed only to shout, and the twisted Mentat could hear. If only everyone else obeyed him as well—Rabban, the Mother Superior, even that smug Suk doctor Yueh. . . .

As expected, the feral man danced in on tiptoes, moving with rubbery limbs. He carried a sealed parcel in his arms, right on time. The Baron's engineers had promised results, and every one of them knew he would flay them alive if they failed him.

"Your new suspensors, my Baron." De Vries bowed and extended the container toward his master's lumbering hulk. "If you strap them about your waist, they will decrease your body weight and allow you to move with unaccustomed freedom."

Reaching out with pudgy hands, the Baron tore open the package. "The freedom I *used* to have." Inside, linked together on a chain belt, were small globes of self-contained suspensors, each with its own power pack. While he didn't think he would fool anyone, at least the suspensor belt would help hide the depth of his infirmity. And make others wonder . . .

"They may require a bit of practice to use—"

"They'll make me feel fit and healthy again." The Baron grinned as he held the suspensor globes in front of him, then fastened the belt around his grotesquely swollen waist—how had his belly grown so large? He toggled on the suspensor globes, one by one. With each additional hum, he felt the weight lessening from his feet, his joints, his shoulders. "Ahhh!"

The Baron took a long step and bounded across the room like an explorer on a low-gravity world. "Piter, look at me! Ha, ha!" He landed on one foot, then sprang into the air again, leaping nearly to the ceiling. Laughing, he bounced once more, then spun on his left foot like an acrobat. "This is so much better."

The twisted Mentat hovered by the door, wearing a self-satisfied smile.

The Baron landed again and swept his cane from side to side with a whistling sound like an athletic fencer. "Exactly as I had hoped." He smacked the cane hard on the unyielding desk surface.

"The parameters may take some getting used to, my Baron. Don't overextend yourself," the Mentat cautioned, knowing the Baron would do exactly the opposite.

With the footwork of a gross ballet dancer, Baron Harkonnen crossed the room and clapped an astonished Piter de Vries paternally on the cheeks, then moved toward the high, open balcony.

As de Vries watched the big man's foolishly overconfident movements, he imagined that the Baron would misjudge his bounding strides and sail off the edge of the Keep tower and into open sky. *I can only hope.*

The suspensors would hinder his descent somewhat, but they could only lessen the immense weight. The Baron would strike the distant pavement at a slightly decreased velocity— but he would splatter across the streets, nonetheless. *An unexpected bonus.*

Since de Vries was responsible for watching over the family's various assets, including hidden spice stockpiles such as the one on Lankiveil, the Baron's demise would enable him to shift ownership to himself. Dimwitted Rabban wouldn't know what was happening.

Perhaps a nudge in the right direction—

But the big man caught himself on the balcony rail and rebounded, settling into an enthusiastic pause. He stared across the smoky streets and sprawling buildings. The metropolis looked black and grimy, industrial buildings and administrative towers that had sunk their roots into Giedi Prime. Beyond the city lay even dirtier agricultural and mining villages, squalid places that were barely worth the trouble of keeping in line. Far below, like lice crawling the streets, workers milled about between labor shifts.

The Baron hefted his cane. "I don't need this anymore." He took one last look at the silver maw of the symbolic sandworm on its head, ran his swollen fingers along the smooth wood of the shaft—then hurled the walking stick out into open space.

He leaned over the railing to watch it drop, spinning and dwindling, toward the streets below. He held out a childish hope that it might strike someone on the head.

Buoyed by the globes on his belt, the Baron returned to the main room, where a disappointed Piter de Vries looked toward the abrupt edge of the balcony. The Mentat knew he could never scheme against the Baron, for he would be discovered and executed. The Baron could always obtain another Mentat from the Bene Tleilax, perhaps even a new de Vries ghola grown from his own dead cells. His only hope lay in a fortuitous accident . . . or an acceleration of the effects of the Bene Gesserit disease.

"Now nothing can stop me, Piter," the Baron said, delighted. "The Imperium had better watch out for Baron Vladimir Harkonnen."

"Yes, I suppose so," the Mentat said.

If you surrender, you have already lost. If you refuse to give up, though, no matter the odds against you, at least you have succeeded in trying.

—DUKE PAULUS ATREIDES

IF HE WAS TO RESCUE HIS SISTER, GURNEY HALLECK KNEW HE HAD TO ACT alone.

He planned carefully for two months, aching to move, knowing Bheth was suffering every moment, every night. But his scheme would be doomed to fail if he didn't take every possibility into account. He obtained crude maps of Giedi Prime and laid out his route to Mount Ebony. It seemed very far away, farther than he had ever traveled in his life.

He was tense, fearing the villagers would notice his activities, but they staggered through their days with gazes downcast. Even his parents said little to him, noticing nothing of his moods, as if their son had disappeared along with their daughter.

Finally, as prepared as he was ever going to be, Gurney waited until darkness. And then he simply . . . left.

With a sack of krall tubers and vegetables slung over one shoulder and a harvesting knife tucked into his belt, he made his way across the patchwork fields. He hid from roads and patrols, sleeping during the day, traveling under the wan moonlight. He doubted searchers would come after him. The Dmitri villagers would assume that the troublemaker had been snatched away in the middle of the night by Harkonnen torturers; with any luck, they'd be afraid to report his disappearance at all.

Several nights, Gurney managed to slip aboard unmanned cargo transports that crawled westward across the landscape, heading in the correct direction. Their hulking forms levitated along without stopping, all through the night. The transports took him hundreds of kilometers, allowing him to rest and brood and wait until he could find the military compound.

During long hours, he listened to the throb of suspensor engines that dragged produce or minerals to processing centers. He longed for his baliset, which he'd been forced to abandon back at home, for it was too bulky to carry on his mission. When he had the instrument, no matter how much the overlords took from his family, he could still make his own music. He missed those days. Now he just hummed to himself, all alone.

Finally, he saw the looming cone of Mount Ebony, the stark and blackened remnant of a volcano whose cliffs had broken off at sharp angles. The rock itself was black, as if covered with tar.

The military compound was a jigsaw puzzle of evenly spaced buildings, all square, all undecorated. It looked like an insect warren established uphill and upwind from the slave pits and obsidian mines. Between the fenced-in slave pits and the regimented military encampment lay a hodgepodge of buildings, support facilities, inns . . . and a small pleasure house to entertain the Harkonnen troops.

So far Gurney had made his way undetected. The Harkonnen masters could not conceive that a downtrodden laborer with little education and few resources would dare to strike out across Giedi Prime on his own, would venture to spy upon the troops with a personal goal in mind.

But he had to make his way into the place where Bheth must be imprisoned. Gurney hid and waited, observing the military compound and trying to formulate his plan. He came up with few alternatives.

Still, he wouldn't let that stop him.

A LOWBORN, UNEDUCATED man could never hope to pass himself off as someone who belonged there, so Gurney could not infiltrate the pleasure house. Instead he chose a daring raid. He grasped a metal pipe taken from a refuse pile and held his harvesting knife in the other hand. Stealth would be sacrificed for speed.

He charged through a side door of the pleasure house and ran to the administrator, a crippled old man wired into a chair at the front table. "Where's Bheth?" the intruder yelled, surprised to hear his own voice after so long. He thrust the point of his blade under the old man's sinewy chin. "Bheth Halleck, where is she?"

Gurney reeled for a moment. What if Harkonnen pleasure houses never bothered with the names of their women? Trembling, the old man saw death in Gurney's blazing eyes and the scars on his face. "Chamber twenty-one," he said in a croak.

Gurney dragged the administrator, chair and all, into a closet and locked him in. Then he raced up the hall.

A few surly customers stared at him, some half-dressed in Harkonnen uniforms. He heard screams and thumps from behind closed doors, but he had no time to investigate the atrocities. His concentration focused only on one thing. *Chamber twenty-one. Bheth.*

His vision tunneled down to a pinpoint until he located the door. His audacity had bought him a little time, but it would be only moments before Harkonnen soldiers were called. He didn't know how fast he could get Bheth out and into hiding. Together, they could race across the landscape, vanish into the wilderness. After that, he didn't know where they would go.

He couldn't think. He only knew that he had to try.

The number was scribed on the lintel in Imperial Galach. He heard a scuffle inside. Using his muscular shoulder, Gurney battered the door. It splintered at the jamb and caved in with a heavy thud.

"Bheth!" Letting out a wild roar, he rushed into the dimly lit chamber, knife in one hand, metal club in the other.

From the bed she gave a muffled cry, and he turned to see her tied up with thin metal cables. Thick grease had been smeared over her breasts and lower body like war paint, and two naked Harkonnen soldiers lurched back from their activities like startled snakes. Both men held strangely shaped tools, one of which sparked and sizzled.

Gurney didn't want to imagine what they'd been doing, had forced himself not to contemplate the sadistic tortures that Bheth endured daily. His roar became a strangled cry in his throat as he saw her—and froze in shock. The vision of his sister's humiliation, the tragic sight of what had happened to her in the intervening four years, doomed his rescue attempt to failure.

He hesitated only an instant, his jaw dropping. Bheth had changed so much, her face drawn and aged, her body wiry and bruised . . . so different from the silken seventeen-year-old he had known. During the fraction of a second that Gurney stood motionless, his angry momentum stalled.

It took the Harkonnen soldiers only a heartbeat to leap from the bed and fall upon him.

Even without their gauntlets, boots, or body armor, the men pummeled him to the floor. They knew exactly where to strike. One of the men jabbed a sparking device against his throat, and his entire left side went numb. He thrashed uncontrollably.

Bheth could only make wordless, breathy sounds as she struggled against the wires that held her to the bed. Oddly, he noticed a long, thin scar tracing a white line along her throat. She had no larynx.

Gurney couldn't see her anymore as his vision turned crimson. He heard heavy footsteps and shouts thundering down the halls. Reinforcements. He couldn't get up.

With a sagging heart, he realized he had failed. They would kill him and probably murder Bheth, too. *If only I hadn't hesitated.* That instant of uncertainty had defeated him.

One of the men looked down, lips drawn in a rictus of fury. Spittle ran from the left corner of his mouth, and his blue eyes, which might have been handsome at another time, on another person, glared at him. The guard snatched the harvesting knife and the metal pipe from Gurney's limp hands and held them both up. Grinning, the Harkonnen soldier tossed the knife aside—but kept the pipe.

"We know where to send you, lad," he said.

He heard Bheth's odd whispering again, but she could form no words.

Then the guard swung the metal pipe down on Gurney's head.

Dreams are as simple or as complicated as the dreamer.

—LIET-KYNES,
In the Footsteps of My Father

AS ARMED MEN LED THE TWO YOUNG FREMEN DEEPER INTO A WARREN within the glacial mountainside, Liet-Kynes held his tongue. He studied details, trying to understand who these fugitives were. Their threadbare purple-and-copper uniforms seemed to have been modeled after military fashion.

The tunnels had been chewed into walls of permafrost-cemented dust and lined with a clear polymer. The air remained cold enough that Liet could see his own breath, a dramatic reminder of how much moisture left his lungs each time he exhaled.

"So, are you smugglers?" Warrick asked. At first his eyes remained downcast with embarrassment to have been caught so easily, but soon he was intrigued and looked around.

Dominic Vernius glanced back at them as they kept pace. "Smugglers . . . and more, lads. Our mission goes beyond mere profit and self-interest." He did not seem angry. Beneath the mustache, bright white teeth flashed in a sincere grin. His face possessed an open quality, and his bald pate shone like polished wood. His eyes contained hints of sparkle, but what might have been a good-natured personality now held an emptiness, as if a large part of the man had been stolen and replaced with something far inferior.

"Aren't you showing them too much, Dom?" said a pock-faced man whose right eyebrow was a waxy burn scar. "It's always been just us, who've proved our loyalty with blood—no outsiders. Right, Asuyo?"

"Can't say I trust the Fremen any less than that Tuek man, and we do business with him, eh?" said one of the other men—a lean veteran with a shock of bristly gray-white hair. On his worn overalls and uniform, he had painstakingly added old insignia of rank and a few scraps of medals. "Tuek sells water, but he has an . . . *oily* quality to him."

The bald smuggler continued deeper into the complex without pausing. "Johdam, these lads found *us* without me showing them a thing. We've been sloppy—just be glad it was Fremen, instead of Sardaukar. Fremen don't have any more love for the Emperor than we do, right, lads?"

Liet and Warrick looked at each other. "Emperor Shaddam is far away, and he knows nothing of Dune."

"He knows nothing of honor, either." A storm crossed Dominic's face, but he calmed himself by changing the subject. "I've heard that the Imperial Planetologist has gone native, that he's become a Fremen himself and talks about remaking the planet. Is this true? Does Shaddam support these activities?"

"The Emperor is not aware of any ecological plans." Liet withheld his true Fremen identity, said nothing about his father, and introduced himself by his other appellation, "My name is . . . Weichih."

"Well, it's good to have grandiose, impossible dreams." Dominic looked distant for a moment. "We all have them."

Liet was not certain what the big man meant. "So why are you hiding here? Who are you?"

The others deferred to Dominic. "We've been here fifteen years now, and this is only one of our bases. We have a more important one off-world, but I still have a soft spot for our first hiding hole on Arrakis."

Warrick nodded. "You have created your own sietch here."

Dominic stopped at an opening where broad plaz windows looked down into a deep chasm between the towering cliffs. On the flat, gravelly bottom of the fissure, a fleet of mismatched ships sat parked in regimented order. Around one of the lighters, small figures hurried to load cases of cargo, preparing for lift-off.

"We have a few more amenities than a sietch, lad, and a more cosmopolitan outlook." He studied the two Fremen. "But we must retain our secrets. What tipped you off, lads? Why did you come here? How did you see through our camouflage?"

When Warrick started to speak, Liet cut him off to say, "And what do we receive in exchange for telling you this?"

"Your lives, eh?" Asuyo said gruffly. His gray-white hair bristled.

Liet shook his head, standing firm. "You could kill us even after we pointed out all the mistakes you've made. You're outlaws, not Fremen—why should I trust your word?"

"Outlaws?" Dominic gave a bitter laugh. "The laws of the Imperium have caused more damage than any single person's treachery . . . except perhaps that of the Emperor himself. Old Elrood and now Shaddam." His haunted eyes held their distant, unfocused look. "Damned Corrinos . . ." Taking one step away from the cliff-wall windows, he paused again. "You lads aren't thinking of turning me in to the Sardaukar, are you? I'm sure there's still an incredible bounty on my head."

Warrick looked at his friend. Both wore puzzled expressions. "We don't even know who you are, sir."

Some of the smugglers chuckled. Dominic let out a sigh of relief, then showed a flash of disappointment. He puffed up his chest. "I was a hero of the Ecazi Revolt, married one of the Emperor's concubines. I was overthrown when invaders took over my world."

The politics and the vastness of the Imperium were far beyond Liet's Fremen experience. Occasionally, he longed to journey off-planet, though he doubted he would ever have the opportunity.

The bald man stroked the polymer-lined walls. "Being inside these tunnels always reminds me of Ix . . ." His voice, wistful and empty, trailed off. "That's why I chose this place, why I keep coming back here from our other base."

Dominic emerged from his reverie, as if surprised to see his fellow smugglers still there. "Asuyo, Johdam—we'll take these lads to my private office." With a wry smile, he looked back at the two young men. "It's modeled after a chamber in the Grand Palais, as close as I could remember it. I didn't have time to take blueprints when we packed up and fled."

The bald man marched ahead, reciting the story of his life, as if it were dry text from a history filmbook. "My wife was murdered by Sardaukar. My son and daughter now live in exile on Caladan. Early on, I made one raid against Ix and almost died in the process. Lost a lot of my men, and Johdam barely pulled me out alive. Since then I've been in hiding, doing what I could to hurt those sligs, the Padishah Emperors and the Landsraad turncoats who betrayed me."

They passed storage hangars where equipment hid under tarpaulins, workbenches and mechanical bays where machines lay strewn about in various stages of disassembly or repair. "But my work hasn't amounted to much more than vandalism, wrecking Corrino monuments, defacing statues, staging embarrassing stunts . . . being a general nuisance to Shaddam. Of course, with his new daughter Josifa—that's four girls and no son, no heir—he's got more problems than I can make for him."

Behind him, pock-faced Johdam growled, "Causing trouble for the Corrinos has become our way of life."

Asuyo scratched his bristly hair and spoke in a harsh voice, "We all owe Earl Vernius our lives many times over—and we're not about to let any harm come to him. I gave up my commission, my benefits, even a decent rank in the Imperial military to join this motley group. We won't let any Fremen pups give away our secrets, eh?"

"You can trust the word of a Fremen," Warrick said, indignantly.

"But we haven't *given* our word," Liet pointed out, his eyes narrow and hard. "*Yet.*"

They reached a room appointed clumsily with fine trappings, as if a man with no cultural finesse had gathered items he could remember, but which didn't entirely fit together. Faux-gold coins overflowed from chests, making the room look like a pirate's treasure house. The casual treatment of the commemorative pieces—struck with Shaddam's face on one side and the Golden Lion Throne on the other—gave the impression that the bald man did not know what else to do with all the money he had stolen.

Dominic ran a callused hand through a bowl of shimmering emerald spheres, each the size of his small fingernail. "Moss pearls from Harmonthep. Shando always loved these, said the color was a perfect shade of green." Unlike Rondo Tuek, the bald man did not appear to revel in his private trappings for their own sake, but he drew comfort from the memories they brought him.

After sending Johdam and Asuyo away, Dominic Vernius sat down in a padded purple chair, indicating cushions on the opposite side of a low table for his visitors. Colors ranging from scarlet to crimson flowed like puddles across the sleek wood surface.

"Polished bloodwood." Dominic rapped the low table with his knuckles, causing a burst of color to spread out across the grain. "The sap still flows when heated by warm lights, even years after the tree was cut down." He stared at the walls and hangings. Several crude sketches of people hung there in expensive frames, as if Dominic had drawn them from too-clear memories but with too little artistic training.

"My men fought with me in the bloodwood forests on Ecaz. We killed many rebels there, torched their base deep in the forest. You saw Johdam and Asuyo—they were two of my captains. Johdam lost his brother there, in the forests. . . ." He took a long, shuddering breath. "That was back when I willingly shed blood for the Emperor, when I swore my allegiance to Elrood IX and expected a reward in return. He offered me anything I wanted, and I took the one thing that angered him."

Beside him, Dominic reached into a glazed pot filled with golden commemorative coins. "Now I do everything I can against the Emperor."

Liet frowned. "But Elrood has been dead for many years, since I was a baby. Shaddam IV now sits on the Golden Lion Throne."

Warrick sat next to his friend. "We don't hear much news of the Imperium, but even I know that."

"Alas, Shaddam is as bad as his father." In his hands, Dominic played with several of the faux-gold coins, jingling them together. He sat up straight, as if he suddenly realized how many years had passed, how long he'd been hiding. "Very well, then, listen to me. We are of course indignant and offended that you have trespassed here. Two lads . . . what are you, sixteen?" A smile wrinkled the leathery skin on Dominic's cheeks. "My men are embarrassed that you found us out. I would very much like for you to go outside and show us what you noticed. Name your price, and I'll meet it."

Liet's mind whirled as he considered the resources and skills this group had. Treasure lay all around, but neither of them could use baubles like the green pearls. Some of the tools and equipment might be useful. . . .

Being cautious and thinking through the consequences, Liet did a very Fremen thing. "We will agree, Dominic Vernius—but I stipulate that we hold your obligation in abeyance. When I wish to receive a boon from you, I will ask—as will Warrick. For now, we will instruct your men in how to make your hideout invisible." Liet smiled. "Even to Fremen."

BUNDLED UP, THE smugglers followed as the two young men indicated the imperfectly covered tracks, the discoloration in the glacial cliffside wall, the too-obvious paths that led up the rock slope. Even when the Fremen pointed out these things, some of the smugglers still couldn't see what should have been plain to them. Still, Johdam scowled and promised to make the suggested changes.

Dominic Vernius stood breathing cold air and shaking his head in amazement. "No matter how much security one adds to a home, there are always ways to breach it." His lips drew downward in a frown. "Generations of planners tried to develop perfect isolation on Ix. Only our royal family understood the whole system. What a monumental waste of effort and solaris! Our underground cities were supposed to be impregnable, and we grew lax in our security. Just like these men here."

He clapped Johdam on the back. The pock-faced veteran frowned and went back to his work.

The big bald man sighed once more. "At least my children got away." His face screwed up in an expression of disgust. "Damn the filthy Tleilaxu and damn House Corrino!" He spat on the ground, startling Liet. Among the Fremen, spitting— offering the body's water—was a gesture of respect given only to an honored few. But Dominic Vernius had used it as a curse.

Strange ways, Liet thought.

The bald man looked at the two young Fremen. "My main base off-planet probably suffers from similar flaws, too." He leaned closer. "Should either of you ever wish to come with me, you could inspect our other facilities. We make regular runs to Salusa Secundus."

Liet perked up. "Salusa?" He recalled his father's stories of growing up there. "I've heard it is a fascinating world."

From where he worked off to one side, Johdam let out a disbelieving laugh. He rubbed a sweat-itch at his scarred eyebrow. "It sure doesn't look like the capital of the Imperium anymore." Asuyo shook his head in agreement.

Dominic shrugged. "I am the leader of a renegade House, and I vowed to strike against the Imperium. Salusa Secundus seemed a good place to hide. Who would think to look for me on a prison planet, under the Emperor's closest security?"

Pardot Kynes had spoken of the terrible Salusan disaster caused by the rebellion of an unnamed noble family. They had gone renegade and unleashed forbidden atomics on the capital planet. A few members of House Corrino survived, including Hassik III, who had rebuilt the dynasty and restored Imperial government on a new world, Kaitain.

Pardot Kynes had been less interested in history or politics than in the natural order of things, how the world had been changed from paradise to hell by the holocaust. The Planetologist claimed that with sufficient investment and hard work, Salusa Secundus could be restored to its former climate and glory.

"Someday, perhaps, I would like to behold such an . . . interesting place." *A world that so affected my father.*

With a loud, booming laugh, Dominic pounded Liet on the back. It was a gesture of camaraderie, though Fremen rarely touched each other except during knife fights. "Pray you never have to, boy," the smuggler leader said. "Pray you never have to."

Water is the image of life. We came from water, adapted from its all-encompassing presence . . . and we continue to adapt.

—IMPERIAL PLANETOLOGIST PARDOT KYNES

"OUT HERE, WE FREMEN HAVE NONE OF YOUR COMFORTS, LADY FENRING," the Shadout Mapes said as she scurried ahead on short legs. Her steps were so precise and careful that she did not even kick up dust on the moonlit hardpan. In contrast with the humid conservatory, the bone-dry night retained very little of the day's heat. "You are cold?"

She glanced back at willowy, blonde-haired Margot, who walked proudly in front of the Rutii priest. Mapes wore her jubba hood. Stillsuit filters dangled beside her face, and her dark eyes reflected the light of Second Moon.

"I am not cold," Margot said, simply. Wearing only her glitterslick housedress, she adjusted her metabolism to compensate.

"And those thin-soled slippers you wear," the priest scolded from behind her. "Unsuited for desert travel."

"You did not give me time to dress for our journey." Like all Reverend Mothers, she maintained thick calluses on her feet from the fighting exercises they were required to perform each day. "If the shoes wear out, I will go barefoot."

Both Fremen smiled at her calm audacity. "She does maintain a good pace," Mapes admitted. "Not like other water-fat Imperials."

"I can go faster," Margot offered, "if you like."

Taking this as a challenge, the Shadout Mapes trotted along at a military cadence, not breathing hard at all. Margot followed every footstep, barely perspiring. A nightbird streaked overhead with a piercing cry.

The unpaved road led out of Arrakeen toward the village of Rutii in the distance, nestled within knuckled foothills of the Shield Wall. Avoiding the town lights, Mapes turned onto a faint path that climbed into the rocky elevations.

Rimwall West loomed before them, a craggy megalith that marked this boundary of the Shield Wall. The small party began to climb, at first over a gentle slope of rock, then up a steep, narrow path that skirted an immense slide area.

The Fremen moved with speed and surefootedness in the shadows. Despite her training in balance and endurance, Margot tripped twice on the unfamiliar terrain and had to be steadied by the others. This seemed to please the guides.

More than two hours had passed since leaving the comfort and safety of the Residency at Arrakeen. Margot began to tap her bodily reserves, but still showed no sign of weakness. *Did our lost Sisters travel this way?*

Mapes and the priest spoke strange words in a language that Margot's deep memories told her was Chakobsa, a tongue spoken by Fremen for dozens of centuries, since their arrival on Arrakis. As she recognized one of the Shadout's phrases, Margot responded, "The power of God is indeed great."

Her remark agitated the priest, but his short-statured companion smiled wisely. "The Sayyadina will speak with her."

The path forked several times, and the Fremen woman led the way up, then down, or laterally in tight switchbacks, before ascending again. Margot identified the same places in the frosty moonlight, and realized they were guiding her back and forth in an effort to confuse and disorient her. With her Bene Gesserit mental skills, Margot would remember the way back, in exact detail.

Impatient and curious, she wanted to scold the Fremen for

taking her on such an unnecessarily tedious route, but decided not to reveal her ability. After years of waiting, she was being led into their secret world, into a place where no outsiders were ever taken. Mother Superior Harishka would want her to observe every detail. Perhaps Margot would finally acquire the information she had sought for so long.

On a ledge, Mapes pressed her chest against the cliff and inched along a narrow path over a sheer dropoff, clinging with fingertips. Without hesitation, Margot did the same. The lights of Arrakeen twinkled in the distance, and the village of Rutii huddled far below.

Several meters ahead now, Mapes suddenly disappeared into the rock face. Margot discovered a small cave entrance, barely large enough for a person to enter. Inside, the space grew broader to the left, and in the dim light she saw tool marks on the walls where Fremen had widened the cavern. The dense odors of unwashed bodies touched her nostrils. Ahead, the Shadout beckoned.

When the priest caught up, Mapes unfastened a doorseal and swung a camouflaged door inward. Now, unmuffled by seals and doors, voices could be heard, mixed with the hum of machinery and the rustle of many people. Glowglobes tuned to dim yellow bobbed in the air currents.

Mapes passed through a fabric-covered doorway into a room where women worked power looms, weaving long strands of hair and desert cotton into fabrics. The warm air held a heavy human musk and waftings of melange-incense. All eyes watched the regal, blonde visitor.

The weaving room opened into another chamber, where a man tended a metal pot suspended over a cooking fire. Firelight danced on the Shadout's wrinkled face and imparted a feral look to her deep blue eyes. Margot observed everything, storing details for her later report. She had never imagined the Fremen could hide such a population, such a settlement.

Finally, they emerged into a larger, dirt-floored chamber filled with desert plants, sectioned off by paths. She recognized saguaro, wild alfalfa, creosote, and poverty grasses. An entire botanical testing ground!

"Wait here, Lady Fenring." Mapes strode ahead, accompanied by the priest. Alone, Margot bent to examine the cacti, saw glossy ears, firm flesh, pale new growth. Somewhere in another cavern she heard voices and resonating chants.

At a slight sound she looked up to see an ancient woman in a black robe. Standing by herself on one of the garden pathways, arms folded over her chest, the strange woman was withered and wiry, as tough as shigawire. She wore a necklace of sparkling metal rings, and her dark eyes looked like shadowed pits gouged into her face.

Something about her demeanor, her *presence*, reminded Margot of a Bene Gesserit. On Wallach IX, Mother Superior Harishka was approaching the two-century mark, but this woman looked even older, her body saturated with spice, her skin aged by climate more than years. Even her voice was dry. "I am Sayyadina Ramallo. We are about to begin the Ceremony of the Seed. Join us, if you are truly who you say you are."

Ramallo! I know that name. Margot stepped forward, ready to cite the secret code phrases to identify her awareness of the Missionaria Protectiva work. A woman named Ramallo had disappeared into the dunes a full century ago . . . the last of a series of Reverend Mothers to vanish.

"No time for that now, child," the old woman interrupted her. "Everyone is waiting. With you among us, they are as curious as I am."

Margot followed the Sayyadina into a vast cavern that thronged with thousands upon thousands of people. She had never imagined such a huge enclosure within the high rocks— how had they eluded detection from the constant Harkonnen patrols? This wasn't just a squalid settlement, but an entire hidden city. The Fremen had far more secrets, and far greater plans, than even Hasimir Fenring suspected.

A wall of unpleasant scents assailed her. Crowded close, some of the Fremen wore dusty cloaks; others were in still-suits, open at the collars within the body-humid cave. Off to one side stood the priest who had brought her from Arrakeen.

I'm certain they left no sign of our departure from the conservatory. If they mean to kill me now, no one will ever know what happened—just like the other Sisters. Then Margot smiled to herself. *No, if I am harmed, Hasimir will find them.* The Fremen might think their secrets were safe, but even they could be no match for her Count, should he focus his efforts and intellect on tracking them down.

The Fremen might doubt that, but Margot did not.

As the last of the desert people streamed into the cavern from several entrances, Ramallo took Margot's hand in her sinewy grip. "Come with me." The withered Sayyadina led the way up stone steps to a rock platform, where she faced the crowd.

The cavern fell silent except for a rustle of clothes, like bat wings.

With some trepidation, Margot took a position beside the old woman. *I feel like a sacrifice.* She used breathing exercises to calm herself. Wave upon wave of impenetrable Fremen eyes stared at her.

"Shai-Hulud watches over us," Ramallo said. "Let the watermasters come forward."

Four men made their way through the crowd. Each pair carried a small skin sack between them. They placed the sloshing containers at the feet of the Sayyadina.

"Is there seed?" Ramallo asked.

"There is seed," the men announced, in unison. They turned and departed.

Opening the top of one of the sacks, Ramallo splashed liquid onto both hands. "Blessed is the water and its seed." She brought her hands out, trickling blue fluid as if the droplets were liquid sapphires.

The words and the ceremony startled Margot, for they resembled the Bene Gesserit poison ordeal through which a Sister was transformed into a Reverend Mother. A few chemicals—all deadly poisons—could be used to induce the terrible agony and mental crisis upon a Sister. Adapted from the Missionaria Protectiva? Had the vanished Bene Gesserit brought even this secret to the Fremen? If so, what else did the desert people know about the Sisterhood's plans?

Ramallo unfastened the sack's coiled spout and pointed its end toward Margot. Showing no glimmer of doubt, Margot dropped to her knees and took the tube in her hands, then hesitated.

"If you are truly a Reverend Mother," Ramallo whispered, "you will drink this exhalation of Shai-Hulud without harm to yourself."

"I am a Reverend Mother," Margot said. "I have done this before."

The Fremen maintained their deep, reverent silence.

"You have never done *this* before, child," the old woman said. "Shai-Hulud will judge you."

The sack reeked of familar spice odor, but with an underlying bitterness. The acrid blue liquid seemed to roil with death. Though she had passed the Agony to become a Reverend Mother, Margot had nearly died in the process.

But she could do it again.

Beside her, the Sayyadina uncoiled the drinking tube on the second sack. She took a sip from the tube, and her eyes rolled back in her head.

I must not fear, Margot thought. *Fear is the mind-killer* . . . In her mind she recited the entire Litany Against Fear, then sucked on the straw, drawing in just a drop. The barest bit of moisture, touching the tip of her tongue.

It struck her with a shockingly vile taste, like a hammer, all the way to the back of her skull. Poison! Her body recoiled, but she forced herself to concentrate on her own chemistry, altered a molecule here, added or subtracted a radical there. It required all of her skills.

Margot released the tube. Her consciousness floated, and time stopped its eternal, cosmic progression. She let her body, her trained Bene Gesserit abilities take over and begin to alter the chemistry of the deadly poison. Margot understood what she had to do, breaking the chemical down into something useful, creating a catalyst that would transform the rest of the liquid in the sacks. . . .

The taste changed to sweetness in her mouth.

Every action she had taken up to that point in her life lay spread like a tapestry for her to observe. Sister Margot Rashino-Zea, now Lady Margot Fenring, examined herself in minute detail, every cell of her body, every nerve fiber . . . every thought she'd ever experienced. Deep in her core, Margot found that terrible dark place she could never see, the place that fascinated and terrified all of her kind. Only the long-anticipated Kwisatz Haderach could look there. The *Lisan al-Gaib*.

I will survive this, she told herself.

Margot's head reverberated as if a gong had been struck inside it. She saw a distorted image of Sayyadina Ramallo wavering in front of her. Then one of the watermasters came forward and pressed the tip of the tube into Margot's mouth, collecting the drop of transformed liquid, which he then dipped into the contents of the sack. Beside her, the ancient woman released her grip on the second tube, and other watermasters spread the transformed poison from one container to another like firestarters touching flaming brands to a field of dry grass.

People thronged to the sacks to receive droplets of the catalyzed drug, brushing the moistness against their lips. Ramallo said, somewhere in Margot's consciousness, "You have helped make it possible for them."

Strange. This was so different from anything in her experience . . . but not so different after all.

Slowly, like a dreamer dancing inside her own consciousness, Margot felt herself return to the stone-walled chamber, with the drug-induced vision only a flickering memory. Fremen continued to touch their fingers to the hanging droplets, tasting, moving to the side so that others could partake. Euphoria spread like dawnlight in the cavern.

"Yes, once I was a Reverend Mother," Ramallo told her, at long last. "Many years ago I knew your Mother Superior."

Still fogged by reverberations of the powerful drug, Margot couldn't even act shocked, and the old woman nodded. "Sister Harishka and I were classmates . . . long, long ago. I joined the Missionaria Protectiva and was sent here with nine other Reverend Mothers. Many of our order had been lost before, absorbed into the Fremen tribes. Others simply died in the desert. I am the last. It is a harsh life on Dune, even for a trained Bene Gesserit. Even with melange, which we have come to understand, and appreciate, in new ways."

Margot looked deeply into Ramallo's eyes and saw understanding there.

"Your message spoke of the *Lisan al-Gaib*," Ramallo said, her voice quavering. "He is close, is he not? After these thousands of years."

Margot kept her voice low as the Fremen became wilder with the ecstasy of their ritual. "We hope within two generations."

"These people have waited a long time." The Sayyadina surveyed the euphoria in the room. "I can reveal Bene Gesserit matters to you, child, but I have a dual allegiance. I am also a Fremen now, sworn to uphold the values of the desert tribes. Certain confidences cannot be revealed to any outworlder.

One day I must choose a successor—one of the women here, no doubt."

Ramallo bowed her head. "The sietch tau orgy is a merging point of Bene Gesserit and Fremen. Long before the Missionaria Protectiva arrived here, these people had discovered how to partake of the awareness-spectrum narcotic in primitive, simple ways."

In the shadows of the great chamber the Fremen moved apart, and together, fogged with the drug, some raised to an inner peace and ecstasy, some driven to members of the opposite sex in frenzied coupling. A sloppily painted canvas of reality settled over them, turning their harsh lives into a dream image.

"Over the centuries, Sisters like myself guided them to follow new ceremonies, and we adapted the old Fremen ways to our own."

"You've accomplished a great deal here, Mother. Wallach IX will be eager to learn of it."

While the Fremen orgy continued, Margot felt as if she were floating, numb and separate from it all. The ancient woman raised a clawlike hand in benediction, to release her back into the outside world. "Go and report to Harishka." Ramallo displayed a wispy smile. "And give her this gift." She removed a small boundbook from a pocket of her robe.

Opening the volume, Margot read the title page: *Manual of the Friendly Desert*. Beneath that, in smaller letters, it read, "The place full of life. Here are the *ayat* and *burhan* of Life. Believe, and al-Lat shall never burn you."

"This is like the *Azhar Book*," Margot exclaimed, surprised to see an edition adapted to Fremen ways. "Our Book of Great Secrets."

"Give my sacred copy to Harishka. It will please her."

AWED NOW BY her presence, the Rutii priest took Margot back to the Residency at Arrakeen. She arrived shortly before dawn, just as the sky began to pale into soft orange pastels, and slipped into her bed. No one in the household—other than the Shadout Mapes—knew she had ever gone. Excited, she lay awake for hours. . . .

Several days later, her head full of questions, Margot climbed the trail back to the cave, following her crystal-clear memory map. In bright sunlight she traversed the steep trail into Rimwall West, made her way across the narrow ledge to the opening of the sietch. The heat slowed her.

Slipping inside the cool cave shadows, she found that the doorseal had been removed. She walked through the chambers, finding them empty. No machinery, no furnishings, no people. No proof. Only odors lingered. . . .

"So, you don't entirely trust me after all, Sayyadina," she said aloud.

For a long while Margot remained in the cavern where the tau orgy had taken place. She knelt where she had consumed the Water of Life, feeling the echoes of long habitation there. All gone now. . . .

The next day Count Hasimir Fenring returned from his desert inspections with the Baron Harkonnen. At dinner, basking in her presence, he asked his lovely wife what she had done in his absence.

"Oh, nothing, my love," she responded with a carefree toss of her honey-gold hair. She brushed her lips across his cheek in a tender kiss. "I just tended my garden."

I stand in the sacred human presence. As I do now, so should you stand some day. I pray to your presence that this be so. Let the future remain uncertain for that is the canvas to receive our desires. Thus the human condition faces its perpetual tabula rasa. We possess no more than this moment where we dedicate ourselves continuously to the sacred presence we share and create.

—Bene Gesserit Benediction

"THIS IS HOW WE TEST HUMANS, GIRL."

Behind the barrier of her desk, Reverend Mother Gaius Helen Mohiam looked like a stranger, her face stony, her eyes black and merciless. "It is a death-alternative challenge."

Instantly tense, Jessica stood before the Proctor Superior. A skinny girl with long, bronze hair, her face bore the seeds of genuine beauty that would soon flower. In back of her, the Acolyte who had delivered the Reverend Mother's summons closed the heavy door. It locked with an ominous click.

What kind of test does she have in mind for me?

"Yes, Reverend Mother?" Summoning all of her strength, Jessica kept her voice calm and still, envisioning a shallow pool of sound.

With a recent promotion, Mohiam had acquired her additional title as Proctor Superior of the Mother School on Wallach IX. Mohiam had her own private office, with antique books sealed in a clearplaz humidity case. On her wide desk sat three silver trays, each containing a geometric object: a green metal cube, a brilliant red pyramid, a golden sphere. Streaks of light shot from the surfaces of the objects, bouncing between them. For a long moment, Jessica stared at the hypnotic dance.

"You must listen to me carefully, girl, to every word, every inflection, every nuance. Your very life depends on this."

Jessica lowered her eyebrows. Her green-eyed gaze shifted to the older woman's tiny, birdlike eyes. Mohiam seemed nervous and fearful, but why?

"What are those?" Jessica pointed at the unusual articles on the desk.

"You're curious, are you?"

Jessica nodded.

"They are whatever you think they are." Mohiam's voice was as dry as a desert wind.

Synchronized, the objects rotated, so that each one revealed a dark, dark hole in its surface—a hole that corresponded in shape with the object itself. Jessica focused on the red pyramid, with its triangle-shaped opening.

The pyramid began to float toward her. *Is this real, or all illusion?* Startled, she opened her eyes wide and stared, transfixed.

The other two geometric shapes followed, until all three floated in front of Jessica's face. Brilliant beams darted and arced, spectral streaks of color that made barely audible snappings and flowings.

Jessica's curiosity mingled with fear.

Mohiam made her wait for many seconds, then said in an iron voice, "What is the first lesson? What have you been taught since you were a little girl?"

"Humans must never submit to animals, of course." Jessica allowed a thread of anger and impatience to infiltrate her voice; Mohiam would know it was intentional. "After all you have trained in me, Proctor Superior, how can you suspect I am not human? When have I ever given you cause—"

"Silence. *People* are not always *humans*." She came around the desk with the grace of a hunting cat and peered at Jessica through the sparkling light between the cube and the pyramid.

The girl felt a nervous tickle in her throat, but didn't cough or speak. From experience with this instructor, Jessica knew something more was coming. And it did.

"Ages ago, during the Butlerian Jihad, most people were merely organic automatons, following the commands of thinking machines. Beaten down, they never questioned, never resisted, never *thought*. They were people, but had lost the spark that made them human. Still, a core of their kind resisted. They fought back, refused to give up, and ultimately prevailed. They alone remembered what it was to be human. We must never forget the lessons of those perilous times."

The Reverend Mother's robes rustled as she moved to one side, and suddenly her arm moved with an astonishing flash of speed, a blur of motion. Jessica saw a fingertip needle poised at her cheek, just below her right eye.

The girl did not flinch. Mohiam's papery lips formed a smile. "You know of the gom jabbar, the high-handed enemy that kills only animals—those who behave out of instinct instead of discipline. This point is coated with meta-cyanide. The tiniest prick, and you die."

The needle remained motionless, as if frozen in air. Mohiam leaned closer to her ear. "Of the three objects before you, one is pain, another is pleasure, and the third is eternity. The Sisterhood uses these things in a variety of ways and combinations. For this test, you are to select the one that is most profound to you and experience it, if you dare. There will be no other questions. This is the entire test."

Without moving her head, Jessica shifted her gaze to study each item. Utilizing her Bene Gesserit powers of observation— and something more, the source of which she did not know— she sensed pleasure in the pyramid, pain in the box, eternity in the sphere. She had never undergone a test like this before, and had never heard of it, though she knew of the gom jabbar, the legendary needle developed in ancient times.

"This is the test," Reverend Mother Mohiam said. "If you fail, I will scratch you."

Jessica steeled herself. "And I will die."

LIKE A VULTURE, the leathery proctor hovered beside the girl, watching every flicker of eye movement, every twitch. Mohiam could not let Jessica see her own anguish and dread, but she knew she had to carry out the test.

You must not fail, my daughter.

Gaius Helen Mohiam had trained Jessica since her youth, but the girl did not know her heritage, did not know her importance to the Sisterhood's breeding program. She did not know that Mohiam was her mother.

Beside her, Jessica had turned ashen with concentration. Sweat sparkled on her smooth forehead. Mohiam studied the patterns on the geometric shapes, saw that the girl still had several levels to go within her mind. . . .

Please, child, you must survive. I cannot do this again. I am too old.

Her first daughter by the Baron had been weak and defective; following a terrible prophetic dream, Mohiam had killed the infant herself. It had been a true vision, Mohiam was certain; she saw her place at the culmination of the Sisterhood's millennia-long breeding program. But she also learned through startling prescience that the Imperium would suffer great pain and death, with planets burned, a near-total genocide . . . if the breeding scheme were to go awry. If the wrong child were born in the next generation.

Mohiam had already murdered one of her daughters, and she was willing to sacrifice Jessica, too. If necessary. Better to kill her than to allow another terrible jihad to occur.

The poisoned silver needle hovered a hairbreadth from Jessica's creamy skin. The girl trembled.

———

JESSICA CONCENTRATED WITH all her might, staring ahead but seeing only words in her mind, the Litany Against Fear. *I must not
fear. Fear is the mind-killer. Fear is the little death that brings total
obliteration.*

As she took a calming breath, she wondered, *Which do I
choose? The wrong decision and I die.* She realized she had to go
deeper, and in an epiphany, saw how the three geometric objects were positioned in the human journey: the pain of birth,
the pleasure of a life well lived, the eternity of death. She was
to select the most profound, Mohiam had said. But only one?
How could she start anywhere but the beginning?

Pain first.

"I see you have chosen," Mohiam said, watching the girl's
right hand lift.

Cautiously, Jessica inserted her hand into the green cube,
through the hole in one side of it. Instantly, she felt her skin
burning, scorching, her bones filling with lava. Her fingernails were flaking off one by one, peeled away by the ferocious
heat. She had never in her life even imagined such agony. And
it continued to build.

I will face my fear, and allow it to pass over me and through me.

With a supreme effort, she resigned herself to living without her hand, blocked off the nerves. She would do it, if she
must. But then logic imposed itself, even with the agony. She
could not recall seeing stump-wristed Sisters in the halls of the
Mother School. And if all Acolytes were required to face tests
such as this . . .

When the fear has passed, there will be nothing.

A distant, analytical part of her brain realized that she did
not smell cooking flesh, either, did not see wisps of gray
smoke, did not hear the crackle and pop of sizzling fat in the
meat of her hand.

Only I will remain.

Fighting for control of her nerves, Jessica shut off the pain. From her wrist to her elbow, she felt only cold numbness. Her hand no longer existed; the agony no longer existed. Deeper, deeper. Moments later, she had no physical form whatsoever, having separated herself entirely from her body.

Out of the hole in the green box came a mist. Like incense.

"Good, good," Mohiam whispered.

The mist—a manifestation of Jessica's awareness—floated into a hole of a different shape, the entrance to the red pyramid. Now a jolt of pleasure suffused her, intensely stimulating but so shocking that she could hardly bear it. She had gone from one extreme to another. She trembled, then flowed and surged, like the ascension of a tsunami on a vast sea. Higher and higher the great wave mounted, crested. . . .

But the mist of her awareness, after riding the top of a powerful wave, suddenly cascaded down it, tumbling away . . . falling. . . .

The images vanished, and Jessica felt the thin fabric shoes on her feet, a clammy, sweating sensation of skin against material, and the hardness of the floor beneath. Her right hand . . . She still couldn't feel it, and couldn't see it, either, or even a stump at the wrist, for only her eyes were able to move.

Glancing to the right, she saw the poisoned needle hovering at her cheek, the deadly gom jabbar with the golden sphere of eternity visible beyond. Mohiam held firm, and Jessica centered her vision on the sharp silver tip, the glinting central point of the universe poised like a distant star. A prick of the needle and Jessica would enter the sphere of eternity, in mind and body. There would be no return. The girl felt no pain or pleasure now, only a numbed stillness as she hovered on the precipice of a decision.

A realization came to her: *I am nothing.*

"Pain, pleasure, eternity . . . all interest me," Jessica murmured at last, as if from a great distance, "for what is one without the others?"

Mohiam saw that the girl had passed the crisis, survived the test. An animal would not have been able to comprehend such intangibles. Jessica sagged, visibly shaken. The poisoned needle withdrew.

For Jessica, the ordeal was over quite suddenly. All of it had been imagined, the pain, the pleasure, the nothingness. All accomplished through Bene Gesserit mind-control, the tremendous ability of the Sisterhood to direct another person's thoughts and actions. A test.

Had her hand really gone into the green cube? Had she become a mist? Intellectually, she didn't think so. But when she flexed the fingers of her hand, they were stiff and sore.

Her robes smelling of musty perspiration, Mohiam trembled, then regained her composure. She gave Jessica the briefest hug, and then her demeanor became formal again.

"Welcome to the Sisterhood, human."

I fought in great wars to defend the Imperium and slew many men in the Emperor's name. I attended Landsraad functions. I toured the continents of Caladan. I managed all the tedious business matters required to run a Great House. And still the best of times were those I spent with my son.

—DUKE PAULUS ATREIDES

WHEN THE DUCAL WINGBOAT CAST OFF FROM THE DOCKS AND MOVED OUT into the sea, Leto stood at the bow and turned back to gaze at the ancient edifice of Castle Caladan, where House Atreides had ruled for twenty-six generations.

He could not recognize faces in the high windows, but he saw a small silhouette on a high balcony. *Kailea.* Despite her resistance to him taking young Victor, not yet two and a half, on this trip, she had indeed come to see them off in her silent way. Leto took heart from that.

"Could I take the helm?" Rhombur's rounded face wore a hopeful smile. His unruly, straw-colored hair blew in the freshening breeze. "I've never piloted a big wingboat before."

"Wait until we reach open sea." Leto looked at the exiled Prince with a mischievous smile. "That might be safest. I seem to remember you crashing us against the reefs once."

Rhombur flushed. "I've learned a lot since that time. Uh, common sense, especially."

"Indeed you have. Tessia has been a good influence on you." When the mousy-haired Bene Gesserit concubine had accompanied Rhombur to the docks, her arm in his, she had passionately kissed him farewell.

In contrast, Kailea had refused to leave the Castle for Leto. At the rear of the vee-shaped craft, little Victor giggled, running his hands through the cold spray while the ever-attentive guard captain, Swain Goire, kept watch. Goire kept the boy amused while remaining alert to protect him.

Eight men accompanied Leto and Victor on this happy-go-lucky voyage. In addition to Rhombur and Goire, he also brought with him Thufir Hawat, a pair of guards, a boat captain, and two fishermen, Gianni and Dom, friends of Leto's from the docks with whom he'd played as a boy. They would go fishing; they would see the seaweed forests and kelp islands. Leto would show his son the wonders of Caladan.

Kailea had wanted to keep her boy locked within the Castle, where Victor would be exposed to nothing worse than a common cold or a draft. Leto had listened to her complaints in silence, knowing that the boat trip was not the root of her objection, merely the current manifestation. It was the same old problem. . . .

Perhaps Chiara's muttered comments had finally convinced Kailea that Leto was to blame for her unacceptable situation. "I want to be more than an exile!" she had shouted during their last evening together (as if that had something to do with the fishing trip).

Leto stifled the urge to remind Kailea that her mother had been murdered, her father remained a hunted fugitive, and her people were still enslaved by the Tleilaxu—while she herself was a Duke's lady, living in a castle with a fine, healthy son and all the wealth and trappings of a Great House. "You should not complain, Kailea," he said, his voice dark with anger.

Though he could not placate her, Leto did want the best for their son.

Now, under cloud-studded skies, they breathed fresh ocean air and cruised far from land. The wingboat cut through the water like a knife blade through jellied pundi rice.

Thufir Hawat stood attentive inside the deckhouse; he scanned the signal-ranging systems and weather patterns, always concerned that some danger might befall his beloved Duke. The Master of Assassins kept himself in powerful shape, his skin leathery, his muscles like cables. His sharp Mentat mind could see the wheels within wheels of enemy plots. He studied third- and fourth-order consequences that Leto, or even Kailea with her shrewd business mind, could not comprehend.

In early afternoon the men cast nets. Though he was a life-long fisherman, Gianni made it no secret that he preferred a nice big steak for dinner along with good Caladan wine. But out here, they had to eat what the sea provided.

As the nets came up full of flopping, squirming creatures, Victor raced to inspect the beautiful fish with their multicolored scales. Ever watchful, Goire stood conscientiously next to the child, steering him away from the ones with poisonous spines.

Leto selected four fat butterfish, and Gianni and Dom took them to the galley to clean them. Then he knelt beside his son, helping the curious boy to gather the leftover struggling fish. Together, they tossed them overboard, and Victor clapped his hands as they watched the sleek shapes dart into the water.

Their course took them into floating continents of inter-linked sargasso weed, a greenish-brown desert that extended as far as the eye could see. Broad rivers flowed through breaks in the weed. Flies buzzed about, laying eggs in glistening water droplets; black-and-white birds hopped from leaf to leaf, devouring shrimps that wriggled through the warm surface layers. The pungent smell of rotting vegetation filled the air.

When the men anchored in the seaweed, they talked and sang songs. Swain Goire helped Victor cast a fishing line over the side, and though his hooks tangled in the seaweed, the delighted boy managed to pull up several silvery finger-fish. Victor ran into the cabin with the slippery fish to show his father, who applauded his son's fishing prowess. After such an exhausting day, the boy crawled into his bunk shortly after sunset and fell asleep.

Leto played a few gambling games with the two fishermen; though he was their Duke, Gianni and Dom did nothing to help Leto win. They considered him a friend . . . exactly as Leto wished. Later, when they told sad stories or sang tragic songs, Gianni wept at the slightest hint of sentiment.

Then, far into the night, Leto and Rhombur sat on deck in the darkness, just talking. Rhombur had recently gotten a terse, coded message that C'tair Pilru had received the explosives, but no word as to how they would be put to use. The Prince longed to see what the rebels were doing in the Ixian caverns, though he could not go there. He didn't know what his father would have done in the situation.

They spoke of Leto's continuing diplomatic efforts in the Moritani-Ecazi standoff. It was slow, difficult going. They were faced not only with resistance from the feuding parties but from Emperor Shaddam himself, who seemed to resent the Atreides intrusion. Shaddam believed that by stationing a legion of Sardaukar on Grumman for a few years he had already solved the problem. In reality it had only delayed the hostilities. With the Imperial troops gone now, tensions were mounting again. . . .

During a long moment of silence, Leto watched Captain Goire, which brought to mind another one of his friends and fighters. "Duncan Idaho has been on Ginaz for four years now."

"He'll become a great Swordmaster." Rhombur stared across the seaweed desert, where furry murmons set up a bubbly chorus, singing challenges to each other across the darkness. "And after so many years of tough training, he'll be a thousand times more valuable to you. You'll see."

"Still, I miss having him around."

THE NEXT MORNING Leto awoke into a dewy gray dawn. Breathing deeply, he felt refreshed and full of energy. He found Victor still sleeping, the corner of a blanket wrapped around one clenched hand. In his own bunk Rhombur yawned and stretched, but gave no sign that he meant to follow Leto out onto the deck. Even on Ix, the Prince had never been an early riser.

The wingboat captain had already pulled up anchor. At Havat's direction—did the Mentat ever sleep?—they coasted down a wide channel through the seaweed toward open water again. Leto stood on the foredeck enjoying a silence broken only by the hum of the wingboat's engines. Even the weed-hopping birds were still. . . .

Leto noted strange colorations in the clouds out at sea, a moving clump of flickering lights unlike anything he had seen before. From his seat in the midships deckhouse, the captain increased engine power and the wingboat raced along, picking up speed.

Leto sniffed, detected a metallic scent of ozone, but with an added sourness. He narrowed his gray eyes, ready to call the boat captain. The dense cluster of electrical activity moved against the breezes, darting along low to the water . . . as if alive.

Approaching us.

With a thrill of concern, he stepped backward into the deckhouse. "Do you see it, Captain?"

The older man did not take his eyes from the steering column or the phenomenon racing toward them. "I've been watching it for ten minutes, my Lord—and in that time it's closed half the distance."

"I've never seen anything like that before." Leto stood beside the captain's chair. "What is it?"

"I've got my suspicions." The captain's expression betrayed concern and fear; he yanked the throttle lever and the engines roared louder than ever. "I'm thinking we should run." He pointed to the right, away from the approaching lights.

Leto brought an edge of ducal command to his voice, Stripping away the friendliness he had built over the past day. "Captain, explain yourself."

"It's an elecran, Sire. If you ask me."

Leto laughed once, then stopped. "An elecran? Isn't that just a myth?" His father, the Old Duke, had liked to tell stories as the two of them sat by an open beach fire, with the night illuminated only by flickering flames. "You'd be amazed at what's in that sea, boy," Paulus had said, pointing toward the dark water. "Your mother wouldn't want me to tell you this, but I think you should know." He would take a long, thoughtful puff on his pipe and begin his tale. . . .

Now the wingboat captain shook his head. "They're rare, my Lord, but they do exist."

And if such an elemental creature was indeed real, Leto knew what destruction and death it could bring. "Turn the boat, then. Set a course away from the thing. Maximum speed."

The captain slewed them to starboard, churning a white wake in the still water, tilting the deck at an angle steep enough to tumble the men from their bunks below. Leto gripped a cabin rail until his knuckles turned white.

Thufir Hawat and Swain Goire hurried into the deckhouse, demanding to know the reason for the emergency. As Leto pointed aft, the men stared through the mist-specked plaz of the windows. Goire cursed with colorful language he never used around Victor. Hawat's brow furrowed as his complex Mentat mind analyzed the situation and plucked the information he needed from his storehouse of knowledge. "We are in trouble, my Duke."

The flashing lights and stormy appearance of the strange creature came closer on their stern, picking up speed, causing steam to boil off the water. The boat captain's forehead glistened with sweat. "It's seen us, Sire." He jammed the engine hrottle down so hard it nearly broke off in his hand. "Even in his wingboat we can't outrun it. Better prepare for an attack."

Leto sounded the alarm. Within seconds, the other guards appeared, followed by the two fishermen. Rhombur carried Victor, who, frightened by the commotion, clung to his uncle.

Hawat stared aft, narrowing his eyes. "I don't know how to fight a myth." He looked at his Duke, as if he had failed in some way. "Nevertheless, we will try."

Goire rapped on a bulkhead of the deckhouse. "This boat won't shelter us, will it?" The guard appeared ready to fight anything the Duke identified as an enemy.

"An elecran is a cluster of ghosts from men who died in storms at sea," said the fisherman Dom, his voice uncertain as he leaned out of the deckhouse while the others went out onto the aft deck to face the creature.

His brother Gianni shook his head. "Our grandmother said it's the living vengeance of a woman scorned. A long time ago, a woman went out during a thunderstorm and screamed curses at the man who had left her. She was struck by lightning, and that's how the elecran was born."

It hurt Leto's eyes to look at the towering elecran, a squid of electricity formed by vertical bolts of power and tendrils of gas. Lightning skittered across its surface; mist, steam, and ozone surrounded it like a shield. As the creature approached the wingboat, it swelled in volume, absorbing seawater like a great geyser.

"I've also heard it can only keep its shape, keep itself alive, so long as it stays in contact with the water," the boat captain added.

"That information is more useful," Hawat said.

"Vermilion hells! We're not getting that bloody thing out of the water," Rhombur said. "I hope there's another way to kill it."

Hawat barked a quick order, and the two Atreides guards

drew their lasrifles, weaponry brought aboard at the warrior Mentat's insistence. At the time, Leto had wondered how they could possibly need such firepower on a simple fishing trip; now he was glad. Dom and Gianni took one look at the threatening knot of energy and scrambled belowdecks.

Swain Goire, with a glance behind him to make sure Victor was with Rhombur, raised his own weapon. He was the first to open fire off the stern of the speeding boat, sending out a hot, pulsing blast of light. The energy struck the elecran and dissipated, causing no harm. Thufir Hawat fired, as did the second Atreides guard.

"No effect!" the Mentat bellowed into the rising buzz. "My Duke—remain in the safety of the cabin."

Even inside, Leto could feel the heat in the air, smell the burned salt and crisped seaweed. Bolts of primal power crackled through the elecran's fluid body, and it loomed closer to the wingboat, a cyclone of raw power. With a single strike, it could shatter the vessel and electrocute every person aboard.

"There is no safety, Thufir," Leto shouted back. "I will not let that thing have my son!" He glanced at the boy, who grasped Rhombur around the neck.

As if to flaunt its power, one crackling tendril bent down and touched the wooden side of the boat like a priest giving a blessing. Part of the craft's metal trim blasted free as hot sparks danced along every conductive contact. The boat's engines sputtered and died.

The captain tried to restart the engines, was rewarded with only rasping, metallic sounds.

Goire appeared ready to hurl himself bodily into the crackling mass, if it would do anything to help. As the boat stopped running, the men continued to fire their lasguns at the core of the elecran, though with no more effect than a thrown table knife. But Leto realized they were targeting the wrong place. The boat, with no power, was turning, the bow coming around toward the monster.

Spotting his opportunity, Leto left the deckhouse and ran toward the wingboat's pointed bow. Hawat cried out to restrain his Duke, but Leto raised a hand to forestall his intervention. Audacity had always been an Atreides hallmark. He had to pray the boat captain's folk wisdom was not composed entirely of ridiculous stories.

"Leto! Don't do it!" Rhombur said, clutching Victor tightly to his chest. The boy screamed and squirmed, trying to pummel his way free of his uncle's grasp so he could run to his father.

Leto shouted at the monster and waved his hands, hoping to distract the thing, act as bait. "Here! To me!" He had to save his son as well as his men. The captain was still trying to start the engines, but they wouldn't switch on. Thufir, Goire, and the two guards hurried to join Leto on the foredeck.

The Duke watched the elecran swell. As it towered like an oncoming tsunami in the air, the creature maintained only a tenuous contact with the salt water that gave it corporeal existence. A lingering static charge made Leto's hair rise, as if a million tiny insects were crawling on his skin.

The timing would have to be precise. "Thufir, Swain— point your lasguns at the *water below it*. Turn the ocean to steam." Leto raised both arms, offering himself. He had no weapon, nothing with which to threaten the creature.

The fearsome elecran glowed brighter, a crackling mass of primal energy that rose high above the water. It had no face, no eyes, no fangs—its entire body was composed of death.

Hawat barked the order just as Leto dove facefirst to the wooden deck. Two lasguns blasted the water into froth and steam at the base of the crackling ribbon of lightning. Clouds of white mist boiled up all around.

Leto rolled aside, trying to reach the shelter of a high gunwale. The two Atreides guards also opened fire, vaporizing the waves around the flickering creature.

The elecran thrashed, as if surprised, trying to draw itself back down to the seawater that boiled away underneath it. It gave an unearthly cry and struck the boat twice more with spasmic lightning bolts. Finally, when its connection had been completely severed, the elecran lost all integrity.

In a brilliant flashing and sparking explosion, it dissipated into nothing, returning to the realms of myth. A shower of water splattered the deck, tingling and effervescent as if it still contained a shred of the elecran's presence. Hot droplets pelted Leto. The stench of ozone made breathing difficult.

The ocean became peaceful again, calm and quiet. . . .

DURING THE WINGBOAT'S subdued return to the docks, Leto felt exhausted, yet content that he had solved the problem and saved his men—and, most of all, his son—without a single casualty. Gianni and Dom were already formulating the stories they would tell on stormy nights.

Lulled by the drone of the engines, Victor fell asleep on his father's lap. Leto stared out at the water curling past them. He stroked the boy's dark hair and smiled at the innocent face. In Victor's features he could see the Imperial bloodlines that had been passed to Leto through his mother—the narrow chin, the intense, pale gray eyes, the aquiline nose.

As he studied the dozing boy, he wondered if he loved Victor more than he loved his concubine. At times, he wondered if he still loved Kailea at all—especially during the past difficult year, as their life together had grown sour . . . slowly, inexorably.

Had his father felt the same about his wife Helena, trapped as he was in a relationship with a woman whose expectations were so different from his own? And how had their marriage degenerated so far, to the lowest possible level? Few people knew that Lady Helena Atreides had fostered the death of the Old Duke, arranging to have him killed by a Salusan bull.

Caressing his son gently so that he did not wake, Leto

vowed never to let Victor be exposed to such great danger again. His heart swelled as if it would burst with love for the boy. Perhaps Kailea had been right. He shouldn't have taken their child out on this fishing trip.

Then the Duke narrowed his eyes and rediscovered the steel of leadership. Realizing the cowardice in his thoughts, Leto reversed himself. *I cannot be overly protective of him.* It would be a serious mistake to coddle this child. Only by facing perils and challenges—as Paulus Atreides had made Leto do— could the young man become strong and intelligent, the leader he needed to be.

He looked down and smiled at Victor again. *After all,* Leto thought, *this boy may be Duke someday.*

He saw the dim gray coastline emerge from the morning shore mist, then Castle Caladan and its docks. It would feel good to be home.

Body and mind are two phenomena, observed under different conditions, but of one and the same ultimate reality. Body and mind are aspects of the living being. They operate within a peculiar principle of synchronicity wherein things happen together and behave as if they are the same . . . yet can be conceived of as separate.

—Staff Medical Manual,
Ginaz School

IN THE RAINY LATE MORNING DUNCAN IDAHO WAITED WITH HIS CLASS-mates on yet another training ground, yet another island in the sprawling chain of isolated classrooms. Warm droplets poured down on them from the oppressive tropical clouds. It always seemed to be raining here.

The Swordmaster was sweaty and fat, dressed in volumi-nous khakis. A red bandanna cinched around his enormous head made his mahogany-red hair spike upward in rain-dampened points. His eyes were hard little darts, a brown so dark the irises were difficult to distinguish from the pupils. He spoke in a high, thin voice that squeaked out of a voice-box buried beneath enormous jowls.

When he moved, though, Swordmaster Rivvy Dinari did so with the grace and speed of a raptor in the final arc of a killing blow. Duncan saw nothing jovial about the man and knew not to underestimate him. The roly-poly appearance was a carefully cultivated feint. "I am a legend here," the huge instructor had said, "and you will come to know it."

In the second four years of the Ginaz curriculum, the train-ees numbered less than half of those from the first day when Duncan had been forced to wear a heavy suit of armor. A handful of students had already died in the merciless training; many more had resigned and departed. "Only the best can be

Swordmasters," the teachers said, as if that explained all the hardships.

Duncan defeated other students in combat or in the thinking exercises that were so essential to battle and strategy. Before leaving Caladan he had been one of the best young fighters for House Atreides—but had never imagined he knew so little.

"Fighting men are not molded by coddling," Swordmaster Mord Cour had droned, one afternoon long ago. "In real combat situations, men are molded through extreme challenges that push them to their limits."

Some of the scholarly Swordmasters had spent days lecturing on military tactics, the history of warfare, even philosophy and politics. They engaged in battles of rhetoric rather than blades. Some were engineers and equipment specialists who had trained Duncan how to assemble and disassemble any kind of weapon, how to create his own killing devices out of the most meager supplies. He learned about shield use and repair, the design of large-scale defensive facilities, and battle plans for large- and small-scale conflicts.

Now, the drumming rain beat its inescapable cadence on the beach, the rocks, the students. Rivvy Dinari didn't seem to notice a single droplet. "For the next six months you will memorize the samurai warrior code and its integral philosophy of *bushido*. If you insist on being oil-slick rocks, I will be rushing water. I will wear away your resistance until you learn everything I am able to teach you." He shifted his piercing gaze like staccato weapons fire so that he seemed to address every student individually. A raindrop hung on the end of his nose, then fell away to be replaced by another one.

"You must learn honor, or you deserve to learn nothing at all."

Unintimidated, the ill-humored lordling Trin Kronos interrupted the rotund man. "Honor will win no battles for you unless every combatant agrees to abide by the same terms. If you bind yourself with nonsensical strictures, Master, you can be beaten by any opponent willing to bend the rules."

After hearing that, Duncan Idaho thought he understood some of the brash, provocative actions Viscount Moritani had taken during his conflict with Ecaz. The Grummans didn't play by the same rules.

Dinari's face flushed dark red. "A victory without honor is no victory."

Kronos shook his head, flinging rainwater away. "Tell that to the dead soldiers on the losing side." His friends standing next to him muttered their congratulations at his riposte. Though soaked and bedraggled, somehow they all maintained their haughty pride.

Dinari's voice grew more strident. "Would you give up all human civilization? Would you rather become wild animals?" The enormous man stepped closer to Kronos, who hesitated, then backed away into a puddle. "Warriors of the Ginaz School are respected across the Imperium. We produce the finest fighters and the greatest tacticians, better even than the Emperor's Sardaukar. And yet do we need a military fleet in orbit? Do we need a standing army to drive off invaders? Do we need a stockpile of weapons so that we can sleep well at night? No! Because we follow a code of honor and all the Imperium respects us."

Kronos either ignored or failed to notice the murderous edge in the Swordmaster's eyes. "Then you have a blind spot: your overconfidence."

Silence hung for a long moment, broken only by the constant tattoo of pattering rain. Dinari put a ponderous weight into his words. "But we have our *honor*. Learn to value it."

IT WAS POURING again, as it had been for months. Rivvy Dinari ambled between the ranks of trainees; despite his bulk, the Swordmaster moved like a breeze across the muddy ground.

f you are eager to fight, you must rid yourself of anxiety. If ou are angry at your enemy, you must rid yourself of anger. nimals fight like animals. Humans fight with *finesse*." He im- aled Duncan with his dart-sharp gaze. "Clear your mind."

Duncan did not breathe, did not blink. Every cell in his ody had frozen to a standstill, every nerve locked in stasis. A vet breeze caressed his face, but he allowed it to blow past him; the constant downpour drenched his clothes, his skin, his ones—but he imagined that it flowed through him.

"Stand without any movement—not the blink of an eye, nor any swelling of your chest, nor the tiniest twitch of a sin- gle muscle. *Be a stone. Remove yourself from the conscious uni- erse.*"

After months of Dinari's rigorous instruction, Duncan knew how to slow his metabolism to a deathlike state known as *funestus*. The Swordmaster called it a purification process to prepare their minds and bodies for the introduction of new fighting disciplines. Once achieved, *funestus* gave him a sensa- tion of peace unlike any previous experience, reminding him of his mother's arms, of her sweet, whispering voice.

Wrapped in the trance, Duncan focused his thoughts, his imagination, his drive. An intense brilliance filled his eyes, but he maintained his hold and refused to blink.

Duncan felt a sharp pain in his neck, the prick of a needle. "Ah! You still bleed," Dinari exclaimed, as if it were his job to destroy as many candidates as possible. "So, too, will you bleed in battle. You are not in a perfect state of *funestus*, Dun- can Idaho."

He struggled to achieve the meditative state in which the mind commanded its *chi* energy, remaining in a state of rest while totally prepared for battle. He sought the highest level of concentration, without the contamination of unnecessary and confusing thoughts. He felt himself going deeper, heard Rivvy Dinari's continuing verbal onslaught.

"You carry one of the finest blades in the Imperium, the

sword of Duke Paulus Atreides." He loomed over the candidate, who struggled to maintain his focus, his serenity. "But you must earn the right to use it in battle. You have acquired fighting skills, yet you have not demonstrated mastery over your own thoughts. Overintellectualizing slows and dulls reactions, dampens a warrior's instincts. Mind and body are one—and you must fight with both."

The corpulent Swordmaster glided around him, slowly circling. Duncan fixed his gaze ahead.

"I see every tiny crack of which even you are not aware. If a Swordmaster fails, he doesn't just let himself down—he imperils his comrades, disgraces his House, and brings dishonor upon himself."

Duncan felt another needle prick his neck, heard a satisfied grunt. "Better." Dinari's voice faded as he moved along to inspect the others in turn. . . .

As the relentless rain streamed down on him, Duncan maintained *funestus*. Around him the world grew silent, like the quiet before a storm. Time ceased to hold any meaning for him.

"Ay-eee . . . Huhh!"

At Dinari's call, Duncan's consciousness began to float, as if he were a boat in a fast-moving river, and the bulky Swordmaster had him in tow. He submerged and continued forward, pushing through metaphorical water toward a destination that lay far beyond his mind. He had been in this mental stream many times . . . the journey of *partus* as he went to the second step in the sequence of meditation. He washed away all that was old so he could begin anew, like a child. The water was fresh and clean and warm all around him, a womb.

Duncan accelerated through the liquid, and the boat that was his soul tilted upward. The darkness diminished, and presently he saw a glow above him, becoming brighter. The sparkling light became a watery brilliance, and he saw himself as a tiny mote swimming upward.

"Ay-eee . . . Huhh!"

At Dinari's second cry, Duncan surged out of the metaphorical water back into tropical rain and sweet air. He gasped for breath, and coughed along with the other students—only to find himself entirely dry, his clothes, his skin, his hair. Before he could express his astonishment, the rain began to soak his clothes again.

With clasped hands, the obese Swordmaster gazed at the gray heavens, letting raindrops pour over his face like a cleansing baptism. Then he tilted his head down and gazed from face to face, showing supreme pleasure. His students had reached *novellus*—the final stage of organic rebirth required before they could begin a complex new teaching.

"To conquer a fighting system you must let it conquer you. You must give yourself to it totally." The loose, wet ends of Swordmaster Dinari's red bandanna, tied behind his head, drooped down his neck. "Your minds are like soft clay upon which impressions may be made."

"We will learn now, Master," the class intoned.

The Swordmaster said solemnly, "*Bushido*. Where does honor begin? Ancient samurai masters hung mirrors in each of their Shinto temples and asked adherents to look deeply into them to see their own hearts, the variegated reflections of their God. It is in the heart where honor is nurtured and flourishes."

With a meaningful glance over at Trin Kronos and the other Grumman students, he continued. "Remember this always: Dishonor is like a gash on a tree trunk—instead of disappearing with age, it enlarges."

He made the class repeat this three times before he went on. "The code of honor was more valuable to a samurai than any treasure. A samurai's word—his *bushi no ichi-gon*—was never doubted, nor is the word of any Swordmaster of Ginaz."

Dinari finally smiled at them, showing pride at last. "Young samurai, first you will learn basic moves with empty hands.

When you have perfected these techniques, weapons will be added to your routines." With his black-dart eyes, he looked at them all sharply enough to make them afraid.

"The weapon is an extension of the hand."

A WEEK LATER, the exhausted students retired to cots inside their tents on the rugged north shore. Rain spattered their shelters, and trade winds gusted all night long. Fatigued from the rigorous fighting, Duncan settled down to sleep. Tent fittings rattled, metal eyelets clanked against rope ties in a steady rhythm that made him drowsy. At times, he thought he would never be completely dry again.

A booming voice startled him. "Everyone out!" He recognized the timbre of Dinari's voice, but the big man's tone conveyed something new, something ominous. Another surprise training exercise?

The students scrambled out of the tents into the downpour, some clad in shorts, some wearing nothing at all. Without hesitation, they lined up in their usual formations. By now they didn't even feel the rain. Glowglobes bobbed in the wind, swaying at the ends of suspensor tethers.

Still dressed in khakis, an agitated Swordmaster Dinari paced in front of the class like a stalking animal. His footsteps were heavy and angry; he didn't care that he splashed in the muddy puddles. Behind him, the engine of a landed ornithopter whined as its articulated wings thumped in the air.

A red strobelight on top of the aircraft illuminated the figure of the slender, bald woman Karsty Toper, who had met Duncan upon his first arrival on Ginaz. Wearing her usual black martial-arts pajama, now rain-soaked, she clutched a glistening diplomatic plaque that was impervious to moisture. Her expression looked hard and troubled, as if she were barely able to contain disgust or outrage.

"Four years ago, a Grumman ambassador murdered an

cazi diplomat after being accused of sabotaging Ecazi fog-wood trees, and then Grumman troops engaged in a criminal carpet-bombing of Ecaz. These heinous and illegal aggressions violated the Great Convention, and the Emperor stationed a legion of Sardaukar on Grumman to prevent further atrocities." Toper paused, waiting for the implications to sink in.

"The forms must be obeyed!" Dinari said, sounding greatly offended.

Karsty Toper stepped forward, holding up her crystal document like a cudgel. Rain streamed down her scalp, her temples. "Before removing his Sardaukar from Grumman, the Emperor received promises from both sides agreeing to cease all aggressions against one another."

Duncan looked around at the other students, seeking an answer. No one seemed to know what the woman was talking about or why the Swordmaster seemed so angry.

"Now, House Moritani has struck again. The Viscount reneged on the pact," Toper said, "and Grumman—"

"They have broken their word!" Swordmaster Dinari interrupted.

"And Grumman agents have kidnapped the brother and eldest daughter of Archduke Armand Ecaz and publicly executed them."

The gathered students muttered their dismay. Duncan could tell, though, that this was no mere lesson in inter-House politics for them to learn. He dreaded what was about to come.

On Duncan's right, Hiih Resser shifted uneasily on his feet. He wore shorts, no shirt. Two rows back, Trin Kronos appeared to be smugly satisfied at what his House had done.

"Seven members of this class are from Grumman. Three are from Ecaz. Though these Houses are sworn enemies, you students have not permitted such enmity to affect the work of our school. This is to your credit." Toper pocketed her diplomatic plaque.

The wind whipped the tails of Dinari's bandanna around his head, but he stood as sturdy as an enormous oak tree. "Though we have not been part of this dispute, and we avoid Imperial politics altogether, the Ginaz School cannot tolerate such dishonor. It shames me even to spit the name of your House. All Grummans, step forward. Front and center!"

The seven students did as they were told. Two (including Trin Kronos) were nude, but stood at attention with their companions as if they were fully dressed. Resser looked alarmed and ashamed; Kronos actually raised his chin in indignation.

"You are faced with a decision," Toper said. "Your House has violated Imperial law and dishonored itself. After your years here on Ginaz, you understand the appalling seriousness of this offense. No one has ever been kicked out of this school for purely political reasons. Therefore, you may either denounce the insane policies of Viscount Moritani, here and now—or be expelled immediately and permanently from the academy." She pointed toward the waiting ornithopter.

Trin Kronos scowled. "So, after all your words about *honor*, you ask us to give up loyalty to our House, our families? Just like that?" He glared at the fat Swordmaster. "There can be no honor without loyalty. My eternal allegiance is to Grumman and to House Moritani."

"Loyalty to an unjust cause is a perversion of honor."

"Unjust cause?" Kronos stood flushed and indignant in his nakedness. "It is not my place to challenge the decisions of my Lord, sir—*nor is it yours*."

Resser looked straight forward, did not glance at his fellows. "I choose to be a Swordmaster, sir. I will stay here." The redhead fell back into line beside Duncan, while the other Grummans glared at him as if he were a traitor.

Prompted by Kronos, the remaining six refused to yield. The Moritani lordling growled, "You insult Grumman at your own peril. The Viscount will never forget your meddling." His words were full of bluster, but neither Swordmaster Dinari nor Karsty Toper seemed impressed.

The Grummans stood proud and arrogant, though obviously disturbed to be put in such a position. Duncan sympathized with them, realizing that they, too, had selected a course of honor—a different form of honor—since they refused to abandon their House, regardless of the accusations. If he were thrust into a choice between the Ginaz School and loyalty to House Atreides, he would have chosen Duke Leto without hesitation. . . .

Given only minutes to dress and gather their possessions, the Grumman students boarded the 'thopter. The wings went to full extension, then began a powerful flapping rhythm as the craft flew through the rain over the dark water until its red strobe faded like a dying star.

The Universe is a place inaccessible, unintelligible, completely absurd . . . from which life—especially rational life—is estranged. There is no place of safety, or basic principle upon which the Universe depends. There are only transitory, masked relationships, confined within limited dimensions, and bound for inevitable change.

—Meditations from Bifrost Eyrie,
Buddislamic Text

RABBAN'S SLAUGHTER OF THE FUR WHALES IN TULA FJORD WAS ONLY THE first in a chain of disasters to strike Abulurd Harkonnen.

On a sunny day when the ice and snow had begun to thaw after a long, hard winter, a terrible avalanche buried Bifrost Eyrie, the greatest of the mountain retreats built by reclusive Buddislamic monks. It was also the ancestral home of House Rabban.

The snow came down like a white hammer, sweeping away everything in its path. It crushed buildings, buried thousands of religious devotees. Emmi's father, Onir Rautha-Rabban, sent a plea for help directly to Abulurd's main lodge.

With knotted stomachs, Abulurd and Emmi took an ornithopter, leading larger transports filled with local volunteers. He piloted with one hand, while clutching her fingers with his other. For a lingering moment, he studied the strong profile of his wife's wide face, and her long black hair. Though she wasn't beautiful in any classic sense, he never tired of looking at her, or of being with her.

They traveled along the folded coastline, then deep into the rugged mountain ranges. Many of the isolated retreats had no roads leading to the crags in which they nestled. All raw materials were extracted from the mountains; all supplies and people came via 'thopter.

Four generations ago, a weak House Rabban had surrendered planetary industrial and financial rights to the Harkonnens, on the condition that they be allowed to live in peace. The religious orders built monasteries and focused their energies on scriptures and sutras in an attempt to understand the subtlest nuances of theology. House Harkonnen couldn't have cared less.

Bifrost Eyrie had been one of the first cities built like a dream of Shangri-La in the backbone ranges. Chiseled stone buildings were situated on cliffs so high that they remained above Lankiveil's perpetual cloud level. Viewed from meditation balconies, the peaks floated like islands on a sea of white cumulus. The towers and minarets were covered with gold painstakingly extracted from distant mines; every flat wall surface was etched with friezes or intaglios depicting ancient sagas and metaphors for moral choices.

Abulurd and Emmi had been to Bifrost Eyrie many times, to visit her father or just to go on retreats when they needed relaxation. Upon returning to Lankiveil after seven years on dusty Arrakis, he and his wife had required a month at Bifrost Eyrie just to cleanse their minds.

And now an avalanche had nearly destroyed that great monument. Abulurd didn't know how he could bear to see it.

They sat together tensely as he flew the ornithopter high, holding the vehicle steady in bucking air currents. Since there were few landmarks and no roads, he relied on coordinates for the 'thopter's navsystems. The craft came over one razorback range and into a glacier-filled bowl, then up a rugged black slope to where the city should have been. The sunlight was dazzling.

With her jasper-brown eyes Emmi looked ahead, counting peaks and orienting herself, before she pointed, still not releasing his hand from her tightening grip. Abulurd recognized a few glittering gold spires, the milky-white stones that held up the magnificent buildings. Fully a third of Bifrost Eyrie had been *erased*, as if a giant broom of snow had smoothed everything over, obliterating any obstruction, whether cliff or building or praying monk.

The 'thopter landed in what had been the town square, now cleared as a staging area for rescue and salvage parties. The surviving monks and visitors had swarmed out onto the snowfield: The robed figures used makeshift tools and even bare hands to rescue survivors, but mostly to recover frozen bodies.

Abulurd climbed out of the 'thopter and reached up to help his wife down; he was afraid her legs might be shaking as much as his were. Although cold gusts cast ice crystals like gritty sand in their faces, the tears that sprang to Abulurd's pale eyes were not caused by the wind.

Seeing them arrive, the barrel-chested burgomaster, Onir Rautha-Rabban, came forward. His mouth opened and closed above a bearded chin, but he remained speechless. Finally he just threw his thick arms around his daughter and gave Emmi a long hug. Abulurd embraced his father-in-law.

Bifrost Eyrie had been famed for its architecture, for prismatic crystal windows that reflected rainbows back into the mountain. The people who dwelled there were artisans who crafted precious items sold off-world to affluent, discriminating customers. Most famed of all were the irreplaceable books of delicate calligraphy and illuminated manuscripts of the enormous Orange Catholic Bible. Only the wealthiest Great Houses in the Landsraad could afford a Bible hand-lettered and embellished by the monks of Lankiveil.

Of particular interest had been the singing crystal sculptures, harmonic quartz formations taken from cave grottoes, arranged carefully and tuned to proper wavelengths, so that the resonance of one crystal, when tapped, would set up a vibration in the next, and the next, in a harmonic wave, a music unlike any other in all the Imperium. . . .

"More work crews and transports are on their way," Abulurd said to Onir Rautha-Rabban. "They're bringing equipment and emergency supplies."

"All we can see is grief and tragedy," Emmi said. "I know it's too soon for you to think clearly now, Father, but if there's anything else we can do—"

The square-shouldered man with the gray beard nodded. "Yes, there is, my daughter." Onir looked Abulurd straight in the eye. "Our tithe to House Harkonnen is due next month. We'd sold enough crystals, tapestries, and calligraphy, and we had the proper amount of solaris set aside. But now—" He gestured to the ruins from the avalanche. "It's all buried in there somewhere, and what money we have we'll need in order to pay for . . ."

In the original agreement between Houses Rabban and Harkonnen, all of the religious cities on Lankiveil agreed to pay a specified sum each year. As a result they were free of other obligations and left alone. Abulurd held up his hand. "Not to worry."

Despite his family's tradition of harshness, Abulurd had always done his best to live well, to treat others with the respect they deserved. But ever since his son's whale hunt had ruined the breeding grounds in Tula Fjord, he found himself slipping into a dark, deep hole. Only the love he shared with Emmi maintained him, providing him with strength and optimism.

"You can have all the time you need. What's important now is to find any survivors, and to help you rebuild."

Onir Rautha-Rabban looked too devastated even to weep. He stared at the people working on the mountainside. The sun was bright overhead, and the sky a clear blue. The avalanche had painted his world a pristine white, covering the depth of misery it brought.

ON GIEDI PRIME, in the private chamber where he often went to brood with his nephew and his Mentat, Baron Harkonnen reacted to the news with appropriate indignation. In the midst of clutter, he bounced in his suspensor mechanism, while the others sat in chairdogs. A new, mostly ornamental walking stick rested against the chair, close at hand in case he needed to snatch it up and strike someone. This stick featured a Harkonnen griffin on its head, unlike the sandworm head of the one he had thrown off the balcony.

Decorative pillars rose in each corner of the room, squared off in a jumbled architectural style. A dry fountain sat in one corner. There were no windows—the Baron rarely bothered looking at the view anyway—and the polished tile felt cold against his bare feet, which touched the floor like a whisper, thanks to his suspensors. In one corner of the room, a pole bearing the drooping banner of House Harkonnen lay tilted against the wall, tossed there casually and never righted.

The Baron glowered over at Glossu Rabban. "Your father's showing his soft heart and his soft head again."

Rabban flinched, afraid he might be sent back to talk sense into Abulurd. He wore a padded sleeveless jacket of maroon leather that left his muscular arms bare. His close-cropped reddish hair had been smashed into a cowlick from the helmet he often wore. "I wish you wouldn't keep reminding me that he's my father," he said, trying to deflect the Baron's anger.

"For four generations the income stream from Lankiveil's monasteries has been unbroken. That was our agreement with House Rabban. They always pay. They know the terms. And now, because of a little"—the Baron snorted—"*snowfall*, they're going to shirk their tithe? How can Abulurd blithely wave his hands and excuse his subjects from their tax obligations? He is the planetary governor, and he has responsibilities."

"We can always make the other cities pay more," Piter de Vries suggested. He twitched as additional possibilities occurred to him. He got up from the chairdog and moved across the chamber toward the Baron; the loose-fitting robe curled around him as he glided with the grace and silence of a vengeful ghost.

"I don't agree with setting a precedent like this," the Baron said. "I prefer our finances all neat and tidy—and Lankiveil has managed to remain clean until now." He reached over to a side table and poured himself a snifter of kirana brandy. He sipped it, hoping the smoky-tasting liquid would burn the ache from his joints. Since being fitted with his belt-mechanism the Baron had gained even more weight from reduced activity. His physical body felt like a burden hanging on his bones.

The Baron's skin bore an aroma of eucalyptus and cloves from the oils he added to his daily bath. The massage boys had rubbed ointments deep into his skin, but his deteriorating body still felt miserable.

"If we go easy on one city, it'll lead to an epidemic of manufactured disasters and excuses." He pursed his generous lips in a pout, and his spider-black eyes flicked over to Rabban.

"I can understand why you're displeased, Uncle. My father's a fool."

De Vries raised a long, bony finger. "If I may make a point, my Baron. Lankiveil is lucrative because of its whale fur trade. Virtually all of our profit comes from that one industry. The few trinkets and souvenirs from these monasteries bring a nice price, yes . . . but overall, the income is insignificant. On general principle, we require them all to pay, but we don't *need* them." The Mentat paused.

"Your point being?"

He raised his bushy eyebrows. "The point being, my Baron, that in this particular instance we can afford to . . . shall we say, make a point of the matter."

Rabban began to laugh, a booming chuckle similar to his uncle's. His exile on Lankiveil still rankled.

"House Harkonnen controls the fief of Rabban-Lankiveil," the Baron said. "With fluctuations in the spice market, we need to ensure our absolute control in every moneymaking enterprise. Perhaps we've been lax in watching over my half-brother's activities. He may feel he can be as lenient as he wishes, and that we'll ignore him. This sort of thinking needs to stop."

"What are you going to do, Uncle?" Rabban leaned forward, and his thick-lidded eyes narrowed.

"It's what *you* are going to do. I need someone familiar with Lankiveil, and someone who understands the requirements of power."

Rabban swallowed with anticipation, knowing what was coming.

"You're going back there," the Baron ordered. "But this time not in disgrace. This time you have a job to do."

The Bene Gesserit tell no casual lies. Truth serves us better.

—BENE GESSERIT CODA

ON AN OVERCAST MORNING, DUKE LETO SAT ALONE IN THE COURTYARD OF Castle Caladan, staring at an untouched breakfast of smoked fish and eggs. A magnaboard containing metal-impregnated paper documents rested by his right hand. Kailea seemed to be attending to fewer of the daily business matters. So much to do, and none of it interesting.

Across the table lay the remains of Thufir Hawat's meal; the Mentat had eaten hurriedly and departed to tend to the security details required for the day's affair of state. Leto's thoughts kept wandering to the Heighliner that had entered orbit and the shuttle that would soon come down to the surface.

What do the Bene Gesserit want of me? Why are they sending a delegation to Caladan? He'd had nothing further to do with the Sisterhood since Rhombur had taken Tessia as his bound-concubine. Their representative wanted to speak to him about an "extremely important matter," yet refused to reveal anything further.

His stomach knotted, and he hadn't slept well the night before. The insanity of the Moritani-Ecazi conflict weighed constantly on his mind. While he had gained stature in the Landsraad for his determined diplomatic efforts, he was sickened by the recent kidnapping and execution of the Archduke's family members. Leto had met Armand Ecaz's daughter Sanyá, found her attractive, had even considered her a good marriage prospect. But Grumman thugs had killed Sanyá and her uncle.

He knew this would not be solved without further bloodshed.

Leto watched a bright orange-and-yellow butterfly flutter above a vase of flowers at the center of the table. For an instant the pretty insect made him forget his troubles, but the questions seeped back into his awareness.

Years ago, at his Trial by Forfeiture, the Bene Gesserit had offered him assistance, though he knew better than to expect unfettered generosity. Thufir Hawat had given Leto a warning he already knew too well: "The Bene Gesserit aren't errand girls for anyone. They made this offer because *they* wanted to, because it benefits *them* somehow."

Hawat was right, of course. The Sisterhood was adept at securing information, power, and position. A Bene Gesserit of Hidden Rank was married to the Emperor; Shaddam IV kept an ancient Truthsayer at his side at all times; another Sister had wed Shaddam's Spice Minister, Count Hasimir Fenring.

Why have they always been so interested in me? he wondered.

The butterfly landed on the magnaboard beside his hand, showing off its beautiful patterned wings.

Even with advanced Mentat abilities, Hawat could provide no useful projections regarding the Sisterhood's motives. Perhaps Leto should ask Tessia—Rhombur's concubine usually gave straightforward answers. But even though Tessia was now part of the Atreides household, the young woman remained loyal to the Sisterhood. And no organization kept its secrets better than the Bene Gesserit.

With a flash of color, the butterfly danced in the air in front of his eyes. He extended a hand, palm up—and to his surprise the creature landed on it, perching so lightly that he barely felt a thing.

"Do you have the answers I'm looking for? Is that what you're trying to tell me?" The butterfly had placed its complete faith in him, trusting that Leto wouldn't harm it. So it was, too, with the sacred trust the good people of Caladan placed in him. The butterfly darted off and dropped to the ground, seeking dew in the shade of the breakfast table.

Suddenly a house servant appeared, stepping into the courtyard. "My Duke, the delegation has arrived early. They are already at the spaceport!"

Leto stood abruptly, knocking the magnaboard off the table. It tumbled onto the cool flagstones. The servant hurried to pick it up, but Leto brushed him aside when he saw that the butterfly had been crushed beneath it. His own carelessness had killed the delicate creature. Disturbed, he knelt beside it for several seconds.

"Are you all right, my Lord?" the servant asked.

Leto straightened, brushed off the magnaboard, and assumed a stoic expression. "Inform the delegation that I will meet them in my study, instead of at the spaceport."

As the servant hurried off, Leto lifted the dead butterfly and laid it between two magnaboard sheets. Though the insect's body had been crushed, the exquisite wings remained intact. He would have the creature encased in clearplaz, so that he could always remember how easily beauty could be destroyed in a moment of carelessness. . . .

WITH HIS BLACK uniform, green cape, and ducal badge of office in place, Leto rose from his elacca wood desk. He bowed as five black-robed Sisters entered, led by a severe-faced, gray-haired woman with hollow cheeks and bright eyes. His gaze shifted to a bronze-haired young beauty beside her, then focused back on the leader.

"I am Reverend Mother Gaius Helen Mohiam." The woman's face showed no hostility, nor did it ease into a smile.

"Thank you for allowing us to speak with you, Duke Leto Atreides."

"Normally I do not grant visits on such short notice," he said with a cool nod. Hawat had advised him to keep the women off-balance, if possible. "However, since the Sisterhood does not often ask for my indulgence, I can make an exception." A household servant closed the doors of the private study as Leto gestured to his warrior Mentat. "Reverend Mother, may I present Thufir Hawat, my Security Commander?"

"Ah, the famous Master of Assassins," she said, meeting his gaze.

"An informal title only." Rigid with suspicion, Hawat bowed slightly. Tension hung thick in the air, and Leto did not know how to cut it.

As the women took seats in deep-cushioned chairs, Leto found himself captivated by the young girl with bronze hair, who remained standing. Perhaps seventeen years old, her intelligent green eyes were widely set on an oval face that had a slightly upturned nose and generous lips. She carried herself with a regal bearing. Had he seen her before? He wasn't certain.

When Mohiam looked at the young girl, who stood straight and rigid, they exchanged hard stares, as if some strain existed between them. "This is Sister Jessica, a very talented Acolyte, trained in many areas. We would like to present her to your household, with our compliments."

"*Present* her to us?" Hawat said with a hard edge in his voice. "As a servant, or as your spy?"

The girl looked at him sharply, but quickly covered her indignation.

"As a consort, or just a sounding board for ideas. That is for the Duke to decide." Mohiam calmly ignored the Mentat's accusatory tone. "Bene Gesserit Sisters have proven their value as advisors to many Houses, including House Corrino." She kept her attention firmly on Leto, though it was clear she remained aware of every movement Hawat made. "A Sister may observe, and draw her own conclusions . . . but that does not make her a spy. Many nobles find our women to be fine companions, beautiful, skilled in the arts of—"

Leto cut her off. "I already have a concubine, who is the mother of my son." He glanced at Hawat, saw the Mentat analyzing the new data.

Mohiam gave him a knowing smile. "An important man such as yourself may have more than one woman, Duke Atreides. You have not yet chosen a wife."

"Unlike the Emperor, I do not maintain a harem."

The other Sisters looked impatient, and the Reverend Mother let out a long sigh. "The traditional meaning of the word 'harem,' Duke Atreides, included all the women for whom a man bore responsibility, including his sisters and mother as well as concubines and wives. There was no implied sexual connotation."

"Word games," Leto growled.

"Do you wish to play word games, Duke Leto, or strike a bargain?" The Reverend Mother glanced over at Hawat as if considering how much to say in front of the Mentat. "A matter involving House Atreides has come to our attention. It concerns a certain plot perpetrated against you years ago."

With a barely perceptible jerk, Hawat focused his attention. Leto leaned forward. "What plot, Reverend Mother?"

"Before we reveal this vital information to you, we must arrive at an understanding." Leto wasn't the slightest bit surprised. "Is it so much we ask in return?" Because of the urgency of the situation, Mohiam thought it might be necessary to use Voice on him, but the Mentat would surely recognize it. Jessica remained standing to one side, on display. "Any other nobleman would be glad to have this lovely child as part of his retinue . . . in any capacity."

Leto's thoughts whirled. *It's clear they want to have someone here on Caladan. For what purpose? Just to exert influence? Why would they bother? Tessia is already here, if they need a spy so badly. House Atreides has respect and influence, but is not particularly powerful in the Landsraad.*

Why have I come to their notice?

And why are they so insistent upon this particular girl?

Leto came around in front of the desk and gestured to Jessica. "Come here." The young woman glided across the small study. A head shorter than the Duke, with unblemished and radiant skin, she gave him a long, importunate look.

"I've heard that all Bene Gesserit are witches," he said, as he ran a finger through the bronze silkiness of her hair.

She met his gaze and responded in a soft voice. "But we have hearts and bodies." Her lips were softly sensual, inviting.

"Ah, but what have your heart and body been trained to do?"

She fended off his question in a tranquil tone. "Trained to be loyal, to offer the comforts of love . . . to have children."

Leto glanced at Thufir Hawat. No longer in a Mentat trance, the leathery warrior nodded, indicating that he did not object to the bargain. In their private discussions, however, the two had planned an aggressive tack with the delegation, to see how the Bene Gesserit would respond under pressure, to keep them off-balance so the Mentat could observe. This appeared to be the opportunity they had discussed.

"I don't believe the Bene Gesserit ever give without taking," Leto snapped, in sudden fury.

"But, my Lord—" Jessica could not complete the sentence, because he snatched a jewel-handled knife from a sheath at his waist and held the blade to her throat, pulling her tightly against him in a hostage position.

Her Bene Gesserit companions did not move. They gazed at Leto with unnerving serenity, as if they thought Jessica could kill him herself if she so chose. Mohiam watched with impenetrable birdlike eyes.

Jessica tilted her head back, exposing more of her soft, smooth throat. It was the way of D-wolves, as she had been taught in the Mother School: Bare your throat in total submission, and the aggressor backs away.

The tip of Leto's blade pressed into her skin ever so slightly, but not enough to draw blood. "I don't trust what you offer."

Jessica remembered the command Mohiam had whispered in her ear just before they stepped off the shuttle in the Cala Municipal Spaceport. "Let the chain be unbroken," her stern mentor had said. "You must give us the female child we require."

Jessica hadn't been told where she fitted into the Sisterhood's breeding programs, and it was not her position to ask. Many young girls were assigned as concubines for various Great Houses, and she had no reason to believe she was any different from the others. She respected her superiors and worked hard to show this, but sometimes Mohiam's unbending ways chafed her. They'd had an argument on the way here, and the remnants of it still hung in the air.

Leto whispered in her ear: "I could kill you now." But he could not hide from her, or any of the Sisters, that his anger was feigned. Years ago, as a test, she had studied this dark-haired man as she hid in balcony shadows on Wallach IX.

She pressed her neck against the blade. "You are not a casual killer, Leto Atreides." He withdrew the edge, but kept his arm around her waist as she said, "You have nothing to fear from me."

"Do we have a deal, Duke Leto?" Mohiam asked, unruffled by his behavior. "I assure you, our information is quite . . . revealing."

Leto didn't like being cornered, but he stepped away from Jessica. "You say a plot has been perpetrated against me?"

A smile worked at the wrinkled corners of the Reverend Mother's mouth. "First you must agree to the contract. Jessica stays here and is to be treated with due respect."

Leto and his warrior Mentat exchanged glances. "She can live in Castle Caladan," he said finally, "but I do not agree to take her into my bed."

Mohiam shrugged. "Use her as you wish. Jessica is a valuable and useful resource, but do not waste her talents." *Biology will take its course.*

"Reverend Mother, what is your vital information?" Hawat demanded.

Clearing her throat, Mohiam replied, "I speak of an incident some years back, in which you were falsely accused of attacking two Tleilaxu ships. We have learned that Harkonnens were involved."

Both Leto and Hawat stiffened. The Mentat's brows furrowed in deep concentration as he awaited further data.

"You have proof of this?" Leto asked.

"They used an invisible warship to fire upon the Tleilaxu vessels, implicating you, in an attempt to start an Atreides-Tleilaxu war. We have the wreckage of the craft in our possession."

"An *invisible* ship? I've never heard of such a thing."

"Nonetheless it exists. We have the prototype, the only one of its kind. Fortunately, the Harkonnens experienced technical problems, which contributed to its . . . crash . . . near our Mother School. We have also determined that the Harkonnens are unable to manufacture another such ship."

The Mentat studied her. "Have you analyzed the technology?"

"The nature of what we discovered cannot be revealed. Such a fearsome weapon could wreak tremendous havoc in the Imperium."

Leto barked a short laugh, elated that he finally had an answer to the question that had nagged him for fifteen years. "Thufir, we'll take this information to the Landsraad, and clear my name once and for all. Reverend Mother, provide us with all of your evidence and documentation—"

Mohiam shook her head. "That is not part of our bargain. The tempest has abated, Duke Leto. Your Trial by Forfeiture is over, and you have been acquitted of the charges."

"But not cleared. Some of the Great Houses still suspect I was involved. You could provide conclusive proof of my innocence."

"Does that mean so much to you, Duke Leto?" Her eyebrows rose. "Perhaps you could find a more effective way to spend this coin. The Sisterhood will not support such an endeavor simply to bolster your pride or salve your conscience."

Leto felt helpless and very young in the face of Mohiam's intense stare. "How can you come to me with information like that and expect me not to act on it? If I have no proof of what you say, then your information is meaningless."

Mohiam frowned, and her dark eyes glittered. "Come now, Duke Leto. Is House Atreides interested only in trappings and documents? I thought you valued the truth for itself. I have given you the truth."

"So you say," Hawat answered coldly.

"The wise leader understands patience." Ready to depart, Mohiam signaled to her companions. "One day you will discover the best way to use the knowledge. But take heart. Simply understanding what truly occurred in that Heighliner should be worth a great price to you, Duke Leto Atreides."

Hawat was about to object, but Leto held up his hand. "She's right, Thufir. Those answers are quite valuable to me." He looked over at the bronze-haired girl. "Jessica can stay here."

The man who gives in to adrenaline addiction turns against all humanity. He turns against himself. He runs away from the workable issues of life and admits a defeat which his own violent actions help to create.

—CAMMAR PILRU, Ixian Ambassador in Exile
Treatise on the Downfall of Unjust Governments

THE SECRET SHIPMENT OF EXPLOSIVES ARRIVED INTACT, PASSED BY bribed off-world delivery crews, hidden among crates, delivered to a specific loading dock in the cave openings in the cliffs of the port-of-entry canyon.

Working with the loaders, C'tair spotted the subtle markings and diverted the innocuous-looking container, as he had done many times before. When he uncovered the cleverly packaged explosive wafers, though, he was astounded. There must be a thousand of them! Other than handling instructions for the charges, there was no message, coded or otherwise, and no source information, but C'tair knew the identity of the sender anyway. This was far more than Prince Rhombur had ever sent before. C'tair felt renewed hope, and the burden of tremendous responsibility.

Only a few other wary, independent rebels remained underground, and they kept to themselves, trusting no one. C'tair was that way himself. Other than Miral Alechem, he felt all alone in his fight, even though Rhombur—and the Tleilaxu—apparently thought there was a much larger, more organized resistance.

These explosives would make up for that.

During his youth, Prince Rhombur Vernius had been a pudgy boy; C'tair remembered him as something of a good-natured buffoon, who spent more time collecting geological specimens than learning statecraft or Ixian industrial processes. There had always seemed to be time.

But everything had changed when the Tleilaxu came. *Everything*.

Even in exile, Rhombur still had pass-codes and connections with the shipping administration by which raw materials came into the manufacturing city. He had been able to smuggle vital supplies underground, and now these explosive wafers. C'tair vowed to make each one count. Now, his primary concern was to hide the demolitions material before sluggish Ixian suboids discovered the package's true contents.

Wearing the stolen uniform of an upper-level worker, he transported the shipment of explosives into the stalactite city on a suspensor cart with other everyday deliveries. He did not hurry toward his hiding place. At all times he kept his expression bland and passive, making no conversation, barely responding to comments or insults made by the Tleilaxu Masters.

When he finally reached the appropriate level and ducked through the camouflaged entrance into his sensor-shielded room, C'tair piled the black, rough-textured wafers, then lay back on his cot, breathing heavily.

This would be his first major strike in years.

He closed his eyes. Moments later he heard a click at the door, footsteps, and a rustling noise. He didn't move or look because the sounds were familiar, a small bit of comfort for him in an uncomfortable world. He smelled her faint, sweet scent.

For months he had been living with Miral Alechem. They had clung to each other's companionship after making love in a darkened tunnel, hushed and nervous, while hiding from a Sardaukar patrol. In his years as an Ixian patriot, C'tair had resisted the urge for any sort of a personal relationship, spurning close contact with other human beings. It was too dangerous, too distracting. But Miral had the same burning goals, the same needs. And she was so beautiful. . . .

Now he heard her set something down on the floor with a soft thump. She kissed his cheek. "I got a few things, some high-energy wire, a laser pack, a—" He heard her indrawn gasp of breath.

C'tair smiled, kept his eyes closed. She'd spotted the piles of wafers.

"I got a few things, too." Abruptly, he sat up and explained how he'd come by the explosives, and how they worked. Each black wafer, the size of a small coin and honeycombed with compressed detonation beads, packed enough power to blow up a small building. With just a handful of them, placed correctly, they could cause tremendous, large-scale damage.

Her fingers moved close to the pile, hesitated. She looked at him with her large, dark eyes, and as she did, he thought about her, as he often did. Miral was the best person he'd ever met. It was admirable the way she took risks comparable to his own. She hadn't seduced him, hadn't enticed him at all. Their relationship had just happened. They were right for each other.

He thought briefly of his youthful crush on Kailea, the daughter of Earl Vernius. That had been a fantasy, a game, which might have become real if Ix had not fallen. Miral, though, was all the reality he could endure.

"Don't worry," he assured her. "It takes a detonator to set them off." He pointed to a small red box filled with needle-set timing devices.

She took one of the wafers in each hand, inspecting it like a Hagal jeweler with a new firegem. C'tair could imagine the possibilities streaming through her mind, stress points in the city, places where the explosives would cause the most pain and damage to the invaders.

"I've already chosen a few targets," he said. "I was hoping you'd help out."

She replaced the wafers carefully, then dropped with him onto the cot in an embrace. "You know I will." Her breath was hot in his ear. They could hardly wait to get their clothes off.

After making love with an intensity fanned by their great plans, C'tair slept for more hours than he usually allowed himself. When he was rested and ready, he and Miral went through the motions repeatedly in order to ensure that every connection was made, all procedures and safeguards set. After they had rigged several charges in the shielded room, they took the remaining explosives and stepped to the sealed doorway, checking the scanners to make certain the outer corridor was empty.

With sadness, C'tair and Miral bade a silent farewell to the shielded chamber that had been C'tair's desperate hiding place for so long. Now it would serve one last purpose, enabling them to deliver a stinging blow to the invaders.

The Bene Tleilax would never know what hit them.

C'TAIR STACKED THE boxes one at a time with other crates necessary for whatever experiments the Tleilaxu conducted inside their high-security research pavilion. One of the boxes was rigged with explosive wafers, a shipment that looked just like the others being loaded onto the automated rail system. The package would be delivered right into the heart of their secret lair.

He did not waste a glance on the booby-trapped crate. He simply stacked it with all the others, then surreptitiously set the timer, and hurried to add another container. One of the suboid laborers stumbled, and C'tair picked up the man's designated crate and lifted it onto the railcar bed to avoid a delayed departure. He had given himself a sufficient window of opportunity, but still found it hard not to let his nervousness show. Miral Alechem was in the passageway beneath another building. She would be setting charges at the base of the immense structure that had Tleilaxu offices on upper levels; by now she should have made good her escape.

With a humming sound, the loaded pallet shuddered into motion and cruised along the rail, picking up speed toward the laboratory complex. C'tair longed to know what went on behind those blind windows; Miral had not been able to find out, and neither had he. But he would be satisfied just to cause damage.

The Tleilaxu, for all their bloody repressions, had grown lax over sixteen years. Their security measures were laughable . . . and he would now show them the error of their ways. This strike had to be significant enough to make them reel, because the next attempt would not be so easy.

Staring after the railcar, C'tair suppressed a smile of anticipation. Behind him, workers prepped a new, empty pallet car with more supplies. He glanced up at the grotto ceiling, at the gossamer buildings protruding like inverted islands through the projected sky.

Timing was crucial. All four bombs had to go off close together.

This would be as much a psychological victory as a material one. The Tleilaxu invaders must come to the conclusion that a large and coordinated resistance movement was responsible for these attacks, that the rebels had a widespread membership and an organized plan.

They must never guess that there are only two of us.

In the wake of an outrageous success, others might begin their own struggles. If enough people took action, it would make the large-scale rebellion a self-fulfilling prophecy.

He drew a deep breath and turned back to the other waiting crates. He dared not show any out-of-the-ordinary behavior. Overhead, surveillance pods moved about constantly, lights blinking, transeye cameras imaging every movement.

He did not glance at his chronometer, but he knew the time was close.

When the first explosion shuddered through the cavern floor deep underground, the dull-brained workers paused in their tasks and looked at each other in confusion. C'tair knew that the detonation at the disposal pits should have been sufficient to collapse the rooms, to twist and destroy the conveyor belts. Perhaps the rubble would even seal the tops of the deep magma shafts.

Before anyone could notice the smug expression on his face, the stalactite buildings in the ceiling exploded.

Inside his sensor-shielded bolt-hole within the administrative levels, a cluster of explosive wafers tore out entire levels of the bureaucratic complex. One wing of the Grand Palais was wrecked, left hanging by long girders and broken reinforced strands.

Debris rained into the center of the cavern, and workers fled in panic. A bright light and swirling cloud of rock powder spread from the torn ceiling chambers.

Blaring alarms echoed against the stone walls like thunder. He hadn't heard such a racket since the initial suboid uprising years ago. Everything was working perfectly.

In feigned horror, he backed away with the rest of the Ixian laborers, standing among them for implied protection, lost in the crowd. He smelled the dust of building materials and the stench of fear around him.

He heard a distant explosion, from the direction of the building where Miral worked, and knew she was clever enough to have gotten away before setting it off. Then at last, precisely as he had hoped, the loaded pallet car arrived inside the loading dock of the secret research pavilion. The final set of explosive wafers erupted in streaks of fire and black clouds of smoke. The sounds of the detonation rang out like a space battle within the thick walls.

Fires began to spread. Armed Sardaukar troops rushed about like heat-maddened beetles, trying to find the source of the concerted attack. They fired at the sky ceiling, just to express their anger. Alarms rattled the walls. Over the PA system, Tleilaxu Masters screamed incomprehensible orders in their private language, while the work crews muttered in subdued fear.

But even in the chaos C'tair recognized a strange look on some of the Ixian faces: a sort of satisfaction, a sense of wonder that such a victory could have occurred. They had long ago lost their heart for fighting.

Now, perhaps they could regain it.

At last, C'tair thought as he blinked in dull-eyed shock, trying to cover his smile. He squared his shoulders, but quickly let them sag as he sought to recapture the demeanor of a defeated and cooperative prisoner.

At last a true blow had been struck against the invaders.

There exists no way of exchanging information without making judgments.

—Bene Gesserit Axiom

FROM THE BALCONY OF HER PRIVATE APARTMENT, JESSICA OBSERVED HER frumpy, apple-cheeked lady-in-waiting in the practice yard near the west guardhouse. She watched as the breathless woman chattered with Thufir Hawat, using too many hand gestures as she spoke. Both of them glanced up at her window.

Does the Mentat think I am stupid?

In the month that Jessica had lived on Caladan, her every need had been met with cold precision, as a respected guest but no more. Thufir Hawat had personally seen to her comforts, placing her in the former apartments of the Lady Helena Atreides. After being sealed for so many years, the chambers had needed to be aired out, but the fine furniture, the pool-bath and sunroom, the complete wardrobe were all more than she required. A Bene Gesserit needed very little in the way of comfort and luxury.

The Mentat had also arranged for Jessica's busybody lady-in-waiting, who flitted around her like a moth, finding little tasks that kept her close to Jessica at all times. Obviously, one of Hawat's spies.

Abruptly, Jessica had dismissed the woman from service that very morning, giving her no reason. Now she sat back to await the repercussions. Would the Master of Assassins come himself, or would he send a representative? Would he even understand her intended message? *Don't underestimate me, Thufir Hawat.*

From the balcony, she saw him break from his discussion with the disgraced woman. Moving with confidence and strength, he strode away from the west guardhouse toward the Castle proper.

A strange man, that Mentat. While still at the Mother School, Jessica had memorized Hawat's background, how he'd spent half his life at a Mentat training center, first as a student and later as a philosopher and theoretical tactician, before being purchased for the newly titled Duke Paulus Atreides, Leto's father.

Using her Bene Gesserit powers of observation, Jessica studied the leathery, confident man. Hawat wasn't like other graduates of the Mentat Schools, the introverted types who shied away from personal contact. Instead, the deadly man was aggressive and crafty, with a fanatic loyalty to House Atreides. In some ways his deadly nature resembled that of the Tleilaxu-twisted Piter de Vries, but Hawat was the ethical opposite of the Harkonnen Mentat. It was all very curious. . . .

Similarly, she had noticed the old Master of Assassins scrutinizing her through his Mentat logic filter, processing bits of data about her and arriving at unsubstantiated conclusions. Hawat could be very dangerous indeed.

They all wanted to know why she was here, why the Bene Gesserit had chosen to send her, and what she meant to do.

Jessica heard a heavy-knuckled rap on the door, and answered it herself. *Now we shall see what he has to say. Enough games.*

Hawat's lips were moist with sapho juice, and the deep-set brown eyes showed concern and agitation. "Please explain why you were dissatisfied with the servant I chose for you, my Lady."

Jessica wore a lavender soosatin singlesuit, which showed

off the curves of her slender body. Her makeup was minimal, only a bit of lavender around the eyes and lip tint to match. Her expression had no softness at all. "Given your legendary prowess, I'd thought you would be a man of greater subtlety, Thufir Hawat. If you are going to spy on me, choose someone a little more competent in the wiles of espionage."

The bold comment surprised him, and he looked at the young woman with heightened respect. "I am in charge of the Duke's security, my Lady, tending to his personal safety. I must take whatever actions I feel are required."

Jessica closed the door, and they stood in the entry, close enough for a killing blow—by either of them. "Mentat, what do you know of the Bene Gesserit?"

A slight smile etched his leathery face. "Only what the Sisterhood permits outsiders to know."

With raised voice, she snapped, "When the Reverend Mothers brought me here, Leto became my sworn master as well. Do you think I pose a danger to him? That the Sisterhood would take direct action against a Duke of the Landsraad? In the history of the Imperium, are you aware of a single instance in which such a thing has happened? It would be suicide for the Bene Gesserit." She flared her nostrils. "Think, Mentat! What is your projection?"

After a heavy moment, Hawat said, "I am unaware of any such instance, my Lady."

"And yet you stationed that clumsy wench to keep me under surveillance. Why do you fear me? What do you suspect?" She stopped herself from using Voice, which Hawat would never forgive. Instead, she added a quieter threat. "I caution you, do not attempt to lie to me." *There, let him think I am a Truthsayer.*

"I apologize for the indiscretion, my Lady. Perhaps I am a bit . . . overzealous in protecting my Duke." *This is a strong young woman*, Hawat thought. *The Duke could do much worse.*

"I admire your devotion to him." Jessica noticed that his

eyes had grown softer, but without evidence of fear, merely a bit more respect. "I have been here only a short time, while you have served three generations of Atreides. You bear a scar on your leg from a Salusan bull, from one of the Old Duke's early encounters, do you not? It is not easy for you to accommodate something new." She took the faintest step away from him, letting a trickle of regret enter her voice. "So far your Duke has treated me more like a distant relative, but I hope he will not find me displeasing in the future."

"He does not find you displeasing at all, my Lady. But he has already chosen Kailea Vernius as a partner. She is the mother of his son."

It had not taken Jessica long to learn that there were fractures in the relationship. "Come now, Mentat, she is not his bound-concubine, and not his wife. Either way, he has given the boy no birthright. What message are we to derive from that?"

Hawat stood rigid, as if offended. "Leto's father taught him to use marriage only to gain political advantage for House Atreides. He has many prospects in the Landsraad. He has not yet calculated the best match . . . though he is considering."

"Let him consider, then." Jessica signaled that the conversation was over. She waited for him to turn, and then she added, "Henceforth, Thufir Hawat, I prefer to choose my own ladies-in-waiting."

"As you wish."

After the Mentat had departed, Jessica assessed her situation, thinking of long-term plans rather than her mission for the Sisterhood. Her beauty could be enhanced by Bene Gesserit seduction techniques. But Leto was proud and individualistic; the Duke might guess her intentions and would resent being manipulated. Even so, Jessica had a job to do.

In fleeting moments she had noticed him looking at her with guilt in his eyes—particularly after fights with Kailea.

Whenever Jessica tried to take advantage of those moments, though, he quickly grew cold and pulled away.

Living in the Lady Helena's former quarters did not help, either. Leto was reluctant to go there. Following the death of Paulus Atreides, the enmity between Leto and his mother had been extreme, and Helena had gone to "rest and meditate" in a remote religious retreat. To Jessica it smacked of banishment, but she had found no clear reasons in the Atreides records. Being placed in these rooms could act as an emotional barrier between them.

Leto Atreides was certainly dashing and handsome, and Jessica would have no trouble accepting his company. In fact, she *wanted* to be with him. She chided herself whenever such feelings came over her—as they did too frequently. She could not allow emotions to sway her; the Bene Gesserit had no use for love.

I have a job to do, she reminded herself. Jessica would bide her time and wait for just the right moment.

Infinity attracts us like a floodlight in the night, blinding us to the excesses it can inflict upon the finite.

—Meditations from Bifrost Eyrie,
Buddislamic Text

FOUR MONTHS AFTER THE AVALANCHE DISASTER, ABULURD HARKONNEN and his wife embarked on a well-publicized visit to the recovering mountain city. The Bifrost Eyrie tragedy had struck to the heart of Lankiveil and drawn the populace together.

Steadfast companions, he and Emmi had shown their combined strength. For years now Abulurd had preferred to be a behind-the-scenes ruler, not even claiming the specific title that was his due. He wanted the people of Lankiveil to govern themselves, to help each other according to their hearts. He saw the various villagers, hunters, and fishermen as a great extended family, all with common interests.

Then, speaking with quiet confidence, Emmi convinced her husband that a public pilgrimage as acting planetary governor would draw attention to the plight of the mountain stronghold. The burgomaster, Onir Rautha-Rabban, would welcome them.

Abulurd and Emmi rode in a formal transport flanked by servants and retainers, many of whom had never been far from the whaling villages. The three ornithopters passed slowly inland over glaciers and snow-covered mountains, toward the line of crags in which the monastery city nestled.

With the sun sparkling off snow and ice crystals from protruding mountaintops, the world appeared pristine and peaceful. Ever an optimist, Abulurd hoped the Bifrost inhabitants could now look forward to an even stronger future. He had written a speech that imparted basically the same message; though he had little experience addressing large crowds, Abulurd looked forward to delivering this communication. He'd already practiced twice in front of Emmi.

On a plateau in front of the sheer cliffs of Bifrost Eyrie, the governor's procession landed, and Abulurd and his entourage disembarked. Emmi walked at her husband's side, looking regal in a heavy blue cape. He took her arm.

The construction teams had made amazing progress. They had sliced away the intruding fan of snow and excavated the buried buildings. Because most of the wonderful architecture had been destroyed or defaced, the broken buildings were now covered with a webwork of scaffolding. Skilled stonemasons worked round-the-clock to add block upon block, rebuilding and glorifying the retreat. Bifrost Eyrie would never be the same . . . but perhaps it could be even better than before, like a phoenix rising from the snowfield.

Stocky Onir Rautha-Rabban came out to meet them, dressed in gilded robes lined with sable whale fur. Emmi's father had shaved off his voluminous gray beard after the disaster; whenever he looked in a reflecting glass, he wanted to be reminded of how much his mountain city had lost. This time his broad, squarish face seemed content, lit with a fire that had not been present the last time they'd been together.

With the arrival of their planetary governor, workers climbed down from scaffoldings and picked their way along packed snowfield paths into the large square. When completed, the towering buildings would look down upon the square like gods from on high; even incomplete, the soaring stonework remained impressive.

The weather had cooperated since the avalanche, but in another month or two, the hard snap of winter would force them to cease: their efforts and huddle within the stone buildings for half a year. Bifrost Eyrie would not be finished this season. With the magnitude of construction work, perhaps it would never be complete. But the people would continue to build, enhancing their prayer in stone to the skies of Lankiveil.

When the crowds had gathered, Abulurd raised his hands to speak, rehearsing again in his mind. Then all the words drained from his mind to be replaced with nervousness. Looking like a queen beside him, Emmi reached out to touch his arm, giving her support. Then she whispered his opening lines, helping him remember what he needed to say.

"My friends," he said loudly, grinning with embarrassment, "Buddislamic teachings encourage charity, hard work, and assistance to those in need. There can be no better example of heartfelt cooperation than what you volunteers are doing now to rebuild—"

The gathered people began to murmur, gesturing toward the sky and whispering among themselves. Abulurd hesitated again, turning to look over his shoulder. Just then, Emmi cried out.

A formation of black ships appeared in the azure sky, swooping toward the mountains, attack craft that bore the griffin of House Harkonnen. Abulurd's brows knitted, more in puzzlement than alarm. He looked over at his wife. "What does this mean, Emmi? I did not call for any ships." But she had no better idea than he did.

Seven fighters roared low, engines cracking through the air with sonic booms. Abulurd felt a flash of annoyance, afraid the thunderous sound would provoke fresh avalanches—until the ships' gunports opened. The people of the mountain stronghold began milling back and forth in confusion, shouting. Some ran, searching for shelter. Abulurd could not understand what he was seeing.

Three of the sleek craft slowed to a hover over the square where the villagers were gathered. Lasguns extended, targeted.

Abulurd waved his hands, trying to get the pilots' attention. "What are you doing? There must be some mistake."

Emmi pushed him away from the speaking podium, where he was a prime target. "There's no mistake."

The villagers scrambled for cover as the vessels settled down to land in the square. Abulurd was convinced the pilots would have landed right on top of the crowd if the spectators had not moved fast enough. "Stay here," he said to Emmi as he strode toward the trio of landed ships to demand answers.

The four remaining vessels circled in the air and came back. With a buzzing crackle of static, hot lasgun beams lanced out to slice scaffolding from the stone buildings like a fisherman gutting his catch.

"Stop!" Abulurd shouted to the skies, clenching his fists— but none of the military men could hear him. These were Harkonnen troops, loyal to his own family, but they were attacking *his* people, the citizens of Lankiveil. "Stop!" he repeated, reeling backward from the shockwaves.

Emmi grabbed him and pulled him aside as one of the ships swooped low, creating a sharp, hot wind with its passage.

More lasgun fire lanced out, this time targeting the milling mass of people. The blasts slew dozens in a single sweep.

Chunks of ice toppled from the glaciers, crystalline blue-white blocks that fell in a flash of steam as they were cauterized from the main mass. Half-completed buildings were crushed under the onslaught as lasgun beams chopped them to bits.

The four attack craft came around a third time while the other vessels powered down and stabilized on the ground. Their doors hissed open, and Harkonnen troops boiled out, wearing dark blue commando assault uniforms, insulated against the cold.

"I am Abulurd Harkonnen, and I order you to stop!" After quick glances in his direction, the soldiers ignored him.

Then Glossu Rabban stepped out of the craft. Weapons

bristled from his belt and military insignia covered his shoulders and breast. An iridescent black helmet made him look like a gladiator in an ancient coliseum.

Recognizing his grandson, Onir Rautha-Rabban raced forward, his hands clasped in front of him, beseeching. His face was splotched with anger and horror. "Please stop! Glossu Rabban, why are you doing this?"

At the other side of the square, the ground troops withdrew lasrifles and opened fire on screaming villagers, who had no place to go. Before the old burgomaster could reach Rabban on the boarding ramp, soldiers grabbed him and dragged him away.

His face stormy, Abulurd marched toward Rabban. Harkonnen troops moved to block his way, but he snapped, "Let me pass."

Rabban looked over at him with cold metal eyes. His thick lips were drawn into a satisfied line above his blocky chin. "Father, your people must learn that there are worse things than natural disasters." He raised his chin a notch. "If they find excuses to avoid paying their tithes, they will face an *unnatural* disaster—me."

"Call them off!" Abulurd raised his voice even as he felt completely impotent. "I am governor here, and these are *my* people."

Rabban looked at him in disgust. "And they need an example to understand the kind of behavior that's expected of them. It's not a complicated issue, but obviously you don't provide the proper inspiration."

Harkonnen soldiers dragged the struggling Onir Rabban toward an abrupt cliff edge. Emmi saw what they meant to do and screamed. Abulurd whirled to see that they had brought his father-in-law to the sheer, ice-frosted precipice. The chasm below ended only in a soup of clouds.

"You can't do that!" Abulurd said, aghast. "That man is the lawful leader of this village. He's your own grandfather."

Smiling, Rabban whispered the words, with no emotion, no sense of command. "Oh, wait. Stop." There was no chance the troops could hear him. They already had their orders.

The Harkonnen guards grabbed the burgomaster by both arms and held him like a loose sack of cargo at the brink. Emmi's father cried out, his arms and legs flailing. He looked over at Abulurd, his face filled with disbelief and horror. Their eyes met.

"Oh, dear me, please, no," Rabban whispered again, with a grin curving his lips.

Then the soldiers shoved the old man over, and he disappeared into the void.

"Too late," Rabban said with a shrug.

Emmi fell to her knees, retching. Abulurd, who couldn't decide whether to comfort her or rush forward to strike his son, remained paralyzed.

With a clap of his meaty hands, Rabban called out, "Enough! Fall in!"

Loud signals came from the landed battleships. With military precision, the Harkonnen troops marched back to their ships in perfect ranks. They left wailing survivors who scurried over to the bodies, searching for companions, loved ones, anyone who might need medical attention.

On the ramp of the flagship, Rabban studied his father. "Be thankful I was willing to do your dirty work. You've used too light a touch on these people, and they've grown lazy."

The four flying vessels completed one more attack run, which devastated another building, causing it to collapse in a rumble of rock dust. Then they flew off, regrouping in a formation in the sky.

"If you force my hand again, I'll have to show a little more muscle—all in your name, of course." Rabban turned about and strode back into his command ship.

Appalled and disoriented, Abulurd stared in utter horror at the obliteration, the fires, the awful cauterized bodies. He heard a mounting scream like a song of mourning—and realized it came from his own throat.

Emmi had staggered over to the cliff edge and stood sobbing as she stared down into the bottomless clouds where her father had disappeared.

The last Harkonnen ships lifted into the sky on suspensors, leaving scorch marks on the clearing in front of the now-devastated mountain city. Abulurd sank to his knees in utter despair. His mind filled with a roaring hum of disbelief and a bright agony dominated by the smug expression of Glossu Rabban.

"How could I have ever sired such a monster?" He knew he would never find an answer to that question.

Love is the highest achievement to which any human may aspire. It is an emotion that encompasses the full depth of heart, mind, and soul.

—Zensunni Wisdom from the Wandering

LIET-KYNES AND WARRICK SPENT AN EVENING TOGETHER NEAR SPLINTERED Rock in Hagga Basin. They had raided another one of the old botanical testing stations for usable equipment, taking inventory of a few tools and records the desert had preserved for centuries.

For two years following their return from the south polar regions, the young men had accompanied Pardot Kynes from sietch to sietch, checking the progress of old and new plantings. The Planetologist maintained a secret greenhouse cave at Plaster Basin, a captive Eden to demonstrate what Dune *could* become. Water from catchtraps and windstills irrigated the shrubs and flowers. Many Fremen had received samples grown in the Plaster Basin demonstration project. They took sweet pieces of the fruit as a holy communion, closing their eyes and breathing deeply, relishing the taste.

All of this Pardot Kynes had promised . . . and all of this he had given them. He was proud that his visions were becoming reality. He was also proud of his son. "One day you will be Imperial Planetologist here, Liet," he said, nodding solemnly.

Though he spoke with passion about awakening the desert, bringing in grasses and biodiversity for a self-sustaining ecosystem, Kynes could not teach any subject in an orderly or structured fashion. Warrick hung on every word he said, but the man often began with one topic, then rambled on to other subjects at his whim.

"We are all part of a grand tapestry, and we each must follow our own threads," Pardot Kynes said, more pleased with his own words than he should have been.

Oftentimes he would recount the stories of his days on Salusa Secundus, how he had studied a wilderness no one else had bothered with. The Planetologist had spent years on Bela Tegeuse, seeing how the hardy plant life flourished despite the dim sunlight and acidic soil. There had also been journeys to Harmonthep, III Delta Kaising, Gammont, and Poritrin—and the dazzling court on Kaitain, where Emperor Elrood IX had given him this assignment on Arrakis.

Now, as Liet and Warrick made their way from Splintered Rock, a heavy wind picked up—a *heinali* or man-pusher. Bending into the stinging gusts, Liet pointed to the lee of a rock outcropping. "Let us set up our shelter there."

His dark hair bound in a shoulder-length ponytail, Warrick trudged forward, head lowered, already removing his Fremkit pack. Working together, they soon had a protected, camouflaged camp and hunkered down to talk far into the night.

In two years, the young men had told no one about Dominic Vernius and his smuggler base. They had given their word to the man, and kept it a secret between themselves. . . .

They were both eighteen and expected to marry soon—but Liet, dizzy with the hormones of his age, could not choose. He found himself more and more attracted to Faroula, the willowy, large-eyed, but tempestuous daughter of Heinar, the Naib of Red Wall Sietch. Faroula was trained in the lore of the herbalist, and would, one day, be a well-respected healer.

Unfortunately for him, Warrick desired Faroula as well, and Liet knew that his blood-brother was more likely to gather the courage to ask the Naib's daughter before he could make his own clumsy move.

The two friends fell asleep listening to the whispering fingernails of sand blown against their tent. . . .

The following dawn, when they climbed out, knocking powdery dust from the sphincter opening of the tent, Liet stared across the expanse of Hagga Basin. Warrick blinked in the bright light. *"Kull wahad!"*

The night windstorm had blown the dirt clear of a broad white playa, the salty remnants of an ancient dried sea. Scoured clean, the lake bed wavered in the rising heat of the day. "A gypsum plain. A rare sight," Liet said, then added in a mutter, "My father would probably run down and do tests."

Warrick spoke in a low, awed voice. "It is said that he who sees *Biyan*, the White Lands, can make a wish and it is sure to be granted." He fell silent and moved his lips, expressing his deepest, most private desires.

Not to be outdone, Liet uttered his own fervent thoughts in a rush. He turned to his friend and announced, "I wished that Faroula would be my wife!"

Warrick gave him a bemused smile. "Bad luck, my bloodbrother—I wished for the same thing." With a laugh, he clapped Liet on the shoulder. "It seems that not all wishes can come true."

AT DUSK THE two met Pardot Kynes as he arrived at Sine Rock Sietch. The sietch elders solemnly went through a greeting ceremony, pleased with what they had accomplished. Kynes accepted their welcome with brusque good grace, offhandedly forgoing many of the formal responses in his eagerness to inspect everything himself.

The Planetologist went to inspect their plantings under bright glowglobes that simulated sunlight within crannies of rock. The sand had been fertilized with chemicals and human feces to create a rich soil. The people of Sine Rock grew mesquite, sage, rabbitbush, even a few accordion-trunked saguaros, surrounded by scrubby grasses. Groups of robed women went from plant to plant as if in a religious ceremony, adding cupfuls of water so the plants could thrive.

The stone walls of Sine Rock's blocked-off canyon retained a bit of moisture every morning; dew precipitators along the top of the canyon recaptured lost water vapor and returned it to the plants.

In the evening, Kynes walked from planting to planting, bending over to study leaves and stems. He'd already forgotten that his son and Warrick had come to meet him. His warrior escort, Ommun and Turok, stood guard, willing to give their lives should anything threaten their Umma. Liet noticed his father's intense concentration and wondered if the man ever realized the sheer loyalty he inspired among these people.

At the mouth of the narrow canyon, where a few boulders and rocks provided the only barrier against open desert, Fremen children had tethered bright glowglobes that shone onto the sand. Each child carried a bent metal rod extracted from a Carthag refuse dump.

Enjoying the private stillness of the gathering night, Liet and Warrick squatted on a rock to watch the children. Warrick sniffed and looked behind them toward the artificial sunlight on the bushes and cacti. "The little Makers are drawn to the moisture like iron filings to a magnet."

Liet had seen the activity before, had done it himself as a boy, but was still fascinated to see the young ones poking about to capture sandtrout. "They have easy pickings."

One of the young girls bent to let a small drop of saliva fall onto the end of her metal staff; then she extended the rod over the sands. The miniature tethered glowglobes cast deep shadows on the uneven ground. Creatures stirred under the surface, rising out of the dust.

The sandtrout were shapeless fleshy creatures, soft and flexible. Their bodies were pliable when alive, yet they turned hard and leathery when dead. Many little Makers were found strewn about the site of a spice blow, killed in the explosion; many more burrowed to capture the released water, sealing it away to protect Shai-Hulud.

One of the sandtrout extended a pseudopod toward the glistening tip of the rod. When it touched the girl's saliva, the Fremen child turned the metal stick, as if to capture a self-moving flow of taffy. She raised her rod, taking the sandtrout out of the ground, and twirled it to keep the amorphous little Maker suspended in the air. The other children giggled.

A second child caught another sandtrout and both hurried back to the rocks, where they played with their prizes. They could poke and tug the soft flesh, teasing out a few droplets of sweet syrup, a special treat that Liet himself had loved in his youth.

Though tempted to try his own hand at the game, Liet reminded himself that he was an adult now, a full member of the tribe. He was the son of Umma Kynes; the other Fremen would frown to see him engage in frivolous play.

Warrick sat on the rock beside him, wrapped in his thoughts, watching the children and thinking of a future family of his own. He looked up into the purpling sky. "It is said that storm season is the time for lovemaking." He wrinkled his brow, then placed his narrow chin in his hands, deep in concentration. He had begun to grow a thin beard.

Liet smiled; he still kept his own face clean-shaven. "It is time for both of us to choose a mate, Warrick." They held Faroula in their thoughts, and the Naib's daughter led them on, feigning aloofness while enjoying their attentions. Liet and Warrick brought her special treasures from the desert whenever they could.

"Perhaps we should make our selection the Fremen way." Warrick withdrew from his belt a pair of polished bone slivers as long as knives. "Shall we throw tally sticks to see who may court Faroula?"

Liet had his own pair of the gambling markers; he and his friend had spent many camp nights challenging each other. Tally sticks were slender carvings with a scale of random numbers etched along the sides, high numbers mixed with low ones. The Fremen threw bone tallies into the sand, then read off the number of the depth; whoever achieved the highest score won. It required finesse as well as plain luck.

"If we played tally sticks, I would beat you, of course," Liet said offhandedly to Warrick.

"I doubt that."

"In any event, Faroula would never abide by the throw of the bones." Liet sat back against the cool rock wall. "Perhaps it is time for the *ahal* ceremony, where a woman chooses her mate."

"Do you think Faroula would choose me?" Warrick said wistfully.

"Of course not."

"In most things I trust your judgment, my friend—but not in this."

"Perhaps I shall ask her myself when I return," Liet said. "She couldn't want a better husband than me."

Warrick laughed. "In most challenges, you are a brave man, Liet-Kynes. But when facing a beautiful woman, you are a shameful coward."

Liet drew a deep, indignant breath. "I have composed a love poem for her. I mean to write it down on spice paper and leave it in her chamber."

"Oh?" Warrick teased. "And would you have the nerve to sign it with your own name? What is this beautiful poem you've written?"

Liet closed his eyes and recited:

Many nights I dream beside open water,
hearing the winds pass high;
Many nights I lie by the snake's den
and dream of Faroula in summer heat;

I see her baking spice bread on red-hot sheets of iron;
And braiding water rings into her hair.
The amber fragrance of her bosom
strikes my innermost senses;
Though she torments and oppresses me,
I would have her no other way;
She is Faroula, and she is my love.

A storm wind rages through my heart;
Behold the clear water of the qanat, gentle and shimmering.

Liet opened his eyes, as if emerging from a dream.

"I've heard better," Warrick said. "I've *written* better. But you show promise. You might find a woman to accept you after all. But never Faroula."

Liet feigned offense. In silence, the two watched the Fremen children continue to capture sandtrout. Deeper in the canyon, he knew his father rambled on about ways to increase plant growth, how to add supplementary vegetation to improve the turnover and retain nitrates in the soil. *He's probably never played with a sandtrout in his life*, Liet thought.

He and Warrick thought of other things and stared into the night. Finally, after a long silence, both spoke at once, their words tumbling over each other. Then the two laughed and agreed. "Yes, we will both ask her when we return to Red Wall Sietch."

They clasped hands, hoping . . . but secretly relieved that they had taken the decision out of their own hands.

AMID THE BUSTLE of Heinar's Sietch, the Fremen greeted the return of Pardot Kynes.

Young Faroula pressed her hands against her narrow waist, watching the party file past the moisture-sealed doorways. Her long dark hair hung in silky loops strung with water rings down to her shoulders; her face was narrow and elfin-looking. Her large eyes were midnight pools below her striking eyebrows. A slight flush danced along her tanned cheeks.

She regarded Liet first, then Warrick. Her face held a stern expression with only the faintest upturn of lips to show that she was secretly pleased, rather than offended, by what the two young men had just asked her.

"And why should I choose *either* of you?" Faroula regarded both suitors for a long moment, making them squirm with the agony of anticipation. "What makes the two of you so confident?"

"But . . ." Warrick struck his chest. "I have raided many Harkonnen troops. I have ridden a sandworm down to the south pole. I have—"

Liet interrupted him. "I've done everything Warrick has— and *I* am the son of Umma Kynes, his heir and successor as Planetologist. There may be a day when I leave this planet to visit the Imperial Court on Kaitain. I am—"

Faroula impatiently dismissed their bluster. "And I am the daughter of Naib Heinar. I can have any man I choose."

Liet groaned deep in his throat, his shoulders sagging. Warrick looked at his friend, but drew himself up, trying to recapture his bravado. "Well, then . . . choose!"

Faroula laughed, covered her mouth, and restored her tight expression. "You both have admirable qualities . . . a few of them, at least. And I suppose if I don't make up my mind soon, you'll end up killing yourselves trying to show off for me, as if I asked for escapades like that." She tossed her head, and her long hair jingled with the bound water rings.

She put a finger to her lips, pondering. Her eyes glinting with mirth, she said, "Give me two days to decide. I must think on this." When they refused to move, her voice became crisper. "Don't just stand there ogling me! You must have work to do. One thing I tell you: I'll never marry a lazy husband."

Both Liet and Warrick nearly tripped as they scrambled to find something important-looking to occupy themselves.

AFTER WAITING FOR two long, agonizing days, Liet discovered a wrapped note in his room. He tore open the spice paper, his heart pounding and sinking at the same time: If Faroula had chosen him, wouldn't she come to tell him herself? But as his eyes scanned the words she had written, his breath came fast and cold in his throat.

"I wait in the distant Cave of Birds. I will give myself to whichever man reaches me first."

That was all the note said. Liet stared at it for a few moments, then ran through the sietch passages until he reached Warrick's quarters. He pulled aside the curtain-hanging and saw his friend frantically packing a satchel and a Fremkit.

"She's issued a *mihna* challenge," Warrick said, over his shoulder.

It was a test in which Fremen youths proved themselves worthy of manhood. The two looked at each other, frozen for a moment, their gazes locking.

Then Liet whirled and rushed back to his own quarters. He understood too well what he had to do.

It was a race.

It is possible to become intoxicated with rebellion for rebellion's sake.

—DOMINIC VERNIUS,
Ecaz Memoirs

EVEN TWO YEARS IN A HARKONNEN SLAVE PIT DID NOT BREAK THE SPIRIT of Gurney Halleck. The guards considered him a difficult prisoner, and he wore that fact like a badge of honor.

Though beaten and pummeled regularly, his skin bruised, his bones cracked, his flesh slashed—Gurney always recovered. He came to know the inside of the infirmary well, to understand the miraculously fast ways the doctor could patch up injuries so the slaves could work again.

Following his capture at the pleasure house, he had been thrown into the obsidian mines and polishing pits, where he had been forced to work harder than his worst days of digging trenches for krall tubers. Still, Gurney did not miss the easier duty. At least he would die knowing he had *tried* to fight back.

The Harkonnens did not bother to ask questions about who he was or why he had come here; they saw him as no more than another functioning body to perform tasks. The guards believed they had subdued him, and nothing else mattered to them. . . .

Initially, Gurney had been assigned to the cliffs of Mount Ebony, where he and his crewmates used sonic blasters and laser-heated handpicks to chip away slabs of blue obsidian, a translucent substance that seemed to suck light from the air.

Gurney and his fellow laborers were chained together with cuffs that could extrude shigawire to sever their limbs if they struggled.

The work crew climbed up narrow mountain paths in the frosty dawn and worked through long days of battering sun. At least once a week, some slaves were killed or maimed by falling volcanic glass. The crew supervisors and guards didn't care. Periodically, they just made new sweeps around Giedi Prime to harvest additional slaves.

After surviving his stint on the cliffs, Gurney was transferred to a work detail in the processing pits, where he waded in emulsifying solutions to prepare small pieces of obsidian for shipment. Wearing only thick trunks, he worked up to his waist in foul-smelling gelatinous liquid, some sort of lye and abrasive with a mild radioactive component that activated the volcanic glass. The treatment made the finished product shimmer with a midnight-blue aura.

To his bitter amusement, he learned that rare "blue obsidian" was sold only by the gem merchants of Hagal. Though assumed to be from the crystal-rich mines of Hagal itself, the source of the valuable obsidian was a carefully held secret. House Harkonnen had been quietly providing the glowing volcanic glass all along, fetching a premium price for their resources.

Gurney's body became a patchwork of small cuts and slashes. His unprotected skin soaked up the foul, burning solution. No doubt it would kill him within a few years, but his chances of survival in the slave pits were slim anyway. After Bheth had been taken six years ago, he'd given up on any sort of long-term planning. Nonetheless, as he slogged through the liquid, churning the knife-edged chunks of obsidian, he kept his face lifted toward the sky and the horizon, while the other slaves stared into the muck.

Early one morning, the work supervisor stood on his podium with odor-filters plugged into his nostrils. He wore a tight-fitting blue tunic that displayed his scrawny chest and the rounded paunch of his belly.

"Stop daydreaming down there. Listen up, all of you." He raised his voice, and Gurney heard something strange in the timbre of the words. "A noble guest is coming to inspect our operations. Glossu Rabban, the Baron's designated heir, will oversee our quotas, and likely demand more work from you lazy worms. Get ahead of yourselves today, because tomorrow you'll have a vacation while you stand at attention to be inspected."

The work supervisor scowled. "And don't think this isn't an honor. I'm surprised Rabban's even willing to put up with your stink."

Gurney narrowed his eyes. The ignominious thug Rabban coming here? He began to hum a song to himself, one of the acidly satirical tunes he had sung in the Dmitri tavern before the initial Harkonnen attack:

> *Rabban, Rabban, the blustering brute,*
> *No brain in his head but rotten fruit.*
> *His muscles, his brawn*
> *Make a thinking man yawn.*
> *Without the Baron, he's destitute!*

Gurney couldn't help smiling, but kept his face turned away from the work supervisor. It wouldn't do to let the man notice any amusement in a slave's expression.

He couldn't wait to see the lumbering bully face-to-face.

WHEN RABBAN AND his escort arrived, they carried so many weapons Gurney had to restrain a chuckle. What was he afraid of? A bunch of work-weakened prisoners who had been battered into submission for years?

The guards had activated the cores of the cuffs so that razor-edged shigawire dug into his wrists, reminding him that a sharp jerk could slice all the way to the bone. The enhanced restraints were meant to keep the prisoners cooperative, perhaps even respectful, in front of Rabban.

The ancient man bound to Gurney had such angular joints that he had an insectlike appearance. His hair had fallen out in patches, and he jittered with a neurological disorder. He had no comprehension of what was going on around him, and Gurney pitied the fellow, wondering whether this might be his own fate one day . . . if he lived that long.

Rabban wore a black-leather uniform, padded to emphasize his muscular physique and broad shoulders. A blue Harkonnen griffin adorned his left breast. His black boots were polished to a high gloss, his thick belt studded with ornamental brass. Rabban's broad face had a ruddy appearance, as if it had been sunburned too often, and he wore a black military helmet that gleamed in the hazy sunlight. Holstered at his hip was a shining flèchette pistol accompanied by packs of spare needle cartridges.

A nasty inkvine whip hung at his waist; no doubt Rabban would look for any opportunity to use it. Blackish-red fluid inside the long-dead stem flowed like still-living blood, causing the spiked strands to twist and curl in reflex. Its juice—a poisonous substance that had commercial properties for coloring and dyeing—could cause a great deal of pain.

Rabban gave no droning speeches in front of the slaves. It wasn't his job to inspire them, merely to terrify the supervisors to squeeze out more productivity. He had already seen the slave-pit operations, and now he moved up and down the line of prisoners, offering no encouragement.

The work manager followed, jabbering in a voice made thinner by the odor-filters jammed into his nostrils. "We've done everything possible to increase efficiency, Lord Rabban. We're feeding them a bare minimum of nourishment to keep them functioning at peak performance. Their clothing is inexpensive but durable. It lasts for years, and we can reuse it when prisoners die."

Rabban's stony face showed no pleasure whatsoever.

"We could install machinery," the work supervisor suggested, "to do some of the menial tasks. That would improve our output—"

The beefy man glared. "Our objective is not merely to improve production. Destroying these men is every bit as important." He glared at them all from a position close to Gurney and the jittering, spidery old man. Rabban's close-set eyes locked on to the pathetic prisoner.

In one fluid motion he drew the flèchette pistol and fired a round point-blank at the old man. The prisoner barely had time to raise his arms in a warding gesture; the spray of silvery-needle projectiles chopped through his wrists and plunged through his heart, dropping him dead before he could even squawk.

"Frail people are a drain on our resources." Rabban took a step away.

Gurney didn't have time to think or plan, but saw in an impulsive instant what he could do to strike back. Jamming a wad of the dead prisoner's durable tunic around his own wrists to keep the wire from cutting the skin, Gurney stood up with a roar, yanking with all his might. The rag-muffled shigawire dug and cut against his padded wrists and sliced the rest of the way through the mangled, nearly severed wrists of the dead man.

Using one of the dead prisoner's detached hands like a handle, he lunged toward an astonished Rabban, gripping the shigawire like a razor-fine garrote. Before Gurney could slice open the burly man's jugular, Rabban moved with surprising speed. Gurney overbalanced and succeeded only in knocking the flèchette pistol out of the other man's hand.

The work supervisor shrieked and backed away. Rabban,

seeing his pistol gone, lashed out with his inkvine whip, striking Gurney across the face on his cheek and jaw, barely missing his eye with one of the thorny strands.

Gurney had never imagined a whip could hurt so much, but as the blazing cuts registered on his nerves, the inkvine juice seared like potent acid. His head exploded in a nova of pain that tunneled through his skull and into the core of his mind. He dropped the old man's still-bleeding hand, letting it dangle from the shigawire bond on one of his own wrists.

Gurney toppled backward. The nearby guards rushed in; his fellow prisoners shrank away in terror, clearing a wide area. The guards closed in to kill Gurney, but Rabban held up a broad hand for them to stop.

Writhing, Gurney felt only the inkvine pain in his cheek and neck while Rabban's face burned into his vision. He might be slain soon—but for now, at least, he could hold on to his hatred for this . . . this *Harkonnen*.

"Who is this man? Why is he here, and why did he attack me?" Rabban glared at the work supervisor, who cleared his throat.

"I . . . I'd have to check our records, my Lord."

"Then check the records. Find out where he came from." Rabban fashioned a thick-lipped smile. "And see if he has any family left alive."

Gurney summoned to mind the insipid words of his sarcastic song: *Rabban, Rabban, the blustering brute* . . .

But as he looked up into the broad, ugly face of the Baron's nephew, he realized that Glossu Rabban would have the last laugh after all.

What is each man but a memory for those who follow?

—DUKE LETO ATREIDES

ONE EVENING, DUKE LETO AND HIS CONCUBINE HAD BEEN SHOUTING AT ONE
another for more than an hour, and Thufir Hawat was troubled. He stood in the ducal wing, just down the hall from the
closed door of Leto's bedroom. If either of them emerged,
Hawat could slip down one of the side passageways that honeycombed the Castle. No one knew the back corridors and
secret ways better than the Mentat.

Something crashed in the bedroom. Kailea's voice rose
over the Duke's deeper, equally furious tones. Hawat didn't
hear everything they said . . . nor did he need to. As Security
Commander, he was responsible for the Duke's personal well-
being. He didn't want to intrude, but in the present atmosphere his primary concern was the potential for violence
between Leto and his concubine.

The Duke shouted, exasperated, "I don't intend to spend
my life arguing with you about what cannot be changed."

"Then why don't you just have Victor and me killed? That
would be your best solution. Or send us away to a place where
you don't have to think about us—like you did to your
mother."

Hawat couldn't hear Leto's response, but he understood all
too well why the young Duke had banished Lady Helena.

"You're no longer the man I fell in love with, Leto," Kailea continued. "It's Jessica, isn't it? Has the witch seduced you yet?"

"Don't be ridiculous. In the year and a half she's been with us I've never visited her bed once—though I have every right to do so."

Several moments of silence ensued. The Mentat waited in a state of tension.

Kailea finally said with a sarcastic sigh, "Same old refrain. Keeping Jessica here is *just politics*. Refusing to marry me is *just politics*. Hiding your involvement with Rhombur and the rebels on Ix is *just politics*. I'm sick of your politics. You're as much a schemer as any in the Imperium."

"I'm not a schemer. It's my enemies who plot against me."

"The words of a true paranoid. Now I understand why you haven't married me and made Victor your rightful heir. It's a Harkonnen plot."

Leto's reasonable tones slipped into open rage. "I never promised you marriage, Kailea, but for your sake I never even took another concubine."

"What does it matter, if I'm never to be your wife?" Choking laughter punctuated the scorn in Kailea's words. "Your 'faithfulness' is one more show you put on to appear honorable—*just politics*."

Leto sucked in a sharp breath, as if the words had been a physical blow. "Perhaps you're right," he agreed in a voice as icy as a Lankiveil winter. "Why did I bother?" The bedroom door slammed open, and Hawat melted into the shadows. "I am neither your pet, nor a fool, Kailea—I am the Duke."

Leto strode down the hallway, muttering and cursing. Behind the partially open door, Kailea began sobbing. Soon she would call Chiara, and the plump old woman would comfort her through the long night.

Remaining out of sight, Hawat followed his Duke down one corridor and then another—until Leto stepped boldly into Jessica's apartment without knocking.

———

INSTANTLY ALERT FROM her Bene Gesserit training, Jessica summoned light from a blue glowglobe. The shadowy cocoon retreated around her.

Duke Leto!

Sitting up in the four-poster bed that had long ago belonged to Helena Atreides, she made no attempt to cover herself. She wore a pink nightgown of slick merh-silk, cut low. A faint scent of lavender hung in the air from a pheromone emitter cleverly concealed at the ceiling joint. This night, as always, she had prepared carefully . . . in the hope that he would come to her.

"My Lord?" She saw his troubled, angry expression as he stepped into the light. "Is everything all right?"

Leto's gray gaze darted around, and he breathed deeply, trying to control the adrenaline, the uncertainty, the determination that warred within him. Beads of perspiration covered his brow. His black Atreides jacket hung askew, as if he had tugged it hurriedly over his shoulders.

"I am here for all the wrong reasons," he said.

Jessica slid out of bed and draped a green robe over her shoulders. "Then I must accept those reasons and be grateful for them. May I get you anything? How can I help you most?" Though she had waited so many months for him, she felt little triumph—only concern at seeing him so distressed.

The tall, hawk-featured man removed his jacket and sat on the edge of the bed. "I'm in no condition to present myself to a Lady."

Moving close to him, she massaged his shoulders. "You are the Duke, and this is your Castle. You may present yourself in any manner you please." Jessica touched his dark hair, and ran her fingers sensually along his temples.

As if imagining a dream, he closed his eyes, then snapped

them open again. She drew her finger down his cheek and placed it against his lips to silence any words. Her green eyes danced. "Your condition is perfectly acceptable to me, my Lord."

When she loosened the clasps on his shirt, he sighed and allowed her to nudge him toward the bed. Mentally and physically exhausted, torn by his own guilt, he lay facedown on the rich coverings that smelled of rose petals and coriander. He seemed to sink into the soft, pliant sheets, and allowed himself to drift away.

Her delicate hands slid across his bare skin, and she worked her fingers into the tight muscles of his back, as if she had done this for him a thousand times before. To Jessica, it felt as if this moment in eternity had always been meant to be, that Leto was destined to be here, with her.

At last, he rolled over to face her. When their eyes met, Jessica saw fire there again, except it did not smolder with anger this time. Nor did it fade. He took her in his arms and pressed his lips to hers in a long, passionate kiss.

"I'm glad you are here, my Duke," she said, remembering all the methods of seduction the Sisterhood had taught her, but with the realization that she genuinely cared about him, that she meant what she was saying.

"I shouldn't have waited so long, Jessica," he said.

AS KAILEA WEPT, she felt more anger at her own failure than sorrow at feeling Leto slip through her fingers. He had disappointed her so much—Chiara had reminded her again and again of her own worth, her noble birthright, the future she deserved. Kailea despaired that these hopes were gone forever.

House Vernius was not entirely dead, and its survival might very well depend on her. She was stronger than her brother, whose support of the rebels was little more than a pipe dream.

Deep inside she felt a steely will: House Vernius would only survive through *her* efforts, and ultimately through the bloodline of her son Victor.

She was determined to gain royal status for him. All of her love, all of her dreams, rested on the boy's fortunes.

Finally, far into the lonely night, she fell into a fitful sleep.

IN ENSUING WEEKS, Duke Leto sought Jessica more and more often, and he began to consider her his concubine. Sometimes he came into her room without a word and made love to her with feral intensity. Then, sated, he would hold her for hours and talk.

Using Bene Gesserit skills, Jessica had studied him for sixteen months, educating herself in the concerns of Caladan. She knew the daily difficulties Leto Atreides faced in running an entire planet, managing the affairs of a Great House, attending to Landsraad matters, keeping pace with the political and diplomatic machinations in the Imperium.

Jessica knew exactly what to say, precisely how to advise him without pushing. . . . Gradually, he came to see her as more than just a lover.

She tried not to think of Kailea Vernius as her rival, but the other woman had been wrong to push this proud nobleman too hard, trying to bend him to her will. Duke Leto Atreides was not a man to be forced into anything.

He sometimes spoke of his hardening feelings toward Kailea as he and Jessica went for long walks along the cliff-side path. "You are within your rights, my Lord." The young woman's tone was soft, like a summer breeze over a Caladan sea. "But she seems so sad. I wish something could be done for her. She and I might have become friends."

He looked at her with a perplexed expression as the wind blew his dark hair. "You're so much better than she is, Jessica. Kailea feels only venom toward you."

She had seen the Ixian woman's deep pain, the tears she tried to conceal, the dagger glares she hurled at Jessica. "Your point of view can be distorted by circumstance. Since the fall of House Vernius, she's had a difficult life."

"And I made it better for her. I risked my own family fortune to keep her and Rhombur safe when their House went renegade. I've shown her every consideration, but she always wants more."

"You once felt affection for her," Jessica said. "She bore your child."

He smiled warmly. "Victor . . . ah, that boy has made every moment with his mother worthwhile." For several minutes he gazed out to sea, without saying anything. "You are wise beyond your years, Jessica. Maybe I will try one more time."

She didn't know what had come over her, and regretted sending him back to Kailea. Mohiam would have chastised her for that. But how could she not encourage him to think kindly about the mother of his son, a woman he had loved? Despite her Bene Gesserit training, which required keeping a tight rein on one's passions, Jessica found herself becoming deeply attached. Perhaps too deeply.

But she had another attachment as well, one going back much longer in her lifetime. With her Bene Gesserit reproductive skills, she could have manipulated Leto's sperm and her eggs during their very first night together, thus conceiving the daughter her superiors had instructed her to produce. Why, then, hadn't she done as she'd been commanded? Why was she delaying?

Jessica felt an inner turmoil over this issue, that forces within her were warring for control. Clearly the Bene Gesserit were on one side, a whispering presence insisting that she fulfill her obligations, her vows. But what opposed them? It wasn't Leto himself. No, it was something much larger and more significant than the love of two people in a vast universe.

But she had no idea what it might be.

———

THE NEXT DAY, Leto visited Kailea in the tower apartments where she spent most of her time, widening the gulf between them. As he entered, she turned toward him, ready to flare with anger, but he sank down beside her on a settee. "I'm sorry we see things so differently, Kailea." He took her hands firmly in his. "I cannot change my mind about marriage, but that doesn't mean I don't care for you."

She pulled away, instantly suspicious. "What's the matter? Did Jessica turn you out of her bed?"

"Not at all." Leto considered telling Kailea what the other woman had said to him, but reconsidered. If she thought Jessica was behind anything, she wouldn't accept it. "I have arranged to send a gift to you, Kailea."

Despite herself, she brightened; it had been a long time since Leto had brought her expensive baubles. "What is it? Jewelry?" She reached for the pocket of his jacket, where he used to hide rings, brooches, bracelets, and necklaces for her; in earlier days, he had made her search his clothes for new baubles, a game that often turned into foreplay.

"Not this time," Leto said with a bittersweet smile. "You are accustomed to a family home much more elegant than my austere Castle. Do you remember the ballroom in the Grand Palais on Ix, with its indigo walls?"

Kailea looked at him, puzzled. "Yes, rare blue obsidian—I haven't seen anything like it in years." Her voice grew wistful and distant. "I remember as a child, being dressed in my ball gown and looking into the translucent walls. The layers within layers made reflections look like ghosts. Light from chandeliers gleamed like stars in the galaxy."

"I have decided to install a veneer of blue obsidian in the ballroom of Castle Caladan," Leto announced, "and also here in your chambers. Everyone will know I did it just for you."

Kailea didn't know what to think. "Is this to salve your conscience?" she challenged, daring him to contradict her. "Do you think it's so easy?"

He shook his head slowly. "I have gone beyond anger, Kailea, and feel only affection for you. Your blue obsidian has already been ordered from a Hagal merchant, though it will take a few months to arrive."

He went to the door, paused. She remained silent, then finally drew in a long breath as if it required a great effort for her to speak.

"Thank you," she said, as he left.

A man may fight the greatest enemy, take the longest journey, survive the most grievous wound—and still be helpless in the hands of the woman he loves.

—Zensunni Wisdom from the Wandering

BREATHLESS WITH ANTICIPATION, LIET-KYNES FORCED HIMSELF TO MOVE methodically, to make no errors. Though excited about racing for Faroula's hand, if he did not prepare properly for the *mihna* challenge, he could find his death instead of a wife.

Heart pounding, he dressed in his stillsuit, fitting it out to retain every drop of moisture, checking all the connections and seals. He rolled his pack, including extra water and food, and took the time to inventory the items in his Fremkit: still-tent, paracompass, manual, charts, sandsnorkel, compaction tools, knife, binoculars, repair pack. Finally, Liet gathered the Maker hooks and thumpers he'd need to summon a worm for the trek across the Great Flat and Habbanya Erg to Habbanya Ridge.

The Cave of Birds was an isolated stopping point for Fremen on their travels, for those with no permanent sietch. Faroula must have departed two days earlier, summoning her own worm as few Fremen women could do. She would know the cave was empty. She would be there waiting for Liet, or Warrick—whoever arrived first.

Liet bustled around the room adjacent to his parents' chambers. His mother heard the frantic movements even at such a late hour and moved the hangings aside. "Why are you preparing for a journey, my son?"

He looked at her. "Mother, I am off to win myself a wife."

Frieth smiled, her thin lips turning up on her tanned and weathered face. "So Faroula has issued the challenge."

"Yes—and I must hurry."

Moving with quick, deft fingers, Frieth rechecked the fastenings on his stillsuit and tied the Fremkit to his back as Liet unfolded charts printed on spice paper so that he could review geography known only to the Fremen. He studied the topography of the desert, the rock outcroppings, the salty basins. Weather records showed where wind patterns and storms were likely to strike.

Warrick had a head start, he knew, but his impetuous friend would not have taken as many precautions. Warrick would rush into the challenge and trust his Fremen skills. But unexpected problems took time and resources to resolve, and Liet invested these few additional minutes to save time later.

His mother kissed him briefly on the cheek. "Remember, the desert is neither your friend nor your enemy . . . simply an obstacle. Use it to your advantage."

"Yes, Mother. Warrick knows that, too."

Pardot Kynes was nowhere to be found . . . but then, he rarely was. Liet could be gone and return again to Red Wall Sietch before the Planetologist even understood the importance of his son's contest.

When he emerged from the moisture-sealed sietch doors to stand on the rugged ridge, Liet took in the vista of sweeping sands lit by the rising moons. He could hear the throbbing beat of a distant thumper.

Warrick was already out there.

Liet rushed down the steep path toward the open basin, but paused again. Sandworms had broad, well-defined territories, which they defended fiercely. Warrick was already calling a great beast, and it would be a long time before Liet could lure a second worm into the same area.

Knowing that, he hiked higher instead, crossed the saddle

of the ridge, and descended the other side of the mountains picking his way toward a shallow basin. Liet hoped he could summon a good Maker there, a better one than his friend obtained.

As he climbed down the rugged slope, using hands and feet, Liet studied the landscape ahead and found a long dune that faced the open desert. That would be a good place to wait. He planted a thumper downslope and set it working without a delayed timer. He'd have several minutes to plow through the loose sand up the backface of the dune. In the darkness, it would be difficult to see the oncoming ripples of wormsign.

Listening to the *thump, thump, thump* of the device, he removed tools from his kit, stretched out the telescoping whip-rods and Maker hooks, then strapped the goads to his back. Always before, when he'd called worms, there had been spotters and helpers, people to assist him should difficulties arise. But for this challenge, Liet-Kynes had to do everything himself. He completed each step according to the familiar ritual. He fastened cleats to his boots, removed the ropes—and hunkered down to wait.

On the other side of the ridge, Warrick would already be mounted and racing across the Great Flat. Liet hoped he could make up for lost time. It would take two, perhaps three, days to reach the Cave of Birds . . . and much could happen in that time.

He dug his fingertips into the sand and sat absolutely motionless. The night had no wind, no sounds other than the thumper, until finally he heard the static hiss of moving sand, the rumble of a leviathan deep beneath the dunes attracted by the steady beat of the thumper. The worm came closer and closer, with a crest of sand in front of it.

"Shai-Hulud has sent a big Maker," Liet said with a long sigh.

The worm circled toward the thumper. Its huge, segmented

ack rode high, encrusted with debris; the wide ridges were ike canyons.

Liet froze in awe before scrambling across the slipping and, holding Maker hooks in both hands. Even through his tillsuit nose plugs, he smelled sulfur, burned rock, and the otent, acrid esters of melange that oozed from the worm.

He raced along as the beast swallowed the thumper. Before he worm could bury itself again, Liet lashed out with one of he Maker hooks, securing its glistening end into the leading edge of a ring segment. With all his strength he pulled, spreading the segment to expose pinkish flesh too tender to touch the abrasive sands. Then he held on.

Avoiding irritation to the stinging wound between its segments, the worm rolled upward and carried Liet with it. He reached out with his other hand, slapping down a second Maker hook and embedding it deeper along the segment. He pulled again to widen the gap.

The worm rose in a reflex action, flinching from this further annoyance.

Normally, additional Fremen riders would open more ring segments, but Liet was alone. Digging his cleats into the hard flesh of Shai-Hulud, he climbed higher, then planted spreaders to keep the segment open. The worm rose out of the sand, and Liet tapped with his first goad to turn the worm around and head onto the sprawling plain of the Great Flat.

Liet held his ropes, finished planting his hooks, and finally stood to look back at the sinuous arc of the worm. The Maker was huge! An air of dignity hung about this one, a sense of great antiquity that went to the very roots of the planet itself. Never before had he seen such a creature. He could ride this one for a long time, at great speed.

He might yet have a chance of overtaking Warrick. . . .

His worm raced across the shifting sands as the two moons rose higher. Liet studied his course, using the stars and constellations, following the tail of the mouse pattern known as

Muad'Dib, "the one who points the way," so that he alway knew his direction.

He crossed the rippling track of what might have been an other great Maker plowing across the Great Flat—likely Wa rick's own worm, since Shai-Hulud rarely traveled on th surface unless provoked. Liet hoped that luck was on his side

After many hours, the race took on a monotonous familiar ity, and drowsiness filled him. He could doze if he lashed him self to the worm, but Liet didn't dare. He had to remain awake to guide the leviathan. If Shai-Hulud strayed from the direc course, Liet would lose time—and he could no longer affore that.

He rode the monster all through the night until the lemor color of dawn tinged the indigo skies, washing away the stars He kept an alert eye for Harkonnen patrol 'thopters, though he doubted they would come so far below the sixty-degree line.

He rode through the morning until, at the hottest point of the day, the enormous worm trembled, thrashed, and fough every attempt to keep it going. It was ready to drop from ex haustion. Liet dared not push it any harder. Worms could be ridden to death, and that would be a bad omen, indeed.

He steered the long, slithering beast toward an archipelago of rock. Releasing the hooks and spreaders, he sprinted along the ring segments and leaped to safety seconds before the lumbering worm wallowed into the sand. Liet dashed toward the low rocks, which were the only strip of dark coloration in a monotony of whites, tans, and yellows, a barricade that sep-arated one vast basin from another.

He huddled under a camouflaged, heat-reflective blanket and set a timer from his Fremkit to allow himself one full hour of sleep. Though his instincts and external senses re-mained alert, he slept deeply, regaining energy.

When he awoke, he climbed over the barrier of rocks to the edge of the vast Habbanya Erg. There Liet planted his second thumper and called another worm—a much smaller one, but still a formidable creature that would take him farther on his journey. He rode through the afternoon.

Toward dusk, Liet's sharp eyes picked up a faint coloration on the shaded sides of the dunes, a pale, gray-green where tendrils of grass wove their roots to stabilize the shifting sands. Fremen had placed seeds here, nurtured them. Even if only one out of a thousand sprouted and lived long enough to re-produce, his father was making progress. Dune would be green again, one day.

During the hypnotic thrumming of the worm's passage, hour after hour, he could hear his father lecturing: "Anchor the sand, and we take away one of the wind's great weapons. In some of the climatic belts of this planet, the winds don't top a hundred klicks per hour. These we call 'minimum-risk spots.' Plantings on the downwind side will build up the dunes, creating larger barriers and increasing the size of these minimum-risk spots. In that way, we can achieve another tiny step toward our goal here."

Half-asleep, Liet shook his head. *Even here, all alone in this vast wasteland, I can't escape the great man's voice . . . his dreams, his lectures.*

But Liet had hours left to travel. He had not seen Warrick yet, knew that there were many routes across the wasteland. He did not relent or decrease his speed. Finally, he made out a wavering dark smudge on the far horizon: Habbanya Ridge, where lay the Cave of Birds.

WARRICK LEFT HIS last worm behind and sprinted with renewed energy up the rocks, using his hands and *temag* boots to climb an unmarked trail. The rocks were greenish-black and ocher-red, baked and weathered by the harsh storms of Arrakis. Blowing sands had scoured the face of the cliff, leaving pock-marks and crannies. He couldn't see the cave opening from here—nor should he be able to, since the Fremen could not risk outside eyes spotting it.

He had traveled well and called good worms. He had never rested, feeling the need to reach Faroula first, to claim her hand . . . but also to outperform his friend Liet. It would make a good story for their grandchildren. Already, the Fremen sietches would be talking of the great worm race, how Faroula had issued such an unusual challenge for her *ahal*.

Warrick climbed hand over hand, finding footholds and fingerholds, until he reached a ledge. Near the camouflaged opening, he found a narrow, scuffed footprint from a woman's boot. Faroula's, for certain. No Fremen would have left such a mark accidentally; she had intended to leave that trace. It was her message that she was there, waiting.

Warrick hesitated, drew a deep breath. It had been a long journey, and he hoped Liet was safe. His blood-brother might be approaching even now, since tall rocks blocked Warrick's view of the surrounding desert. He didn't want to lose his friend, not even over this woman. Fervently, he hoped there would not be a fight.

But he still wanted to be first.

Warrick stepped inside the Cave of Birds, forming a clear silhouette near the edge of the opening. Inside the rough rock cavern, the shadows blinded him. Finally, he heard a woman's voice, silken words sliding along the walls of the cave.

"It's about time," Faroula said. "I've been waiting for you."

She didn't say his name, and for a moment Warrick remained motionless. Then Faroula came to him, elfin-faced, her legs and arms long and lean and muscular. Her overlarge eyes seemed to bore into him. She smelled of sweet herbs and potent scents other than melange. "Welcome, Warrick . . . my husband." Taking his hand, she led him deeper into the cave.

Nervous, struggling for the right words, Warrick held his head high and removed the stillsuit plugs from his nostrils while Faroula worked at the fastenings of his boots. "Here I redeem the pledge thou gavest," he said, using the ritual words of the Fremen marriage ceremony. "I pour sweet water upon thee in this windless place."

Faroula picked up the next phrase. "Naught but life shall prevail between us."

Warrick leaned closer. "Thou shalt live in a palace, my love."

"Thy enemies shall fall to destruction," she promised him.

"Surely well do I know thee."

"Truly well."

Then they spoke together, in unison. "We travel this path together, which my love has traced for thee."

At the end of the blessing and the prayer, they smiled at one another. Naib Heinar would perform a formal ceremony when they returned to Red Wall Sietch, but in the sight of God and in their own hearts, Warrick and Faroula had become married. They stared into each other's eyes for a long time, before withdrawing deeper into the cool darkness of the cave.

LIET ARRIVED PANTING, his boots skittering pebbles along the path as he climbed to the opening of the cave—only to stop when he heard movement within, voices. He hoped it was just that Faroula had brought a companion with her, a maidservant perhaps, or a friend . . . until he recognized the second voice as a man's.

Warrick.

He heard them complete the wedding prayer, and knew that according to tradition, they were married and she was now his friend's wife. No matter how much Liet longed for Faroula, despite the wish he had made upon seeing the mysterious white *Biyan*, she was lost to him now.

Silently, he turned and left the ledge to sit in the rock shadows sheltered from the sun. Warrick was his friend, and he accepted defeat gracefully and privately, but with the deepest sadness he could imagine. It would take time and strength to get over this.

Liet-Kynes waited for an hour, staring across the desert. Then, without venturing inside the cave, he climbed back down to the sand and summoned a worm to take him home.

Political leaders often don't recognize the practical uses of imagination and innovative new ideas until such forms are thrust under their noses by bloody hands.

—CROWN PRINCE RAPHAEL CORRINO,
Discourses on Galactic Leadership

AT THE HEIGHLINER CONSTRUCTION SITE IN THE DEEP CAVERNS OF IX, glowglobes shed garish shadows and searing reflections along girders. Beams glimmered through a haze of caustic smoke from burned solder and fused alloys. Work bosses shouted commands; heavy structural plates slammed together with a din that echoed off the rock walls.

The downtrodden laborers worked as little as possible, hindering progress and diminishing Tleilaxu profits. Even months after the beginning of construction, the old-design Heighliner had not progressed beyond a skeletal framework.

In disguise, C'tair had joined the construction crew, welding girders and support trusses to reinforce the cavernous cargo bay. Today, he needed to be out in the open grotto, where he could see the artificial sky overhead.

Where he could watch the latest step in his desperate plan. . . .

After the major set of explosions he and Miral had set off two years ago, the Masters had become even more repressive, but the Ixians were immune to further hardships. Instead, the example of these two resistance fighters gave their people the strength to endure. Enough "rebels," acting alone or in small groups with sufficient determination, constituted a formidable army—and it was a fighting force that no amount of repression could stop.

Cut off and unaware of the situation inside Ix, Prince Rhombur continued to send explosives and other supplies for the resistance, but only one small additional shipment had found its way to C'tair and Miral. The Masters opened and inspected every container. The workers at the port-of-entry canyon had changed, and the ship pilots had been replaced. All of C'tair's surreptitious contacts were now lost, and he was isolated again.

Still, he and Miral had been heartened to see random windows broken, internal cargoes disrupted, and work productivity diminished even further from its already-disgraceful pace. Just a week before, a man who had no connections to politics, who had never called attention to himself, was caught painting garish letters all along a highly traveled corridor: DEATH TO TLEILAXU SLIGS!

Now C'tair did a graceful catwalk along a cross-girder to reach a floating pad, where he picked up a sonic welder. He ascended via lift platform to the top framework of the Heighliner and looked down the kilometers-long grotto. Below him, surveillance pods avoided the framework of the Heighliner and studied labor troops under the cavern lights. The others on C'tair's construction squad continued their tasks, unaware of what was about to happen. A welder in coveralls moved closer to C'tair, and with a quick peripheral glance he noted that it was Miral, in her own disguise. They would see this together.

Any moment now.

The embedded holoprojectors in the artificial sky flickered; clouds from the Tleilaxu homeworld were dotted with skyscraper islands that protruded downward, glittering with light. Once, those buildings had appeared to be crystal stalactites; now the fairyland structures looked like old, chipped teeth set into the rock of the Ixian crust.

With Miral standing nearby, C'tair squatted on the girder, listening to hammering construction sounds that echoed with tinny reverberations. He looked up like an ancient wolf staring at the moon. *Waiting.*

Then the illusory picture of the sky shifted, distorted, and changed color, as if the alien clouds were gathering in a false storm. The holoprojectors flickered and shifted to project a completely different image, one taken from faraway Caladan. The close-up of a face filled the sky like a titanic god-head.

Rhombur had changed greatly during eighteen years of exile. He looked much more mature, more regal, with a hard edge to his stare and determination in his deep voice.

"I am Prince Rhombur Vernius," the projection boomed, and everyone stared upward, gaping in awe. His mouth was as large as a Guild frigate, his lips opening and closing to dispense words like commandments from on high. "I am the rightful ruler of Ix, and I will return to lead you from your suffering."

Gasps and cheers erupted from all the Ixians. From their perch, C'tair and Miral saw Sardaukar moving about in confusion, and Commander Garon shouting to his troops to impose order. On balconies high above, Tleilaxu Masters emerged, gesturing. Guards raced back into the administrative buildings.

C'tair and Miral enjoyed the moment, allowing themselves an exchange of bright smiles.

"We did it," she said, words that were heard only by him in the confusion around them.

It had taken the pair weeks to study the systems well enough to hijack the projector controls. No one had thought to prepare for such a clever sabotage, such a manipulative invasion of their daily environment.

In the solitary shipment that got through, Rhombur Vernius had smuggled the recorded message, hoping they could secretly disseminate it to loyal Ixians. The Prince had suggested talking posters or coded message bursts inside the regular communication systems of the underground city.

But the enterprising guerrilla couple had chosen to do something far more memorable. To Miral's credit, this had been her idea, and C'tair had perfected many of the details.

Rhombur's face was wide and squarish, his eyes glittering with a passion any other exiled leader would envy. His blond hair had just the right ragged edge to give him a noble, yet disheveled, appearance. The Prince had learned a great deal about statecraft during his years with House Atreides.

"You must rise up and overthrow these foul slave masters. They have no legal right to give you orders or manipulate your daily lives. You must help me return Ix to its former glory. Remove this disease called the Bene Tleilax. Band together and use whatever means necessary to—"

Rhombur's words cut off, stuttering, as someone worked the override controls in the main administrative complex, but the Prince's voice crackled through again, insistent, "—shall return. I merely await the proper time. You are not alone. My mother was murdered. My father has vanished from the Imperium. But my sister and I remain, and I watch Ix. I intend to—"

Rhombur's image twisted and finally faded into static. A darkness blacker than imaginable night settled on the underground grotto. The Tleilaxu had chosen to shut down the whole sky rather than let Prince Rhombur complete his speech.

But C'tair and Miral continued smiling in the inky shadows. Rhombur had said enough, and his listeners would imagine a grander rallying cry than anything the exiled Prince could have actually said.

Within seconds, white-hot glowglobes burst into luminescence, emergency lights that dazzled like harsh suns inside the cavern. Alarms sounded, but already the downtrodden Ixians chattered among themselves, inspired. Now they attributed the explosions to the power of Prince Rhombur. They had seen the continued disruptive activities, and this projected speech was the grandest gesture of all. It was true, they thought. Perhaps Prince Rhombur even walked among them in disguise! House Vernius would return and drive away the evil Tleilaxu. Rhombur would bring happiness and prosperity back to Ix.

Even the suboids were cheering below. With bitter wryness C'tair remembered that these dull bioengineered workers had been among those responsible for driving out Earl Vernius. Their foolish unrest and unwise gullibility in believing Tleilaxu promises had led to the overthrow in the first place.

C'tair didn't mind, though. He would accept any ally who was willing to fight.

Sardaukar troops swarmed out, weapons evident, shouting for everyone to return to their dwellings. Booming loudspeakers declared an immediate crackdown and full martial law. Rations would be cut in half, work shifts would be increased. The Tleilaxu had done it all many times before.

Following Miral and others, C'tair climbed down from the Heighliner girders to the safety of the cavern floor. The more the invaders squeezed, the more outraged the Ixians would become, until at last they would reach the eruption point.

Commander Cando Garon, the leader of Imperial troops on Ix, shouted through a voice-projector in battle-language. Sardaukar fired blasts into the air to frighten the laborers. C'tair moved among his companions on the construction squad, meekly allowing himself to be herded into a holding area. At random, some would be detained and questioned— but no one could prove his involvement, or Miral's. Even if both of them were executed for this, their grand gestures had been worth everything.

C'tair and Miral, widely separated in the throng, did as they were told, following the angry orders of Sardaukar guards. When C'tair heard workers whispering to each other, repeating the words of Rhombur Vernius, his joy and confidence reached its peak.

Someday . . . someday soon, Ix would be restored to its people.

Enemies strengthen you; allies weaken.

—EMPEROR ELROOD IX,
Deathbed Insights

AFTER HE RECOVERED FROM THE INKVINE BEATING, GURNEY HALLECK worked for two months with a sluggish sense of inner dread, worse than he had ever experienced in the slave pits. An ugly scar ran along the side of his jaw, thrashing lines that throbbed a beet-red color and continued to hurt. Though the actual wound had healed, the toxic residue still pulsed with neural fire, as if an intermittent lightning bolt lay buried within his cheek and jaw.

But that was only pain. Gurney could endure that. Physical injuries meant very little to him anymore; they had become part of his existence.

He was more frightened by the fact that he had been punished so *minimally* after he'd attacked Glossu Rabban. The burly Harkonnen had whipped him, and the guards had beaten him afterward so that he'd needed three days in the infirmary . . . but he had experienced much worse for only minor infractions. What did they really have in mind?

He remembered the dull gleam of calculated cruelty in Rabban's close-set eyes. "Check the records. Find out where he came from. And if he has any family left alive." Gurney feared the worst.

With the other slaves he wandered through the days mechanically, hunched over with a growing anticipation and horror in the pit of his stomach. He worked alternately on the cliffs of Mount Ebony and in the obsidian-processing vats. Cargo ships landed near the garrison and the slave pits, hauling away containers filled with glowing, sharp-edged volcanic glass to be distributed by House Hagal.

One day a pair of guards unceremoniously hauled him from the vats. He dripped with dark suspension fluids. Half-clad, splattering oily liquid on the uniformed guards, Gurney stumbled out into the open square where Glossu Rabban had inspected the prisoners, where Gurney had attacked him.

Now he saw a low platform on the ground, and in front of it, a single chair. No chains, no shigawire bindings . . . just the chair. The sight struck terror into his heart. He had no idea what might be in store for him.

Guards shoved him into the chair, then stepped away. A doctor from the prison infirmary stood at attention nearby, and a group of Harkonnen soldiers marched into the square. The other slaves continued working in the pits and tanks, so Gurney knew the impending event was personal . . . a spectacle arranged only for him.

That made it infinitely worse.

The more Gurney showed his agitation, the more pleasure the guards took in refusing to answer him. So he fell silent, as the thick processing liquid dried into a crackling film on his skin.

The familiar doctor stepped up, holding a small yellow vial with a tiny needle at one end. Gurney had seen those yellow vials in the infirmary, stored in a transparent case, but he'd never had occasion to receive one. The doctor slapped the pointed end against the prisoner's neck as if he were crushing a wasp. Gurney jerked up, throat clenched, muscles straining.

Warm numbness spread like hot oil through his body. His arms and legs grew leaden. He twitched a few times, then couldn't move at all. He couldn't turn his neck, couldn't grimace, couldn't blink or even move his eyes.

The doctor shifted the chair and twisted Gurney's head as if positioning a mannequin, forcing him to stare at the low platform in front of him. Gurney suddenly realized what it was.

A *stage*. And he would be compelled to watch something.

From one of the outbuildings Glossu Rabban emerged, fully dressed in his finest uniform and accompanied by the work supervisor, who also wore a dark, clean uniform. The scrawny, potbellied man had eschewed his nostril filters for the occasion.

Rabban stepped in front of Gurney, who wanted nothing more than to leap to his feet and throttle the man. But he couldn't move. The paralysis drug held him like a vise, so he simply put as much hatred into his eyes as he could manage.

"Prisoner," Rabban said, his thick lips wearing an obscene smile. "Gurney Halleck of the village Dmitri. After you attacked me, we took the trouble to find your family. We've heard from Captain Kryubi about the obnoxious little songs you were singing in the tavern. Even though no one had seen you in the village for years, they never thought to report your disappearance. A few of them, before they died under torture, said that they assumed we'd taken you away in the night. The fools."

Gurney felt panicked now, with fluttering dark wings in his mind. He wanted to demand answers about his tired and unambitious parents . . . but he feared Rabban would tell him anyway. He could barely breathe. His chest muscles spasmed, fighting the paralysis. As his blood boiled and his rage grew, he was unable to draw in more breath. His head began to buzz from lack of oxygen.

"Then all the pieces fell into place. We learned about how your sister had been assigned to the pleasure houses . . . and you just couldn't accept the natural order of things." Rabban shrugged his broad shoulders; his fingers strayed meaningfully to his inkvine whip, but did not pull it free. "Everyone else knows his place on Giedi Prime, but you don't seem to know yours. So we've decided to provide a reminder, just for you."

He gave a theatrically heavy sigh that emphasized his disappointment. "Unfortunately, my troops were a bit too . . . enthusiastic . . . when they asked your parents to join us here. I'm afraid your mother and father did not survive the encounter. However . . ."

Rabban raised one hand, and the guards hurried to the supply shack. Out of his field of view, Gurney heard a scuffle and then a woman's wordless cry, but he could not turn to see. He knew it was Bheth.

For a moment his heart skipped a beat just to know she was still alive. He'd thought the Harkonnens might have killed her after his capture in the pleasure house. But now he knew in his soul that they'd only been saving her for something much worse.

They dragged her, thrashing and struggling, onto the wooden platform. She wore only a baggy, torn shirt. Her flaxen hair was long and wild, her eyes wide with fear, and even more so once she caught sight of her brother. Again, he saw the white scar on her throat. They had stolen Bheth's ability to sing or to talk . . . and had destroyed her ability to smile.

Their gazes locked. Bheth couldn't speak. Paralyzed, Gurney could not say anything to her, or even flinch.

"Your sister knows her place," Rabban said. "In fact, she served us rather well. I checked through the records to come up with an exact number. This little girl has provided pleasure to 4,620 of our troops." Rabban patted Bheth on the shoulder. She tried to bite him. He clenched his fingers and tore off the shift she wore.

The guards forced her naked onto the platform—and Gurney couldn't move. He wanted to shut his eyes, but the paralysis prevented him. Though he understood what she had been forced to do for the past six years, seeing her nakedness again offended and appalled him. Her body was bruised, her skin a patchwork of dark colors and thin scars.

"Not many women at our pleasure houses last as long as she has," Rabban said. "This one has a strong will to live, but her time is at an end. If she could speak, she'd tell us how very happy she is to give this one last service to House Harkonnen—providing a lesson to you."

Gurney strained with all of his might, trying to force his muscles to move. His heart pounded, and heat pulsed through his body. But he could not so much as wiggle a finger.

The work supervisor went first. He opened his robes, and Gurney had no recourse but to watch as the potbellied man raped Bheth on the stage. Then came five of the other guards, performing at Rabban's command. The broad-shouldered brute observed Gurney as much as he observed the spectacle on the stage. Inside his mind, Gurney flew into a rage, then wished fervently to be allowed to retreat, to call down black sleep upon himself. But he didn't have that option.

Rabban himself went last, taking the greatest pleasure. He was forceful and brutal, though by then Bheth had been abused nearly into unconsciousness. As he finished, Rabban locked his hands around Bheth's neck, around the white scar. She struggled again, but Rabban twisted her head, forcing her to look over at her brother as he squeezed his hands around her throat. He thrust once more inside her, viciously, and then the muscles in his arms went tense. He squeezed harder, and Bheth's eyes bulged.

Gurney had no choice but to watch as she died in front of him. . . .

Doubly satisfied, Rabban stood, stepped back, and re-dressed himself in his uniform. He smiled at both of his victims. "Leave her body here," he said. "How long will her brother's paralysis last?"

The doctor approached quickly, unmoved by what he had just seen. "Another hour or two at that small dosage. Any more of the *kirar* would have put him into a hibernation trance, and you didn't want that."

Rabban shook his head. "Let's leave him here to stare at her until he can move again. I want him to consider the error of his ways."

Laughing, Rabban departed and the guards followed. Gurney remained alone in the chair, completely unshackled. He could not cease staring at the motionless form of Bheth sprawled on the platform. Blood trickled from her mouth.

But even the paralysis that gripped Gurney's body could not prevent the tears that spilled from his eyes.

The mystery of life is not a problem to be solved, but a reality to be experienced.

—Meditations from Bifrost Eyrie,
Buddislamic Text

FOR A YEAR AND A HALF, ABULURD HARKONNEN REMAINED A BROKEN MAN. He hid his face in shame from the horror of what his son had done. He accepted the blame and the guilt, but he could not bear to meet the haunted eyes of the good people of Lankiveil.

As he had feared, after Rabban's slaughter of Bjondax whales in Tula Fjord, the fishing had gone bad; villages were abandoned as the fishermen and fur whale hunters moved on. Left exposed to the elements, the wooden settlements remained empty, a string of ghost towns in rocky coves.

Abulurd had dismissed his servants, and he and Emmi shut down the main lodge, leaving it like a tombstone to memorialize their once-idyllic way of life. They departed from the grand old building in hopes that one day the good times would return. For now, he and his wife lived in their small dacha out on an isolated spit of land that extended into the blood-tainted waters of the fjord.

Emmi, who had been so hale and hearty with laughing eyes and a commonsense smile, now seemed old and tired, as if the knowledge of their corrupted son sapped her remaining strength. She had always been firmly anchored in the world, like a bed'rock, but her foundation had been badly eroded.

Glossu Rabban was forty-one years old, an adult responsible for his own horrific actions. Yet Abulurd and Emmi feared *they* had done something wrong, that they had not instilled in him the proper sense of honor and love for a ruled people. . . .

Rabban had personally led the attack that obliterated Bifrost Eyrie. Abulurd had watched the man stand by as guards hurled his own grandfather off the cliffs. By slaughtering the whales in Tula Fjord, he had single-handedly destroyed the economy of the entire coast. From a CHOAM representative, they'd learned how Rabban delighted in torturing and killing innocent victims in the grim slave pits of Giedi Prime.

How can this man be any offspring of mine?

During the time spent in their lonely dacha, Emmi and Abulurd tried to conceive another son. It had been a difficult decision, but he and his wife finally realized that Glossu Rabban was no longer their child. He had cut himself off forever from their love. Emmi had made up her mind, and Abulurd could not refuse her.

While they could not undo the damage Rabban had caused, they could perhaps have another son, one to be raised right. Though she was strong and healthy, Emmi was past her prime years, and the Harkonnen bloodline had never spawned a large number of children.

Victoria—the first wife of Dmitri Harkonnen—had given him only one son, Vladimir. After a bitter divorce, Dmitri had married the young and beautiful Daphne, but their first child, Marotin, had been severely retarded, a terrible embarrassment who died at the age of twenty-eight. Daphne's second son, Abulurd, was a bright boy who became his father's favorite. They had laughed and read and played together. Dmitri had taught Abulurd about statecraft, reading to him from the historical treatises of Crown Prince Raphael Corrino.

Dmitri never spent much time with his eldest child, but his bitter ex-wife Victoria taught her son much. Though they had the same father, Vladimir and Abulurd could not have been more different. Unfortunately, Rabban took after the Baron more than his own parents. . . .

Following months of self-imposed isolation, Abulurd and Emmi took their boat down the gnarled coast to the nearest village, where they intended to buy fresh fish, vegetables, and supplies that the dacha's stores didn't offer. They wore home-spun shawls and thickly padded tunics without the ceremonial jewelry or fine trimmings of their station.

When Abulurd and his wife first walked through the market, he hoped they would be treated as mere villagers, unrec-ognized. But the people of Lankiveil knew their leader too well. They welcomed him with painfully wholehearted greet-ings.

Seeing how the villagers looked at him with understand-ing, Abulurd realized he'd been wrong to isolate himself. The natives needed to see *him* as much as he needed the company of his citizens. What had happened at Bifrost Eyrie was one of the great tragedies of Lankiveil's history, but Abulurd Har-konnen could not give up hope entirely. In the hearts of these people, a bright flame continued to burn. Their welcome did much to fill the emptiness within him. . . .

Over the next few months, Emmi spoke to women in the villages; they knew of their governor's desire to have another son, someone who would be raised here and not as a . . . *Harkonnen*. Emmi refused to give up hope.

A strange chance occurred one week while they shopped, filling their baskets with fresh greens and smoked fish wrapped in salted sheets of kelp. As they moved along the stalls, chat-ting with fish vendors and shell carvers, Abulurd noticed an old woman standing at the end of the market. She wore the pale-blue robes of a Buddislamic monk; gold embroidery on the trim and copper bells at her neck signified that this woman had reached her religion's higher orders of enlightenment, one of the few females to do so. She stood rigid as a statue, no taller than the other villagers . . . yet somehow the woman's *presence* made her stand out like a monolith.

Emmi stared with her dark eyes, transfixed, and finally

stepped forward with hope and wonder on her face. "We've heard of you." Abulurd looked at his wife, wondering what she meant.

The old monk threw back her hood to reveal a freshly shaved scalp, which was pink and mottled, as if unaccustomed to exposure to the cold; when she furrowed her brow, the parchmentlike skin on her long face wrinkled up like crumpling paper. But she spoke in a voice that had resonant, hypnotic qualities. "I know what you desire—and I know that Buddallah sometimes grants wishes to those He deems worthy."

The old woman leaned closer as if her words were a secret to be shared only with them. The copper bells at her neck jingled faintly. "Your minds are pure, your consciences clear, and your hearts worthy of such a reward. You have already suffered much pain." Her eyes became hard like a bird's. "But you must want a child badly enough."

"We do," Abulurd and Emmi said in such perfect unison that it startled them. They looked at each other and chuckled nervously. Emmi grasped her husband's hand.

"Yes, I see your sincerity. An important beginning." The woman murmured a quick blessing over the two. Then, as if it were a supernatural nod from Buddallah Himself, the soup of gray clouds thinned, allowing a streak of sunlight to shine down on the village. The others in the market stared at Abulurd and Emmi with curious, hopeful expressions.

The monk reached into her sky-blue robes and withdrew several packets. She held them up, clutching the edges with the barest tips of her fingers.

"Extracts of shellfish," she said. "Mother-of-pearl ground together with diamond dust, dried herbs that grow only during the summer solstice up in the snowfields. These are extremely potent. Use them well." She extended three packets to Abulurd and the same to Emmi. "Brew them into tea and drink deeply before your lovemaking. But have a care that you do not waste yourselves. Watch the moons, or look at your charts if the clouds are too thick."

The old monk carefully explained the most fortuitous phases of the moon, the times in the monthly cycle best suited for conceiving a child. Emmi nodded, clutching the packets in her fingers as if they were great treasure.

Abulurd felt a wave of skepticism. He'd heard of folk remedies and superstitious treatments, but the look of delight and hope on his wife's face was so great that he dared not voice any doubts. He promised himself that for *her* he would do everything this strange old woman suggested.

In an even quieter voice, but without the slightest embarrassment, the withered woman told them in explicit detail of certain enhancement rituals they must perform to heighten their sexual pleasure and to increase the possibility of sperm uniting with a fertile egg. Emmi and Abulurd listened, and each agreed to do as they had been instructed.

Before returning to their boat and leaving the village market behind, Abulurd made certain to pick up a current lunar chart from a vendor.

IN THE BLACK of night at their isolated dacha, they lit the rooms with candles and built a roaring fire in the fireplace so that their home was filled with warm, orange light. Outside, the wind had died away into deep silence like a held breath. The water in the fjord was a dark mirror reflecting the clouds above. The brooding mountains rose sheer from the waterline, their peaks lost in the overcast sky.

In the distance, around the curve of the cove, they could make out the silhouette of the main lodge, its windows shuttered, its doors barred. The rooms would be cold and frosty, the furniture covered, the cupboards empty. The abandoned villages were quiet, silent memories of bustling times before all the fur whales had gone away.

Abulurd and Emmi lay on their honeymoon bed made of amber-gold elacca wood carved with beautiful fern designs. They wrapped themselves in plush furs and slowly made love with more passionate attention than they had experienced in years. The bitter taste of the old monk's strange tea lingered in their throats and filled them each with a heathen arousal that made them feel young again.

Afterward, as they lay contented in each other's arms, Abulurd listened to the night. In the distance, quiet but echoing over the still waters and sheer rock walls, he thought he heard the calls of lonely Bjondax whales hovering at the entrance to the cove.

Abulurd and Emmi took that as a good omen.

HER MISSION ACCOMPLISHED, Reverend Mother Gaius Helen Mohiam discarded her Buddislamic robes, wrapped up the tiny ornamental bells she had worn at her throat, and packed them all away. Her scalp itched, but her hair would soon grow back.

She removed the contact lenses that disguised the color of her eyes, and the makeup that made her look older, then added lotions to the rough skin on her face to help her recover from the harsh winds and cold of Lankiveil.

She had been here for more than a month, collecting data, studying Abulurd Harkonnen and his wife. One time, when they were in the village following their too-predictable weekly routine, she had slipped north and broken into their dacha, collecting hairs, skin scrapings, discarded nail clippings, anything to help her determine the precise biochemistry of these two. Such things provided her with all the information she needed.

Sisterhood experts had analyzed all the probabilities and determined how to improve the odds of Abulurd Harkonnen having another child, a *boy* child. The Kwisatz Haderach breeding program needed these genetics, and the actions of

Glossu Rabban proved him too unruly—not to mention too old—to be a fitting mate for the daughter Jessica had been commanded to bear by Leto Atreides. The Bene Gesserit needed another male Harkonnen alternative.

She went to the Lankiveil spaceport and waited for the next scheduled shuttle. For once, unlike her experience with the vile Baron, she was not coercing others to conceive a child they did not wish to have. Abulurd and his wife desired another son more than anything else, and Mohiam was happy to use the Sisterhood's expertise to manipulate their chances.

This new child, Glossu Rabban's younger brother, would have an important destiny ahead of him.

The work to which we have set ourselves is the liberating of the imagination, and the harnessing of the imagination to man's physical creativity.

—FRIEDRE GINAZ,
Philosophy of the Swordmaster

LATE AFTERNOON ON YET ANOTHER GINAZ ISLAND, WITH STRETCHES OF sloping green land, fences of black-lava boulders, and grazing cattle. Thatch-and-frond huts stood in clearings studded with mounds of pampas grass that waved in the wind; canoes lay on smooth beaches. Out on the water, the white flecks of sails dotted the lagoons.

The fishing boats made Duncan Idaho think fondly of Caladan . . . his home.

The remaining students had spent a grueling day of martial-arts instruction, practicing the art of balance. Trainees fought with short knives while standing amidst sharpened bamboo stakes in the ground. Two of his classmates had been seriously injured when they'd fallen onto the stakes. Duncan had sliced open his hand, but he ignored the stinging red gash. It would heal.

"Wounds make better lessons than lectures," the Swordmaster had remarked, without sympathy.

Now the students took a break for mail call. Duncan and his comrades stood around a wooden platform in front of their interim barracks, waiting as Jeh-Wu, one of their first training masters, called out names and distributed message cylinders and nullentropy parcels. The humidity made Jeh-

Wu's long black dreadlocks hang like drooping vines around his iguana-like face.

It had been two years since the terrible, rainswept night during which Trin Kronos and the other Grumman students were expelled from the Ginaz School. According to infrequent news reports reaching the trainees, Emperor Shaddam and the Landsraad had never agreed on the penalties to be assessed against Grumman for kidnapping and murdering members of the Ecazi noble family. Unrestrained, Viscount Moritani continued his considerable saber rattling, while several other allied Houses began subtle machinations to portray him as the injured party in the quarrel.

Increasingly the name of Duke Atreides was mentioned with admiration. Leto had originally tried to be an intermediary in the conflict, but had now grown unflagging in his support for Archduke Ecaz, and had marshaled agreement among the Great Houses to curb Grumman aggression. Duncan was proud of his Duke, and wished he knew more about what was going on outside in the galaxy. He wanted to return to Caladan and stand by Leto's side.

In his years on Ginaz, Duncan had grown close to Hiih Resser, the only Grumman who'd had the nerve to condemn his planet's aggression. House Moritani had severed all ties with Resser for what they considered his betrayal. Resser's tuition was now paid out of an Imperial hardship fund, since his adoptive father had publicly disowned him at the Viscount's court.

Now, as Duncan stood beside the redhead at mail call, it was clear that the young man knew he would receive no offworld messages, not then, not ever again. "You might be surprised, Hiih. Don't you have an old girlfriend who would write to you?"

"After six years? Not likely."

After the expulsion of the Moritani loyalists, Duncan and

Resser spent even more of their free time together, playing pyramid chess and reverse poker, or hiking, or swimming in the wild surf. Duncan had even written to Duke Leto, suggesting that the young Grumman trainee might be a candidate for employment with House Atreides.

Resser, like Duncan, had been orphaned before the age of ten. He'd been adopted by Arsten Resser, one of the principal advisors to Viscount Hundro Moritani. Resser had never gotten along well with his adoptive father, especially during his rebellious teen years. Following a family tradition for alternate generations, the redhead had been sent away to Ginaz; Arsten Resser had been convinced the renowned academy would break the spirit of his difficult adoptive son. Instead, Hiih Resser was thriving and had learned much.

Hearing his name called, Duncan stepped forward to accept a heavy package. "Melange cakes from your mommy?" Jeh-Wu teased.

Earlier, Duncan would have flown into a rage and attacked the man for his teasing, ripping out one dreadlock after another like stalks of celery. Now, he used cutting words instead. "My mother was killed by Glossu Rabban on Giedi Prime."

Jeh-Wu looked suddenly uncomfortable. Resser put a hand on Duncan's shoulder and pulled him back into the line. "Something from your home?" He prodded the package. "You're lucky to have anyone who cares about you."

Duncan looked at him. "I've made Caladan my home, after what the Harkonnens did to me." He remembered what Leto had said to him, on their last morning at breakfast, when the Duke had given him the marvelous sword: "Never forget compassion."

Impulsively, Duncan extended the parcel, noting the red hawk crest on the wrapping. "You can have whatever it is. The food, at least—any holophotos or messages are mine."

Resser accepted the parcel with a grin while Jeh-Wu continued to distribute letter cylinders. "Maybe I'll share it with you, and maybe I won't."

"Don't challenge me to a duel, because you'll lose."

The other young man muttered good-naturedly, "Sure, sure."

The pair sat on a stairway of the interim barracks, looking out at fishing boats in the lagoon. Resser tore open the wrapping with more enthusiasm than Duncan could have summoned. Removing one of several sealed containers, he gazed through clearplaz at the orange-colored slices inside. "What's this?"

"Paradan melon!" Duncan grabbed for the container, but Resser snapped it out of his reach and scrutinized it skeptically. "You haven't heard of paradan? Sweetest treat in the Imperium. My favorite. If I'd known they were sending me that—" Resser handed the container back to him, and Duncan opened it. "Haven't seen any in a year. They had some crop failures, a plankton bloom that caused shortages."

He handed a slice of preserved fruit to Resser, who took a small bite and forced himself to swallow. "Way too sweet for me."

Greedily, Duncan tasted another piece, followed by two more before he closed the container. To cheer Resser, he found some delicious Cala pastries made of brown pundi rice and molasses, wrapped in spice paper.

Finally, he removed three messages from the bottom of the package, handwritten on parchment that bore the seal of House Atreides. Greetings from Rhombur, encouraging him to keep his hopes up . . . a note from Thufir Hawat expressing how much the Mentat looked forward to having Duncan share his work at Castle Caladan . . . a message from Leto promising to consider Hiih Resser for a position in the Atreides House Guard, if the redhead completed his training satisfactorily.

Resser had tears in his eyes when his friend let him read the notes. He looked away, trying to keep Duncan from seeing.

With an arm around his companion's shoulders, Duncan said, "No matter what House Moritani does, you'll still find a place. Who would dare challenge House Atreides, knowing that we have *two* Swordmasters?"

That night Duncan was so homesick he couldn't sleep, so he took the Old Duke's sword outside the barracks and practiced in the starlight, dueling with imaginary opponents. It had been such a long time since he'd seen the rolling blue seas of Caladan . . . but he still remembered his chosen home, and how much he owed to House Atreides.

Nature has moved inexplicably backward and forward to produce this marvelous, subtle Spice. One is tempted to suggest that only divine intervention could possibly have produced a substance which in one aspect extends human life and in another opens the inner doors of the psyche to the wonders of Time and Creation.

—HIDAR FEN AJIDICA,
Laboratory Notes on the Nature of Melange

AT THE UNDERGROUND XUTTUH SPACEPORT, RESEARCH DIRECTOR HIDAR Fen Ajidica watched Fenring's shuttle lift off from the canyon wall, a wide rift in the crust of the planet. Ostensibly a scenic gorge when viewed from above, the fissure provided access to the secure worlds below. Fenring's craft dwindled to a speck in the cold, blue sky.

Good riddance! He could always hope that the meddling Imperial observer might die in a spacecraft explosion, but unfortunately, again, he reached orbit safely.

Ajidica turned back into the tunnels, taking a lift tube down into the deep levels. He'd had enough fresh air and open sky for one day.

The Spice Minister's unannounced inspection visit had consumed two days . . . wasted time, as far as the Master Researcher was concerned. He was anxious to get back to his long-term artificial spice experiments, which were nearing their final phase. *How am I to accomplish anything with that man breathing down my neck?*

To make matters worse, a Tleilaxu representative was scheduled to arrive in a week—now it seemed as if Ajidica's own people didn't trust him. They took their reports back to the Masters on the sacred home planet, who discussed it in the

438 — BRIAN HERBERT AND KEVIN J. ANDERSON

central *kehl*, the highest holy council of his people. *More in*
spections. More interference.

But I have almost achieved my goal. . . .

Pursuant to the Master Researcher's precise instructions,
his laboratory assistants had prepared an important modification in the new axlotl tanks, the sacred biological receptacles
in which counterfeit spice variations were grown. With those
adjustments, he could proceed to the next stage: actual testing, and then the production of amal.

Inside the sealed research pavilion, Hidar Fen Ajidica and
his team had been much more successful than he'd dared reveal to the weasel Fenring or even to his own people. Within
another year, two at the most, he expected to solve the elusive
riddle. And then he would activate the plan he'd already set in
motion, stealing the secret of amal and putting it to his own
uses.

By that time, not even the legions of Sardaukar secretly
stationed here could stop him. Before they realized anything,
Ajidica would slip away with his prize, destroying the laboratories in his wake. And keeping the artificial spice for himself.

Of course, there were other things that could interfere
with Ajidica's grand scheme—unknowns. Spies were in operation on Xuttuh; the Sardaukar and Ajidica's own security force
had located and executed more than a dozen from the various
Houses Major. But there had been rumors of a covert Bene
Gesserit woman at work here, too. He wished those witches
would mind their own business.

On the railcar ride back to his high-security facility, the
Master Researcher popped a red lozenge into his mouth and
chewed it. The medication, which treated his phobia of being
underground, tasted like rotten slig meat from a fouled tank.
He wondered why pharmacists couldn't formulate drugs that
tasted better. Surely it was only a matter of additives?

Ahead, the research pavilion was comprised of fifteen
white buildings connected by overpasses, conveyors, and track

systems, all surrounded by powerful defense mechanisms and reinforced one-way windows. Sardaukar troops protected the complex.

Ajidica had adapted Tleilaxu genetic science to the advanced manufacturing facilities left behind when House Vernius had been driven away. The victors had commandeered stockpiles of raw materials and, through intermediaries, obtained additional resources off-world. In exchange for their lives, a number of Ixian factory managers and scientists had aided in this process.

The railcar came to a smooth stop at the pavilion walls. After working his way through cumbersome security procedures, Ajidica stepped onto a clean white platform. From there he took a lift tube to the largest, scan-muffled section, where new "candidates" were fitted to modified axlotl tanks. Every Ixian survivor wanted to know what occurred inside the secret facility, but no one had any evidence. Only suspicions, and mounting fears.

In the research pavilion, Ajidica had the most advanced fabrication facility in the Imperium, including elaborate materials-handling systems for transporting samples. The experimental nature of Project Amal required a broad spectrum of chemicals and specimens and the disposal of large quantities of toxic waste, all of which he was able to do with unparalleled efficiency. He'd never had access to anything so advanced on Tleilax itself.

Ajidica passed through a biosecurity doorway, entered an immense room where workers were finishing the rough connections in the floor, preparing for the new, still-living axlotl tanks that would be brought in.

My tests must continue. When I have learned the secret, I will control the spice, and I can destroy all of those devils who depend on it.

Freedom is an elusive concept. Some men hold themselves prisoner even when they have the power to do as they please and go where they choose, while others are free in their hearts, even as shackles restrain them.

—Zensunni Wisdom from the Wandering

INTENTIONALLY, GURNEY HALLECK BROKE THE STIRRING EQUIPMENT IN THE obsidian-processing vat, which caused a rupture in the container. Polishing liquid gushed all over the already-mucky ground. He stood back and braced himself for the punishment he knew would come.

The first step in his cold, desperate escape plan.

Predictably, the guards rushed forward, raising their spark-clubs and gauntleted fists. In the two months since Bheth's murder, the Harkonnens were sure they'd snuffed out any candle of resistance in this blond-haired man. Why they didn't simply kill him, Gurney wasn't sure. Not because they admired his spirit, or because he was so tough. Instead, they probably got a sadistic pleasure from tormenting him and letting him come back for more.

Now he needed to be injured severely enough to require medical attention. He wanted the guards to hurt him worse than usual, breaking a few ribs, perhaps. Then the medics would treat him in the infirmary and ignore him as he healed. That was when Gurney would make his move.

He fought back when the guards attacked, flailing and clawing at them. Other prisoners would have surrendered meekly—but if Gurney hadn't struggled, they would have been suspicious. So he resisted fiercely and, of course, the guards won. They punched and kicked him and hammered his skull against the ground.

Pain and blackness swam up around him with a nauseating thickness, but the guards, filled with adrenaline now, did not relent. He felt bones crack. He coughed blood.

As Gurney fell into oblivion, he feared that he'd gone too far, that they might actually kill him this time. . . .

FOR DAYS, THE workers in the slave pits had been loading a shipment of blue obsidian. The fenced-off cargo hauler lay waiting on the landing field, its hull plates ion-scarred from many trips up to orbit and back. Guards watched the shipment, but without much attention. No man came to the heart of a slave pit willingly, and as far as the guards were concerned no treasure in the universe would tempt even the greediest of thieves.

This large order had been commissioned through Hagal merchants by Duke Leto Atreides. Even Gurney knew that the Atreides had been generations-long adversaries of House Harkonnen. Rabban and the Baron took a smug delight in knowing that they were selling such an expensive shipment to their greatest adversary.

Gurney cared only that the cargo was due to leave soon . . . and that he meant to follow it far away from the slave pits.

When he finally swam back out of his agony-filled stupor, he found himself in an infirmary bed. The sheets were stained from previous patients. The doctors wasted little effort to keep the slaves alive; it simply wasn't cost-effective. If the injured prisoners could be healed with a minimum of time and attention, then they would be sent back to work. If they died . . . Harkonnen sweeps would pick up replacements.

As full awareness returned, Gurney lay motionless, careful not to moan or call attention to himself. On an adjacent cot, a man writhed in pain. Through slitted eyes, Gurney saw that the bandaged stump of the man's right arm was soaked with blood. He wondered why the doctors had bothered. As soon as the potbellied work supervisor saw the maimed slave, he would order his termination.

The man cried out, either from horrible pain or an awareness of his fate. Two medical techs held him down and injected him with a hissing spray—no mere tranquilizer. Within moments he gurgled and fell silent. Half an hour later, uniformed men hauled the body away, humming a rhythmic marching tune as if they did this all day long.

A doctor loomed over Gurney, checking him, poking; though he made appropriate moans and weak mewling sounds, he did not stir from feigned unconsciousness. The doctor snorted and shuffled away. Over the years, the medical techs had already spent far too much time tending Gurney Halleck's repeated injuries, as far as they were concerned.

When the lights went out in the slave-pit complex for nighttime shutdown, the infirmary droned into a low stupor. The doctors indulged in their own chemical addictions, semuta or other drugs from the pharmacy stores. They made a final perfunctory check of the still-comatose patient. Gurney groaned, pretending to be trapped in nightmare-wracked sleep. One doctor hovered over him for a moment with a needle, perhaps a painkiller but more likely a sedative, then shook his head and went away. Maybe he wanted Gurney to sweat if he woke up in the night. . . .

As soon as the medical techs left, Gurney opened his eyes and touched his bandages, assessing his injuries. He wore only a tattered beige hospital smock, patched and frayed—like his own body.

He had numerous bruises and clumsily stitched gashes and cuts. His head ached: a cracked skull or at least a severe concussion. But even as he'd fought back, Gurney had been careful to protect his limbs. He could still move.

He swung his bare feet off the edge of the bed onto the cold, gritty infirmary floor. Nausea rose within him, but passed. When he inhaled deeply, his ribs ached like a fire of broken glass. But he could live with that.

He took several staggering steps across the room. The techs kept dim glowglobes burning in case of an emergency. All around, patients snored or whimpered in the night, but no one noticed him. The inkvine scar along the side of his face throbbed, threatening an encore of terrible pain, but Gurney ignored it. *Not now*.

Standing in front of the sealed medicine cabinet, he saw a rack containing needle-tipped ampoules of *kirar*, the drug Rabban had used to make him sit paralyzed and helpless during the prolonged rape and murder of Bheth. Gurney jiggled the cabinet door, then snapped the latch, trying to minimize the damage so that the doctors wouldn't immediately see what he had done.

Not knowing the proper dosage, he grabbed a handful of the yellow ampoules. Each container was like a wasp made of smooth polymers. He turned away, paused. If anyone spotted the broken cabinet and the missing ampoules, they might guess what he had in mind—so Gurney took handfuls of other potent drugs as well, painkillers and hallucinogens, which he tossed into the medical incinerator, keeping only a few painkillers for himself, just in case he needed them. The Harkonnens would assume someone had stolen a variety of drugs, not just the *kirar*.

He searched for clothes, found a bloodstained surgical uniform and decided it was better than his hospital gown. Wincing from the pain of moving his unhealed body, he dressed, then found some energy capsules but no solid food. He swallowed the oval tablets, not knowing how long he might need them to sustain him. Crouching low, he jimmied open the infirmary door and slipped out into the darkness, a shadow among shadows.

Gurney bypassed the crackling, electricity-laced fences that surrounded the compound, a system designed more for intimidation than for security. The barriers were easy enough to break through. Bright glowglobes spread garish pools of light across the pitted landing area, but the globes were tuned and positioned badly, leaving large islands of murky gloom.

Flitting from one dark patch to another, Gurney approached the bulky containers that sat unguarded, filled with obsidian. He worked open a metal hatch that squeaked. He hesitated, but any delay would only invite more attention, so he thrust himself into the chute. As quietly as he could, he let the hatch fall back shut.

He slid down a rough metal ramp that caught and tore his stolen garment, until he landed on the mounds of chemically treated blue obsidian. The sides were rough-edged glass, but Gurney didn't care about a few extra cuts and scratches. Not after all he'd been through. He took care not to sustain any deep cuts.

He wallowed deeper. Each chunk of obsidian was the size of his fist or larger, but they were ragged and mismatched. Many pieces came in wide, glossy slabs. This bin was nearly full, and the crews would top it off in the morning with a final load before launching the cargo hauler. Gurney tried to cover himself enough to avoid being seen.

The weight of the volcanic glass pressed down as he shoveled it over the top of his head. Already, he could barely breathe. The cuts burned his skin, but he slowly worked his way deeper, pressed into a corner so that at least two sides were solid metal. He tried to push support pieces around him that would hold some of the load above. The oppressive weight would only get worse when additional obsidian was poured on top of him, but he would survive somehow . . . and even if he didn't, he could accept his fate. Dying in an attempt to escape from the Harkonnens was better than living under their boot.

When he had managed to slough loose obsidian chunks over the large flat piece above his head, he stopped. He couldn't see anything, not even the faint blue glow from the activated glass. Already, breathing was nearly impossible. He shifted his arm just enough to bring out the yellow ampoules of *kirar*. He took a deep breath to fill his lungs.

One dose of the paralysis drug had not placed him into a suffiently deep coma, but three would probably kill him. Holding them in one hand, he jabbed two ampoules into his thigh at the same time. The others he kept beside him, in case he needed additional doses en route.

Paralysis spread with a rush, a flood crashing through his muscle tissue. The drug would put him into a hibernation coma, reduce his breathing and his bodily needs to the fringes of death itself. Maybe, if he was lucky, it would even keep him alive. . . .

Though Duke Leto Atreides did not know he had a stow-away in his shipment, Gurney Halleck owed his passage off Giedi Prime to the ruler of Caladan, the enemy of the Har-konnens.

If he survived long enough to reach the off-world distribu-tion center on Hagal, Gurney hoped to escape while the blue obsidian was being reloaded for cutting, polishing, and trans-port. He would get away and find passage off-planet again if necessary. After lasting on Giedi Prime for all these years, he doubted any place in the Imperium could be worse.

Gurney conjured an image of his unwitting benefactor, the Duke of House Atreides, and felt a smile struggling to form on his face before the hibernation crashed around him.

Heaven must be the sound of running water.

—Fremen Saying

LIET-KYNES RETURNED TO THE ANTARCTIC SMUGGLER BASE THREE YEARS after he and Warrick had stumbled across it. Now that he'd lost all hope of winning the woman he loved, he had nothing to lose. At long last, Liet intended to claim his promised payment from Dominic Vernius. He would ask the smuggler leader to take him away from Dune, to bring him to another world, far from here.

Even before a proud, grinning Warrick had returned from the Cave of Birds with his beautiful new wife, Liet had desperately wanted to do his best to congratulate the couple. When spotters on the ridge above the sietch had signaled the arrival of a worm bearing two riders, Liet withdrew into his own chambers to meditate and pray. He loved his blood-brother, and Faroula as well, and he would not harbor any hard feelings or ill will. The Fremen had a saying, "Every faintly evil thought must be put aside immediately before it takes root."

At the moisture-sealed entrance to Red Wall Sietch, he had embraced Warrick, not bothered by the dust and potent odor of spice and sweat from so many hours on the back of a worm. He noted a sweet sparkle of happiness all around his friend.

For her part, Faroula looked content; she greeted Liet formally, as befitted a newly married woman. Liet smiled at them, but his bittersweet greeting became lost in the flood of congratulations from well-wishers, including the raspy voice of Heinar, Faroula's father and the Naib of the sietch.

Rarely had Liet-Kynes traded upon his father's fame, but for the nuptial celebration he had obtained a basket of fresh fruits from the greenhouse cave at Plaster Basin: oranges, dates, and figs, as well as a cluster of tart *li* berries, native to Bela Tegeuse. He'd placed the gift in the empty chamber Warrick and Faroula would share, and it was waiting for them when they retired for the evening.

Through it all, Liet-Kynes had come out a stronger man.

Over the following months, though, he could not pretend there had been no changes. His best friend now had other commitments. He had a wife, and soon—by the grace of Shai-Hulud—a family. Warrick could not spend as much time on commando raids.

Even after a full year, the heartache did not diminish. Liet still wanted Faroula more than any other woman, and he doubted he would marry, now that he had lost her. If he stayed at Red Wall Sietch any longer, his sadness might turn to bitterness—and he did not want to feel envy toward his friend.

Frieth understood her son's feelings. "Liet, I can see that you need to leave this place for a time."

The young man nodded, thinking of the long trek down to the south polar regions. "It would be best if I devote myself to . . . to other work." He volunteered to deliver the next spice bribe to Rondo Tuek, an arduous journey that few others undertook willingly.

"It is said that echoes are not only heard by the ears," Frieth said. "Echoes of memory are heard with the heart." Smiling, his mother placed a lean hand on his shoulder. "Go where you must. I will explain everything to your father."

Liet said his farewells to the sietch, to Warrick and Faroula. The other Fremen could sense his disquiet and his restlessness. "The son of Umma Kynes wishes to go on a *hajj*," they said, treating his journey as if it were some holy pilgrimage. And perhaps it was a kind of vision-quest, a search for inner peace and purpose. Without Faroula, he needed to find another obsession that would drive him.

He had lived in the shadow of Pardot Kynes all his life. The Planetologist had trained Liet to be his successor, but the young man had never scrutinized his heart to determine if that was a path he wanted to take.

Young Fremen men often chose the profession of their fathers, but that was not carved in stone. The dream of reawakening Dune was a powerful one that inspired—and *required*—intense passions. Even without his nineteen-year-old son, Umma Kynes had his devoted lieutenants Stilgar, Turok, and Ommun, as well as the secondary leaders. The dream would not die, no matter what Liet decided.

He could be in charge of them someday . . . but only if he threw himself wholeheartedly into the problem. *I will go away and try to understand the purpose that burns in the heart of my father.*

He had decided to go back to Dominic Vernius.

WITH THE FREMEN ability to retrace footsteps across rugged or featureless ground, Liet-Kynes stared at the antarctic wilderness. He had already delivered his cargo of distilled spice essence for surreptitious shipment to Guild agents. But instead of returning to his sietch, instead of going to inspect the palmaries as was expected of him, Liet headed deeper into the polar regions in search of the smugglers.

Presently he stood under the dim, slanting light, trying to pick out any unevenness on the towering glacier wall that would indicate the warren of caves. He was pleased to see that the smugglers had made all the camouflage modifications he and Warrick had suggested. Behind the tall line of ice-impregnated rock, he would find a deep chasm, at the bottom of which lay Dominic's smuggler ships.

He strode toward the base of the cliff. His hands were numb, and his cheeks burned from the cold. Since he did not know how to enter the base, he searched for a passage and hoped the refugees would see him and take him inside—but no one emerged.

Liet spent an hour trying to make himself seen, even shouting and waving his arms, until finally a small opening cracked beside him and several glaring men came out, pointing lasguns.

Calmly, young Liet-Kynes raised his chin in the air. "I see you're as vigilant as ever," he said sarcastically. "It looks like you need my help more than I had anticipated." As the men continued to hold their weapons on him, Liet frowned and then pointed to one pock-faced man with a missing eyebrow and another old veteran with a shock of bristly gray-white hair. "Johdam, Asuyo—do you not recognize me? I am older and taller, with a bit of a beard, but not so different than I was."

"All Fremen look alike," pock-scarred Johdam growled.

"Then all smugglers have bad eyesight. I am here to see Dominic Vernius." Now they either had to kill him for his knowledge or take him inside. Liet marched into the tunnels, and the smugglers sealed the entrance behind him.

As they passed the observation wall inside the cliff stronghold, he looked down into the chasm that sheltered their landing field. Groups of men scurried like rock ants, loading supplies into the ships.

"You're preparing for an expedition," Liet said.

Both veterans gave him stony looks. Asuyo, with his gray-white hair even bristlier than before, puffed his chest to display a few new cobbled-together medals and rank insignia he had added to his jumpsuit . . . but no one seemed impressed but him. Johdam continued to look bitter and skeptical, as if he had lost much already and expected to lose the rest soon.

They took a powered lift down to the base of the crevasse, and walked out into the gravel-packed basin. Liet recognized the towering figure of Dominic Vernius, his shaved scalp gleaming in the dim polar light. The smuggler leader saw the visitor's stillsuit and immediately recognized him. He waved a broad hand and strode over.

"So, lad, are you lost again? Did you have a harder time finding our place, now that we have hidden ourselves better?"

"It was harder to get your men to notice *me*," Liet said. "Your sentries must be sleeping."

Dominic laughed. "My sentries are busy loading ships. We have a Heighliner to catch, docking space already reserved and paid for. What can I do for you? We are in somewhat of a hurry at the moment."

Liet drew in a deep breath. "You promised me a favor. I have come to make my request of you."

Though he was taken aback, Dominic's eyes twinkled. "Very well. Most people awaiting a payment don't take three years to make up their minds."

"I have many skills, and I can be a valuable member of your team," Liet said. "Take me with you."

Dominic looked startled, then grinned. He clapped Liet on the shoulder with a blow hard enough to fell a herd beast. "Step aboard my flagship, and we'll talk about it." He gestured up the ramp of a reentry-scarred frigate.

Dominic had strewn rugs and possessions around his private cabin to make the place look like home. The renegade Earl gestured for Liet to take a seat in one of the suspensor chairs. The fabric cushion was worn and stained, as if it had seen decades of hard use, but Liet didn't mind. Off to one side of Dominic's writing desk shimmered a solido holophoto of a beautiful woman.

"Make your case, lad."

"You said you could use a Fremen to tighten up security at your Salusa Secundus base."

Dominic's smooth forehead wrinkled. "A Fremen would be a welcome addition." He turned toward the image of the beautiful woman, which shimmered as if smiling at him no matter where he moved. "What do you think, Shando, my love? Shall we let the lad take a trip with us?"

Dominic stared at the holo as if expecting an answer. An eerie feeling crept down Liet's spine. Then the Ixian Earl turned back to him, smiling. "Of course we will. I made a bargain, and your request is perfectly reasonable . . . although one might question your sanity." Dominic scratched a droplet of sweat at his temple. "Anyone who *wants* to go to the Emperor's prison planet obviously needs a little more happiness in his life."

Liet pressed his lips together, but didn't provide details. "I have my reasons." Dominic didn't push the matter.

Years ago, his father had been deeply affected by what he saw on Salusa Secundus, by the planetary scars that remained even centuries after the holocaust. On a quest to understand his own motivations, to set the course for his life, Liet needed to go there, too. Perhaps if he spent time on Salusa among the rugged rocks and unhealed wounds, he could understand what had sparked his father's lifelong interest in ecology.

The big smuggler clasped Liet's hand in a brisk handshake. "Very well, that's done with. What was your name again?"

"To outsiders, I am known as Weichih."

"All right, Weichih, if you are to be a member of our team, you'll have to do your share of the work." Dominic led him out of the captain's quarters to the ramp, and then outside.

Around them, smugglers sweated and grunted, out of breath. "Before the day is out, we take off for Salusa Secundus."

Look inside yourself and you can see the universe.

—Zensunni Aphorism

ARRAKIS. THIRD PLANET IN CANOPUS SYSTEM. A MOST INTRIGUING PLACE.

Guild Navigator D'murr gazed through plaz windows from his chamber, a mere speck inside the huge Heighliner. Far beneath his vessel, beyond a dirt-brown veil of wind-whipped dust, lay Arrakis, sole source of the melange that enabled him to see along the intricate pathways of the universe.

Such pleasure the spice gives me.

A tiny shuttle burned upward through the planet's atmosphere from the south pole, broke free, and reached the great ship in orbit. When the shuttle docked, a surveillance camera showed D'murr a group of passengers disembarking into the Heighliner's atmospheric-controlled community areas.

Though many other Spacing Guild workers crewed the vessel, as Navigator, D'murr had to watch all things, at all times. This was his ship, his home and workplace, his responsibility.

Within his sealed chamber, the familiar hiss of orange melange gas was barely audible. In his grossly deformed body, D'murr could never walk upon the desert planet, could never, in fact, leave the security of his tank. But just being near Arrakis calmed him in a primal way. With his higher-order brain he attempted to develop a mathematical analogy for his sensation, but it would not come into clear focus.

Before entering Guild service, D'murr Pilru should have done more with his life while he was still human. But now it was too late. The Guild had taken him so quickly—so unexpectedly—after he'd passed their entrance examination. There'd been no time for saying proper goodbyes, for wrapping up his human affairs.

Human.

How wide a definition did the word encompass? The Bene Gesserit had spent generations grappling with that exact question, with all the nuances, the ranges of intellect and emotion, the exalted achievements, the dismal failures. D'murr's physical form had altered significantly since he joined the Guild . . . but how much did that matter? Had he and all other Navigators transcended the *human* condition, to become something altogether different?

I am still human. I am no longer human. He listened to his own troubled, vacillating thoughts.

Through the surveillance transeye, D'murr watched the new passengers, rugged men in dark clothing, walk into the main passenger lounge. Suspensor-borne travel bags floated behind them. One of the men, ruddy-featured, with a voluminous mustache and a clean-shaven head, seemed oddly familiar. . . .

I still remember things.

Dominic Vernius. Where had he been all these years?

The Navigator uttered a command into the glittering speaker globe by his tiny V-mouth. The screen showed the names of the passengers, but none was familiar. The exiled Earl Vernius was traveling under an alias, despite the Guild's absolute assurances of confidentiality.

He and his companions were bound for Salusa Secundus.

A buzzer sounded inside the navigation chamber. All shuttles were secured in their berths. Guild crewmen sealed the entry hatches and monitored the Holtzman engines; an army of experts prepared the Heighliner for departure from polar orbit. D'murr hardly noticed.

Instead, he thought of halcyon days on Ix, of the bucolic time he'd spent with his parents and twin brother in the Grand Palais of Earl Vernius.

Useless detritus of the mind.

As Navigator, he made higher-order calculations and reveled in dimensional mathematics. He transported Heighliners filled with passengers and cargo across vast distances. . . .

Yet suddenly he found himself blocked, distracted, unable to function. His intricate brain lost focus in the midst of precious equations. Why had his mind, the remnant of his lost self, insisted on recognizing that man? An answer surfaced, like a creature emerging from the depths of a dark sea: Dominic Vernius represented an important part of D'murr Pilru's past. His human past . . .

I want to fold space.

Instead, images of bygone Ix rolled across his mind: scenes of splendor in the Vernius court with his brother C'tair. Pretty girls in expensive dresses smiling; even the Earl's lovely young daughter. *Kailea.* His brain, large enough to enfold the universe, was a storehouse of all he had been, and all he would become.

I have not finished evolving.

The faces of the Ixian girls shifted, becoming the glowering countenances of his instructors in Navigation School on Junction. Their sealed chambers clustered around his, their tiny dark eyes piercing him for his failure.

I must fold space!

For D'murr this was the ultimate sensual experience, of his mind and body and the multiple dimensions available to him. He had given himself to the Guild, much as primitive priests and nuns once gave themselves to their God, abstaining from sexual relations.

Finally he left the tiny stall-point of human recollection and expanded to encompass the star systems, stretching to reach them and beyond. As D'murr guided the Heighliner through foldspace, the galaxy became his woman . . . and he made love to her.

FOR C'TAIR, THE PLEASURES OF HIS LIFE WITH MIRAL ALECHEM WERE short-lived. Following the holoprojection of Rhombur, they had separated for security purposes, finding different bolt-holes in which to live. They hoped to maximize the odds of at least one of them surviving and continuing their important work. By prior arrangement, they met regularly for furtive looks and muffled words in the cafeteria in which she worked.

On one occasion, however, when he arrived at the appointed time, a different, dull-eyed woman stood at Miral's position in the food-distribution line. He took his plate of sliced vegetable matter and sat down at the table they usually shared.

C'tair watched the line, but Miral did not appear. Still staring, he ate in concerned silence. Finally, when he took his empty dishes back to where workers scrubbed them for the next shift, he asked one of the food workers, "Where is the woman who was here three days ago?"

"Gone," came the gruff answer. The older woman with a squarish face frowned. "Is that your business?"

"I meant no offense." He bowed, taking one step backward. A Tleilaxu guard looked over, noticed the discussion. His rodent eyes narrowed, and C'tair moved with careful steps, focused in his demeanor so that he called no further attention to himself.

Something had happened to Miral, but he dared not press the issue. He could ask no one.

When the guard walked over and spoke to the old food-server, C'tair increased his pace just enough so that he disappeared into a milling crowd, then ducked to a side shaft, descended into the suboid tunnels, and hurried out of sight. He could feel impending doom pressing around him.

Something had gone terribly wrong. They had captured Miral, and now C'tair was alone again—without an organized resistance, without someone to cover for him and help in his private rebellion. Stripped of outside resources, what chance did he have? Had he been deluding himself all these years?

He'd worked alone before, had sheltered his emotions, but now his heart was filled with longing for her. At times he wished he'd never gotten involved with Miral, because now he worried about her constantly. But in the quietest hours, when he lay alone in his bed, he was thankful for the moments of love they had shared.

He never saw her alive again.

LIKE ANGRY WASPS protecting a hive, the Tleilaxu instituted a brutal crackdown far more repressive than any they had previously enacted. They executed thousands of workers on mere suspicion, just to heighten their reign of terror. It soon became clear that the invaders did not care if they exterminated the entire Ixian population. They could wipe the slate clean, and bring in their own people: gholas, Face Dancers, whomever they chose.

Soon the rebellious Ixian spirit was crushed all over again. C'tair had not struck a blow for six months. In a close call, he had escaped from a Sardaukar trap only by surprising them with a handheld needlegun. Afraid the Tleilaxu might trace his fingerprints or genetic patterns, he had lived in constant fear of arrest.

Nothing ever got better.

After he'd projected Prince Rhombur's smuggled message, communication with the outside had been blocked off more vigorously than before. No observers or messages were allowed. All independent shipping captains and transportation workers were turned away. He had no way of sending even the briefest message back to Rhombur in exile on Caladan. Ix became little more than a black box that produced technology for CHOAM customers. Under Tleilaxu supervision, much of the work was inferior and there had been cancellations, adversely affecting sales revenues. This was only small consolation to C'tair.

Cut off again, he was unable to find allies, unable to steal the equipment he needed. In his new bolt-hole, only a few components remained, enough that he could perhaps use his rogo transmitter a final time or two. He would make a desperate request to his ethereal Navigator brother for assistance.

If nothing else, C'tair vowed that someone had to know what was happening here. Miral Alechem had been his only glimmer of friendship or emotional warmth, and she had vanished from his life. He feared the worst must have happened to her. . . .

He had to transmit his message, had to find a listener. For all his enthusiasm, Rhombur had not been able to do enough. Perhaps D'murr, with his skills as a Guild Navigator, could locate the long-lost Earl of Ix, Dominic Vernius. . . .

C'tair's dirty clothes smelled of sweat and grease. His body had been too long without rest or decent food. Hungry, he huddled in the back of an armored storage container that held sealed crates of rejected Ixian chronometers, timepieces that could be programmed to accommodate any planet in the Imperium. The instruments had been set aside for recalibration, and had gathered dust for years. The Tleilaxu had no use for frivolous technological toys.

Working under the dim light of a fading palmglobe, C'tair

reassembled the stored components of his rogo transmitter. He felt the ice of fear in his bloodstream, not because he was concerned he might be caught by Tleilaxu snoopers, but because he feared the rogo would not function. It had been a year since he'd tried to use the communications device, and this was his last set of pristine silicate crystal rods.

He wiped a drop of sweat from his shaggy hair and inserted the rods into the receptacle. The battered transmitter had been repaired many times. With each use, C'tair strained the jury-rigged systems—as well as his own brain—to the limit.

As youths, he and his twin had shared a perfect rapport, a brotherly connection that had allowed them to complete each other's sentences, to look across the room and know what the other sibling was thinking. Sometimes his longing to recapture that empathy was almost too strong to bear.

Since D'murr became a Navigator, the brothers had grown farther and farther apart. C'tair had done his best to maintain that fragile thread, and the rogo transmitter allowed the two minds to find a common ground. But over the years the rogo had faltered, and finally the machine was on the verge of breaking down completely . . . as was C'tair.

He slipped in the last rod, set his jaw with determination, and activated the power source. He hoped the armored walls of the cargo container would prevent any leakage that Tleilaxu scanners could detect. After setting off his explosive wafers two years ago, he no longer had his scan-shielded chamber. As a result, his risks grew greater every day.

Commander Garon and his Sardaukar were searching for him, and others like him, narrowing the possibilities, getting closer.

C'tair placed receptors against his skull, smeared on a dab of gel to improve the contact. In his mind, he tried to summon a connection with D'murr, seeking the thought patterns that had once been so identical to his own. Though they still shared a common origin, D'murr was vastly changed . . . to such a degree that the twins were now almost members of different species.

He sensed a tickle in his consciousness, and then a startled but sluggish recognition.

"D'murr, you must listen to me. You must hear what I am saying."

He felt a receptiveness in the images, and he saw in his mind the face of his brother, dark-haired, large-eyed, a snub nose, with a pleasant smile. Exactly as C'tair remembered him from their days in the Grand Palais, when they had attended diplomatic functions and both had flirted with Kailea Vernius.

But behind the familiar image, the startled C'tair saw a strange and distorted shape, a gross, startling shadow of his brother with an enlarged cranium and stunted limbs, suspended forever in a tank of rich melange gas.

C'tair drove the image back and focused again on the human face of his twin, whether or not it was real.

"D'murr, this could be the last time we speak." He wanted to ask his brother for any news of the outside Imperium. What of their father, Ambassador Pilru, in his exile on Kaitain? If alive, the Ambassador was still trying to rally support, C'tair theorized, but after so many years it would be a lost, almost pathetic, cause.

C'tair had no time for chatting. He needed to communicate the urgency and desperation of the Ixian people. All other forms of communication had been cut off—but D'murr, through his Guild connections, had another outlet, a tenuous thread across the cosmos.

Someone must understand how desperate our situation is!

Frantically, C'tair talked at length, describing everything the Tleilaxu had done, listing the horrors inflicted by Sardaukar guards and fanatics upon the captive Ixians.

"You must help me, D'murr. Find someone to take up our cause in the Imperium." Rhombur Vernius already knew the situation, and though the Prince had done what he could with secret Atreides backing, that had not been enough. "Find Dominic Vernius—he could be our only chance. If you remember me, if you remember your human family and friends . . . your people . . . *please help us*. You are the only hope we have left."

In front of him, only half-seeing with his eyes because his mind was so far away, stretched across the paths of foldspace to his brother, C'tair saw smoke curling from the rogo transmitter. The silicate crystal rods began to shiver and crack. "Please, D'murr!"

Seconds later, the rods shattered. Sparks sizzled from cracks in the transmitter, and C'tair tore the connectors from his temples.

He jammed a fist into his mouth to cut off a scream of pain. Tears filled his eyes, squeezed out by the pressure in his brain. He touched his nose, then his ears, and felt blood leaking from ruptures inside his sinuses. He sobbed and bit his knuckles hard, but the agony was a long time subsiding.

Finally, after hours of dazed pain, he looked at the blackened crystals in his transmitter and wiped the blood from his face. Sitting up and waiting for the throbbing to fade, he found himself smiling despite his hurt and the damaged rogo.

He was sure he had gotten through this time. The future of Ix depended on what D'murr could do with the information.

Beneath a world—in its rocks, its dirt and sedimentary overlays—there you find the planet's memory, the complete analog of its existence, its ecological memory.

—PARDOT KYNES,
An Arrakis Primer

IN TIGHT FORMATION, ARMORED IMPERIAL PRISON SHIPS DROPPED OUT OF the Heighliner hold and fell toward the festering planet like an airborne funeral procession.

Even from space, Salusa Secundus looked gangrenous, with dark scabs and a filmy cloud layer like a torn shroud. According to official press releases, new convicts sent to Salusa had a sixty-percent mortality rate in the first Standard Year.

After the new cargo of prisoners and supplies had been shuttled down to guarded unloading points, Spacing Guild crewmen held the bay doors open long enough for another battered frigate and two unmarked fast lighters to emerge. Leaving no record of their passage, Dominic Vernius and his men proceeded to the planet through a gap in the satellite surveillance net.

Liet-Kynes sat in a passenger seat of the frigate, fingers pressed to the cool pane of the viewplaz. His eyes were as wide as those of a Fremen child on his first worm ride. *Salusa Secundus!*

The sky was a sickly orange, streaked by pallid clouds even in the noon brightness. Ball lightning bounced across the heavens, as if invisible titans were playing electrical ninepins.

Avoiding Imperial detection beacons, Dominic's frigate

skimmed across the puckered and cracked wastelands as it headed for its landing area. They crossed expanses of vitrified rock that sparkled like lakes, but were actually puddles of granite-glass. Even after so many centuries, only sparse brown grass pried upward through the blasted fields, like the clawed fingers of men buried alive.

Between one heartbeat and the next, Liet understood how his father had been so profoundly moved by the unhealed wounds of this forsaken place. He made a low sound in his throat. When Dominic turned toward him with a curious expression, Liet explained, "In ancient times the Zensunni people—the Fremen—were slaves here for nine generations." Staring at the blistered landscape, he added in a quiet voice, "Some say you can still see their blood staining the soil and hear their cries carried on the wind."

Dominic's broad shoulders sagged. "Weichih, Salusa has endured more than its share of pain and misery."

They approached the outskirts of a once-sprawling city that now looked like an architectural scar. Stumps of buildings and blackened milk-marble columns lay as detritus of the splendor that once held dominion here. Off in the scabrous hills, a new wall zigzagged around a portion of reasonably intact structures, the remains of an abandoned city that had survived the holocaust.

"That wall was meant to enclose the prison population," Dominic said, "but after it broke down and the prisoners escaped, the functionaries and administrators sealed up the barrier again and lived inside it, where they felt protected." He coughed out a snorting laugh. "Once the prisoners realized they were better off in a place where they were at least fed and clothed, they tried to break back in."

He shook his shaved head. "Now, the toughest ones have learned to make their own lives out here. The others just die. The Corrinos imported dangerous beasts—Laza tigers, Salusan bulls, and the like—to keep the survivors in check. Convicted criminals are just . . . abandoned here. No one expects to leave."

Liet studied the landscape with a Planetologist's eye, trying to remember everything his father had taught him. He could smell a sour dampness in the air, even in this desolate place. "Seems to be enough potential, enough moisture. There could be ground cover, crops, livestock. Someone could change this place."

"The damned Corrinos won't allow it." Dominic's face darkened. "They like it this way, as a suitable punishment for anyone who dares to defy the Imperium. Once prisoners get here, a cruel game begins. The Emperor likes to see who toughens up the best, who survives the longest. In his Palace, members of the Royal Court place bets on renowned prisoners, as to who will survive and who won't."

"My father didn't tell me that," Liet said. "He lived here for years when he was younger."

Dominic gave a wan smile, but his eyes remained dark and troubled. "Whoever your father is, lad, he must not know everything." The weary exile guided the frigate above the rubble of the outer city, to a broken hangar where the roof had sagged into a spiderweb of rusted girders. "As the Earl of Ix, I prefer to be underground. No need to worry about aurora storms down there."

"My father also told me about aurora storms."

The frigate descended into the dark hole in the hangar—and kept going down into cavernous warehouse spaces. "This used to be an Imperial repository, reinforced for long-term storage." Dominic switched on the ship's running lights, splashing yellow beams into the air. A settling dust cloud looked like gray rain.

The two mismatched lighters swooped in beside the frigate and landed first. Other smugglers emerged from within the hidden base to lock down the craft. They unloaded cargo, tools, and supplies. The pilots of the small ships hurried over to stand by the frigate ramp, waiting for Dominic to emerge.

As he followed the bald leader down, Liet sniffed, still feeling naked without stillsuit or nose plugs. The air smelled dry and burned, tinged with solvents and ozone. Liet longed for the rough warmth of natural rock, like a comfortable sietch; too many of the walls around him were covered with artificial sheets of metal or plastone, concealing chambers beyond.

On a ramp that circled the landing zone, a well-muscled man appeared. He bounded down a stairway to the ground with a smooth and feral grace, though his body was lumpy and unwieldy-looking. A startling, beet-red inkvine scar marred his squarish face, and his stringy blond hair hung at an odd angle over his left eye. He looked like a man who had been broken and then reassembled without instructions.

"Gurney Halleck!" Dominic's voice echoed in the landing chamber. "Come and meet our new comrade, born and raised among the Fremen."

The man grinned wolfishly and came over with startling swiftness. He extended a broad palm and tried to crush Liet's hand with his grip. He quoted a passage that Liet recognized from the Orange Catholic Bible, "Greet all those whom you would have as friends, and welcome them with your heart as well as your hand."

Liet returned the gesture, speaking a traditional Fremen response in the ancient language of Chakobsa.

"Gurney comes to us from Giedi Prime," Dominic said. "He stowed away on a shipment bound for my old friend Duke Leto Atreides, then switched ships on Hagal, moving through commercial hubs and spaceports, until he fell in with the right comrades."

Gurney gave an awkward shrug. He was sweaty, his clothes disheveled from rigorous sword practice. "By the hells, I continued to dig myself deeper, hiding in more and more miserable places for half a year before I finally found these thugs . . . at the very bottom."

Liet narrowed his eyes suspiciously, ignoring the good-natured banter. "You come from Giedi Prime? The Harkonnen world?" His fingers strayed toward his belt, where he kept his crysknife sheathed. "I have killed a hundred Harkonnen devils."

Gurney detected the movement, but locked gazes with the bearded young Fremen. "Then you and I will be great friends."

LATER, WHEN LIET sat with the smuggler band in the drinking hall of the underground base, he listened to the discussions, the laughter, the gruffly exchanged stories, the boastings and outright lies.

They opened expensive bottles of a rare vintage and passed around snifters of the potent amber liquid. "Imperial brandy, lad," Gurney said, handing a glass to Liet, who had trouble swallowing the thick liqueur. "Shaddam's private stock, worth ten times its weight in melange." The scarred man gave him a conspiratorial wink. "We swapped a shipment from Kirana, took the Emperor's personal goods for ourselves, and replaced them with bottles of skunk-vinegar. I expect we'll hear about it soon."

Dominic Vernius entered the hall, and all the smugglers greeted him. He had changed into a sleeveless jerkin made of maroon merh-silk lined with black whale fur. Floating like ghosts near him were several holo-images of his beloved wife, so that he could see her no matter which way he turned.

It was warm and comfortable inside the stronghold, but Liet hoped to spend time outside, exploring the Salusan landscape as his father had done. First, though, Liet had promised to use his Fremen skills to study the hidden base, to help disguise it and protect it from observers—though he agreed with

Dominic that few people would bother to look for a hideout here.

No one *willingly* came to Salusa Secundus.

On the wall of his hideout mess hall, Dominic kept a centuries-old map, depicting the way this world had been in its glory days as the magnificent capital of an interstellar empire. Lines were drawn in gold metal, palaces and cities marked with jewels, ice caps made of tiger's-breath opal, and inlaid seas of petrified Elaccan bluewood.

Dominic claimed (from his own imagination rather than any documentary evidence) that the map had belonged to Crown Prince Raphael Corrino, the legendary statesman and philosopher from thousands of years ago. Dominic expressed relief that Raphael—"the only good Corrino of the bunch," as far as he was concerned—had never lived to see what had happened to his beloved capital. All of that fairy-tale magnificence, all the dreams and visions and good deeds, had been wiped away by nuclear fire.

Gurney Halleck strummed his new baliset and sang a mournful song. Liet listened to the words, finding them sensitive and haunting, evoking images of bygone people and places.

O for the days of times long past,
Touch sweet nectar to my lips once more.
Fond memories to taste and feel . . .
The smiles and kisses of delight
And innocence and hope.

But all I see are veils and tears
And the murky, drowning depths
Of pain and toil and hopelessness.
It's wiser, my friend, to look another way,
Into the tight, and not the dark.

Each man took his own meaning from the song, and Liet noticed tears at the edges of Dominic's eyes, while his gaze was directed at the holo-portraits of Shando. Liet flinched at the naked emotion that was so rare among the Fremen.

Dominic's distant gaze was only partly focused on the be-jeweled map on the wall. "Somewhere in Imperial records, undoubtedly covered with dust, is the name of the renegade family that used forbidden atomics to devastate a continent here."

Liet shuddered. "What were they thinking? Why would even a renegade do such a terrible thing?"

"They did what they had to do, Weichih," Johdam snapped, rubbing the scar on his eyebrow. "We cannot know the price of their desperation."

Dominic sagged deeper into his chair. "Some Corrinos—damn them and their descendants—were left alive. The surviving Emperor, Hassik III, moved his capital to Kaitain . . . and the Imperium goes on. The Corrinos go on. And they took an ironic pleasure in turning the hellhole of Salusa Secundus into their private prison world. Every member of that renegade family was hunted down and brought here to suffer horrible deaths."

The bristly-haired veteran Asuyo nodded gravely. "It's said that their ghosts still haunt this place, eh?"

Startled, Liet recognized that the exiled Earl Vernius saw reminders of himself in that desperate, long-forgotten family. Though Dominic seemed good-natured, Liet had learned the depths of pain this man had endured: his wife murdered, his subjects crushed under a Tleilaxu yoke, his son and daughter forced to live in exile on Caladan.

"Those renegades long ago . . ." Dominic said with a strange light in his eyes, "they weren't as thorough as I'd have been with the killing."

A Duke must always take control of his household, for if he does not rule those closest to him, he cannot hope to govern a planet.

—DUKE PAULUS ATREIDES

SHORTLY AFTER THE NOONDAY MEAL, LETO SAT ON THE CARPETED FLOOR of the playroom, bouncing his four-and-a-half-year-old son on his knee. Though he had grown big for the game, Victor still squealed with unbounded glee. Through armor-plaz windows the Duke could see the blue Caladan sky kissing the sea at the horizon, with white clouds scudding above.

Behind him, Kailea watched from the doorway. "He's too old for that, Leto. Stop treating him like a baby."

"Victor doesn't seem to agree." He bounced the dark-haired boy even higher, eliciting louder giggles.

Leto's relationship with Kailea had improved in the six months since he'd installed the fabulously expensive blue obsidian walls. Now the dining hall and Kailea's private tower chambers echoed the splendor of the Grand Palais. But her mood had darkened again in recent weeks, as she brooded (no doubt egged on by Chiara) over how much time he spent with Jessica.

Leto no longer paid any attention to her complaints; they ran off him like spring rain. In sharp contrast, Jessica demanded nothing from him. Her kindness and occasional suggestions energized him and allowed him to perform his duties as Duke with compassion and fairness.

For Kailea's sake, and for Victor's as well, Leto would no harm her reputation on Caladan. The people loved thei Duke, and he let them maintain their illusions of fairy-tal happiness in his Castle—much the same way Paulus ha feigned a pleasant marriage with Lady Helena. The Old Duk had called it "bedroom politics," the bane of leaders all acros the Imperium.

"Oh, why do I make the effort to talk with you at all, Leto?' Kailea said, still standing at the playroom doorway. "It's lik arguing with a stone!"

Leto stopped bouncing Victor and looked over at her, his gray eyes hard. He kept his voice carefully neutral. "I didn't realize you were making much of an effort."

Muttering an insult under her breath, Kailea whirled and stalked down the corridor. Leto pretended not to notice she had left.

Spying her blond-haired brother carrying a baliset over one shoulder, Kailea hurried to catch up with him. But upon seeing her, Rhombur just shook his head. He held up a wide hand to forestall what he knew would be a flood of complaints.

"What is it now, Kailea?" He touched one hand to the baliset strings. Thufir Hawat had continued teaching him how to play the nine-stringed instrument. "Have you found something new to be angry about, or is it a subject I've heard before?"

His tone took her aback. "Is that any way to greet your sister? You've been avoiding me for days." Her emerald eyes flashed.

"Because all you do is complain. Leto won't marry you . . . he plays too rough with Victor . . . uh, he spends too much time with Jessica . . . he should take you to Kaitain more often . . . he doesn't use his napkin right. I'm tired of trying to mediate between you two." He shook his head. "To top it all off, it seems to irritate you that I'm completely content with

Tessia. Stop blaming everyone else, Kailea—your happiness is your own responsibility."

"I've lost too much in my life to be happy." She raised her chin.

Now Rhombur actually looked angry. "Are you really too self-centered to see that I've lost as much as you have? I just don't let it eat at me every day."

"But we didn't *have* to lose it. You can still do more for House Vernius." She was ashamed of his ineffectiveness. "I'm glad our parents aren't here to see this. You're a pitiful excuse for a Prince, brother."

"Now that does sound a little like Tessia, though the way she says it isn't so grating."

She fell silent as Jessica emerged from a passageway and turned toward the playroom. Kailea flashed the other concubine a dagger-glare, but Jessica smiled congenially. After entering the playroom to join Leto and Victor, she closed the door behind her.

Looking back at Rhombur, Kailea snapped, "My son Victor is the future and hope of a new House Atreides, but you can't understand that simple fact."

The Ixian Prince just shook his head, deeply saddened.

"I TRY TO be pleasant to her, but it's no use," Jessica said, inside the playroom. "She hardly says a word to me, and the way she looks at—"

"Not again." Leto heaved a perturbed sigh. "I know Kailea's causing damage to my family, but I can't find it in my heart to just send her away." He sat on the floor, while his son played with toy groundcars and ornithopters. "If it weren't for Victor—"

"Chiara is always whispering something to her. The results are obvious. Kailea is a powder keg, ready to explode."

Holding a model 'thopter in his hands, Duke Leto looked up at Jessica helplessly. "Now you're showing spite of your own, Jessica. I'm disappointed in you." His face hardened. "Concubines do not rule this House."

Because he knew Jessica had spent years in Bene Gesserit training, Leto was surprised to see all color drain from her face. "My Lord, I . . . didn't mean it that way. I'm so sorry." Bowing, she backed up and left the room.

Leto stared blankly at the toy, then at Victor. He felt completely lost.

A short while later, concealed like a shadow, Jessica observed Kailea in the Castle foyer, whispering to Swain Goire, the household guard who spent much of his time watching over Victor. Goire's loyalty and dedication to the Duke had always been clear, and Jessica had seen how much he adored his young ward.

Goire seemed uneasy about receiving so much attention from the ducal concubine; seemingly by accident, Kailea brushed her breasts against his arm, but he pulled away.

Having been schooled in the intricate ways of human nature by the Bene Gesserit, Jessica was only surprised that Kailea had taken so long to attempt this petty revenge against Leto.

TWO NIGHTS LATER, unnoticed even by Thufir Hawat, Kailea slipped quietly into Goire's bedroom.

We create our own future by our own beliefs, which control our actions. A strong enough belief system, a sufficiently powerful conviction, can make anything happen. This is how we create our consensus reality, including our gods.

—REVEREND MOTHER RAMALLO,
Sayyadina of the Fremen

THE SWORDMASTER PRACTICE HALL ON THE NEW GINAZ ISLAND WAS SO opulent that it would not have been out of place in any Landsraad ruling seat or even in the Imperial Palace on Kaitain.

When Duncan Idaho stepped onto the gleaming hardwood floor, a veneer of light and dark strips laid down and polished by hand, he looked around in wonder. A dozen reflected images stared back at him from beveled floor-to-ceiling mirrors, bounded by intricately wrought gold frames. It had been seven years since he'd seen surroundings this fine, in Castle Caladan, where he'd trained under Thufir Hawat in the Atreides hall.

Wind-bowed cypress trees surrounded the magnificent training facility on three sides, with a stony beach on the fourth. The ostentatious building was startling in its stark contrast with the students' primitive barracks. Run by Swordmaster Whitmore Bludd, a balding man with a purple birthmark on his forehead, the ornamentation of this practice hall would have made shaggy-haired Mord Cour laugh.

Though an accomplished duelist, foppish Bludd considered himself a noble and surrounded himself with fine things, even on his remote Ginaz island. Blessed with an inexhaustible family fortune, Bludd had spent his own money to make this fencing facility the most "civilized" place in the entire archipelago.

The Swordmaster was a direct descendant of Porce Bludd, who had fought valiantly in the Butlerian Jihad. Prior to the battle exploits that had bought him fame and cost him his life, Porce Bludd transported war-orphaned children to sanctuary planets, paying the tremendous costs out of his huge inheritance. On Ginaz, Whitmore Bludd never forgot his heritage— or allowed others to forget, either.

As Duncan stood with the others in the echoing hall— smelling lemon and carnauba oil, seeing splinters of light from chandeliers and mirrors—the finery seemed foreign to him. Paintings of dour-looking Bludd noblemen lined the walls; a massive fireplace befitting a royal hunting lodge reached to the ceiling. A fully stocked armory held racks of swords and fencing paraphernalia. The palatial decor implied an army of servants, but Duncan saw no other souls besides the trainees, the assistant instructors, and Whitmore Bludd himself.

After permitting the students to gape in astonishment and uncertainty, Swordmaster Bludd strutted in front of them. He wore billowy lavender pantaloons bound at the knees, and gray hose down to short black boots. The belt was wide, with a square buckle the size of his hand. His blouse shirt had a high, restrictive collar, long ballooning sleeves, tight cuffs, and lace trimmings.

"I will teach you fencing, Messieurs," he said. "No brutish nonsense with body shields and kindjal daggers and power packs. No, most vehemently no!" He withdrew a whip-thin blade with a bell-shaped handguard and a triangular cross section. He swished it in the air. "Fencing is the sport—no, the *art* of swordsmanship with a blunted blade. It is a dance of mental reflexes, as well as of the body."

He thrust the flexible épée into a scabbard at his side, then ordered all of the students to change into fancy fencing outfits: archaic musketeer costumes with studded buttons, lacy cuffs, ruffles, and cumbersome billows—"the better to display the beauty of fencing," Bludd said.

By now, Duncan had learned never to hesitate in following instructions. He pulled on knee-high calfskin boots with cavalier spurs, and slipped into a blue-velvet shortcoat with a lace collar and voluminous white sleeves. He donned a rakish, broad-brimmed felt hat with the variegated pink plume of a Parella peacock tucked into its band.

Across the room, he and Hiih Resser made eyes and faces at each other, amused. The attire seemed better suited to a holiday masque than to fighting.

"You will learn to fight with finesse and grace, Messieurs." Whitmore Bludd strutted back and forth, immensely pleased with all the finery around him. "You will see the artistry in a fine duel. You will turn every movement into an art form." The foppish but powerfully built Swordmaster picked at a speck of lint on his ruffled shirt. "With only a year left in your training, one assumes you have the potential to rise above animal attacks and cloddish brawls? We will not lower ourselves to barbarism here."

Morning sunlight passed through a high, narrow window and glinted off Duncan's pewter buttons. Feeling foolish, he examined himself in the wall mirror, then found his usual place in formation.

When the remaining students lined up on the hardwood practice floor, Swordmaster Bludd inspected their uniforms with many sighs and disapproving noises. He smoothed wrinkles, while scolding the young men for incorrectly buttoned cuffs and criticizing their attire with surprising seriousness.

"Terran musketeer fencing is the fifteenth fighting discipline you will learn. But knowing the moves does not mean you understand the *style*. Today you will compete against one another, with all the grace and chivalry that fencing demands. Your épées will not be blunted, and you will wear no protective masks."

He indicated racks of fencing swords between each bank of mirrors on the wall, and the students moved forward to arm themselves; all the blades were identical, ninety centimeters long, flexible, and sharp. The students toyed with them. Duncan wished he could use the Old Duke's sword, but the fabulously tooled weapon was made for a different kind of fighting. Not fencing.

Bludd sniffed, then swished his thin épée in the air to recapture their attention. "You must fight to your fullest ability— but I insist that there be no injuries or blood on either opponent. Not so much as a scratch—no, most vehemently no! And certainly no damage to the clothes. Learn the perfect attack, and the perfect defense. Lunge, parry, riposte. Practice supreme control. You are each responsible for your fellows." He swept his ice-blue gaze across the trainees, and his birthmark darkened on his forehead. "Any man who fails me, anyone who causes a wound or allows himself to be injured, will be disqualified from the next sequence of competitions."

Duncan drew deep, calming breaths, centering himself to face the challenge.

"This is a test of your artistry, Messieurs," Bludd said, pacing the polished floor in his black boots. "This is the delicate dance of personal combat. The goal will be to score touchés upon your opponent's person without cutting him."

The spotlessly clean Swordmaster picked up his feathered hat and set it firmly on his head. He indicated marked combat rectangles inlaid into the beautiful parquet floor. "Prepare to fight."

DUNCAN QUICKLY DEFEATED three comparatively easy opponents, but his fourth adversary, Iss Opru—a smooth stylist from Al-Dhanab—made himself a difficult target. Even so, the dark-skinned Opru had insufficient skill in offense to match his defense, and Duncan outscored him by a single point.

In a nearby combat box, a student buckled at the knees,

and bled from a wound in his side. The assistant trainers rushed in and removed him on a litter. His opponent, a Terrazi with shoulder-length hair, scowled at his stained blade, awaiting his punishment. Whitmore Bludd snagged the Terrazi student's sword and viciously flogged his backside with it, as if it were a metal whip. "Both of you are a disgrace to your training—him for allowing the wound, you for not exercising sufficient restraint." Without protest, the Terrazi stumbled to the losers' bench.

Now, two liveried servants—the first Duncan had seen—rushed in to clean up the blood and polish the parquet in preparation for the next match. The fighting continued.

Duncan Idaho, along with Resser and two other perspiring finalists, stood panting in the center of the practice hall, awaiting their final dueling assignments. Frustrated and uncomfortable, they had come to loathe their extravagant costumes, but so far none of the finalists had been scratched, none of the heavy fabric had been torn.

"Idaho and Resser over here! Eddin and al-Kaba, there!" Swordmaster Bludd called out, designating combat rectangles on the floor.

Obediently, the students moved into position. Resser eyed Duncan, sizing him up as a foe instead of as a friend. Duncan crouched, flexing his knees and balancing on the balls of his feet. Leaning forward with his arm slightly bent, he extended the épée toward Resser, then drew back in a brief salute. With a confident look, the redheaded Grumman did the same. Evenly matched, they had dueled one another many times in full protective gear, with other weapons. Duncan's speed usually compensated for lanky Resser's superior height and reach. But now they had to follow Bludd's rules of fencing, inflict or receive no scratches, not even damage the expensive, anachronistic outfits.

Bouncing on his feet to stay loose, Duncan said nothing.

The flexible sword would do the talking for him. Perspiration prickled his black hair beneath the felt hat and the distracting peacock plume. He stared up at his freckled opponent.

"*En garde*," Bludd said. His blue eyes flashed as he raised his blade.

At the signal to begin, Resser lunged forward. Duncan parried, deflecting his opponent's blade with a sound like singing chimes, then took half a step to the right and delivered a precise riposte, skillfully diverted by the tall Grumman. Swords clattered together, steel skimming steel, as the two felt each other out.

Both men were sweating, panting, their expressions fading into blank stares as they moved back and forth within the clear boundaries of dark wood on the parquet floor. So far Resser had done nothing unexpected, as usual. Duncan hoped he could use that trait to defeat his opponent.

As if sensing the direction of his friend's thoughts, the redhead began to fight with the fury of a warrior possessed, scoring one touché on Duncan and then two, careful not to damage his opponent but also relying on Duncan to mount a perfect defense.

Duncan had never seen such energy in his friend, and he struggled to elude a series of vicious thrusts. He backed up, waiting for the flurry of activity to ebb. Sweat ran down his cheek.

Still, Resser pressed on at a frantic pace, as if under the influence of a stimulant. Their swords clattered loudly. Duncan could spare no fraction of his attention to note the progress of the other match, but heard shouting and a final clang of blades that told him the two other contestants had finished.

Swordmaster Bludd gave Duncan's match the full weight of his scrutiny.

The redhead's point touched him on his padded shirt, then seconds later on the forehead. Resser was scoring points, leaving no scratches, following the rules. Four points now, and with five he would win the match. *If this had been a fight to the death, I would be dead now.*

Like a carrion bird waiting for a feast, Bludd watched every move.

Under Resser's onslaught, Duncan's muscles seemed to be slowing, holding him back and preventing him from applying his normal skills. He looked at the épée in his right hand and dredged up resources and strength within himself, drawing upon everything he had learned in seven years on Ginaz. *I fight for House Atreides. I can win.*

Resser danced deftly around him with the épée, making him look foolish. Duncan's breathing slowed, and his heart rate diminished. *Maximize chi*, he thought, visualizing the energy that flowed along precise paths in his body. *I must become a complete Swordmaster to defend my Duke—not make a pretty performance to please these instructors.*

Resser ceased scoring as Duncan danced away. The *chi* within him mounted, building pressure, waiting for the right moment to be released. Duncan focused the energy, aiming it. . . .

Now he was on the attack. He confused the lanky redhead with moves synthesized from various fighting disciplines. He whirled, kicked, used his free hand as a weapon. They both staggered outside the boundaries of the fencing area, then back into the rectangle. Duncan attacked again. A fist to the side of Resser's head, knocking off the feathered cap, a kick to the stomach—all without drawing blood.

Stunned, Resser thudded to the floor. Duncan knocked his rival's sword away and leaped on top of him, placing the tip of his own blade at the Grumman's throat. *Victory!*

"Gods below! What are you doing?" Swordmaster Bludd shoved Duncan off Resser. "You clod!" He grabbed the flexible sword away, and slapped Duncan twice across the face. "This isn't a street brawl, fool. We're doing musketeer fencing today. Are you an animal?"

Duncan rubbed his face where he'd been struck. In the heat of combat he had fought for survival, ignoring the frivolous restrictions imposed by the instructor.

Bludd slapped Duncan several more times, harder each time, as if the student had personally insulted him. In the background, Resser kept saying, "It's all right—I'm not hurt. He bested me, and I couldn't defend myself." Humiliated, Duncan backed away.

Bludd's rage did not subside. "You may think you're the best student in the class, Idaho—but you're a failure in my eyes."

Duncan felt like a small child being backed into a corner by an adult with a strap. He wanted to fight back, wanted to stand up to this ridiculous-looking man, but didn't dare.

He recalled the ill-tempered Trin Kronos using the same reasoning with fat Swordmaster Rivvy Dinari. *If you are bound by nonsensical strictures, you'll be beaten by any opponent witting to bend the rules.* His primary purpose was to defend his Duke against any possible threat, not to play fencing games in costumes.

"Think about why you're a failure," Whitmore Bludd thundered, "and then explain it to me."

Tell that to the dead soldiers on the losing side.

Duncan thought hard. He did not want to echo the shameful thinking of the spoiled Kronos, though it made more sense than he had realized before. Rules could be interpreted differently, depending on the purpose they served. In some situations there was no absolute good or evil, simply points of view. In any event, he knew what his instructor wanted to hear.

"I am a failure because my mind is imperfect."

His answer seemed to surprise the muscular man, but a bemused smile gradually formed on Bludd's face. "Correct enough, Idaho," he said. "Now get over there with the other losers."

Challenge: Time?
Answer: A brilliant, many-faceted gem.
Challenge: Time?
Answer: A dark stone, reflecting no visible light.

—Fremen wisdom,
from The Riddle Game

WITH HIS BALISET SLUNG BY A LEATHER STRAP OVER ONE SHOULDER, Rhombur Vernius hiked down the steep zigzag trail to the bottom of the black cliff. Castle Caladan loomed high over the rock face, stretching toward the billowing cumulus clouds and the cerulean sky. A strong early-afternoon breeze caressed his face.

Behind him, in one of those soaring Castle towers, his sister spent too much time brooding. As he paused to look back, he saw Kailça up there now, standing on her balcony. With forced cheer, he waved to her, but she did not respond. For months they had hardly spoken to one another. This time he shook his head and decided not to let her usual rebuff bother him. His sister's expectations outweighed her reality.

It was a warm spring day, with gray gulls soaring on thermals over the whitecaps. Like one of the poor village fishermen, Rhombur wore a short-sleeved blue-and-white-striped shirt, fishing dungarees, and a blue cap jammed over his blond hair. Tessia sometimes walked along the shore with him, while other times she let him ponder by himself.

With Kailea's dark moods in mind, the Ixian Prince descended a wooden stairway that cantilevered out over the cliff. He took care on the rough, moss-covered section of trail. It was a treacherous route, even in good weather: A careless misstep and he could tumble to the rocks below. Hardy green shrubs clung to crevices on the sheer rock face, along with orange and yellow succulents. Duke Leto, like his father before him, preferred to leave the path essentially natural, with minimal maintenance. "The life of a leader should not be too soft," the Atreides men liked to say.

Rather than discussing his concerns with Tessia, Rhombur decided to soothe his troubled spirits by spending time on a small boat, drifting alone and playing the baliset. Not confident of his musical abilities, he preferred to practice away from the Castle anyway, where no critical ears could hear him.

After traversing a black-shingle downslope to the main dock, he took a steep wooden stairway down to a finger pier where a white motorboat bobbed gently in the waves. A purple-and-copper Ixian insignia marked the bow above letters that named the craft after his missing father: *Dominic*.

Each time Rhombur saw the name, he dreamed that his father might still be alive, somewhere in the Imperium. The Earl of House Vernius had disappeared—and with the passage of time all hope of locating him had faded. Dominic had never sent word, made no contact at all. *He must be dead.*

Rhombur unslung the baliset and laid the instrument on the dock. A cleat on the stern of the boat was missing one bolt, so he climbed aboard and opened a toolbox in the cockpit, where he found another bolt and a ratchet to tighten it down.

He liked to maintain his own boat, and sometimes hours would pass as he worked on it, sanding, painting, lacquering, replacing hardware, installing new electronics and fishing accessories. It was all so different from the pampered life he'd led on Ix. Now, as he stepped back onto the dock and made the simple repair, Rhombur wished he could be the leader that his father had been.

The chances of that seemed virtually nil.

Though Rhombur had made efforts to help the mysterious rebels on Ix, he hadn't heard from them in over a year, and some of the weapons and explosives he'd sent had come back undelivered, despite bribes paid to transport workers. Even the most highly paid smugglers had been unable to infiltrate the material into the cavernous underground city.

No one knew what was going on there. C'tair Pilru, his primary contact with the freedom fighters, had fallen silent. Like Dominic himself, C'tair might be dead, the valiant struggle crushed with him. Rhombur had no way of knowing, no means of breaching the intense Tleilaxu security.

Hearing footsteps on the dock, Rhombur was surprised to see his sister approaching. Kailea wore a showy dress of silver and gold; a ruby clasp secured her copper-dark hair. He noticed that both of her shins were red and bruised, and that the hem of her dress was soiled.

"I tripped on the trail," she admitted. She must have run after him, hurrying to catch up.

"You don't often come down to the docks." He forced a smile. "Would you like to go out on the boat with me?"

When Kailea shook her head, her curls bounced against her cheeks. "I'm here to apologize, Rhombur. I'm sorry I've been so mean to you, avoiding you, hardly saying anything at all."

"And glaring at me," he added.

Her emerald eyes flashed, before she caught herself and softened. "That, too."

"Apology accepted." He finished tightening down the cleat, then climbed back into the cockpit of the *Dominic* to put the tools away.

She remained on the dock after he stepped aboard. "Rhombur," Kailea began in a plaintive tone that was only too familiar. It meant she wanted something, though her face was all innocence. "You and Tessia are so close—I just wish I had the same relationship with Leto."

"Relationships require maintenance," he said. "Uh, like this boat. With some time and care, you could repair things between you two."

Her mouth twisted in a grimace of distaste. "But isn't there anything more *you* can do about Leto? We can't go on this way forever."

"Do *about* him? It sounds like you want to dispose of him."

His sister did not answer directly. "Victor should be his legal heir, not a bastard without name, title, or property. There must be something different you can say to Leto, something more you could try."

"Vermilion hells, Kailea! I've tried fifty different times and fifty different ways, and he always turns me down. It's already driven a wedge between us. Because of you, I may have lost my best friend."

The glow of sunshine on her skin looked like distant firelight. "What does mere friendship matter, when we're talking about the future of House Vernius—the Great House of our forefathers? Think about the *important* things, Rhombur."

His expression turned to stone. "You've turned this into a problem, when it never had to be. You alone, Kailea. If you couldn't accept the limitations, why did you agree to become Leto's concubine at all? You two seemed so happy at first. Why don't you apologize to him? Why not simply accept reality? Why don't *you* make an effort?" Rhombur shook his head, stared at the fire-jewel ring on his right hand. "I'm not going to question Leto's decisions. I may not agree with his reasons, but I understand them. He is Duke Atreides, and we owe him the respect of following his wishes."

Kailea's expression, which she had been keeping under control, changed to a disdainful sneer. "You're not a Prince. Chiara says you're not even a *man*." She lifted one foot and stomped at the baliset, but in her rage lost her balance and dealt it only a glancing blow. The instrument skidded off the dock into the water, where it floated behind the boat.

Swearing, Rhombur leaned out over the edge of the dock and retrieved the baliset, as Kailea whirled and left. While drying the instrument with a towel, he watched her climb the steep path back to the Castle, half-running and half-walking. She stumbled, got back up, and kept going, trying to maintain her dignity.

No wonder Leto preferred the calm, intelligent Jessica. Kailea, once so sweet and kind, had become hard and cruel. He didn't know her anymore. He sighed. *I love her, but I don't like her.*

It requires a desperate and lonely sort of courage to challenge the accepted wisdom upon which social peace of mind rests.

—CROWN PRINCE RAPHAEL CORRINO,
In Defense of Change in the Face of Tradition

THE TOWERING GOVERNMENT BUILDINGS OF CORRINTH, THE CAPITAL CITY of Kaitain, rose around Abulurd Harkonnen like a drug-induced fantasy. In his wildest dreams he had never visualized so many soaring edifices, jeweled inlays, and polished slabs of precious stone.

On Giedi Prime, where he'd grown up under the watchful eye of his father, Dmitri, cities were crowded, with dirty settlements erected for function and industry rather than beauty. But here, it was quite different. Colorful chime kites were tethered to the tall buildings, writhing on breezes in the perpetually blue skies. Prismatic ribbons drifted across the sky and shed rainbows on the flagstones below. Kaitain was obviously more concerned with form than substance.

Within an hour, the sunny dazzle of perfect skies made Abulurd dizzy, causing an ache in the back of his skull. He longed for the overcast skies of Lankiveil, the damp breezes that cut right to the bone, and the warm embrace of Emmi.

But Abulurd had an important task to perform, an appointment at the daily Landsraad Council meeting. It seemed a mere formality, but he was determined to do it, for the sake of his family and his infant son, and it would change his life forever. Abulurd longed for the days to come.

He strode along the promenade under banners of Great

and Minor Houses that flapped precisely in the gentle winds. The imposing buildings seemed even more massive and powerful than the cliffs bounding the fjords of Lankiveil.

He had taken care to wear his grandest whale fur cloak adorned with precious jewels and hand-worked scrimshaw amulets. Abulurd had come to Corrinth as a legal representative of House Harkonnen to reclaim his title as subdistrict governor of Rabban-Lankiveil. It had always been his right, but never before had it mattered to him.

Because he walked without an escort or a retinue of sycophants, the clerks and functionaries dismissed Abulurd as not deserving of notice. They looked out the windows, sat on balconies, or bustled to and fro with important documents scribed on ridulian crystal sheets. To them, he was invisible.

When seeing him off at the Lankiveil spaceport, Emmi had coached him, making him rehearse for her. According to the rules of the Landsraad, Abulurd had the authority to request an audience and to file his documents. The other nobles would see his request as minor . . . trivial, even. But it meant so much to him, and he had put it off for too long.

During the months of Emmi's pregnancy, happy again, they had reopened the main lodge and tried to bring life and color back into their lives. Abulurd subsidized industries, even seeded the waters with fish so that boatmen could earn a livelihood until the Bjondax whales chose to return.

Then, five months ago, Emmi had quietly given birth to a healthy baby boy. They named him Feyd-Rautha, partly in honor of his grandfather Onir Rautha-Rabban, the slain burgomaster of Bifrost Eyrie. When Abulurd held the baby in his arms, he saw quick, intelligent eyes and an insatiable curiosity, exquisite features, and a strong voice. In his heart this was now his only son.

Together, he and Emmi had searched for the old Buddislamic monk who had been responsible for the pregnancy. They wanted to thank her and have her bless the healthy infant, but they could find no trace of the wizened woman in sky-blue robes and gold embroidery.

Now, on Kaitain, Abulurd would do something to benefit his new son more than a simple monk's blessing could ever accomplish. If it went well, little Feyd-Rautha would have a different future, untainted by the crimes in House Harkonnen's extended history. He would grow up to be a *good* man.

Standing tall, Abulurd entered the Landsraad Hall of Oratory, passing beneath a mottled coral archwork that rose over his head like a bridge across a mountain chasm. Upon arriving at the capital world, he had made an appointment with an Imperial scribe to add his name to the agenda. When Abulurd refused to bribe the functionary, though, the scheduling secretary was unable to find a slot open until the end of a long session, three days hence.

So Abulurd had waited. He despised bureaucratic corruption and preferred to inconvenience himself rather than bow to the unfortunate standards of Shaddam IV's court. He disliked long-distance travel, would rather have stayed home tending his own affairs or playing board games with Emmi and the household staff, but the requirements of noble status forced him to do many things he came to regret.

Perhaps today he would change all that for the better.

Within the Hall of Oratory, meetings were held by representatives of the Great and Minor Houses, CHOAM directors, and other important officials who had no noble titles. The business of the Imperium continued daily.

Abulurd expected his appearance to draw little attention. He'd not forewarned his half-brother, and knew that the Baron would be upset when he found out, but Abulurd continued into the enormous hall, proud and confident—and more nervous than he had ever been in his life. Vladimir would simply have to accept this.

The Baron had other problems and obligations. His health had failed greatly over the years, and he'd put on such an enormous amount of weight that he now walked with the aid of suspensors. How the Baron kept going despite all that, Abulurd didn't know; he understood little of the engines that drove his half-brother.

Abulurd quietly took a seat in the gallery and called up the agenda to see that the meetings had already fallen an hour behind the time slots—which was to be expected, he supposed. So he waited, straight-backed on the plastone bench, listening to dull business resolutions and minor adjustments to laws that he didn't pretend to care about or even understand.

Despite the light shining through stained-glass windows and the heaters mounted under the cold stone, this enormous hall had a sterile feel to it. He just wanted to go home. When they finally called his name, Abulurd emerged from his distraction and marched toward the speaker's podium. His knees were shaking, but he tried not to show it.

On their high bench, the council members sat in formal gray robes. Glancing over his shoulder, Abulurd saw empty seats in the section where formal Harkonnen representatives should have been. No one had bothered to attend this minor daily meeting, not even Kalo Whylls, the longstanding ambassador from Giedi Prime, No one had thought to inform Whylls that the day's business would involve House Harkonnen.

Perfect.

He faltered as he remembered the last time he'd intended to address a group of people—his citizens rebuilding Bifrost Eyrie, and the horrors that had befallen them before he could speak his piece. Now, Abulurd drew a deep breath and prepared to address the Chairman, a lean man with long braided hair and hooded eyes. He could not remember which House the Chairman belonged to.

Before Abulurd could speak, however, the Master of Arms rattled off his name and titles in a long and droning sequence.

Abulurd hadn't known so many words could follow his name, since he was a relatively unimportant person in the faufreluches system. But it did sound impressive.

None of the sleepy members of the council appeared the least bit interested, however. They passed papers among themselves.

"Your Honors," he began, "sirs, I have come to make a formal request. I have filed the appropriate paperwork to reclaim the title that is due me as subdistrict governor of Rabban-Lankiveil. I have effectively served in this capacity for years, but I never . . . submitted the proper documents."

When he began to lay forth his reasoning and his justification in a voice rising with passion, the Council Chairman raised a hand. "You have followed the formal procedures required for a hearing, and the necessary notices have been dispatched." He shuffled through the documents in front of him. "I see the Emperor has received his notice as well."

"That is correct," Abulurd said, knowing that the message intended for his own half-brother had been sent by a slow, circuitous Heighliner route—a necessary sleight of hand.

The Chairman held up a single sheet of parchment. "According to this you were removed from your position on Arrakis by the Baron Harkonnen."

"Without my objection, your Honor. And my half-brother has filed no objection to my petition today." This was true enough. The message was still en route.

"Duly noted, Abulurd Harkonnen." The Chairman looked down. "Nor, I see, does the Emperor object."

Abulurd's pulse accelerated as he watched the Chairman study the papers, the legal notices. *Have I forgotten something?*

Finally, the Chairman lifted his gaze. "Everything is in order. Approved."

"I . . . I have a second request," Abulurd announced, somewhat unsettled that things had gone so rapidly and smoothly. "I wish to formally renounce my Harkonnen name."

This caused a brief titter among the attendees.

He summoned the words he had rehearsed so many times with Emmi and imagined her there beside him. "I cannot condone the actions of my family members," he said, without naming them. "I have a new son, Feyd-Rautha, and I wish him to be raised untainted, without the black mark of a Harkonnen name."

The Council Chairman leaned forward, as if really seeing Abulurd for the first time. "Do you fully understand what you're doing, sir?"

"Oh, absolutely," he said, surprised at the strength in his voice. His heart swelled with pride at what he had just said. "I grew up on Giedi Prime. I am the second surviving son of my father, Dmitri Harkonnen. My half-brother, the Baron, rules all Harkonnen holdings and does as he chooses. I ask only to keep Lankiveil, the place I call my home."

His voice softened, as if he thought a compassionate argument might move the bored men listening to his speech. "I want no part of galactic politics or ruling worlds. I served my years on Arrakis and found that I didn't like it. I have no use for riches, power, or fame. Let such things remain in the keeping of those who desire them." His voice choked in his throat. "I want no more blood on my hands, and none for my new son."

The Chairman rose solemnly and stood tall in his gray robes. "You renounce all affiliation with House Harkonnen forever, including the rights and privileges pertaining thereto?"

Abulurd nodded vigorously, ignoring the muttering voices around the chamber. "Absolutely and without equivocation." These people would have a great deal to talk about for days to come, but it mattered nothing to him. By then he would be on his way back home to Emmi and their baby. He wanted nothing, only a normal, quiet life and personal happiness. The rest of the Landsraad could continue without him. "Henceforth, I will take my wife's honored name of Rabban."

The Council Chairman rapped his sonic gavel, which echoed with a boom of finality through the hall. "So noted. The council approves your request. Notification will be sent immediately to Giedi Prime and to the Emperor."

While Abulurd stood stunned by his good fortune, the Sergeant at Arms called the next representative, and he found himself ushered out of the way. Rapidly leaving the building, he put the Hall of Oratory behind him. Outside, sunshine splashed his face again and he heard the tinkle of fountains and the music of chime kites. His step had a new lightness, and he grinned foolishly.

Others might have trembled at the momentous decision he had just made, but Abulurd Rabban felt no fear. He'd achieved everything he'd hoped to accomplish, and Emmi would be so pleased.

He raced to pack up the few possessions he'd brought with him and headed for the spaceport, anxious to return to quiet, isolated Lankiveil, where he could begin a new and better life.

There is no such thing as a law of nature. There is only a series of laws relating to man's practical experience with nature. These are laws of man's activities. They change as man's activities change.

—PARDOT KYNES, An Arrakis Primer

EVEN AFTER SIX MONTHS ON SALUSA SECUNDUS, LIET-KYNES STILL MAR-veled at the wild and restless landscape, the ancient ruins and the deep ecological wounds. As his father had said, it was . . . fascinating.

Meanwhile, in his underground hideout, Dominic Vernius studied records and pored over stolen reports of CHOAM activities. He and Gurney Halleck scrutinized Spacing Guild manifests to determine how best to sabotage business dealings in ways that would cause the most harm to the Emperor. His occasional contacts and spies who gave him scant details of the Ixian situation had vanished. He had once received occasional intelligence from his lost ancestral home, but finally even that source had dried up.

Dominic's reddened eyes and frown-creased face showed how little sleep he had been getting.

For himself, Liet finally saw beyond the intrigues of the desert people and interclan rivalries for control of spice sands. He observed the politics between Great and Minor Houses, shipping magnates, and powerful families. The Imperium was far more vast than he had imagined.

He also began to grasp the magnitude of what his father had accomplished on Dune, and felt a growing respect for Pardot Kynes.

Wistful at times, Liet imagined what it would take to re turn Salusa to the glory it had enjoyed long ago, as the foca point of the Imperium. There was so much left to understand here, so many questions still unanswered.

With some well-placed weather installations, along with hardy colonists willing to replant prairies and forests, Salusa Secundus might live and breathe again. But House Corrino refused to invest in such an enterprise, no matter what rewards they might reap. In fact, it seemed that their effort was directed toward keeping Salusa *the same* as it had been for all these centuries.

Why would they do that?

As a stranger on this world, Liet spent most of his free time with a pack and survival gear, wandering across the ravaged landscape, avoiding the ruins of long-destroyed cities where prisoners inhabited the ancient Imperial government buildings: towering museums, immense halls, great chambers with collapsed ceilings. In all the centuries Salusa had been a Corrino prison world, no one had tried to rebuild. Walls were leaning or tumbled over; roofs had huge holes.

Liet had devoted his first weeks to studying the underground smuggler base. He instructed the hardened veterans in how to erase traces of their presence, how to alter the collapsed hangar so that it looked as if it were inhabited by only a few feral refugees, attracting nothing more than a cursory glance. When the smugglers were safely hidden, and Dominic satisfied, the young Fremen went out exploring on his own, as his father had done. . . .

Moving with great care so as not to dislodge pebbles or crumbled dirt that might leave a mark of his presence, Liet climbed a ridge to look down upon a basin. Through binoculars he saw people moving under the crackling sunlight: soldiers in mottled tan and brown uniforms, desert camouflage used by the Emperor's Sardaukar troops. Extravagant war games, again.

A week ago, he'd watched the Sardaukar root out a nest of prisoners barricaded in an isolated ruin. Liet had been hiking nearby and saw the Imperials attack with all their might, wearing full body shields, using flamethrowers and primitive weapons against the convicts. The one-sided battle had gone on for hours, as well-trained Sardaukar fought hand-to-hand against hardened prisoners who boiled out of the stronghold.

The Emperor's men had slaughtered many prisoners, but some had fought back extremely well, even taking down several Sardaukar, commandeering their weapons, and prolonging the fight. When only a few dozen of the best fighters remained holed up and ready to die, the Sardaukar planted a stun-bomb. After the troops fell back behind barricades, a pulse beacon of intense light, coupled with the motivational force of a Holtzman field, knocked the surviving prisoners unconscious . . . allowing the Sardaukar to swarm inside.

Liet had wondered why the Imperial soldiers didn't just plant a stunner in the first place. Later, he wondered if the Sardaukar might have been culling the prisoners, selecting the best candidates. . . .

Now, days later, some of those surviving captives stood out on the scorched basin wearing tattered, mismatched clothes, the remnants of prison uniforms. Around them, the Sardaukar formed regimented lines, a human grid. Weapons and pieces of heavy equipment were parked at strategic positions around the perimeter, tethered down with metal spikes and chains.

The men seemed to be training, prisoners and Sardaukar alike.

As he crouched on the top of the ridge, Liet felt vulnerable without his stillsuit. The dry taste of thirst scratched in his mouth, reminding him of the desert, of his home, but he had no catchtube at his neck for a sip of water. . . .

Earlier that day they had distributed another load of melange smuggled from Dune, selling it to escaped prisoners who hated the Corrinos as much as Dominic did. In the common room, Gurney Halleck had raised a cup of spice-laced coffee in a salute to his leader. He strummed an F-sharp chord on his baliset, added a minor chord, and then sang in his bold, gruff voice (which, though not melodious, was at least exuberant)—

Oh, cup of spice
To carry me
Beyond my flesh,
To a distant star.
Melange, they call it—
Melange! Melange!

The men cheered, and Bork Qazon, the Salusan camp cook, poured him a fresh cup of spice coffee. The broad-shouldered Scien Traf, formerly an Ixian engineer, patted Gurney on the back, and the onetime merchant Pen Barlow, ever-present cigar in his mouth, laughed boisterously.

The song had made Liet want to walk on the spice sands himself, to savor the pungent cinnamon odor as it wafted up from a sandworm he rode. Perhaps Warrick would come to escort him back to Red Wall Sietch, once they returned from Salusa. He hoped so. It had been too long since he'd seen his friend and blood-brother.

Warrick and Faroula had been married for nearly a year and a half. Perhaps by now she was even carrying his child. Liet's life would have been so different if only he had won her hand instead. . . .

Now, though, he crouched in the rocks of a high ridge on a different planet, spying on the mysterious movements of Imperial troops. Liet adjusted the binocular's high-definition oil lenses for the best possible view. As the Sardaukar drilled across the barren basin, he studied the speed and precision with which they moved.

Still, Liet thought, a desperate group of well-armed Fremen might be able to defeat them. . . .

Finally, the surviving prisoners were led out onto the training field in front of new Sardaukar barracks, alloy tentments clustered like bunkers on the open flat, metal sides reflecting hazy sunlight. The soldiers seemed to be testing the prisoners, challenging them to keep up with their exercises. When one man faltered, a Sardaukar killed him with a purple blast from a lasgun; the others didn't pause.

Liet-Kynes turned his gaze from the military drills to the bilious sky, which bore ominous patterns he'd been taught to recognize. The air looked soupy as it roiled a deep orange edged with streaks of green, as if from indigestion. Clumps of ball lightning drifted across the sky. Clusters of static like huge snowflakes channeled the flow of wind toward the basin.

From stories told by Gurney Halleck and the other smugglers, Liet knew the dangers of being exposed in an aurora storm. But part of him—the curious part he'd inherited from his father—watched in awed fascination as the electrical and radioactive disturbance flowed closer. The tempest was accompanied by tendrils of exotic color, ionized air and cone-shaped funnels known as the hammer-wind.

Uneasy at being so exposed, he found cracks in the outcropping behind him. The talus caves provided enough shelter for any resourceful Fremen to wait out the harsh weather, but the troops below were unprotected. Did they have the gall to think they could survive against such raw, elemental power?

Seeing the clouds and discharges approach, the ragged prisoners began to break ranks, while the uniformed troops stood firm. The commander barked orders, apparently telling them to return to their places. Seconds later, a powerful gust of precursor wind nearly toppled the craggy-faced man from his wobbly, levitating platform. The tall leader shouted for everyone to fall back to their metal bunkers.

The Sardaukar marched in lockstep, perfectly trained.

Some of the prisoners tried to emulate the soldiers, while others just fled into the reinforced shelters.

The aurora storm struck only moments after the last of the tentments had been sealed. Like a living thing, it ripped across the basin, flashing multicolored lightning. A great fist of hammer-wind pounded the ground; another slammed into one of the tentments, flattening the metal-walled shelter and crushing everyone inside.

Boiling, crackling air swept toward the ridge. Although this was not his planet, Liet had understood the potentially lethal nature of storms since childhood. He ducked down from his exposed vantage, slid along the rocks until he could worm his way between two tall boulders and deep into a crack of rock. Within moments, he heard the demonic howling, the crackle of air, the discharges of ball lightning, the pounding slams of hammer-wind.

In the narrow slice of visible sky between the rocks, Liet watched a kaleidoscope of colors that flashed with retina-searing glare. He huddled back, but sensed he was as safe as he could be.

Breathing calmly, patiently waiting for the storm to blow over, he stared at the frenzied intensity of the aurora storm. Salusa exhibited many similarities with Dune. Both were harsh worlds, with unforgiving lands, unforgiving skies. On Dune, ferocious storms could also reshape the landscape, crushing a man into the ground or stripping flesh from his bones.

Somehow, though, unlike this place, those terrible winds made sense to him, linked as they were to the mystery and grandeur of Dune.

Liet wanted to leave Salusa Secundus, to return to his homeworld with Dominic Vernius. He needed to live in the desert again—where he belonged.

———

WHEN THE TIME was right, Dominic Vernius took part of his smuggling crew back in his frigate, accompanied by the two small lighters. Dominic piloted his own flagship, guiding the vessel into its assigned berth in the hold of the Guild Heighliner.

The renegade Earl went to his stateroom to relax and contemplate. Though he'd spent years operating in the shadows of the Imperium, a gadfly to annoy Shaddam IV, he had never struck a clear and decisive blow. Yes, he had stolen a shipment of the Emperor's commemorative coins, and he'd floated the hilarious balloon caricature over the pyramid stadium on Harmonthep. Yes, he had scrawled the snide hundred-meter-tall message on the granite canyon wall ("Shaddam, does your crown rest comfortably on your pointy head?"), and he had defaced dozens of statues and monuments as well.

But to what end? Ix was still lost, and he had no new information on the situation there.

Early in his self-imposed exile, Dominic had rallied his troops, men selected because of their loyalty in past campaigns. Remembering how they had defeated the Ecazi rebels years before, he had led a small force, heavily armed and well trained, in a raid against the new Tleilaxu stronghold.

With weapons and the advantage of surprise, Dominic had hoped to blast his way in and overthrow the invaders. At the port-of-entry canyon, he and his men rushed from their ships, firing lasguns. But they had encountered astonishing defenses from the Emperor's own Sardaukar. The damned Corrinos! Why were their troops still involved here?

Years ago, the element of surprise had been turned against Dominic, and the crack Imperial soldiers killed fully a third of his men. He himself had been hit in the back by debris from a lasgun blast and left for dead; only Johdam had dragged him back to one of their ships, in which they beat a desperate retreat.

In Dominic's secret stronghold at the south pole of Arrakis, his men had nursed him back to health. Since he had taken precautions to conceal the identity of the avenging attack force—to avoid repercussions against the Ixian people should the assault fail, or against his children on Caladan—the Tleilaxu had never learned who had come after them.

As a result of the debacle, Dominic had sworn to his men that he would never again try to recapture his hereditary world in a military action, which could only end poorly.

Out of necessity, Dominic had decided to settle for other means.

His sabotage and vandalism, however, had been largely ineffectual, no more than tiny blips on House Corrino balance sheets, or Imperial embarrassments. Shaddam IV didn't even know that the outcast Earl Vernius was involved.

Though he continued the struggle, Dominic felt worse than dead—he was *irrelevant*. He lay back in his cabin on the frigate, assessing everything he had achieved . . . and all that he'd lost. With a solido holo-portrait of Shando standing on a pedestal nearby, he could look at her and almost imagine she was still there, still with him.

Their daughter, Kailea, must be an attractive young woman by now. He wondered if she was married, perhaps to someone in the court of Leto Atreides . . . certainly not to the Duke himself. The Atreides emphasis on political marriages was well-known, and the Princess of a renegade House had no dowry. Likewise, though Rhombur was old enough to become the Earl of House Vernius, the title was valueless.

With immense sadness sagging his shoulders, he gazed at the holo-image of Shando on the pedestal. *And in his grief, she spoke to him.*

"Dominic . . . Dominic Vernius. I know your identity."

Startled, he sat up, wondering if he had descended into a labyrinth of madness. Her mouth moved mechanically. The holo of her face turned, but her expression did not change. Her eyes did not focus on him. The words continued.

"I am using this image to communicate with you. I must present a message from Ix."

Dominic trembled as he approached the image. "Shando?"

"No, I am the Navigator of this Heighliner. I have chosen to speak through this holo-image because it is difficult to communicate otherwise."

Reluctant to believe this, Dominic fought back superstitious fear. Just seeing the likeness of Shando move, seeing her face come alive again, infused him with a trembling awe he had not experienced in a long time. "Yes, whoever you are. What is it you want of me?"

"My brother, C'tair Pilru, sends these words from Ix. He begs me to give you this information. I can do no more than instruct you."

Her lips moving faster, and using a different voice this time, Shando's holo-image repeated the words C'tair had sent in a desperate message to his Navigator brother. In growing horror, Dominic listened, and learned the extent of damage the Tleilaxu usurpers had inflicted on his beloved world and its people.

Rage simmered within him. When he had begged for assistance during the first Tleilaxu attacks, damnable old Emperor Elrood IX had stalled, thereby guaranteeing the defeat of House Vernius. Bitter at their loss, Dominic only wished the old man hadn't died before he could find a way to kill him.

But now Dominic realized the Imperial plan was much broader, much more insidious. At its core, the entire Tleilaxu takeover had been an Imperial plot, with Sardaukar troops still enforcing it nearly twenty years later. Elrood had set up the conflict from the start, and his son Shaddam perpetuated the scheme by oppressing the remaining subjects of House Vernius.

Presently the voice from the Shando-likeness changed again, returning to the more ponderous and disconnected words of the Navigator. "On my route in this vessel, I can take you to Xuttuh, formerly known as Ix."

"Do it," Dominic said, with hatred icing his heart. "I wish to see the horrors for myself, and then I"—he put a hand to his breast, as if swearing a vow to Shando—"I, Lord Dominic, Earl of House Vernius, will avenge the suffering of my people."

When the Heighliner went into orbit, Dominic met with Asuyo, Johdam, and the others. "Return to Arrakis. Go to our base and continue our work. I'm taking one of the lighters." He stared at the pedestal as if he could still see his wife there. "I have business of my own."

The two veterans expressed their surprise and confusion, but Dominic pounded his fist on the table. "No further argument! I have made my decision." He glared at his men, and they were amazed to see such a transformation in his personality.

"But where are you going?" Liet asked. "What do you plan to do?"

"I am going to Ix."

One uses power by grasping it lightly. To grasp with too much force is to be taken over by power, thus becoming its victim.

—Bene Gesserit Axiom

THE BARON DID NOT TAKE THE NEWS ABOUT HIS HALF-BROTHER AT ALL well.

At the Harko City Spaceport, men were loading his private frigate with the amenities, supplies, and personnel he would need for a trip to Arrakis. In order to keep spice operations running smoothly, he had to spend months at a time on the desert hellhole, squeezing his fist to prevent smugglers and the accursed Fremen from getting out of hand. But, after the damage Abulurd had done years ago, the Baron had turned the most economically important planet in the Imperium back into a huge moneymaker. House profits were increasing steadily.

And now, just when everything seemed to be going his way, he had to deal with *this*! Abulurd, for all his stupidity, had an incredible knack for doing precisely the wrong thing, every time.

Piter de Vries, sensing his superior's displeasure, approached with mincing steps, wanting to assist—or to *appear* to be doing so. But he knew better than to come too close. For years he had survived by avoiding the Baron's wrath, longer than any of his master's previous Mentats. In his younger, leaner days, Vladimir Harkonnen had been capable of lashing out like a cobra and striking a person in the larynx to cut off his breathing. But now he had grown so soft, so corpulent that de Vries could easily slither out of the way.

Simmering, the Baron sat in the Keep's stone-walled accounting room. His oval blackplaz table looked polished enough to ice-skate on. A huge globe of Arrakis stood in one corner, an art object any noble family would have coveted. But rather than show it off at Landsraad gatherings or blue-blood social events, the Baron kept it in his private room, savoring the globe for himself.

"Piter, what am I to do?" He gestured toward a cluster of message cylinders newly arrived via bonded Courier. "The CHOAM Corporation demands an explanation, warning me in none-too-subtle terms that they expect shipments of whale fur to continue from Lankiveil despite the 'change in ruler-ship.'" He snorted. "As if I would *decrease* our quotas! They remind me that spice production on Arrakis is not the only vital commodity House Harkonnen controls. They've threatened to revoke my CHOAM directorship if I fail to meet my obligations."

With a flick of his wrist he hurled a copper-sheathed message cylinder at the wall. It clanged and clattered, leaving a white nick on the stone.

He picked up a second cylinder. "Emperor Shaddam wants to know why my own half-brother would renounce the Harkonnen name and take the subdistrict governorship for himself."

Again he hurled the cylinder at the wall. It struck with a louder *clink* beside the first white mark. He picked up a third. "House Moritani on Grumman offers covert military support in case I wish to take direct action." The third cylinder struck the wall. "House Richese, House Mutelli—all curious, all laughing behind my back!"

He continued to throw message cylinders until his table was clear. One of the metal tubes rolled toward Piter, and he picked it up. "You didn't open this one, my Lord."

"Well, do it for me. It probably says the same as all the others."

"Of course." The Mentat used one of his long fingernails to cut the seal on the capsule, and slid the cap off. Bringing out a piece of *instroy* paper, he scanned it, his tongue darting over his lips. "Ah, from our operative on Caladan."

The Baron perked up. "Good news, I hope?"

De Vries smiled as he translated the cipher. "Chiara apologizes for her inability to get messages out before this, but she is making progress with the concubine, Kailea Vernius, turning her against the Duke."

"Well, that's something anyway." The Baron rubbed his fat chin. "I would have preferred word of Leto's assassination. Now that would have been really good news!"

"Chiara likes to do things in her own way, at her own pace." The *instroy* message faded, and de Vries balled it up, then tossed it and the cylinder aside. "We aren't sure how far she'll go, my Lord, for she has certain . . . standards . . . in royal matters. Spying is one thing; murder is quite another, and she's the only one we could get past Thufir Hawat's security."

"All right, all right." The two of them had been over this before. The Baron pushed himself up from his seat. "At least we're throwing a bit of sand in the Duke's eye."

"Perhaps we should do more than that to Abulurd?"

Aided by the suspensor system at his waist, the fat man misjudged the strength of his own flabby arms and nearly flew off his feet. Wisely, de Vries said nothing about that, and absorbed data so that he could perform a proper Mentat analysis as soon as his master demanded it.

"Perhaps." The Baron's face reddened. "Abulurd's older brother Marotin was an idiot, you know. Literally, I mean. A drooling, brain-damaged moron who couldn't even dress himself, though his mother simpered over him, as if Marotin was worth the resources expended to keep him alive." His jowly face was blotched with pent-up rage.

"Now it seems that Abulurd is just as brain-damaged, but in a more subtle way." He slammed his flat palm down on the oily blackplaz surface, leaving a handprint that would gradually be broken down by self-cleaning systems in the furniture.

"I didn't even know his bitch Emmi was pregnant. Now he's got another son, a sweet little baby—and Abulurd's robbed the child of his birthright." The Baron shook his head. "You realize, that boy could be a leader, another Harkonnen heir . . . and his foolish father takes it all away."

With his master's frustration building, de Vries took extra care to stay out of reach, on the opposite side of the oval table. "My Lord, as near as I can tell, Abulurd has followed the precise forms of law. According to Landsraad rules he is allowed to request, and receive, a concession that few of us would even have considered. We may not think it wise, but Abulurd was within his rights as part of House Harkonnen—"

"*I* am House Harkonnen!" the Baron roared. "He doesn't have any rights unless I say so." He came around the desk. The Mentat stood frozen, afraid the corpulent man might attack him after all. Instead, he bobbed toward the door of the chamber. "We go to see Rabban."

They walked through the echoing halls of the blocky Keep to an external armored lift that dropped them from the Keep's spiked pinnacles down to an enclosed arena. Glossu Rabban worked with the House Guard to prepare for the evening's scheduled gladiatorial combat, a tradition the Baron had established as a precursor to each of his long journeys to Arrakis.

Inside the arena, silent slaves cleaned the tiers of seats, polishing and sweeping away debris. The Baron's great contests always drew large crowds, and he used such spectacles to impress guests of other Great Houses. Heavy durasteel doors at the gladiator-pit level remained closed, trapping caged beasts for combat. Hirsute, shirtless workers hosed down the empty pens of slain creatures or slaves, then dusted them with odor-suppressants.

Sweating, though he didn't appear to be doing any work, Rabban stood in the midst of the men. Wearing a sleeveless jerkin of studded leather, he rested his hands at his waist, pursed thick lips, and glowered at the activity. Other laborers raked the sand of the arena floor, sifting out bone fragments and shattered blades.

Kryubi, captain of the House Guard, directed his soldiers. He decided where to station each armed man to provide an appropriately impressive military presence for the upcoming festivities.

Buoyed by his suspensor belt, the Baron glided down the waterfall of steps, passed through a spiked iron gate, and emerged on the stained arena floor. His feet barely touched the ground, giving his walk a ballet-like grace. Piter de Vries followed him with similar dancing steps.

Kryubi stepped up and saluted. "My Baron," he said, "everything is prepared. We shall have a spectacular event tonight."

"As always," de Vries said, a smile twisting his sapho-stained lips.

"How many beasts do we have?" the Baron asked.

"Two Laza tigers, my Lord, a deka-bear, and one Salusan bull."

With glittering black eyes the Baron studied the arena and nodded. "I'm weary this evening. I don't want a long combat. Release the beasts and all five chosen slaves at once. We'll have a free-for-all."

Kryubi gave a brisk salute. "As you wish, my Lord."

The Baron turned to his Mentat. "The blood will fly tonight, Piter. Maybe it will distract me from what I'd like to do to Abulurd."

"Do you prefer to be merely distracted, my Baron?" the

508 — BRIAN HERBERT AND KEVIN J. ANDERSON

Mentat asked. "Or do you prefer . . . satisfaction? Why not have your revenge on Abulurd?"

A moment of hesitation, then: "Revenge will do quite nicely, Piter. Rabban!"

His nephew turned to see the Baron and his Mentat standing there. On stocky legs, Rabban marched across the arena floor to the two men.

"Did Piter tell you what your fool father has done now?"

Rabban's expression contorted. "Yes, Uncle. Sometimes I can't understand how such a clod can get through the day."

"It's true that we don't understand Abulurd," de Vries said. "But one of the important laws of statecraft suggests that to utterly defeat one's enemy, one *must* understand him, learn his weaknesses. Learn where it will hurt the most."

"Abulurd's entire brain is his weakness," the Baron mumbled, his tone dark. "Or maybe just his bleeding heart."

Rabban chuckled, too loudly.

The Mentat held up one long finger. "Consider this. His infant son, Feyd-Rautha Rabban, is now his greatest vulnerability. Abulurd has taken an extraordinary step in order to—as he puts it—'see that the child is raised in a proper fashion.' Apparently, this means a great deal to him."

The Baron looked at his broad-shouldered nephew. "We wouldn't want Rabban's little brother turning out like Abulurd, would we?"

Rabban glowered at the possibility.

De Vries continued, his voice as smooth as oiled ice. "And so, what is the most terrible thing we could do to Abulurd under these circumstances? What would cause him the greatest pain and despair?"

A cold smile crossed the Baron's face. "Brilliant question, Piter. And for that, you shall live another day. Two days, in fact—I feel generous."

Rabban's expression remained blank; he still hadn't caught on. Finally, he began to snigger. "What should we do, Uncle?"

The Baron's voice became sickly sweet. "Why, we must do everything possible to make sure that your new little brother is 'raised properly.' Naturally, knowing the consistently bad decisions your father has made, we cannot in good conscience allow Abulurd *Rabban* to corrupt this boy." He looked over at the Mentat. "Therefore, we must raise him ourselves."

"I shall prepare the documents immediately, my Lord Baron," de Vries said with a smile.

The Baron shouted for Kryubi to attend them, then turned to his nephew. "Take all the men you need, Rabban. And don't be too secretive about it. Abulurd must understand full well what he has brought upon himself."

*No one has yet determined the power of the human species . . .
what it may perform by instinct, and what it may accomplish
with rational determination.*

—Mentat Objective Analysis of Human Capabilities

GUIDED BY DOMINIC VERNIUS, THE LIGHTER SLIPPED UNDER THE IXIAN DE-
tection grid, masked by clouds. He cruised low across the pristine surface of his lost homeworld, drinking in the sight of the
mountains and waterfalls, the dark pine forests clinging to
granite slopes.

As the former lord of Ix, Dominic knew a thousand ways to
get inside. He hoped at least one of them still worked.

Fighting back tears of dread, he flew onward, intent on his
destination. The Imperium knew Ix for its industry and technology, for the marvelous products it exported through
CHOAM distributors. Long ago, House Vernius had chosen
to leave the surface unspoiled, burying unsightly production
facilities deep underground, which greatly enhanced security
and protected valuable Ixian secrets.

Dominic remembered the defensive systems he himself
had designed and established, as well as those put in place generations before. The threat of technological espionage from
rivals such as Richese had always been sufficient for the Ixians
to keep up their guard. Surely the Tleilaxu usurpers had instituted their own safeguards, but they would not have found all
of Dominic's personal tricks. He had hidden them too well.

An organized assault team might be doomed to failure, but

Earl Vernius was confident that by himself he could still get back inside his own world. He had to see it with his own eyes.

Although each of the hidden openings into the subterranean realms made for weak spots in overall security, Dominic had understood the need for emergency exits and secret routes known only to himself and his family. Deep within the crustal city of Vernii—his beloved capital city—there had been numerous shielded chambers, hidden tunnels, and escape hatches. Dominic's children, along with young Leto Atreides, had used those bolt-holes during the bloody overthrow. Now Dominic would use one of the many long-hidden back doors to slip *in*.

He flew the lighter over a series of poorly concealed ventilation shafts, from which steam emerged like thermal geysers. Elsewhere out on the flat plains, large shafts and cargo platforms opened to allow shipments of materials, mostly outbound. In this deep, forested canyon, narrow guarded ledges and hollows allowed occasional ships to land. Dominic scanned the terrain as he cruised along until he spotted the subtle markings, the fallen trees, the stains on rugged rock walls.

The first disguised entry door was sealed up, the tunnel filled with what must have been meters of solid plascrete. The second door was booby-trapped, but Dominic spotted the explosive connections before he entered his pass-code. He didn't try to disarm the device. He flew off again.

Dominic dreaded what he might find below in his once-beautiful city. In addition to the horrifying message passed along from the Ixian patriot C'tair Pilru, his own bribed investigators had brought rumors about conditions on Ix. Yet he had to *know* what the Tleilaxu and the damned Corrinos had done to his cherished planet.

Then they would all pay.

Next, Dominic landed the lighter in a small hollow surrounded by dark firs. Hoping he remained within the surveillance grid, he stepped out and stood still, smelling the cold clear air, the spicy pungency of copper-pine needles, the wet sharpness of rushing water. In the grottoes beneath him, under a kilometer of rock, the air would be warm and thick, redolent of chemicals and a crowded populace. He could almost hear and feel familiar sounds, a faint buzz of activity, a barely discernible vibration under his feet.

He located the brush-covered hatch opening of the escape shaft and operated the controls after careful inspection for further traps and explosives. If the Tleilaxu had found this one, then they had been thorough indeed. But he found no sign. Then he waited, hoping the systems still functioned.

At last, after the brisk wind had raised goose bumps on his flesh, a self-guided lift chamber rose up, ready to take him deep into the network of caves to a secret personal storeroom at the rear of what had once been the Grand Palais. It was one of several rooms that he had set up in his younger days for "contingencies." That had been before the Ecazi Revolt, before he had married . . . long before the Tleilaxu takeover. It was safe.

Whispering Shando's name, Dominic closed his eyes. The chamber descended at frightening speed, and now he hoped that C'tair's sabotage efforts hadn't damaged these hidden systems. He took deep breaths, summoning images from his past on the projection screen of his eyelids. He longed to return to the magical underground city—but feared the harsh reality that awaited him.

When the lift chamber came to a stop, Dominic emerged holding a compact lasgun. He also had a flèchette pistol in a shoulder holster. The dark storeroom smelled of dust and the mildew of inactivity. No one had been there for a long time.

He moved about carefully, went to the hidden locker where he'd stored a pair of nondescript coveralls worn by mid-level workers. Hoping the Tleilaxu had not made drastic changes in work uniforms, he dressed and slipped the lasgun into a custom-fitted holster strapped to his skin, beneath the clothing.

Disguised and hoping for the best, knowing he could not turn back, Dominic crept through the dim corridors and located a plaz-walled observation deck. After two decades, he took his first look at the reshaped city beneath the ground.

He blinked in disbelief. The magnificent Grand Palais had been stripped, all the glittering marble taken away, one entire wing destroyed in an explosion. The immense building now looked like a warehouse with injured shadows of greatness, now an ugly warren of bureaucratic offices. Through panes of windowplaz he saw disgusting Tleilaxu going about their business like cockroaches.

Across the projected sky, he watched oblong devices studded with blinking lights cruising in random paths, studying all movement. *Surveillance pods*. Military equipment designed by Ixians to be sent into battle zones. Now the Tleilaxu used that same technology to spy on *his* people, to keep them cowering in fear.

Sickened, Dominic moved to other observation decks in the grotto ceiling, slipping in and out of groups of people. He stared at their haunted eyes and gaunt faces, trying to remind himself that these were *his people*, rather than images from a nightmare. He wanted to talk to them, to reassure them that he would do something, and soon. But he could not reveal his identity. He did not know enough about what had occurred there since he and his family had gone renegade.

These loyal Ixians had depended on Dominic Vernius, their rightful Earl, but he had failed them. He had fled, leaving all of them to their own fates. A feeling of unbearable guilt overwhelmed him; his stomach knotted.

With cold calculation, Dominic stared across the cavernous city, looking for the best observation points, pinpointing heavily guarded industrial facilities. Some were shut down and

514 — BRIAN HERBERT AND KEVIN J. ANDERSON

abandoned, others surrounded by buzzing security fields. On the grotto floor, suboids and Ixian inhabitants worked together like downtrodden slaves.

Lights flared on the balconies of the freakishly altered Grand Palais. Public address speakers boomed out, the words reverberating and synchronized so that echoes rippled like force waves up and down the grotto.

"People of Xuttuh," said an accented voice in Galach, "we continue to find parasites in our midst. We will do what we must to obliterate this cancer of conspirators and traitors. We Bene Tleilax have generously provided for your needs and granted you a part in our holy mission. Therefore, we will punish those who would distract you from your sacred tasks. You must understand and accept your new place in the universe."

Down on the grotto floor, Dominic could see squads of soldiers rounding up work gangs. The troops wore the distinctive gray-and-black uniforms of Sardaukar and carried deadly Imperial weapons. So, Shaddam no longer even tried to hide his involvement. Dominic seethed.

On a Grand Palais balcony, a pair of terrified prisoners flanked by Sardaukar were nudged forward by robed Tleilaxu Masters. The speaker boomed again. "These two were captured in the act of committing sabotage against essential industries. During interrogation they identified other conspirators." An ominous pause followed. "You may anticipate further executions within the week."

Only a few isolated voices in the throng dared to cry out in protest. High above, Sardaukar guards pushed the thrashing prisoners to the brink of the balcony. "Death to those who oppose us!" The guards—Imperial guards—shoved them over the edge, and the crowds scattered below. The victims fell across the gulf of empty air, with hideous shrieks that ended abruptly.

In horrified fury, Dominic stared. Many times he had stood

on that balcony to deliver orations. He had addressed his subjects from there, praising them for their work, promising greater rewards for productivity. The balcony of the Grand Palais should have been a place for the people to see the kindness of their leaders—not an execution platform.

Below, shots rang out, and the sizzle of lasgun fire. The Sardaukar clamped down, enforcing order among the angry and restless populace.

The voice from the speakers crackled out a final punishment. "For the next three weeks, rations will be reduced by twenty percent. Productivity will remain the same, or further restrictions will be imposed. If volunteers come forward to identify additional conspirators, our rewards will be generous."

With a swish of robes, the smug Tleilaxu Masters turned about and followed the Sardaukar guards back into the desecrated Palais structure.

Outraged, Dominic wanted to charge into the city and open fire on the Sardaukar and the Tleilaxu. But alone, a surreptitious spy, he didn't have the firepower to accomplish more than a token attack—and he dared not expose his identity in such a futile gesture.

His jaw ached as he ground his teeth together. Gripping the railing, he realized that he had stood on this very observation platform, long ago, with his new bride, Lady Shando. Holding hands, they had gazed across the immense cavern at the fairyland structures of Vernii. She had been bright-eyed, wearing elegant clothes from the Imperial Court at Kaitain.

But the Emperor had never forgotten the insult of her departure from his concubine service. Elrood had waited many years for his chance at revenge, and all of Ix had paid for it. . . .

Dominic's chest clenched. He'd had it all: wealth, power, a prosperous world, a perfect wife, a fine family. Now the cavern city was severely wounded, with barely a hint remaining of its former splendor.

"Oh, look what they've done, Shando," he whispered in a morose voice, as if he were a ghost along with her. "Look what they've done."

He remained in the city of Vernii for as long as he dared, letting the wheels of reprisal turn in his mind. By the time he made ready to depart, Dominic Vernius knew exactly what he would do to strike back.

History would never forget his vengeance.

Power and deceit are tools of statecraft, yes. But remember that power deludes the ones who wield it—making them believe it can overcome the defects of their ignorance.

—COUNT FLAMBERT MUTELLI,
early speech in Landsraad Hall of Oratory

ONCE AGAIN, ABULURD ENJOYED THE PEACEFUL NIGHTS ON LANKIVEIL. HE had no regrets about renouncing his powerful family connections. He was content.

Roaring fires in the hearths of the great rooms warmed the restored and redecorated main lodge in Tula Fjord. Lounging in the common area adjacent to the big kitchen, he and Emmi felt satisfied, their stomachs full from a large feast of grupper paella they had shared with the servants to celebrate being together again. Most of the original staff had been located and brought back. Finally, Abulurd looked forward to the future.

That very morning two Bjondax whales had been seen at the mouth of the fjord, testing the waters. Fishermen reported that recent catches were the best in over a year. The normally dismal weather had turned sharply cold and dusted the cliffs with a clean blanket of snow; even under the cloudy night skies, the whiteness added a pearly overtone to the shadows.

Baby Feyd-Rautha sat on a handwoven carpet beside Emmi. Good-natured, the boy was prone to giggles and a variety of facial expressions. Clinging to one of his mother's fingers as she held him upright, Feyd began to take his first wobbly steps, testing his balance. The bright child already had a small vocabulary, which he employed often.

In celebration, Abulurd considered bringing out a few old instruments and calling for folk music, but before he could do so he heard a grating noise outside, the hum of engines. "Are those boats?" When the servants fell silent, he could indeed make out the sounds of aquatic motors.

The fishmistress, who was also their cook, had brought a large basin into the sitting room adjacent to the common area, where she used a flat knife to pry open stoneclams and shuck the meat into a pot of salted broth. Hearing the commotion outside, she wiped her hands on a towel and looked over her shoulder through the windowplaz. "Lights. Boats coming up the fjord. Movin' too fast, if you ask me. Dark outside—they could hit somethin'."

"Turn up the house glowglobes," Abulurd commanded. "We need to welcome our visitors." Outside, a wreath of illumination blazed around the wooden structure, shedding a warm glow onto the docks.

Three seacraft roared along the rocky waterline, arrowing straight for the main lodge. Emmi clutched baby Feyd. Her wide, normally calm face carried a ripple of uneasiness, and she looked at her husband for reassurance. Abulurd made a soft gesture to quell her fears, though he felt a knot forming in his own stomach.

He opened the big wooden doors just as the armored boats lashed up against the docks. Uniformed Harkonnen soldiers disembarked onto the quay, their heavy bootsteps like cannon fire. Abulurd took a step backward as the troops marched up the steep stairs toward him, weapons shouldered but ready for use.

Abulurd sensed that all of his peace was about to end.

Glossu Rabban strode onto the dockboards; with brisk stomping footsteps, he followed the vanguard of armed men.

"Emmi, it's . . . it's *him*." Abulurd couldn't utter his son's name. More than four decades separated Glossu Rabban from his young sibling, in whom the parents now placed all their hopes. The baby seemed incredibly vulnerable—Abulurd's household had no defenses.

On impulse, reacting foolishly, Abulurd swung shut the heavy door and barred it, which only served to provoke the oncoming soldiers. They opened fire and blasted the century-old barricade. Abulurd scrambled back to protect his wife and child. The aged wood smoked and splintered, falling to one side with a dreadful sound like a headsman's ax.

"Is this how you welcome me, Father?" Rabban gave a gruff laugh as he stepped through the smoke and over the wreckage.

The servants began to move about in a flurry. Behind the basin of salted broth, the fishmistress held her little shellfish knife as a pathetic weapon. Two manservants emerged from the back rooms with spears and fishing knives, but Abulurd raised his hands to keep them calm. The Harkonnen soldiers would slaughter them all, just like at Bifrost Eyrie, if he didn't handle this properly.

"Is this how you *ask* for a welcome, Son?" Abulurd gestured to the wreckage of the door. "With armed soldiers and military boats arriving in the middle of the night?"

"My uncle has been teaching me how to make an entrance."

The men in blue Harkonnen livery stood motionless, weapons in plain view. Abulurd didn't know what to do. He looked at his wife, but she sat by the roaring fire, clutching the baby close. By the hunted look in her eyes, Abulurd knew she was wishing she'd hidden the child somewhere in the main lodge.

"Is that my new little brother, Feyd-Rautha? A prissy-sounding name." Rabban shrugged, "But if he's my own flesh and blood . . . I suppose I *have* to love him."

Holding the child even tighter, Emmi tossed her straight hair behind her shoulders, hair that was still black despite her advancing years. She met Rabban's gaze with hard eyes, angry at what she saw and torn by a few scraps of love for her own son, whom she could not abandon. "Let us hope that blood is all you two share. You did not learn to be cruel in this house, Glossu. Not from me, and not from your father. We always loved you, even after you caused us so much pain." Surprisingly, she stood and took a step toward him, and Rabban flushed with flustered anger as he inadvertently took a step back. "How could you have turned out the way you have?"

He glowered at her.

Emmi lowered her voice, as if she were asking herself the question, not him. "We are so disappointed in you. Where did we go wrong? I don't understand it."

Her wide, plain face softened with love and pity, but hardened again as Rabban burst out in cruel laughter to cover his own unease. "Oh? I'm disappointed in you two as well. My own parents, and you didn't even invite me to the naming ceremony of my little brother." He stepped forward. "Let me hold the brat."

Emmi drew back, protecting her good son from the bad. Rabban feigned a look of sadness, then strode closer. The Harkonnen troops raised their weapons and advanced.

"Leave your mother alone!" Abulurd said. One of the soldiers put up a single hand and stopped him from rushing forward.

Rabban turned to him. "I can't sit idly by and let my own brother be corrupted by an embarrassing weakling like you, Father. Baron Vladimir Harkonnen, your half-brother and head of our Great House, has already filed documents and received full Landsraad approval to raise Feyd-Rautha in his own household on Giedi Prime." One of the guards took out an ornate scroll of imprinted saarti parchment and tossed it on the floor at Abulurd's feet. Abulurd could only stare at it. "He has adopted the boy formally and legally as his foster son."

Smiling at his parents' horrified expressions, Rabban said, "In the same manner that he has already adopted *me*. I am his heir-designate, the na-Baron. I'm a Harkonnen as pure and proper as the Baron himself." He extended his thick arms. The troops kept their weapons steady, but Emmi backed closer to the fire. "See, you have nothing to worry about."

Jerking his head to one side, Rabban signaled two of the nearest men, who opened fire on the fishmistress where she stood, still holding the little curved knife. During Rabban's brief stay in the main lodge, the husky woman had cooked many meals for him. But now the lasgun beams cut her down before she could even scream; the fishmistress dropped her knife and tumbled forward into the basin. Clams turned over, and sour-smelling water spilled onto the wooden floor.

"How many more of them will you force me to kill, Mother?" he inquired, almost plaintively, still reaching out with his thick-fingered hands. "You know I'll do it. Now give me my brother."

Emmi's gaze flicked from Rabban's to all of the terrified household servants, to the baby boy, and then to Abulurd, who did not have the courage to meet her eyes. He could only make a strangled cry in his throat.

Though she gave him no sign of surrender, Rabban pulled the infant roughly from her numb arms, and she did not resist—out of fear that all the other people in the house would be slaughtered just the way the Harkonnen troops had slaughtered the innocent workers at Bifrost Eyrie.

Unable to bear the thought of her baby being taken away, Emmi gave a small gasp, as if the anchors that had always given her strength and stability had just been severed. The child began to cry upon seeing the broad, stony face of his much older brother.

"You can't do this!" Abulurd said, still unwilling to push his way past the armed guards. "I am planetary governor here. I will contest this with the Landsraad."

"You have no legal rights whatsoever. We didn't contest your meaningless title as planetary governor, but when you renounced your Harkonnen name, you forfeited your position, all nice and tidy." Rabban held the struggling baby at arm's length as if he didn't know what to do with a child. The parchment legal document still lay untouched on the floor. "You are effectively *nothing*, Father. Nothing at all."

Taking the boy, he headed back toward the smoking ruins of the door. Abulurd and Emmi, both wild with grief, screamed after him, but the guards turned around, pointing their weapons.

"Oh, don't kill anyone else," Rabban said to them. "I'd rather hear a houseful of whimpering as we leave."

The soldiers marched down the steps to the docks, where they boarded the armored boats. Abulurd held Emmi tightly, rocking her back and forth, and they supported each other like two trees fallen together. Both of their faces were streaked with tears, their eyes wide and glassy. The servants in the house wailed in anguish.

Rabban's military boats cruised off across the black waters of Tula Fjord. Abulurd gasped, unable to breathe. Emmi shuddered in his arms and he tried to comfort her, but he felt utterly helpless, ineffective, and crushed. She stared at her open, callused hands, as if expecting to see her baby there.

Off in the distance, though he knew it was only his imagination, Abulurd thought he could hear the child crying even over the roar of the departing boats.

Never be in the company of anyone with whom you would not want to die.

—Fremen Saying

WHEN LIET-KYNES RETURNED FROM SALUSA SECUNDUS TO THE SMUGGLER base at Dune's south pole, he found his friend Warrick awaiting him.

"Look at you!" the taller Fremen said with a laugh. Warrick threw back his hood as he rushed across the crunching gravel at the bottom of the hidden chasm. He embraced Liet and pounded him sharply on the back. "You're water-fat and . . . *clean.*" He sniffed deprecatingly. "I see no mark of the stillsuit upon you. Have you washed all the desert from yourself?"

"I'll never get the desert out of my blood." Liet clasped his friend. "And you . . . you've grown."

"The happiness of married life, my friend. Faroula and I have a son now, named Liet-chih in your honor." He smacked a fist into his palm. "And I've continued to fight the Harkonnens every day, while you've grown pampered and soft among these outsiders."

A *son.* Liet felt a twinge of sadness for himself, but it passed, replaced by genuine joy for his friend and gratitude for the honor of the name.

The smugglers unloaded their cargo with little conversation or banter. They were uneasy and sullen because Dominic Vernius had not accompanied them back to Arrakis. Johdam and Asuyo shouted orders for stowing the material they had brought from Salusa Secundus. Gurney Halleck had remained behind on Salusa, to supervise the smuggler operations there.

Warrick had been at the antarctic base for five days now, eating the smugglers' food, telling the men how to survive the deserts of Dune. "I don't think they'll ever learn, Liet," he whispered with a snort. "No matter how long they live here, they'll still be off-worlders."

As they strode back into the main tunnels, Warrick shared his news. Two times in a row, he had taken the spice bribe down to Rondo Tuek, trying to find out when his friend would return. It had seemed a long time. "What ever drove you to go to a place like Salusa Secundus?"

"A journey I had to take," Liet responded. "My father grew up there, and spoke of it so often. But I'm back now, and I intend to stay. Dune is my home. Salusa was just . . . just an interesting diversion."

Pausing, Warrick scratched his long hair; it was matted and kinked from many hours under a stillsuit hood. No doubt Faroula kept his water rings for him, as a wife should do. Liet wondered what the elfin young woman looked like now. "So, will you return to Red Wall Sietch, Liet—where you belong? Faroula and I miss you. It makes us sad that you feel the need to stay apart from us."

With a hard swallow, Liet admitted, "I was foolish. I wanted time alone to consider my future. So many things have changed, and I have learned so much." He forced a smile. "I think I comprehend my father better now."

Warrick's blue-within-blue eyes widened. "Who would question the Umma Kynes? We simply do his bidding."

"Yes, but he's *my* father, and I wanted to understand him."

From a high vantage inside the frozen walls, they gazed across the layered terraces of the dust-impregnated ice cap. "Whenever you're ready, my friend, we can summon a worm and return to the sietch." Warrick pursed his lips to squelch an expression of mirth. "*If* you remember how to put on your stillsuit."

Liet snorted and went to his locker, where he had stored the desert equipment. "You may have beaten me in our race to the Cave of Birds"—he shot a sidelong glance at his taller friend—"but I can still call a larger worm."

They bade farewell to the other smugglers. Although the hardened old men had been Liet's companions for almost a year, he did not feel close to them. They were military, loyal to their commander and accustomed to regimented training. They talked endlessly of bygone days and battles on far-off worlds, of leading charges beside Earl Vernius for the glory of the Imperium. But their passions had soured, and now they simply did what they could to annoy Shaddam. . . .

Liet and Warrick trekked across the antarctic wasteland, avoiding the dirt and grit of the water merchant's industries. Warrick looked back at the cold, unmarked terrain. "I see you've taught them a few things, even beyond what we showed them the first time. Their stronghold is not quite so obvious as before."

"You noticed, eh?" Liet said, pleased. "With a good Fremen teacher, even *they* can learn the obvious."

Reaching the desert boundary at last, they planted their thumper and summoned a worm. Soon, they headed due north into the wild flatlands where dust and storms and capricious weather patterns had always discouraged Harkonnen patrols.

As their mount plowed through the sands, taking them toward the equatorial regions, Warrick spoke at great length. He seemed happier and more filled with stories and good-natured anecdotes than ever before.

Still feeling a dull pain in his heart, Liet listened to his friend talk about Faroula and their son, their life together, a trip they had taken to Sietch Tabr, a day spent in Arrakeen, how one day they wanted to go to the greenhouse demonstration project in Plaster Basin. . . .

All the while, Liet found himself daydreaming. If only he'd called a larger worm, or driven it harder, or rested less, he might have arrived first. Both young men had made the same wish upon the *Biyan*, the uncovered white lake bed, so long ago—to marry the same girl—and only Warrick's wish had been granted.

It was the will of Shai-Hulud, as Fremen would say; Liet had to accept it.

At night, they made camp, then sat on a dune crest, where they tossed tally sticks into the sand. Afterward, watching the stars glide silently overhead in the darkness, they sealed themselves inside the stilltent. With the soft feel of the desert beneath him, Liet-Kynes slept better than he had in months. . . .

They traveled hard and fast. Two days later, Liet found himself longing to see Red Wall Sietch again: to greet his mother, Frieth, to tell his father what he had seen and done on Salusa Secundus.

But that afternoon, Liet stared across the sands at a brownish-tan smudge on the horizon. He removed his stillsuit plugs and inhaled deeply, smelling ozone, and his skin tingled with static electricity in the air.

Warrick frowned. "It's a big storm, Liet, approaching rapidly." He shrugged with forced optimism. "Perhaps it will just be a *heinali* wind. We can brave it."

Liet kept his thoughts to himself, not wishing to give voice to unpleasant suspicions. Evil possibilities spoken aloud could attract the evil itself.

But as the knot of weather grew closer and louder, rising ominously tall and brown in the sky, Liet stated the obvious. "No, my friend, it is a Coriolis storm." Grimly, he clamped his mouth shut. He remembered his experience years before in the meteorological pod with his father, and more recently in he aurora storm on Salusa Secundus. But this was worse, much worse.

Warrick looked over at him and gripped a ridge on the worm's back. "*Hulasikali Wala*. The wind of the demon in the open desert."

Liet studied the oncoming cloud. At the highest levels, the murk was caused by tiny dust particles blown to great altitudes, whereas closer to the ground, the winds would pick up the heavier, scouring sand. *Hulasikali Wala*, he thought. This was the Fremen term for the most powerful of all Coriolis storms. *The wind that eats flesh.*

Beneath them, the sandworm became agitated and restless, reluctant to continue. As the deadly storm approached, the creature would dive to safety underground no matter how many spreaders and Maker hooks they applied to open its body segments.

Liet scanned the wind-fuzzed dunes that spread like an endless ocean in all directions. Open, unbroken desert. "No mountains, no shelter."

Warrick didn't answer, continuing to search for the slightest irregularity across the spreading paleness. "There!" He stood atop the worm's back and pointed with one outstretched finger. "A small outcropping. Our only chance."

Liet squinted. Already the wind slapped irritating dust in his face. He saw only a tiny fleck of brownish black, a knob of rock like a misplaced boulder jutting out of the sands. "Doesn't look like much."

"It is all we have, my friend." Warrick thrashed with his goad sticks to turn the worm toward the tiny embankment before the Coriolis storm hit.

A flurry of high-velocity grit whipped their faces, scratched at their eyes. They kept their stillsuit plugs firmly pressed into their nostrils and their mouths clamped tight, then pulled hoods forward to cover their faces, but Liet still felt as if the grit penetrated the pores of his skin.

The hoarse wind whispered in his ears and then grew louder, like the breath of a dragon. The increasing electrical fields nauseated him, gave him a pounding headache, which would only decrease if he grounded himself well on the sand. An impossibility out here.

As they approached the tiny cluster of rocks, Liet's heart sank. He could see it now, a mere elbow of hardened lava exposed by scouring winds. Barely the size of a stilltent with rough edges, cracks, and crannies. Certainly not large enough to shelter both of them.

"Warrick, this will not work. We must find another way."

His companion turned to him. "There is no other way."

The sandworm reared and thrashed, resisting the direction Warrick wanted it to take. As they approached their unlikely sanctuary, the storm rose above them as a great brown wall in the sky. Warrick released his hooks. "Now, Liet! We must trust to our boots, and skills . . . and to Shai-Hulud."

Letting go of the ropes, Liet plucked his Maker hooks free and leaped. The worm dove into the sand, tunneling with a vengeance; Liet scrambled off its rough back, jumping away from the wake of soft sand.

The Coriolis storm rushed toward them with a dry, swishing sound, scouring the ground and howling like an angry creature. Liet could no longer differentiate between desert and sky.

Fighting against the wind, they scrambled onto the rock. Only one crevice was deep enough for a man to huddle inside, pull down his cloak, and hope to be shielded from the ravenous blasting sand.

Warrick looked at it, then faced the oncoming storm. He raised his head high. "You must take the shelter, my friend. It is yours."

Liet refused. "Impossible. You're my blood-brother. You have a wife and child. You must go back to them."

Warrick gazed at him with a cold but distant glare. "And

you are the son of Umma Kynes. Your life is worth more than mine. Take the shelter before the storm kills us both."

"I won't let you sacrifice your life for me."

"I won't give you the choice." Warrick turned to step off the rock, but Liet grabbed his arm and yanked him back.

"No! How do Fremen choose in situations like this? How do we decide the best way to preserve water for our tribe? I say your life is worth more because you have a family. You say I'm worth more just because of who my father is. We cannot resolve this in time."

"Then God must choose," Warrick said.

"All right, then." Liet snatched a tally stick from the sash at his side. "And you must abide by the decision." When Warrick frowned, Liet swallowed hard as he added, "And so must I."

They both removed their sticks, turned to the soft dune, shielding the angle of their throw from the blasting wind. The storm beast came closer and louder, a roiling universe of eternal darkness. Warrick threw first, the pointed end of his bone dart embedding itself into the soft surface. *Seven.*

As Liet threw his own bone stick, he thought, if he won, his friend would die. And if he lost, he himself would die. But he could think of no other way.

Warrick strode out to kneel where the sticks had landed. Liet hurried to see. His friend wouldn't cheat, which was anathema to Fremen. But he didn't trust Warrick's watering eyes, which stung from the blowing dust. His tally stick stood at an angle, revealing the mark of *nine.*

"You have won." Warrick turned to him. "You must get inside the shelter, my friend. We have no time to delay, no time to argue."

Liet blinked moisture from his irritated eyes and shuddered. His knees felt weak, ready to collapse in despair. "This can't be. I refuse to accept it."

"You have no choice." Warrick gave him a push toward the rock. "These are the vagaries of nature. You've heard your father talk about it often enough. The environment has its hazards, and you and I . . . we have been unfortunate this day."

"I cannot do this," Liet moaned, digging in his bootheels, but Warrick shoved him violently, knocking him backward onto the rock.

"Go! Don't make me die for nothing!"

Shaking, Liet moved trancelike toward the crack in the rock. "Come in here with me. Together, we can share the shelter. We'll squeeze in."

"Not enough room. Look with your own eyes."

The storm's howling rose to a crescendo. Dust and sand pelted them like bullets. The two shouted at each other though they stood only a few steps apart. "You must take care of Faroula," Warrick said. "If you argue with me and die out here, too, who will watch over her? And my son?"

Knowing he was defeated, knowing there was nothing else he could do, Liet embraced his friend. Then Warrick pushed him down into the crack. Liet squirmed and struggled, trying to squeeze deeper, hoping there might be enough space for Warrick to have partial shelter at least. "Take my cloak! Cover yourself. It might protect you."

"Keep it, Liet. Even you will have a hard time surviving this." Warrick gazed down at him. His cloak and stillsuit whipped about from the angry wind. "Think of it this way—I shall be a sacrifice to Shai-Hulud. My life will perhaps gain a bit of kindness for you."

Liet found himself crushed against the rocks, barely able to move. He could smell the atmospheric electricity from the sand tempest, saw it crackling in the oncoming dustwall. This was the greatest violence that Dune could hurl at them, far worse than anything found on Salusa Secundus, or anywhere else in the universe.

Liet reached up, extending his hand; without a word, Warrick grasped it. Already Liet could feel the harsh abrasives against his skin. The wind tore at him like tiny teeth. He wanted to pull Warrick closer, to give him at least a partial shelter in the crack, but his friend refused; he had already made up his mind that he had no chance.

The gale blew louder, with hissing, shrieking claws. Liet could not keep his eyes open, and tried to shrink farther into the unyielding rock.

In a huge burst of the storm, Warrick's hand was torn from his. Liet tried to surge up, to grab him and pull him back, but the rock held him pinned and the wind slammed him down. He could see nothing except the roiling Coriolis forces. Dust blinded him.

Warrick's scream could not even be heard over the gale.

AFTER HOURS OF enduring hell itself, Liet emerged. His body was covered with powdery dust, his eyes red and barely able to see, his clothes torn from the rocks and the probing fingers of wind. His forehead burned.

He felt sick, sobbed in despair. Around him, the desert looked clear and pristine, renewed. Liet kicked out with his *temag* boots, wanting to destroy all of it in his anger and grief. But then he turned.

Impossibly, he saw the dark figure of a man, a silhouette standing high on a sand dune, a tattered cloak blowing about him. His stillsuit showed gaps where it had been mangled.

Liet froze, wondering if his eyes had deceived him. A mirage? Or had the ghost of his friend returned to haunt him? No, this truly was a man, a living being turned away from him.

Warrick.

Gasping, crying out, Liet staggered across the powdery sand, leaving deep footprints. He climbed, laughing and crying at the same time, unable to believe his eyes. "Warrick!"

The other Fremen stood unmoving. He did not rush to greet his friend, and simply faced away, staring northward toward home.

Liet could not imagine how Warrick had survived. The Coriolis storm destroyed anything in its path—but somehow this man remained standing. Liet cried out again and stumbled to the top of the dune. He regained his balance and rushed to his friend, grasping his arm. "Warrick! You're alive!"

Warrick turned slowly to face him.

The wind and sand had torn away half of his flesh. Warrick's face was scoured off in patches, his cheeks gone to expose long teeth. His eyelids were stripped, leaving a round, blind stare unblinking in the sunlight.

The backs of Warrick's hands revealed exposed bone, and the sinews in his throat moved up and down like pulleys and ropes as he worked his jaw and spoke in a monstrous, garbled voice.

"I have survived, and I have *seen*. But perhaps it would have been better if I had simply died."

If a man can accept his sin, he can live with it. If a man cannot accept personal sin, he suffers unbearable consequences.

> —Meditations from Bifrost Eyrie,
> Buddislamic Text

IN THE MONTHS AFTER THE KIDNAPPING OF HIS INFANT SON, ABULURD HAR-konnen drove himself nearly mad. A broken man, he cut himself off from his world once again. All the servants were dismissed. He and his wife loaded a single ornithopter with only their most important possessions.

Then they burned the main lodge to the ground, reducing all of its memories to embers and smoke. The walls, roof, and support beams blazed brightly. The framework roared and crackled like a funeral pyre into the murky skies of Lankiveil. The large wooden building had been Abulurd and Emmi's home for decades, their place of happiness and warm recollections. But they left without once looking back.

He and Emmi flew across the mountains until they set down in one of the silent mountain cities, a place named Veritas, meaning "truth." Resembling a fortress, the Buddislamic community had been built under a sheltering granite overhang, a shelf of rock that jutted out from the main mountain mass. Over the centuries, monks had deepened the hollow, digging a warren of tunnels and private cells where devoted followers could sit and think.

Abulurd Harkonnen had a good deal to ponder, and the monks accepted him without question.

While not devoutly religious, nor even following the forms

of Buddislam, Abulurd and Emmi spent much time together in silence. They gave one another solace after all the pain and grief. They sought to understand why the universe insisted on striking out at them. But neither of them could find an answer.

Abulurd believed he had a good heart, that he was fundamentally a good person. He tried to do everything right. Yet somehow he found himself in a pit of demons.

One day, he sat in his stone-walled chamber, where the light was dim and flickering, shed by burning candlepots that sent perfumed smoke into the air. Auxiliary thermal heaters hidden in the rock niches warmed the air. He huddled in loose, plain garments, not in prayer but deep in contemplation.

Kneeling beside him, Emmi stroked the sleeve of his tunic. She had been writing poetry, the structured verse found in the Buddislamic sutras, but the words and metaphors were so sharp and painful that Abulurd could not read them without feeling the sting of tears. She set her parchment and calligraphy pens aside, leaving the stanza unfinished.

Now, both stared into the flickering candles. Somewhere in the halls of Veritas, monks were singing, and the vibrations of their chants traveled through the stone. The muffled sounds became hypnotic tones without distinction.

Abulurd thought of his father, a man who had looked much like him, with long hair, a muscular neck, and a lean body. Baron Dmitri Harkonnen had always worn loose-fitting clothes to make himself appear more imposing than he really was. He'd been a hard man, willing to face difficult decisions in order to advance his family fortunes. Each day was an effort to increase the wealth of House Harkonnen, to raise his family's standing in the Landsraad. Receiving the siridar-fief of Arrakis had elevated the stature of the Harkonnen name among the noble families.

Over the millennia since the Battle of Corrin, the Harkonnen bloodline had earned a well-deserved reputation for cruelty—but Dmitri had been less harsh than most of his predecessors. His second wife, Daphne, had softened him a great deal. In later years, Dmitri became a changed man, laughing exuberantly, showing his love for his new wife and spending time with his youngest son, Abulurd. He even cared for severely retarded Marotin, when earlier generations of Harkonnens would have simply slain the infant under the guise of mercy.

Unfortunately, the more affectionate Dmitri became, the harsher his eldest son, Vladimir grew, as if in reaction. Vladimir's mother, Victoria, had done her best to instill a power lust in her son.

We are so different.

Meditating in the stone chamber, focused on the subtle, shifting colors of candle flames, Abulurd did not regret failing to follow in his half-brother's footsteps. He had neither the heart nor the stomach for the deeds that so delighted the Baron.

As he listened to the distant vibrations of the monks' music, Abulurd considered his family tree. He'd never understood why his father had christened him *Abulurd*, a name fraught with scorn and infamy since the aftermath of the Butlerian Jihad. The original Abulurd Harkonnen had been banished for cowardice after the Battle of Corrin, forever disgraced.

It had been the final victory of humans against the thinking machines. At their last stand on the legend-shrouded Bridge of Hrethgir, Abulurd's long-dead namesake had done something to bring down censure from all the victorious parties. It had created the original rift between Harkonnen and Atreides, a blood feud that had lasted for millennia. But details were sketchy, and proof nonexistent.

What did my father know? What did that other Abulurd really do at the Battle of Corrin? What decision did he make at the Bridge?

Perhaps Dmitri had not considered it a matter for shame.

Perhaps the victorious Atreides had merely rewritten history, changed the story after so many centuries in order to blacken the Harkonnen reputation. Since the Great Revolt, myths had collected like barnacles on history, obscuring the truth.

With a shudder, Abulurd drew a deep breath, smelling the candlepot incense inside their tiny room.

Sensing her husband's uneasiness, Emmi stroked the back of his neck. She gave him a bittersweet smile. "It will take some time," she said, "but I think in this holy place we may find some small measure of peace."

Abulurd nodded and swallowed hard.

He clasped Emmi's hand and brought it to his lips, kissing the weathered skin of her knuckles. "I may have been stripped of my wealth and power, dearest. I may have lost both of my sons . . . but I still have you. And you are worth more than all the treasures in the Imperium." He closed his pale blue eyes. "I just wish we could do something to make amends to Lankiveil, to all these people who have suffered so much simply because of who I am."

In anguish he pressed his lips together, and his eyes shimmered with a thin sheen of tears that could not block the images: Glossu Rabban covered with whale blood and blinking in the spotlight at the end of the dock . . . Bifrost Eyrie devastated by Rabban's troops . . . the disbelieving expression on Onir Rautha-Rabban's face just before the guards flung him off the cliff . . . even the poor fishmistress—Abulurd remembered the smell of her burned flesh, the crash of the overturned bucket, water spilled on the hardwood floor, soaked up by the apron of the dead woman as she sprawled in it. The baby crying. . . .

Had it been so long ago that life had been good and peaceful? How many years had it been since he'd gone on a friendly whale hunt with the native fishermen, when they had hunted down an albino whale. . . .

With a start he recalled the artificial iceberg, the illicit and enormous spice stockpile hidden in the arctic waters. A Harkonnen treasure hoard greater than any wealth these people could imagine. That stockpile had been placed right under Abulurd's nose, no doubt by his own half-brother.

Now, in the stone-walled room, he stood up quickly and smiled. Abulurd could not suppress his sheer delight. He looked over at his wife, who couldn't comprehend his excitement.

"I know what we can do, Emmi!" He clapped his hands, thrilled at the prospect. At last he had found a way to make reparations to the hardworking people, whom his own family had so terribly wronged.

ABOARD A CARGO-CARRYING ice-cutter that had filed no trip plan and transmitted no locator signal, Abulurd led a group of Buddislamic monks, a whale fur crew, and his former household servants on an expedition. They cruised through the ice-clogged waters, listening to chunks grind against each other like mortar stones.

A night mist of suspended ice crystals drifted across the waters, diffusing the boats searchlights as the craft forged ahead, seeking the anchorage of the artificial iceberg. Using sounding apparatus and scanners, they searched the waters, mapping out the floating mounds. Once they knew what they were looking for, tracking down the impostor became simple enough.

In the hours before dawn, the craft tied up against the polymer sculpture that looked so much like crystalline ice. The awestruck workers, whalers, and monks crept like trespassers into the corridors that extended beneath the water. Inside, untouched for years, sat container after container of the precious spice melange, covertly removed from Arrakis and hidden here. An Emperor's ransom.

Early in his long reign, Elrood IX had established severe restrictions against illegal stockpiles such as this. If the cache were ever discovered, the Baron would be punished, with an immense fine levied and perhaps the loss of his CHOAM directorship, or forfeiture of the quasi-fief of Arrakis itself.

For a few moments of desperate hope, Abulurd had considered blackmailing his half-brother, demanding the return of his baby boy under threat of revealing the illegal spice stockpile. No longer a Harkonnen, Abulurd had nothing to lose. But he knew that wouldn't work in the long run. No, *this* was the only way to bring some sort of closure, to salvage some good from a nightmare.

Using suspensor pallets and a fire-brigade line, the furtive crew spent hours loading their cargo ship with melange, all the way to the top decks. Though disgraced, Abulurd still retained his title as subdistrict governor. He would send feelers out to his former contacts. He would find smugglers and merchants to help him dispose of this stockpile. It would take months, but Abulurd intended to liquidate it for hard solaris, which he would distribute as he saw fit. To benefit his people.

He and Emmi had considered, but discarded, the idea of spending heavily on a military defense system for Lankiveil. Even with all of this spice, they realized, they could not hope to build anything to oppose the combined might of House Harkonnen. No, they had a better idea in mind.

While sitting alone in the warm closeness of their monastic cell, he and Emmi had developed an elaborate plan. It would be a monumental task to distribute such enormous wealth, but Abulurd had his trusted assistants, and knew he would succeed.

The spice money would be sent through cities and villages, dispersed to hundreds of mountain strongholds and fishing towns. The people would rebuild their Buddislamic temples. They would upgrade old whale fur–processing equipment, widen streets and docks. Every native fisherman would receive a new boat.

The money would be doled out in thousands of small pieces, and it would be completely unrecoverable. The spice stockpile would increase the standard of living for the poor people of this planet—*his* citizens—giving them comforts they'd never imagined possible in their hard lives.

Even when the Baron discovered what his half-brother had done, he could never reclaim the ill-gotten fortune. It would be like trying to recapture the sea with an eyedropper. . . .

As the ice-cutter raced back to the rocky fjord villages, Abulurd stood at the bow, smiling into the frigid mist and shivering with anticipation. He knew how much good he would do with this night's effort.

For the first time in years, Abulurd Harkonnen felt deeply proud.

The capacity to learn is a gift;
The ability to learn is a skill;
The willingness to learn is a choice.

—REBEC OF GINAZ

TODAY, THE SWORDMASTER TRAINEES WOULD LIVE OR DIE BASED ON WHAT they had learned.

Standing beside an assortment of weapons, the legendary Mord Cour conferred in low tones with junior training master Jeh-Wu. The testing field was damp and slick from a light rain earlier that morning. The clouds still hadn't drifted away.

Soon I will be a Swordmaster, both in body and mind, Duncan thought.

Those who passed—survived?—this phase would still face an intense battery of oral examinations covering the history and philosophy of the fighting disciplines they had been studying. Then, the victors would return to the main administration island, view the sacred remains of Jool-Noret, and go back home.

As Swordmasters.

"A tiger on one arm and a dragon on the other," Mord Cour called out. His silvery hair had grown a full ten centimeters since Duncan had last seen him on the barren volcanic island. "Great warriors find a way to overcome any obstacle. Only a truly great warrior can survive the Corridor of Death."

Of the original 150 trainees in the class, only 51 remained—and each failure taught Duncan a lesson. Now he and Hiih Resser, arguably the top students, stood side by side, as they had for years.

"Corridor of Death?" The tip of Resser's left ear had been cut off in a knife-fighting exercise; since he thought the scar made him look like a battle-hardened veteran, the redhead had decided never to undergo any cosmetic surgery to repair the damage.

"Just hyperbole," Duncan said.

"You think so?"

Taking a deep, calm breath, Duncan focused on the comforting presence of the Old Duke's sword in his hand. The pommel's inlaid rope pattern gleamed in sunlight. *A proud blade*. He vowed to be worthy of it, and was glad to carry the sword now.

"After eight years, it's too late to quit," he said.

Enclosed by a shield-fence, the outdoor training course was hidden from the gathered trainees. To survive the obstacles and reach the end of the course they would have to react to assassin meks, solido holo-illusions, booby traps, and more. This would be their final physical test.

"Come forward and choose your weapons," Jeh-Wu called.

Duncan buckled two short knives to his belt, along with the Old Duke's sword. He hefted a heavy mace, but exchanged it for a long battle lance.

Jeh-Wu tossed his dark dreadlocks and stepped forward. Though his voice was hard, it held a hint of compassion. "Some of you might consider this final test cruel, worse than any real combat situation could possibly be. But fighting men must be tempered in a fiery forge of true dangers."

While he waited, Duncan thought of Glossu Rabban, who had showed no mercy hunting human prey on Giedi Prime. Real monsters like the Harkonnens could devise sadistic exercises far worse than anything Jeh-Wu might imagine. He took a deep breath, tried to stop the self-defeating flow of fear, and instead visualized himself *surviving* the ordeal.

"When Ginaz delivers a Swordmaster to a noble House," old Mord Cour continued, "that family depends on him with their lives, their safety, their fortunes. Since you bear this responsibility, no test can be too difficult. Some of you will die today. Do not doubt it. Our obligation is to release only the best fighters in the Imperium. There can be no turning back."

The gates opened. Attendants boomed out names, one at a time, from a list, and several of the trainees stepped through, disappearing behind the solid-front barricade. Resser was among the first to be called.

"Good luck," Resser said. He and Duncan clasped in the half handshake of the Imperium, and then he was summoned. Without looking back, the redhead slipped through the ominous doorway.

Eight years of rigorous training culminated in this moment.

Duncan waited behind other toughened students, some oily with nervous sweat, some blustering with bravado. More trainees passed through the gate. His stomach knotted with anticipation.

"Duncan Idaho!" one of the attendants finally thundered. Through the opening, Duncan could see the previous student evading weapons that came at him from all directions. The young man whirled, dodged, stutter-stepped, then disappeared from view among the obstacles and meks.

"Come on, come on. It's easy," the heavyset attendant growled. "We've already had a couple of survivors today."

Duncan uttered a silent prayer and ran forward into the unknown. The gate slammed shut behind him with an ominous clank.

Focused on what he was doing, letting his mind settle into a fugue state of instant reaction, he heard a blur of voices filling his mind: Paulus Atreides telling him he could accomplish anything he set his mind to; Duke Leto counseling him to take the high ground, the moral course, never to forget compassion; Thufir Hawat telling him to watch all points in a full hemispherical perimeter around his body.

Two meks loomed on either side of the corridor, metal monsters with glittering sensor-eyes that followed his every movement. Duncan began to dash past, then stopped, made a feint, dove and tumbled by.

Watch all points. Whirling, Duncan swung backward with his lance, heard it strike edged metal, deflecting one of the meks' weapons, a thrown spear. *Perfect perimeter*. Warily, he danced forward on the balls of his feet, maintaining balance, ready to dart in any direction.

The words of his school instructors came to him: shaggy-haired Mord Cour, iguana-faced Jeh-Wu, enormously fat Rivvy Dinari, pompous Whitmore Bludd, even stern Jamo Reed, keeper of the prison island.

His tai-chi instructor had been an attractive young woman, her body so flexible that it appeared to be composed entirely of sinew. Her soft voice had a hard edge. "Expect the unexpected." Simple words, but profound.

The fighting machines contained mechanisms triggered by eye-sensors that followed his rapid/cautious movements. But, in compliance with Butlerian strictures, the meks could not think like him. Duncan rammed the metal butt of his lance into one mek, then whirled and did the same to the other. He spun away in a gymnastics maneuver, barely eluding impaler-knives that stabbed at him.

As he crept along, he studied the wooden path under his bare feet, looking for pressure pads. Blood spattered the floorboards; off to the side of the course he saw part of a mangled body; he did not take time to identify it.

Farther ahead, he blinded meks with thrown knives that shattered their glassy eyes. Some he toppled with powerful kicks. Four were only holoprojections, which he detected by noticing subtle differences in light and reflection, a trick Thufir Hawat had taught him.

One of the island instructors had been a mere boy with a baby face and a killer's instincts . . . a ninja warrior who taught stealth methods of assassination and sabotage, the supreme skill of melting into the slightest shadows and striking in absolute silence. "Sometimes the most dramatic statement can be made with an unseen touch," the ninja had said.

Synthesizing eight years of training, Duncan drew parallels between the various disciplines, similarities of method—and differences. Some techniques were clearly useful for what he faced at that moment, and his mind raced to sort them out, selecting appropriate methods for each challenge.

Darting past the last of the deadly meks, his heart pounded against the inside of his chest. Duncan scrambled down the slope to the rugged shore, following course markers, still bounded by the shield-fence. Glowing red suspensors directed him over a frothy blue-white pool of geysers and volcanic hot springs, but waves from the aquamarine sea lapped over the rim of the rocky bowl, cooling the temperature to just below scalding.

Duncan dove in and stroked down to underwater lava tubes bubbling with mineral water. Already desperate for air, he swam through the heated water until he emerged in another steaming hot spring where fierce-looking meks plunged in to attack him.

Duncan fought like a wild animal—until he realized that his mission was to *get through* this Corridor of Death, not to subdue all opponents. He blocked kicks, drove meks back, and broke free to dash along the trail, toward the jungle highlands and the next phase. . . .

Across a deep chasm hung a narrow rope bridge, a difficult challenge of balance, and Duncan knew it would get worse. In the middle of the span, solido-projected holo-beasts appeared, ready to attack him. He slashed out with his lance, battered them with his rigid hands.

But Duncan didn't fall. *A student's worst enemy is his own mind.* Panting, he focused his thoughts. *The challenge is to con-*

trol fear. I must never forget that these are not real adversaries, no matter how solid their blows feel.

He had to use every skill he had learned, assemble the diverse techniques—and survive, just like a real battle. The Ginaz School could teach methods, but no two combat situations were identical. *A warrior's greatest weapons are mental and physical agility, coupled with adaptability.*

Concentrating on the direct route across the chasm, he took one step after another. Using his spear to knock aside the unreal opponents, he reached the opposite end of the rope, sweating and exhausted, ready to drop.

But he pushed on. Toward the end.

Through a short, rocky gorge—the perfect place for an ambush—he sprinted along a planked path, pounding a steady rhythm on it with bare feet. He saw pits and trapdoors. Hearing a burst of gunfire, he rolled and tumbled, then sprang back to his feet. A spear flew at him, but Duncan used his lancc for leverage and vaulted over the obstacle, spinning his body in a blur.

As he landed, a glimmer of motion streaked toward his face. With lightning speed he whipped the lance staff in front of his eyes, felt two sudden, sharp impacts in the wood. A pair of tiny flying meks had embedded themselves in the shaft, like self-motivated arrowheads.

He saw more blood on the deck, and another butchered body lying on the ground. Though he was not supposed to think of fallen comrades, he regretted the loss of even one talented student who had made it through so much training . . . only to fall there, in the last challenge. *So close.*

Sometimes he caught glimpses of Ginaz observers beyond the crackling shield-fence, keeping pace with him, other Swordmasters, many of whom he remembered. Duncan didn't dare permit himself to wonder how his fellow students had fared. He didn't know if Resser was still alive.

So far he had used the knives and the lance, but not the Old Duke's sword, which remained at his side. It was a reassuring presence, as if Paulus Atreides accompanied him in spirit form, whispering advice along the way.

"Any young man with balls as big as yours is a man I must have as part of my household!" the Old Duke had once told him.

With the vanquished meks behind him, blocked on both sides by the shield-fence, Duncan faced the final obstacle—a huge sunken cauldron of burning oil, a vat spanning the path, blocked on both sides by the shield-fence. The end of the Corridor of Death.

He coughed in the acrid smoke, covered his mouth and nose with his shirt fabric, but he still couldn't see. Blinking away irritated tears, he studied the buried cauldron, which looked like a hungry demon's mouth. A narrow rim encircled the vat, slippery with splatters of oil, thick with noxious vapors.

The final obstacle. Duncan would have to pass it somehow.

Behind him, a high metal gate shot up across his path, preventing him from returning the way he had come. It was barbed with shigawire, unclimbable.

I never intended to turn back anyway.

"Never argue with your instincts, boy," Paulus Atreides had counseled him. Based on a gut feeling, the Old Duke had taken the young refugee into his household, despite knowing that Duncan had come from a Harkonnen world.

Duncan wondered if he could possibly vault over the cauldron, but he couldn't see the far side through the shimmering flames and smoke-smeared air. What if the cauldron was not really round, but distorted, to trap a student making assumptions? Tricks within tricks.

Was the vat only a holoprojection? But he felt the heat, coughed in the smoke. He threw his lance, and it clanked against the metal side.

Hearing a heavy ratchet and the rumble of metal plates behind him, he turned to see the huge gate sliding toward him. If he didn't move, the barrier would push him into the cauldron.

Drawing the Old Duke's sword, he swished it through the air. The weapon seemed entirely useless. *Think!*

Expect the unexpected.

He studied the shield-fence on his right, the shimmer of the force field. And remembered his shield-training sessions on Caladan with Thufir Hawat. *The slow blade penetrates the body shield, but it must move at just the right speed, not too fast and not too slow.*

He stroked the Duke's sword in the air for practice. Could he breach the flickering fence and tumble through? If a slow blade penetrated the shield, the energy of the barrier could be moved, changed, shifted. The sharp point of the sword could distort the field, puncture an opening. But how long would a shield remain compromised, if penetrated by a sword? Could he push his body through the temporary opening before the shield closed again?

Behind him, the barbed gate ground closer, nudging him toward the burning cauldron. But he would not go.

Duncan visualized how he would accomplish what he had in mind. His options were limited. He stepped toward the pulsing barrier and stopped where he could smell the ozone and feel the crackle of energy on his skin. He tried to remember one of the prayers his mother had sung to him, before Rabban had murdered her. But he could recall only fragments that made no sense.

Gripping the Old Duke's heavy sword, Duncan leaned into the shield-fence and pierced it as if it were a wall of water, then dragged the blade up, feeling the ripples of the field. It reminded him of gutting a fish.

Then he pushed himself forward, following the sword point, dropping through the resistance—and fell in a wave of dizziness onto a rough surface of black lava. He rolled and landed on his feet, still gripping the sword, ready to fight the Swordmasters if they challenged him for breaking the rules. Suddenly he was safe from the cauldron and the moving gate.

"Excellent! We have another survivor." Frizzy-haired Jamo Reed, released from prison-island duty, rushed up to embrace Duncan in a bearlike hug.

Swordmaster Mord Cour and Jeh-Wu weren't far behind, wearing alien expressions of delight on their faces. Duncan had never seen either of them look so pleased.

"Was that the only way out?" he asked, trying to catch his breath as he looked at Swordmaster Cour.

The old man gave a boisterous laugh. "You found one of twenty-two ways, Idaho."

Another voice intruded. "Do you want to go back and search for the other possibilities?" It was Resser, grinning from ear to scarred ear. Duncan slipped the Old Duke's sword into its scabbard and clapped his friend on the back.

How to define the Kwisatz Haderach? The male who is everywhere simultaneously, the only man who can truly become the greatest human of all of us, mingling masculine and feminine ancestry with inseparable power.

—Bene Gesserit Azhar Book

BENEATH THE IMPERIAL PALACE, IN A NETWORK OF PERIMETER WATER lanes and connected central pools, two women swam in black sealsuits. The younger of the pair stroked slowly, staying back to help the older whenever she faltered. Their impermeable suits, slick as oil and warm as a womb, offered flexibility while modestly covering the chest, midriff, and upper legs.

Despite the fact that some Bene Gesserit women wore common clothing, even exquisite gowns for special occasions such as Imperial balls and gala events, they were counseled to keep their bodies covered on an everyday basis. It helped to foster the mystique that kept the Sisters apart.

"I can't . . . do what . . . I used to," Reverend Mother Lobia wheezed, as Anirul helped her into the largest of seven central pools, a steaming water-oasis, scented with salts and herbs. Not so long ago, Truthsayer Lobia had been able to outswim Anirul quite easily, but now, at more than one hundred seventy years old, her health had been declining. Warm condensation dripped from the arched stone ceiling overhead, like a tropical rain.

"You're doing fine, Reverend Mother." Anirul held the ancient woman's arm and helped her up a stone stairway.

"Don't ever lie to a Truthsayer," Lobia said with a wrinkled

550 — BRIAN HERBERT AND KEVIN J. ANDERSON

smile. Her yellowing eyes danced, but she was gasping for air. "Especially not the Emperor's Truthsayer."

"Surely the Emperor's wife deserves a bit of leniency?"

The old woman chuckled.

Anirul helped her into a flowform chair, handed her a plush karthan-weave towel. Lobia lay back with the towel over her and pressed a button to activate the chair's skin massage. She sighed as the electric fields pulsed her muscles and nerve endings.

"Preparations have been made for my replacement," Lobia said in a sleepy voice, over the hum of the chair. "I've seen the names of the candidates. It will be good to go back to the Mother School, though I doubt I will ever see it again. On Kaitain, the climate is so perfect, but I long for the cold and the damp of Wallach IX. Odd, don't you think?"

Anirul perched on the edge of her chair, seeing the age on the Truthsayer's face, heard the ever-present murmur of crowded lives within herself. As the secret Kwisatz Mother, Anirul lived with a clear and strident presence of Other Memory inside her head. All the lives down the long path of her heritage spoke in her, telling her things that even most Bene Gesserit did not know. Lobia, with all her years, didn't know as much about *age* as Anirul.

I am wise beyond my years. This was not hubris; it was more a sensation of the weight of history and events that she bore with her.

"What will the Emperor do without you around, Reverend Mother? He relies on you to learn who lies and who tells the truth. You're no ordinary Truthsayer, by any historical measure."

Beside her, soothed by the massage cycle, Lobia fell asleep.

As she relaxed, Anirul pondered layers of secrecy within the Sisterhood, the strict compartmentalization of information. The dozing Truthsayer beside her was one of the most powerful women in the Imperium, but even Lobia didn't know the true nature of Anirul's duties—knew very little, in fact, about the Kwisatz Haderach program.

On the other side of the underground pool chambers, Anirul watched her husband, Shaddam, emerge from a steam room, dripping and wrapped in a karthan towel. Before the door closed she saw his companions, two naked concubines from the royal harem. The women had all begun to look alike to her, even with her Bene Gesserit powers of observation.

Shaddam didn't have much of a sexual appetite for Anirul, though she certainly knew techniques to please him. In accordance with the Mother Superior's command, she had recently delivered a fourth daughter to him, Josifa. He had grown more furious with each girl-child, and now he turned to concubines and ignored her. Realizing that Shaddam lived under the ponderous weight of Elrood's long reign, Anirul wondered if her husband dallied with so many concubines because he was trying to compete with his father's ghost. Was he keeping score?

As the Emperor walked pompously from the steam room toward one of the cold pools, he turned away from his wife and dove in with a small splash. Surfacing, he stroked efficiently toward the water lanes. He liked to swim the Palace perimeter at least ten times a day.

She wished Shaddam paid as much attention to running the Imperium as he did to his own diversions. Occasionally Anirul tested him in subtle ways, and found that he knew far less than she did about the interfamilial alliances and manipulations around him. A grave gap in his knowledge. Shaddam had been increasing the ranks of his Sardaukar corps, though not enough, and without any overall plan. He liked to style himself as a soldier and even wore the uniform—but he didn't have the edge, the military vision, or the talent for moving his toy soldiers around the universe in a productive manner.

Hearing a high-pitched squeal, Anirul saw a tiny black

shape in the stone rafters above the waterways. With a fluttering of wings, a distrans bat swooped toward her with yet another message from Wallach IX. The tiny creature had been transported and set free on Kaitain, where it had homed in on her. Old Lobia didn't stir, and Anirul knew Shaddam wouldn't return for at least half an hour. She was alone.

Adjusting her vocal cords, the Kwisatz Mother matched the cry of the bat. It swooped down and landed on her damp, upturned palms. She stared at its ugly muzzle, the sharp teeth, the eyes like tiny black pearls. Focusing her attention, Anirul emitted another squeak, and the bat responded with a staccato chitter, a burst of compact signals encoded on the nervous system of the rodent messenger.

Hearing this, Anirul slowed it down in her mind; even Truthsayer Lobia didn't know the code. The high-pitched tone became a series of clicks and bursts, which she translated and sorted.

It was a report from Mother Superior Harishka, updating her on the culmination of ninety generations of careful genetic planning. Sister Jessica, the secret daughter of Gaius Helen Mohiam and Baron Vladimir Harkonnen, remained unsuccessful in her sacred mission to bear an Atreides daughter. Was she refusing, delaying intentionally? Mohiam had said the young girl was spirited, loyal but occasionally stubborn.

Anirul had expected the next daughter in the genetic path to be conceived by now—the penultimate child who would be mother to their secret weapon. Yet for some time, Jessica had been sleeping with Duke Leto Atreides—but still she had not become pregnant. Intentional on her part? The attractive young woman had tested as fertile, and she was an adept seductress; Duke Leto Atreides had already sired one son.

What is taking her so long?

Not good news. If the long-awaited Harkonnen/Atreides daughter was not born soon, Mother Superior would summon Jessica back to Wallach IX and find out why.

Anirul considered letting the bat fly free, but decided not to risk it. With a clench of her fingers, she broke the creature's fragile neck and disposed of the winged carcass in a matter-recycler behind the pool chamber.

Leaving Lobia to sleep in her massage chair, Anirul hurried back upstairs, into the Palace.

You carve wounds upon my flesh and write there in salt!

—Fremen Lament

DESPITE THE FACT THAT LIET-KYNES HAD NO MEDICINES OTHER THAN A simple first-aid pack in his Fremkit, Warrick survived.

Blinded by grief and guilt, Liet lashed the near-dead man high onto the back of a worm. During the long journey back to the sietch, Liet shared his own water, did his best to repair Warrick's ravaged stillsuit.

Within Red Wall Sietch, there was much wailing and weeping. Faroula, who had considerable skill in the uses of healing herbs, never left her husband's side. She tended him hour after hour as he lay in a blind stupor, clinging to the threads of life.

Though his face was bandaged, Warrick's skin could never regrow. Liet had heard that the genetic wizards of the Bene Tleilax could create new eyes, new limbs, new flesh, but the Fremen would never accept such a healing miracle, not even for one of their own. Already, the sietch elders and fearful children made warding signs near the curtain hangings of Warrick's chambers, as if to fend off an ugly demon.

Heinar, the old one-eyed Naib, came to see his disfigured son-in-law. Kneeling beside her husband's pallet, Faroula looked stricken; her elfin face, once so quick to flash a smile or snap a witty retort, was now drawn; her intense and curious eyes were wide with helplessness. Though Warrick had not died, she wore a yellow nezhoni scarf, the color of mourning.

Proud and grieving, the Naib called a council of sietch elders, at which Liet-Kynes told the stern men exactly what had
happened, giving his testament so that the Fremen could understand and honor the great sacrifice Warrick had made. The
young man should have been considered a hero. Poems should
have been written and honorific songs sung about him. But
Warrick had made one terrible mistake.

He had not died when he should have.

Heinar and the council somberly made preparations for a
Fremen funeral. It was only a matter of time, they said. The
mutilated man could not possibly survive.

Nonetheless, he did.

Covered with salves, Warrick's wounds stopped bleeding.
Faroula fed him, often with Liet looking on, desperately wishing he could do something helpful. But even the son of Umma
Kynes could not perform the miracle his friend needed. Warrick's son Liet-chih, too young to understand, remained in the
care of his mourning grandparents.

Though Warrick looked like a half-rotted carcass, there
was no smell of infection about him, no yellowish suppura-
tion of wounds, no gangrene. In a most curious manner he
was healing, leaving patches of exposed bone. His staring, lidless eyes could never close in a peaceful sleep, though the
night of blindness was always with him.

Standing with Faroula in the midst of her vigil, Liet whispered to his friend, telling stories of Salusa Secundus, recalling
the times the two had raided Harkonnen troops, when they
had acted as bait to kill the enemy scouts who'd poisoned the
wells of Bilar Camp.

Still, Warrick lay unmoving, day after day, hour after hour.

Faroula bowed her head and said in a voice that barely
managed to escape her throat, "What have we done to offend
Shai-Hulud? Why are we punished like this?"

During the heavy silence in which Liet tried to find an answer for her, Warrick stirred on the pallet. Faroula gasped and

took a half step back. Then her husband sat up. His lidless eyes flickered, as if focusing on the far wall.

And he spoke, moving the sinews that held his jaws together. His teeth and his corrugated tongue stirred, forming harsh words.

"I have seen a vision. Now I understand what I must do."

FOR DAYS WARRICK shambled, slow but determined, through the passageways of the sietch. Blinded by the sand, he found his way by touch, seeing with inner mystical eyes. Keeping to the shadows, he looked like a mockery of a corpse. He spoke in a low, papery voice, but his words had a compelling edge.

People wanted to run, but could not tear themselves away as he intoned, "When I was engulfed by the storm, at the moment I should have encountered death, a voice whispered to me from the sand-laden wind. It was Shai-Hulud himself, telling me why I must endure this tribulation."

Faroula, still wearing yellow, tried to drag her husband back to their quarters.

Though the Fremen avoided speaking to him, they were drawn to listen. If ever a man could receive a holy vision, might it not be Warrick, after what he had endured in the maw of a storm? Was it just a coincidence that he had lived through what no other man had ever survived? Or did it prove that Shai-Hulud had plans for him, a thread in a cosmic tapestry? If ever they had seen a man touched by the fiery finger of God, Warrick was such a one.

Staring ahead, he walked compulsively into the chambers where Heinar sat on a mat with the Council of Elders. The Fremen fell silent, unsure how to respond. Warrick stood just inside the chamber doorway.

"You must drown a Maker," he said. "Call the Sayyadina, and have her witness the ceremony of the Water of Life. I must transform it . . . so that I may proceed with my work."

He turned away with his shuffling gait, leaving Heinar and his companions appalled and confused.

No man had ever taken the Water of Life and survived. It was a substance for Sayyadinas, a magical, poisonous concoction that was fatal to anyone not prepared.

Unswerving, Warrick walked into a common chamber where adolescents trampled raw spice in tubs; unmarried women curded melange distillate for the production of plastics and fuel. Against the walls, the *whing* and *slap* of a power loom made a hypnotic rhythm. Other Fremen labored meticulously on stillsuits, repairing and checking the intricate mechanisms.

Solar-powered cookstoves heated a healthy gruel and mash, which the sietch members ate for a light midday meal; larger feasts occurred only after sundown, when dusk had cooled the desert. An old man with a nasal voice sang a sad lament, recounting the centuries of aimless journeys the Zensunni had endured before finally arriving on the desert planet. Liet-Kynes sat listlessly with two of Stilgar's guerrilla fighters, drinking spice coffee.

All activity stopped when Warrick arrived and began to talk. "I have seen a green Dune, a paradise. Even Umma Kynes does not know the grandeur that Shai-Hulud revealed to me." His voice was like a cold wind through an open cave. "I have heard the Voice from the Outer World. I have had a vision of the *Lisan al-Gaib*, for whom we have waited. I have seen the way, as promised by legend, as promised by the Sayyadina."

The Fremen murmured at his audacity. They had heard the prophecy, knew that such a one was foretold. The Sayyadinas had taught it for centuries, and legend had passed from tribe to tribe, generation to generation. The Fremen had waited so long that some were skeptical, but others were convinced—and fearful.

"I must drink the Water of Life. I have seen the path."

Liet led his friend away from the communal chamber, back

to his own rooms, where Faroula sat talking with her father. Looking up at her husband as he entered, her face was drawn with resignation and her eyes red with weeks of grieving. On a carpet nearby, her baby son began to cry.

Seeing Warrick and Liet together, the old Naib turned back to his daughter. "This is as it must be, Faroula," Heinar said. "The elders have decided. It is a tremendous sacrifice, but if . . . if he is *the one*, if he is truly the *Lisan al-Gaib*, we must do as he says. We will give him the Water of Life."

LIET AND FAROULA both tried to talk Warrick out of his obsession, but the scarred man persisted in his belief. He stared with lidless eyes, but could not meet their gaze. "It is my *mashhad* and my *mihna*. My spiritual test and my religious test."

"How do you know it wasn't just strange sounds you heard in the wind?" Liet insisted. "Warrick, how do you know you're not being deceived?"

"Because I *know*." And in the beatific face of his conviction, they had no choice but to believe him.

Old Reverend Mother Ramallo journeyed from a distant sietch to preside over the ceremony, to prepare. Fremen men took their captive small worm, only ten meters in length, and wrestled it down, drowning it in water taken from a qanat. As the worm died and exhaled its poisonous bile, the Fremen gathered the liquid into a flexible jug and prepared it for the ceremony.

In the midst of the commotion, Planetologist Kynes returned from his plantings, but was so focused on his own concerns that he did not grasp the significance of the event, only that it was important. He voiced awkward apologies to his son, expressing sadness over what had happened to Warrick . . . but Liet could see that planet-scale calculations and assessments continued in the back of his mind. His terraforming project could not rest for one moment, not even for the chance that Warrick might be the long-foretold messiah who would unify the Fremen into a fighting force.

The population of Red Wall Sietch gathered in their huge meeting chamber. High above, on the open platform where Heinar addressed his tribe, Warrick stepped forth. The disfigured man was accompanied by the Naib and the powerful Sayyadina who had served these people for several generations. Old Ramallo looked as toughened and hard as a desert lizard who would hold her own against a hunting hawk.

The Sayyadina summoned the watermasters and intoned the ritual words; the Fremen repeated them, but with a greater anxiety than usual. Some truly believed Warrick was everything he claimed to be; others could do no more than hope.

Murmurs filled the chamber. Under normal circumstances, partaking in the tau orgy was a joyous event, celebrated only at times of great import: after a victory against Harkonnens or the discovery of a huge spice deposit or surviving a natural disaster.

This time, though, the Fremen knew what was at stake.

They looked at the mutilated face of Warrick as he stood, impassive and determined. They watched with hope and fear, wondering if he would change their lives . . . or fail horribly, as had other men in generations past.

In the audience Liet stood beside Faroula and her baby, observing from the foremost tiers. Her lips were tight in a tense frown, her eyes closed in fearful anticipation. Liet could sense fear radiating from her, and he wanted to comfort her. Was she afraid that the poison would kill her husband . . . or rather afraid that he might survive and continue his painful daily life?

Sayyadina Ramallo finished her benediction and handed the flask to Warrick. "Let Shai-Hulud judge now if your vision is true—if you are the *Lisan al-Gaib*, whom we have sought for so long."

"I have seen the *Lisan al-Gaib*," Warrick said, then lowered his voice so that only the old woman could hear. "I did not say it was me."

The exposed bones and tendons on Warrick's hands moved as he grasped the flexible nozzle and tilted it toward his lips. Ramallo squeezed the sides of the bag, squirting a gush of poison into Warrick's mouth.

He swallowed convulsively, then swallowed again.

The Fremen audience fell silent, a humming mass of humanity who tried to comprehend. Liet thought he could hear their hearts beating in unison. He experienced the whisper of each indrawn breath, sensed the blood pounding in his own ears. He waited and watched.

"The hawk and the mouse are the same," Warrick said, peering into the future.

Within moments, the Water of Life began to do its work.

ALL OF WARRICK'S previous suffering, all the terrible anguish he had endured in the storm and afterward, were only prelude to the horrific death that awaited him. The poison pervaded the cells of his body, setting them afire.

The Fremen believed that the disfigured man's spiritual vision had deluded him. He raved and thrashed. "They do not know what they have created. Born of water, dies in sand!"

Sayyadina Ramallo stepped back, like a predatory bird seeing prey turn on her. *What does this mean?*

"They think they can control him . . . but they are deluded."

She chose her words carefully, interpreting them through her ancient, half-forgotten filter of the Panoplia Propheticus. "He says he can see where others cannot. He has seen the way."

"*Lisan al-Gaib!* He will be everything we dreamed." Warrick retched so hard that his ribs cracked like kindling. Blood came from his mouth. "But nothing like we expected."

The Sayyadina raised her clawlike hands. "He has seen the *Lisan al-Gaib*. He is coming, and he will be everything we dreamed."

Warrick screamed until he had no more voice to utter a sound, twitched and kicked and thrashed until he had no more muscle control, until his brain was eaten away. The villagers of Bilar Camp had consumed heavily diluted Water of Life, and had still died in terrible agony. For Warrick, even such an insane death would have been a mercy.

"The hawk and the mouse are the same!"

Unable to help him, the Fremen could only watch in appalled dismay. Warrick's death convulsions lasted for hours and hours . . . but Ramallo took far longer to interpret the disturbing visions he had seen.

The stone is heavy and the sand weighty; but a fool's wrath is heavier than them both.

—DUKE LETO ATREIDES

WHEN A GRIM AND UNSETTLED DOMINIC VERNIUS RETURNED TO THE POLAR base on Arrakis, his men rushed to greet him. Seeing the man's expression, though, they knew their leader did not bear welcome news.

Under the bald pate and heavy brow, his eyes were haunted, deep-set in shadowed hollows; his once-bronzed skin had aged prematurely, as if all the color and spirit had been scrubbed from him, leaving him with only an iron will. His last thread of hope had been severed, and now vengeance burned in his gaze.

Bundled in a heavy synfur coat open at the front to reveal his mat of white chest hair, the veteran Asuyo stood on the landing platform, his expression lined with concern. He scratched his bristly shock of hair. "What is it, Dom? What's happened, eh?"

Dominic Vernius just stared at the towering walls of the crevasse that rose like a fortress around him. "I have seen things no Ixian should have to witness. My beloved world is as dead as my wife."

In a daze, he walked from his empty ship into the warren of passages that his men had drilled into the frozen walls. More smugglers greeted him, asked him for tidings . . . but he continued without answering. In confusion, the men whispered.

Aimless, Dominic wandered from one passage to another. He trailed his fingertips along the polymer-sealed walls, imagining the caves of Ix. Coming to a stop, he drew a deep breath, and let his gaze fall half-closed. Through sheer force of will, he tried to summon the glory of House Vernius behind his eyelids, the wonders of the underground city of Vernii, the Grand Palais, the inverted stalactite buildings of crystalline architecture.

Despite centuries of fierce competition from Richese, Ixians had been the undisputed masters of technology and innovation. But in only a few years the Tleilaxu had gutted those accomplishments, closed access to Ix, even driven off the Guild Bank, causing financiers to deal through off-world headquarters of Tleilaxu choosing. . . .

In his prime, during the revolt on Ecaz, Dominic Vernius had given everything for his Emperor. He'd fought and sweated and bled to defend Corrino honor. So long ago, as if in another lifetime . . .

Back then, the Ecazi separatists had seemed to be misguided dreamers, violent yet naive guerrillas who needed to be crushed into submission, lest they set a bad precedent for other uneasy worlds in the galactic Imperium.

Dominic had lost many good men in those struggles. He had buried comrades. He had seen the painful deaths of soldiers who followed his orders into battle. He remembered rushing across the stubbled field of a burned forest beside Johdam's brother, a brave and fast-thinking man. Yelling, weapons pointed ahead, they had fired into the nest of resistance fighters. Johdam's brother had dropped to the ground. Dominic thought he'd tripped on a blackened root, but when he bent to pull the other man to his feet, he found only a smoldering neck stump from a photonic artillery blast. . . .

Dominic had won the battle that day, at the cost of nearly a third of his men. His troops had succeeded in wiping out the Ecazi rebels, and for that, he had received accolades. The fallen soldiers had received mass graves on a planet far from their homes.

The Corrinos did not deserve such sacrifices.

The CHOAM directorship of House Vernius had been expanded because of his great deeds. At the victory celebrations, with a very young Archduke Ecaz seated once again on the Mahogany Throne, he'd been a revered guest on Kaitain. At Elrood's side, Dominic had strolled through halls brimming with crystal, precious metals, and polished woods. He'd sat at feasting tables that seemed to stretch for kilometers, while crowds outside cheered his name. He'd stood proudly below the Golden Lion Throne while the Emperor presented him with the Medal of Valor, and other medals for his lieutenants.

Dominic had emerged as a famous hero from those battles, earning the undying loyalty of his men—as they had shown him for years now, even here in this squalid place. No, the Corrinos deserved none of that.

What are you thinking, Dominic? The voice seemed to whisper in his head, a soft musical tone that was oddly familiar . . . yet nearly forgotten.

Shando. But it could not be. *What are you thinking, Dominic?*

"What I saw on Ix drove away the last vestiges of my fear. It killed my restraint," he said aloud, but in a quiet voice so that no one heard him . . . no one but the ethereal presence of his lovely Lady. "I've decided to do something, my love—something I should have done twenty years ago."

IN THE MONTHS-LONG antarctic day, Dominic did not mark the passage of hours or weeks on his chronometer. Shortly after he returned from Ix, with plans formed like stone sculptures in his mind, he went out alone. Dressed in worker's clothes, he requested an audience with the water merchant, Rondo Tuek.

The smugglers paid handsomely for Tuek's silence every month, and the industrial baron arranged secret connections with the Guild for transport to other worlds. Dominic had never been interested in turning a profit and only stole solaris from the Imperial treasury in order to sabotage the Corrino name, so he'd never regretted paying the bribes. He spent what was necessary to do what he needed to do.

None of the off-worlders at the water-processing factory recognized him, though some gave Dominic disapproving glances when he strode into the complex and insisted on seeing the water merchant.

Tuek recognized him, but did not manage to cover his expression of shock. "It's been years since you've shown your face here."

"I need your help," Dominic said. "I want to purchase more services."

Rondo Tuek smiled, his wide-set eyes glimmering. He scratched the thick tuft of hair on the left side of his head. "Always happy to sell." He gestured to a corridor. "This way, please."

As they rounded a bend, Dominic saw a man approaching. His heavy white parka was open at the front, and he carried a plex-file pack, which he flipped through as he walked. He had his head down.

"Lingar Bewt," Tuek said, his tone bemused. "Watch out or he'll run into you."

Though Dominic tried to avoid him, the man wasn't paying attention and brushed against Dominic anyway. Bewt leaned over to retrieve a dropped plex-file. His face, bland and round, was deeply tanned. He looked soft around the chin and the belly—definitely not military material.

As the preoccupied man hurried on his way, Tuek said,

"Bewt handles all my accounting and shipping. Don't know what I'd do without him."

Inside Tuek's locked personal offices, Dominic barely noticed the treasures, the wall hangings, the artwork.

"I require a transport ship. Unmarked, a heavy hauler. I need to get it on board a Heighliner with no mention of my name."

Tuek folded his splayed hands together and blinked repeatedly. A slight tic in his neck caused his head to twitch from side to side. "You've found a large strike, then? How much spice did you get?" The squat man leaned forward. "I can help you sell it. I have my connections—"

Dominic cut him off. "Not spice. And there's no percentage in it for you. This is a . . . personal matter."

Disappointed, Tuek sat back, his shoulders slumping. "All right, then. For a price—which we can negotiate—I'll find a big hauler. We will provide whatever you require. Let me contact the Guild and arrange for passage aboard the next Heighliner. Where's your final destination?"

Dominic looked away. "Kaitain, of course . . . the den of the Corrinos." Then he blinked and sat up stiffly. "But then, that's none of your business, Tuek."

"No," the water merchant agreed, shaking his head. "None of my business." A troubled expression crossed his face, and he distracted his guest as he shuffled papers and attended to the useless business cluttering his office. "Come back in a week, Dominic, and I will give you all the equipment you need. Shall we establish a price now?"

Dominic turned away, not even looking at him. "Charge me whatever is fair." Then he walked to the door, anxious to get back to his base.

AFTER DOMINIC SUMMONED his men into the largest chamber in his base, he spoke in a somber, cadaverous voice as he described the horrors he had witnessed on Ix. "Long ago when I brought you here, I took you from your homes and your lives, and you agreed to join me. We allied ourselves against the Corrinos."

"With no regrets, Dom," Asuyo interrupted.

Dominic made no acknowledgment, but continued in his droning voice. "We meant to become wolves, but instead we were only gnats." He rested his large hands on the tabletop and drew a long, slow breath. *"That's about to change."*

Without explanation, the renegade Earl left the room. He knew where he had to go and what he had to do. These men could follow him or not. It was their choice, because this was his battle. No one else's. It was well past time to bring an accounting to House Corrino.

He penetrated deep into the cold fortress, down dim corridors where the floors were coated with grit and dust. Few people came there; it had been years since he himself had set foot in the armored storehouses.

Don't do it, Dominic. The whispering voice prickled the back of his head again. A chill ran down his spine. It sounded so much like Shando, his conscience trying to make him reconsider. *Don't do it.*

But the time for any choice in the matter had long since passed. The thousands of years of Corrino rule following the Butlerian Jihad had left a deep scar on the glorious timelines. The Imperial House did not deserve it. At the watershed of the old Empire, that other renegade family—whatever their names had been, whatever their motivations—had not finished the job. Though Salusa Secundus lay destroyed, the other renegades had not done enough.

Dominic would take vengeance one step further.

At the sealed doors of the deepest storage chamber, he keyed in the proper code before slapping his palm against the scanner plate. No one else had access to this vault.

When the doors slid open, he saw the collection of forbidden weaponry, the family atomics that had been House Vernius's last resort, held in reserve for millennia. The Great Convention absolutely forbade the use of such devices, but Dominic no longer cared. He had nothing to lose.

Absolutely nothing.

After the Tleilaxu overthrow, Dominic and his men had retrieved the secret stockpile from a moon in the Ixian system and brought it here. Now, he ran his gaze over the whole array. Sealed in gleaming metal containers were warheads, planet-killers, stone burners, devices that would ignite the atmosphere of a world and transform Kaitain into a tiny, short-lived star.

It was time. First, Dominic would visit his children on Caladan to see them one last time, to say goodbye. Before this he hadn't wanted to risk calling attention to them or incriminating them . . . Rhombur and Kailea had been granted amnesty while he was a hunted fugitive.

But he would do it just this once, with utmost discretion. It was appropriate to do that after all these years. Then he would strike his final blow and become the victor after all. The entire corrupt bloodline of the Corrinos would become extinct.

But the voice of Shando in his conscience was filled with sadness and regret. Despite all they'd been through, she didn't approve. *You always were a stubborn man, Dominic Vernius.*

Innovation and daring create heroes. Mindless adherence to outdated rules creates only politicians.

—VISCOUNT HUNDRO MORITANI

THE EVENING AFTER THE CORRIDOR OF DEATH ORDEAL, THE GATHERED Swordmasters sat in a large dining tent with the 43 surviving members of the original class of 150. These students were now treated as colleagues, finally awarded the respect and camaraderie of fighting men.

But at such a cost . . .

Rich, cold spice beer was served in tall mugs. Off-world hors d'oeuvres lay spread on porcelain dishes. The proud old instructors were congratulatory, wandering among the rugged trainees they had shaped for eight years. Duncan Idaho thought the students' revelry carried a hysterical tinge. Some of the young men sat in shock, moving little, while others drank and ate with wild abandon.

In less than a week they would regroup at the main island's administration building, where they still had to face a final round of oral examinations, a formal checking of the intellectual knowledge they had absorbed from the Swordmasters. But after the murderous obstacle course, answering a few questions seemed anticlimactic.

Released from their pent-up tension, Duncan and Resser drank too much. Over years of rigorous training, they had consumed only meager fare to toughen them up, and they had developed no tolerance for alcohol. The spice beer hit them hard.

Duncan found himself growing maudlin as he remembered the struggles, the pain, and all his fallen schoolmates. *What a waste . . .*

Resser reeled from his triumph, full of celebration. He knew his adoptive father had expected him to fail all along. After separating from his fellow Grumman students and refusing to quit his training, the redhead had won as many psychological battles as physical ones.

Long after the yellow moons had passed overhead, leaving a wake of sparkling stars, the party broke up. The students—bruised, scarred, and drunk—wandered off one at a time, forsaking further revelry to face battles with impending hangovers. Inside the main huts, dishes and glasses were broken; nothing remained to eat or drink.

Hiih Resser walked barefoot with Duncan into the island darkness. They wandered from the big house toward the cluster of lodging huts farther down the broad white beach, their steps uneven on the rough ground.

Duncan clapped a hand on his friend's shoulder in a brotherly gesture, but also to help keep his balance. He couldn't understand how the enormous Swordmaster Rivvy Dinari managed to walk with such grace.

"So, when all this is over, will you come with me to see Duke Leto?" Duncan formed his words carefully. "Remember, House Atreides would welcome two Swordmasters, if Moritani doesn't want you."

"House Moritani doesn't want me, not after Trin Kronos and the others left the school," Resser said. Duncan noted no tears in his friend's eyes.

"Strange," Duncan said. "They could have celebrated with us tonight, but they made their own choices." The pair walked down the slope toward the beach. The sleeping huts seemed very far away, and blurry.

"But I still have to go back there, to face my family, to show them what I accomplished."

"From what I know of Viscount Moritani, that sounds dangerous. Suicidal, even."

"Nevertheless, I still have to do it." In the shadows he turned to face Duncan, and his somber mood slipped away. "Afterward, I'll come to see Duke Atreides."

He and Duncan peered through the darkness, stumbling around as they tried to adjust their eyes. "Where are those huts?" They heard people ahead and a clank of weapons. Warning signals went off in Duncan's fogged mind, but too slowly for him to react.

"Ah there, it's Resser and Idaho." A blazing light stabbed his eyes like luminous ice picks, and he raised his hand to shield against the glare. "Get them!"

Disoriented and surprised, Duncan and Resser bumped into each other as they turned to fight back. A group of unrecognizable, dark-clad warriors fell on them in an ambush, carrying weapons, sticks, clubs. Unarmed, Duncan called upon the skills Ginaz had taught him, defending himself next to his friend. At first he wondered if this was some kind of additional test, a last surprise the Swordmasters had sprung after lulling their students with the celebration.

Then he saw a blade, felt it slash a long shallow wound in his shoulder—and he no longer held back. Resser yelled, not in pain but in anger. Duncan spun with fists and feet, lashing out. He heard an arm crack, felt one of his toenails gouge open a sinewy throat.

But the mob of opponents pounded Duncan's head and shoulders with stunsticks; one attacker struck the base of his skull with an old-fashioned club. With a grunt, Resser tumbled to the soft ground, and four men piled on top of him.

Drunk and maddeningly sluggish, Duncan tried to throw off his attackers to help his comrade, but they struck him at the temples with the stunsticks, flooding his mind with blackness. . . .

———

WHEN HE CAME to consciousness, struggling with a sour gag in his mouth, Duncan saw a seaskimmer beached nearby on the dark shore. Farther out, with no running lights, the shadowy hulk of a much larger boat bobbed in the waves. His captors threw him unceremoniously aboard the skimmer. The limp form of Hiih Resser tumbled beside him.

"Don't try to get free of those shigawire bindings unless you want to lose your arms," a deep voice growled in his ear. He felt the fiber biting into his skin.

Duncan ground his teeth, trying to chew through the gag. On the beach he saw pools of blood, weapons broken and discarded into the rising tide. The attackers carried the wrapped forms of eleven men, obviously dead, onto the narrow skimmer. So, he and Resser had fought well, like true Swordmasters. Perhaps they weren't the only captives.

The shadowy men shoved Duncan into a crowded, stinking lower deck, where he bumped into other bound men on the floorboards, some of his comrades from class. In the darkness he saw fear and rage in their eyes; many were bruised and beaten, the worst injuries patched with rag bandages.

With only a faint groan, Resser awoke beside him. From the glint in his friend's eyes, Duncan knew the redhead had assessed the situation, too. Thinking alike, they rolled together at the bottom of the skimmer, back to back. With numb fingers they worked carefully at each other's bonds, trying to break free. One of the shadowy men uttered a curse and kicked them apart.

At the front of the skimmer, men spoke in low tones with heavy accents. *Grumman accents.* Resser continued to struggle against his bonds, and one of the men kicked him again. The motor started, a low purr, and the small craft got under way, heading out into the waves.

Farther out at sea, the ominous dark boat waited for them.

How easily grief becomes anger, and revenge gains arguments.

—PADISHAH EMPEROR HASSIK III,
Lament for Salusa Secundus

IN A DOME-ROOFED CHAMBER OF HIS RESIDENCY AT ARRAKEEN, HASIMIR
Fenring contemplated a difficult mind-teaser puzzle: a holo-
representation of geometrical shapes, rods, cones, and spheres
that fitted together and balanced perfectly . . . but only when
all of the electropotentials were evenly spaced.

During his youth, he had played similar games in the Imperial Court of Kaitain; Fenring usually won. In those years, he'd
learned much about politics and conflicting powers—learning
more, in fact, than Shaddam ever had. And the Crown Prince
had realized it.

"Hasimir, you're much more valuable to me away from the
Imperial Court," Shaddam had said when sending him away. "I
want you on Arrakis watching over those untrustworthy Harkonnens and making sure my spice revenues are untouched—
at least until the damned Tleilaxu finish their amal research."

Rich yellow sunlight drizzled through the dome windows,
distorted by house shields that diverted the day's heat while
protecting the mansion against possible mob attacks. Fenring
simply couldn't abide the high temperatures on Arrakis.

For eighteen years now, Fenring had built his power base in
Arrakeen. At the Residency, he lived with all the comforts and
pleasures he could wring from this dustbowl. He felt content
enough in his position.

He placed one shimmering puzzle stick above a tetrahedron, almost let go, then adjusted the piece to precisely the correct location.

Willowbrook, the slack-jawed chief of his guard force, chose that moment to stride in and clear his throat, shattering Fenring's concentration. "The water merchant Rondo Tuek has requested an audience with you, my Lord Count."

In disgust, the Count switched off the pulsing puzzle before the separate pieces could tumble across the table. "What does *he* want, hmmm?"

"'Personal business,' he called it. But he stressed that it is important."

Fenring tapped long fingers on the tabletop where the brain-teaser puzzle had glowed moments before. The water merchant had never requested a private audience. *Why would Tuek come here now? He must want something.*

Or he knows something.

Typically, the odd-looking merchant attended banquets and social functions. Knowing the true seat of power on Arrakis, he provided Fenring's household with extravagant amounts of water, more than the Harkonnen overlords received in Carthag.

"Ahhh, he's aroused my curiosity. Send him in, and see that we're not disturbed for fifteen minutes." The Count pursed his lips. "Hmmm-mm, after that, I'll decide whether or not I want you to take him away."

Moments later, the lumpy-shouldered Tuek entered the domed chamber with a rolling gait, swinging his arms as he walked. He swiped a hand across his rusty-gray hair, smoothing it into place with sweat, then bowed. The man looked flushed from ascending so many stairs; Fenring smiled, approving of Willowbrook's decision to make him climb rather than offering the private lift that would have brought him directly to this level.

Fenring remained at his table, but did not motion for the

visitor to sit; the water merchant stood in his formal silver robe, wearing a gaudy necklace of dust-pitted platinum links around his throat, no doubt sandstorm-scoured in a rough attempt at Arrakis art.

"Do you have something for me?" Fenring inquired, flaring his nostrils. "Or do you wish something *from* me. hmmm-ah?"

"I can provide you with a name, Count Fenring," Tuek said without prettying his words. "As for what I wish in return—" He shrugged his lumpy shoulders. "I expect you will pay me as you see fit."

"So long as our expectations are commensurate. What is this name . . . and why should I care?"

Tuek leaned forward like a tree about to fall. "It's a name you haven't heard in years. I suspect you'll find it interesting. I know the Emperor will."

Fenring waited, but not patiently. Finally, Tuek continued. "The man has kept a low profile on Arrakis, even as he does his best to disrupt your activities here. He wishes revenge on the entire Imperial House, though his original quarrel was with Elrood IX."

"Oh, everyone had a quarrel with Elrood," Fenring said. "He was a hateful old vulture. Who *is* this man?"

"Dominic Vernius," Tuek replied.

Fenring sat straight up, his bright, overlarge eyes widening further. "The Earl of Ix? I thought he was dead."

"Your bounty hunters and Sardaukar never caught him. He has been hiding here on Arrakis, with a few other smugglers. I do a little business with them now and then."

Fenring sniffed. "You didn't inform me immediately? How long have you known?"

"My Lord Fenring," Tuek said, sounding overly reasonable, "Elrood signed the vendetta papers against the renegade House, and he's been dead for many years. As far as I could tell, Dominic seemed to be causing no harm. He'd already lost everything . . . and other problems demanded my attention."

The water merchant took a deep breath. "Now, however, matters have changed. I feel it's my duty to inform you, because I know you have the Emperor's ear."

"And what exactly has changed, hmmm?" In the back of Fenring's mind, wheels were turning. House Vernius had disappeared long ago. Lady Shando had been killed by Sardaukar hunters. Exiled on Caladan, the Vernius children were considered no threat.

But an angry and vengeful Dominic Vernius could cause damage, especially so close to the precious spice sands. Fenring had to ponder this.

"Earl Vernius requested a heavy transport. He seemed . . . extremely disturbed, and may be planning a strike of some sort. In my opinion, this might mean an assassination plot against the Emperor. That was when I knew I had to come to you."

Fenring raised his eyebrows, wrinkling his forehead. "Because you thought *I* would pay you a greater reward than Dominic's bribes add up to?"

Tuek spread his hands and responded with a deprecating smile, but did not deny the accusation. Fenring respected the man for that. Now at least everyone's motivations were clear.

He ran a finger along his thin lips, still pondering. "Very well, Tuek. Tell me where to find the renegade Earl's hiding place. Explicit details, please. And before you depart, see my exchequer. Make a list of everything you require, every desire or reward you could imagine—and then I'll choose. I'll grant you whatever I believe your information was worth."

Tuek didn't quibble, but bowed. "Thank you, Count Fenring. I am pleased to be of service."

After providing the known details of the smugglers' antarctic facility, Tuek backed toward the door just as Willowbrook reentered, precisely at the end of fifteen minutes.

"Willowbrook, take my friend to our treasure rooms. He

knows what to do, hmmm? For the rest of the afternoon, leave me in peace. I have much thinking to occupy me."

After the men departed and the door to the chamber slid shut, Fenring paced, humming to himself, alternately smiling and frowning. Finally, he switched on his brain-teaser puzzle again. It would help him relax so that he could focus his thoughts.

Fenring enjoyed plots within plots, spinning wheels concealed within wheels. Dominic Vernius was an intelligent adversary, and most resourceful. He had eluded Imperial detection for years, and Fenring thought it would be most satisfying to let the renegade Earl have a hand in his own destruction.

Count Fenring would keep his eyes open, extending the spiderweb, but he would let Vernius make the next move. As soon as the renegade had everything in place for his own plans, then Fenring would strike.

He would enjoy giving the outlaw nobleman just enough rope to hang himself. . . .

Paradise on my right, Hell on my left, and the Angel of Death behind me.

—Fremen Conundrum

TRUE TO HIS WORD, THE WATER MERCHANT OBTAINED AN UNMARKED hauler for Dominic Vernius. Absent-minded Lingar Bewt piloted it from Carthag to the antarctic ice-mining facility and, with a sheepish smile, handed over the control card for the ship. Dominic, accompanied by his lieutenant Johdam, flew the battered craft back toward the secret landing field in the crevasse. The former Earl of Ix remained silent for most of the journey.

The heavy hauler was old and made strange groaning sounds as it cruised low through the atmosphere. With a curse, Johdam slapped the control panels. "Damned slug. Probably won't function for more than a year, Dom. It's junk."

Dominic gave him a distant look. "It'll be good enough, Johdam." Years ago, he'd been there when Johdam's face was burned by a backlash flame. Then the veteran had saved Dominic's life during the first abortive raid on Ix, hauling him from the line of Sardaukar fire. Johdam's loyalty would never flag, but now it was time for Dominic to set him free, to give the man back his life.

When Johdam's skin flushed with anger, the burn-scar tissue looked pale and waxy. "Have you heard how many solaris Tuek charged us for this wreckage? If we'd had equipment like this on Ecaz, the rebels could have beaten us by throwing rocks."

They had broken Imperial law together for years—but Dominic had to do the rest alone. He felt oddly content with his decision and kept his voice even and calm. "Rondo Tuek knows we will no longer pay him our usual bribes. He wants to make as much profit as he can."

"But he's cheating you, Dom!"

"Listen to me." He leaned close to his lieutenant in the adjacent seat. The heavy hauler vibrated as it came in for a landing. "It does not matter. Nothing matters. I just need enough . . . to do what I must do."

Sweat glistened on Johdam's scarred face as the craft came to a stop at the bottom of the crevasse. The lieutenant moved with tight, jerky gestures as he stomped down the landing ramp. Dominic could see the uncertainty and helplessness in the man's face. He knew Johdam was not furious merely with what the water merchant had done, but also at what Dominic Vernius planned to do. . . .

Dominic longed to liberate Ix and his people, doing something positive to make up for all the wrongs that had been done by the Tleilaxu invaders and their Sardaukar allies. But he could not accomplish that. Not now.

In his power he had only the capability for destruction.

The former Ixian Ambassador, Cammar Pilru, had made repeated pleas to the Landsraad, but by now the man had merely become a tiresome joke. Even Rhombur's efforts— probably made with secret Atreides support—had amounted to nothing. The problem had to be destroyed at its heart.

Dominic Vernius, former Earl of Ix, would send a message that the entire Imperium would never forget.

AFTER MAKING HIS decision, Dominic had taken his men deep into the fortress and opened the storage vault. Staring at the stored atomics, the smugglers froze; they had all dreaded this day. They'd served with the renegade Earl long enough that they needed no detailed explanations. The men stood inside the cold corridors, leaning against the polymer-lined walls.

"I will go to Caladan first, then alone to Kaitain," Dominic had announced. "I have written a message for my children, and I mean to see them again. It has been far too long, and I must do this thing." He looked at each one of the smugglers in turn. "You men are free to do as you wish. I suggest you liquidate our stockpiles and abandon this base. Go back to Gurney Halleck on Salusa, or just return to your families. Change your names, erase all records of what we did here. If I succeed, there will no longer be a reason for our band to exist."

"And the whole Landsraad will be out for our blood," Johdam growled.

Asuyo tried to talk Dominic out of it, using a military tone, an officer reasoning with his commander—but he would not listen. Earl Vernius had nothing to lose, and a great deal of vengeance to gain. Perhaps if he obliterated the last of the Corrinos, his own ghost and Shando's could rest peacefully.

"Load these weapons on board the cargo hauler," he said. "I will pilot it myself. A Guild Heighliner arrives in two days." He gazed at them all, his expression flat and emotionless.

Some of the men wore stricken looks. Tears welled in their eyes, but they knew better than to argue with the man who had commanded them in countless battles, the man who had once run all the industries on Ix.

Without friendly banter or conversation, the men took suspensor grapples and began to drag out the atomics, one load at a time. They did not move with haste, dreading the completion of their task.

Without eating or drinking, Dominic observed the progress all day long. Metal-encased warheads were carried out on pallets and then guided through tunnels to the crevasse landing field.

He daydreamed about seeing Rhombur and talking with

him about leadership; he wanted to hear Kailea's aspirations. It would be so good to see them both again. He tried to imagine what his children looked like now, their faces, how tall they were. Did they have families of their own, his grandchildren? Had it really been more than twenty years since he'd seen his son and daughter, since the fall of Ix?

There would be some risk, but Dominic had to take the chance. They would want him to do it. Every precaution would be taken. He knew how difficult this would be emotionally, and he promised himself he would be strong. If Rhombur found out what he was up to—should he tell his son?—the Prince would want to join the effort and fight in the name of Ix. What would Kailea's reaction be? Would she try to talk her brother out of going? Probably.

Dominic decided it would be best not to reveal his plans to his children, for that could only cause problems. Best to see his son and daughter without telling them anything.

There might be one more child, too, whom Dominic wished he could locate. His beloved Shando had given birth to a son out of wedlock before marrying Dominic. The child, borne secretly when she was a concubine in the Imperial Palace, had been Elrood Corrino's, but had been taken away from her shortly after its birth. In her position, Shando had not been able to keep her son and, despite her persistent requests for information, she never learned what had happened to him. He just disappeared.

UNABLE TO BEAR watching the preparations, Asuyo and Johdam worked at transferring the treasury reserve and supplies into the hands of the men. Old Asuyo had made a point of removing his medals and rank insignia, throwing them on the ground. Everyone would have to depart from the base at once and scatter to the far corners of the Imperium.

Muttering to himself, Johdam inventoried the stockpile of

spice they had collected, and with two other men, led an expedition back to the water merchant's industrial facility. There, they intended to convert the remaining merchandise into liquid credit, which they would use to buy passage, identities, and homes for themselves.

In his final hours, Dominic removed possessions from his quarters, giving away meaningless treasures, keeping only a few things he wanted at his side. The holo-portraits of Shando and keepsakes of his children meant more to him than any wealth. He would give them back to Rhombur and Kailea, so they had some memento of their parents.

Smelling the cold brittleness inside what had been his home for so many years, Dominic noticed details he hadn't seen since building the fortress. He studied cracks in the wall, uneven lumps on the floor and ceiling . . . but he felt only failure and emptiness inside. He knew of only one way to fill that void—with blood. He would make the Corrinos pay.

Then his children, and the people of Ix, would be proud of him.

When all but three hover-warheads and a pair of stone burners had been moved aboard the heavy hauler, Dominic walked out into the wan antarctic sunshine, a slice of light that carved into the deep fissure. He had planned every step of his attack on the Imperial capital. It would be a complete surprise—Shaddam wouldn't even have time to hide under the Golden Lion Throne. Dominic would make no grandiose speeches, would not revel in his triumph. No one would know of his arrival. Until the end.

Elrood IX was already dead, and the new Padishah Emperor had only a Bene Gesserit wife and four young daughters. It would not be difficult to exterminate the Corrino bloodline. Dominic Vernius would sacrifice his life to destroy the Imperial House that had ruled for thousands of years, since the Battle of Corrin—and he would call it a bargain.

He drew a deep breath into his barrel chest. He turned his head, looking up the sheer canyon walls of the fissure, saw Johdam's shuttle land, returning from his errand at Tuek's water factory. He didn't know how long he stood like a statue as his men moved around him, taking inventory of the atomic stockpile.

A voice startled him out of his concentration. Johdam rushed red-faced toward him, his parka hood tossed back. "We've been betrayed, Dom! I went to the water merchant's facility—and it's abandoned. All the off-worlders are gone. The factory is closed down. They packed up and left in a hurry."

Panting, Asuyo added, "They don't want to be around, sir, because *something is going to happen*." His entire demeanor had changed: even without his medals, Asuyo looked like a military officer again, ready for a bloody engagement.

Some of the smugglers cried out in rage. Dominic's expression turned stony and grim. He should have expected this. After all the years of cooperation and assistance, Rondo Tuek could still not be trusted.

"Gather what you can. Go to Arsunt or Carthag or Arrakeen, but leave before the end of the day. Change your identities." Dominic gestured toward the old heavy hauler. "I want to get the last warheads and take off. I still intend to go about my mission. My children are waiting for me."

LESS THAN AN hour later, during the final preparations for evacuation and departure, the military ships arrived—an entire wing of Sardaukar in attack 'thopters, cruising low. They dropped concussion bombs that fractured the frozen walls. Wide lasgun beams flashed the cliffs into steam and dust, liberating the ice in the matrix and sending boulders tumbling down into melted craters.

The Sardaukar vessels tilted their wings to dive like predatory fish into the chasm. They dropped more explosives, destroying four transport ships parked on the loose gravel.

Determined, Asuyo rushed to their nearest 'thopter and leaped inside. He fired up the jet engines, as if already confident of receiving another medal for bravery. As he rocketed upward, the 'thopter's weapon turrets brightened. Asuyo spared a few breaths over the comsystem to curse Tuek's treachery and the Sardaukar, too. Before he could get off a shot, though, two Imperial ships blew him into a smudge of fire and greasy smoke in the sky.

Troop carriers landed on the flat ground, and armed fighting men surged out like maddened insects, carrying hand weapons and knives.

With precise accuracy, Sardaukar forces turned the engine pods of Dominic's loaded heavy hauler to slag. The family atomics—suspected by the Sardaukar to be aboard—were now stranded. The banished Earl could never take off, never reach Kaitain. And seeing the swarm of Imperial troops, Dominic knew that he and his smuggler band would never get away.

Bellowing like a military commander again, Johdam led his final charge. The men ran recklessly, firing mismatched weapons into the oncoming Sardaukar troops. Using knives or bare hands, the Emperor's fighters slew every smuggler they encountered. To them, this activity was little more than practice, and they seemed to be doing it for the sheer enjoyment.

Johdam retreated with his few surviving men back to the tunnels where they could barricade themselves and defend. In a frightening flash of déjà vu from the Ecazi rebellion, Dominic watched a Sardaukar las-blast take off Johdam's head, just like his brother's. . . .

Dominic had only one chance. It would not be the victory he had anticipated, and Rhombur and Kailea would never know about it . . . but given the alternative of total failure, he chose another desperate measure. He and his men were going to die anyway.

For honor, he wanted to stay beside his troops, to fight to the death with each one of them—in what would ultimately be a futile gesture. They knew it, and so did he. The Sardaukar were representatives of the Emperor—giving Dominic Vernius the opportunity to strike a deadly, symbolic blow. For Ix, for his children, for himself.

As concentrated fire began to bring down the walls of the chasm in mounds of slumping mud and stone, Dominic ducked inside the base. Some of his men followed, trusting him to lead them to shelter. Silent and grim, he offered no reassurances.

The Sardaukar penetrated the facility, advancing in attack formation through the passages, cutting down anyone they saw. They had no need to take captives for interrogation.

Dominic retreated into the inner passageways, down toward the vault. It was a dead-end corridor. The frightened men behind him now understood what he meant to do.

"We'll hold them as long as we can, Dom," one man promised. He and a partner took up positions on either side of the corridor, their meager weapons drawn and ready. "We'll give you enough time."

Dominic paused for just a moment. "Thank you. I won't let you down."

"You never have, sir. We all knew the risks when we joined you."

He reached the open door to the armored storage chamber just as a loud explosion rang out behind him. The walls collapsed, breaking through the polymer sheath and sealing him and his men down there. But he had never intended to leave anyway.

The Sardaukar would cut their way through the barrier within minutes. They had smelled the blood of Dominic Vernius and would not stop until they had him in their hands.

He allowed himself a mirthless smile. Shaddam's men were in for a surprise.

Dominic used the palm lock to seal the vault doors, even as he saw the collapsed barricade glowing with inner heat. Solid walls muffled the sounds behind him.

Shielded by the heavy vault door, Dominic turned to look at the remaining items in his atomic stockpile. He chose one of the stone burners, a smaller weapon whose yield could be calibrated to destroy an entire planet, or just wreak havoc in a specified area.

The Sardaukar began hammering on the thick door as he removed the stone burner from its case and studied the controls. He never thought he'd need to understand these weapons. They were meant as doomsday devices, never to be used—whose mere existence should have been a sufficient deterrent against overt aggression. Under the Great Convention, any use of atomics would bring down the combined military forces of the Landsraad to destroy the offending family.

The men out in the corridor were already dead. Dominic had nothing left to lose.

He tamped down the fuel consumption of the stone burner and set the activation mechanism to vaporize only the vicinity of the base. No need to wipe out all the innocents on Arrakis.

That was the sort of thing only a Corrino would do.

He felt like an ancient sea captain going down with his ship. Dominic harbored only one regret: that he hadn't had a chance to say his farewells to Rhombur and Kailea after all, to tell them how much he loved them. They would have to carry on without him.

Through a blur of tears, he thought he saw a shimmering image of Shando again, her ghost . . . or just his wishful desires. She moved her mouth, but he couldn't tell if she was scolding him for his recklessness—or welcoming him to join her.

The Sardaukar cut their way through the frozen wall itself, bypassing the thick door. As they entered the vault, smug and victorious, Dominic did not fire at them. He simply looked down at the scant remaining time on the stone burner.

The Sardaukar saw it, too.

Then everything turned white-hot.

If God wishes thee to perish, He causes thy steps to lead thee to the place of thy demise.

—Cant of the Shariat

OF ALL THE COVERT ATTEMPTS C'TAIR PILRU HAD MADE DURING TWENTY years as a guerrilla fighter on Ix, he had never dared to disguise himself as one of the Tleilaxu Masters. Until now.

Desperate and alone, he could think of nothing else to do. Miral Alechem had vanished. The other rebels were dead, and he had lost all contact with his outside supporters, the smugglers, the transport officials willing to accept bribes. Young women continued to disappear, and the Tleilaxu operated with complete impunity.

He hated them all.

With cold calculation, C'tair waited in a deserted corridor up in the office levels and killed the tallest robed Master he could find. He preferred not to resort to murder to achieve his aims, but he did not shrink from it, either. Some actions were necessary.

Compared to the blood on the hands of the Tleilaxu, his heart and conscience remained clean.

He stole the gnomish man's clothes and identity cards and prepared to discover the secret of the Bene Tleilax research pavilion. Why was Ix so important that the Emperor would send his Sardaukar here to support the invaders? Where had all the captive women been taken? It had to be more than simple politics, more than the petty revenge of Shaddam's father against Earl Vernius.

The answer must lie within the high-security laboratory.

Miral had long suspected an illegal biological project, one that operated with covert Imperial support—perhaps even something that went against the strictures of the Butlerian Jihad. Why else would the Corrinos be willing to risk so much, for so long? Why else had they invested so heavily here, while overall Ixian profits diminished?

Determined to discover the answers, he donned the robes of the slain Tleilaxu Master, shifting the folds and cinching the maroon sash to hide the dark stain of drying blood. Then he disposed of the body, dumping it into the reopened field-lined shafts to the molten core of the planet. Where the garbage was supposed to go.

In a secret storeroom, he applied chemicals to his face and hands to leach the remaining color from his already-pale flesh, and smeared wrinkling substances on his face to give himself the gray-skinned, shriveled appearance of a Tleilaxu overlord. He wore thin-soled slippers to keep his height down, and hunched over a little. He wasn't a large man, and he was aided by the fact that the Tleilaxu were not the most observant of people. C'tair needed to be most wary of the Sardaukar.

He checked his records, memorizing the passwords and override commands he had hoarded for years. His identity cards and signal jammers should be sufficient to get him past any scrutiny. *Even there.*

Taking on a hauteur to complete his masquerade, he emerged from his hidden chamber into the expansive grotto. He strode to the front of a crowd and stepped aboard a linked transport. After slipping his card through the scanner port, he punched in the location for the sealed research pavilion.

The private bubble closed around him and detached itself from the rest of the transport system. The vessel cruised in midair above the crisscrossed paths of surveillance pods. None of the transeyes turned toward him. The transport bubble recognized his right to travel to the laboratory complex. No alarms were raised. No one paid attention to him.

Below, workers moved about in their labors, guarded by an increasing number of Sardaukar. They did not bother to look up at the vessels drifting across the enclosed grotto sky.

One step at a time, C'tair passed through successive guarded gates and security fields, and finally into the hivelike industrial mass. The windows were sealed, the corridors glowing with an orange-tinged light. The stuffy air was warm and humid, with a putrid undertone of rotting flesh and unpleasant human residue.

Huddled in his disguise, he walked along, trying to conceal the fact he was lost and uncertain of his destination. C'tair didn't know where the answers might lie, but he dared not hesitate or look confused. He didn't want anyone to take notice of him.

Robed Tleilaxu moved from chamber to chamber, absorbed in their work. They pulled hoods over their ears and heads, so C'tair did the same, glad for the added camouflage. He withdrew a sheaf of ridulian-crystal reports written in a strange code that he could not decipher, and pretended to study them.

He turned down corridors at random, changing course whenever he heard other people approaching. Several gnomish men marched past him, speaking to each other in heated voices in their private Tleilaxu language, gesturing with long-fingered hands. They paid no attention to C'tair.

He located biological laboratories, research facilities with plazchrome-plated tables and surgical scanners—visible through open doorways that seemed to be protected by special scanning devices that he didn't want to try to penetrate. Nothing, however, provided him with the answers he needed.

Breathing hard and sweating with tension, he followed main corridors that led toward the heart of the research pavilion.

Finally, C'tair found a higher level, an open-windowed observation gallery. The corridor behind him was empty. The air smelled metallic with chemicals and disinfectants, a scrubbed, sterile environment.

And a faint but distinct odor reminiscent of *cinnamon*.

He peered through the broad window into the huge central gallery of the laboratory complex. The vast chamber was large enough to be a spacecraft hangar, holding tables and coffin-sized containers . . . row upon row of "specimens." He stared in horror at the pipes and sample tubes, at all the bodies. All the *women*.

Even knowing how vile the Tleilaxu were, never before had he imagined such a nightmarish reality. The shock dried his unshed tears to a stinging acid. His mouth opened and closed, but he could form no words. He wanted to vomit.

In the gigantic complex below he saw at last what the Tleilaxu criminals were actually doing to the women of Ix. And *one of them, barely recognizable, was Miral Alechem!*

Staggering with revulsion, he tore himself away. He had to escape. The sheer weight of what he'd seen threatened to crush him. It was impossible, impossible, *impossible*! His stomach knotted, threatening to double him over—yet he dared not show any weakness.

Unexpectedly, a guard and two Tleilaxu researchers rounded the corner and came toward him. One of the researchers said something in an unrecognizable guttural language. C'tair didn't respond. He staggered away.

Alarmed, the guard shouted after him. C'tair stumbled down a side corridor. He heard an outcry, and his need for survival burned away his stunned malaise. After penetrating this far, he had to get out. No other outsider suspected what he had now seen with his own eyes.

The truth was far worse than anything he could have imagined.

Bewildered and desperate, C'tair worked his way back to the lower levels, aiming for the external security grids. Behind him, guards rushed toward the observation galleries he had just left behind, but the Tleilaxu had not yet sounded an all-out alarm. Perhaps they didn't want to disrupt their daily routine . . . or maybe they simply couldn't believe that one of the foolish Ixian slaves had managed to penetrate their tightest security.

The research pavilion wing he had destroyed with wafer-bombs three years ago had been entirely rebuilt, but the self-guiding supply rail had been moved to a different portal. He raced over there, hoping to slip through lighter security.

Summoning a transport bubble, he climbed inside, using his stolen identity card and brusquely dismissing one of the guards who tried to question him. Then C'tair drifted away from the security installation toward the nearest work complex, where he could shuck his disguise and melt in among the other laborers again.

Before long, he heard a strident alarm raised behind him, but by now he had escaped the compound and the Tleilaxu secret police. He alone carried a hint of what the invaders were actually doing, why they had come to Ix.

The knowledge did not comfort him, though. Now he felt a despair deeper than any he had experienced since beginning his fight.

Treachery and quick-thinking will defeat hard-and-fast rules any day. Why should we be afraid to seize the opportunities we see?

—VISCOUNT HUNDRO MORITANI,
Response to Landsraad Court Summons

ON THE HEAVING DECK OF THE UNMARKED BOAT, A WILD-EYED GIANT GAZED down on his captives. "Look at the would-be Swordmasters!" He laughed hard enough that they could smell his reeking breath. "Weaklings and cowards, pampered by rules. Against a few stunsticks and a squad of half-trained soldiers, what good are you?"

Duncan stood on deck next to Hiih Resser and four other Ginaz students, nursing cuts and bruises, not to mention skull-splitting hangovers. They had been released from their shigawire bindings, but a squad of heavily armed soldiers in yellow Moritani livery waited nearby, holding an assortment of weapons. Overhead, the knotted gray sky brought darkness a full hour before its time.

The deck of the dark boat was wide and clear, like a practice floor, but slick with spray from drizzle and whitecaps that washed over the rails. The Swordmaster trainees kept their balance, as if this were just another exercise, while their Grumman captors held on to stay-ropes and support rails; some of them looked a bit seasick. Duncan, though, had lived for a dozen years on Caladan, and he felt completely comfortable on a boat. Loose equipment had been tied down in the rough seas. He saw nothing nearby that could provide a weapon for the prisoners.

The ominous boat headed out through the channels of the archipelago. Duncan wondered how even Grummans dared to do such a thing. But House Moritani had already flouted the rules of kanly and launched inexcusably vicious attacks on Ecaz. After the Ginaz School had expelled the Grumman students in disgrace, no doubt their anger had been stoked. As the only one to remain behind, Hiih Resser would face worse treatment than any of his companions. Looking at the redhead's bruised and swollen face, Duncan could see that Resser understood as much.

Standing before them, the huge man had a braided black beard from cheekbones to chin, dark hair that cascaded over broad shoulders. Teardrop fire-jewels dangled from his ears. Entwined into his beard were bright green extrusions like small branches; the ends were lit in slow-burning embers so that foul gray smoke curled around his face. Two shiny maula pistols were tucked into his waistband. He had identified himself only as Grieu.

"What good has all this uppity training done for you? You get drunk, you get complacent, and you stop being supermen. I'm glad my son pulled out early, without wasting any more time."

Another wiry young man in a yellow Moritani tunic stepped out of the main cabins. With a sinking heart, Duncan recognized Trin Kronos as he took his place beside the black-bearded man. "We came back to help you celebrate the completion of your training, and to show you that not everyone needs eight years to become adept at fighting."

With his beard smoldering, Grieu said, "So, let's see how well you fight. My people need a little practice."

The Moritani-uniformed men and women moved with an animal grace. They carried swords, knives, spears, crossbows, even pistols. Some wore martial-arts outfits, others wore the more fanciful garb of Terran musketeers or swashbuckling pirates, as if in mockery of the Ginaz training islands. As another joke, they tossed two blunt wooden swords to the captives; Resser caught one, and Klaen, a musically inclined student from Chusuk, caught the other. The toys were laughably inadequate against maula pistols, flèchette guns, and arrows.

At a signal from the hirsute Grieu, Trin Kronos stepped in front of the battered Ginaz students and raked his deprecating gaze over them. He paused in front of Resser, then Duncan, and finally moved on to the next student, Iss Opru, a dark-skinned native of Al-Dhanab. "This one first. As a warmup."

Grieu grunted in approval. Kronos shoved Opru out of line, to the center of the deck. The other fighters stood tense and waiting.

"Get me a sword," Kronos said, without looking over his shoulder. His eyes remained locked with Opru's. Duncan saw that the student had automatically crouched in a perfect fighting stance, ready to react. The Grummans clearly felt they had all the advantages.

Once he held the long blade, Trin Kronos provoked the dark-skinned captive, waving its sharp point in his face, swishing it expertly across the top of his head so that hairs were sliced away. "What are you going to do about this, sword-boy? I've got a weapon, and you don't."

Opru did not flinch. "I *am* a weapon."

As Kronos continued to advance and taunt, Opru suddenly ducked under the blade and chopped the edge of his hand against his opponent's wrist; the sneering young man cried out and dropped his weapon. With a fluid motion, Opru snatched the pommel before the sword hit the floor, rolled away, and sprang to his feet.

"Bravo," the giant said, while Kronos howled and nursed his wrist. "Son, you've got a lot to learn." Grieu shoved the young man away. "Stay back so you don't get hurt even more."

Opru clutched his stolen sword, knees bent, ready to fight. Duncan tensed, with Resser beside him, waiting to see how this game would play out. The other captives coiled, ready to attack.

Opru circled at the center of the deck, keeping the blade pointed, weaving, ready to strike. He stayed on his toes, kept his gaze moving, intent on the black-bearded giant.

"Isn't that pretty?" Grieu strode around to get a better view. Acrid smoke twined around his face from the embers in his beard. "Look at his perfect form, right out of a textbook. You dropouts should have stayed in school, and then you might have looked good, too."

With his uninjured arm, Trin Kronos yanked one of the maula pistols from his father's belt. "Why prefer form over substance?" He pointed the pistol. "I prefer to *win*." And fired.

In an instant of shock, the captives understood that they would all be executed. Without hesitation, before Iss Opru's body had crumpled to the wet deck, the Swordmaster trainees launched into an all-out offensive with violent, sudden abandon. Two of the smug Grummans died from broken necks before they even realized the captives had begun to attack.

Resser rolled to his right, and a wild projectile hit the deck and ricocheted off into the swollen waves. Duncan dove in the opposite direction as the Moritani soldiers hauled out all their weapons.

The mob of Grumman fighters closed in behind the giant Grieu, then fanned out around the remaining captives. Individuals broke off from the swarm to attack the students at the center and then retreated under a hail of defensive blows and spinning kicks.

The giant whistled in mock appreciation. "Now *that* is style."

Klaen, the Chusuk student, ran forward with a blood-curdling yell, launching himself at the nearest of the two men holding cocked crossbows. He held up the wooden blade to catch two crossbow quarrels and then slashed sideways, gouging out the eyes of an enemy who did not back away quickly enough; the blinded Grumman fell screaming to the deck. Behind Klaen, a second student—Hiddi Aran of Balut—shadowed him, using the Chusuk man as a shield in a repeat of an exercise they had run a year before. This time Klaen knew he would be sacrificed.

Both men with crossbows fired their quarrels over and over again. Seven bolts skewered Klaen's shoulders, chest, stomach, and neck. But still his momentum drove him forward, and as he collapsed, Hiddi Aran leaped over his falling comrade and slammed his body into the nearest crossbow archer. With a speed that broke bones, he tore the crossbow out of the hands of his attacker. One quarrel remained in the bow, and he spun in a fluid motion to shoot the second archer through the hollow of his throat.

He dropped the now-empty crossbow and snatched the second one out of the dying archer's hands before it could strike the deck—only to face an explosion of fire as the big, bearded Grieu drew his second maula pistol and placed a projectile through the middle of the Balut student's forehead.

Gunfire erupted all around them, and Grieu bellowed in a voice like an avalanche, "Don't shoot each other, idiots!" The command came too late: one Grumman fell with a projectile in his chest.

Before Hiddi Aran had stopped moving, Duncan dove across the slippery deck to the Chusuk student's arrow-studded body, yanked one of the crossbow bolts out of the corpse's chest, and lunged toward the nearest Moritani. The enemy swung a long sword at him, but in a fraction of a second, Duncan was through his guard, rising up to drive the already-bloody shaft under the enemy's chin and up through the soft palate. Sensing movement, he grabbed the convulsing man around the chest and spun him so that his back absorbed the impact of three shots fired at Duncan.

With only his dull wooden sword, Hiih Resser yowled an intimidating scream and flailed with the blade. Using wiry, powerful muscles, he smacked the nearest Grumman on the head so hard he heard the skull crack even as his wooden blade shivered into long, sharp splinters. As the Grumman sagged, Resser spun about to jam the splintered end of the toy sword into the eye of another attacker, through the thin bone into the man's brain.

The remaining student—Wod Sedir, nephew of the King of Niushe—delivered a sharp kick to send a smoking maula pistol up into the air. His opponent had fired it repeatedly, but missed his weaving target. Wod Sedir followed through with his heel under the Grumman's jaw, shattering his neck, then grabbed the pistol as it fell and turned toward the other Grummans—but the pistol clicked on an empty charge. Within seconds, he became a pincushion of flèchette needles.

"Goes to show you," Grieu Kronos said, "the gunman beats the swordsman every time."

After less than thirty seconds, Duncan and Resser found themselves side by side, at the edge of the boat. The only ones left.

The Moritani murderers closed in on the survivors, brandishing an arsenal of weapons. They hesitated, looked to their leader for direction.

"How well can you swim, Resser?" Duncan asked, looking over his shoulder at the heaving swells of dark water.

"Better than I can drown," the redhead said. He saw the men draw their projectile pistols, weighed the possibility of being able to grab one of the enemy and drag the man over the side of the boat. But he dismissed it as impossible.

From a safe distance, the Grummans took aim. With a sudden movement of his arm, Duncan knocked Resser back into the railing and lunged after him. Both of them tumbled overboard into the churning sea, far from any visible land, just as the gunfire rang out. Needle flèchettes and blundering maula projectiles blasted the side of the boat, sending up a shower of splinters. In the water, silver needles hissed and stung like a swarm of wasps, but both young men had already plunged deep, far out of sight.

The armed attackers rushed to the ruined side of the boat and stared over into the roiling sea. But they spotted nothing. The undertow must have been horrific.

"Those two are lost," Trin Kronos said with a scowl, nursing his wrist.

"Aye," the big, bearded Grieu answered. "We'll have to dump the bodies of the others where they'll be found."

All technology is suspect, and must be considered potentially dangerous.

—BUTLERIAN JIHAD,
Handbook for Our Grandchildren

WHEN THE TERRIBLE NEWS REACHED THE SMUGGLER BASE ON SALUSA SE-cundus, Gurney Halleck had spent the day alone outside the ruined prison city. Working on a ballad about this desolate planet, he sat atop the remains of an ancient wall, strumming on his baliset. Bricks around him had melted into glassy curves from an ancient wave of atomic heat.

He gazed across a rise, imagining the lavish Imperial structure that might have stood here long ago. His rough but powerful voice drifted beyond the scrub brush and dry land to the accompaniment of the baliset. He paused to shift to a minor key for the mood it imparted . . . and then tried again.

The sickly-colored clouds and the hazy air put him in the proper frame of mind. For his melancholy music he'd actually been thankful for the weather, though the remaining men in the underground fortress grumbled about the capricious storms.

This hellhole was better than the slave pits of Giedi Prime any day.

A gray ornithopter approached from the south, an unmarked craft that belonged to the smugglers, beating its wings through the sluggish sky. Gurney watched out of the corner of his eye as it landed on a salt pan beyond the ancient ruins.

He concentrated on the images he wanted to evoke in his

ballad, the pomp and ceremony of the royal court, the exotic peoples who had journeyed here from distant planets, the finery of their raiment and manners. All gone now. Focusing his thoughts inward, he rubbed the inkvine scar on his jaw. Echoes of bygone times began to tint the perpetual dreariness of Salusa with their glorious colors.

He heard distant shouts and saw a man running up the slope toward him. It was Bork Qazon, the camp cook, waving his arms and yelling. Streaks of food covered the front of his apron. "Gurney! Dominic is dead!"

Stunned, he swung his baliset over his shoulder and dropped to the ground. Gurney swayed on his feet as Qazon told him the tragic news that had been brought in by 'thopter—that Dominic Vernius and all of their comrades had died in an atomic incident on Arrakis, apparently while under attack by Sardaukar.

Gurney couldn't believe it. "The Sardaukar . . . used atomics?"

Once word got back to Kaitain, Imperial Couriers would spread the news as Shaddam wanted it remembered. The Emperor would write his own distorted history, falsely painting Dominic as a heinous criminal who had been at large for decades.

The cook shook his head, his eyes red, his wide mouth slack. "My guess is Dom did it himself. He'd planned to use the family stockpile in a suicide attack on Kaitain."

"That's crazy."

"He was desperate."

"Atomics—against the Emperor's Sardaukar." Gurney shook his head, then knew he had decisions to make. "I have a feeling this isn't over, Qazon. We need to clear this camp out, fast. We've got to disperse. They'll be after all of us now, with a vengeance."

———

THE NEWS OF their leader's death hit the men hard. Just as this wounded world could never regain its past glory, neither could the remnants of the smuggler band. The men could not continue without Dominic. The renegade Earl had been their driving force.

As darkness fell, they sat around a strategy table discussing where they would go next. Several suggested Gurney Halleck as their new leader, now that Dominic, Johdam, and Asuyo were all dead.

"It's not safe to remain here," said Qazon. "We don't know what the Imperials have learned about our operations. What if they took prisoners and interrogated them?"

"We've got to set up a new base to continue our work," another man said.

"*What* work?" asked one of the oldest veterans. "We banded together because Dom called us. We've lived together for *him*. And he's not here anymore."

While the smugglers debated, Gurney's thoughts drifted to the children of their fallen leader, who lived as guests of House Atreides. When he smiled, the inkvine scar wrinkled with a flare of residual pain. He put it out of his mind and instead thought of the irony: the Atreides Duke had also unknowingly rescued *him* from the Harkonnen slave pit, by ordering a shipment of blue obsidian at exactly the right time. . . .

He made up his mind. "I'll not be joining any of you at a new base. No, I'm bound for Caladan. I intend to offer my services to Duke Leto Atreides. That's where Rhombur and Kailea Vernius are."

"You're crazy, Halleck," slope-shouldered Scien Traf said, chewing on a splinter of resinous wood. "Dom insisted that we stay away from his children, so as not to put them in danger."

"The danger died with him," Gurney said. "It's been twenty years since the family went renegade." He narrowed his blue eyes. "Depending on how fast the Emperor moves, perhaps I can get to those two children before they hear the tainted version of events. Dominic's heirs need to know what really happened to their father, not the garbage the official Couriers will report."

"They're not children," Bork Qazon pointed out. "Rhombur's in his mid-thirties now."

"Aye," Pen Barlow agreed. He took a deep puff on his cigar, exhaled dark smoke. "I remember when they were knee-high to a chairdog, little urchins running around the Grand Palais."

Gurney stood up and rested his baliset on his shoulder. "I'll go to Caladan and explain everything." He nodded to all of them. "Some of you will want to continue the trade, no doubt. Take the remainder of the equipment with my blessing. I . . . I don't want to be a smuggler any longer."

ARRIVING AT THE Cala Municipal Spaceport, Gurney Halleck carried only a single bag with a few changes of clothes, a wrapped bundle of solari coins—his share of the smuggling profits—and his beloved baliset. He also brought news and remembrances of Dominic Vernius—enough, he hoped, to gain entrance to the ducal Castle.

During the foldspace journey he'd drunk too much and gambled in the Heighliner casino decks, pampered by Wayku attendants. He'd met an attractive woman from Poritrin, who thought Gurney's songs and good humor more than made up for his scarred face. She stayed with him for several days until the Heighliner went into orbit over Caladan. Finally, he had kissed her goodbye and marched off for the shuttle.

On cool, moist Caladan he spent his money quickly to make himself presentable. Without land or family, he'd never had anything to save it for. "Money was invented to spend," he always said. It would have been a foreign concept to his parents.

After passing through a series of security checkpoints, Gurney at last stood in the Castle's reception hall, watching as a stocky man and a beautiful young woman with copper-dark hair approached him. He could see traces of Dominic in their features. "You are Rhombur and Kailea Vernius?"

"We are." The man had tousled blond hair and a broad face.

"The guards said you know our father?" Kailea asked. "Where has he been all these years? Why didn't he ever send us a message?"

Gurney gripped his baliset, as if it gave him strength. "He was killed on Arrakis in a Sardaukar attack. Dominic ran a smuggler base there, and another on Salusa Secundus." He fidgeted, accidentally strummed a single chord, then nervously thumbed another one.

Rhombur slumped into a chair, almost missed the seat, then caught his balance. Staring straight ahead, blinking and blinking, he reached out with his hand, fumbling to find Kailea's. She grasped his.

Uncomfortable, Gurney continued, "I worked for your father, and . . . and now I have no place else to go. I thought I should come to you and explain where he's been these past two decades, what he's done—and why he had to stay away. He thought only of protecting you."

Tears streamed down the faces of the Vernius children. After the murder of their mother, years ago, the news fit an all-too-familiar pattern. Rhombur opened his mouth to say something, but no words came out, and he closed it again.

"I'll place my skills with a blade against any man in the Atreides House Guard," Gurney said. "You have powerful enemies out there, but I won't let you come to harm. It's what Dominic would have wanted."

"Please be more specific." Another man emerged from a side entrance on Gurney's right, tall and lean, with dark hair and gray eyes. He wore a black military jacket with a red hawk crest on the lapel. "We want the full story, no matter how painful it is."

"Gurney Halleck, this is Duke Leto Atreides," Rhombur said dully, after wiping the tears from his eyes. "He knew my father, too."

Leto received a hesitant handshake from the scarred, sullen-looking visitor. "I'm sorry to bring such terrible tidings," Gurney said. He gazed at Rhombur and Kailea. "Recently, Dominic infiltrated Ix again, after receiving some disturbing news. And what he witnessed there . . . horrified him so much that he came back a broken man."

"There were many ways to get back in," Rhombur said. "Emergency access points that only the Vernius family knew. I remember them myself." He turned back to Gurney. "But what was he trying to do?"

"As near as I can tell, he was making preparations to attack Kaitain with the Vernius family atomics. But the Emperor's Sardaukar learned of the plan, and they ambushed our base first. Dominic set off a stone burner and destroyed them all."

"Our father's been alive all this time," Rhombur said, then looked at Leto. His gaze searched the arched entrances, the long Castle halls, as if he hoped to see Tessia. "He's been alive, but he never told us. I wish I could have fought at his side, just once. I should have been there."

"Prince Rhombur—if I may call you that," Gurney said, "everyone who *was* there is now dead."

THE SAME TRANSPORT that delivered Gurney Halleck also brought a formal diplomatic Courier from Archduke Armand Ecaz. The woman had close-cropped maroon hair and wore the respected, age-old uniform trimmed with braids and decked with dozens of pockets.

She tracked down Leto where he stood in the banquet hall,

chatting with some of the household staff who polished the expensive wall of blue obsidian to a warm luster. Thanks to Gurney Halleck, Leto now knew the blue obsidian came not from Hagal, but from Harkonnen slave pits. Even so, Gurney had asked him not to tear it down.

Leto turned and greeted the Courier, but in a brisk series of businesslike moves, she presented identification, delivered a sealed message cylinder, then waited while the Duke processed a thumbprint receipt. She spoke very little.

Fearing more bad news—when had a Courier brought anything else?—both Thufir Hawat and Rhombur came into Leto's presence from opposite doorways. Leto met their questioning looks with the unopened cylinder.

Duke Leto yanked out one of the heavy side chairs from the dining table, scraping the feet across the stone floor. Workers continued to polish the obsidian wall. With a sigh, Leto slumped into the seat and cracked open the cylinder. His gray eyes scanned the words while the Prince and the Mentat waited in silence.

Finished, Leto looked up at the portrait of the Old Duke hanging on one wall, facing the stuffed head of the Salusan bull that had killed him in the Plaza de Toros. "Well, this is something to consider." He did not explain further, as if he'd rather have advice from long-dead Paulus.

Rhombur fidgeted. "What is it, Leto?" His eyes were still red around the edges.

Setting the cylinder on the table, the Duke caught it before it could roll off. "House Ecaz has formally suggested a marriage alliance with Atreides. Archduke Armand offers the hand of his second daughter Ilesa." He tapped the cylinder with the finger that bore the ducal signet ring. The Archduke's eldest daughter had been killed by Moritani's Grummans. "He's also included a list of Ecazi assets and a suggested dowry."

"But no image of the daughter," Rhombur said.

"I've already seen her. Ilesa is beautiful enough." He spoke in a distracted tone, as if such matters would not affect his decision.

Two of the household servants paused in their polishing, astonished to hear the news, then returned to their labors with increased vigor.

Hawat's brow furrowed. "No doubt the Archduke is also concerned about the renewed hostilities. An Atreides alliance would make Ecaz far less vulnerable to Moritani aggression. The Viscount would think twice about sending in Grumman troops."

Rhombur shook his head. "Uh, I told you the Emperor's simple fix would never solve the problem between those two Houses."

Leto stared off into the distance, his thoughts spinning. "Nobody ever disagreed with you, Rhombur. At the moment, though, I think the Grummans are more upset with the Ginaz School. Last I heard, the academy publicly provoked Viscount Moritani in the Landsraad by calling him a coward and a mad dog."

Hawat looked grave. "My Duke, shouldn't we distance ourselves from this? The dispute has gone on for years—who knows what they will do next?"

"We're too far in it, Thufir, not just by our friendship with Ecaz, but now Ginaz as well. I can no longer remain neutral. Having examined records of the Grumman atrocities, I've added my voice to a Landsraad vote calling for censure." He allowed himself a personal smile. "Besides, I was thinking of Duncan at the time."

"We must study the marriage offer carefully," the Mentat said.

"My sister's not going to like this," Rhombur muttered.

Leto sighed. "Kailea hasn't liked anything I've done for years. I am Duke. I must think about what's best for House Atreides."

———

LETO INVITED GURNEY Halleck to dine with them that evening.

For hours in the afternoon, the brash smuggler refugee had challenged and brawled with several of the best Atreides fighters—and had actually beaten most of them.

Now, in the quieter hours, Gurney proved to be a master storyteller, reciting tale after tale of Dominic Vernius's exploits to eager listeners. At the long table in the banquet hall, he was seated between the mounted Salusan bull's-head and the painting of the Old Duke dressed as a matador.

In a somber voice, the scarred smuggler told of his bone-deep hatred of the Harkonnens. He even talked again about the shipment of blue obsidian, some of which adorned the banquet hall, that had allowed him to escape from the slave pits.

Later, in another demonstration of his swordsmanship, Gurney used one of the Old Duke's swords against an imaginary opponent. He had little finesse, but considerable energy and remarkable accuracy.

Nodding to himself, Leto glanced at Thufir Hawat, who pursed his lips in approval. "Gurney Halleck," Leto said, "if you would like to remain here with the Atreides House Guard, I would be honored to have you."

"Pending a thorough background check, of course," Hawat added.

"Our weapons master, Duncan Idaho, is away at school on Ginaz, though we expect him back soon. You can assist in some of his duties."

"Training to be a Swordmaster? I wouldn't want to intrude on his job." Gurney grinned, rippling the inkvine scar on his jaw. He extended a beefy hand toward Leto. "For the sake of my memories of Dominic, I would like to serve here, by the children of Vernius."

Rhombur and Leto each gripped his hand, welcoming Gurney Halleck to House Atreides.

The seats of power inevitably try to harness any new knowledge to their own desires. But knowledge can have no fixed desires— neither in the past nor in the future.

—DMITRI HARKONNEN,
Lessons for My Sons

BARON VLADIMIR HARKONNEN HAD MADE A LIFETIME CAREER OF SEEKING new experiences. He dabbled in hedonistic pleasures—rich foods, exotic drugs, deviant sex—discovering things he had never done before.

But a *baby* in Harkonnen Keep . . . how would he handle that?

Other Houses of the Landsraad adored children. A generation ago, Count Ilban Richese had married an Imperial daughter and spawned eleven offspring. Eleven! The Baron had heard insipid songs and heartwarming tales that fostered a false impression of the joy of laughing children. He had trouble understanding it, but out of duty for his House, for the future of all Harkonnen businesses, he vowed to do his best. He would be a role model for young Feyd-Rautha.

Barely over a year old, the boy had grown too confident in his walking skills, stumbling across rooms, running long before he had total balance, resilient enough to keep going even when he bumped into something. Bright-eyed Feyd had an insatiable curiosity, and he pried into every storage area, every cabinet. He picked up any movable object and usually stuck it in his mouth. The baby startled easily and cried incessantly.

Sometimes the Baron snapped at him, trying to get some

sort of response other than gurgling nonsensical words. It was no use.

After breakfast one day he took the child out onto the high balcony of a tall turret of Harkonnen Keep. Little Feyd looked across the crowded industrial city to see the ruddy morning sun through a haze of smoke. Beyond the boundaries of Harko City, mining and agricultural villages produced raw material to keep Giedi Prime functioning. But the populace remained unruly, and the Baron had to exercise tight control, making examples, providing the necessary discipline to keep them in their place.

As the Baron let his thoughts ramble, his attention drifted from the child. Surprisingly fast, Feyd charged with his tiptoe-stumble gait to the edge of the balcony, where he leaned between the rails. The Baron, spluttering in indignant shock, lurched forward. Light yet clumsy under the motivation of his suspensor belt, he snatched the child just before Feyd leaned too far over the deep, deep drop.

He snarled obscenities at the toddler, holding him at eye level. "How can you do such a foolish thing, idiot child? Don't you understand the consequences? If you fall, you'd be nothing more than a smear on the streets below!"

All that carefully cultivated Harkonnen blood wasted . . .

Feyd-Rautha looked at him wide-eyed, then made a rude sound.

The Baron hustled the boy back inside. As a safety measure, he removed one of the suspensor globes from his own belt and attached it to the child's back. Though he now walked with a little more difficulty, feeling the strain on his degenerating muscles and heavy arms and legs, at least Feyd was under control. Bobbing along half a meter in the air, the child seemed to find it amusing.

"Come with me, Feyd," the Baron said. "I want to show you the animals. You'll enjoy them."

Feyd drifted along in tow as his uncle plodded, panting and

wheezing, through the corridors and down flights of stairs until he reached the arena level. The baby giggled and laughed while he floated along. The Baron nudged his shoulders every few minutes to keep him moving. Feyd's pudgy little arms and legs waved about as if he were swimming in the air.

In the cage levels surrounding the gladiator arena, Baron Harkonnen lugged the child through low tunnels with sloping ceilings made out of wattle and daub, a primitive stick-and-mud construction that gave the place the feel of an animal's lair. A rich, moist odor of wildness filled the enclosed tunnels. Barred chambers held rotten hay and manure from creatures bred and trained to fight against the Baron's chosen victims. The roars and snarls of tortured animals echoed off the walls. Claws scraped on stone floors. Enraged beasts crashed against the bars.

The Baron smiled. It was good to keep predators on edge.

The beasts were a delight to watch; with their teeth, horns, and claws they could tear a man to bloody shreds. Still, the most interesting battles took place between human opponents, professional soldiers against desperate slaves who had been promised freedom, though none ever received it. Any slave who fought well enough to defeat a trained Harkonnen killer was worth keeping around to fight again and again.

As he continued through the dim tunnels, the Baron looked down at the fascinated face of little Feyd. In the child he saw a future full of possibilities, another heir to House Harkonnen who might outperform his blockheaded brother Rabban. That one, while strong and vicious, didn't have the devious mind the Baron preferred.

His burly nephew was still useful, though. In fact, Rabban had performed many brutal tasks that even the Baron found distasteful. Too often, though, he acted like little more than a . . . muscle-minded tank-brain.

The motley pair stopped at one cage, where a Laza tiger prowled back and forth, its feline pupils narrowed to slits, its triangular nose flaring as it smelled tender flesh and warm blood. These hungry beasts had been favorites in gladiatorial combat for centuries. The tiger was a mass of muscle, every fiber filled with killing energy. Its keepers fed it just enough to maintain its peak strength . . . keeping the tiger ready to feast on the torn flesh of fresh victims.

Suddenly, the beast crashed into the bars of the cage, its dark lips curled and long fangs bared. The abused tiger hurled itself at the barrier again, reaching out a paw filled with saber claws.

Startled, the Baron backed away and yanked Feyd with him. The child, bobbing on his suspensor globe, continued to drift backward until he struck the wall, which startled him more than the roaring predator itself. Feyd wailed with such exuberance that his face turned purple from the effort.

The Baron grasped the child's shoulders. "There, there," he said in a brusque but soothing tone. "Be quiet now. It's all right." But Feyd continued to shriek, enraging his uncle. "Be quiet, I said! There's nothing to cry about."

The baby felt otherwise and continued his loud crying.

The tiger roared and threw himself against the bars, slashing the air.

"Silence, I command!" The Baron didn't know what to do. He'd never been instructed in how to handle babies. "Oh, stop it!" But Feyd only cried louder.

Oddly, he thought of the two daughters he had sired with the Bene Gesserit witch Mohiam. During his disastrous confrontation with the witches on Wallach IX, seven years ago now, he had demanded to have his children returned, but now he realized how much of a blessing it was that the Reverend Mothers had raised these . . . immature creatures themselves.

"Piter!" he shouted at the top of his lungs, then strode to a com-panel on the wall. He hammered it with his bloated fist. "Piter de Vries! Where's my Mentat?"

He shouted until the thin nasal voice of the Mentat responded through the speaker. "I am coming, my Baron."

Feyd continued to cry. When the Baron grasped him again, he found that the baby had filled and soaked his diapers. "Piter!"

Moments later the Mentat scuttled into the tunnels. He must have been close, shadowing the Baron as he always did. "Yes, my Baron?"

As the child wailed without pause for breath, the Baron thrust Feyd into the arms of de Vries. "You take care of him. Make him stop crying."

Taken completely unawares, the Mentat blinked his feral eyes at the littlest Harkonnen. "But my Baron, I—"

"Do as I command! You're my Mentat. You're supposed to know anything I ask you to know." The Baron clenched his jowly jaw and suppressed an amused smile at de Vries's discomfiture.

The Mentat held the smelly Feyd-Rautha at arm's length, grasping the squirming child as if he were some strange specimen. The expression on the thin man's face was worth all of the distress he had just gone through.

"Don't fail me, Piter." The Baron strode away, his gait dragging a bit from the loss of one suspensor globe.

Behind him in the animal tunnels, Piter de Vries held the howling infant with no clue as to how he should proceed.

The haughty do but build castle walls behind which they try to hide their doubts and fears.

—Bene Gesserit Axiom

WITHIN HER PRIVATE CHAMBERS IN CASTLE CALADAN, OUT OF LETO'S VIEW, Kailea mourned the death of her father. Standing at a narrow turret window, she placed her fingers against the cold stone sill and stared out at the gray, churning sea.

Dominic Vernius had been an enigma to her, a brave and intelligent leader who had gone into hiding for twenty years. Had he run from rebellion, left his wife to be killed by assassins, surrendered the birthright of his children? Or had he been working behind the scenes all these years in a fruitless attempt to restore House Vernius to power? And now he was dead. Her father. Such a vibrant, strong man. So difficult to believe. With a sinking feeling, Kailea knew she could never go back to Ix, never regain what was rightfully hers.

And in the midst of this, Leto was considering marriage to yet another Ecaz daughter, a younger sister of the one who'd been kidnapped and murdered by Grummans. Leto wouldn't answer any questions Kailea put to him about this. It was "a matter of state," he'd told her the night before in an arrogant tone—not a matter to be discussed with a mere concubine.

I have been his lover for more than six years. I am the mother of his son—the only one who deserves to be his wife.

Her heart had become an empty place inside of her, a gnawing black cavity that left her with nothing but despair and shattered dreams. Would it never end? After the elder Ecaz daughter had been murdered, Kailea had hoped that Leto might turn to her at long last. But he still harbored dreams of a marital alliance that would strengthen the political, military, and economic power of House Atreides.

Far below, the black cliffs were wet from mist hurled high by the breakers. Seabirds soared, sweeping insects from the air and plunging in pursuit of fish just beneath the waves. Green discolorations of algae and seaweed clung to notches in the rock; the broken reefs at the shore made the waters foam like a boiling cauldron.

My life is cursed, Kailea thought. *Everything that is mine has been stolen from me.*

She turned as matronly Chiara entered her private apartments without knocking. Kailea heard the rattle of cups and containers on an ornate tray, smelled the spice-laced coffee the old woman had brewed for her. The lady-in-waiting still moved with a muscular speed and agility that belied her withered appearance. Chiara set the tray down, trying to muffle the clatter, then picked up the fluted coffeepot and poured a rich brown stream into two cups. She added sugar to her own, cream to Kailea's.

Her heart still heavy, the Ixian Princess took the proffered cup from the woman and drew a delicate sip, trying not to show too much enjoyment. Chiara drank deeply and sat down in one of the chairs, as if she were the equal of the Duke's first concubine.

Kailea's nostrils flared. "You take too many liberties, Chiara."

The lady-in-waiting looked across the edge of her cup at the young woman who should have been a prime marriage prospect to any Great House. "Do you prefer a companion, Lady Kailea, or a mechanical servant? I have always been your friend and confidante. Perhaps you miss the self-motivated meks you once had at your disposal on Ix?"

"Don't presume to tell me my wishes," Kailea said in a bleak voice. "I am grieving for a great man who has died by Imperial treachery."

Chiara's eyes glittered as she pounced. "Yes, and your mother was slain by them as well. You can't count on your brother to do anything but talk—he'll never get back your birthright. You, Kailea"—the matronly woman pointed a big-knuckled finger—"*you* are what remains of House Vernius, the heart and soul of your great family."

"Don't you think I know that?" Kailea turned around again to look out the Castle window. She could not face the old woman, could not face anyone or anything, not even her own fears.

If Leto marries that Archduke's daughter . . . Angrily, she shook her head. It would be worse than having that whore Jessica in the Castle.

The Caladan sea stretched beyond the horizon, and the skies were veiled with clouds that portended only winter gloom. She thought of her precarious position with Leto. He had taken her under his wing when she was just a girl, protected her after her world was destroyed . . . but those times were gone. Somehow the affection, even love, that had blossomed between them had withered and died.

"Naturally you fear that the Duke will accept the proposal and wed Ilesa Ecaz," Chiara added in a sweet voice, compassionate as a long, thin knife. She knew exactly how to prod the sorest spot.

Although preoccupied with Jessica, Leto still came to Kailea's bed, though infrequently, as if out of obligation. And she submitted to him, as if it were her own duty as well. His Atreides honor would never allow him to cast her out entirely, no matter how his feelings had changed. Instead, Leto chose a more subtle punishment by keeping her close to him, yet preventing her from achieving the glory that should have been hers.

Oh, how she wished for sojourns on Kaitain! Kailea longed to wear fine gowns, intricate and precious jewelry; she wanted to be attended by dozens of maidservants—not just one companion who concealed a sharp tongue with a honeyed voice. Glancing over at Chiara, her attention was caught by the blurred reflection of the old woman's features, the carefully coiffed hair that enhanced her noble appearance.

Kailea's gleaming wall of blue obsidian—purchased by Leto at grand expense from Hagal stone merchants—had been a wonderful addition to Castle Caladan. Leto called it her "contemplation surface," where Kailea could see dim shadows of the world around her and think about their implications. Blue obsidian was so rare that few Houses in the Landsraad displayed even a single ornament—and Leto had procured this entire reflecting wall for her, as well as the stones in the banquet hall.

But Kailea frowned. Chiara said that Leto had merely intended to buy her complacency, to make her accept her situation and silence her complaints.

And now Gurney Halleck had told them that the rare substance actually came from Giedi Prime. Ah, the irony! She knew how the news must sting Leto's unfaithful heart.

Chiara watched her lady's expression, knew the often-voiced thoughts that must be passing through her mind . . . and the old woman saw the wedge she needed. "Before Leto can marry this daughter of Archduke Ecaz, you must consider your own dynastic matters, my Lady." She stood beside the blue obsidian wall, and her reflection was distorted, a twisted figure who seemed trapped within the blurred glow of volcanic glass.

"Forget about your father and your brother—and even yourself. You have a son by Duke Leto Atreides. Your brother and Tessia have no children—so Victor is the true heir of House Vernius . . . and potentially of House Atreides as well. If anything were to happen to the Duke before he could take a wife and produce another son, Victor would *become* House Atreides. And since the boy is only six, you would be regent for many years, my Lady. It makes perfect sense."

"What do you mean, if anything 'were to happen' to Leto?" Her heart clenched. She knew exactly what the old woman was suggesting.

Coyly, Chiara finished her coffee, pouring herself a second cup without asking permission. "Duke Paulus was slain in a bullfighting accident. You were there yourself, were you not?"

Kailea recalled the frightful image of the Old Duke fighting a Salusan bull in the Plaza de Toros. The tragic event had thrust Leto into the ducal seat years before his time. She had been a teenager then.

Was Chiara hinting that it had not been an accident? Kailea had heard rumors, quickly hushed—but she'd considered it no more than jealous talk. The old woman withdrew, skirting the issue. "It is not an idea to be considered seriously, I know, my dear. I raise it simply for the sake of argument."

Kailea, though, could not get the insidious thoughts out of her head. She could imagine no other way for a child of her bloodline to lead a Great House of the Landsraad. Otherwise, House Vernius would become extinct. She squeezed her eyes shut.

"If Leto does agree to marry Ilesa Ecaz after all, you will have nothing." Chiara picked up the tray and made as if to leave. She had planted her seeds and done her work. "Your Duke already spends most of his time with that Bene Gesserit whore. Clearly, you mean nothing to him. I doubt he remembers any promises he made to you in moments of passion."

Blinking in surprise at the old woman, Kailea wondered how Chiara could possibly know what bedroom secrets Leto had whispered in her ear. But the thought of Duke Atreides caressing young, bronze-haired Jessica, with her generous mouth and smooth oval face, turned her annoyance with Chiara's impertinence into hatred toward Leto himself.

"You must ask yourself a difficult question, my Lady. Where does your loyalty truly lie? With Duke Leto, or with *your* family? Since he has not seen fit to give you his name, you will always remain a Vernius."

The old woman removed the tray, leaving Kailea with her own lukewarm cup of coffee. Chiara departed without saying farewell, without asking if her Lady needed anything else.

Kailea remained in her chamber, looking over trinkets and baubles that reminded her of the terrible losses she had sustained: her noble House and the finery of the Grand Palais, her chances to join the Imperial Court. With a pang in her heart, she saw one of the sketches she had drawn of her hearty father, bringing to mind Dominic's laughter, how the big bald man had trained her in business matters. Then, with an equal sense of loss, she thought of her son, Victor, and all the things he would never have.

For Kailea, the hardest part was coming to the horrible decision. Once she had made up her mind, though, the rest was just . . . details.

The individual is the key, the final effective unit of all biological processes.

—PARDOT KYNES

FOR YEARS LIET-KYNES HAD YEARNED FOR BEAUTIFUL, DARK-HAIRED Faroula with all his heart. But when he finally faced the prospect of marrying her, he felt only emptiness and a sense of obligation. To be entirely proper, he waited three months after Warrick's death, though both he and Faroula knew their betrothal was a foregone conclusion.

He had made a death vow to his friend.

According to Fremen custom, men took the wives and children of those they vanquished in knife fights or single-handed combat. Faroula, however, was not a *ghanima*, a spoil of war. Liet had spoken with Naib Heinar, professing his love and dedication, citing the solemn promises he'd made to Warrick that he would care for his wife as the most precious of women . . . and accept responsibility for her young son as his own.

Old Heinar had regarded him with his one-eyed gaze. The Naib knew what had transpired, knew the sacrifice Warrick had made during the Coriolis storm. As far as the elders of Red Wall Sietch were concerned, Warrick had perished out in the desert. The visions he claimed to have received from God were obviously false, for he had failed in the testing. Thus, Heinar gave his permission, and Liet-Kynes prepared to marry the Naib's daughter.

Sitting in his room behind the tapestry hangings of dyed

spice fiber, Liet pondered his impending wedding. Fremen superstition did not allow him to see Faroula for two days before the formal ceremony. Both man and wife had to undergo *mendi* purification rituals. The time was spent in beautification and in writing out statements of devotion, promises, and love poems that would later be shared with each other.

Now, though, Liet wallowed in shameful thoughts, wondering if he had somehow caused this tragedy to happen. Was it the fervent desire he'd voiced upon seeing the white *Biyan?* There, he and Warrick had both wished to marry the young woman. Liet had tried to accept his defeat graciously at the Cave of Birds, suppressing the selfish voice in the back of his mind that had never allowed him to forget how much he still wanted her.

Did my secret wishes cause this tragedy to happen?

Now Faroula would be his wife . . . but it was a union born of sadness.

"Ah, forgive me, Warrick, my friend." He continued to sit in silence, waiting for time to tick away, until the hour was at hand and the sietch ceremony would begin. He wasn't looking forward to it, not under these circumstances.

With a rustle of heavy cloth, the door hanging parted and Liet's mother entered. Frieth smiled at him with sympathy and understanding. She carried a stoppered flask that had been ornately embroidered, stitched together out of skins and then sealed with spice resin to keep it waterproof. She held the flask as if it were a precious treasure, a gift of immeasurable price. "I've brought you something, dearest, in preparation for your wedding."

Liet emerged from his troubled thoughts. "I've never seen that before."

"It is said that when a woman feels a special destiny for her child, when she senses great things will come from him, she instructs the midwives to distill and retain the amniotic fluid from the birth. A mother may give this to her son on his wedding day." She extended the flask. "Keep it well, Liet. This is the last commingling of your essence and mine, from the time we shared one body. Now you will commingle your life with another. Two hearts, when joined, may yield the strength of more than two."

Trembling with emotion, he accepted the soft flask.

"It is the greatest gift I could give to you," Frieth said, "on this important . . . but difficult day."

Looking up at her, Liet met her dark eyes with an intent gaze. The emotions she perceived in his face were enough to startle her. "No, Mother—you gave me life, and that is a far greater blessing."

WHEN THE BETROTHED couple stood before the members of the sietch, Liet's mother and the younger women waited in designated spaces, while the elders stepped forward to speak for the young man. The boy Liet-chih, son of Warrick, waited silently beside his mother.

Pardot Kynes, taking a break from his terraforming work, grinned as never before. It surprised him how proud he felt to see his son getting married.

Kynes remembered his own wedding out on the dunes at night. It had been so long ago, shortly after his arrival on Arrakis, and he had spent much of the time in distraction. Unbetrothed Fremen girls had danced like dervishes on the sand, chanting. The Sayyadina had pronounced the words of the ceremony.

His own marriage to Frieth had turned out well enough. He had a fine son, whom he had groomed to take over his work one day. Kynes smiled at Liet—whose name came from, he suddenly remembered, the assassin Uliet, whom Heinar and the elders had sent to kill him, back when the Fremen had considered him an outsider, a stranger with frightful dreams and ways.

But that assassin had seen the grandeur of the Planetologist's vision and had fallen on his own crysknife. The Fremen saw omens in everything, and ever since, Pardot Kynes had been provided with the resources of ten million Fremen at his beck and call. Dune's reshaping—the plantings and the reclamation of the desert—had proceeded at a remarkable pace.

As the couple stood in front of the assemblage, with Liet gazing upon his bride longingly, Pardot felt disturbed at the fixity of his son's attention, the opening of the young man's already-wounded heart. He loved his son in a different way, as an extension of himself. Pardot Kynes wanted Liet to assume the mantle of Planetologist when it was time to pass it on.

Unlike his father, Liet seemed too vulnerable to emotions. Pardot loved his wife well enough, as she performed her traditional role as a Fremen companion, but his work was more important than the marital relationship. He had been captivated by dreams and ideas; he felt the passion for restoring this planet to a lush Eden. But he had never been *engulfed* by a single person.

Naib Heinar performed the ceremony himself, since the old Sayyadina had been unable to travel across the sands. As Kynes listened to the young couple speaking their vows to each other, he felt a strange pall settle over this wedding . . . a heavy worry about his son's mind-set.

Liet: "Satisfy Me as to Thine eyes, and I will satisfy Thee as to Thy heart."

Faroula's answer: "Satisfy Me as to Thy feet, and I will satisfy Thee as to Thy hands."

"Satisfy Me as to Thy sleeping, and I will satisfy Thee as to Thy waking."

And she completed the spoken prayer. "Satisfy Me as to Thy desire, and I will satisfy Thee as to Thy need."

With two sinewy hands, Heinar grasped the palms of the bride and groom, holding them together and raising them up so the entire sietch could see. "You are now united in the Water."

A subdued cheer rose, which grew in intensity until it became heartfelt, happy, and welcoming. Both Liet and Faroula looked relieved. . . .

LATER, AFTER THE celebration, Pardot came to see his son alone in a passageway. Awkwardly, he clasped Liet's shoulders in the semblance of a hug. "I'm so happy for you, my son." He struggled for the proper words. "You must be filled with joy. You have wanted that girl for a long time, haven't you?"

He grinned, but Liet's eyes flashed with anger, as if the elder Kynes had just struck him an unfair blow. "Why do you torment me, Father? Haven't you done enough already?"

Baffled, Pardot stepped back and released his son's shoulders. "What do you mean? I'm congratulating you on your wedding. Is she not the woman you've always wanted to be with? I thought—"

"*Not like this!* How can I be happy with this shadow hanging over us? Perhaps it will go away in a few years, but for now I feel too much pain."

"Liet, my son?"

Pardot's expression must have told Liet all he needed to know. "You don't understand a thing, do you, Father? The great *Umma* Kynes." He laughed bitterly. "With your plantings, and your dunes, and your weather stations, and your climate maps. You are so blind, I pity you."

The Planetologist's mind reeled as he tried to place the angry words into some grid of meaning, like the pieces of a jigsaw puzzle. "Warrick . . . your friend." Then he stopped. "He died accidentally, didn't he, in the storm?"

"Father, you missed it all." Liet hung his head. "I am proud of your dreams for Dune. But you see our entire world as an experiment, just a test bed where you play with theories, where you collect *data*. Don't you see, these aren't experiments? These aren't test subjects—these are *people*. These are the *Fremen*. They have taken you in, given you a life, given you a son. *I am Fremen*."

"Well, so am I." Pardot's tone was indignant.

In a husky tone so low that no one else could hear, Liet said, "You're just using them!"

Pardot, startled, didn't respond.

Liet's voice rose in pitch and volume. He knew the Fremen would hear portions of this argument and would be disturbed at the friction between their prophet and his heir. "You've spoken to me all my life, Father. When I recall our conversations, though, I only remember you reciting reports from botanical stations and discussing new phases of adapted plant life. Have you ever said a thing about my mother? Have you ever talked to me as a *father* rather than as a . . . colleague?"

Liet pounded his own chest. "I do feel your dream. I do see the wonders you've brought in hidden corners of the desert. I do understand the potential that lies beneath the sands of Dune. But even when you do accomplish everything you wish . . . will you bother to notice? Try to put a human face on your plans and see who will reap the benefits of your efforts. Look at the face of a child. Look into the eyes of an old woman. *Live* your life, Father!"

Helpless, Pardot sagged onto a bench against a curved rock wall. "I . . . I've meant well," he said, his voice thick in his throat. His eyes brimmed with tears of shame and confusion as he looked at his son. "You are truly my successor. At times I've wondered if you would ever learn enough about planetology . . . but now I see I was wrong. You understand more things than I can ever know."

Liet sank onto the bench beside his father. Hesitantly the Planetologist reached over and placed a hand on his son's shoulder, more meaningfully this time. In turn, Liet reached up to touch the hand, and looked with Fremen amazement at the *tears* pouring down his father's cheeks.

"You are truly my successor as Imperial Planetologist," Pardot said. "You understand my dream—but with you, it will be even greater, because you have a heart as well as a vision."

Good leadership is largely invisible. When everything runs smoothly, no one notices a Duke's work. That is why he must give the people something to cheer, something to talk about, something to remember.

—DUKE PAULUS ATREIDES

KAILEA SAW HER CHANCE DURING AN INTERMINABLE FAMILY DINNER IN THE grand banquet hall of Castle Caladan. Looking happy, black-haired Leto sat in the ducal chair at the head of the long table while household servants delivered tureens of a spicy fish stew commonly enjoyed by the lower classes of fishermen and villagers.

Leto ate with gusto, savoring the crude dish. Perhaps it reminded him of his childhood running loose on the docks, jumping aboard fishing boats, and avoiding his studies on the leadership of a Great House. As far as Kailea was concerned, Old Duke Paulus had allowed his only heir to spend too much time with commoners and their petty concerns, and not enough time learning political nuances. It was clear to her that Duke Leto had never understood how to run his household and deal with the disparate forces of the Guild, CHOAM, the Emperor, and the Landsraad.

Beside his father, Victor sat on a thickly cushioned chair, raised so that he could eat at the same level. The dark-haired boy slurped his soup, imitating his father while Leto did his best to outdo the six-year-old in making noise. With her elegant background, it especially displeased Kailea how her son tried to copy his father's rough edges. Someday, when the boy became the true Atreides heir and Kailea was regent, she

628 — BRIAN HERBERT AND KEVIN J. ANDERSON

would train him properly so that he might appreciate the obligations of his birthright. Victor would have the best of both House Atreides and House Vernius.

Around the table, the others tore hunks from loaves of bread and drank bitter Caladan ale, though Kailea knew there were plenty of fine wines in the cellar. Laughter and casual conversation drifted, but she didn't participate and instead picked at her food. Several seats away, Gurney Halleck had brought his new baliset to the table and would entertain them during dessert. Because this man had been close to the father neither Kailea nor her brother had known, she felt pleased to have him there . . . despite the fact that Gurney had not been overly friendly toward her.

Sitting across from her, Rhombur seemed perfectly content with his concubine Tessia, and with trying to best Leto in the quantity of fish stew he could consume. In his own chair, Thufir Hawat sat deep in concentration, studying the people around the table, neglecting his meal. The Mentat's gaze slid from face to face, and Kailea tried to avoid eye contact.

Halfway down the table sat Jessica, as if to demonstrate that they were equals in the ducal household. The nerve of that woman! Kailea wanted to strangle her. The attractive Bene Gesserit ate with measured movements, so assured in her position that she exhibited no self-consciousness. She saw Jessica pause and study Leto's face, as if able to read every nuance of expression as easily as words imprinted on a shigawire spool.

This evening Leto had called them all to eat together, though Kailea could think of no special occasion, anniversary, or holiday he meant to celebrate. She suspected the Duke had thought up some wild and inadvisable scheme, one he'd insist upon completing no matter what advice she or anyone else gave him.

Glowglobes hovered above the table like decorations, surrounding the articulated arms of the poison snooper that drifted high above their food, like a hovering insect. The snooper was a necessary device, given the twisted politics of Landsraad feuds.

Leto finished his large bowl of stew and dabbed his mouth with an embroidered linen napkin. He leaned back in the hand-carved ducal chair with a contented sigh. Victor did the same on the high cushions of his own seat; he had finished barely a third of the stew in his small bowl. Having already decided what song to play after dinner, Gurney Halleck looked over at his nine-string baliset leaning against the wall.

Kailea watched Leto's gray eyes, how his gaze drifted from one end of the banquet hall to the other, from the portrait of Paulus Atreides to the mounted bull's-head, its rack of horns still stained with blood. She didn't know what the Duke was thinking, but as she looked across the table, the witchling Jessica met her gaze with green eyes, as if *she* understood what Leto was about to do. Kailea turned away, frowning.

When Leto stood up, Kailea drew a deep sigh. He was about to engage in one of his interminable ducal speeches, trying to inspire them about all the good things in their lives. But if life was so good, why had both of her parents been murdered? Why did she and her brother, the heirs of a Great House, remain in exile, rather than enjoying what should have been theirs?

Two servants hurried forward to remove the soup dishes and leftover bread, but Leto waved them away so that he might speak uninterrupted. "Next week is the twentieth anniversary of the bullfight in which my father was killed." He looked up at the matador portrait. "Consequently, I've been thinking of the grand entertainments Duke Paulus performed for his subjects. They loved my father for that, and I think it's about time *I* created a worthy spectacle, as would be expected from a Duke of Caladan."

Instantly, Hawat raised his guard. "What is it you intend, my Duke?"

"Nothing so dangerous as a bullfight, Thufir." Leto grinned down at Victor, then over at Rhombur. "But I want to do something the people will talk about for a long time to come. I'm leaving soon for the Landsraad Council on Kaitain, to begin a new diplomatic mission in the Moritani-Ecazi conflict, especially now that we might be forming a much stronger alliance with Ecaz."

He paused for a moment, appearing embarrassed. "As a grand send-off, I'm going to take our largest skyclipper on a magnificent procession across the lowlands. My people can look up and see the banners and the colorful airship—and wish their Duke well in his mission. We'll pass above the fishing flotillas, and then inland over the pundi rice farms."

Victor clapped his hands, while Gurney nodded in approval. "Ho! It will be a marvelous sight."

Leaning his elbows on the table, Rhombur rested his square chin in his hands. "Uh, Leto, isn't Duncan Idaho returning soon from Ginaz? Will you be away when he arrives? Or can we combine his homecoming with the same celebration?"

Pondering this, Leto shook his head. "I haven't heard anything in some time. We don't expect him for a couple of months yet."

Gurney thumped a hand on the table. "Gods below! If he's coming to us as a Swordmaster of Ginaz after eight long years of training, the man deserves a reception of his own, don't you think?"

Leto laughed. "Indeed, Gurney! Plenty of time for that when I return. With you, Thufir, and Duncan bearing swords for me, I need never fear a scratch from an enemy."

"There are other ways an enemy can strike, my Lord," Jessica said with a low warning in her voice.

Kailea stiffened, but Leto didn't notice. Instead he looked at the witch. "I'm fully aware of that."

Already, wheels were turning in Kailea's mind. At the conclusion of the meal she excused herself and went to tell Chiara what Leto planned to do.

THAT NIGHT LETO slept on a cot in a hangar of the Cala Municipal Spaceport, while his household staff went about making preparations for the gala event, delivering announcements and gathering supplies. Within a few days the sail-enhanced sky-clipper would begin its grand and colorful procession.

Left alone in her chambers, Kailea summoned Swain Goire and seduced him, as she had done many times in the past. She made love to the guard captain with a feral passion that surprised and exhausted him. He looked so much like Leto, but was such a different man. Afterward, when he had fallen asleep beside her, she stole a tiny code-locked key from a concealed pocket in his thick leather belt, which was curled on the floor. Only rarely used, it would be some time before Goire noticed the missing key.

The following morning, she pressed the small object into Chiara's leathery palm and squeezed the old woman's fingers over it. "This will give you access to the Atreides armory. Move with care."

Chiara's ravenlike eyes sparkled, and quickly she tucked the key into secret folds of her layered garments. "I will handle the rest, my Lady."

War, as the foremost ecological disaster of any age, merely reflects the larger state of human affairs in which the total organism called "humanity" finds its existence.

—PARDOT KYNES,
Reflections on the Disaster at Salusa Secundus

ON THE ADMINISTRATION ISLAND OF GINAZ, THE FIVE GREATEST LIVING Swordmasters met and judged their remaining students in the oral examination phase of their curriculum, grilling them on history, philosophy, military tactics, haiku, music, and more—all according to the exacting requirements and traditions of the school.

But this was a somber, tragic occasion.

The entire school archipelago remained in an uproar, outraged and grieving for the six slain students. Flaunting their barbarity, the Grummans had dumped four of the bodies in the surf near the main training center, where they had washed up on shore. The other two—Duncan Idaho and Hiih Resser—remained missing, likely lost at sea.

On the top floor of the central tower, the Swordmasters sat along the straight side of a semicircular table, their ceremonial swords extended point-outward on the surface in front of them, like the rays of a sun. Each student who stood in front of the table would see the threatening points while he answered rigorous questions.

They had all passed. Now Karsty Toper and the school administration would arrange travel for the successful students to return to their respective homes, where they would apply what they had learned. Some had already gone to the nearby spaceport.

And the Swordmasters were left with the consequences.

Fat Rivvy Dinari sat in the center, drawing out the sword of Duke Paulus Atreides and a jeweled Moritani heirloom knife, found among the possessions of Idaho and Resser. Beside him, Mord Cour hung his gray-maned head. "We have had much experience sending back the keepsakes of fallen students, but never like this."

Sinewy master Jamo Reed, though hardened from overseeing his prison island for many years, could not stop weeping. He shook his head. "If Ginaz students die, it should be during difficult training—not because they are murdered."

Ginaz had lodged formal protests, issuing culturally tailored insults and censures, none of which meant anything to Viscount Hundro Moritani. He had never made satisfactory amends for his brutal attacks on Ecaz. The Landsraad and the Emperor were now holding hearings on the best means of response, with the leaders of many Great Houses traveling to Kaitain in order to speak with the Council. But they had never managed more than censures, fines, and slaps on the hand even for a "mad dog" like the Viscount.

The Grummans believed they could get away with anything.

"I feel . . . violated," Jeh-Wu said, his dreadlocks hanging in disarray. "No one has ever dared to do this sort of thing to a Swordmaster."

Foppish Whitmore Bludd sat up straighter and fiddled with the ruffles on his shirt, the heavy cuffs at his wrists. "I propose that we rename six of our islands after the murdered students. History will remember the dastardly crime, and we will honor the Six."

"Honor?" Rivvy Dinari slapped his fat palm on the tabletop, making the sword blades jangle. "How can you use such a word in this context? I spent three hours last night by Jool-

Noret's burial vault, praying and asking what he would do in such a situation."

"And did he answer you?" Scowling, Jeh-Wu stood up and went to look out the window, at the flat spaceport and the foamy reefs. "Even in his own lifetime, Jool-Noret never taught anybody. He drowned in a tidal wave, and his disciples tried to emulate him. If Noret never helped his closest followers, he certainly won't help us."

Bludd sniffed, looking offended. "The great man taught by example. A perfectly valid technique, for those capable of learning."

"And he had honor, just like the ancient samurai," Dinari said. "After tens of thousands of years, we have grown less civilized. We have forgotten."

Frowning in contemplation, Mord Cour looked over at the obese Swordmaster. "You are forgetting history, Dinari. The samurai may have had honor, but once the British arrived in Japan with guns, the samurai vanished . . . within a generation."

Jamo Reed looked up, his lean face devastated beneath a snowy white cap of frizzy hair. "Please, we must not fight among ourselves or else the Grummans will have beaten us."

Jeh-Wu snorted. "They've already—"

A commotion at the doorway interrupted him. He turned from the window as the other four Swordmasters rose to their feet in shock.

Dirty and disheveled, Duncan Idaho and Hiih Resser pushed past the objections of three uniformed school employees, knocking the men aside in the corridor. The two young men strode into the room, battered and limping, but with a fire in their eyes.

"Are we too late?" Resser asked with a forced grin.

Jamo Reed ran around the table to embrace Duncan, then Resser. "My boys, you are alive!"

Even Jeh-Wu had a relieved and astonished smile on his iguanalike face. "A Swordmaster has no need to state the obvious," he said, but Jamo Reed didn't care.

Duncan's gaze lit on the Old Duke's sword lying on the semicircular table. He took a step forward and looked down at the blood oozing from a gash on his left shin, soaking through the leg of his ill-fitting pants. "Resser and I haven't actually been studying for the past several days . . . but we have been putting your training into practice."

Resser swayed a little, having trouble staying on his feet, but Duncan supported him. After gulping cups of water that Mord Cour gave them, they explained how they had jumped overboard in the rough seas, swimming and helping each other to distance themselves from the large dark boat. Straining their abilities to the limit, clinging to every scrap of knowledge they had learned during eight years of rigorous Swordmaster training, they had remained afloat for hours. They did their best to navigate by the stars, until finally the tides and currents carried them to one of the numerous islands—luckily a civilized one. From there, they had secured minimal first aid and dry clothes, as well as immediate transportation.

Though his good humor had been damaged by the ordeal, Resser still managed to raise his chin. "We would like to formally request a delay in our final examination, sirs—"

"Delay?" Jamo Reed said, with tears in his eyes again. "I suggest a dispensation. Surely these two have proven themselves to our satisfaction?"

Indignant, Whitmore Bludd tugged at his ruffles. "The forms must be obeyed."

Old Mord Cour looked at him skeptically. "Haven't the Grummans just shown us the folly of too blindly following the forms?" The other four Masters turned to Rivvy Dinari for his assessment.

Finally, the huge Swordmaster levered his enormous body

to his feet and gazed at the bedraggled students. He indicated the Old Duke's sword and the ceremonial Moritani dagger. "Idaho, Resser, draw your weapons."

With a clatter of steel, the Swordmasters took up their blades, arranged in a sunburst pattern on the semicircular table. His heart pounding, Duncan picked up the Old Duke's sword from the table, and Resser took the dagger. The five Swordmasters formed a circle, including the two students in the ring, and extended their blades toward the center, placing one atop the other.

"Lay your points on top of the rest," Mord Cour said.

"You are now Swordmasters," Dinari announced in his paradoxically small voice. The huge man sheathed his sword, removed the red bandanna from his spiky mahogany hair, and tied it around Duncan's head. Jamo Reed withdrew another bandanna and cinched it around Resser's red hair.

After eight years, the rush of triumph and relief brought Duncan to near collapse, but through sheer force of will he steadied his knees and remained standing. He and Resser grasped each other's hands in celebration, albeit one tainted by tragedy. Duncan couldn't wait to return to Caladan.

I have not failed you, Duke Leto.

Then a sound like ripping air tore overhead, a succession of sonic booms from descending atmospheric craft. From the reefs that circled the central island, unexpected sirens went off. Much closer, an explosion echoed from the walls of the administration buildings.

The senior Swordmasters sprinted to a balcony that overlooked the complex. Across the channels of still water, two nearby islands glowed with smoky fires.

"Armored airships!" Jamo Reed said. Duncan saw black predatory forms swoop out of the pillars of flame, in steep climbs as they dropped streams of explosives.

Jeh-Wu snarled, tossing his dark hair. "Who would dare attack us?"

To Duncan, the answer seemed obvious. "House Moritani isn't done with us yet."

"It flies in the face of all civilized warfare," Rivvy Dinari said. "They have not declared kanly, have not followed the proper forms."

"After what he has done to us, to Ecaz, what does Viscount Moritani care about the forms?" Resser said in disgust. "You don't understand how his mind works."

More bombs exploded.

"Where's our antiaircraft fire?" Whitmore Bludd sounded more annoyed than outraged. "Where are our 'thopters?"

"No one has ever attacked Ginaz before," Jamo Reed said. "We are politically neutral. Our school serves all Houses."

Duncan could see how these Masters had been blinded by their egos, their rules and forms and structures. Hubris! They had never conceived of their own vulnerabilities—despite what they taught their students.

With a foul stream of expletives, Dinari pushed binoculars against the folds of fat on his face. He flicked the oil-lens settings and, ignoring the oncoming armored craft, scanned the rugged edge of the administrative island. "Enemy commandos are all over that shore, landing opposite the spaceport. Approaching with shoulder-mounted artillery."

"Must have come in by submarine," Jeh-Wu said. "This isn't an impromptu attack—they've been planning it for quite some time."

"Waiting for an excuse," Reed added, a deep frown creasing his tanned face. The attacking airships drew closer, thin black disks shimmering with defensive shields.

To Duncan, the Swordmasters appeared so helpless, almost pathetic, when faced with this unexpected situation. Their hypothetical exercises were far different from reality. Painfully so. He gripped the Old Duke's sword.

"Those ships are unmanned flyovers, made to drop bombs and incendiaries," Duncan said with cool assessment, as a rain of bombs fell from the roaring disks. Buildings blossomed into fire all along the shoreline.

Shouting, the proud Swordmasters ran from the balcony, with Resser and Duncan in their midst. "We need to get to our stations, do what we can to guide the defense!" Dinari's thin voice was sharpened with command.

"The rest of the new trainees are at the spaceport," Resser pointed out. "They can grab equipment and fight back."

Off-balance but struggling to recover, especially in front of the even-more-panicked officials and administrators, Jamo Reed, Mord Cour, and Jeh-Wu charged along the main corridor, while Rivvy Dinari showed how fast he could move his bulk, vaulting down a stairway by holding handrails and leaping from landing to landing. Whitmore Bludd scuttled behind him.

After exchanging quick glances, Duncan and Resser followed the two Swordmasters who'd gone down the stairway. A nearby explosion rocked the administration building, and the young men stumbled. Still, they kept going. Outside, the full-scale attack continued.

The new Swordmasters surged through a door at ground level into the central lobby, joining Dinari and Bludd. Through the armor-plaz windows, Duncan could see buildings burning outside. "We've got to get to your command center," he said to his elders. "We need the equipment to fight. Are there attack 'thopters at the spaceport?"

Resser held his ceremonial Moritani dagger. "I'll fight right here, if they dare send anyone in to face us."

Bludd looked agitated; he had dropped his colorful cloak somewhere on the stairs. "Don't think small. What is their goal? Of course, they'll be after the vault!" In dismay, he nodded toward an ornate black coffin on a dais that dominated the lobby. "Jool-Noret's remains, the most sacred object on all of Ginaz. Can you think of a greater insult to us?" With a flushed face he turned toward his enormous companion. "It would be just like the Grummans to hit us in the heart."

Perplexed, Duncan and Resser looked at each other. They had been steeped in tales about the legendary fighter—but in the face of this bloody attack, the exploding bombs, the screaming civilians rushing for shelter on the island streets, neither of them could care much about the old relic.

Dinari rushed across the floor like a battleship moving at full speed. "To the vault!" he shouted. Bludd and the others tried to keep up with him.

The famous burial vault was surrounded by clear armor-plaz and a shimmering Holtzman-generated shield. Eschewing all arrogant pretenses, the two Swordmasters rushed up the steps and pressed their palms against a security panel. The shield faded, and the armor-plaz barriers lifted.

"We'll carry the sarcophagus," Bludd shouted to Duncan and Resser. "We must keep this safe. It is the very soul of the Ginaz School."

Constantly looking around for attackers in Moritani uniforms, Duncan balanced the Old Duke's sword in his grip. "Take the mummy if you have to, but be quick about it."

Resser stood at his side. "Then we've got to get out of here, and find some ships so we can fight." Duncan hoped that other Ginaz defenses were already rallying to strike back against the attackers.

While the senior Swordmasters, both strong men, lifted the ornate coffin and carried it toward the dubious safety outside, Duncan and Resser cleared the way. Outside, the black disks continued their indiscriminate rain of bombs.

A gun 'thopter with school markings landed in the plaza in front of the administration building; it folded its wings while the engines continued to thrum. Half a dozen Swordmasters leaped from the craft wearing singlesuits and red bandannas, with lasrifles slung over their shoulders.

"We've got Noret's body," Bludd called proudly, gesturing to the 'thopter for assistance. "Come quickly."

Soldiers in yellow Moritani uniforms ran across the plaza.

Duncan shouted a warning, and the Swordmasters fired las-guns at the attackers. The Grumman soldiers responded with their own weapons; two Swordmasters were hit, including Jamo Reed. When an aerial bomb exploded, old Mord Cour sprawled down, injured in the arms and torso by flying stone splinters. Duncan helped the shaggy-haired instructor to his feet and into the safety of the 'thopter.

Just as he got Cour inside, though, a charging attacker knocked Duncan's legs out from under him. The young Swordmaster tumbled to the pavement, rolled, and sprang to his feet again. Before he could extend his sword, a Grumman woman in a yellow martial-arts *gi* dove under his guard, slash-ing at him with claw-knives on her fingers. With his sword useless at such close range, he grabbed the attacker's long hair and jerked back hard enough to hear her neck snap. The assas-sin melted to the ground, limp and twitching.

More Grummans converged on the gun 'thopter. Resser shouted, "Go! Take the damned coffin with you!" He and Duncan whirled to face another opponent.

A bearded man lunged with a sparking electrical spear, but Duncan ducked the blow and spun to one side. His thoughts accelerated as he summoned the proper response from eight years of training. Rage threatened to overtake him, rising in red waves as he remembered the captive students slaughtered on the dark boat. His retinas burned with vivid images of the bombs and fire and the slain innocents.

But he remembered Dinari's admonition: *With anger comes error.* In an instant, he settled on a cold, almost instinctive re-sponse. With sheer force of will, Duncan Idaho slammed steely fingertips under the lunging man's rib cage, breaking skin and piercing his heart.

Then a cagey young man stepped from the fray, lean and muscular, with his injured right wrist sealed in a padded cast. *Trin Kronos.* The surly young lordling grasped a sharp-bladed katana in his good hand. "I thought you two would be feeding the fish, like the other four examples we made." He looked up at the soaring bombers; another huge explosion took down a low building.

"Face *me*, Kronos," Resser said, drawing his ceremonial Moritani dagger. "Or are you too much a coward without your father and a dozen guards armed with heavy weaponry?"

Trin Kronos held his katana, considered, then cast it aside. "Too good a weapon for a traitor. I would have to throw it away after I soiled it with your blood." He withdrew a dueling knife instead. "A dagger is easier to replace."

Resser's cheeks flushed, and Duncan stepped back to watch the two confront each other. "I would never have forsaken House Moritani," Resser said, "if they'd given me anything I could believe in."

"Believe in the cold steel of my blade," Kronos said, with a cruel sneer. "It will feel real enough when it cuts out your heart."

With broken rubble underfoot, the two circled cautiously, not breaking each other's gaze. Resser held up his dagger, maintaining a solid defensive posture, while Kronos jabbed and slashed, aggressive but ineffective.

Resser attacked, withdrew, then swept out his foot in a vicious kick that should have knocked Kronos to the ground, but the Grumman fighter bent backward like a snake, drawing himself away from the redhead's foot. Resser spun all the way around and recovered his balance, deflecting a swift knife blow.

The area around the two combatants was clear. In nearby streets, other Grumman attackers continued to raid, and projectile fire rang out from high windows. At the 'thopter, the Swordmasters struggled with their relic, trying to lift the sarcophagus into their aircraft while fighting off attackers.

Kronos feinted, slashed at Resser's eyes with the tip of his dueling knife, then stabbed for the throat. Resser threw himself to one side, neatly out of range, but his foot came down on a loose chunk of rock; his ankle twisted, and he stumbled.

Kronos was upon him like a lion, pouncing and bringing the knife down, but Resser slapped sideways with his own dagger, knocking the other blade aside with a clang. Then he jabbed upward, sliding the point into his opponent's bicep and tracing a red cut down past the elbow to the forearm.

With a childish cry, Kronos staggered back, looking at the scarlet river pouring down to his uninjured wrist. "Bastard traitor!"

Resser bounced to his feet and focused his stance again, ready to fight. "I'm an orphan, not a bastard." His lips curved in a quick, wan smile.

His arm slick with blood, his knife hand weak, Kronos could see that he had lost the knife fight. His face hardened. Upending his fighting dagger, he brought the pommel down on his thick wrist cast. It split open along a planned seam, and a spring-loaded flèchette pistol popped into his grip. Kronos grinned, thrusting the weapon forward, preparing to fire a full load of the silver flèchettes into Resser's chest. "You still insist on following your absurd rules, don't you?"

"*I* don't," Duncan Idaho said from behind as he thrust mightily with the Old Duke's sword. The point pierced between the shoulder blades of Trin Kronos and emerged from his chest, sliding all the way through his heart. Kronos coughed blood and shivered, astonished at the sharp object that had sprouted from his sternum.

As Kronos slumped dead, he slid off the bloody blade. Duncan stared at his victim and at the sword. "Grummans aren't the only ones who can break the rules."

Resser's face had gone gray, having accepted the inevitability of his death as soon as he saw the pistol hidden in Kronos's cast. "Duncan . . . you stabbed him in the back."

"I saved the life of my friend," Duncan replied. "Given the same options, I would make that choice every time."

Dinari and Bludd finished tying down the sacred relic aboard the 'thopter. Laser arcs filled the air as Ginaz defenders fired with deadly accuracy. The two young men stood exhausted, but the Swordmasters pulled them aboard the 'thopter.

With a great thrust of jets, the gunship surged into the air. The wings reached full extension, transporting the passengers and the body of Jool-Noret away from the main buildings. As Duncan huddled on the metal deck, Rivvy Dinari leaned over to place a thick arm around his shoulders. "You boys had to prove yourselves early."

"What's this attack all about? Wounded pride?" Duncan asked, so angry he wanted to spit. "A foolish reason to begin a war."

"There are rarely good reasons to begin wars," Mord Cour said, hanging his head.

Whitmore Bludd tapped the transparent plaz. "Look out the window."

A swarm of Ginaz gunships fired laser blasts at the enemy aircraft and mowed down troops on the ground. "Our new Swordmasters are at the controls—your fellow students from the spaceport," Cour said.

After a direct hit, one of the unmanned flyovers exploded and plummeted. The Swordmasters raised their fists inside the cramped 'thopter.

The flyover hit the ground in a fireball, and a second vessel crashed into the ocean. Lasbeams struck more of them out of the skies. Duncan's 'thopter dove toward a squad of Grumman commandos rushing back over the water and blasted them, leaving bodies strewn on the ground. The pilot went around for another pass.

"The Grummans expected easy pickings," Whitmore Bludd said.

"And damned if we didn't provide them," Jeh-Wu growled.

Duncan watched the mayhem and tried not to compare the rampant destruction and bloodshed with all the finesse he had learned in eight years at the Ginaz School.

Beware the seeds you sow and the crops you reap. Do not curse God for the punishment you inflict upon yourself.

—Orange Catholic Bible

EMPLOYING INDIGNANT PROPRIETY THAT WOULD HAVE MADE EVEN THE Lady Helena proud, Kailea convinced Leto not to include his son in the grand ducal procession. "I do not want Victor exposed to any danger. That skyclipper isn't safe for a six-year-old boy."

Thufir Hawat proved to be an unexpected ally, agreeing with Kailea's concerns, until finally Leto relented. Exactly as she had hoped. . . .

After the Duke's capitulation, Kailea helped Rhombur to salvage the situation. "You're Victor's uncle. Why don't you two go on . . . a fishing expedition? Take a wingboat along the coast—as long as you're accompanied by enough guards. I'm sure Captain Goire would be happy to join you."

Rhombur brightened. "Maybe we'll go out and collect coral gems again."

"Not with my son," Kailea said sharply.

"Uh, all right. I'll just take him out to the floating paradan melon farms, and maybe to some coves where we can look at the fish."

SWAIN GOIRE MET Rhombur down by the docks as they cleaned out the hold of the small, well-equipped motorboat *Dominic*.

Preparing to be gone for several days, they took bedrolls and food. Behind the Castle, at the spaceport on the outskirts of Cala City, the Duke's crew labored to prepare the enormous skyclipper. Anxious to be off, Leto was utterly absorbed with final arrangements.

As work continued at the boat, Victor became irritable and less than enthusiastic. At first Rhombur thought the boy might still remember the elecran encounter, but instead he saw Victor glance repeatedly up at the plateau where his father was about to embark on his journey. Atreides banners rippled in the air, reflective streamers of green and black.

"I'd rather be with my daddy," Victor said. "Fishing is fun, but riding on a skyclipper is better."

Rhombur leaned against the side of the boat. "I agree, Victor. I wish there was some way for us to join him."

Duke Leto intended to pilot the skyship himself, accompanied by an appropriate escort of five loyal soldiers. With the limited amount of weight allowable in the lighter-than-air vessel, it was not wise to take joyriders.

Swain Goire dropped a crate of provisions outside the bridge house, then wiped sweat from his forehead and smiled at the boy. Rhombur knew that the captain was more dedicated to the boy than to any law or other master. Adoration for Leto's son flickered across Goire's handsome face.

"Uh, Captain, let me ask your opinion." Rhombur looked at Victor, then back at the guard captain. "You've been entrusted with the safety of this child, and you've never once been known to shirk your duties or give anything less than full attention to your assignment."

Goire flushed with embarrassment.

Rhombur continued, "Do you believe my sister's fears that Victor would actually be in danger if he accompanied Leto aboard the skyclipper?"

Laughing, Goire made a dismissive gesture. "Of course not, my Lord Prince. If there was any danger, Thufir Hawat would never allow our Duke to go—and neither would I. Hawat charged me to oversee the security of the clipper itself before it departs, while he and his men scour the flight path for any signs of ambush. It is completely safe, I assure you. I'd stake my life on it."

"My thoughts exactly." Rhombur rubbed his palms together and grinned. "So, is there a particular reason why Kailea should insist that we take a fishing trip rather than go along?"

Pursing his lips, Goire considered the question. He wouldn't meet Rhombur's gaze. "Lady Kailea is sometimes . . . excessive in her concern for the boy. I believe she imagines threats where there are none."

Little Victor looked from one man to the other, not understanding the nuances of the discussion.

"Spoken with true candor, Captain. I can't imagine why you haven't been promoted!" Then Rhombur lowered his voice to a stage whisper. "Uh, why don't we have Victor join his father, in secret? He shouldn't miss this magnificent procession. He is the Duke's son, after all. He needs to take part in important events."

"I concur . . . but there is the issue of weight ratios. The skyclipper has limited passenger capacity."

"Well, if there's truly no danger, why don't we remove two members of the honor guard so that my dear nephew"— Rhombur squeezed Victor's shoulder—"and I can join the Duke. That still leaves three guards, and I can do my share of fighting to protect Leto, if it comes to that."

Though uneasy, Goire could voice no reasons to counter this suggestion, especially not after he saw the delight on Victor's face. The boy made his resistance melt. "Commander Hawat won't like any change of plans, and neither will Kailea."

"True, but you are in charge of security on the airship itself, correct?" Rhombur brushed aside the concern. "Besides, Victor can't possibly grow into a good leader if he is sheltered from every splinter and bruise. He needs to get out and learn from life—no matter what my sister says."

Goire bent in front of the delighted boy, treating him like a little man. "Victor, tell me true. Do you want to go fishing, or—"

"I want to go on the skyclipper. I want to be with my father and see the world." His eyes were filled with determination.

Goire stood up. For a moment he held Victor's gaze, wanting to do anything in his power to make the boy happy. "That's all the answer I needed. It's decided, then." He looked back toward the spaceport where the dirigible waited. "I'll go make the arrangements."

AFRAID HER MANNERISMS might give something away, Kailea sequestered herself in one of the towers of Castle Caladan, feigning illness. She'd already said her formal goodbye to a preoccupied Leto, then hurried away before he could look into her eyes . . . not that he paid much attention to her anyway.

A cheering crowd watched the ducal procession as it prepared to lift off into the blue Caladan sky. The Atreides hawk was painted in brilliant red across the swollen side of the skyclipper, which would be followed by smaller but similarly designed airships, all colorfully decorated. The skyclipper deployed sails to catch the winds, and strained against its tethers like a mammoth, turgid bee. Atreides banners fluttered in a light breeze.

The bulk of the airship was empty space, enclosed pockets of buoyant gas, but the tiny passenger compartment in the belly had been filled with provisions. Guiding sails flapped out like butterfly wings at the sides. Thufir Hawat had checked the proposed route himself, trudging down roads and dispatching guards and inspectors to ensure that no assassins had secreted themselves along the way.

Biting her lip, Kailea watched from the high window that faced inland, where she could see the colorful aircraft. Though she only faintly heard the fanfare playing to see Leto off, she saw figures standing on podiums, waving before they climbed aboard the skyclipper.

Her stomach knotted.

She admonished herself for not obtaining a pair of binoculars . . . but that might have raised suspicions. A foolish worry; the household servants would simply have assumed that she wanted to watch her "beloved" Leto depart on his historic procession. The people of Caladan knew nothing of the dark side of their relationship; in their naïveté, they imagined only romantic stories. . . .

With a pang in her heart and a sense of inevitability, Kailea watched the work crews release the tethers. Raised by suspensor-assisted floats, the skyclipper drifted gracefully into the air currents. The sluggish craft had propulsion systems that could be used in an emergency, but Leto preferred to let the giant vessel move with the winds, whenever possible. Smaller companion ships followed.

Though alone, Kailea Vernius tried to clear all expression from her face, all emotion from her mind, not wanting to recall the good times she'd had with her noble lover. She had waited long enough, and she knew in her soul that it would never happen the way she'd wanted it.

Rhombur, despite his dabbling with a few rebels, had accomplished *nothing* on Ix. Nor had their father, in all his years of supposed underground struggle against House Corrino. Dominic was dead, and Rhombur was content to be Leto's anonymous sidekick, enthralled with his plain Bene Gesserit woman. He had no ambitions at all.

And Kailea couldn't accept that.

She gripped the stone windowsill, watching the glorious procession of airships drift over Cala City and away to the lowlands. The commoners would stand knee-deep in their marshy fields and look up to see the Duke's passage. Kailea's lips formed a firm, straight line. Those pundi rice farmers would get much more of a sight than they expected. . . .

Chiara had told her the details of the plan only after it had already been initiated. Having once been the mistress of a munitions expert, Chiara had personally set a trap, using linked explosives stolen from the Atreides armory. There would be no chance of survival, no hope of rescue.

Feeling helpless dread, Kailea closed her eyes. The wheels had been set in motion, and nothing she could do would prevent the disaster now. *Nothing.* Soon her son would be the new Duke, and she would be his regent mother. *Ah, Victor, I am doing this for you.*

Hearing footsteps, she was surprised to see Jessica appear at the door to her room, already returned from the launching of the ducal ship. Kailea stared at her rival with a stony expression. Why couldn't *she* have accompanied Leto? That would have solved even more of her problems.

"What is it you want?" Kailea said.

Jessica looked slender and delicate—yet Kailea knew that no young woman with Bene Gesserit training could ever be helpless. The witch could probably kill Kailea in an instant with her weirding ways. She promised herself she would get rid of this seductress as soon as the weight and responsibility of House Atreides fell across her shoulders.

I will be regent for my son.

"Now that the Duke has gone and left us alone, it is time for us to talk." Jessica watched Kailea's reaction. "We've avoided it for too long, you and I."

Kailea felt as if every nerve on her face and in her fingers, every twitch and gesture were being dissected through this upstart's scrutiny. It was said that a Bene Gesserit could read minds, though the witches themselves denied it. Kailea shuddered, and Jessica took a step deeper into the room.

"I'm here because I want privacy," Kailea said. "My Duke has departed, and I wish to be alone."

Jessica's brow furrowed. Her green eyes stared intently, as if she had already detected something wrong. Kailea turned away, feeling naked. How could this young woman expose her so easily?

"I thought it would be better if we did not leave so much unspoken between us," Jessica continued. "Leto may decide to marry soon. And it won't be to either of us."

But Kailea did not want to hear any of it. *Does she wish to make peace with me? To ask my permission to love Leto?* The thought brought a flickering smile to her face.

Before Kailea could respond, she heard footsteps again, booted feet. Swain Goire lunged into the room. He looked unsettled, his formal uniform disheveled. He stopped for a moment upon seeing Jessica there in the chamber, as if she were the last person he had expected to encounter with Kailea.

"Yes, Captain, what is it?" Kailea snapped.

He fumbled for words, unconsciously touched his thick belt, then flickered to the tiny uniform pocket where he usually kept his coded armory key. "I . . . I have misplaced something, I fear."

"Captain Goire, why aren't you with my son?" Kailea vented anger toward him in hopes of distracting Jessica. "You and Prince Rhombur were scheduled to depart on your fishing trip hours ago."

The handsome guard avoided her gaze, while Jessica stared at both of them, recording each movement. Kailea's heart froze. *Does she suspect? And if so, what will she do about it?*

"I . . . seem to have lost an important piece of equipment, my Lady," he stammered, looking very embarrassed. "I've been unable to find it, and now I am growing concerned. I intend to search for it in every possible place."

Kailea stepped closer to him, her face flushed. "You didn't answer my question, Captain. You three should have gone fishing. Did you delay my son's trip so he could watch his father depart?" She touched a finger to her frowning lips. "Yes, I can see how Victor would have enjoyed watching the airships. But take him now. I don't want him to miss the fishing trip with his uncle. He was very excited about it."

"Your brother requested a slight change of plans, my Lady," Goire said, uncomfortable with Jessica's presence, and at being caught in his mistake. "We'll schedule another fishing trip for next week, but Victor wanted so much to accompany Duke Leto. This sort of procession is very rare. I didn't have the heart to refuse him."

Kailea whirled, aghast. "What do you mean? Where is Victor? Where's Rhombur?"

"Why, they're aboard the skyclipper, my Lady. I will inform Thufir Hawat—"

Kailea rushed to the window, but the huge airship and its companions had already drifted far out of sight. She battered her fist on the transparent plaz of the window, and let out a loud, keening wail of despair.

Every man dreams of the future, though not all of us will be there to see it.

—TIO HOLTZMAN,
Speculations on Time and Space

ABOARD THE SKYCLIPPER, LETO RELAXED IN THE COMMAND SEAT. THE SHIP rose high above the city and drifted over the surrounding agricultural areas. So peaceful, gentle, quiet. He moved the rudders, but allowed the winds their whim. In utter silence and perfect grace, they cruised over lush terrain at the head of the procession of ships. He looked down upon broad rivers, thick forests, and marshes where standing pools glittered.

Victor stared wide-eyed out the viewing windows, pointing at sights and asking a thousand questions. Rhombur answered, but deferred to Leto when the name of a landform or clustered village exceeded his knowledge.

"I'm glad you're here, Victor." Leto good-naturedly mussed the boy's hair.

Three guards were stationed aboard, one in the main cabin and the others at the fore and aft exits. They wore black uniforms, with the red hawk epaulets of the Atreides honor guard. Since he had replaced one of their members for this trip, Rhombur wore the same uniform; even Victor, who had also replaced a guard because of weight limitations on the skyclipper, wore the epaulets on his replica of the Duke's black jacket. On the boy, the epaulets were oversized, but he insisted on wearing them.

Rhombur began to sing folk songs, rhymes he'd picked up from locals. In recent months he and Gurney Halleck had shared baliset duets, playing tunes and singing ballads. At the moment, Rhombur simply enjoyed singing in his rough voice, without any accompaniment.

Hearing a familiar chanty, one of the guards joined in. The man had grown up on a pundi rice farm before joining the Atreides troops, and still remembered the songs his parents had taught him. Victor tried to sing along, too, adding the intermittent but not always correct words of a chorus when he thought he remembered them.

Though large, the sail-driven skyclipper was an easy craft to handle, a vessel made for leisurely voyages. Leto promised himself that he would do this more often. Perhaps he'd take Jessica with him . . . or even Kailea.

Yes, Kailea. Victor should see his mother and father spend more time together, regardless of their political or dynastic differences. Leto still had feelings for her, though she had rebuffed him at every turn. Remembering how cruel his own parents had been to one another, he did not want to leave such a legacy for Victor.

It had been an oversight at first, worsened by his stubbornness when Kailea began making unreasonable demands about marriage—but he realized he *should* have at least made her his bound-concubine and given their son the Atreides name. Leto had not yet decided to accept Archduke Ecaz's formal offer of marriage to Ilesa, but one day he would certainly find a politically acceptable match for himself among the Landsraad candidates.

Still, he loved Victor too much to deny the boy's status as firstborn. If he designated the child as his official heir, perhaps Kailea would warm to him.

Eventually bored with the singing and the skyclipper's ponderous pace, Victor craned his neck upward to look at the rippling sails outside. Leto let him handle the control grip for a few moments, turning the rudder. The boy was thrilled to see the skyclipper's nose nudging in response to his commands.

Rhombur laughed. "You'll be a great pilot someday, boy— but don't let your father teach you. I know more about piloting than he does."

Victor looked from his uncle to his father, and Leto laughed to see him ponder the comment with such seriousness. "Victor, ask your uncle to tell you how he set our coracle on fire once, then crashed it into a reef."

"You *told* me to crash it into the reef," Rhombur said.

"I'm hungry," Victor said, not surprising Leto at all. The boy had a hearty appetite, and was growing taller every day.

"Go look in the storage cabinets in the back of the bridge deck," Rhombur said. "That's where we keep our snacks." Anxious to explore, Victor ran to the rear of the deck.

The skyclipper passed over pundi rice paddies, soggy green fields separated by sluggish canals. Barges drifted along below them, filled with sacks of the native grain. The sky was clear, the winds gentle. Leto could not imagine a better day for flying.

Victor stood on a ledge to reach the topmost cabinets, rummaging among the shelves. He studied iconic images on the labels; he couldn't read all the Galach words, but recognized letters and understood the purposes of certain things. He found dried meats, and uluus, wrapped berry pastries as a special dessert for the evening. He gobbled one package of uluus, which satisfied his immediate hunger, but he continued to poke about.

With the curiosity of a child, Victor moved to a bank of storage pockets built into the gondola's lower wall against the dirigible sack that made up the bulk of the skyclipper. Identifying the red symbol, he knew that these were emergency supplies, first-aid equipment, medicines. He had seen such things before, watching in awe as House surgeons bandaged cuts and scrapes.

Opening the first-aid pocket, he withdrew medical supplies, scrutinized gauze wrappings and pill packets. A loose cover plate on the back wall rattled intriguingly, so he popped it out to find another compartment even deeper within. Inside a sheltered wall behind the emergency supplies, Victor found something with blinking lights, a glowing counter, impedance-transfer mechanisms connected to clusters of red energy-storage containers, all strung together.

Fascinated, he stared for a long time. "Uncle Rhombur! Come see what I found!"

Smiling tolerantly, Rhombur strode across the deck, ready to do his best to explain whatever the child had encountered.

"There, behind the doctor kits." Victor pointed with a small finger. "See, it's bright and pretty."

Rhombur stood behind the boy, bent over to squint. Proud and proprietary, Victor reached deeper inside. "Look at how all the lights blink. I'll get it so you can see better."

The boy grasped the device, and Rhombur suddenly sucked in a sharp breath. "No, Victor! That's a—"

Duke Leto's son jostled the impedance leads, and activated the tamper-lock timer.

The explosives detonated.

Knowledge is pitiless.

—Orange Catholic Bible

WHEN FLAMES ERUPTED FROM THE AFT END OF THE SKYCLIPPER COCKPIT, the shock wave slammed into Leto like a meteor.

A burned and broken mass of flesh smashed into the front viewing wall beside him, then dropped to the floor. Too large for a child, too small to be a man—a whole man—it left a smear of blackened bodily fluids.

Searing heat roared around him as the air crackled with flames. The rear of the dirigible blazed, engulfed in orange fire.

Yelling uselessly in horrified confusion, Leto wrestled the rudder controls as the wounded skyclipper bucked and reared. Out of the corner of his eye, he couldn't stop looking at the broken form beside him.

It twitched. Who was it? He didn't want to know.

A parade of awful images assaulted his retinas, one at a time, lasting the merest fraction of a second. Behind him, he heard a screaming wail that changed abruptly, then dwindled as the flailing silhouette of a man was sucked through a gaping blast hole torn in the bottom of the cabin. The man's entire body was in flames. It had to be either Rhombur or one of the three guards.

Victor had been at the center of the explosion. . . .
Gone forever.

The crippled skyclipper began to plummet, losing buoyancy as the flammable gas was consumed inside the dirigible's body. The fabric tore away, and yellow-white fire towered higher. Smoke filled the cockpit.

Leto's flesh was hot, and he knew his fine black uniform would soon be in flames. Beside him, the wreck of the unidentified body made a mewling sound of pain. . . . He seemed to have the wrong *number* of arms and legs, and his face was a bloody mass of twisted, unrecognizable flesh.

The skyclipper was crashing.

Below, pundi rice paddies spread out in sinuous rivers, jewel-like ponds, and peaceful villages. The people had gathered, waving pennants to greet his passage. But now, seeing the fireball overhead like the hammer of God, they scrambled for shelter as the skyclipper died in the air. The smaller escort craft flurried around the flaming vessel, but they could do nothing but follow.

Leto tore his mind from its stunned paralysis—*Rhombur! Victor!*—when suddenly he saw that the airship was hurtling toward one of the farming villages. He would crash in the midst of the gathered people.

Like an animal, he wrestled with the rudders to change the angle of descent, but the flames consumed the hydraulic systems, ate away the buoyant enclosure. Most of the villagers scattered like a panicked herd; others stared helplessly, realizing they could never get away in time.

Knowing in his heart that Victor must be dead, Leto was tempted just to let himself vanish in the bright flames and the explosion. He could close his eyes and lean back, allowing gravity and heat to crush and incinerate him. How simple it would be just to give up. . . .

But when he saw all those people down there—some of them children like Victor—Leto forced back his despair, leaned forward, and fought the controls. There had to be some way to alter course and avoid the village.

"No, no, no . . ." he moaned deep in his throat.

Leto felt no physical pain, only grief that ripped through his heart like a knife. He could not bear to consider all he had lost, could not waste a moment of reflexes and skill. He was fighting for the lives of the people who believed in him and relied on him.

At last one of the rudders turned, and the skyclipper's nose tipped upward the barest fraction of a degree. Tearing open an emergency panel below his controls, Leto saw that his hands were red and blistered. All around, the flames grew hotter and hotter. But he reached inside and tugged on the curved red levers with all his strength, hoping the escape cables and controls remained active.

As the blaze in the rear of the skyclipper increased, metal clamps thumped open. The tattered dirigible sack split free, disconnected from the cockpit cabin. Guidance sails broke away and flew off in the winds, some singed, some already on fire, like flaming kites without strings.

The cockpit cabin dropped off, and the remainder of the dirigible sack—suddenly freed of the weight of passengers and the thick-walled cabin—rose like a comet blazing in the sky. Correspondingly, the self-contained cabin dropped at a steeper angle. Glider wings extended, snapping into place, braking the descent. Damaged suspensor mechanisms struggled to function.

Leto pushed hard against the control grip. The hot air seemed to be melting his lungs with every breath he gasped. The tangled trees bordering soft islands in the rice marshes rose up at him. Their thorns were stiff fingers with sharpened ends, a forest of claws. He loosed a wordless howl. . . .

Even the Old Duke's end in the bullring would never be remembered as more spectacular than this final flash of glory. . . .

At the last possible instant, Leto added just a little lift and power, as much as he could wring from the damaged suspensors and engines. He skimmed past the crowded village, singeing ramshackle roofs, and crashed into the rice marshes beyond.

The cockpit cabin hit the saturated ground like an ancient artillery shell. Mud, water, and shattered trees sprayed up into the air. The walls folded and collapsed.

The impact hurled Leto from his seat into the front bulkhead, and then dropped him back down to the floor. Brownish water poured through ruptures in the cabin until finally, with a groan and a shriek, the wreckage came to a rest.

Leto slipped into peaceful darkness. . . .

The greatest and most important problems of life cannot be solved. They can only be outgrown.

—SISTER JESSICA,
private journal entry

IN A LIGHT TROPICAL RAIN, THE SURVIVORS AMONG THE SENIOR SWORD-masters strode along the explosion-pocked pavement of what had formerly been the historic central plaza of the Ginaz School.

Duncan Idaho, already battle-proven, stood in their midst; he had discarded his torn tunic. Beside him, Hiih Resser kept his shirt on, though it was drenched in blood—mostly not his own. Both of them were full-fledged Swordmasters now, but they had no desire to celebrate their triumph.

Duncan just wanted to go home, to Caladan.

Though it had been more than a day since the Grumman sneak attack, fire and rescue crews still worked in the rubble, using sleek dogs and trained ferrets to sniff for signs of life. But buried survivors were few.

The central plaza's once-lovely fountain had been demolished by shrapnel. Smoking debris lay all around. The odor of death and fire lingered in the air, not dissipated by the sea breezes.

The Moritani soldiers had intended only a damaging hit-and-run strike; they had made no preparations—and had no stomach—for a prolonged battle. Shortly after the Ginaz fighters rallied their weapons for defense, the Grummans left their fallen soldiers behind. They abandoned their damaged aircraft and rushed back to waiting frigates. No doubt, Viscount Moritani was already publicly justifying his heinous actions—and privately celebrating his sneak attack, no matter how much blood it had cost his own men.

"We study and teach fighting, but Ginaz is not a military world," Whitmore Bludd said; his fine clothing looked all the worse now, soot-stained and bedraggled. "We strive to remain independent of political matters."

"We made assumptions and got caught sleeping," Jeh-Wu said, turning his perpetual sarcasm on himself for once. "We would have killed any new student for such blind arrogance. And we are guilty of it ourselves."

Weary to the bone, Duncan looked at the men who had once been so proud, and saw how defeated they looked.

"Ginaz should never have been a target for aggression." Rivvy Dinary bent over to pick up a mangled strip of metal, once part of an ornamental clockwork sculpture. "We assumed—"

"You *assumed*," Duncan cut him off, and they had no answer.

DUNCAN AND HIS redheaded friend took the body of Trin Kronos and dumped it out into the crashing surf near the main training center—the same spot where the kidnappers had dropped the corpses of their other four victims. The gesture seemed right, the appropriate symbolic response, but the pair took no satisfaction from it.

Now, the gathered fighting men shook their heads in dismay as they inspected the damaged administration building. Duncan vowed to never forget the arrogance of the Swordmasters, how it had led to so much trouble. Even the ancients understood the danger of hubris, of the pride before the fall; had men learned nothing in all these thousands of years?

Like his companions, Duncan now wore a Swordmaster's

khaki uniform and red bandanna. Black bands encircled their left arms, in honor of more than a hundred Swordmasters who had died in the Moritani assault.

"We relied on Imperial law to protect us," an injured Mord Cour said, sounding weak and small. He seemed very different from the man who had taught the drama of epic poetry and made students weep as he recited legendary stories. Both of his arms were bandaged. "But the Grummans didn't care. They have flouted our most sacred traditions, spat upon the very foundation of the Imperium."

"Not everyone plays by the rules," Duncan said, unable to suppress his bitterness. "Trin Kronos told us himself. We just didn't listen to him." Rivvy Dinari's jowly face flushed.

"House Moritani will get a slap on the wrist," Jeh-Wu said, his lips puckered into a frown. "They'll be fined, perhaps embargoed—and they will continue to laugh at us."

"How can anyone respect the prowess of Ginaz now?" Bludd groaned. "The school is disgraced. The damage to our reputation is immense."

Mord Cour stared up at the hazy sky, and his long gray hair hung like a shroud around his head. "We must remake the school. Just like the followers of Jool-Noret did, after their Master drowned."

Duncan studied the grizzled old Swordmaster, remembered the man's tumultuous lifetime after his village had been wiped out, how he had lived a feral life in the mountainsides of Hagal, then returned to join—and slay—the bandits who had killed his neighbors and family. If anyone could accomplish such a dramatic resurrection, Cour could.

"We will never be so helpless again," Rivvy Dinari promised, his voice filled with emotion. "Our Premier has promised to station two full combat units here, and we are acquiring a squad of minisubs to patrol the waters. We are Swordmasters, righteous in our prowess—and this enemy caught us completely unprepared. We are ashamed." With a graceful move, he kicked a twisted scrap of metal, sending it clattering into the street. "Honor is slipping away. What is the Imperium coming to?"

Overwhelmed by his own thoughts, Duncan stepped around a splash of blood on the pavement, which glistened in the warm rain. Resser bent to look at it, as if he could draw some information from the rusty puddle, some indication of whether the fallen victim was enemy, or ally, or bystander.

"A lot of questions need to be asked," Bludd said, his voice edged by suspicion. "We must dig deeply enough to find out what really happened." He puffed out his chest. "And we will. I'm a soldier first and an educator second."

His companions grunted in agreement.

Seeing something sparkle in a pile of rubble, Duncan stepped over debris to retrieve it. He pulled out a silver bracelet, wiped it on his sleeve. Tight clusters of charms hung from the band . . . tiny swords, Guild Heighliners, ornithopters. Rejoining the others, Duncan handed it to Dinari.

"Let us hope it didn't belong to a child," the bulky man said.

Duncan had already seen four dead children dragged from the debris, the sons and daughters of school employees. The final death toll would be in the thousands. Could it all be traced back to the single insult of expelling Grumman students, which had been a justifiable act in response to House Moritani's outrageous attack on innocent Ecazi civilians . . . which had been caused by the assassination of an ambassador at a banquet on Arrakis . . . which in turn had been provoked by suspected crop sabotage?

But the Grumman students had made their own choices about staying or leaving. It was all so senseless. Trin Kronos had lost his life over it, and too many others with him. When would it end?

Resser still intended to return to Grumman, though it seemed suicidal for him to do so. He had his own demons to face there, but Duncan hoped he would survive them, and eventually make his way to Duke Leto. After all, Resser was a Swordmaster.

A few of the Swordmasters halfheartedly suggested offering their services as mercenaries for Ecaz. Some of the Masters insisted that they regain their honor first. Skilled fighters were needed on Ginaz to rebuild the decimated school faculty. The famed academy would be years recovering from this.

But, while Duncan felt a deep sense of loss and anger for what had happened here, his first allegiance was to Duke Leto Atreides. For eight years Duncan had been forged in fire like the layered steel of a sword. And that sword was sworn to House Atreides.

He would return to Caladan.

Why look for meaning where there is none? Would you follow a path you know leads nowhere?

—Query of the Mentat School

THE NIGHTMARES WERE BAD, BUT WAKING WAS INFINITELY WORSE.

When Leto returned to consciousness in the infirmary, the night nurse greeted him, telling him he was lucky to be alive. Leto didn't feel so lucky. Seeing his dismal expression, the male nurse with heavy spectacles said, "There is some good news. Prince Rhombur survived."

Leto took a deep, agitated breath. His lungs felt as if he had swallowed ground glass. He tasted blood in his saliva. "And Victor?" He could hardly get the words out.

The nurse shook his head. "I'm sorry." After a somber pause, the man added, "You need more rest. I don't want to trouble you with details about the bomb. There is time enough for that later. Thufir Hawat is investigating." He reached into a pocket of his smock. "Let me give you a sleeping capsule."

Leto shook his head vehemently, extended a warding hand. "I'll go back to sleep on my own." *Victor is dead!*

Not entirely satisfied, but deferring to the royal patient, the nurse told him not to get out of bed. A voice-activated call-unit hovered in the air over the bed. Leto just had to speak into it.

Victor is dead. My son! Leto had known it already . . . but now he had to face the terrible reality. *And a bomb. Who could have done such a thing?*

Despite the medical orders, the stubborn Duke watched the night nurse go into a room across the corridor to tend another patient. Rhombur? From his bed, Leto could just see one edge of an open doorway.

Ignoring the pain, Leto pulled himself to a sitting position on the infirmary bed. Moving like a damaged Ixian mek, he levered himself up from crisp sheets that smelled of perspiration and bleach and swung his legs over the side of the bed. His bare feet touched the floor.

Where was Rhombur? Everything else could wait. He needed to see his friend. *Someone has killed my son!* Leto felt a surge of anger, and a sharp pain across the top of his head.

His vision focused to a pinprick, and he concentrated on a tiny goal in front of him as he took one step, then a second. . . . His ribs were bandaged, and his lungs burned. Plaskin salve made his face feel stiff, like soft stone. He had not looked in a mirror to see the extent of the damage. He didn't worry about scars, didn't care at all. Nothing could heal the deep, irreparable damage to his soul. Victor was dead. *My son, my son!*

Incredibly, Rhombur had survived, but where was he?

A bomb on the skyclipper . . .

Leto took one more step, then another away from the diagnostic apparatus beside the bed. Outside, a cold storm blew, splattering raindrops like pellets against the sealed windows behind him. The infirmary lights were dimmed in the gloomy night. He staggered out of the room.

Reeling in the doorway of the room across the corridor, he grasped the jamb to maintain his balance, then blinked before he stumbled toward brighter light inside, where the glowglobes were whiter, colder. The large room was divided by a dark curtain that waved slightly in the shadows. Sharp odors assailed him from chemicals and cold air-purification systems.

Disoriented, he didn't consider consequences or implications. He only knew for certain, like a tolling bell in his mind, that Victor was *gone*. Killed in flames or sucked out with the explosion. Was it a Harkonnen assassination plot against House Atreides? A vengeful attack by the Tleilaxu against Rhombur? Someone trying to eliminate Leto's heir?

It was difficult for the Duke to explore such matters through the fuzz of pain medications, through the stupor of grief. He could barely maintain the mental energy to proceed from one moment to the next. Despair was like a soaked blanket, smothering him. Despite his determination, Leto was sorely tempted to fall into a deep, comforting well of surrender.

I must see Rhombur.

He slid the curtain open, passed through. In low light, a coffin-shaped life-support pod was hooked up to tubes and pipes. Leto focused his efforts and took laboring steps, cursing the pain that caused his movements to falter. A mechanically operated bellows pumped oxygen into the sealed chamber. Rhombur lay within.

"Duke Leto!"

Startled, he noticed the woman who stood beside the life-support pod, wrapped in Bene Gesserit robes, surrounding herself with dark colors like shadows. Tessia's drawn face was leached of its sharp humor and quiet loveliness, drained of life.

He wondered how long Rhombur's concubine had maintained her vigil here. Jessica had told him of Bene Gesserit techniques that allowed Sisters to remain awake for days. Leto realized that he didn't even know how much time had passed since he'd been pulled from the smashed wreckage of the cockpit chamber. From the haggard look on Tessia's face, he doubted she had rested a moment since the disaster.

"I . . . I came to see Rhombur," he said.

Tessia took a half step backward, and pointed toward the pod. She did not assist Leto, and he finally made it on his own to the plazchrome side of the vessel. He leaned heavily against the cool, polished metal seams.

Breathing hard, Leto bent his head but kept his eyes closed

until the dizziness passed and the pain subsided . . . and until he built up his nerve to look upon what had happened to his friend.

He opened his eyes. And recoiled in horror.

All that remained of Rhombur Vernius was a smashed head and most of a spinal column, part of a chest. The rest—limbs, skin, some organs—had been ripped away by the force of the blast or crisped to cinders by engulfing flames. Mercifully, he remained in a coma. This was the torn mass of flesh he had seen on the deck of the skyclipper.

Leto tried to think of an appropriate prayer from the O.C. Bible. His mother would have known exactly what to say— though she had always resented the presence of the Vernius children. Lady Helena would claim this was a righteous punishment from God, because Leto had dared to take in the refugees from a sacrilegious House.

Life-support systems and power packs kept Rhombur alive, trapping his tormented soul inside this scrap of body that still clung to his existence.

"Why?" Leto said to himself. "Why did this happen? Who did this to him? To Victor? To me?"

He looked up and saw Tessia's stony expression. She must be using all of her Bene Gesserit training just to contain her own anguish.

Although she'd been an arranged concubine, Rhombur had genuinely loved her. The two had allowed their match to blossom into what it could be—unlike Leto's relationship with Kailea, and unlike his parents, whose marriage had never engendered true affection.

"Thufir Hawat and Gurney Halleck have been at the crash site for days," Tessia said. "They are investigating the wreckage to determine the responsible party. You are aware of the bomb?"

Leto nodded. "Thufir will find the answers. He always

does." He forced the words from his mouth, driving himself to ask the question he dreaded most. "And Victor's body—?"

Tessia looked away. "Your son was . . . found. The guard captain, Swain Goire, immediately preserved as much as possible . . . though I can't think what purpose that might serve. Goire . . . loved the boy, too."

"I know he did," Leto said.

He stared down at the strange red-and-pink shape inside the life-support pod, unable to recognize his friend. So closely did the chamber resemble a coffin that Leto could almost envision pulling away the wires, sealing the top, and burying it. *Maybe that would be best.*

"Is there anything we can do for him—or is this just a futile exercise?"

He could see the muscles bunch in Tessia's cheeks, and her sepia eyes hardened, blazing with cold fire. Her voice dropped to a breathless whisper. "I can never give up hope."

"My Lord Duke!" The night nurse's alarmed voice carried a scolding tone as he entered the room. "You must not be up, sir. You must recover your strength. You are grievously injured, and I cannot permit you—"

Leto lifted a hand. "Don't speak to me of grievous injuries as I stand here beside the life-support pod of my friend."

The nurse's gaunt face flushed, and he nodded jerkily on a long thin neck, like a wading bird's. But he touched Leto's sleeve with a delicate, scrubbed hand. "Please, my Lord. I am not here to compare wounds. My aim is to see that the Duke of House Atreides heals as quickly as possible. That is *your* duty, too."

Tessia touched the life-support pod, and her gaze met Leto's. "Yes, Leto. You have responsibilities still. Rhombur would never permit you to throw everything away because of his condition."

Leto allowed himself to be guided out of the room, taking

careful steps as the night nurse led him back to his bed. He knew intellectually that he must regain his strength, if only to enable him to understand the disaster.

My son, my son! Who has done this thing?

LOCKED IN HER chambers, Kailea wailed for hours. Refusing to speak to anyone, she did not come out to see the Duke, her brother, or anyone else. But in truth, she could not face herself, the monstrous guilt, the unredeemable shame.

It would be only a matter of time before Thufir Hawat and his relentless investigation uncovered her culpability. For now, no one had expressed any suspicions against her . . . but soon the gossip would begin, whispered along the cool stone halls of Castle Caladan. People would wonder why she was avoiding Duke Leto.

And so, after learning the schedule of medications—and determining when Leto would be least likely to detect the murderous guilt in her eyes—Kailea unbolted the door of her chambers and walked unsteadily toward the infirmary rooms. At dusk, the light visible through stone-framed windows had turned the cloud banks coppery in the sky, like her hair. But she saw no beauty in the sunset, only shadows inside the walls.

Medical technicians and the doctor bustled about, making way for her, backing out of the room to give her privacy with the Duke. The sympathy on their faces tore at her heart.

"He has suffered a relapse, Lady Kailea," the doctor said. "We've had to administer more drugs for his pain, and now he may be too sleepy to say much."

Kailea stood with forced hauteur. Her puffy red eyes dried as she steeled herself. "Nevertheless, I will see him. I shall stand by Leto Atreides as long as I am able, trusting that he knows I am there."

The doctor courteously found something else to do outside the room.

Her footsteps leaden, one hesitant pace at a time, Kailea moved closer to the bedside. The room smelled of injuries and pain, of medicines and despair. She looked down at Leto's bruised, burned face and tried to recall her anger toward him. She thought again of the terrible things Chiara had told her, the myriad ways Leto Atreides had betrayed all of her hopes, destroying her dreams.

Still, she remembered vividly the first time they had actually made love, practically by accident after the Duke had been drinking too much Caladan ale with Goire and the guards. Laughing, Leto had spilled a mug on himself, and then ambled out into the hall. There he encountered Kailea, who'd been unable to sleep and had been prowling the Castle. Noting his condition, she'd scolded him gently and led him into his private chambers.

She had intended to help him into bed and then leave. Nothing more, though she had fantasized about it many times. His own attraction for her had been so plain, for so long. . . .

After all they'd been through, how could she possibly have convinced herself to hate him?

As she stared at him now, lying injured and motionless, she recalled how he had loved to play with his son. She had refused to see how much he'd adored the boy, because she hadn't wanted to believe it.

Victor! She squeezed her eyes shut and pressed her hands against her face. Tears flowed over her palms.

Leto stirred and half awoke, focusing on her with groggy, red-rimmed eyes. It took him a long moment, but finally he recognized her. His face seemed free of walls and the hardness of leadership, showing only naked emotion. "Kailea?" he said in a drawn-out croak.

Not daring to respond, she bit her upper lip. What could she possibly say? He knew her too well . . . he would *know*!

"Kailea . . ." His voice filled with absolute anguish. "Oh,

Kailea, they've killed Victor! Someone has killed our beautiful son. Oh, Kailea . . . who could have done such a thing? Why?"

He struggled to keep his gray eyes open, fighting the fog of drugs in his system. Kailea jammed her fist into her mouth, biting on the knuckles until blood flowed.

Unable to face him any longer, she whirled and fled the room.

IN A RAGE, Swain Goire strode up the long steps to the isolated tower chambers. Two Atreides House guards stood outside the entrance to Kailea's private rooms.

"Step aside," Goire commanded.

But the guards refused to move. "The Lady Kailea has given us orders," said the Levenbrech-ranked officer on the left, flicking his gaze away, afraid to oppose his commanding officer. "She wishes to be alone in her grief. She has not eaten or accepted any visitors. She—"

"Who gives you orders, Levenbrech? A concubine, or the commander of our Lord Duke's troops?"

"You, sir," answered the soldier on the right, looking at his companion. "But you put us in an awkward position."

"You're dismissed, both of you," Goire barked. "Go now. I will bear the responsibility." Then he said in a softer voice, as if to himself, "Yes, I bear the responsibility."

He threw open the door, strode inside, and slammed it behind him.

Kailea wore a pale old sleeping garment. Her coppery hair hung in disarray, and her eyes were red and puffy. She knelt on the stone floor, forsaking the chairs, ignoring the cold wet draft from the open window. The fireplace lay gray and dark in the palpable gloom of the chamber.

Red scratches etched parallel lines on her cheeks, as if she had tried to claw out her eyes but had lost the nerve. With a shadowed gaze she looked up at him, her expression filled with pathetic hope as she saw someone who might offer sympathy.

Kailea raised herself from the floor, little more than a ghost of herself. "My son is dead, my brother mangled beyond recognition." Her face looked like a skull. "Swain, *my son is dead.*" She took a step toward him and extended her hands, as if hoping for comfort. Her expressive mouth twisted in a parody of a pleading smile, but he stood rigid.

"My armory key was stolen," he said. "Taken from my uniform belt shortly after Leto announced his plans for a ducal procession."

She stopped barely a meter from her lover. "How can you think of such things when—"

"Thufir Hawat will learn what has happened!" Goire roared. "I know now who took the key, and I know what it means. Your actions condemn you, Kailea." He shuddered, wanting to tear her heart out with his bare hands. "Your own son! How could you do this?"

"Victor is dead," she wailed. "How can you think I planned that?"

"You meant to kill the Duke alone, didn't you? I saw your panic when you learned that Rhombur and Victor had joined him in the skyclipper. Most of the household already suspects your hand in this."

His eyes blazed and his muscles tightened, but he remained immobile as a statue. "And you have made me responsible, too. Skyclipper security was my duty, but I was slow to realize the importance of the missing key. I kept convincing myself I had only misplaced it, refused to consider other possibilities . . . I should have raised an alarm."

He hung his head, continued to speak while he stared at the floor. "I should have confessed our affair to my Duke long before this, and now you have soaked my hands with blood, as well as your own." His nostrils flared as he looked at her in revulsion, and his vision turned crimson. The room spun around him. "I betrayed my Duke many times, but this is the worst of all. I could have prevented Victor's death if only . . . ah, poor, sweet child."

Kailea's clawlike hands darted forward and grasped the hilt of the dueling dagger at Goire's waist. She snatched it out of its sheath and held it up, her eyes glazing. "If you are so miserable in your guilt, Swain, then fall on your knife like a good warrior, like a loyal Atreides soldier. Take it. Thrust the blade into your heart so that you can no longer feel the pain."

Dully, he looked at the outstretched dagger, but refused to move toward it. Instead, after a long intense moment, he turned away . . . as if taunting Kailea to plunge the blade into his back. "Honor demands justice, my Lady. True justice—not an easy way out. I will face my Duke with what I have done." He looked over his shoulder as he strode toward the doorway. "Worry about your own guilt."

She held the dagger in her hands as Goire left. After he closed the door, he heard Kailea wailing, pleading for him to come back. But the captain closed his ears to her cries and marched purposefully from the tower.

WHEN KAILEA DEMANDED to see her lady-in-waiting, Chiara scuttled into the room, terrified but not daring to tarry. Wind whistled through the open tower window, along with the sounds of surf crashing against the rocks far below. Kailea stared out into the distance, the breezes whipping her pale garment like a funeral shroud around her.

"You . . . summoned me, my Lady?" The old woman hovered close to the doorway, allowing her shoulders to slump in an appearance of meek submission. She wished she had thought to bring a tray of spice coffee or Kailea's favorite sweetmeats, a peace offering to calm the animal fires within the distraught woman.

"Shall we discuss your foolish plan, Chiara?" Kailea's voice sounded hollow and frighteningly cold. She turned, and her expression carried death.

The lady-in-waiting's instincts told her to flee the Castle, to disappear into Cala City and take a transport back to Giedi Prime. She could throw herself upon the mercy of Baron Harkonnen and boast about how much anguish she had caused the Duke, albeit with only partial success.

But Kailea held her paralyzed, like a snake mesmerizing its prey.

"I . . . I am terribly sorry, my Lady." Chiara bowed, then began to grovel. "I mourn for the innocent blood that was shed. No one could have foreseen that Victor and Rhombur would join the procession. They were never supposed to—"

"Silence! I want none of your excuses. I know everything that happened, everything that went wrong."

Like a steel trap closing, Chiara clamped off further words. She felt a deeper nervousness, sensing how alone they were in this chamber. If only the guards had remained at their posts as she'd ordered, if only Chiara had thought to arm herself before coming here.

So many things had been unforeseen.

"As I think back over the years, Chiara, I recall so many comments you made, all those insidious suggestions. Now their meaning grows clear, and the weight of evidence is an avalanche against you."

"What . . . what do you mean, my Lady? I have done nothing but serve you since—"

Kailea cut her off. "You were sent here to sow discord, weren't you? You have been trying to turn me against Leto since the day we met. Who do you work for? The Harkonnens? House Richese? The Tleilaxu?" Sunken eyes and scarred cheeks dominated her blank and emotionless face. "No matter, the result is the same. Leto has survived . . . and my son is dead."

She took a step toward the old woman, and Chiara used

her most compassionate voice like a shield. "Your grief is making you think and say terrible things, my dear. This has all been a dreadful mistake."

Kailea stepped closer. "Be thankful for one thing, Chiara. For many years I considered you my friend. Victor died swiftly and painlessly, unsuspecting. For that, I grant you your own merciful death."

She yanked out the dueling dagger she had taken from Swain Goire. Chiara lurched backward, raising her fingers in a warding gesture. "No, my Lady!"

But Kailea did not hesitate. She drove forward, plunging the blade deep into Chiara's chest. She withdrew and struck again to be sure she had pierced the traitorous woman's heart. Then she let the knife fall with a clatter to the floor as a gurgling Chiara sagged like a pile of rags onto the tiles.

Blood splashed the eerily beautiful blue obsidian wall, and Kailea straightened, looking at her own dim reflection there. She stared for a long moment, not liking what she saw.

With ponderous steps, Kailea went to the open window. The biting cold numbed her skin, and yet all of her flesh felt wet, as if with blood. Holding the stone edges of the windowsill, she stared out into the cloud-laden sky to the distant horizon made smooth by the seas of Caladan. Below, the foaming infinity of waves snarled around the base of the tall cliff.

The marvelous stalactite city inside the crust of Ix shone in her memory. It had been so long since she'd danced in the reflective halls of the Grand Palais, showing off her finest merh-silk dresses. She had stood with her brother and the Pilru twins looking out upon the immense grotto where Heighliners were built.

Like a prayer, Kailea Vernius brought to mind everything she had read and all the images she had seen of the Imperial Court at Kaitain, the spectacular palace, the tiered gardens, the chime kites. She had longed to spend her life in the dazzling glamor that should have accompanied her station—

Princess of a Great House of the Landsraad. But in all her life, Kailea had never achieved the heights or the wonders that she desired.

Finally, leaving only dark memories behind her, she climbed onto the windowsill and spread her wings to fly. . . .

Humans must never submit to animals.

—Bene Gesserit Teaching

THOUGH ABULURD FORMALLY RETAINED THE TITLE OF SUBDISTRICT GOVERnor of Lankiveil, in name at least, Glossu Rabban controlled the planet and its economy. It amused him to let his father keep the title, as that didn't change who was really in power.

What could the old fool do anyway, holed up in a cliffside monastery?

Rabban despised the planet's dreary skies, cold temperatures, and primitive people with their smelly *fish*. He hated it because the Baron had forced him to spend years here after his botched mission on Wallach IX. But mostly, he hated the place because his father loved it so much.

Secure on Lankiveil, Rabban finally decided to inspect the remote spice stockpile they'd hidden decades before. He liked to check the hoards periodically, to be certain they were secure. All records had been erased, all witnesses eliminated. No proof existed that the Baron had secreted away so much melange during his early tenure on Arrakis.

Rabban mounted an expedition, coming out of orbit to set down on the northern landmass where he had spent two years in the industrial port cities and the whale fur–processing plants. Now, with ten of his soldiers, he navigated the icechoked northern seas in a boat commandeered from one of the fisheries. His scanners and technicians knew where to search for the artificial iceberg. Rabban let them do their work while he huddled in his cabin and drank too much kirana brandy. He would come out on deck when the goal was sighted, but he had no interest in smelling the salty fog or freezing his fingertips until it was necessary.

The synthetic iceberg was perfection to the naked eye, exactly like any other floating arctic block. When the boat anchored, Rabban shouldered his way to the front of his troops. He stepped aboard the polymer-based iceberg, operated the hidden hatch, and entered the hollow blue tunnels.

Only to find the enormous storehouse completely empty.

When Rabban let out a deep bellow, the sound echoed through the cold tunnels. "Who did this?"

Later, the boat roared off to the south, leaving the faux iceberg behind. Rabban stood at the bow, so hot with anger that the wet and cold no longer affected him. The craft raced down to the rocky fjords, where Harkonnen soldiers swarmed into pathetic little fishing villages. The settlements looked much nicer than Rabban remembered them: the houses new, the equipment shiny and functional. The fishing boats and tackle, as well as the storehouses, were modern and well cared for, full of off-world imports.

The soldiers wasted no time in grabbing villagers and torturing one after another until the same answer surfaced again and again. Rabban had suspected even before he heard the name uttered through bloody lips and broken teeth.

Abulurd.

He might have known.

IN THE CLIFF city of Veritas, a cold winter snap came on. The Buddislamic monks used fresh water from deep mountain springs to enhance the structure and beauty of their remarkable monastery.

Abulurd's scarred heart had recovered as much as it ever

would. Wearing warm robes and thick gloves, he held a flexible hose and spigot that sprayed a sparkling mist onto the edge of the cave opening.

His breath gushed out in a cloud of steam, and the skin of his cheeks felt so cold it was bound to crack. But he smiled as he sprayed the hose, adding to the prismatic sheetwall of ice. The barricade built up slowly, like a curtain around the front of their overhanging grotto. The translucent, milky-white barrier hung down, a dome that reflected and sparkled in sunlight, yet blocked the winds that whipped around the crags. Chimes and weathervanes jangled outside the grotto and up along the cliffs, gathering power and making music at the same time.

Abulurd shut off the water flow and pulled back on the spigot so that monks could run forward with broken chunks of colored glass, which they positioned in the freezing water to create a kaleidoscope of brilliant hues. They stepped back, and Abulurd sprayed water again, coating the colored glass chips. As the frozen curtain grew, the studded jewels added rainbows to the city under the overhang.

After the ice barrier had been extended another half meter, the abbot of Veritas sounded a gong, calling a halt to the efforts. Abulurd shut off the water and sat back, exhausted but proud of what he had accomplished.

He stripped off his thick gloves and slapped the padded jacket to break away the crusting of ice. Then he opened his body covering to let out the warm steam-sweat and stepped into a portable dining enclosure with clearplaz windows.

When several monks arrived to feed the workers, Emmi came up to him carrying a stone bowl of hot soup. Abulurd patted the bench beside him, and his wife sat to share lunch with her husband. The broth was delicious.

Suddenly, through the dining enclosure he saw the ice curtain shatter inward with a blaze of lasgun fire. Broken shards crunched to the grotto floor, then slid down the outer cliff.

After a second round of weapons fire, a Harkonnen attack craft became visible hovering in front of the overhang, weapons still smoking as it cleared away space so that it could drive under the shelf ceiling.

The monks scrambled about, yelling. One dropped a hose, and fresh water gushed across the cold stone floor.

Abulurd felt sick with a horrible sense of déjà vu. He and Emmi had come to Veritas to lead a life of peace, in secret. They wanted no contact with the outside world, especially not with the Harkonnens. Especially not with their elder son.

The attack craft scraped across the rock floor as it landed. The hatch hissed open, and Glossu Rabban was the first out, flanked by soldiers who bristled with weapons—though none of the monks in Veritas would ever have resorted to violence, not even to defend one of their own. Rabban wore his inkvine whip.

"Where is my father?" he demanded as he led his men toward the dining enclosure. His voice sounded like two rocks crashing together. The intruders ripped the thin plaz door open, allowing a cold wind inside.

Abulurd stood up, and Emmi grabbed him in a gesture so abrupt that she upended the bowl of hot soup. It tumbled to the polished floor and shattered. Steam rose from the spilled broth into the cold air.

"I'm here, Son," Abulurd said, standing tall. "There's no need to break anything else." His mouth was dry with fear, his throat constricted. The monks backed away, and he was glad the others did not try to speak, because Glossu Rabban—his demonic *son*—had no qualms about opening fire on innocents.

The burly man swiveled as if his waist were on ball bearings. His heavy eyebrows furrowed, forming a hood that shadowed his face. He marched forward, fists coiled. "The spice stockpile—what have you done with it? We tortured the people in your fishing village." His eyes danced with pleasure.

"Everyone gave your name. And then we tortured some more, just to be sure of the matter."

Abulurd stepped forward, putting distance between himself and Emmi and the other monks. His gray-blond hair hung limp over his ears with sweat from his labors. "I used the stockpile to help the people of Lankiveil. After all the hurt you've caused, you owe it to them." He had intended to prepare for this eventuality, to set up an effective passive defense system that would protect them from Harkonnen rage. He'd hoped Rabban wouldn't notice the missing spice until he'd had a chance to prepare the monks. But he hadn't gotten around to it soon enough.

Emmi hurried across the floor, her face flushed, her straight black hair thrown back. "Stop this! Leave your father alone."

Rabban didn't even turn his head, didn't take his eyes from Abulurd's. Instead, he lashed out with one muscular arm and struck his mother squarely in the center of her face. She staggered back, clutching her nose as blood poured between her fingers and down her cheeks.

"How *dare* you strike your mother!"

"I'll strike whomever I please. You don't seem to understand who has the power here. You don't know how pathetically weak you are."

"I'm ashamed of what you've become." Abulurd spat on the floor in disgust.

Rabban was unimpressed. "What have you done with our spice stockpile? Where have you taken it?"

Abulurd's eyes flashed fire. "For once, Harkonnen money has done some good, and you'll never get it back."

Moving with the speed of a viper, Rabban grabbed Abulurd's long-fingered hand and yanked it toward him. "I'm not going to waste time with you," he said, his voice deep and threatening. With a vicious twist, he snapped Abulurd's index finger, breaking it like a dry stick. Then he broke the thumb.

Abulurd reeled with the pain. Emmi staggered to her feet and screamed. Blood streamed down her mouth and chin.

"What have you done with the spice?" Quickly, efficiently, Rabban broke two fingers on his father's other hand for good measure.

Abulurd looked at his son, his gaze steady, thrusting away the pain that howled through his broken hands. "I distributed all the money through dozens of intermediaries. We spent the credits here on Lankiveil. We built new buildings, bought new equipment, purchased food and medical supplies from off-world merchants. We've taken some of our people off-planet to better places."

Rabban was incredulous. "You spent *all* of it?" There had been enough melange hidden away to finance several large-scale wars.

Abulurd's laugh was a thin, slightly hysterical sound. "A hundred solaris here, a thousand there."

Now the steam seemed to boil out of Rabban, deflating him—because he understood that his father undoubtedly could have done exactly as he claimed. If so, the Harkonnen spice hoard was truly gone. Rabban could never retrieve it. Oh, he might squeeze a bit of repayment here and there from the villagers, but he would never reclaim everything they had lost.

The tides of rage threatened to burst a blood vessel in Rabban's brain. "I'll kill you for this." His voice held a cold tone of absolute certainty.

Abulurd stared into the wide, hate-filled face of his son—a complete stranger. Despite all Rabban had done, after all the corruption and evil, Abulurd still remembered him as a mischievous boy, still remembered when Emmi had held him as a baby.

"You will not kill me." Abulurd's voice was stronger than he imagined it could be. "No matter how vile you are or how many twisted things the Baron has taught you, you cannot commit such a heinous act. I am your own father. You are a human being—not a beast."

This triggered the last avalanche of uncontrolled emotions. With both hands, Rabban grasped his father around the throat. Emmi screamed and threw herself at their deranged son, but she might have been a blown leaf. Rabban's powerful hands squeezed and *squeezed*.

Abulurd's eyes bulged, and he reached up to fight back with his broken fingers.

Rabban's thick lips curved upward in a smile. He crushed Abulurd's larynx and snapped his neck. With a frown of disgust, he released his grip and let his father's corpse tumble to the rock floor as the monks and his own mother gasped and screamed.

"From now on I shall be called *Beast*." Pleased with the new name he had chosen, Rabban signaled for his men to accompany him. Then he strode back to the ships.

To keep from dying is not the same as "to live."

—Bene Gesserit Saying

EVEN THE DREARIEST ROOM IN CASTLE CALADAN WAS AN IMPROVEMENT over the infirmary, and Leto had been moved to the exquisitely appointed Paulus Suite. The change of location, despite its landmines of memory, was meant to help him recover.

But every day seemed the same, gray and endless and hopeless.

"Thousands of messages have come in, my Duke," Jessica said with forced cheer, though her heart ached for him. She used just the slightest hint of manipulative Voice. She pointed to cards, letters, and message cubes on a nearby table. Bouquets of fragrant flowers adorned the room, battling the antiseptic odors of medicinals. Some children had drawn pictures for their Duke. "Your people grieve with you."

Leto didn't respond. He stared ahead, his gray eyes without luster. A white newskin wrap was secured to his forehead, a second application to repair scar tissue. Quicknit amplifier packs were attached to one shoulder and both of his legs, and an intravenous line dangled from one arm. He noticed none of it.

The burned and mangled body of Rhombur remained connected to a life-support pod back in the hospital. The Prince still clung to life, though he might have been better off in the morgue. Survival like this was worse than death.

At least Victor is at peace. And Kailea, too. He felt only pity for her, sickened at what she had been driven to do.

Leto turned his head slightly in Jessica's direction. His face bore an overwhelming sadness. "The medics have done as I commanded? You're certain?" Under Leto's strict orders, his son's recovered corpse had been placed in cryogenic suspension in the morgue. It was a question he asked each day; he seemed to forget the answer.

"Yes, my Duke—it has been done." Jessica held up one of the packages from well-wishers, trying to take his mind from the unbearable pain. "This is from a widow on the Eastern Continent, who writes that her husband was a civil servant in your employ. Look closely at the holophoto—she is holding a plaque you gave her, in honor of her husband's lifelong service to House Atreides. Now her young sons are eager to work for you." Jessica stroked his shoulder, then touched the sensor to shut off the holophoto. "Everyone wants you to get well."

Outside, on the steep paths and roads leading to Castle Caladan, citizens had come to place candles and flowers along the entire walkway. Mountains of blossoms were piled beneath his windows, so that the heady, sweet perfume rose with the sea breezes. People sang where he could hear them; some played the harp or baliset.

Jessica wished Leto could go out and face the well-meaning crowd. She wanted him to sit in his tall ducal chair in the courtyard and hear the people's petitions, their complaints, their praises. He could wear the garments of his duties, looking larger than any normal human, as the Old Duke had taught him. Leto needed to distract himself enough to move forward in life again, and perhaps the momentum of day-to-day existence would even begin to heal his shattered heart. The business of leadership.

His people needed him.

Hearing a shrill cry outside the window, Jessica saw a large sea hawk, with tethers dangling from its clawed feet as it spread its red-tinged wings. Below stood a teenage boy hold-ing the tether, looking hopefully up at the tiny Castle window. Jessica had seen Leto talking with the young man on occasion, one of the villagers the Duke had befriended. The sea hawk flew past Leto's room again, peering inside, as if the bird could serve as eyes for all the concerned people gathered below.

The Duke's face sank into deepest melancholy, and Jessica gazed upon him with love. *I can't shelter you from the world, Leto.* She had always marveled at his strength of character: Now she worried about the fragility of his spirit. Though stubborn and grim, Duke Leto Atreides no longer had the will to live. This man she admired so much was effectively dead, despite the healing of his body.

She couldn't bear to let him give up and die—not only be-cause of her Bene Gesserit mandate to conceive his daughter, but because she longed to see Leto whole and happy again. Silently, she promised to do everything in her power for him. She murmured a Bene Gesserit prayer, "Great Mother, watch over those who are worthy."

IN THE DAYS afterward, she sat and talked with Leto constantly. He responded to Jessica's quiet, undemanding attentions and slowly, gradually, began to improve. Color returned to the Duke's narrow, handsome face. His voice grew stronger, and he began to carry on longer conversations with her.

Still, his heart was dead. He knew about Kailea's treachery, the murder of her lady-in-waiting, and how the woman he'd once loved had thrown herself out of a high window. But he could feel no rage toward her, no obsession for revenge . . . only a sick sadness. The spark of life and passion had gone from his eyes.

But Jessica wouldn't give up, and she wouldn't let him do so, either.

She set up a bird feeder on the balcony outside his window,

and Leto often watched the wrens, rock sparrows, and finches. He even named certain birds that came back again and again; for a man who had no Bene Gesserit training, the Duke's ability to distinguish among similar creatures impressed her.

One morning, almost a month after the skyclipper explosion, he said to Jessica, "I want to see Victor." His voice sounded peculiar, low but emotionally charged. "I can face it now. Take me to him, please."

They locked gazes. In the woodsmoke-gray of his eyes, Jessica saw that nothing could dissuade him.

Jessica touched his arm. "He is . . . much worse than Rhombur. You don't have to do this, Leto."

"Yes, Jessica . . . yes, I do."

DOWN IN THE vault Jessica thought the boy's crushed body looked almost peaceful, preserved in its cryogenic case. Perhaps it was because Victor, unlike Rhombur, was safe in a realm where pain could no longer reach him.

Leto opened the doorseals and shivered as he reached through the frosty mist. He placed his strong right hand on the boy's wrapped chest. Whatever he said to his dead son, he did so privately, because no words came forth. His lips barely moved.

Jessica saw Leto's sorrow. He and Victor could spend no more time together; he would never have a chance to be the father the boy deserved.

She placed an arm on Leto's shoulder to comfort him. Her heart raced and she fought to calm herself, using Bene Gesserit techniques. She was unsuccessful, though; she heard a murmuring and agitation deep within her psyche, in the most distant reaches of her mind. What was it? It couldn't be the echoes of Other Memory, for she was not yet a Reverend Mother. But she sensed that the ancient Sisters were troubled by something of such grave concern that it transcended normal bounds. *What is happening here?*

"There can be no doubt now," Leto said, as if in a trance. "House Atreides is cursed . . . and has been since the days of Agamemnon."

As she drew Leto reluctantly from the morgue, Jessica needed to reassure him, to tell him he was mistaken. She wanted to remind the Duke of how much his family had accomplished, how greatly he was respected throughout the Imperium.

But the words wouldn't come. She had known Rhombur, Victor, and Kailea. She could not argue with Leto's fears.

We are always human and carry the whole burden of being human.

—DUKE LETO ATREIDES

WINDBLOWN RAIN PELTED THE WINDOWS OF LETO'S ROOM, AS THOUGHTS battered his mind. A downpour slashed the stone walls, and wind whistled through a poorly sealed window frame. The storm echoed his mood.

Alone in the suite, Leto sat shivering in a tall chair that seemed to overwhelm him. Behind closed eyelids, he pictured Victor's face, the boy's black hair and brows, the insatiable curiosity, the quick and generous laughter . . . the child-sized ducal jacket and overlarge epaulets he'd been wearing at the time of his death.

Leto's eyes adjusted to the darkness, and he imagined shadow-shapes around the room. *Why couldn't I have helped my son?*

He hung his head and spoke aloud now, conversing with ghosts. "If there was the slightest thing I could do for Victor, I would sell every Atreides holding." His grief threatened to overwhelm him.

Noises intruded, a pounding at his sealed chamber door that was so loud and heavy, he knew it must be Thufir Hawat. Leto moved slowly, his body aching, without energy. His eyes were red and scratchy; at any other time he could have summoned enough courtesy to greet his Master of Assassins . . . but not now, not so late at night.

Hawat opened the door. "My Duke," he said, crossing the room and extending a silvery message cylinder. "This document just arrived at the spaceport."

"More condolences? I thought we'd already heard from every House in the Landsraad." Leto could not focus his eyes. "I don't dare hope that this could be *good* news?"

"No, my Duke." Hawat's leathery face seemed to sag in on itself. "It is from the Bene Tleilax." He placed the cylinder into Leto's trembling hands.

Scowling, Leto broke the seal, then stared at the brief message, wicked in its simplicity, awful in its promises. He had heard of such possibilities, sinister practices that brought a shudder of revulsion to any moral man. *If only it could be true.* He had avoided even considering the Tleilaxu—but now the vile little gnome-men had made their offer directly.

Hawat waited, ready to serve his Duke, barely concealing his dread.

"Thufir . . . they have offered to grow a ghola of Victor, bring him back from his dead cells, so that . . . so that he can be alive again."

Even the Mentat could not hide his astonishment. "My Lord! You must not consider—"

"The Tleilaxu could do it, Thufir. I could have my son back."

"At what cost? Do they even name their price? This bears an ill stamp upon it, sir, mark my words. Those loathsome men destroyed Ix. They threatened to kill you during the Trial by Forfeiture. They have made no secret of their hatred for House Atreides."

Leto stared at the message cylinder. "They still believe I fired upon their ships inside the Heighliner. Now, thanks to the Bene Gesserit, we know the true perpetrator. We could tell the Tleilaxu about the Harkonnens and their invisible attack ship—"

The Mentat stiffened. "My Lord, the Bene Gesserit have

refused to give us proof. The Tleilaxu will never believe you without evidence."

Leto's voice sounded small, and desperate. "But Victor has no other chance. When it comes to my son, I will deal with anyone, pay any price." He longed to hear the boy's voice again, to see his smile, to feel the touch of the small hand in his own.

"I must remind you that while a ghola may be an exact copy in all respects, the new child would have none of Victor's memories, none of his personality."

"Even so, would that not be better than having only memories and a corpse? And this time, I will legitimize him and make him my rightful heir."

The thought filled him with sorrow beyond measure. Would a ghola Victor grow up normally, or would he be tainted by the knowledge of what he was? What if the Bene Tleilax—so skilled in creating twisted Mentats—did something to the boy's genetic makeup? A hidden plot to strike back at Duke Atreides through the person he loved most.

But Leto would risk even damnation . . . for Victor. He was helpless in the face of the decision. He had no choice.

Hawat's voice was gruff and strained. "My Lord, as your Mentat—and as your friend—I advise you against this rash course of action. It is a trap. You know the Tleilaxu mean to bind you in their poisonous web."

Flinching from residual twinges of pain, Leto stepped closer to the old Master of Assassins. Hawat backed away when he saw the mad fury in the Duke's reddened eyes. He seemed not to have heard any of the objections.

"Thufir, I can entrust this mission to no one but you." He drew a deep breath; desperation coursed like flame through his bloodstream. "Contact the Tleilaxu. Inform them I wish . . ." He could hardly say it. ". . . I wish to learn their terms." His thin smile sent a shudder down Hawat's back. "Think of it, Thufir. I'll have my son again!"

The old warrior placed a sinewy hand on Leto's shoulder. "Rest, my Duke, and consider the implications of what you suggest. We dare not bare our throats in such a way to the Bene Tleilax. Imagine the cost. What will they demand in return? I advise against this. Such an idea is not possible."

Refusing to be swayed, Leto shouted at him. "I am the Duke of House Atreides. I alone determine what is *possible* here."

The torment of his shattered life made his mind reel, blurring his concentration. There were dark circles under his eyes. "We are talking about my son—my dead son!—and I command you to do as I say. Make the request of the Tleilaxu."

THE DAY OF Duncan Idaho's return should have been a cause for great celebration, but the skyclipper tragedy had cast a pall of sorrow over all of Caladan.

At the Cala Municipal Spaceport, a greatly changed Duncan disembarked and breathed deeply of the salty air. He gazed around with sparkling eyes and an eager expression. At the head of an Atreides honor guard, he saw Thufir Hawat in a black uniform coat adorned with military medals, a dressy ambassadorial outfit. Such formality! Red-uniformed attendants moved to the ramp door escorting the passengers to processing stations.

As Hawat stood at the ramp's edge, he hardly recognized the new arrival. Duncan's youthful black curls had grown thick and coarse, and his smooth complexion was ruddy and tanned. Far more muscular than he had been, the young man moved with athletic grace, and wariness mixed with confidence. Proudly, he wore Ginaz khakis and a red bandanna; the Old Duke's sword hung smartly at his side, a bit more battered but newly polished and sharpened.

"Thufir Hawat, you haven't changed at all, you old Mentat!" Duncan hurried forward to clasp the warrior's hand.

"You, on the other hand, have changed a great deal, young Idaho. Or should I call you *Sword*master Idaho? I remember the streetwise scamp who threw himself on the mercy of Duke Paulus. I do believe you're a little taller."

"And wiser, too, I pray."

The Mentat bowed. "I am afraid that events here have forced us to defer a welcoming celebration for you. Allow one of my men to accompany you back to the Castle. Leto will be cheered to see your face right now. Sergeant Vitt, would you please escort Duncan to the Duke?"

Hawat marched past the Swordmaster up the ramp and boarded the shuttle himself, ready to depart for the Heighliner in orbit. Seeing the young man's perplexed expression, Hawat realized that Duncan knew nothing about the tragedy yet. He had never met Leto's son, either, though undoubtedly he had learned of the boy through correspondence.

The Mentat added in the bleakest of tones, "Sergeant Vitt will explain everything."

The sergeant, a powerfully built man with a chestnut goatee, gave a formal nod. "I'm afraid this will be the saddest story I have ever told." Without further explanation, Hawat boarded the shuttle, carrying a satchel of documents from the Duke to the Tleilaxu Masters.

Sliding his tongue along the inside of his mouth, the Mentat felt a sore area where a minuscule injector had been implanted; the device would emit a tiny but powerful spray burst of antiseptics, antitoxins, and antibiotics with each bite of food he took. He had been ordered to meet face-to-face with the Tleilaxu, and not even a Master of Assassins could imagine what sorts of diseases and poisons the hated people might attempt to use on him.

Hawat was determined not to let them take advantage of the situation, despite the Duke's rigorous instructions. He disagreed vehemently with Leto's desperate, unwise course of action, but he was honor-bound to do his best.

———

BEHIND A CONFINEMENT field in the dungeons of Castle Caladan, Swain Goire stared into darkness, thinking of other times, other places. Wearing only a thin prison uniform, he shivered in the dank air.

Where had his life gone so drastically wrong? He'd struggled so hard to better himself; he'd sworn loyalty to the Duke; he'd loved Victor so much. . . .

Seated on his cot he cradled the hypo-injector in his hand, rubbing a thumb along the cool plaz surface of the handle. The scarred smuggler Gurney Halleck had slipped it to him, providing the disgraced guard captain with an easy way out. At any moment Goire could inject poison into his bloodstream. If only he had the courage . . . or the cowardice.

In his mind's eye, years melted away as if cut by a lasbeam. Goire remembered growing up in poverty on Cala Bay, earning money for his mother and two younger sisters by crewing on fishing boats; he had never even known his father. By the age of thirteen, Goire had obtained work as a cook's assistant in Castle Caladan, cleaning stoves and storage chambers, mopping floors, scrubbing grease from the oven walls. The chef had been stern but good-hearted, and had helped the young man.

When Goire turned sixteen, shortly after the Old Duke's death, he'd begun training in the House Guard and rose through the ranks until he became one of Duke Leto's most trusted men. He and Leto were within months of the same age . . . and through different paths they'd come to love the same woman: Kailea Vernius.

And Kailea had ruined them both before plunging to her own death.

During Thufir Hawat's deep interrogation, Goire had offered no excuses. He'd confessed everything, had even searched for additional crimes to increase his own culpability.

He'd hammered himself with guilt, hoping either to survive the worst of the pain . . . or die from it at last. Because of his foolishness, he allowed Kailea access to his armory key, enabling Chiara to obtain the explosives. He never plotted to kill the Duke, for he loved him and still did.

Then Gurney Halleck had brought him the poison, saying with no sympathy whatsoever, "Take the only course open to you, the course of honor." He left the hypo-injector in Goire's cell, then departed.

Goire ran a finger along the shaft of the deadly needle. He could prick his finger and end his ruined life. He took a deep breath, closed his eyes. Tears streamed down his cheeks, and he tasted their saltiness.

"Swain, wait." Glowstrips brightened along the ceiling. Opening his eyes, he saw the sharp needle. His hands were shaking. Slowly, he turned toward the voice.

The containment field faded, and Duke Leto Atreides stepped forward, with Halleck close behind, looking unsettled. Goire froze, holding the injector in front of him. The very sight of his Duke—still bandaged, barely recovered from his worst injuries—was nearly enough to strike him dead. Goire sat helpless, ready to accept any punishment Leto decreed.

The Duke did the most terrible thing imaginable. He took the injector away.

"Swain Goire, you are the most pitiable of men," Leto said in a low voice, as if his own soul had been swept away. "You loved my son and were sworn to protect him, and yet you contributed to Victor's death. You loved Kailea, and thus betrayed me with my own concubine even as you claimed to love me. Now Kailea is dead, and you can never hope to regain my faith."

"Nor do I deserve to." Goire looked into Leto's gray eyes, already feeling the anguish of the deepest hells.

"Gurney wants you put to death—but I'm not going to

allow that," Leto said, each word like a physical blow. "Swain Goire, I sentence you to *live* . . . to live with what you have done."

Stunned, the man said nothing for a long moment. Tears poured from his eyes. "No, my Duke. Please, no."

Gurney Halleck glared at Goire ferociously, dangerously, as Leto spoke. "Swain, I do not believe you will ever betray House Atreides again—but your life in Castle Caladan is over. I will send you into exile. You'll depart with nothing, carrying only your crimes."

Spluttering, Halleck could contain himself no longer. "But, Sire! You can't let this traitor live, after what he has done! Is that *justice*?"

Leto gave him a hard, cold look. "Gurney, this is justice in the purest possible sense . . . and one day my people will realize it, that there was no more fitting punishment."

Stricken, Goire slumped back against the cold wall. He drew in a long breath, stifling a moan. "One day, my Lord, they will call you Leto the Just."

No one person can ever know everything that is in the heart of another. We are all Face Dancers in our souls.

—Tleilaxu Secret Handbook

UNDER THE SUN OF THALIM, THE BENE TLEILAX CLOSED OFF THEIR WORLDS to outsiders, but allowed select representatives to land in specific quarantined areas, which had been swept clean of sacred objects. As soon as Thufir Hawat departed, the Tleilaxu would disinfect every surface he had touched.

The main city of Bandalong was fifty kilometers from the spaceport complex, across a plain that showed no roads or rail lines. As the shuttle descended through the carnelian daytime sky, Hawat studied the huge sprawl and guessed that Bandalong contained millions of people. But the Mentat, an outsider, could never go there. He would attend to his business in one of the approved buildings at the spaceport proper. And then he would return to Caladan.

Hawat was one of a dozen passengers aboard the descending craft, half of whom were Tleilaxu; the others appeared to be businessmen coming to purchase biological products such as new eyes, healthy organs, twisted Mentats, or even a ghola, as Hawat had been commanded to do.

When he stepped out onto the platform, a gray-skinned man hurried to intercept him. "Thufir Hawat, Mentat to the Atreides?" The gnomish man flashed sharp teeth when he smiled. "I am Wykk. Come this way."

Without offering a handshake or awaiting a response,

Wykk curtly led Hawat down a spiraling walkway to a subterranean watercourse, where they boarded an automated boat. Standing on deck, they grasped handrails as the craft sped across the muddy water, leaving a considerable wake behind them.

After disembarking, Hawat ducked to follow his guide into a seedy lobby in one of the spaceport's perimeter buildings. Three Tleilaxu men stood talking; others hurried across the lobby. He saw no women anywhere.

A robo delivery machine—of Ixian manufacture?—clanked across the worn and scratched floor, came to a stop in front of Wykk. The Tleilaxu man removed a metal cylinder from a tray, handed it to the Mentat. "This is your room key. You must remain in the hotel." Hawat noted hieroglyphics on the cylinder that he didn't recognize, and a number in Imperial Galach.

"In one hour you will meet the Master here." Wykk designated one of the doorways, through which an array of tables could be seen. "If you do not arrive for the meeting, we will send hunters to find you."

Hawat stood stiff and formal, resplendent in his Atreides military regalia. "I will be punctual."

His assigned quarters featured a sagging bed, stained sheets, and vermin droppings on the windowsills. With a handheld apparatus, Thufir scanned the room for bugging devices, but found none—which probably only meant they were too subtle for his scanner to detect, or of an esoteric construction.

He reported for his meeting ten minutes early and found the restaurant even filthier than the room: soiled tablecloths, dirty place settings, streaked glasses. A din of conversation filled the air in a language he didn't understand. Every aspect of this place had been designed to make visitors feel unwelcome, to encourage them to leave as soon as possible.

Hawat intended to do just that.

Wykk emerged from behind a counter and led him to a table beside a wide plaz window. Another diminutive man already sat there, spooning lumpy soup into his mouth. Wearing a red jacket with billowing black pants and sandals, the man looked up without bothering to wipe away the food that dripped from his chin.

"Master Zaaf," Wykk said, indicating a chair across the small table, "this is Thufir Hawat, a representative from the Atreides. Regarding our proposal."

Hawat brushed crumbs from the chair before he sat at a table built too small for a man of his size. He did not allow himself to express any revulsion.

"Especially for our off-world guests, we have prepared a delicious slig chowder," Zaaf said.

A mute serving slave arrived with a tureen, and ladled soup into a bowl. Another slave slopped bloody slabs onto plates in front of both men. No one bothered to identify the meat.

Always security-conscious, Hawat glanced around, saw no poison snoopers. His own defenses would have to be sufficient. "I am not particularly hungry, considering the difficult message I carry from my Duke."

With powerful little hands, Master Zaaf set to work on a chunk of the rare steak, stuffing it into his mouth. He made rude noises as he ate, as if trying to offend Hawat.

Zaaf wiped a sleeve across his chin. With glittering black eyes, he glowered up at the much taller Mentat. "It is customary to share meals during such negotiations." He traded his own plate and soup bowl for Hawat's, and began again. "Eat, eat!"

Hawat used a knife to cut off a small piece of meat. He ate only as much as politeness required, and felt the implanted mist injector in his mouth doing its work with each bite. He swallowed, with difficulty.

"Trading plates is an old tradition," Zaaf said, "our way of checking for poison. In this case you—as the guest—should have insisted on it, not me."

"I will keep that in mind," Hawat responded, then pressed on with his instructions. "We recently received an offer from the Tleilaxu to grow a ghola of my Duke's son, who was killed in a terrible accident." Hawat removed a folded document from his jacket pocket, passed it across the table, where it became stained with grease and blood. "Duke Atreides has asked me to inquire as to your terms in the matter."

Zaaf only half glanced at the document, then set it aside to concentrate on his steak. He finished as much of the meal as he wanted to eat, then washed it all down with murky liquid from a cup. Grabbing the Atreides document, he rose to his feet. "Now that we have ascertained your interest, we will determine what we believe will be an acceptable price. Remain in your room, Thufir Hawat, and await our answer."

He leaned close to the still-seated Mentat, and Hawat saw the purest hatred for the Atreides boiling behind the pupils. "Our services will not come cheap."

We as humans tend to make pointless demands of our universe, asking meaningless questions. Too often we make such queries after developing an expertise within a frame of reference which has little or no relationship to the context in which the question is asked.

—Zensunni Observation

IN A RARE AFTERNOON OF RELAXATION, WHILE SUNNING HIMSELF ON THE patio of his Richesian estate, Dr. Wellington Yueh's mind remained preoccupied with thoughts of nerve patterns and circuit diagrams. Overhead, the artificial laboratory moon of Korona glided along in low orbit, a bright ornament that crossed the sky twice daily.

After the passage of eight years, Yueh had nearly forgotten his unpleasant experiences diagnosing Baron Vladimir Harkonnen. The Suk doctor had accomplished so much in the meantime, and his own researches were far more interesting than a mere disease.

Investing the Baron's extravagant payment in laboratory facilities around his new estate on Richese, Yueh had made great advances in cyborg development. As soon as he had solved the biological-nerve/electronic-receptor problem, the next steps followed in rapid succession. New techniques, new technologies, and—to the Richesians' delight—new commercial opportunities.

Already Premier Ein Calimar had begun to make tidy profits from the cyborg endeavor, quietly selling Yueh's designs for bionic limbs, hands, feet, ears, even optical-sensor eyes. It was exactly the boost the failing Richesian economy needed.

The grateful Premier had bestowed upon the doctor a

stately villa and vast acreage on the lovely Manha Peninsula, along with a full complement of servants. Yueh's wife, Wanna, enjoyed the home, especially the library and meditation pools, while the doctor himself spent most of his time in the research facilities.

After taking a sip of a sweet blossom tea, the mustachioed doctor watched a white-and-gold ornithopter land on a wide expanse of lawn by the water's edge. A man in a trim white suit stepped out and walked up a gentle slope toward him, moving at a good pace despite his advanced years. Sunlight gleamed from golden lapels.

Yueh rose from his sunning chair and bowed. "To what do I owe the honor of this visit, Premier Calimar?" Yuen's aged body was lean and wiry, his long dark hair bound in a ponytail by a single silver ring.

Calimar took a seat at a nearby shaded table. Listening to recorded birdsong from speakers in the bushes, he waved away a servant who arrived with a tray of drinks. "Dr. Yueh, I would like you to consider the Atreides matter, and the grievously injured Rhombur Vernius."

Yueh stroked his long mustaches. "It is an unfortunate case. Most sad, from what my wife tells me. Prince Rhombur's concubine is also a Bene Gesserit, like my Wanna, and her message sounded quite desperate."

"Yes, and perhaps you could help him." Calimar's eyes sparkled behind his spectacles. "I'm certain it would fetch an extravagant price."

Yueh resented the request, feeling languid here on his estate but remembering how much he still wanted to research, how much he had to do. He did not want to move his facilities, especially not to watery Caladan. But he had begun to grow bored in this business park of a planet, with few challenges beyond refining the original work he had commenced years ago.

He considered Rhombur's injuries. "I have never done such

a complete replacement on a human body." He ran a thin finger along his purplish lips. "It will be a formidable task, requiring a good deal of my time. Perhaps even a permanent assignment to Caladan."

"Yes, and Duke Atreides will pay for everything." Behind his thin spectacles, Calimar's eyes continued to shine. "We cannot pass up an opportunity like this."

THE MAIN HALL of Castle Caladan seemed too large, as did the ancient ducal chair, from which Paulus Atreides had spent so many years ministering to his people. Leto seemed unable to fill the vast spaces around him, or in his heart. But still, he had ventured out of his room. That much, at least, was progress.

"Duncan Idaho has brought a most disturbing matter to my attention, Tessia." Leto stared at the slender woman who stood before him, her mousy brown hair cut boyishly short. "Did you make arrangements for a Suk doctor to come here? A cyborg specialist?"

Wearing a velglow robe, Tessia shifted on her feet and nodded. She did not take her sepia eyes from him, showing a strength like steel that skirted the edges of defiance.

"You told me to find any way to help him, if I could. I have done so. This is Rhombur's only chance." Her face flushed. "Would you deny it to him?"

Dressed in a black-and-red Atreides uniform, the new Swordmaster Duncan Idaho stood at one side, scowling. "Did you speak on the Duke's behalf, and make promises without discussing them? You're just a concubine—"

"My Duke gave me permission to take any necessary steps." Tessia turned to Leto. "Would you rather we left Rhombur as he is now? Or would you prefer we asked the Tleilaxu to grow replacement body parts for him? My Prince would choose to die, if that were the only other option. Dr. Yueh's new cyborg work offers us another chance."

While Duncan continued to scowl, Leto found himself nodding. He shuddered at the thought of how much of his friend's body would be replaced with synthetic parts. "When is this Suk doctor scheduled to arrive?"

"In a month. Rhombur can stay on life support that long, and Dr. Yueh requires the time to build components to match Rhombur's . . . losses."

Leto took a deep breath. As his father had instructed him so many times, a leader must always remain in control—or give the impression that he is. Tessia had acted ambitiously, spoken in his name, and Duncan Idaho was right to be upset. But there had never been any question as to whether Leto would spend every solari in the House Atreides coffers to help Rhombur.

Tessia straightened, and the fierce love in her eyes was genuine. Duncan cautioned, though, "There are political complexities you must remember, Sire. Vernius and Richese have been rivals for generations. There may be a plot afoot."

"My mother was born a Richese," Leto pointed out, "and therefore so am I, by distaff lineage. Count Ilban, a mere figurehead on Richese, wouldn't dare strike against my House."

Duncan's forehead wrinkled in thought. "Cyborgs are composite living forms, with machine-body interfaces."

Tessia remained stony. "So long as none of the parts simulate the workings of the human *mind*, we have nothing to fear."

"There is always something to fear," Duncan said, thinking of the unexpected ambush and slaughter on Ginaz. Gruff and stern, he sounded like Thufir Hawat now, who had not yet returned from his negotiations with the Tleilaxu. "Fanatics do not examine evidence rationally."

Leto was not entirely recovered from his injuries. He heaved a tired sigh and raised a hand to silence the young man before he could make another argument. "Enough, Duncan, Tessia. Of course we'll pay. If there's a chance to save Rhombur, we must do it."

ON AN OVERCAST afternoon, Leto sat in his study trying to concentrate on the business of Caladan. For years, even when their relationship had soured, Kailea had done more work than Leto had ever realized. He sighed and went over the numbers again.

Thufir Hawat strode in, fresh from the spaceport. Deeply troubled, the Mentat thumped a sealed message cylinder on the desk and stepped back, as if in disgust. "From the Tleilaxu, Sire. These are their terms."

Duke Leto lifted the cylinder, looked pensively at Hawat, searching for any hint, any reaction. Suddenly apprehensive, he pried off the cap. A sheet of tan paper fell out as supple as if it had been made from human skin. He scanned the words quickly; his pulse quickened.

"To the Atreides: After your unprovoked attack on our transport ships and your devious escape from true justice, the Bene Tleilax have awaited an opportunity such as this."

The palms of his hands were moist and clammy as he continued. Leto knew Hawat disagreed with his idea to offer the Tleilaxu information about the invisible Harkonnen attack ship. If too many people learned about the dangerous technology, it could fall into the wrong hands. For the time being, the wreckage seemed safe enough with the Bene Gesserit, who had no military aspirations of their own.

One thing was certain, though: The Tleilaxu would never believe him without proof.

"We can return your son to you, but you must pay a price. Not in solaris, spice, or other valuables. Instead, we demand that you surrender Prince Rhombur Vernius to us—the last of the Vernius bloodline and the only person who continues to threaten our possession of Xuttuh."

"No . . ." Leto whispered. Hawat stared at him like a grim statue.

He continued to read. "We give our guarantees and assurances that Rhombur will not be physically harmed, but you must make a choice. Only this way can you have your son back."

Hawat seethed with anger as Leto finished reading. "We should have expected this. I should have predicted it."

Leto spread the parchment out in front of him and spoke in a small voice, "Leave me to consider this, Thufir."

"Consider it?" Hawat looked at him in surprise. "My Duke, you cannot possibly entertain—" Seeing Leto's glare, the Mentat fell silent. With a brief bow, he departed from the study.

Leto stared at the terrible terms until his eyes burned. For generations, House Atreides had stood for honor, for the course of righteousness and integrity. He felt a deep obligation to the exiled Prince.

But for Victor . . . *Victor.*

Wouldn't Rhombur be better off dead, anyway? Better off without inhuman cyborg replacements? As Leto considered this, he felt a dark stillness in his soul. Would history judge him severely for selling Rhombur to his sworn enemies? Would he become known as Leto the Betrayer instead of Leto the Just? It was an impossible conundrum.

The intense loneliness of leadership enveloped him.

In his soul of souls, at the deepest core where only he could look and find absolute truth, Duke Leto Atreides wavered.

Which is more important, my closest friend or my son?

The ego is only a bit of consciousness swimming upon the ocean of dark things. We are an enigma unto ourselves.

—The Mentat Handbook

IN HER OWN APARTMENT, JESSICA LAY BESIDE DUKE LETO ON THE WIDE bed, trying to soothe his nightmares. A number of scars on his chest and legs required additional newskin wraps to repair them completely. Much of Leto's body had healed, though the tragedy festered in him, along with the terrible decision he had to make.

His friend or his son?

Jessica was sure that seeing a ghola of Victor each day would only worsen his pain, but she had been unable to say this to him. She searched for the right words, the right moment.

"Duncan is upset with me," Leto said, pushing away from her to gaze into her clear green eyes. "So is Thufir, and probably Gurney, too. Everyone challenges my decisions."

"They are your advisors, my Lord," she said, treading cautiously. "They are required to counsel you."

"In this matter, I've had to tell them to keep their opinions to themselves. This is my decision to make, Jessica—but what am I to do?" The Duke's face darkened with anger, and his eyes misted over. "I have no other options, and only the Tleilaxu can do it. I . . . I miss my son too much." His eyes begged for her understanding, her support. "How can I choose—how can I say no? The Tleilaxu will bring Victor back."

"At the cost of Rhombur . . . and perhaps the price of your soul," she said. "To sacrifice your friend for a false hope—I fear that will be your downfall. Please don't do this, Leto."

"Rhombur should have died in the crash."

"Perhaps. But that was in God's hands, not yours. He still lives. Despite everything, he still has the *will* to live."

Leto shook his head. "Rhombur will never recover from his injuries. *Never.*"

"Dr. Yueh's cyborg work will give him a chance."

He glowered at her, suddenly defensive. "What if the robotic enhancements don't work? What if Rhombur doesn't *want* them? Maybe he's better off dead."

"If you give him to the Tleilaxu, they will never allow him a simple death." She paused, and in a gentle tone suggested, "Perhaps you should go see him again. Look down at your friend and listen to what your heart tells you. Look at Tessia, look into her eyes. Then talk to Thufir and Duncan."

"I don't need to explain myself to them, or to anyone else. I am Duke Leto Atreides!"

"Yes, you are. And you are a man, too." Jessica fought to control her emotions. She stroked his dark hair. "Leto, I know you're only acting out of love, but sometimes love can guide a person in the wrong direction. Love can blind us to the truth. You're on the wrong path, my Duke, and you know it in your heart."

Although he turned away from her, she did not relent. "You must never love the dead more than the living."

THUFIR HAWAT, CONCERNED as always, accompanied the Duke to the infirmary, where Rhombur's life-support pod bristled with fittings for intravenous tubes, catheters, and scanners. The whir and hum of machinery filled the room, stirring the smell of chemicals.

Hawat lowered his voice. "This can only lead to your ruin,

my Duke. Accepting the Tleilaxu offer would be a betrayal, a dishonorable course of action."

Leto folded his arms across his chest. "You have served House Atreides for three generations, Thufir Hawat, and you dare to question my honor?"

The Mentat pressed ahead. "The medical attendants are attempting to establish a means of communicating with Rhombur's brain while he remains in the life-support pod. Soon he will be able to speak again, and tell you in his own words—"

"The decision is mine to make, Thufir." Leto's eyes seemed darker than usual, like thunderheads. "Will you do as I ask, or must I obtain a more obedient Mentat?"

"As you command, my Duke." Hawat bowed. "However, it would be better to let Rhombur die now, rather than permit him to fall into the hands of the Tleilaxu."

By prior arrangement, Yuen's cyborg team was scheduled to arrive soon to begin the complex process of rebuilding Rhombur part by part, establishing proper machine-body interfaces. In an amalgamation of engineering and medical technology, the Suk doctor would weave machine into tissue, and tissue into machine. New and old, hard and soft, lost abilities restored. If Leto permitted it to proceed, Dr. Yueh and his team would be playing God.

Playing God.

The Bene Tleilax did that, too. Using other techniques, they could bring back what had been lost, what had died. They required only a few cells, carefully preserved. . . .

Taking a deep breath, Leto stepped to the life-support pod, where he looked down at the bandaged horror, the burned remnants of his longtime friend. He reached for the curved glass that showed the unrecognizable man inside. His fingers touched the slick surface, trembling with a strange mixture of fear and fascination. Tears streamed down his cheeks.

A cyborg. Would Rhombur hate Leto for that, or thank him? At least he would still be alive. In a manner of speaking.

Rhombur's body was so twisted and mangled that it no longer seemed human. Fittings had been customized for the mass of flesh and bone; narrow fragments of raw tissue lay exposed around the edges of tubings and covers. One side of the face and brain had been crushed, and only a single blood-shot eye remained . . . unfocused. The eyebrow was blond, the only suggestion that this was truly Prince Vernius.

Never love the dead more than the living.

Leto placed a hand on the clearplaz barrier; he saw Rhombur's finger stubs and a heat-fusion of metal and flesh where his fire-jewel ring had once been.

"I won't let you down, friend," Leto promised in a whisper. "You can count on me to do the right thing."

IN THE BARRACKS of the Atreides House Guard, two men sat at a rough wooden table, passing a bottle of pundi rice wine between them. Though initially strangers, Gurney Halleck and Duncan Idaho already conversed like lifelong friends. They had a great deal in common, especially an intense ha-tred of the Harkonnens . . . and an unbridled love for Duke Leto.

"I'm deeply concerned about him. This ghola matter . . ." Duncan shook his head. "I do not trust gholas."

"Nor do I, lad."

"That creature would be a pale reminder of the saddest time Leto has ever experienced, without memories of its for-mer life."

Gurney tilted his cup for a long, thoughtful swig of wine, then lifted his baliset from beside the table and began to strum. "And the cost—to sacrifice Rhombur! But Leto would not listen to me."

"Leto is not the same person I knew before."

Gurney stopped strumming. "And who would be . . . after all that pain?"

———

THE TLEILAXU MASTER Zaaf arrived on Caladan, accompanied by two bodyguards and hidden weapons. Haughty and self-confident, he strode up to Thufir Hawat in the main hall of Castle Caladan and looked up at the much taller Mentat.

"I have come for the body of the boy, so that we can prepare it for our axlotl tank." Zaaf narrowed his eyes, utterly confident that Leto would bow to their demands. "I have also made arrangements to transport the life-support pod of Rhombur Vernius back to the medical and experimental facilities on Tleilax."

Noting the sly upward curl of the mouth, Hawat knew that these fiends would commit atrocities upon Rhombur's ragged body. They would experiment, grow clones from the living cells, then perhaps torture the clones as well. Eventually this terrible decision would come back to haunt Leto. Death for his friend would be preferable to that.

The Tleilaxu representative twisted the knife deeper. "My people can do much with the genetics of both the Atreides and Vernius families. We are looking forward to many. . . . options."

"I have advised the Duke against this course of action." Hawat knew he must face Leto's wrath, but old Paulus had often said, "Any man—even the Duke himself—must choose the welfare of House Atreides over his own."

Hawat would offer his resignation from service, if necessary.

At that moment Leto walked into the room, looking more self-confident than the Mentat had seen him for many weeks. Gurney Halleck and Jessica followed him. With an inexplicable strength showing on his face, the Duke looked at Hawat, then bowed slightly in formal diplomatic greeting to the Tleilaxu Ambassador.

"Duke Atreides," Zaaf said, "it is possible this business arrangement can bridge the gulf between your House and my people."

Leto looked down his hawkish nose at the little man. "Unfortunately, that bridge will never be built."

Hawat readied himself as the Duke stepped forward, close to Zaaf. Gurney Halleck also looked ready for murder. He exchanged uneasy glances with Hawat and Jessica. When the Tleilaxu bodyguards tensed, the warrior Mentat made ready for a quick, bloody battle in the large echoing chamber.

With a scowl, the Tleilaxu representative said, "Are you reneging on our agreement?"

"I made no agreement to break. I have decided that your price is too high, for Rhombur, for Victor, and for my own soul. Your trip here has been in vain." The Duke's voice remained strong and firm. "There will be no ghola made of my firstborn son, and you will not have my friend, Prince Vernius."

Stunned, Thufir, Gurney, and Jessica looked on.

Leto's face had an impenetrable hardness, and a new resolve. "I understand your continued, petty desire for revenge against me, even though the Trial by Forfeiture exonerated me of all charges. I have sworn that I did not attack your ships inside the Heighliner, and the word of an Atreides is worth more than all the laws in the Imperium. Your refusal to believe me shows your own foolishness."

The Tleilaxu man appeared outraged, but Leto continued with a sharp, cold voice that stopped Zaaf before he could utter a sound. "I have learned the explanation behind the attack. I know who did it, and how. But since I have no tangible proof, informing you would accomplish nothing. The Bene Tleilax have no interest in the truth, anyway—only in the price you can extract from me. *And I will not pay it.*"

At a whistle from Hawat, the ever-alert Atreides House

Guard rushed in and took control of the Tleilaxu bodyguards, while Gurney and Hawat stepped forward on either side of a spluttering Master Zaaf.

"I'm afraid we do not require the services of the Tleilaxu. Not today, not ever," Leto said, and then turned, dismissing him rudely. "Go home."

Hawat took great pleasure in escorting the indignant man out of the Castle.

The individual is shocked by the overwhelming discovery of his own mortality. The species, however, is different. It need not die.

—PARDOT KYNES,
An Arrakis Primer

OF ALL THE ECOLOGICAL DEMONSTRATION PROJECTS PARDOT KYNES HAD established, the sheltered greenhouse cave at Plaster Basin was his favorite. With his lieutenant Ommun and fifteen hard-working Fremen followers, Kynes summoned an expedition to visit the site.

Though it wasn't on his regular schedule of plantings or inspections, Pardot simply wanted to see the cave with the running water, hummingbirds, moisture dripping from ceiling rock, fresh fruit, and bright flowers. It all represented his vision of Dune's future.

The group of Fremen took a worm east across the sixty-degree line that surrounded the northern inhabited areas. In his long years here, Kynes had never learned to become a sandrider, so Ommun rigged up a palanquin for him. The Planetologist rode like an old woman but without embarrassment; he had nothing to prove.

Once, long ago, when Liet had been only a year old, Pardot had taken his wife, Frieth, and their child to Plaster Basin. A woman who rarely displayed amazement or outright wonder, Frieth had been dumbstruck when she first saw the greenhouse cave, the thick foliage, the flowers and birds. Just before that, though, on the way up the rugged mountainside to the hidden cavern, they had been attacked by a Harkonnen patrol.

Frieth, thinking fast and using her Fremen training, had saved the lives of her husband and son.

Kynes paused in his plodding procession of thoughts and scratched his beard, wondering if he had ever thanked her for that. . . .

Since the day of his son's wedding to Faroula, when Liet had chastised him for his distraction and unintentional coldness, Kynes had done a great deal of thinking, assessing what he had accomplished in his life: his years on Salusa Secundus and Bela Tegeuse, his astonishing summons to Elrood's Court at Kaitain, his two decades here as Imperial Planetologist. . . .

He had spent his career delving into explanations, seeing the convoluted tapestry of the environment. He understood the ingredients, from the power of water and sun and weather to organisms in the soil, plankton, lichens, insects . . . how it was all connected to human society. Kynes understood how the pieces fit, at least in general terms, and he was among the best Planetologists in the Imperium. He'd been called a "world reader," selected for this most important assignment by the Emperor himself.

And yet how could he consider himself a *detached* observer? How could he stand apart from the complex web of interactions that ran each planet, each society? He was himself a piece of the grand scheme, not an impartial experimenter. There could be no "outside" to the universe. Scientists had known for thousands of years that an observer affects the outcome of an experiment . . . and Pardot Kynes himself had certainly affected the changes on Dune.

How could he have forgotten that?

After Ommun helped him to dismount from the worm within walking distance of Plaster Basin, they led him to the black-and-greenish ridge that enclosed the cave. Kynes imitated their random-walk motions until his legs ached. He would never truly be a Fremen, unlike his son. Liet had all the knowledge of planetology his father had given him, but the young man also understood Fremen society. Liet was the best of both worlds. Pardot only wished the two of them got along better.

Taking broad strides, Ommun led the way up the rugged slope. Kynes had never been able to see the actual trail in the rocks, but tried to place his boots in the same crannies, on the same flat stones, as his lieutenant did.

"Quickly, Umma Kynes." Ommun reached down with his hand. "We must not tarry here in the open."

The day was hot, the sun blistering the cliffside—and he remembered running for shelter from a Harkonnen patrol with Frieth, long ago. How many years had it been?

Kynes stepped up onto a broad ledge and then around an elbow of brown rock until he saw the camouflaged entrance seal that prevented moisture loss from the cave. They stepped through.

Kynes, Ommun, and the fifteen Fremen stood inside, stomping their *temag* boots and shaking off windblown dust from their days of travel across the desert. Automatically, Kynes yanked the nose plugs from his nostrils; the other Fremen did the same, inhaling extravagant breaths of the moisture and plants. He let his eyes fall half-closed, smelled the ambrosia of blooming flowers and fruits and fertilizers, of thick green leaves and dispersed pollens.

Four of the Fremen helpers had never been there before, and they rushed forward like pilgrims reaching a long-sought shrine. Ommun looked around, sniffing deeply, proud to have been part of this sacred project from the beginning. He tended Kynes like an old mother, making certain the Planetologist had everything he needed.

"These workers will replace the team already here," Ommun said. "We have smaller shifts now, because this place has survived—as you said it would. Plaster Basin is an ecosystem of its own. Now we are required to do less work to keep it healthy."

Kynes smiled proudly. "As it should be. One day all of Dune will be like this, self-sustaining and self-renewing." He laughed, a short burst of sound. "Then what will you Fremen do to keep yourselves busy?"

Ommun's nostrils flared, callused from perpetually wearing nose plugs. "This is not yet our world, Umma Kynes. Not until we rid it of the hated Harkonnens."

Kynes blinked and nodded. He'd given little thought to the political aspect of the process. He had seen this only as an ecological problem, not a human one. Yet another thing he had missed. His son was right. The great Pardot Kynes had tunnel vision, seeing far into the future along a certain path . . . but missing all the hazards and distractions along the way.

He had done the important ecological work, though. He had been the prime mover, starting what he hoped would be a planetwide avalanche of change. "I'd like to see this entire world caught up in a net of plants," he said. Ommun made a wordless sound of agreement: Anything the prophet Kynes said was important and worth remembering. They strolled deeper into the moist cavern to view the gardens.

The Fremen knew their duties, and they would continue the plantings, even if it took centuries. Through the geriatric qualities of their melange-filled diet, some of the younger ones might actually see the grand plan come to fruition; Kynes was satisfied just to observe the indications of change.

The Plaster Basin project was a metaphor for all of Dune. His plan was now so firmly established in the Fremen psyche that it would continue even without his guidance. These hardy people had been infected by the dream, and the dream would not die.

From now on, Kynes would be little more than a figurehead, the prophet of ecological transformation. He smiled softly to himself. Perhaps now he could make time to see the people around him, get to know his wife of twenty years, and spend more time guiding his son. . . .

Deep inside the cave, he examined dwarf trees laden with lemons, limes, and the sweet round oranges known as portyguls. Ommun walked beside him, looking over the irrigation systems, the fertilizers, the progress of the plantings.

Kynes remembered showing Frieth the portyguls when he'd first brought her here, and the look of pleasure on her face when she tasted the honey-sweet orange flesh. It had been one of the most marvelous experiences in her entire life. Now Kynes stared at the fruit and knew he would have to take some of them back for her.

When was the last time I brought her a gift? He couldn't remember.

Ommun went over to the limestone walls, touching them with his fingers. The chalky rock was soft and wet, unaccustomed to so much dampness. With his keen eyes, he followed disturbing traceries along the wall and ceiling, fracture lines that should not have been there.

"Umma Kynes," he said. "These cracks concern me. The integrity of this cave is . . . suspect, I believe."

As the two of them watched, one of the cracks grew visibly, jagging left and then right in a fine black lightning bolt.

"You're right. The water is probably making the rock expand and settle over . . . how many years now?" The Planetologist raised his eyebrows.

Ommun calculated. "Twenty, Umma Kynes."

With a popping, shattering sound, a crack spread across the ceiling . . . and then others, in a chain reaction. The Fremen workers looked up in fear, then glanced over at Kynes, as if the great man could somehow avert disaster.

"I believe we should get everyone out of the cave. *Now*." Ommun took the Planetologist's arm. "We must evacuate until we are sure this is safe."

Another loud boom sounded deep within the mountain, a grinding of rock as broken slabs shifted and tried to find a new stable point. Ommun tugged at the Planetologist, while the other Fremen scurried toward the exit.

But Kynes hesitated, pulling his arm free of his lieutenant's grasp. He had promised himself to give Frieth some of the ripe portyguls, to show her that he did indeed love and appreciate her . . . despite his inattentiveness for many years.

He hurried to the small tree, and plucked some of the orange fruit. Ommun rushed back to take him away. Kynes cradled the portyguls against his chest, very glad that he had remembered to do this one important thing.

STILGAR BROUGHT THE news to Liet-Kynes.

In her sietch quarters, Faroula was sitting at a table with her young son Liet-chih, cataloging the jars of herbs she had gathered over the years, sealing the pots with resin and verifying the potency of the substances. On a bench near his new wife and adopted child, Liet-Kynes read through a purloined document that detailed the location of Harkonnen spice and military stockpiles.

Stilgar held back the privacy curtain, waited like a statue. He stared at the far wall, not blinking his deep blue eyes.

Immediately, Liet sensed something was wrong. He had fought beside this man, raided Harkonnen supplies, killed enemies. When the Fremen commando did not speak, Liet stood. "What is it, Stil? What's happened?"

"Terrible news," the man finally answered, his words like cold lead dropping heavily onto the ground. "Your father, Umma Kynes, has been killed in a cave-in at Plaster Basin. He and Ommun and most of the work crew were trapped when the ceiling collapsed; The mountain fell on them."

Faroula gasped. Liet found that all words had been stolen

from him. "But that can't be," he finally said. "He had more work left to do. He had—"

She dropped one of her small jars. It shattered, spilling powdered green leaves in a pungent splash pattern across the worn floor. "Umma Kynes has died among the plants that were his dream," she said.

"A fitting end," Stilgar said.

For some time, Liet was speechless. Thoughts whirled in his head, memories and wishes as he listened to his wife and Stilgar, and knew that the labors of Pardot Kynes must continue.

The Umma had trained his disciples well. Liet-Kynes himself would proceed with the vision. From what Faroula had just said, he could already see how the story of the prophet's tragic death, his martyrdom, would be passed from Fremen to Fremen. And it would grow with each retelling.

A fitting end, indeed.

He remembered something his father had told him, "The symbolism of a belief can survive far longer than the belief itself."

Stilgar said, "We could not collect the water of the dead for our tribe. Too much dirt and rock covered the bodies. We must leave them in their tomb."

"As it should be," Faroula said. "Plaster Basin shall be a shrine. Umma Kynes died with his lieutenant and his followers, giving his body's water to the planet he loved."

Stilgar narrowed his eyes and looked down his chiseled nose at Liet. "We will not let the Umma's vision die with him. *You* must continue his work, Liet. The Fremen will listen to the Umma's son. They will follow your commands."

In a daze, Liet-Kynes nodded, wondering if his mother had already been told the news. Trying to be brave, he straightened his shoulders as the deeper implications penetrated his mind. Not only would he continue to be the emissary for the

Fremen in the terraforming project . . . now he had an even greater, more far-reaching responsibility. His father had filed the appropriate documents long ago, and Shaddam IV had approved them without comment.

"I am the Imperial Planetologist now," he announced. "By my vow, the transformation of Dune will continue."

The man faced with a life-and-death decision must commit himself, or he will remain caught in the pendulum.

—From "In My Father's House,"
by the Princess Irulan

THE STATUE OF LETO'S PATERNAL GREAT-GRANDFATHER, DUKE MIKLOS Atreides, stood tall in the courtyard of the Cala City Hospital, stained by time and moss and guano. As Leto passed the serene visage of an ancestor he had never known, he nodded in habitual respect, then hurried up a set of wide marblecrete stairs.

Though he limped slightly, Leto was substantially recovered from his physical injuries. Once again, he was able to face each day without the smothering blackness of despair. By the time he reached the uppermost floor of the medical building, he was hardly winded at all.

Rhombur was *awake*.

The Duke's personal physician, who had continued to treat Rhombur until the impending arrival of the cyborg team, greeted him. "We have begun to communicate with the Prince, my Lord Duke."

White-coated medical attendants stood around the life-support pod and its elaborate tubes, injection bags, and blood-purification pumps. Machinery hummed and whirred, as it had for months. But it was different now.

Stopping Leto before he could rush forward, the doctor said, "There was, as you know, severe trauma to the right side of the Prince's head, but the human brain is a remarkable instrument. Already Rhombur's cerebellum has shifted control functions to new regions. Information is flowing through the neural pathways. I believe this will make the work of the cyborg team considerably easier."

Tessia leaned over the coffin-shaped pod, stared inside. "I love you, Rhombur—you never needed to worry about that."

In response, synthesized, humming words droned from a speakerbox. "I . . . love . . . you . . . too . . . And . . . always . . . will." The words were distinct and precise, unmistakable but with a pause between each, as if Rhombur still hadn't accustomed himself to the speech process.

The Duke stared, transfixed. *How could I have even considered giving you over to the Tleilaxu?*

The sleek pod lay open, revealing Rhombur's scarred lump of skin and bone, bristling with tubes, wires, and connections. The doctor said, "At first we could only speak to him by using an Ixian code . . . pulses and taps. But now, we've managed to link the voice synthesizer up to his speech center."

The Prince's remaining eye was open, showing life and awareness. For long moments Leto stared into Rhombur's nearly unrecognizable face, and he could think of nothing to say.

What is he thinking? How long has he known what happened to him?

Synthesized words poured out of the speaker beside the pod. "Leto . . . friend . . . How . . . are . . . coral . . . gem . . . beds . . . this . . . year? Have . . . you . . . been . . . diving . . . lately?"

Almost giddy with relief, Leto chuckled. "Better than ever, Prince—we'll go out again together . . . *soon*." Suddenly a wash of tears stung his eyes. "I'm sorry, Rhombur—you don't deserve anything but the truth."

The lump of Rhombur's body didn't move, and Leto saw only a few spasmodic muscle twitches beneath his skin. The artificial voice from the speaker conveyed no emotions, no inflections.

"When . . . I . . . am . . . a . . . cyborg . . . we . . . can . . . build . . . a . . . special . . . suit. We'll . . . go . . . diving . . . again. Wait . . . and . . . see."

Somehow, the exiled Prince had accepted the dramatic changes to his body, even the prospect of cyborg replacements. His good heart and infectious optimism had helped Leto through the darkest times after the Old Duke's death. Now Leto would be there for Rhombur.

"Remarkable," the doctor said.

Rhombur's eye did not waver from Leto. "I . . . want . . . a . . . Harkonnen . . . beer."

Leto laughed. On his left, Tessia clutched his arm. The hideously injured Prince would still go through oceans of pain, both physical and mental.

Rhombur seemed to sense Leto's gloom, and his speech improved, a little. "Don't . . . be . . . sad . . . for me. Be happy. I . . . look . . . forward to . . . my . . . cyborg parts." Leto leaned closer. "I . . . *am* Ixian . . . No . . . stranger . . . to machines!"

It all seemed so unreal to Leto, so impossible. And yet, it was happening. Over the centuries, cyborg attempts had always failed when the body rejected its synthetic parts. Psychologists claimed the human mind refused to accept such a drastic intrusion by mechanicals. The deep-seated fear dated back to the machine-induced horrors of pre-Butlerian days. Supposedly, this Suk doctor Yueh, with his intensive research program on Richese, had solved such problems, Only time would tell.

But even if the components worked as promised, Rhombur would function little better than the stiff old Ixian meks. The adjustment would not be easy, and delicate control would never be possible. In the face of his injuries and disabilities, would Tessia abandon him and return to the Sisterhood?

In his youth, Leto had listened with rapt attention as Paulus and his veteran soldiers told of severely injured men performing incredible feats of bravery. The triumph of the human spirit over insurmountable odds. Leto had never seen anything like that firsthand.

Rhombur Vernius was the bravest man Leto had ever met.

TWO WEEKS LATER, Dr. Wellington Yueh arrived from Richese, accompanied by his cyborg-development team of twenty-four men and women, and two shuttle loads of medical equipment and supplies.

Duke Leto Atreides personally supervised as his men helped the party disembark. Fussy about details, the stylus-thin Yueh barely took time to introduce himself before he scurried about the spaceport, attending to the arriving cargo cases of instruments and the prosthetic parts that would ultimately be fitted onto Rhombur's salvageable flesh and bones.

Groundtrucks transported personnel and cargo to the infirmary center, where Yueh insisted upon seeing the patient immediately. The Suk doctor looked over at Leto as they entered the hospital. "I will make him whole again, sir, though it will take some time for him to get used to his new body."

"Rhombur will do everything you ask."

Inside the room, Tessia still had not left Rhombur's side. Yueh moved smoothly over to the life-support pod, studied connections, diagnostic readings. Then he looked down at the injured Prince, who regarded him with his bizarre single eye, set in grossly wounded flesh.

"Prepare yourself, Rhombur Vernius," Yueh said, stroking his long mustaches. "I intend to begin the first surgical procedure tomorrow."

Rhombur's synthetic voice floated across the room, smoother now that he had practiced using it. "I look forward . . . to shaking . . . your hand."

Love is an ancient force, one that served its purpose in its day but is no longer essential for the survival of the species.

—Bene Gesserit Axiom

LOOKING DOWN FROM THE SEA CLIFF, LETO SAW THE HOUSE GUARD ARrayed on the beach where he had ordered them to take up positions. He had given them no reason. Concerned about the Duke's mental state, Gurney, Thufir, and Duncan had been watching him like Atreides hawks, but Leto knew how to sidetrack them.

The golden sun rode high overhead in a clear blue sky, yet still a shadow hung over him. The Duke wore a short-sleeved white tunic and blue dungarees, comfortable clothes with no trappings of his office. He drew a deep breath and stared. Maybe he could just be a *man* for a short while.

Jessica hurried up behind him, wearing a low-cut aqua singlesuit. "What are you thinking, my Lord?" Her face showed deep concern, as if she feared he might jump to his death, as Kailea had done. Perhaps Hawat had sent her up here to check on him.

Seeing the grouped men on the beach, Leto gave a wan smile. No doubt they would try to catch him in their own arms if he tumbled off the cliff.

"I am distracting the men, so I can get away." He looked at her oval face. With her Bene Gesserit training, Jessica would not be so easily fooled—and he knew better than to try. "I've had enough talk, advice, and pressure . . . I need to escape to where I can have peace."

She touched his arm.

"If I don't preoccupy them," he said, "they will insist upon sending a retinue of guards to accompany me." Below, Duncan Idaho began to drill the troops in techniques he had learned at the Ginaz School. Leto turned from the view. "Now, perhaps, I can get away."

"Oh? Where are we going?" Jessica asked, fully confident. Leto frowned at her, but she cut him off before he could object to her presence. "My Lord, I will not allow you to go alone. Would you rather have the full complement of guards, or just me?"

He considered her words and, with a sigh, gestured toward the green-roofed 'thopter hangars at the edge of the nearby landing fields. "I suppose you're less objectionable than an entire army."

Jessica followed as he crossed the dry grasses. Grief still radiated from him in waves. That he'd even considered the foul price demanded by the Tleilaxu in exchange for a ghola of Victor showed her how close to the edge of madness he had gone. But in the end, Leto had made the right decision.

She hoped it was his first step toward healing.

Inside the hangar building were a number of ornithopters, some with engine covers open; mechanics stood on suspensor platforms, working on them. Leto walked purposefully to an emerald-hulled 'thopter with red Atreides hawks on the undersides of the wings. Built low to the ground, it had a two-seat cockpit in a front-back arrangement instead of the standard face-front or side-by-side configurations.

A man in gray coveralls had his head inside the engine compartment, but emerged when the Duke approached. "Just a couple of final adjustments, my Lord." He had a shaved upper lip, and a silver-flecked beard encircled his face, giving him a simian appearance.

"Thank you, Keno." Distracted, Leto stroked the side of the sleek vessel. "My father's racing 'thopter," he said to Jessica. "He called it *Greenhawk*. I trained on her, went out with him and did loops, dives, and rolls." He allowed himself a bittersweet smile. "Used to drive Thufir crazy, seeing the Duke and his only heir taking such risks. I think my father did it just to irritate him."

Jessica examined the unusual craft. Its wings were narrow and upswept, with the nose split into two aerodynamic sections. The mechanic finished his adjustments and closed the engine cover. "All ready to go, sir."

After helping Jessica into the rear-facing seat, Duke Leto climbed into the front. A safety harness snicked into place over her lap, another over his own. Turbines hissed on, and he taxied the sleek aircraft out of the hangar onto a broad ocher tarmac. Keno waved after them. Warm wind whipped through Jessica's hair until the plexplaz cockpit cover slid shut.

Leto touched the controls, working busily, expertly—intent on prepping the 'thopter, ignoring Jessica. The green wings shortened for jet-boost takeoff, their delicate interleavings meshing together. The turbines roared, and the craft launched straight up.

Extending the wings to beetle stubs, Leto banked sharply to the left, then low over the beach, where his soldiers waited in formation. With startled faces they looked up as the Duke flew by, dipping the wings.

"They'll see us flying north along the coastline," Leto shouted back to Jessica, "but after we're out of sight, we'll go west. They won't . . . they won't be able to follow us."

"We'll be alone." Jessica hoped the Duke's mood would improve with this sojourn into the wilderness, but she would stay by him regardless.

"I always feel alone," Leto answered.

The ornithopter turned, crossed over pundi rice lowlands and small farm buildings. The wings extended to full soaring length and began to beat like the appendages of a great bird. Below them were river orchards, the narrow Syubi River, and a modest mountain of the same name—the highest point on the plain.

They flew west all afternoon without seeing another aircraft. The landscape changed, becoming more rugged and mountainous. After sighting a village by an alpine lake, Leto studied the instruments and changed his heading. Soon the mountains gave way to grassy plains and sheer canyons. Presently, Leto stubbed the wings and banked hard right to descend into a deep river gorge.

"Agamemnon Canyon," Leto said. "See the terraces?" He pointed to one side. "They were built by ancient Caladanian primitives, whose descendants still live here. They're rarely seen by outsiders." Observing intently, Jessica spotted a brown-skinned man with a narrow, dark face before he ducked out of sight into a rock hollow.

Leto steered away from the cliff face and continued down, toward a broad river with surging white water. In the waning daylight, they flew low over the rushing current, through the narrow winding gorge. "It's beautiful," Jessica said.

In an offshoot canyon, the river dwindled, leaving creamy sand beaches. Wings fully tucked, the ornithopter set down on a bank of sand with a soft lurch. "My father and I used to come fishing here." Leto opened a hatch on the side of the 'thopter and brought out a spacious autotent, which set itself up and shot stabilizing stakes into the sand. They set up an airpad and a double sleeping envelope and brought their luggage and foodpaks in.

For a while they sat together on the riverbank and talked, while the shadows of late afternoon settled over the gorge and the temperature dropped. They snuggled closer, and Jessica leaned her bronze hair into the side of his neck. Large fish jumped while swimming upstream, against the current.

Leto maintained his somber silence, causing her to pull

back and look into his smoky gray eyes. Feeling the muscles in his hand tighten up, she leaned close, gave him a long kiss.

Against her explicit training in the Sisterhood, all the lectures Mohiam had given her, Jessica found herself breaking one of the primary rules of the Bene Gesserit. Despite her intentions, despite her loyalty to the Sisterhood, Jessica had actually allowed herself to fall in love with this man.

They held each other, and for a long while Leto gazed out onto the river. "I still have nightmares," he said. "I see Victor, Rhombur . . . the flames." He pressed his face into his hands. "I thought I could escape the ghosts by coming way out here." He looked at her, his expression bleak. "I shouldn't have allowed you to come with me."

Wind gusts began to whip through the narrow canyon, snapping the tent fabric, and knotted clouds crawled overhead. "We'd better get inside before the storm comes." He hurried over to close the 'thopter hatch, and just as he returned a hard rain began to fall. He barely escaped getting drenched.

They shared a warm foodpak inside the tent, and later, when Leto lay back on the double sleeping pad, still troubled, Jessica moved close and began kissing his neck. Outside, the storm grew louder, more demanding of their attention. The tent flapped and rattled, but Jessica felt safe and warm.

As they made love that stormy night, Leto clung to her like a drowning man grasping a life raft, hoping to find some island of safety in a hurricane. Jessica responded to his desperation, afraid of his intensity, hardly able to cope with his outpouring of love. He was like a storm himself, uncontrolled and elemental.

The Sisterhood had never taught her about anything like this.

Emotionally torn, but determined, Jessica finally gave Leto the most precious gift she had left to offer. Manipulating her own body chemistry in the Bene Gesserit way, she envisioned his sperm and her egg merging . . . and allowed herself to conceive a child.

Though she had been given explicit instructions from the Sisterhood to produce only a daughter, Jessica had delayed and reconsidered, spending month after month contemplating this most important of decisions. Through it all she came to the realization that she could no longer bear to watch Leto's anguish. She had to do this one thing for him.

Duke Leto Atreides would have another son.

How will I be remembered by my children? This is the true measure of a man.

—ABULURD HARKONNEN

WITHIN SIGHT OF THE BARON'S SQUARE-WALLED KEEP, THE INDUSTRIAL floatcraft rose high in the gloomy sky.

Inside the floatcraft's large cargo hold, directly over its gaping, open hatch, Glossu Rabban hung spread-eagled. Shackles secured his wrists and ankles, but little else kept him from falling into the open sore of Harko City. His blue uniform was torn, his face bruised and bloodied from the scuffle with Captain Kryubi's troopers when they'd subdued him, pursuant to the Baron's orders. It had taken six or seven of the burliest guards to control the "Beast," and they had not been gentle. Now, on chains, the brutish man thrashed from side to side, looking for something to bite, something to spit at.

Steadying himself against a rail while the wind whipped up through the yawning hatch, Baron Harkonnen gazed dispassionately down at his nephew. The obese Baron's spider-black eyes were like deep holes. "Did I give you permission to kill my brother, Rabban?"

"He was only your half-brother, Uncle. He was a fool! I thought we would be better off—"

"Don't try to do any *thinking*, Glossu. You aren't good at it. Answer my question. Did I give you permission to kill a member of the Harkonnen family?"

When the response didn't come quickly enough, the Baron moved a lever on a control panel. The shackle on Rabban's left ankle sprang open, leaving the leg to dangle out over open space. Rabban writhed and screamed, unable to do anything. The Baron found the technique a primitive but effective method of increasing fear.

"No, Uncle, I did not have your permission!"

"No, *what*?"

"No, Uncle . . . I mean no, my Lord!" The blocky man grimaced in pain while he struggled for the correct words, trying to understand what his uncle wanted.

The Baron spoke into a com-unit to the floatcraft operator. "Take us over my Keep and hover fifty meters above the terrace. I think the cactus garden there could use some fertilizer."

Looking up with a pitiful expression, Rabban declared, "I killed my father because he was a weakling. All his life, his actions brought dishonor on House Harkonnen."

"Abulurd wasn't strong, you mean . . . not like you and me?"

"No, my Lord Baron. He didn't measure up to our standards."

"So now you have decided to call yourself Beast. Is that correct?"

"Yes, Un—I mean, yes, my Lord."

Through the open hatch, Baron Harkonnen could see the Keep's spires. Directly below them was a garden terrace where he sometimes liked to sit and eat sumptuous meals in privacy, in the midst of the spiny desert growths. "If you look below, Rabban—yes, I believe you have a good view now—you can see a certain modification I made to the garden earlier today."

As he spoke, the metal tips of army lances emerged from the dirt beside thorn-saguaro and chocatilla. "See what I planted for you?"

Dangling from the three remaining shackles, Rabban twisted to look. His face filled with terror.

"Note the bull's-eye arrangement of the tips. If I drop you

just right, you will be impaled in the exact center. If I miss by a little, we can still earn points for the hit, since every lance has a scoring number written on it." He stroked his upper lip. "Hmm, perhaps we can even introduce slave-dropping as an event for our arena crowds. Quite an exciting concept, don't you think?"

"My Lord, please don't do this. You need me!"

With emotionless eyes, the Baron looked down at him. "Why? I have your little brother, Feyd-Rautha. Perhaps I'll make *him* my heir-designate. By the time he's your age, he certainly won't make as many mistakes as you have."

"Uncle, please!"

"You must learn to pay close attention to what I say, at all times, *Beast*. I never make idle chatter."

Rabban squirmed, and the chains jingled. Cold, smoky air drifted into the floatcraft as he tried desperately to think of what to say. "You want to know if it's a good game? Yes, uh, my Lord, it's most ingenious."

"So I'm a smart man to devise it? Much smarter than *you*, correct?"

"Infinitely smarter."

"Then don't ever try to oppose me. Is that understood? I'll always be ten steps ahead of you, ready with surprises that you could never imagine."

"I understand, my Lord."

Relishing the abject terror he saw in his nephew's face, the Baron said, "Very well. I shall release you now."

"Wait, Uncle!"

The Baron touched a button on the control panel, and both arm shackles opened, so that Rabban dropped upside down into open air, held by only the right ankle band. "Ooops. Do you think I hit the wrong button?"

Screaming: "No! You're teaching me a lesson!"

"And have you learned that lesson?"

"Yes, Uncle! Let me come back. I will always do what you say."

Into the com-unit, the Baron said, "Take us to my private lake."

The floatcraft glided over the estate until it was directly over the grimy waters of a man-made pond. Following previous orders, the operator descended to ten meters over the water.

Seeing what lay in store for him, Rabban tried to pull himself up by the single shackle. "This isn't necessary, Uncle! I've learned—"

The rest of Rabban's words were lost in a clatter of chain as the remaining shackle was released. The burly man fell, flailing and screaming, a long way down into the water.

"I don't think I've ever had the opportunity to ask," the Baron shouted through the opening as Rabban went under. "Can you swim?"

Kryubi's men were stationed around the lake with rescue equipment, just in case. After all, the Baron couldn't risk the life of his only trained heir. Though he would never admit it to Rabban, he was actually pleased at the loss of bleeding-heart Abulurd. It took guts to do what he had done to his own father—guts and ruthlessness. Good Harkonnen traits.

But I'm even more ruthless, the Baron thought as the floatcraft glided back to its landing field. *I've just demonstrated that, to keep him from trying to kill me. "Beast" Rabban must prey only on the weak. And only when I say so.*

Still, the Baron faced a much greater challenge; his body continued to decline each day. He'd been taking imported energy supplements, and they helped to keep the weakness and bloating in check—but it was becoming necessary to consume more and more pills to achieve the same benefit, with unknown side effects.

The Baron sighed. It was so difficult to medicate himself, when there weren't any good doctors around. How many had he killed now for their incompetence? He'd lost count.

Some say that the anticipation of a thing is better than the thing itself. In my view, this is utter nonsense. Any fool can imagine a prize. I desire the tangible.

—HASIMIR FENRING,
Letters from Arrakis

THE CONFIDENTIAL MESSAGE CAME TO THE RESIDENCY AT ARRAKEEN VIA A tortuous route from one Courier to another, Heighliner to Heighliner—as if Master Researcher Hidar Fen Ajidica wanted to delay delivering the news to Hasimir Fenring.

Very odd, since the Tleilaxu had already delayed for twenty years.

Eager to read the contents of the cylinder, already planning a series of punishments if Ajidica dared to make more excuses, Fenring scuttled to his private study dome on the rooftop level of the mansion.

What whining lies will that little gnome tell now?

Behind shimmering shield windows that dulled the harsh edges of sunlight, Fenring went through the tedious process of decoding the message, humming to himself all the while. The Courier cylinder had been genetically keyed to his touch alone, such a sophisticated technique that he wondered if the Tleilaxu were showing off their abilities for him. The little men were not incompetent . . . merely annoying. He expected the letter to be filled with further requests for laboratory materials, more empty promises.

Even decoded, the words made no sense—and Fenring saw that they were masked by a secondary encryption. He felt a flash of impatience, then spent ten more minutes stroking the words again.

As the true text finally emerged, Fenring stared with his overlarge eyes. He blinked twice, then read Ajidica's note again. Astounding.

His guard chief Willowbrook appeared at the doorway, curious about the important delivery. He was aware of the Count's frequent plots and secret work for Shaddam IV, but knew not to ask too many questions. "Would you like me to summon a light lunch, Master Fenring?"

"Go away," Fenring said without looking over his shoulder, "or I will have you assigned to the Harkonnen headquarters in Carthag."

Willowbrook left promptly.

Fenring sat back with the message in his hands, flash-memorized every word, and then destroyed the tough paper. He would very much enjoy relaying the news to the Emperor. *At last*. His thin lips curled in a smile.

Even before the death of Shaddam's father, this plan had been set in motion. Now, after decades, that work had finally come to fruition.

"Count Fenring, we are pleased to report that the final sequence of development appears to meet our expectations. We are confident that Project Amal has succeeded, and the next round of rigorous tests will prove it. We expect to go into full-scale production within a few months.

"Soon, the Emperor will have his own inexpensive and inexhaustible supply of melange—a new monopoly that will place the great powers of the Imperium at his feet. All spice-harvesting operations on Arrakis will become irrelevant."

Trying to suppress his satisfied grin, Fenring stepped to the window and gazed out onto the dusty streets of Arrakeen, at the impossible aridity and heat. In the masses of people, he picked out blue-uniformed Harkonnen troops, brightly-attired water merchants and grimy spice crews, haughty preachers and ragged beggars, an economy based solely on one commodity. *Spice*.

Soon, none of that would matter to anyone. Arrakis, and natural melange, would become an obsolete historical curiosity. No one would care about this desert planet anymore . . . and he could move on to other, more important things.

Fenring drew a long, deep breath. It would be good to get off this rock.

Though death will cancel it, life in this world is a glorious thing.

— DUKE PAULUS ATREIDES

A MAN SHOULD NOT HAVE TO ATTEND THE FUNERAL OF HIS OWN CHILD.

Standing erect on the bow of the Atreides funeral barge, Duke Leto wore a formal white uniform, stripped of all insignia to symbolize the loss of his only son. At his side, Jessica had draped herself in a black Bene Gesserit robe, but it could not hide her beauty.

Behind them a cortege of boats followed the funeral barge, all of them decked in colorful flowers and ribbons to celebrate the life of a boy whose days had been cut tragically short. Atreides soldiers lined the decks of the escort boats, holding ceremonial metal shields that flashed when the sun broke through the cloud-scudded sky.

Sadly, Leto gazed past the gilded hawk prow, shading his eyes to look across the waters of Caladan. Victor had loved the oceans. In the distance, where the sea faded into the curved horizon, Leto saw flickering storms and bright sky-sparkles, perhaps a congregation of elecrans come to usher the lad's soul to a new place beneath the waves. . . .

For generations of Atreides, life itself had been revered as the ultimate blessing. The Atreides counted what a man did when he was *alive*—events he could experience with clarity and enjoy with all of his senses. A person's accomplishments held far more significance than any shadowy afterlife. The tangible was more important than the intangible.

Oh, how I miss you, my son.

In the brief years he had shared with Victor, he'd tried to instill strength in the boy, just as his own father had done for him. Each person must have the ability to rely on himself, to help his comrades but never to lean on them too much.

I need all my strength today.

A man should not have to attend the funeral of his own child. The natural order had been disrupted. Though Kailea had not been his wife, and Victor had not been the official ducal heir, Leto could not think of a more terrible thing to befall a person. Why had he been the one to survive, the one to endure the knowing, the awful sense of loss?

The cortege of boats set course for the coral gem beds far offshore, where Leto and Rhombur had gone diving years ago, where Leto would have taken his own son one day. But Victor hadn't been given enough time; Leto could never fulfill all the promises he'd made to the boy, both in words and in his heart. . . .

The Atreides funeral barge rose several tiers high, an impressive floating monument. On the top level, giant kabuzu shell cressets, fifteen meters tall, burned whale oil. Up there Victor's body lay in a golden coffin surrounded by his favorite things—a stuffed Salusan bull toy, a feathered *vara* lance with a rubber tip, filmbooks, games, seashells he had collected from the shore. Representatives of many Great Houses had also sent wrapped gifts. The baubles and keepsakes nearly engulfed the child's tiny, preserved body.

Bright flowers, green-and-black pennants, and long ribbons decorated the gilded tiers. Donated paintings and artists' renderings depicted a proud Duke Leto holding his newborn son high overhead, then later teaching the boy how to bullfight . . . fishing with him on one of the docks . . . protecting him from the attack of the elecran. Other images showed Victor on his mother's lap, doing school lessons, or running while holding a whistle-kite by its string. And then, poignantly, several empty panels, left blank to represent what Victor had not done in his life and never would.

Reaching the reefs, crewmen set anchors to keep the barge in place. The boats took up positions encircling the funeral barge; Duncan Idaho piloted a small motorboat around to the bow and tied up alongside.

Atreides soldiers began clanging their ceremonial shields in a mounting crescendo that carried across the waves. Duke Atreides and Jessica stood together with their heads bowed. The brisk wind blew in their faces, stinging Leto's eyes, ruffling Jessica's dark robe.

After a long moment the Duke straightened and drew a deep breath of sea air to drive back a tide of tears. He looked up at the top level of the barge, where his son lay. A shaft of bright sunlight flashed on the golden coffin.

Slowly, Leto raised his hands to the heavens.

The clashing of shields ceased, and a hush fell over the assemblage. Waves lapped against the boats, and far overhead a lone seabird called. The engine of Duncan Idaho's motorboat purred steadily.

In one of the Duke's hands he held a transmitter, which he activated. The flaming cressets tipped in toward Victor and poured burning oil over his coffin. Within seconds the top level of the wooden barge caught on fire.

Duncan helped Jessica into the motorboat, then Leto joined them. They untied from the funeral barge and drifted away as the roaring fire grew brighter and hotter.

"It is done," Leto said, not taking his eyes from the flames while Duncan maneuvered the boat into position in the circle of larger boats.

As the Duke watched his son's funeral pyre consume the entire barge in a splash of yellow-and-orange light, he murmured to Jessica, "I can never again think fondly of Kailea. Now you alone provide the strength I need to survive." He had already sent his regrets to Archduke Armand Ecaz declining the offer of marriage to his daughter Ilesa—at least for the time being—and the Archduke had quietly withdrawn the offer.

Deeply touched by his words, Jessica promised herself that she would never press Leto for a commitment that he was not willing to offer. It was enough that she had the trust of the Duke she loved. *And you are my only man*, she thought to herself.

She dared not let the Sisterhood know about the baby boy she carried in her womb, not until it was too late for them to interfere. Mohiam had given her explicit instructions, without explaining the Bene Gesserit's grand plans for the daughter Jessica had been ordered to bear.

But Leto wanted another son so badly. . . . After the funeral she would tell him she was pregnant—and no more. He deserved to at least know that, so that he could hope for another son.

As they drifted away from the rising flames on the funeral barge, Duke Leto felt determination strengthen his heart. Though he believed in Jessica, trusted and deeply loved her, he had too many scars from the tragedies, and knew he must always maintain a dignified distance.

His father had taught him this, that an Atreides Duke always lived in a different world from his women. As the leader of a Great House, Leto's primary obligation was to his people, and he could not allow himself to get too close to anyone.

I am an island, he thought.

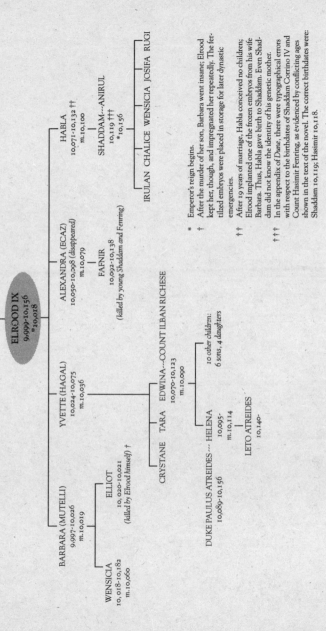

FONDIL III ("THE HUNTER")

ELROOD IX
9,999-10,156
*10,018

BARBARA (MUTELLI)
9,997-10,026
m.10,019

ELLIOT
10,020-10,021
(killed by Elrood himself) †

WENSICIA
10,018-10,182
m.10,060

YVETTE (HAGAL)
10,024-10,075
m.10,036

CRYSTANE   TARA

EDWINA...COUNT ILBAN RICHESE
10,070-10,123
m.10,090

DUKE PAULUS ATREIDES ... HELENA
10,089-10,156   10,095-
                        m.10,114

10 other children:
6 sons, 4 daughters

LETO ATREIDES
10,140-

ALEXANDRA (ECAZ)
10,050-10,098 (disappeared)
m.10,079

FAFNIR
10,092-10,138'
(killed by young Shaddam and Fenring)

HABLA
10,071-10,132 ††
m.10,100

SHADDAM...ANIRUL
10,119 ††† *10,156

IRULAN CHALICE WENSICIA JOSIFA RUGI

* Emperor's reign begins.

† After the murder of her son, Barbara went insane; Elrood kept her, though, and impregnated her repeatedly. The fertilized embryos were placed in storage for later dynastic emergencies.

†† After 19 years of marriage, Habla conceived no children; Elrood implanted one of the frozen embryos from his wife Barbara. Thus, Habla gave birth to Shaddam. Even Shaddam did not know the identity of his genetic mother.

††† In the appendix of Dune, there were typographical errors with respect to the birthdates of Shaddam Corrino IV and Count Hasimir Fenring, as evidenced by conflicting ages shown in the text of the novel. The correct birthdates were: Shaddam 10,119; Hasimir 10,118.

EXPLORE THE WORLDS OF DEL REY BOOKS

READ EXCERPTS from hot new titles.

STAY UP-TO-DATE on your favorite authors.

FIND OUT about exclusive giveaways and sweepstakes.

CONNECT WITH US ONLINE!

⊡ ◨ ⬛ @DelReyBooks

RandomHouseBooks.com/DelReyNewsletter